Condition Noted 10/19 mcs

light marks, edges, etc.

THE
BEST
OF
MICHAEL
SWANWICK

THE
BEST
OF
MICHAEL
SWANWICK

MICHAEL SWANWICK

SUBTERRANEAN PRESS 2008

TABLE OF CONTENTS

INTRODUCTION

One autumn day half a lifetime ago, I was visiting my friend Jack Dann at his house in Binghamton, New York. This was long before he emigrated to Australia. He was in a nostalgic mood, and swept a hand toward the tidy shelves holding a copy of every book he'd ever written or had a story appear in. They covered half a wall. Many years earlier, he said, he'd visited Anne McCaffrey—this was before she'd moved to Ireland—and admired her assembled clutch of publications. She'd told him then that someday sooner than he expected, he'd have a similar set of shelves, and that they'd measure out his life.

"It'll happen to you too," Jack said. "They're like a clock, ticking."

At the time, Jack's prediction seemed as simultaneously wonderful and ominous as an Arabian Nights tale.

Now I have my own set of shelves and when I look at them, I can see my life staring back at me. Thus, "The Feast of Saint Janis" and "Ginungagap," aren't just my first two published stories, but the only ones that saw print before that happy day in late 1980 when I married my wife, Marianne Porter. The next year I had the good fortune that both stories made it onto the Nebula ballot, and the even better fortune that they then both lost. I've known writers who won a major award right off the bat, and it took all the joy out of the awards process for them. Every year that they didn't win another felt like a failure to live up to their initial promise.

Winning isn't everything, and sometimes it isn't even anything at all.

"Trojan Horse" has roots deep in my childhood. My father was an engineer for General Electric's aerospace division, and he used to bring home the most wonderful publicity handouts. One day, he gave me an artist's rendering of what a GE lunar colony would look like, shown from the interior of a glass-domed crater. There was a black sky overhead and happy people strolling amid terraced gardens on the crater's inner slopes. The future never looked better. It was pretty much inevitable that someday I'd write about that colony.

"A Midwinter's Tale" was inspired by a show of Marc Chagall's paintings at the Philadelphia Museum of Art. It's one of my favorite stories and an almost-direct gift from the city in which I've spent most of my adult life. "The Edge of the World," however, was based on my senior year of high school in Seven Pines, Virginia. 1968 was a terrifying time to be young. The assassination of Martin Luther King and the resulting arrest of every black student from my school in the riots that followed was only one of many horrifying events that washed through my life that year. Adolescence is hell. I swore that I would remember how it was and write about it someday. Finally I did.

I wrote "Griffin's Egg" because I was about to start on my first fantasy novel, *The Iron Dragon's Daughter*, and knew that I'd be a way from science fiction for years. Rather than find myself using stale ideas when I returned, I threw in every hard-SF invention I'd been saving up for future use. When I came to write the nuclear war, however, the thought of a classic East-West confrontation between the US and the USSR—which everyone had been predicting for all my life—was so damned boring, I just couldn't do it. Which turned out to be a good thing because by the time the book came out (it was part of a series of hardcover novellas commissioned by Century Legend), the Soviet Union had fallen and great swaths of speculative fiction were swept into the dustbin of history.

"The Changeling's Tale" is as close to autobiographical as anything I've ever written. When I was young, I ran off with the elves to become a writer. And I've never looked back.

Years of pleasant incubation went into "North of Diddy-Wah-Diddy," mostly in the form of daydreaming while staring out the window of the train to New York City whenever I went to hobnob with my editors. I still enjoy the trip, but I must confess that I miss the sight of giant centaurs floundering through the toxic marshes of the Fresh Kill Landfill.

"Radio Waves" is set in my neighborhood of Roxborough. The telephone lines in the opening scene run right up my street and the red lights of the Seven Sisters blink benignly down upon me at night. At one point Cobb climbs through my house and sees me sitting on the couch, watching TV. "The Dead," however, is a New York City story, inspired by a show of oil paintings by an old-school American Marxist. My family comes from the Big Apple, and I have many fond and enduring memories of visiting relatives there as a child.

INTRODUCTION

I almost never start a story without knowing how it's going to end, but "Mother Grasshopper" is one of the rare exceptions. It bubbled up from the hindbrain and I had no idea what it was about until two or three pages before the end. All the place names, incidentally, are towns and cities in Pennsylvania.

Shortly after "Radiant Doors" came out, one of my Clarion students dropped by my house, along with his fiancé, to invite Marianne and me to their wedding. His wife-to-be was a rabbi and she took Marianne aside and asked her how she could bear to sleep next to me, knowing I had such things in my head.

Marianne smiled and said, "Oh, they're not in *his* head anymore. They're in *yours*."

Nevertheless, the wedding was lovely, as all weddings should be. There was a klezmer band at the reception afterwards and I danced until I could dance no more.

Almost two decades after my first experience losing a Nebula, "The Very Pulse of the Machine" won a Hugo. By then, I'd lost track of how many Nebulas and Hugos I'd been nominated for and lost (okay, yes, I am bragging here, a little), and was able to accept with pure, unalloyed joy.

I have a particular fondness for "Wild Minds." It dropped into my hands in 1995, during Intersection, the first Worldcon held in Glasgow. I was staying in a cheap B&B high up on Renfrew Street, from which I could see the M8 motorway, a classic of misguided urban planning, cutting through the city like a scar, with abandoned buildings like dead flesh to either side of it. On a panel I said that we'd best embrace neural enhancement with extreme care lest it prove to be an M8 motorway right through the brain. Thus was born a story that I hope says something a little more nuanced than what one usually hears about the Catholic faith in which I was raised.

"Scherzo With Tyrannosaur" was written as a rough sketch for *Bones of the Earth*, to work out the mechanics of time travel and the politics of *in chrono* paleontology. I was so pleased with it that I later rewrote it with a totally different plot, set it in a different part of the Cretaceous, replaced the tyrannosaur with plesiosaurs, and used it as a chapter in the novel. If you read the book you'll see what I mean. It won my second Hugo.

"The Raggle Taggle Gypsy-O" was the result of a reading Ellen Kushner gave at a local bookstore. After the event, she hit me up for a contribution to a planned but ultimately doomed anthology of stories based on folk ballads. Nothing leapt to mind, but since Ellen is a good friend, I said I'd give it a try. So on the drive home, I said to Marianne, "Okay, here's an element for a story—a panel van filled with velociraptors. Give something else that's off the wall."

Without hesitating, she said, "A picnic basket full of dead puppies."

"I can write this sucker!" I crowed.

"The Dog Said Bow-Wow" is probably my single most popular story, due entirely to the characters of Darger and Surplus. I was word-doodling one day, and they simply showed up. After which they insinuated themselves into my life, my career, and (I'm guessing) my ultimate reputation. I've written three full-scale stories and four connected short-shorts about the rogues to date, and I've just recently begun a novel for them. The story won my third Hugo.I took a big chance with "Slow Life," writing hard science fiction about Titan at a time when the Cassini-Huygens probe was en route to Saturn. Subsequent radar mapping of Titan's surface showed it to be very much the way I described it. No credit for that goes to me, however. I was simply extrapolating from what NASA's scientists had said were their best guesses. Turns out they were right. The story won my fourth Hugo.

"Legions in Time" was an homage to A. E. Van Vogt's "Recruiting Station," which was a seminal work for me. It was the first SF story whose author's name I bothered to remember, and one of a handful which convinced me I wanted to become a writer. I didn't mean for it to win a Hugo. But it did. My fifth in six years. You'd think I'd be tired of the things by then. But I wasn't.

I grew up in Winooski, Vermont, the only town in Vermont with no small-town charm whatsoever. It was a mill town before the money went away, and the kids from Burlington, across the river, called those who lived there "river rats," and threw rocks at us. Nevertheless, there's a lot of good things about Vermont, and almost all of them are people. "Triceratops Summer" is about those people.

Finally, there's "From Babel's Fall'n Glory We Fled…" This is my most recent story, and I have no idea what images it will conjure up in years to come. Perhaps the memory of me banging out this introduction and trying to find something to say about it? It'll be interesting to find out.

This book took me more than a quarter of a century to write. It will always be a landmark volume on my growing shelf of books. If I can keep it up for another twenty-seven years, my career is already half-spent. If not…well, not. I wrote these stories as best I could, and with the hope that they would endure. But whether they do or not is out of my hands. Once a story is published, it leaves the writer's control. These stories don't belong to me anymore.

They belong to you. I hope you like them.

THE FEAST OF SAINT JANIS

Take a load off, Janis,
And
You put the load right on me. .
—THE WAIT (TRAD.)

Wolf stood in the early morning fog watching the *Yankee Clipper* leave
Baltimore harbor. His elbows rested against a cool, clammy wall, its
surface eroded smooth by the passage of countless hands, almost certainly
dating back to before the Collapse. A metallic grey sparkle atop the fore-
mast drew his eye to the dish antenna that linked the ship with the geosyn-
chronous *Trickster* seasats it relied on to plot winds and currents.

To many the wooden *Clipper*, with its computer-designed hydrofoils
and hand-sewn sails, was a symbol of the New Africa. Wolf, however,
watching it merge into sea and sky, knew only that it was going home
without him.

He turned and walked back into the rick-a-rack of commercial buildings crowded against the waterfront. The clatter of hand-drawn carts mingled with a mélange of exotic cries and shouts, the alien music of a dozen
American dialects. Workers, clad in coveralls most of them, swarmed
about, grunting and cursing in exasperation when an iron wheel lurched
in a muddy pothole. Yet there was something furtive and covert about
them, as if they were hiding an ancient secret.

Craning to stare into the dark recesses of a warehouse, Wolf collided with
a woman clad head to foot in chador. She flinched at his touch, her eyes glaring above the black veil, then whipped away. Not a word was exchanged.

A citizen of Baltimore in its glory days would not have recognized the city. Where the old buildings had not been torn down and buried, shanties crowded the streets, taking advantage of the space automobiles had needed. Sometimes they were built over the streets, so that alleys became tunnelways, and sometimes these collapsed, to the cries and consternation of the natives.

It was another day with nothing to do. He could don a filter mask and tour the Washington ruins, but he had already done that, and besides the day looked like it was going to be hot. It was unlikely he'd hear anything about his mission, not after months of waiting on American officials who didn't want to talk with him. Wolf decided to check back at his hostel for messages, then spend the day in the bazaars.

Children were playing in the street outside the hostel. They scattered at his approach. One, he noted, lagged behind the others, hampered by a malformed leg. He mounted the unpainted wooden steps, edging past an old man who sat at the bottom. The old man was laying down tarot cards with a slow and fatalistic disregard for what they said; he did not look up.

The bell over the door jangled notice of Wolf's entry. He stepped into the dark foyer.

Two men in the black uniforms of the political police appeared, one to either side of him. "Wolfgang Hans Mbikana?" one asked. His voice had the dust of ritual on it; he knew the answer. "You will come with us," the other said.

"There is some mistake," Wolf objected.

"No, sir, there is no mistake," one said mildly. The other opened the door. "After you, Mr. Mbikana."

The old man on the stoop squinted up at them, looked away, and slid off the step.

The police walked Wolf to an ancient administrative building. They went up marble steps sagging from centuries of footscuffing, and through an empty lobby. Deep within the building they halted before an undistinguished-looking door. "You are expected," the first of the police said.

"I beg your pardon?"

The police walked away, leaving him there. Apprehensive, he knocked on the door. There was no answer, so he opened it and stepped within.

A woman sat at a desk just inside the room. Though she was modernly dressed, she wore a veil. She might have been young; it was impossible to tell. A flick of her eyes, a motion of one hand, directed him to the open door of an inner room. It was like following an onion to its conclusion, a layer of mystery at a time.

A heavyset man sat at the final desk. He was dressed in the traditional suit and tie of American businessmen. But there was nothing quaint or old-fashioned about his mobile, expressive face or the piercing eyes he turned on Wolf.

"Sit down," he grunted, gesturing toward an old overstuffed chair. Then: "Charles DiStephano. Controller for Northeast Regional. You're Mbikana, right?"

"Yes, sir." Wolf gingerly took the proffered chair, which did not seem all that clean. It was clear to him now; DiStephano was one of the men on whom he had waited these several months, the biggest of the lot, in fact. "I represent—"

"The Southwest Africa Trade Company." DiStephano lifted some documents from his desk. "Now this says you're prepared to offer—among other things—resource data from your North American *Coyote* landsat in exchange for the right to place students in Johns Hopkins. I find that an odd offer for your organization to make."

"Those are my papers," Wolf objected. "As a citizen of Southwest Africa, I'm not used to this sort of cavalier treatment."

"Look, kid, I'm a busy man, I have no time to discuss your rights. The papers are in my hands, I've read them, the people that sent you knew I would. Okay? So I know what you want and what you're offering. What I want to know is *why* you're making this offer."

Wolf was disconcerted. He was used to a more civilized, a more leisurely manner of doing business. The oldtimers at SWATC had warned him that the pace would be different here, but he hadn't had the experience to decipher their veiled references and hints. He was painfully aware that he had gotten the mission, with its high salary and the promise of a bonus, only because it was not one that appealed to the older hands.

"America was hit hardest," he said, "but the Collapse was worldwide." He wondered whether he should explain the system of corporate social responsibility that African business was based on. Then decided that if DiStephano didn't know, he didn't want to. "There are still problems. Africa has a high incidence of birth defects." *Because America exported its poisons; its chemicals arid pesticides and foods containing a witch's brew of preservatives.* "We hope to do away with the problem; if a major thrust is made, we can clean up the gene pool in less than a century. But to do this requires professionals—eugenicists, embryonic surgeons—and while we have these, they are second-rate. The very best still come from your nation's medical schools."

"We can't spare any."

"We don't propose to steal your doctors. We'd provide our own students—fully trained doctors who need only the specialized training."

"There are only so many openings at Hopkins," DiStephano said. "or at U of P or the UVM Medical College, for that matter."

"We're prepared to—" Wolf pulled himself up short. "It's in the papers. We'll pay enough that you can expand to meet the needs of twice the number of students we require." The room was dim and oppressive. Sweat built up under Wolf's clothing.

"Maybe so. You can't buy teachers with money, though." Wolf said nothing. "I'm also extremely reluctant to let your people *near* our medics. You can offer them money, estates—things our country cannot afford. And we *need* our doctors. As it is, only the very rich can get the corrective surgery they require."

"If you're worried about our pirating your professionals, there are ways around that. For example, a clause could be written—"Wolf went on, feeling more and more in control. He was getting somewhere. If there wasn't a deal to be made, the discussion would never have gotten this far.

The day wore on. DiStephano called in aides and dismissed them. Twice, he had drinks sent in. Once, they broke for lunch. Slowly the heat built, until it was sweltering. Finally, the light began to fail, and the heat grew less oppressive.

DiStephano swept the documents into two piles, returned one to Wolf, and put the other inside a desk drawer. "I'll look these over, have our legal boys run a study. There shouldn't be any difficulties. I'll get back to you with the final word in—say a month. September twenty-first, I'll be in Boston then, but you can find me easily enough, if you ask around."

"A month? But I thought..."

"A month. You can't hurry City Hall," DiStephano said firmly. "Ms. Corey!"

The veiled woman was at the door, remote, elusive. "Sir."

"Drag Kaplan out of his office. Tell him we got a kid in here he should give the VIP treatment to. Maybe a show. It's a Hopkins thing, he should earn his keep."

"Yes, sir." She was gone.

"Thank you," Wolf said, "but I don't really need..."

"Take my advice, kid, take all the perks you can get. God knows there aren't many left. I'll have Kaplan pick you up at your hostel in an hour."

✹

Kaplan turned out to be a slight, balding man with nervous gestures, some sort of administrative functionary for Hopkins. Wolf never did get the connection. But Kaplan was equally puzzled by Wolf's status, and Wolf took petty pleasure in not explaining it. It took some of the sting off of having his papers stolen.

Kaplan led Wolf through the evening streets. A bright sunset circled the world, and the crowds were much thinner. "We won't be leaving the area that's zoned for electricity," Kaplan said. "Otherwise I'd advise against going out at night at all. Lot of jennie-deafs out then."

"Jennie-deafs?"

"Mutes. Culls. The really terminal cases. Some of them can't pass themselves off in daylight even wearing coveralls. Or chador—a lot are women." A faintly perverse expression crossed the man's face, leaving not so much as a greasy residue.

"Where are we going?" Wolf asked. He wanted to change the subject. A vague presentiment assured him he did not want to know the source of Kaplan's expression.

"A place called Peabody's. You've heard of Janis Joplin, our famous national singer?"

Wolf nodded, meaning no.

"The show is a re-creation of her act. Woman name of Maggie Horowitz does the best impersonation of Janis I've ever seen. Tickets are almost impossible to get, but Hopkins has special influence in this case because— ah, here we are."

Kaplan led him down a set of concrete steps and into the basement of a dull brick building. Wolf experienced a moment of dislocation. It was a bookstore. Shelves and boxes of books and magazines brooded over him, a packrat's clutter of paper.

Wolf wanted to linger, to scan the ancient tomes, remnants of a time and culture fast sinking into obscurity and myth. But Kaplan brushed past them without a second glance and he had to hurry to keep up.

They passed through a second roomful of books, then into a hallway where a grey man held out a gnarled hand and said, "Tickets, please."

Kaplan gave the man two crisp pasteboard cards, and they entered a third room.

It was a cabaret. Wooden chairs clustered about small tables with flickering candles at their centers. The room was lofted with wood beams, and a large unused fireplace dominated one wall. Another wall had obviously been torn out at one time to make room for a small stage. Over a century's accumulation of memorabilia covered the walls or hung from the rafters, like barbarian trinkets from toppled empires.

"Peabody's is a local institution," Kaplan said. "In the twentieth century it was a speakeasy. H.L. Mencken himself used to drink here." Wolf nodded, though the name meant nothing to him. "The bookstore was a front, and the drinking went on here in the back."

The place was charged with a feeling of the past. It invoked America's bygone days as a world power. Wolf half-expected to see Theodore Roosevelt or Henry Kissinger come striding in. He said something to this effect, and Kaplan smiled complacently.

"You'll like the show, then," he said.

A waiter took their orders. There was barely time to begin on the drinks when a pair of spotlights came on, and the stage curtain parted.

A woman stood alone in the center of the stage. Bracelets and bangles hung from her wrists, gaudy necklaces from her throat. She wore large tinted glasses and a flowered granny gown. Her nipples pushed against the thin dress. Wolf stared at them in horrified fascination. She had an extra set, immediately below the first pair.

The woman stood perfectly motionless. Wolf couldn't stop staring at her nipples; it wasn't just the number, it was the fact of their being visible at all. So quickly had he taken on this land's taboos.

The woman threw her head back and laughed. She put one hand on her hip, thrust the hip out at an angle, and lifted the microphone to her lips. She spoke, and her voice was harsh and raspy.

"About a year ago I lived in a row house in Newark, right? Lived on the third floor, and I thought I had my act together. But nothing was going right, I wasn't getting any...action. Know what I mean? No talent comin' around. And there was this chick down the street, didn't have much and she was doing okay, so I say to myself: *What's wrong, Janis?* How come she's doing so good and you ain't gettin' any? So I decided to check it out, see what she had and I didn't. And one day I get up early, look out the window, and I see this chick out there *hustling*! I mean, she was doing the streets at *noon*! So I said to myself, Janis, honey, you ain't

18

even trying. And when ya want action, ya gotta try. Yeah. Try just a little bit harder."

The music swept up out of nowhere, and she was singing: "Try-iii, Try-iii, Just a little bit harder..."

And unexpectedly, it was good. It was like nothing he had ever heard, but he understood it, almost on an instinctual level. It was world-culture music. It was universal.

Kaplan dug fingers into Wolf's arm, brought his mouth up to Wolf's ear. "You see? You see?" he demanded. Wolf shook him off impatiently. He wanted to hear the music.

The concert lasted forever, and it was done in no time at all. It left Wolf sweaty and emotionally spent. Onstage, the woman was energy personi-fied. She danced, she strutted, she wailed more power into her songs than seemed humanly possible. Not knowing the original, Wolf was sure it was a perfect re-creation. It had that feel.

The audience loved her. They called her back for three encores, and then a fourth. Finally, she came out, gasped into the mike, "I love ya, hon-eys, I truly do. But please—no more. I just couldn't do it." She blew a kiss, and was gone from the stage.

The entire audience was standing, Wolf among them, applauding furi-ously. A hand fell on Wolf's shoulder, and he glanced to his side, annoyed. It was Kaplan. His face was flushed and he said, "Come on." He pulled Wolf free of the crowd and backstage to a small dressing room. Its door was ajar and people were crowded into it.

One of them was the singer, hair stringy and out-of-place, laughing and gesturing widely with a Southern Comfort bottle. It was an antique, its label lacquered to the glass, and three-quarters filled with something amber-colored.

"Janis, this is—" Kaplan began.

"The name is Maggie," she sang gleefully. "Maggie Horowitz. I ain't no *dead* blues singer. And don't you forget it."

"This is a fan of yours, Maggie. From Africa." He gave Wolf a small shove. Wolf hesitantly stumbled forward, grimacing apologetically at the people he displaced.

"Whee—howdy!" Maggie whooped. She downed a slug from her bottle. "Pleased ta meecha, Ace. Kinda light for an African, aintcha?"

"My mother's people were descended from German settlers." And it was felt that a light-skinned representative could handle the touchy Americans better, but he didn't say that.

"Whatcher name, Ace?

"Wolf."

"Wolf." Maggie crowed. "Yeah, you look like a real heartbreaker, honey. Guess I'd better be careful around you, huh? Likely to sweep me off my feet and deflower me." She nudged him with an elbow. "That's a joke, Ace."

Wolf was fascinated. Maggie was *alive*, a dozen times more so than her countrymen. She made them look like zombies. Wolf was also a little afraid of her.

"*Hey*. Whatcha think of my singing, hah?"

"It was excellent," Wolf said. "It was"—he groped for words—"in my land the music is quieter, there is not so much emotion."

"Yeah, well I think it was fucking good, Ace. Voice's never been in better shape. Go tell 'em that at Hopkins, Kaplan. Tell 'em I'm giving them their money's worth."

"Of course you are," Kaplan said.

"Well, I *am*, goddammit. Hey, this place is like a morgue! Let's ditch this matchbox dressing room and hit the bars. Hey? Let's party."

She swept them all out of the dressing room, out of the building, and onto the street. They formed a small boisterous group, noisily wandering the city, looking for bars.

"There's one a block thataway," Maggie said. "Let's hit it. Hey, Ace, I'd likeya ta meet Cynthia. Sin, this is Wolf. Sin and I are like one person inside two skins. Many's the time we've shared a piece of talent in the same bed. Hey?" She cackled, and grabbed at Cynthia's ass.

"Cut it out, Maggie." Cynthia smiled when she said it. She was a tall, slim, striking woman.

"Hey, this town is *dead*!" Maggie screamed the last word, then gestured them all to silence so they could listen for the echo. "There it is." She pointed, and they swooped down on the first bar.

After the third, Wolf lost track. At some point he gave up on the party and somehow made his way back to his hostel. The last he remembered of Maggie she was calling after him, "Hey, Ace, don't be a party poop." Then: "At least be sure to come back tomorrow, goddammit."

Wolf spent most of the day in his room, drinking water and napping. His hangover was all but gone by the time evening took the edge off the day's heat. He thought of Maggie's half-serious invitation, dismissed it and decided to go to the Club.

The Uhuru Club was ablaze with light by the time he wandered in, a beacon in a dark city. Its frequenters, after all, were all African foreign service, with a few commercial reps such as himself forced in by the insular nature of American society and the need for polite conversation. It was *de facto* exempt from the power-use laws that governed the natives.

"Mbikana! Over here, lad, let me set you up with a drink." Nnamdi of the consulate waved him over to the bar. Wolf complied, feeling conspicuous as he always did in the Club. His skin stood out here. Even the American servants were dark, though whether this was a gesture of deference or arrogance on the part of the local authorities, he could not guess.

"Word is that you spent the day closeted with the comptroller." Nnamdi had a gin-and-tonic set up. Wolf loathed the drink, but it was universal among the service people. "Share the dirt with us." Other faces gathered around; the service ran on gossip.

Wolf gave an abridged version of the encounter, and Nnamdi applauded. "A full day with the Spider King, and you escaped with your balls intact. An auspicious beginning for you, lad."

"Spider King?"

"Surely you were briefed on regional autonomy—how the country was broken up when it could no longer be managed by a central directorate? There *is* no higher authority than DiStephano in this part of the world, boy."

"Boston," Ajuji sniffed. Like most of the expatriates, she was a failure; unlike many, she couldn't hide the fact from herself. "That's exactly the sort of treatment one comes to expect from these savages."

"Now, Ajuji," Nnamdi said mildly. "These people are hardly savages. Why, before the Collapse they put men on the moon."

"Technology! Hard-core technology, that's all it was, of a piece with the kind that almost destroyed us all. If you want a measure of a people, you look at how they live. These—*yanks*," she hissed the word to emphasize its filthiness, "live in squalor. Their streets are filthy, their cities are filthy, and even the ones who aren't rotten with genetic disease are filthy. A child can be taught to clean up after itself. What does that make them?"

"Human beings, Ajuji."

"Hogwash, Nnamdi."

Wolf followed the argument with acute embarrassment. He had been brought up to expect well from people with social standing. To hear gutter language and low prejudice from them was almost beyond bearing. Suddenly it *was* beyond bearing. He turned his back on them all, and left.

Mbikana! You mustn't—" Nnamdi called after him.

"Oh, let him go," Ajuji cut in, with a satisfied tone, "you mustn't expect better. After all, he's practically one of *them*."

Well maybe he was.

Wolf wasn't fully aware of where he was going until he found himself at Peabody's. He circled the building, and found a rear door. He tried the knob: it turned loosely in his hand. Then the door swung open and a heavy, bearded man in coveralls leaned out. "Yes?" he said in an unfriendly tone.

"Uh," Wolf said. "Maggie Horowitz told me I could drop by."

"Look, pilgrim, there are a lot of people trying to get backstage. My job is to keep them out unless I know them. I don't know you."

Wolf tried to think of some response to this, and failed. He was about to turn away when somebody unseen said, "Oh, let him in, Deke."

It was Cynthia. "Come on," she said in a bored voice. "Don't clog up the doorway." The guard moved aside, and he entered.

"Thank you," he said.

"*Nada*," she replied. "As Maggie would say. The dressing room is that way, pilgrim."

"Wolf, honey!" Maggie shrieked. "How's it going, Ace? Ya catch the show?"

"No, I—"

"You shoulda. I was good. Really good. Janis herself was never better. Hey, gang! Let's split, hah? Let's go somewhere and get down and boogie."

A group of twenty ended up taking over a methane-lit bar outside the zoned-for-electricity sector. Three of the band had brought along their instruments, and they talked the owner into letting them play. The music was droning and monotonous. Maggie listened appreciatively, grinning and moving her head to the music.

"Whatcha think of that, Ace? Pretty good, hey? That's what we call Dead music."

Wolf shook his head. "I think it's well named."

"Hey, guys, you hear that? Wolf here just made a funny. There's hope for you yet, honey." Then she sighed. "Can't get behind it, huh? That's really sad, man. I mean they played *good* music back then; it was real. We're just echoes, man. Just playing away at them old songs. Got none of our own worth singing."

"Is that why you're doing the show, then?" Wolf asked, curious.

Maggie laughed. "Hell, no. I do it because I got the chance. DiStephano got in touch with me—"

"DiStephano? The comptroller?"

"One of his guys, anyway. They had this gig all set up, and they needed someone to play Janis. So they ran a computer search and came up with my name. And they offered me money, and I spent a month or two in Hopkins being worked over, and here I am. On the road to fame and glory." Her voice rose and warbled and mocked itself on the last phrase.

"Why did you have to go to Hopkins?"

"You don't think I was *born* looking like this? They had to change my face around. Changed my voice too, for which God bless. They brought it down lower, widened out my range, gave it the strength to hold on to them high notes and push 'em around."

"Not to mention the mental implants," Cynthia said.

"Oh, yeah, and the 'plants so I could talk in a bluesy sorta way without falling out of character," Maggie said. "But that was minor."

Wolf was impressed. He had known that Hopkins was good, but this—! "What possible benefit is there for them?"

"Beats the living hell out of me, lover-boy. Don't know, don't care, and don't ask. That's my motto."

A long-haired pale young man sitting nearby said, "The government is all hacked up on social engineering. They do a lot of weird things, and you never find out why. You learn not to ask questions."

"Hey, listen, Hawk, bringing Janis back to life isn't weird. It's a beautiful thing to do," Maggie objected. "Yeah. I only wish they could *really* bring her back. Sit her down next to me. Love to talk with that lady."

"You two would tear each other's eyes out," Cynthia said.

"What? Why?"

"Neither one of you'd be willing to give up the spotlight to the other."

Maggie cackled. "Ain't it the truth? Still, she's one broad I'd love to have met. A *real* star, see? Not a goddamned echo like me."

Hawk broke in, said, "You, Wolf. Where does your pilgrimage take you now? The group goes on tour the day after tomorrow; what are your plans?"

"I don't really have any," Wolf said. He explained his situation. "I'll probably stay in Baltimore until it's time to go up north. Maybe I'll take a side trip or two."

"Why don't you join the group, then?" Hawk asked. "We're planning to make the trip one long party. And we'll slam into Boston in just less than a month. The tour ends there."

"That," said Cynthia, "is a real bright idea. All we need is another non-productive person on board the train."

Maggie bristled. "So what's wrong with it?"

"Nothing's wrong with it. It's just a dumb idea."

"Well, *I* like it. How about it, Ace? You on the train or off?"

"I—" He stopped. Well, why not? "Yes. I would be pleased to go along."

"Good." She turned to Cynthia. "*Your* problem, sweets, is that you're just plain jealous."

"Oh, Christ, here we go again."

"Well, don't bother. It won't do you any good. Hey, you see that piece of talent at the far end of the bar?"

"Maggie, that 'piece of talent,' as you call him, is eighteen years old. At most."

"Yeah. Nice though." Maggie stared wistfully down the bar. "He's kinda pretty, ya know?"

Wolf spent the next day clearing up his affairs and arranging for the letters of credit. The morning of departure day, he rose early and made his way to Baltimore Station. A brief exchange with the guards let him into the walled train yard.

The train was an ungainly steam locomotive with a string of rehabilitated cars behind it. The last car had the word PEARL painted on it, in antique psychedelic lettering.

"Hey, Wolf! Come lookit this mother." A lone figure waved at him from the far end of the train. Maggie.

Wolf joined her. "What do you think of it, hah?"

He searched for something polite to say. "It is very impressive," he said finally. The word that leapt to mind was *grotesque*.

"Yeah, there's a methane processing plant nearby. Hey, lookit me! Up and awake at eight in the morning. Can ya take it'? Had to get behind a little speed to do it, though."

The idiom was beyond him. "You mean—you were late waking up?"

"What? Oh, hey, man, you can be—look, forget I said a thing. No." She pondered a second. "Look, Wolf. There's this stuff called 'speed,' it can wake you up in the morning, give you a little boost, get you going. Ya know?"

Awareness dawned. "You mean amphetamines."

"Yeah, well this stuff ain't exactly legal, dig? So I'd just as soon you didn't spread the word around. I mean, I trust you man, but I wanna be sure you know what's happening before you go shooting off your mouth."

"I understand," Wolf said. "I won't say anything. But you know that amphetamines are—"

"Gotcha, Ace. Hey, you gotta meet the piece of talent I picked up last night. Hey, Dave! Get your ass over here, lover."

A young sleepy-eyed blond shuffled around the edge of the train. He wore white shorts, defiantly it seemed to Wolf, and a loose blouse buttoned up to his neck. Giving Maggie a weak hug around the waist, he nodded to Wolf.

"Davie's got four nipples, just like me. How about that? I mean, it's gotta be a pretty rare mutation, hah?"

Dave hung his head, half blushing. "Aw, Janis," he mumbled. Wolf waited for Maggie to correct the boy, but she didn't. Instead she led them around and around the train chatting away madly, pointing out this, that, and the other thing.

Finally, Wolf excused himself, and returned to his hostel. He left Maggie prowling about the train, dragging her pretty-boy after her. Wolf went out for a long lunch, picked up his bags, and showed up at the train earlier than most of the entourage.

The train lurched, and pulled out of the station. Maggie was in constant motion, talking, laughing, directing the placement of luggage. She darted from car to car, never still. Wolf found a seat and stared out the window. Children dressed in rags ran alongside the tracks, holding out hands and begging for money. One or two of the party threw coins; more laughed and threw bits of garbage.

Then the children were gone, and the train was passing through endless miles of weathered ruins. Hawk sat down beside Wolf. "It'll be a slow trip," he said. "The train has to go around large sections of land it's better not to go through." He started moodily at the broken-windowed shells that were once factories and warehouses. "Look out there, pilgrim, *that's* my country," he said in a disgusted voice. "Or the corpse of it."

"Hawk, you're close to Maggie."

"Now if you go out to the center of the continent..." Hawk's voice grew distant. "There's a cavern out there, where they housed radioactive waste. It was formed into slugs and covered with solid gold—anything else deteriorates too fast. The way I figure it, a man with a lead suit could go into the cavern arid shave off a fortune. There's tons of the stuff there." He sighed. "Someday I'm going to rummage through a few archives and go."

"Hawk, you've got to *listen* to me."

Hawk held up a hand for silence. "It's about the drugs, right? You just found out, and you want me to warn her."

"Warning her isn't good enough. Someone has to stop her."

"Yes, well. Try to understand, Maggie was in Hopkins for *three months* while they performed some very drastic surgery on her. She didn't look a thing like she does now, and she could sing but her voice wasn't anything to rave about. Not to mention the mental implants.

"Imagine the pain she went through. Now ask yourself what are the two most effective painkillers in existence?"

"Morphine and heroin. But in my country, when drugs are resorted to, the doctors wean the patients off them before their release."

"That's not the point. Consider this—Maggie could have had Hopkins remove the extra nipples. They could have done it. But she wasn't willing to go through the pain."

"She seems proud of them."

"She talks about them a lot, at least."

The train lurched and stumbled. Three of the musicians had uncrated their guitars and were playing more "Dead" music. Wolf chewed his lip in silence for a time, then said, "So what is the point you're making?"

"Simply that Maggie was willing to undergo the greater pain so that she could become Janis. So when I tell you she only uses drugs as painkillers, you have to understand that I'm not necessarily talking about physical pain." Hawk got up and left.

Maggie danced into the car. "Big time!" she whooped. "We made it into the big time, boys and girls. Hey, let's party!"

The next ten days were one extended party, interspersed with concerts. The reception in Wilmington was phenomenal. Thousands came to see the show; many were turned away. Maggie was unsteady before the first concert, achingly afraid of failure. But she played a rousing set, and was called back time and time again. Finally, exhausted and limp, her hair sticking to a sweaty forehead, she stood up front and gasped, "That's all there is, boys and girls. I love ya and I wish there was more to give ya, but there ain't. You used it all up." And the applause went on and on...

The four shows in Philadelphia began slowly, but built up big. A few seats were unsold at the first concert; people were turned away for the second. The last two were near-riots. The group entrained to Newark for a day's rest and put on a Labor Day concert that made the previous efforts look pale. They stayed in an obscure hostel for an extra day's rest.

Wolf spent his rest day sight-seeing. While in Philadelphia he had hired a native guide and prowled through the rusting refinery buildings at Point Breeze. They rose to the sky forever in tragic magnificence, and it was hard to believe there had ever been enough oil in the world to fill the holding tanks there. In Wilmington, he let the local guide lead him to a small Italian neighborhood to watch a religious festival.

The festival was a parade, led first by a priest trailed by eight altar girls, with incense burners and fans. Then came twelve burly men carrying the flower-draped body of an ancient Cadillac. After them came the faithful, in coveralls and chador, singing.

Wolf followed the procession to the river, where the car was placed in a hole in the ground, sprinkled with holy water, and set afire. He asked the guide what story lay behind the ritual, and the boy shrugged. It was old, he was told, very very old.

It was late when Wolf returned to the hostel. He was expecting a party, but found it dark and empty. Cynthia stood in the foyer, hands behind her back, staring out a barred window at black nothingness.

"Where is everybody?" Wolf asked. It was hot. Insects buzzed about the coal-oil lamp, batting against it frenziedly.

Cynthia turned, studied him oddly. Her forehead was beaded with sweat. "Maggie's gone home—she's attending a mid-school reunion. She's going to show her old friends what a hacking big star she's become. The others?" She shrugged. "Off wherever puppets go when there's no one to bring them to life. Their rooms, probably."

"Oh." Cynthia's dress clung damply to her legs and sides. Dark stains spread out from under her armpits. "Would you like to play a game of chess or—something?"

Cynthia's eyes were strangely intense. She took a step closer to him. "Wolf, I've been wondering. You've been celibate on this trip. Is there a problem? No? Maybe a girlfriend back home?"

"There was, but she won't wait for me." Wolf made a deprecating gesture. "Maybe that was part of the reason I took this trip."

She took one of his hands, placed it on her breast. "But you are interested in girls?" Then, before he could shape his answer into clumsy words, she whispered, "Come on," and led him to her room.

Once inside, Wolf seized Cynthia and kissed her, deeply and long. She responded with passion, then drew away and with a little shove toppled them onto the bed. "Off with your clothes," she said. She shucked her blouse in a complex fluid motion. Pale breasts bobbled, catching vague moonlight from the window.

After an instant's hesitation, Wolf doffed his own clothing. By contrast with Cynthia he felt weak and irresolute, and it irked him to feel that way. Determined to prove he was nothing of the kind, he reached for Cynthia as she dropped onto the bed beside him. She evaded his grasp.

"Just a moment, pilgrim." She rummaged through a bag by the headboard. "Ah. Care for a little treat first? It'll enhance the sensations."

"Drugs?" Wolf asked, feeling an involuntary horror.

"Oh, come down off your high horse. Once won't melt your genes. Give a gander at what you're being so critical of."

"What is it?"

"Vanilla ice cream," she snapped. She unstoppered a small vial and meticulously dribbled a few grains of white powder onto a thumbnail. "This is expensive, so pay attention. You want to breathe it all in with one snort. Got that? So by the numbers: take a deep breath and breathe out slowly. That's it. Now in. Now out and hold."

Cynthia laid her thumbnail beneath Wolf's nose, pinched one nostril shut with her free hand. "Now in fast. Yeah!"

He inhaled convulsively and was flooded with sensations. A crisp, clean taste filled his mouth, and a spray of fine white powder hit the back of his throat. It tingled pleasantly. His head felt spacious. He moved his jaw, suspiciously searching about with his tongue.

Cynthia quickly snorted some of the powder herself, restoppering the vial.

"Now," she said. "Touch me. Slowly, slowly, we've got all night. That's the way. Ahhhh." She shivered. "I think you've got the idea."

They worked the bed for hours. The drug, whatever it was, made Wolf feel strangely clearheaded and rational, more playful and more prone to linger. There was no urgency to their lovemaking; they took their time. Three, perhaps four times they halted for more of the powder, which Cynthia doled out with careful ceremony. Each time they returned to their lovemaking with renewed interest and resolution to take it slowly, to postpone each climax to the last possible instant.

The evening grew old. Finally, they lay on the sheets, not touching, weak and exhausted. Wolf's body was covered with a fine sheen of sweat. He did not care to even think of making love yet another time. He refrained from saying this.

"Not bad," Cynthia said softly. "I must remember to recommend you to Maggie."

"Sin, why do you do that?"

"Do what?"

"We've just—been as intimate as two human beings can be. But as soon as it's over, you say something cold. Is it that you're afraid of contact?"

"Christ." It was an empty syllable, devoid of religious content, and flat. Cynthia fumbled in her bag, found a metal case, pulled a cigarette out, and lit it. Wolf flinched inwardly. "Look, pilgrim, what are you asking for? You planning to marry me and take me away to your big, clean African cities to meet your momma? Hah?

"Didn't think so. So what do you want from me? Mental souvenirs to take home and tell your friends about? I'll give you one; I spent years saving up enough to go see a doctor, find out if I could have any brats. Went to one last year, and what do you think he tells me? I've got red-cell dyscrasia, too far gone for treatment, there's nothing to do but wait. Lovely, hah? So one of these days it'll just stop working and I'll die. Nothing to be done. So long as I eat right, I won't start wasting away, so I can keep my looks up to the end. I could buy a little time if I gave up drugs like this"— she waved the cigarette, and an ash fell on Wolf's chest. He brushed it away quickly— "and the white powder, and anything else that makes life worth living. But it wouldn't buy me enough time to do anything worth doing." She fell silent. "Hey. What time is it?"

Wolf climbed out of bed, rummaged through his clothing until he found his timepiece. He held it up to the window, squinted. "Um. Twelve... fourteen."

"Oh, *nukes.*" Cynthia was up and scrabbling for her clothes. "Come on, get dressed. Don't just stand there."

Wolf dressed himself slowly. "What's the problem?"

"I promised Maggie I'd get some people together to walk her back from that damned reunion. It ended *hours* ago, and I lost track of the time." She ignored his grin. "Ready? Come on, we'll check her room first and then the foyer. God, is she going to be mad."

They found Maggie in the foyer. She stood in the center of the room, haggard and bedraggled, her handbag hanging loosely from one hand. Her face was livid with rage. The sputtering lamp made her face look old and evil.

"Well!" she snarled. "Where have you two been?"

"In my room, balling," Cynthia said calmly. Wolf stared at her, appalled.

"Well, that's just beautiful. That's really beautiful, isn't it? Do you know where I've been while my two best friends were upstairs humping their brains out? Hey? Do you want to know?" Her voice reached hysterical peak. "I was being *raped by two jennie-deafs,* that's where!"

She stormed past them, half-cocking her arm as if she were going to assault them with her purse, then thinking better of it. They heard her run down the hall. Her door slammed.

Bewildered, Wolf said, "But I—"

"Don't let her dance on your head," Cynthia said. "She's lying."

"Are you certain?"

"Look, we've lived together, bedded the same men—I know her. She's all hacked off at not having an escort home. And Little Miss Sunshine has to spread the gloom."

"We should have been there," Wolf said dubiously. "She could have been killed, walking home alone."

"Whether Maggie dies a month early or not doesn't make a bit of difference to me, pilgrim. I've got my own problems."

"A month—? Is Maggie suffering from a disease too?"

"We're all suffering, we all—Ah, the hell with you too." Cynthia spat on the floor, spun on her heel, and disappeared down the hallway. It had the rhythm and inevitability of a witch's curse.

The half-day trip to New York left the troupe with playtime before the first concert, but Maggie stayed in seclusion, drinking. There was talk about her use of drugs, and this alarmed Wolf, for they were all users of drugs themselves.

There was also gossip about the reunion. Some held that Maggie had dazzled her former friends—who had not treated her well in her younger years-had been glamorous and gracious. The predominant view, however, was that she had been soundly snubbed, that she was still a freak and an oddity in the eyes of her former contemporaries. That she had left the reunion alone.

Rumors flew about the liaison between Wolf and Cynthia too. The fact that she avoided him only fed the speculation.

Despite everything the New York City concerts were a roaring success. All four shows were sold out as soon as tickets went on sale. Scalpers made small fortunes that week, and for the first time the concerts were allowed to run into the evening. Power was diverted from a section of the city to allow for the lighting and amplification. And Maggie sang as she had never sung before. Her voice roused the audience to a frenzy, and her blues were enough to break a hermit's heart.

They left for Hartford on the tenth, Maggie sequestered in her compartment in the last car. Crew members lounged about idly. Some strummed guitars, never quite breaking into a recognizable tune. Others talked quietly. Hawk flipped tarot cards into a heap, one at a time.

"Hey, this place is fucking *dead*!" Maggie was suddenly in the car, her expression an odd combination of defiance and guilt. "Let's party! Hey? Let's hear some music." She fell into Hawk's lap and nibbled on an ear.

"Welcome back, Maggie," somebody said.

"*Janis!*" she shouted happily. "The lady's name is Janis!"

Like a rusty machine starting up, the party came to life. Music jelled. Voices became animated. Bottles of alcohol appeared and were passed around. And for the remainder of the two days that the train spent making wide looping detours avoid the dangerous stretches of Connecticut and New York, the party never died.

There were tense undertones to the party, however, a desperate quality in Maggie's gaiety. For the first time, Wolf began to feel trapped, to count the days that separated him from Boston and the end of the tour.

The dressing room for the first Hartford concert was cramped, small, badly lit—like every other dressing room they'd encountered. "Get your ass over here, Sin," Maggie yelled. "You've gotta make me up so I look strung out, like Janis did."

Cynthia held Maggie's chin, twisted it to the left, to the right. Maggie, you don't *need* makeup to look strung out."

"Goddammit, yes I *do*. Let's get it on. Come on, come on—I'm a star, I shouldn't have to put up with this shit."

Cynthia hesitated, then began dabbing at Maggie's face, lightly accentuating the lines, the bags under her eyes.

Maggie studied the mirror. "Now *that's* grim," she said. "That's really grotesque."

"That's what you look like, Maggie."

"You cheap bitch! You'd think *I* was the one who nodded out last night before we could get it on." There was an awkward silence. "Hey, Wolf!" She spun to face him. "What do you say?"

"Well," Wolf began, embarrassed, "I'm afraid Cynthia's..."

"You see? Let's get this show on the road." She grabbed her cherished Southern Comfort bottle and upended it.

"That's not doing you any good either."

Maggie smiled coldly. "Shows what *you* know. Janis always gets smashed before a concert. Helps her voice." She stood, made her way to the curtains. The emcee was winding up his pitch.

"Ladies and gentlemen...Janis!"

Screams arose. Maggie sashayed up to the mike, lifted it, laughed into it.

"Heyyy. Good ta see ya." She swayed and squinted at the crowd, and was off and into her rap. "Ya know, I went ta see a doctor the other week. Told him I was worried about how much drinking I was doing. Told him I'd been drinkin' heavy since I was twelve. Get up in the morning and have a few Bloody Marys with breakfast. Polish off a fifth before lunch. Have a few drinks at dinner, and really get into it when the partying begins. Told him how much I drank for how many years. So I said, 'Look, Doc, none of this ever hurt me any, but I'm kinda worried, ya know? Give it to me straight, have I got a problem?' And he said, 'Man, I don't think you've got a problem. I think you're doing just *fine!*'" Cheers from the audience. Maggie smiled smugly. "Well, honey, *everybody's* got problems, and I'm no exception." The music came up. "But when I got problems, I got an answer, 'cause I can sing dem ole-time blues. Just sing my problems away." She launched into "Ball and Chain," and the audience went wild.

Backstage, Wolf was sitting on a stepladder. He had bought a cup of water from a vendor and was nursing it, taking small sips. Cynthia came up and stood beside him. They both watched Maggie strutting on stage, stamping and sweating, writhing and howling.

"I can never get over the contrast," Wolf said, not looking at Cynthia. "Out there everybody is excited. Back here, it's calm and peaceful. Sometimes I wonder if we're seeing the same thing the audience does."

"Sometimes it's hard to see what's right in front of your face." Cynthia smiled a sad cryptic smile and left. Wolf had grown used to such statements, and gave it no more thought.

The second and final Hartford show went well. However, the first two concerts in Providence were bad. Maggie's voice and timing were off, and she had to cover with theatrics. At the second show she had to order the audience to dance—something that had never been necessary before. Her onstage raps became bawdier and more graphic. She moved her body as suggestively as a stripper, employing bumps and grinds. The third show was better, but the earthy elements remained.

The cast wound up in a bar in a bad section of town, where guards with guns covered the doorway from fortified booths. Maggie got drunk and ended up crying. "Man, I was so blitzed when I went onstage—you say I was good?"

"Sure, Maggie," Hawk mumbled. Cynthia snorted.

"You were very good," Wolf assured her.

"I don't remember a goddamned thing," she wailed. "You say I was good? It ain't fair, man. If I was good, I deserve to be able to remember it. I mean, what's the point otherwise? Hey?"

Wolf patted her shoulder clumsily. She grabbed the front of his dashiki and buried her face in his chest. "Wolf, Wolf, what's gonna *happen* to me?" she sobbed.

"Don't cry," he said. Patting her hair.

Finally, Wolf and Hawk had to lead her back to the hostel. No one else was willing to quit the bar.

They skirted an area where all the buildings had been torn down but one. It stood alone, with great gaping holes where plate glass had been, and large nonfunctional arches on one side.

"It was a fast-food building," Hawk explained when Wolf asked. He sounded embarrassed.

"Why is it still standing?"

"Because there are ignorant and superstitious people everywhere," Hawk muttered. Wolf dropped the subject.

The streets were dark and empty. They went back into the denser areas of town, and the sound of their footsteps bounced off the buildings. Maggie was leaning half-conscious on Hawk's shoulder, and he almost had to carry her.

There was a stirring in the shadows. Hawk tensed. "Speed up a bit, if you can," he whispered.

Something shuffled out of the darkness. It was large and only vaguely human. It moved toward them. "What—?" Wolf whispered.

"Jennie-deaf," Hawk whispered back. "If you know any clever tricks, this is the time to use 'em." The thing broke into a shambling run.

Wolf thrust a hand into a pocket and whirled to face Hawk. "Look," he said in a loud, angry voice. "I've taken *enough* from you! I've got a *knife*, and I don't care *what* I do!" The jennie-deaf halted. From the corner of his eye, Wolf saw it slide back into the shadows.

Maggie looked up with sleepy, quizzical expression. "Hey, what…"

"Never mind," Hawk muttered. He upped his pace, half dragging Maggie after him. "That was arrogant," he said approvingly.

Wolf forced his hand from his pocket. He found he was shivering from the aftershock. "*Nada,*" he said. Then: "That is the correct term?"

"Yeah."

"I wasn't certain that jennie-deafs really existed."

"Just some poor mute with gland trouble. Don't think about it."

Autumn was just breaking out when the troupe hit Boston. They arrived to find the final touches being put on the stage on Boston Commons. A mammoth concert was planned; dozens of people swarmed about making preparations.

This must be how America was all the time before the Collapse," Wolf said, impressed. He was ignored.

The morning of the concert, Wolf was watching canvas being hoisted above the stage, against the chance of rain, when a gripper ran up and said, "You, pilgrim, have you seen Janis?"

"Maggie," he corrected automatically, "No, not recently."

"Thanks," the man gasped, and ran off. Not long after, Hawk hurried by and asked, "Seen Maggie lagging about?"

"No. Wait, Hawk, what's going on? You're the second person to ask me that."

Hawk shrugged. "Maggie's disappeared. Nothing to scream about."

"I hope she'll be back in time for the show."

"The local police are hunting for her. Anyway, she's got the implants; if she can move she'll be onstage. Never doubt it." He hurried away.

The final checks were being run, and the first concertgoers beginning to straggle in, when Maggie finally appeared. Uniformed men held each arm; she looked sober and angry. Cynthia took charge, dismissed the police, and took Maggie to the trailer that served as a dressing room.

Wolf watched from a distance, decided he could be of no use. He ambled about the Commons aimlessly, watching the crowd grow. The people coming in found places to sit, took them, and waited. There was little talk among them, and what here was was quiet. They were dressed brightly, but not in their best. Some carried winejugs or blankets.

They were an odd crew. They did not look each other in the eye; their mouths were grim, their faces without expression. Their speech was low, but with an undercurrent of tension. Wolf wandered among them, eavesdropping, listening to fragments of their talk.

"Said that her child was going to…"

"…needed that. Nobody needed that."

"Couldn't have paid it away…"

"…tasted odd, so I didn't…"

"Had to tear down three blocks…"

"…blood."

Wolf became increasingly uneasy. There was something about their expressions, their tones of voice. He bumped into Hawk, who tried to hurry past.

"Hawk, there is something very wrong happening."

Hawk's face twisted. He gestured toward the light tower. "No time," he said, "the show's beginning. I've got to be at my station." Wolf hesitated, then followed the man up the ladders of the light tower.

All of the Commons was visible from the tower. The ground was thick with people, hordes of ant-specks against the brown of trampled earth. Not a child among them, and that felt wrong too. A gold-and-purple sunset smeared itself three-quarters of the way around the horizon.

Hawk flicked lights on and off, one by one, referring to a sheet of paper he held in one hand. Sometimes he cursed and respliced wires. Wolf waited. A light breeze ruffled his hair, though there was no hint of wind below.

"This is a sick country," Hawk said. He slipped a headset on, played a red spot on the stage, let it wink out. "You there, Patrick? The kliegs go on in two." He ran a check on all the locals manning lights, addressing them by name. "Average life span is something like forty-two—if you get out of the delivery room alive. The birth-rate has to be very high to keep the population from dwindling away to nothing." He brought up all the red and blue spots. The stage was bathed in purple light. The canvas above looked black in contrast. An obscure figure strolled to the center mike.

"Hit it, Patrick." A bright pool of light illuminated the emcee. He coughed, went into his spiel. His voice boomed over the crowd, relayed away from the stage by a series of amps with timed delay synchronization with the further amplification. The crowd moved sluggishly about the foot of the tower, set in motion by latecomers straggling in. "So the question you should ask yourself is why the government is wasting its resources on a goddamned show."

"All right," Wolf said. "Why?" He was very tense, very still. The breeze swept away his sweat, and he wished he had brought along a jacket. He might need one later.

"Because their wizards said to—the damn social engineers and their machines," Hawk answered. "Watch the crowd."

"...Janis!" the loudspeakers boomed. And Maggie was onstage, rapping away, handling the microphone suggestively, obviously at the peak of her form. The crowd exploded into applause. Offerings of flowers were thrown through the air. Bottles of liquor were passed hand over hand and deposited on the stage.

From above it could not be seen how the previous month had taken its toll on Maggie. The lines on her face, the waxy skin, were hidden by the colored light. The kliegs bounced off her sequined dress dazzlingly.

Halfway through her second song, Maggie came to an instrumental break and squinted out at the audience. "Hey, what the fuck's the matter with you guys? Why ain't you *dancing*?" At her cue, scattered couples rose to their feet. "Ready on the kliegs," Hawk murmured into his headset. "Three, four, and five on the police." Bright lights pinpointed three widely separated parts of the audience, where uniformed men were struggling with dancers. A single klieg stayed on Maggie, who pointed an imperious finger at one struggling group and shrieked, "Why are you trying to stop them from dancing? I want them to dance. I *command* them to dance!"

With a roar, half the audience were on their feet. "Shut down three. Hold four and five to the count of three, then off. One—Two—Three! Good" The police faded away, lost among the dancers.

"That was prearranged," Wolf said. Hawk didn't so much as glance at him.

"It's part of the legend. You, Wolf, over to your right." Wolf looked where Hawk was pointing, saw a few couples at the edge of the crowd slip from the light into the deeper shadows.

"What am I seeing?"

"Just the beginning." Hawk bent over his control board.

By slow degrees the audience became drunk and then rowdy. As the concert wore on, an ugly, excited mood grew. Sitting far above it all, Wolf could still feel the hysteria grow, as well as see it. Women shed chador and danced atop it, not fully dressed. Men ripped free of their coveralls. Here and there, spotted through the crowd, couples made love. Hawk directed lights onto a few, held them briefly; in most cases the couples went on, unheeding.

Small fights broke out, and were quelled by police. Bits of trash were gathered up and set ablaze, so that small fires dotted the landscape. Wisps of smoke floated up. Hawk played colored spots on the crowd. By the time darkness was total, the lights and the bestial noise of the revelers combined to create the feel of a witches' Sabbath.

"Pretty nasty down there," Hawk observed. "And all most deliberately engineered by government wizards."

"But there is no true feeling involved," Wolf objected. "It is nothing but animal lust. No—no involvement."

"Yeah." Onstage, Maggie was building herself up into a frenzy. And yet her blues were brilliant—she had never been better. "Not so much different from the other concerts. The only difference is that tonight nobody waits until they go home."

"Your government can't believe that enough births will result from this night to make a difference."

"Not tonight, no. But all these people will have memories to keep them warm over the winter." Then he spat over the edge of the platform. "Ahhh, why should I spout their lies for them? It's just bread and circuses is all, just a goddamned release for the masses."

Maggie howled with delight. "Whee-ew, man! I'm gettin' horny just looking at you. Yeah, baby, get it on, that's right!" She was strutting up and down the stage, a creature of boundless energy, while the band filled the night with music, fast and urgent.

"Love it!" She stuck her tongue out at the audience and received howls of approval. She lifted her Southern Comfort bottle, took a gigantic swig, her hips bouncing to music. More howls. She caressed the neck of the bottle with her tongue.

"Yeah! Makes me horny as sin, 'deed it does. Ya know," she paused a beat, then continued, "that's something I can really understand man. 'Cause I'm just a horny little hippie chick myself. Yeah." Wolf suddenly realized that she was competing against the audience itself for its attention, that she was going to try to outdo everybody present.

Maggie stroked her hand down the front of her dress, lingering between her breasts, then between her legs. She shook her hair back from her eyes, the personification of animal lust. "I mean, shit. I mean, hippie chicks don't even wear no underwear." More ribald howls of applause. "Don't believe me, do ya?"

Wolf stared, was unable to look away as Maggie slowly spread her legs wide and squatted, giving the audience a good look up her skirt. Her frog face leered, and it was an ugly, lustful thing. She lowered a hand to the stage behind her for support, and beckoned. "Come to momma," she crooned.

It was like knocking the chocks out from a dam. There was an instant of absolute stillness, and then the crowd roared and surged forward. An ocean of humanity converged on the stage, smashing through the police lines, climbing up on the wooden platform. Wolf had a brief glimpse of Maggie trying to struggle to her feet, before she was overrun. There was a dazed, disbelieving expression on her face.

"Mother of Sin," Wolf whispered. He stared at the mindless, evil mob below. They were in furious motion, straining, forcing each other in great swirling eddies. He waited for the stage to collapse, but it did not. The audience kept climbing atop it, pushing one another off its edge, and it did not collapse. It would have been a mercy if it had.

A hand waved above the crowd, clutching something that sparkled. Wolf could not make it out at first. Then another hand waved a glittering rag, and then another, and he realized that these were shreds of Maggie's dress.

Wolf wrapped his arms around a support to keep from falling into the horror below. The howling of the crowd was a single chaotic noise; he squeezed his eyes shut, vainly trying to fend it off. "Right on cue," Hawk muttered. "Right on goddamned cue." He cut off all the lights, and placed a hand on Wolf's shoulder.

"Come on. Our job is done here."

Wolf twisted to face Hawk. The act of opening his eyes brought on a wave of vertigo, and he slumped to the platform floor, still clutching the support desperately. He wanted to vomit, and couldn't. "It's—they—Hawk, did you *see* it? Did you see what they did? Why didn't someone—?" He choked on his words.

"Don't ask me," Hawk said bitterly. "I just play the part of Judas Iscariot in this little drama." He tugged at Wolf's shoulders. "Let's go, pilgrim. We've got to go down now." Wolf slowly weaned himself of the support, allowed himself to be coaxed down from the tower.

There were men in black uniforms at the foot of the tower. One of them addressed Hawk. "Is this the African national?" Then, to Wolf: "Please come with us, sir. We have orders to see you safely to your hostel."

Tears flooded Wolf's eyes, and he could not see the crowd, the Commons, the men before him. He allowed himself to be led away, as helpless and as trusting as a small child.

In the morning, Wolf lay in bed staring at the ceiling. A fly buzzed somewhere in the room, and he did not look for it. In the streets iron-wheeled carts rumbled by, and children chanted a counting out game.

After a time he rose, dressed, and washed his face. He went to the hostel's dining room for breakfast.

There, finishing off a piece of toast, was DiStephano.

"Good morning, Mr. Mbikana. I was beginning to think I'd have to send for you." He gestured to a chair. Wolf looked about, took it. There were at least three of the political police seated nearby.

DiStephano removed some documents from his jacket pocket handed them to Wolf. "Signed, sealed, and delivered. We made some minor changes in the terms, but nothing your superiors will object to." He placed the last corner of toast in the side of his mouth. "I'd say this was a rather bright beginning to your professional career."

"Thank you," Wolf said automatically. He glanced at the documents, could make no sense of them, dropped them in his lap.

"If you're interested, the *African Genesis* leaves port tomorrow morning. I've made arrangements that a berth be ready for you, should you care to take it. Of course, there will be another passenger ship in three weeks if you wish to see more of our country."

"No," Wolf said hastily. Then, because that seemed rude, "I'm most anxious to see my home again. I've been away far too long."

DiStephano dabbed at the corners of his mouth with a napkin, let it fall to the tablecloth. "Then that's that." He started rise.

"Wait," Wolf said. "Mr. DiStephano, I...I would very much like an explanation."

DiStephano sat back down. He did not pretend not to understand the request. "The first thing you must know," he said, "is that Ms. Horowitz was not our first Janis Joplin."

"No," Wolf said.

"Nor the second."

Wolf looked up.

"She was the twenty-third, not counting the original. The show is sponsored every year, always ending in Boston on the equinox. So far, it has always ended in the same fashion."

Wolf wondered if he should try to stab the man with a fork, if he should rise up and attempt to strangle him. There should be rage, he knew. He felt nothing. "Because of the brain implants."

"No. You must believe me when I say that I wish she had lived. The implants helped her keep in character, nothing more. It's true that she did not recall the previous women who played the part of Janis. But her death was not planned. It's simply something that—happens."

"Every year."

"Yes. Every year Janis offers herself to the crowd. And every year they tear her apart. A sane woman would not make the offer; a sane people would not respond in that fashion. I'll know that my country is on the road to recovery come the day that Janis lives to make a second tour." He paused. "Or the day we can't find a woman willing to play the role, knowing how it ends."

Wolf tried to think. His head felt dull and heavy. He heard the words, and he could not guess whether they made sense or not. "One last question," he said. "Why me?"

DiStephano rose. "One day you may return to our nation," he said. "Or perhaps not. But you will certainly rise to a responsible position within the Southwest Africa Trade Company. Your decisions will affect our economy." Four men in uniform also rose from their chairs. "When that happens, I want you to understand one thing about your land: *We have nothing to lose.* Good day, and a long life to you, sir."

DiStephano's guards followed him out.

It was evening. Wolf's ship rode in Boston harbor, waiting to carry him home. Away from this magic nightmare land, with its ghosts and walking dead. He stared at it and he could not make it real; he had lost all capacity for belief.

The ship's dinghy was approaching. Wolf picked up his bags.

GINUNGAGAP

Abigail checked out of Mother of Mercy and rode the translator web to Toledo Cylinder in Juno Industrial Park. Stars bloomed, dwindled, disappeared five times. It was a long trek, halfway around the sun.

Toledo was one of the older commercial cylinders, how given over almost entirely to bureaucrats, paper pushers, and free-lance professionals. It was not Abigail's favorite place to visit, but she needed work and 3M had already bought out of her contract.

The job broker had dyed his chest hairs blond and his leg hairs red. They clashed wildly with his green cache-sexe and turquoise jewelry. His fingers played on a keyout, brining up an endless flow of career trivia. "Cute trick you played," he said.

Abigail flexed her new arm negligently. It was a good job, but pinker than the rest of her. And weak of course, but exercise would correct that. "Thanks," she said. She laid the arm underneath one breast and compared the colors. It matched the nipple perfectly. Definitely too pink. "Work outlook any good?"

"Naw," the broker said. A hummingbird flew past his ear, a nearly undetectable parting of the air. "I see here that you applied for the Proxima colony."

"They were full up," Abigail said. "No openings for a gravity bum, hey?"

"I didn't say that," the broker grumbled. "I'll find—hello! What's this?" Abigail craned her neck, couldn't get a clear look at the screen. "There's a tag on your employment record."

"What's that mean?"

"Let me read." A honeysuckle flower fell on Abigail's hair, and she brushed it off impatiently. The broker had an open-air office, framed by hedges and roofed over with a trellis. Sometimes Abigail found the older Belt cylinders a little too lavish for her taste.

"Mmp" The broker looked up. "Bell-Sandia wants to hire you. Indefinite term one-shot contract." He swung the keyout around so she could see. "*Very* nice terms, but that's normal for a high-risk contract."

"High risk? From B-S, the Friendly Communications People? What kind of risk?"

The broker scrolled up new material. "There." He tapped the screen with a finger. "The language is involved, but what it boils down to is they're looking for a test passenger for a device they've got that uses black holes for interstellar travel."

"Couldn't work," Abigail said. "The tidal forces—"

"Spare me. Presumably they've found a way around that problem. The question is, are you interested or not?"

Abigail stared up through the trellis at a stream meandering across the curved land overhead. Children were wading in it. She counted to a hundred very slowly, trying to look as if she needed to think it over.

Abigail strapped herself into the translation harness and nodded to the technician outside the chamber. The tech touched her console, and a light stasis field immobilized Abigail and the air about her while the chamber wall irised open. In a fluid bit of technological sleight-of-hand, the translator rechanneled her inertia and gifted her with a velocity almost, but not quite, that of the speed of light.

Stars bloomed about her, and the sun dwindled. She breathed in deeply and—

—was in the receiver device. Relativity had cheated her of all but a fraction of the transit time. She shrugged out of harness and frog-kicked her way to the lip station's tugdock.

The tug pilot grinned at her as she entered, then turned his attention to his controls. He was young and wore streaks of brown makeup across his chest and thighs—only slightly darker than his skin. His mesh vest was almost in bad taste. But he wore it well, and looked roguish rather than over-dressed. Abigail found herself wishing she had more than a cache-sexe and nail polish on—some jewelry or makeup, perhaps. She felt drab in comparison.

The starfield wraparound held two inserts routed in by synchronous cameras. Alphanumerics flickered beneath them. One showed her immediate destination, the Bell-Sandia base *Arthur C. Clarke*. It consisted of five wheels, each set inside the other and rotating at slightly differing speeds. The base was done up in red-and-orange supergraphics. Considering its distance from the Belt factories, it was respectably sized.

Abigail latched herself into the passenger seat as the engines cut in. The second inert—

Ginungagap, the only known black hole in the sun's gravity field, was discovered in 2023, a small voice murmured. *Its presence explained the long-puzzling variations in the orbits of the outer planets. The* Arthur C. Clarke *was*

"Is this necessary?" Abigail asked.

"Absolutely," the pilot said. "We abandoned the tourist program a year or so ago, but somehow the rules never caught up. They're very strict about the regs here." He winked at Abigail's dismayed expression. "Hold tight a minute while—" His voice faded as he tinkered with the controls.

established forty years later and communications with the Proxima colony began shortly thereafter. Ginungagap

The voice cut off. She grinned thanks. "Abigail Vanderhoek."

"Cheyney," the pilot said. "You're the gravity bum, right?"

"Yeah."

"I used to be a vacuum bum myself. But I got tired of it, and grabbed the first semipermanent contract that came along."

"I kind of went the other way."

"Probably what I should have done," Cheyney said amiably. "Still, it's a rough road. I picked up three scars along the way." He pointed them out: a thick slash across his abdomen, a red splotch beside one nipple, and a white crescent half obscured by his scalp. "I could've had them cleaned up, but the way I figure, life is just a process of picking up scars and experience. So I kept 'em."

If she had thought he was trying to impress her, Abigail would have slapped him down. But it was clearly just part of an ongoing self-dramatization, possibly justified, probably not. Abigail suspected that, tour trips to Earth excepted, the *Clarke* was as far down a gravity well as Cheyney had ever been. Still, he did have an irresponsible boyish appeal. "Take me past the net?" she asked.

Cheyney looped the tug around the communications net trailing the *Clarke*. Kilometers of steel lace passed beneath them. He pointed out a small dish antenna on the edge and a cluster of antennae on the back. "The loner on the edge transmits into Ginungagap," he said. "The others relay information to and from Mother."

"Mother?"

"That's the traditional name for the *Arthur C. Clarke*." He swung the tug about with a careless sweep of one arm, and launched into a long and scurrilous story about the origin of the nickname. Abigail laughed, and Cheyney pointed a finger. "There's Ginungagap."

Abigail peered intently. "Where? I don't see a thing?"

She glanced at the second wraparound insert, which displayed a magnified view of the black hole. It wasn't at all impressive; a red smear against black nothingness. In the starfield it was all but invisible.

"Disappointing, hey? But still dangerous. Even this far out, there's a lot of ionization from the accretion disk."

"Is that why there's a lip station?"

"Yeah. Particle concentration varies, but if the translator were right at the *Clarke*, we'd probably lose about a third of the passengers."

Cheyney dropped Abigail off at Mother's crewlock and looped the tug off and away. Abigail wondered where to go, what to do now.

"You're the gravity bum we're dumping down Ginungagap." The short, solid man was upon her before she saw him. His eyes were intense. His cache-sexe was a conservative orange. "I liked the stunt with the arm. It takes a lot of guts to do something like that." He pumped her arm. "I'm Paul Gerard. Head of external security. In charge of your training. You play verbal Ping-Pong?"

"Why do you ask?" she countered automatically.

"Don't you know?"

"Should I?"

"Do you mean now or later?"

"Will the answer be different later?"

A smile creased Paul's face. "You'll do." He took her arm, led her long a sloping corridor. "There isn't much prep time. The dry run is scheduled in two weeks. Things will move pretty quickly after that. You want to start your training now?"

"Do I have a choice?" Abigail asked, amused.

Paul came to a dead stop. "Listen," he said. "Rule number one. Don't play games with *me*. You understand? Because I always win. Not sometimes, not usually—always."

Abigail yanked her arm free. "You maneuvered me into that," she said angrily.

"Consider it part of your training." He stared directly into her eyes. "No matter how many gravity wells you've climbed down, you're still the product of a near-space culture—protected, trusting, willing to take things at face value. This is a dangerous attitude, and I want you to realize it. I want you to look behind the mask of events. I want you to grow up. And you will."

Don't be so sure. A small smile quirked Paul's face as if he could read her thoughts. Aloud, Abigail said, "That sounds a little excessive for a trip to Proxima."

"Lesson number two," Paul said. "Don't make easy assumptions. You're not going to Proxima." He led her outward—down the ramp to the next wheel, pausing briefly at the juncture to acclimatize to the slower rate of revolution. "You're going to visit spiders." He gesture. "The crewroom is this way."

The crewroom was vast and cavernous, twilight gloomy. Keyouts were set up along winding paths that wandered aimlessly through the workspace. Puddles of light fell on each board and operator. Dark-loving foliage was set between the keyouts.

"This is the heart of the beast," Paul said. "The green keyouts handle all Proxima communications—pretty routine by now. But the blue..." His eyes glinting oddly, he pointed. Over the keyouts hung silvery screens with harsh grainy images floating on their surfaces, black-and-white blobs that Abigail could not resolve into recognizable forms.

"Those," Paul said, "are the spiders. We're talking to them in real time. Response delay is almost all due to machine translation."

In a sudden shift of perception, the blobs became arachnid forms. That mass of black flickering across the screen was a spiderleg and *that* was its thorax. Abigail felt an immediate primal aversion, and then it was swept away by an all-encompassing wonder.

"Aliens?" she breathed.

"Aliens."

They actually looked no more like spiders than humans looked like apes. The eight legs had an extra joint each, and the mandible configuration was all wrong. But to an untrained eye they would do.

"But this is—how long have you—why in God's name are you keeping this a secret?" An indefinable joy arose in Abigail. This opened a universe of possibilities, as if after a lifetime of being confined in a box someone had removed the lid.

"Industrial security," Paul said. "The gadget that'll send you through Ginungagap to *their* black hole is a spider invention. We're trading optical data for it, but the law won't protect our rights until we've demonstrated its use. We don't want the other corporations cutting in." He nodded toward the nearest black-and-white screen. "As you can see, they're weak on optics."

"I'd love to talk…" Abigail's voice trailed off as she realized how little-girl hopeful she sounded.

"I'll arrange an introduction."

There was a rustling to Abigail's side. She turned and saw a large black tomcat with white boots and belly emerge from the bushes. "This is the esteemed head of Alien Communications," Paul said sourly.

Abigail started to laugh, choked it back in embarrassment as she realized that he was not speaking of the cat. "Julio Dominguez, section chief for translation," Paul said. "Abigail Vanderhoek, gravity specialist."

The wizened old man smiled professorially. "I assume our resident gadfly has explained how the communications net works, has he not?"

"Well—" Abigail began.

Dominguez clucked his tongue. He wore a yellow cache-sexe and matching bow tie; just a little too garish for a man his age. "Quite simple, actually. Escape velocity from a black hole is greater than the speed of light. Therefore, within Ginungagap the speed of light is no longer the limit to the speed of communications."

He paused just long enough for Abigail to look baffled. "Which is just a stuffy way of saying that when we aim a stream of electrons into the boundary of the stationary limit, they emerge elsewhere—out of another black hole. And if we aim them *just so*"—his voice rose whimsically— "they'll emerge from the black hole of our choosing. The physics is simple. The finesse is in aiming the electrons."

The cat stalked up to Abigail, pushed its forehead against her leg, and mewed insistently. She bent over and picked it up. "But nothing can emerge from a black hole," she objected.

Dominguez chuckled. "Ah, but anything can fall in, hey? A positron can fall in. But a positron falling into Ginungagap in positive time is only an electron falling out in negative time. Which means that a positron falling into a black hole in negative time is actually an electron falling out in positive time—exactly the effect we want. Think of Ginungagap as being the physical manifestation of an equivalence sign in mathematics."

"Oh," Abigail said, feeling very firmly put in her place. Three white moths flittered along the path. The cat watched, fascinated, while she stroked its head.

"At any rate, the electrons do emerge, and once the data is in, the theory has to follow along meekly."

"Tell me about the spiders," Abigail said, before he could continue. The moths were darting up, sideward, down, a chance ballet in three dimensions.

"The *aliens*," Dominguez said, frowning at Paul, "are still a mystery to us. We exchange facts, descriptions, recipes for tools, but the important questions to not lend themselves to our clumsy mathematical codes. Do they know of love, do they appreciate beauty? Do they believe in God, hey?"

"Do they want to eat us?" Paul threw in.

"Don't be ridiculous," Dominguez snapped. "Of course they don't."

The moths parted when they came to Abigail. Two went to either side; one flew over her shoulder. The cat batted at it with one paw. "The cat's name is Garble," Paul said. "The kids in Bio cloned him up."

Dominguez opened his mouth, closed it again.

Abigail scratched Garble under the chin. He arched his neck and purred all but noiselessly. "With your permission," Paul said. He stepped over to a keyout and waved its operator aside.

"Technically you're supposed to speak a convenience language, but if you keep it simple and nonidiomatic, there shouldn't be any difficulty." He touched the keyout. "Ritual greetings, spider." There was a blank pause. Then the spider moved a hairy leg flickering across the screen.

"Hello, human."

"Introductions: Abigail Vanderhoek. She is our representative. She will ride the spinner." Another pause. More leg waving.

"Hello, Abigail Vanderhoek. Transition of vacuum garble resting garble commercial benefits garble still point in space."

"Tricky translation," Paul said. He signed to Abigail to take over.

Abigail hesitated, then said, "Will you come to visit us? The way we will visit you?"

"No, you see—" Dominguez began, but Paul waved him to silence.

"No, Abigail Vanderhoek. We are sulfur-based life."

"I do not understand."

"You can garble black hole through garble spinner because you are carbon-based life. Carbon forms chains easily, but sulfur combines in lattices or rosettes. Our garble simple form garble. Sometimes sulfur forms short chains.

"We'll explain later," Paul said. "Go on, you're doing fine."

Abigail hesitated again. What do you say to a spider, anyway? Finally, she asked, "Do you want to eat us?"

"Oh, Christ, get her off that thing," Dominguez said, reaching for the keyout.

Paul blocked his arm. "No," he said. "I want to hear this."

Several of the spiderlegs wove intricate patterns. "The question is false. Sulfur-based life derives no benefit from eating carbon-based life."

"You see," Dominguez said.

"But if it were possible," Abigail persisted. "If you *could* eat us and derive benefit. Would you?"

"Yes, Abigail Vanderhoek. With great pleasure."

Dominguez pushed her aside. "We're terribly sorry," he said to the alien. "This is a horrible, horrible misunderstanding. You!" he shouted to the operator. "Get back on and clear this mess up."

Paul was grinning wickedly. "Come," he said to Abigail. "We've accomplished enough here for one day."

As they stared to walk away, Garble twisted in Abigail's arms and leapt free. He hit the floor on all fours and disappeared into the greenery. "Would they really eat us?" Abigail asked. Then amended it to, "Does that mean they're hostile?"

Paul shrugged. "Maybe they thought we'd be insulted if they *didn't* offer to eat us." He led her to her quarters. "Tomorrow we start training for real. In the meantime, you might make up a list of all the ways the spiders could hurt us if we set up transportation and they *are* hostile. Then another list of all the reasons we shouldn't trust them." He paused. "I've done it myself. You'll find that the lists get rather extensive."

*   *   *

Abigail's quarters weren't flashy, but they fit her well. A full starfield was routed to the walls, floor, and ceiling, only partially obscured by a trellis inner-frame that supported foxgrape vines. Somebody had research into her tastes.

"Hi." The cheery greeting startled her. She whirled, saw that her hammock was occupied.

Cheyney sat up swung his legs over the edge of the hammock, causing it to rock lightly. "Come on in." He touched an invisible control, and the starfield blueshifted down to a deep erotic purple.

"Just what do you think you're doing here?" Abigail asked.

"I had a few hours free," Cheyney said, "so I thought I'd drop by and seduce you."

"Well, Cheyney, I appreciate your honesty," Abigail said. "So I won't say no."

"Thank you."

"I'll say maybe some other time. Now get lost. I'm tired."

"Okay." Cheyney hopped down, walked jauntily to the door. He paused. "You said 'later,' right?"

"I said *maybe* later."

"Later. Gotcha." He winked and was gone.

Abigail threw herself into the hammock, redshifted the starfield until the universe was a sparse smattering of dying embers. Annoying creature! There was no hope for anything more than the most superficial of relationships with him. She closed her eyes, smiled. Fortunately, she wasn't currently in the market for a serious relationship.

She slept.

✸

She was falling...

Abigail had landed the ship an easy walk from 3M's robot laboratory. The lab's geodesic dome echoed white clouds to the north, where Nix Olympus peeked over the horizon. Otherwise all—land, sky, rocks—was standard-issue Martian orange. She had clambered to the ground and shrugged on the supply backpack.

Resupplying 3M-RL stations was a gut contract; easy but dull. So perhaps she was less cautious than usual going down the steep rock-strewn hillside, or perhaps the rock would have turned under her no matter how carefully she placed her feet. Her ankle twisted and she lurched sideways, but the backpack had shifted her center of gravity too much for her to be able to recover.

Arms windmilling, she fell.

The rockslide carried her downhill in a panicky flurry of dust and motion, tearing her flesh and splintering her bones. But before she could feel pain, her suit shot her full of a nerve synesthetic, translating sensation into colors:

reds, russets, and browns, with staccato yellow spikes when a rock slammed into her ribs. So that she fell in a whirling rainbow of glorious light.

She came to rest in a burst of orange. The rocks were settling about her. A spume of dust drifted away, out toward the distant red horizon. A large jagged slab of stone slid by, gently shearing off her backpack. Tools, supplies, airpacks, flew up and softly rained down.

A spanner as long as her arm slammed down inches from Abigail's helmet. She flinched and suddenly events became real. She kicked her legs, and sand and dust fountained up. Drawing her feet under her body— the one ankle bright gold—she started to stand.

And was jerked to the ground by a sudden tug on one arm. Even as she turned her head, she became aware of a deep, profound purple sensation in her left hand. It was pinioned by a rock not quite large enough to stake a claim to. There was no color in the fingers.

"Cute," she muttered. She tugged at the arm, pushed at the rock. Nothing budged.

Abigail nudged the radio switch with her chin. "Grounder to Lip Station," she said. She hesitated, feeling foolish, then said, "Mayday. Repeat, Mayday. Could you guys send a rescue party down for me?"

There was no reply. With a sick green feeling in the pit of her stomach, Abigail reached a gloved hand around the back of her helmet. She touched something jagged, a sensation of mottled rust, the broken remains of her radio.

"I think I'm in trouble." She said it aloud and listened to the sound of it. Flat, unemotional—probably true. But nothing to get panicky about.

She took quick stock of what she had to work with. One intact suit and helmet. One spanner. A worldful of rocks, many close at hand. Enough air for—she checked the helmet readout—almost an hour. Assuming the lip station ran its checks on schedule and was fast on the uptake, she had almost half the air she needed.

Most of the backpack's contents were scattered too far away to reach. One rectangular gaspack, however, had landed nearby. She reached for it but could not touch it; squinted but could not read the label on its nozzle. It was almost certainly liquid gas—either nitrogen or oxygen—for the robot lab. But there was a slim chance it was the spare airpack. If it was, she might live to be rescued.

Abigail studied the landscape carefully, but there was nothing more. "Okay, then, it's an airpack." She reached as far as her tethered arm would allow. The gaspack remained a tantalizing centimeter out of reach.

For an instant she was stymied. Then, feeling like an idiot, she grabbed the spanner. She hooked it over the gaspack. Felt the gaspack move grudgingly. Slowly nudged it toward herself.

By the time Abigail could drop the spanner and draw in the gaspack, her good arm was blue with fatigue. Sweat running down her face, she juggled the gaspack to read its nozzle markings.

It was liquid oxygen—useless. She could hook it to her suit and feed in the contents, but the first breath would freeze her lungs. She released the gaspack and lay back, staring vacantly at the sky.

Up there was civilization; tens of thousands of human stations strung together by webs of communication and transportation. Messages flowed endlessly on laser cables. Translators borrowed and lent momentum, moving streams of travelers and cargo at almost (but not quite) the speed of light. A starship was being readied to carry a third load of colonists to Proxima. Up there, free from gravity's relentless clutch, people lived in luxury and ease. Here, however…

"I'm going to die." She said it softly and was filled with wondering awe. Because it was true. She was going to die.

Death was a black wall. It lay before her, extending to infinity in all directions, smooth and featureless and mysterious. She could almost reach out an arm and touch it. Soon she would come up against it and, if anything lay beyond, pass through. Soon, very soon, she would *know*.

She touched the seal to her helmet. It felt grey—smooth and inviting. Her fingers moved absently, tracing the seal about her neck. With sudden horror, Abigail realized that she was thinking about undoing it, releasing her air, throwing away the little time she had left…

She shuddered. With sudden resolve, she reached out and unsealed the shoulder seam of her captive arm.

The seal clamped down, automatically cutting off air loss. The flesh of her damaged arm was exposed to the raw Martian atmosphere. Abigail took up the gaspack and cradled it in the pit of her good arm. Awkwardly, she opened the nozzle with the spanner.

She sprayed the exposed arm with liquid oxygen for over a minute before she was certain it had frozen solid. Then she dropped the gaspack, picked up the spanner, and swung.

Her arm shattered into a thousand fragments.

She stood up.

Abigail awoke, tense and sweaty. She blueshifted the walls up to normal light, and sat up. After a few minutes of clearing her head, she set the walls to cycle from red to blue in a rhythm matching her normal pulse. Eventually the womb-cycle lulled her back to sleep.

"Not even close," Paul said. He ran the tape backward, froze it on a still shot of the spider twisting two legs about each other. "That's the morpheme for 'extreme disgust,' remember. It's easy to pick out, and the language kids say any statement with this gesture should be reversed in meaning. Irony, see? So when the spider says that the strong should protect the weak, it means—"

"How long have we been doing this?"

"Practically forever," Paul said cheerily. "You want to call it a day?"

"Only if it won't hurt my standing."

"Hah! Very good." He switched off the keyout. "Nicely thought out. You're absolutely right; it would have. However, as a reward for realizing this, you can take off early *without* it being noted on your record."

"Thank you," Abigail said sourly.

Like most large installations, the *Clarke* had a dozen or so smaller structures tagging along after it in minimum maintenance orbits. When Abigail discovered that these included a small wheel gymnasium, she had taken to putting in an hour's exercise after each training shift. Today, she put in two.

The first hour she spent shadow-boxing and practicing savate in heavy-gee to work up a sweat. The second hour she spent in the axis room, performing free-fall gymnastics. After the first workout, it made her feel light and nimble and good about her body.

She returned from the wheel gym sweaty and cheerful to find Cheyney in her hammock again. "Cheyney," she said, "this is not the first time I've had to kick you out of there. Or even the third, for that matter."

Cheyney held his palms up in mock protest. "Hey, no," he said. "Nothing like that today. I just came by to watch the raft debate with you."

Abigail felt pleasantly weary, decided uncerebral. "Paul said something about it, but…"

"Turn it on, then. You don't want to miss it." Cheyney touched her wall, and a cluster of images sprang to life at the far end of the room.

"Just what is a raft debate, anyway?" Abigail asked, giving in gracefully.

She hoisted herself onto the hammock, sat beside him. They rocked gently for a moment.

"There's this raft, see? It's adrift and powerless, and there's only enough oxygen on board to keep one person alive until rescue. Only there are three on board—two humans and a spider."

"Do spiders breathe oxygen?"

"It doesn't matter. This is a hypothetical situation." Two-thirds of the image area were taken up by Dominguez and Paul, quietly waiting for the debate to begin. The remainder showed a flat spider image.

"Okay, what then?"

"They argue over who gets to survive. Dominguez argues that he should, since he's human and human culture is superior to spider culture. The spider argues for himself and its culture." He put an arm around her waist. "You small nice."

"Thank you." She ignored the arm. "What does Paul argue?"

"He's the devil's advocate. He argues that no one deserves to live and they should dump the oxygen."

"Paul would enjoy that role," Abigail said. Then, "What's the point to this debate?"

"It's an entertainment. There isn't *supposed* to be a point."

Abigail doubted it was that simple. The debate could reveal a great deal about the spiders and how they thought, once the language types were done with it. Conversely, the spiders would doubtless be studying the human responses. *This could be interesting* , she thought. Cheyney was stroking her side now, lightly but with great authority. She postponed reaction, not sure whether she liked it or not.

Louise Chang, a vaguely highly placed administrator, blossomed in the center of the image cluster. "Welcome," she said, and explained the rules of the debate. "The winner will be decided by acclaim," she said, "with half the vote being human and half alien. Please remember not to base your vote on racial chauvinism, but on the strengths of the arguments and now well they are presented." Cheyney's hand brushed casually across her nipples; they stiffened. The hand lingered. "The debate will begin with the gentleman representing the aliens presenting his thesis."

The image flickered as the spider waved several arms. "Thank you, Ms. Chairman. I argue that I should survive. My culture is superior because of our technological advancement. Three examples. Humans have used translation travel only briefly, yet we have used it for sixteens of garble.

Our black-hole technology is superior. And our garble has garble for the duration of our society."

"Thank you. The gentleman representing humanity?"

"Thank you, Ms. Chairman." Dominguez adjusted an armlet. Cheyney leaned back and let Abigail rest against him. Her head fit comfortably against his shoulder. "My argument is that technology is neither the sole nor most important measure of a culture. By these standards dolphins would be considered brute animals. The aesthetic considerations—the arts, theology, and the tradition of philosophy—are of greater import. As I shall endeavor to prove."

"He's chosen the wrong tactic," Cheyney whispered in Abigail's ear. "That must have come across as pure garble to the spiders."

"Thank you. Mr. Girard?"

Paul's image expanded. He theatrically swigged from a small flask and hoisted it high in the air. "Alcohol! There's the greatest achievement of the human race!" Abigail snorted. Cheyney laughed out loud. "But I hold that neither Mr. Dominguez nor the distinguished spider deserves to live, because of the disregard both cultures have for sentient life." Abigail looked at Cheyney, who shrugged. "As I shall endeavor to prove." His image dwindled.

Chang said, "The arguments will now proceed, beginning with the distinguished alien."

The spider and then Dominguez ran through their arguments, and to Abigail they seemed markedly lackluster. She didn't give them her full attention, because Cheyney's hands were moving most interestingly across unexpected parts of her body. He might not be too bright, but he was certainly good at some things. She nuzzled her face into his neck, gave him a small peck, returned her attention to the debate.

Paul blossomed again. He juggled something in his palm, held his hand open to reveal three ball bearings. "When I was a kid I used to short out the school module and sneak up to the axis room to play marbles." Abigail smiled, remembering similar stunts she had played. "For the sake of those of us who are spiders, I'll explain that marbles is a game played in free-fall for the purpose of developing coordination and spatial perception. You make a six-armed star of marbles in the center..."

One of the bearings fell from his hand, bounced noisily, and disappeared as it rolled out of camera range. "Well, obviously it can't be played here. But the point is that when you shoot the marble just right, it hits the end of one arm and its kinetic energy is transferred from marble to marble along that arm. So that the shooter stops and the marble at the far end of the arm flies away." Cheyney was stroking her absently now, engrossed in the argument.

"Now, we plan to send a courier into Ginungagap and out the spiders' back hole. At least, that's what we say we're going to do.

"But what exits from a black hole is not necessarily the same as what went into its partner hole. We throw an electron into Ginungagap and another one pops out elsewhere. It's identical. It's a direct causal relationship. But it's like the marbles—they're identical to each other and have the same kinetic force. It's simply not the same electron."

Cheyney's hand was still, motionless. Abigail prodded him gently, touching his inner thigh. "Anyone who's interested can see the equations. Now, when we send messages, this doesn't matter. The message is important, not the medium. However, when we send a human being in...what emerges from the other hole will be cell for cell, gene for gene, atom for atom identical. *But it will not be the same person.*" He paused for a beat, smiled.

"I submit, then, that this is murder. And further, that by conspiring to commit murder, both the spider and human races display absolute disregard for intelligent life. In short, no one on the raft deserves to live. And I rest my case."

"Mr. Girard!" Dominguez objected, even before his image was restored to full size. "The simplest mathematical proof is an identity: that A equals A. Are you trying to deny this?"

Paul held up the two ball bearings he had left. "These marbles are identical too. But they are not the same marble."

"We know the phenomenon you speak of," the spider said. "It is as if garble the black hole bulges out simultaneously. There is no violation of continuity. The two entities are the same. There is no death."

Abigail pulled Cheyney down, so that they were both lying on their sides, still able to watch the images. "So long as you happen to be the second marble and not the first," Paul said. Abigail tentatively licked Cheyney's ear.

"He's right," Cheyney murmured.

"No, he's not," Abigail retorted. She bit his earlobe.

"You mean that?"

"Of course I mean that. He's confusing semantics with reality." She engrossed herself in a study of the back of his neck.

"Okay."

Abigail suddenly sensed that she was missing something. "Why do you ask?" She struggled into a sitting position. Cheyney followed.

"No particular reason." Cheyney's hands began touching her again. But Abigail was sure something had been slipped past her.

They caressed each other lightly, while the debate dragged to an end. Not paying much attention, Abigail voted for Dominguez and Cheyney voted for Paul. As a result of a nearly undivided spider vote, the spider won. "I told you Dominguez was taking the wrong approach." Cheyney said. He hopped off the hammock. Look, I've got to see somebody about something. I'll be right back."

"You're not leaving *now*?" Abigail protested, dumbfounded. The door irised shut.

Angry and hurt, she leapt down, determined to follow him. She couldn't remember ever feeling so insulted.

Cheyney didn't try to be evasive; it apparently did not occur to him that she might follow. Abigail stalked him down a corridor, up an inramp, and to a door that irised open for him. She recognized that door.

Thoughtfully, she squatted on her heels behind an untrimmed boxwood and waited. A minute later, Garble wandered by, saw her, and demanded attention. "Scat!" she hissed. He butted his head against her knee. "Then be silent, at least." She scooped him up. His expression was smug.

The door irised open and Cheyney exited, whistling. Abigail waited until he was gone, stood, went to the door, and entered. Fish darted between long fronds under a transparent floor. It was an austere room, almost featureless. Abigail looked, but did not see a hammock.

"So Cheyney's working for you now," she said coldly. Paul looked up from a corner keyout.

"As a matter of fact, I've just signed him to permanent contract in the crewroom. He's bright enough. A bit green. Ought to do well."

"Then you admit that you put him up to grilling me about your puerile argument in the debate?" Garble struggled in her arms. She juggled him into a more comfortable position. "And that you staged the argument for my benefit in the first place?"

"Ah," Paul said. "I knew the training was going somewhere. You've become very wary in an extremely short time."

"Don't evade the question."

"I needed your honest reaction," Paul said. "Not the answer you would have given me, knowing your chances of crossing Ginungagap rode on it."

Garble made an angry noise. "You tell him Garble!" she said. "That goes double for me." She stepped out the door. "You lost the debate," she snapped.

Long after the door had irised shut, she could feel Paul's amused smile burning into her back.

❀

Two days after she returned to kick Cheyney out of her hammock for the final time, Abigail was called to the crewroom. "Dry run," Paul said. "Attendance is mandatory," and cut off.

They crewroom was crowded with technicians, triple the number of keyouts. Small knots of them clustered before the screens, watching. Paul waved her to him.

"There," he motioned to one screen. "That's Clotho—the platform we built for the transmission device. It's a hundred kilometers off. I wanted more, but Dominguez overruled me. The device that'll unravel you and dump you down Ginungagap is that doohickey in the center." He tapped a keyout, and the platform zoomed up to fill the screen. It was covered by a clear transparent bubble. Inside, a spacesuited figure was placing something into a machine that looked like nothing so much as a giant armor-clad clamshell.

"That's Garble," she said indignantly.

"Complain to Dominguez. I wanted a baboon."

The clamshell device closed. The spacesuited tech left in his tug, and alphanumerics flickered, indicating the device was in operation. As they watched, the spider-designed machinery immobilized Gable, transformed his molecules into one long continuous polymer chain, and spun it out in an invisible opening at near-light speed. The water in his body was separated out, piped away, and preserved. The electrolyte balances were recorded and simultaneously transmitted in a parallel stream of electrons. It would reach the spider receiver along with the lead end of the cat-polymer, to be used in the reconstruction.

Thirty seconds passed. Now Garble was only partially in Clotho. The polymer chain, invisible and incredibly long, was passing into Ginungagap. On the far side the spiders were beginning to knit it up.

It all was going well.

Ninety-two seconds after they flashed on, the alphanumerics stopped twinkling on the screen. Garble was gone from Clotho. The clamshell opened, and the remote cameras showed it to be empty. A cheer arose.

Somebody boosted Dominguez atop a keyout. Intercom cameras swivelled to follow. He wavered fractionally, said "My friends," and launched into a speech. Abigail didn't listen.

Paul's hand fell on her shoulder. It was the first time he had touched her since their initial meeting. "He's only a scientist," he said. "He had no idea how close you are to that cat."

"Look, I *asked* to go. I knew the risks. But Garble's just an animal; he wasn't given the choice."

Paul groped for words. "In a way, this is what your training has been about; the reason you're going across instead of someone like Dominguez. He projects his own reactions onto other people. If—"

Then, seeing that she wasn't listening, he said, "Anyway, you'll have a cat to play with in a few hours. They're only keeping him long enough to test out the life-support systems."

There was a festive air to the second gathering. The spiders reported that Garble had translated flawlessly. A brief visual display showed him stalking about Clotho's sister platform, irritable but apparently unharmed.

"There," somebody said. The screen indicated that the receiver net had taken in the running end of the cat's polymer chain. They waited a minute and a half, and the operation was over.

It was like a conjuring trick: the clamshell closed on emptiness. Water was piped in. Then it opened and Garble floated over its center, quietly licking one paw.

Abigail smiled at the homeliness of it. "Welcome back, Garble," she said quietly. "I'll get the guys in Bio to brew up some cream for you."

Paul's eyes flicked in her direction. They lingered for no time at all, long enough to file away another datum for future use, and then his attention was elsewhere. She waited until his back was turned and stuck out her tongue at him.

The tug docked with Clotho, and a technician floated in. She removed her helmet self-consciously, aware of her audience. One hand extended, she bobbed toward the cat, calling softly.

"Get that jerk on the line," Paul snapped. "I want her helmet back on. That's sloppy. That's real—"

And in that instant Garble sprang.

Garble was a black-and-white streak that flashed past the astonished tech, though the airlock, and into the open tug. The cat pounced on the pilot panel. Its forearms hit the controls. The hatch slammed shut, and the tug's motors burst into life.

Crewroom techs grabbed wildly at their keyouts. The tech on Clotho frantically tried to fit her helmet back on. And the tug took off, blasting away half the protective dome and all the platform's air.

The screens showed a dozen different scenes, lenses shifting from close to distant and back. "Cheyney," Paul said quietly. Dominguez was frozen, looking bewildered. "Take it out."

"It's coming right at us!" somebody shouted.

Cheyney's fingers flicked: rap-tap-rap.

A bright nuclear flower blossomed.

There was silence, dead and complete, in the crewroom. *I'm missing something*, Abigail thought. *We just blew up five percent of our tug fleet to kill a cat.*

"*Pull* that transmitter!" Paul strode through the crewroom, scattering orders. "Nothing goes out! You, you, and you"—he yanked techs away from their keyouts—"*off* those things. I want the whole goddamned net shut *down*."

"Paul…" an operator said.

"Keep on receiving." He didn't bother to look. "Whatever they want to send. Dump it all in storage and don't merge any of it with our data until we've gone over it."

Alone and useless in the center of the room, Dominguez stuttered. "What—what happened?"

"You blind idiot!" Paul turned on him viciously. "Your precious aliens have just made their first hostile move. The cat that came back was nothing like the one we sent. They made changes. They retransmitted it with instructions wetwired into its brain."

"But why would they want to steal a tug?"

"*We don't know!*" Paul roared. "Get that through your head. We don't know their motives, and we don't know how they think. But we would have known a lot more about their intentions than we wanted if I hadn't rigged that tug with an abort device."

"You didn't—" Dominguez began. He thought better of the statement.

"—have the authority to rig that device," Paul finished for him. "That's right. I didn't." His voice was heavy with sarcasm.

Dominguez seemed to shrivel. He stared bleakly, blankly, about him, then turned and left, slightly hunched over. Thoroughly discredited in front of the people who worked for him.

That was cold, Abigail thought. She marveled at Paul's cruelty. Not for an instant did she believe that the anger in his voice was real, that he was capable of losing control.

Which meant that in the midst of confusion and stress, Paul had found time to make a swift play for more power. To Abigail's newly suspicious eye, it looked like a successful one, too.

For five days, Paul held the net shut by sheer willpower and force of personality. Information came in but did not go out. Bell-Sandia administration was not behind him—too much time and money had been sunk into Clotho to abandon the project. But Paul had the support of the tech crew and he knew how to use it.

"Nothing as big as Bell-Sandia runs on popularity," Paul explained. "But I've got enough sympathy from above, and enough hesitation and official cowardice, to keep this place shut down long enough to get a message across."

The incoming information flow fluctuated wildly, shifting from subject to subject. Data sequences were dropped halfway through and incomplete. Nonsense came in. The spiders were shifting through strategies in search of the key that would reopen the net.

"When they start repeating themselves," Paul said, "we can assume they understand the threat."

"But we *wouldn't* shut the net down permanently," Abigail pointed out.

Paul shrugged. "So it's a bluff."

They were sharing an aftershift drink in a fifth-level bar. Small red lizards scuttled about the rock wall behind the bartender. "And if your bluff doesn't work?" Abigail asked. "If it's all for nothing—what then?"

Paul's shoulders sagged, a minute shifting of tensions. "Then we trust in the good will of the spiders," he said. "We let them call the shots. And they will treat us benevolently or not, depending. In either case," his voice became dark, "I'll have played a lot of games and manipulated a lot of people for no reason at all." He took her hand. "If that happens, I'd like to apologize." His grip was tight; his knuckles pale.

That night Abigail dreamt she was falling.

Light rainbowed all about her, in a violent splintering of bone and tearing of flesh. She flung out an arm, and it bounced on something warm and yielding.

"Abigail."

She twisted and tumbled, and something smashed into her ribs. Bright spikes of yellow darted up.

"Abigail!" Someone was shaking her, speaking loudly into her face. The rocks and sky went grey, were overlaid by unresolved images. Her eyelids struggled apart, fell together, opened.

"Oh," she said.

Paul rocked back on his heels. Fish darted about in the water beneath him. "There now," he said. Blue-green lights shifted gently underwater, moving in long, slow arcs. "Dream over?"

Abigail shivered, clutched his arm, let go of it almost immediately. She nodded.

"Good. Tell me about it."

"I—" Abigail began. "Are you asking me as a human being or in your official capacity?"

"I don't make that distinction."

She stretched out a leg and scratched her big toe, to gain time to think. She really didn't have any appropriate thoughts. "Okay," she said, and told him the entire dream.

Paul listened intently, rubbed a thumb across his chin thoughtfully when she was done. We hired you on the basis of that incident, you know," he said. "Coolness under stress. Weak body image. There were a lot of gravity bums to choose from. But I figured you were just a hair tougher, a little bit grittier."

"What are you trying to tell me? That I'm replaceable?"

Paul shrugged. "Everybody's replaceable. I just wanted to be sure you knew that you could back out if you want to. It wouldn't wreck our project."

"I don't want to back out." Abigail chose her words carefully, spoke them slowly, to avoid giving vent to the anger she felt building up inside. "Look, I've been on the gravity circuit for ten years. I've been everywhere in the system there is to go. Did you knew that there are less than two thousand people alive who've set foot on Mercury *and* Pluto? We've got a little club; we get together once a year." Seaweed shifted about her; reflections of the floor lights formed nebulous swimming shapes on the walls. "I've spent my entire life going around and around and around the sun, and never really getting anywhere. I want to travel, and there's nowhere left for me to go. So you offer me a way out and then ask if I want to back down. Like hell I do!"

"Why don't you believe that going through Ginungagap is death?" Paul asked quietly. She looked into his eyes, saw cool calculations going on behind them. It frightened her, almost. He was measuring her, passing judgment, warping events into long logical chains that did not take human factors into account. He was an alien presence.

"It's—common sense, is all. I'll be the same when I exit as when I go in. There'll be no difference, not an atom's worth, not a scintilla."

"The *substance* will be different. Eery atom will be different. Not a single electron in your body will be the same one you have now."

'Well, how does that differ so much from normal life?" Abigail demanded. "All our bodies are in constant flux. Molecules come and go. Bit by bit, we're replaced. Does that make us different people from moment to moment? 'All that is body is as coursing vapors,' right?"

Paul's eyes narrowed. "Marcus Aurelius. Your quotation isn't complete, though; it goes on: 'all that is of the soul is dreams and vapors.'"

"What's that supposed to mean?"

"It means that the quotation doesn't say what you claimed it did. If you were to read it literally, it argues the opposite of what you're saying."

"Still, you can't have it both ways. Either the me that comes out of the spider black hole is the same as the one who went in, or I'm not the same person I was an instant ago."

"I'd argue differently," Paul said. "But no matter. Let's go back to sleep."

He held out a hand, but Abigail felt no inclination to accept it. "Does that mean I've passed your test?"

Paul closed his eyes, stretched a little. "You're still reasonably afraid of dying, and you don't believe that you will," he said. "Yeah. You pass."

"Thanks a heap," Abigail said. They slept, not touching, for the rest of the night.

Three days later Abigail woke up and Paul was gone. She touched the wall and spoke his name. A recording appeared. "Dominguez has been called up to Administration," it said. Paul appeared slightly distracted; he had not looked directly into the recorder, and his image avoided Abigail's eyes. "I'm going to reopen the net before he returns. It's best we beat him to the punch." The recording clicked off.

Abigail routed an intercom call through to the crewroom. A small chime notified him of her call, and he waved a hand in combined greeting and direction to remain silent. He was hunched over a keyout. The screen above it came to life.

"Ritual greetings, spider," he said.

"Hello, human. We wish to pursue our previous inquiry: the meaning of the term 'art' which was used by the human Dominguez six-sixteenths of the way through his major presentation."

"That is a difficult question. To understand a definition of art, you must first know the philosophy of aesthetics. This is a comprehensive field of knowledge comparable to the study of perception. In many ways it is related."

"What is the trade value of this field of knowledge?"

Dominguez appeared, looking upset. He opened his mouth and Paul touched a finger to his own lips, nodding his head toward the screen.

"Significant. Our society considers art and science as being of roughly equal value."

"We will consider what to offer in exchange."

"Good. We also have a question for you. Please wait while we select the phrasing." He cut the translation lines, turned to Dominguez. "Looks like your raft gambit paid off. Though I'm surprised they bit at that particular piece of bait."

Dominguez looked weary. "Did they mention the incident with the cat?"

"No, nor the communications blackout."

The old man sighed. "I always felt close to the aliens," he said. "Now they seem—cold, inhuman." He attempted a chuckle. "That was almost a pun, wasn't it?"

"In a human, we'd call it a professional attitude. Don't let it spoil your accomplishment," Paul said. "This could be as big as optics." He opened the communications line again. "Our question is now phrased." Abigail noted he had not told Dominguez of her presence.

"Please go ahead."

"Why did you alter our test animal?"

Much leg waving. "We improved the ratios garble centers of perception garble wetware garble making the animal twelve-sixteenths as intelligent as a human. We thought you would be pleased." ·

"We were not. Why did the test animal behave in a hostile manner toward us?"

The spider's legs jerked quickly, and it disappeared from the screen. Like an echo, the machine said, "Please wait."

Abigail watched Dominguez throw Paul a puzzled look. In the background, a man with a leather sack looped over one shoulder was walking slowly along the twisty access path. His hand dipped into the sack, came out, sprinkled fireflies among the greenery. Dipped in, came out again. Even in the midst of crisis, the trivia of day-to-day existence went on.

The spider reappeared, accompanied by two of its own kind. Their legs interlaced and retreated rapidly, a visual pantomime of an excited conversation. Finally, one of their number addressed the screen.

"We have discussed the matter."

"So I see."

"It is our conclusion that the experience of translation through Ginungagap had a negative effect on the test animal. This was not anticipated. It is new knowledge. We know so little of the psychology of carbon-based life."

"You're saying the test animal was driven mad?"

"Key word did not translate. We assume understanding. Steps must be taken to prevent a recurrence of this damage. Can you do this?"

Paul said nothing.

"Is this the reason why communications were interrupted?"

No reply.

"There is a cultural gap. Can you clarify?"

"Thank you for your cooperation," Paul said, and switched the screen off. "You can set your people to work," he told Dominguez. "No reason why they should answer the last few questions, though."

"Were they telling the truth?" Dominguez asked wonderingly.

"Probably not. But at least now they'll think twice before trying to jerk us around again." He winked at Abigail, and she switched off the intercom.

They reran the test using a baboon shipped out from the Belt Zoological Gardens. Abigail watched it arrive from the lip station, crated and snarling.

"They're a lot stronger than we are," Paul said. "Very agile. If the spiders want to try any more tricks, we couldn't offer them better bait."

The test went smooth as silk. The baboon was shot through Ginungagap, held by the spiders for several hours, and returned. Exhaustive testing showed no tampering with the animal.

Abigail asked how accurate the tests were. Paul hooked his hands behind his back. "We're returning the baboon to the Belt. We wouldn't do that if we had any doubts. But—" He raised an eyebrow, asking Abigail to finish the thought.

"But if they're really hostile, they won't underestimate us twice. They'll wait for a human to tamper with."

Paul nodded.

✸

The night before Abigail's send-off they made love. It was a frenzied and desperate act, performed wordlessly and without tenderness. Afterward they lay together, Abigail idly playing with Paul's curls.

"Gail…" His head was hidden in her shoulder; she couldn't see his face. His voice was muffled.

"Mmmm?"

"Don't go."

She wanted to cry. Because as soon as he said it, she knew it was another test, the final one. And she also knew that Paul wanted her to fail it. That he honestly believed that traversing Ginungagap would kill her, and that the woman who emerged from the spiders' black hole would not be her.

His eyes were shut; she could tell by the creases in his forehead. He knew what her answer was. There was no way he could avoid knowing.

Abigail sensed that this was as close to a declaration of emotion as Paul was capable of. She felt how he despised himself for using his real emotions as yet another test, and how he could not even pretend to himself that there were circumstances under which he would *not* test her so. *This must be how it feels to think as he does,* she thought. *To constantly scrabble after every last implication, like eternally picking at a scab.*

"Oh, Paul," she said.

He wrenched about, turning his back to her. "Sometimes I wish"—his eyes rose in front of his face like claws; they moved toward his eyes, closed into fists—"that for just ten goddamned minutes I could turn my mind *off.* His voice was bitter.

Abigail huddled against him, looped a hand over his side and onto his chest. "Hush," she said.

✸

The tug backed away from Clotho, dwindling until it was one of a ring of bright sparks pacing the platform. Mother was a point source lost in the starfield. Abigail shivered, pulled off her armbands, and shoved them into a storage sack. She reached for her cache-sex, hesitated.

The hell with it, she thought. *It's nothing they haven't seen before.* She shucked it off, stood naked. Gooseflesh rose on the backs of her legs. She swam to the transmittal device, feeling awkward under the distant watching eyes.

Abigail groped into the clamshell. "Go," she said.

The metal closed about her seamlessly, encasing her in darkness. She floated in a lotus position, bobbing slightly.

A light gripping field touched her, stilling her motion. On cue, hypnotic commands took hold in her brain. Her breathing became shallow; her heart slowed. She felt her body ease into stasis. The final command took hold.

Abigail weighed fifty keys. Even though the water in her body would not be transmitted, the polymer chain she was to be transformed into would be two hundred seventy-five kilometers long. It would take fifteen minutes and seventeen seconds to unravel at light speed, negligibly longer at translation speed. She would still be sitting in Clotho when the spiders began knitting her up.

It was possible that Garble had gone mad from a relatively swift transit. Paul doubted it, but he wasn't taking any chances. To protect Abigail's sanity, the meds had wetwired a travel fantasy into her brain. It would blind her to external reality while she traveled.

She was an eagle. Great feathered wings extended out from her shoulders. Clotho was gone, leaving her alone in space. Her skin was red and leathery, her breasts hard and unyielding. Feathers covered her thighs, giving way at the knees to scaley talons.

She moved her wings, bouncing lightly against the thin solar wind swirling down into Ginungagap. The vacuum felt like absolute freedom. She screamed a predator's exultant shrill. Nothing enclosed her; she was free of restrictions forever.

Below her lay Ginungagap, the primal chasm, an invisible challenge marked by a reed smudge of glowing gases. It was inchoate madness, a gibbering impersonal force that wanted to draw her in, to crush her in its embrace. Its hunger was fierce and insatiable.

Abigail held her place briefly, effortlessly. Then she folded her wings and dove.

A rain of X rays stung through her, the scattering of Ginungagap's accretion disk. They were molten iron passing through a ghost. Shrieking defiance, she attacked, scattering sparks in her wake.

Ginungagap grew, swelled, until it swallowed up her vision. It was purest black, unseeable, unknowable, a thing of madness. It was Enemy.

A distant objective part of her knew that she was still in Clotho, the polymer chain being unraveled from her body, accelerated by a translator, passing through two black holes, and simultaneously being knit up by the spiders. It didn't matter.

She plunged into Ginungagap as effortlessly as if it were the film of a soap bubble.

In—

—and out.

It was like being reversed in a mirror, or watching an entertainment run backward. She was instantly flying out the way she came. The sky was a mottled mass of violet light.

The stars before her brightened from violet to blue. She craned her neck, looked back at Ginungagap, saw its disk-shaped nothingness recede, and screamed in frustration because it had escaped her. She spread her wings to slow her flight and—

—was sitting in a dark place. Her hand reached out, touched metal, recognized the inside of a clamshell device.

A hairlike crack of light looped over her, widened. The clamshell opened.

Oceans of color bathed her face. Abigail straightened, and the act of doing so lifted her up gently. She stared through the transparent bubble at a phosphorescent foreverness of light.

My God, she thought. *The stars.*

The stars were thicker, more numerous than she was used to, large and bright and glittery-rich. She was probably someplace significant, a star cluster or the center of the galaxy; she couldn't guess. She felt irrationally happy to simply *be*; she took a deep breath, then laughed.

"Abigail Vanderhoek."

She turned to face the voice and found that it came from a machine. Spiders crouched beside it, legs moving silently. Outside, in the hard vacuum, were more spiders.

"We regret any pain this may cause," the machine said.

Then the spiders rushed forward. She had no time to react. Sharp mandibles loomed before her, then dipped to her neck. Impossibly swift, they sliced through her throat, severed her spine. A sudden jerk, and her head was separated from her body.

It happened in an instant. She felt brief pain, and the dissociation of actually *seeing* her decapitated body just beginning to react. And then she died.

A spark. A light. *I'm alive*, she thought. Consciousness returned like an ancient cathode tube warming up. Abigail stretched slowly, bobbing gently in the air, collecting her thoughts. She was in the sister-Clotho again, not in pain, her head and neck firmly on her shoulders. There were spiders on the platform, and a few floating outside.

"Abigail Vanderhoek," the machine said. "We are ready to begin negotiations."

Abigail said nothing.

After a moment, the machine said, "Are you damaged? Are your thoughts impaired?" A pause, then, "Was your mind not protected during transit?"

"Is that you waving the legs there? Outside the platform?"

"Yes. It is important that you talk with the other humans. You must convey our questions. They will not communicate with us."

"I have a few questions of my own," Abigail said. "I won't cooperate until you answer them."

"We will answer any questions provided you neither garble nor garble."

"What do you take me for?" Abigail asked. "Of course I won't."

Long hours later she spoke to Paul and Dominguez. At her request, the spiders had withdrawn, leaving her lone. Dominguez looked drawn and haggard. "I swear we had no idea the spiders would attack you," Dominguez said. "We saw it on the screens. I was certain you'd been killed…" His voice trailed off.

"Well, I'm alive, no thanks to you guys. Just what *is* this crap about an explosive substance in my bones, anyway?"

"An explosive—I swear we know nothing of anything of the sort."

"A close relative to plastique," Paul said. "I had a small editing device attached to Clotho's translator. It altered roughly half the bone marrow in your sternum, pelvis and femurs in transmission. I'd hoped the spiders wouldn't pick up on it so quickly."

"You actually did," Abigail marveled. "The spiders weren't lying; they decapitated me in self-defense. What the holy hell did you think you were *doing*?"

"Just a precaution," Paul said. "We wetwired you to trigger the stuff on command. That way we could have taken out the spider installation if they'd tried something funny."

"Um," Dominguez said, "this *is* being recorded. What I'd like to know, Ms. Vanderhoek, is how you escaped being destroyed."

"I didn't," Abigail said. "The spiders killed me. Fortunately, they anticipated the situation and recorded the transmission. It was easy for them to re-create me—after they edited out the plastique."

Dominguez gave her an odd look. "You don't—feel anything particular about this?"

"Like what?"

"Well—" He turned to Paul helplessly.

"Like the real Abigail Vanderhoek died and you're simply a very realistic copy," Paul said.

"Look, we've been through this garbage before," Abigail began angrily.

Paul smiled formally at Dominguez. It was hard to adjust to seeing the two in flat black-and-white. "She doesn't believe a word of it."

"If you guys can pull yourselves up out of your navels for a minute," Abigail said, "I've got a line on something the spiders have that you want. They claim they've sent probes through their black hole."

"Probes?" Paul stiffened. Abigail could sense the thoughts coursing through his skull, of defenses and military applications.

"Carbon-hydrogen chain probes. Organic probes. Self-constructing transmitters. They've got a carbon-based secondary technology."

"Nonsense," Dominguez said. "How could they convert back to coherent matter without a receiver?"

Abigail shrugged. "They claim to have found a loophole."

"How does it work?" Paul snapped.

"They wouldn't say. They seemed to think you'd pay well for it."

"That's very true," Paul said slowly. "Oh, yes."

The conference took almost as long as her session with the spiders had. Abigail was bone weary when Dominguez finally said, "That ties up the official minutes. We now stop recording." A line tracked across the screen, was gone. "If you want to speak to anyone off the record, now's your chance. Perhaps there is someone close to you…"

"Close? No." Abigail almost laughed. "I'll speak to Paul alone, though."

A spider floated by outside Clotho II. It was a golden crablike being, its body slightly opalescent. It skittered along unseen threads strung between the open platforms of the spider star-city. "I'm listening," Paul said.

"You turned me into a bomb, you freak."

"So?"

"I could have been killed."

"Am I supposed to care?"

"You damn well ought to, considering the liberties you've taken with my fair white body."

"Let's get one thing understood," Paul said. "The woman I slept with, the woman I cared for, is dead. I have no feelings toward or obligations to you whatsoever."

"Paul," Abigail said. "*I'm not dead.* Believe me, I'd know if I were."

"How could I possibly trust what you think or feel? It could all be attitudes the spiders wetwired into you. We know they have the technology."

"How do you know that *your* attitudes aren't wetwired in? For that matter, how do you know anything is real? I mean, these are the most sophomoric philosophic questions there are. But I'm the same woman I was a few hours ago. My memories, opinions, feelings—they're all the same as they were. There's absolutely no difference between me and the woman you slept with on the *Clarke*."

"I know." Paul's eyes were cold. "That's the horror of it." He snapped off the screen.

Abigail found herself staring at the lifeless machinery. *God, that hurt,* she thought. *It shouldn't, but it hurt.* She went to her quarters.

The spiders had done a respectable job of preparing for her. There were no green plants, but otherwise the room was the same as the one she'd had on the *Clarke*. They'd even been able to spin the platform, giving her an adequate down-orientation. She sat in her hammock, determined to think pleasanter thoughts. About the offer the spiders had made, for example. The one she hadn't told Paul and Dominguez about.

Banned by their chemistry from using black holes to travel, the spiders needed a representative to see to their interests among the stars. They had offered her the job.

Or perhaps the plural would be more appropriate—they had offered her the jobs. Because there were too many places to go for one woman to handle them all. They needed a dozen, in time perhaps a hundred Abigail Vanderhoeks.

In exchange for licensing rights to her personality, the right to make as many duplicates of her as were needed, they were willing to give her the rights to the self-reconstructing black-hole platforms.

It would make her a rich woman—a hundred rich women—back in human space. And it would open the universe. She hadn't committed herself yet, but there was no way she was going to turn down the offer. The chance to see a thousand stars. No, she would not pass it by.

When she got old, too, they could create another Abigail from their recording, burn her new memories into it, and destroy her old body.

I'm going to see the stars, she thought. *I'm going to live forever.* She couldn't understand why she didn't feel elated, wondered at the sudden sense of melancholy that ran through her like the precursor of tears.

Garble jumped into her lap, offered his belly to be scratched. The spiders had recorded him, too. They had been glad to restore him to his unaltered state when she made the request. She stroked his stomach and buried her face in his fur.

"Pretty little cat," she told him. "I thought you were dead."

TROJAN HORSE

I t's all inside my head," Elin said wonderingly. It was trite. A chimney swift flew overhead, and she could feel its passage through her mind. A firefly landed on her knee. It pulsed cold fire, then spread its wings and was gone, and that was a part of her too.

"Please try not to talk too much." The wetware tech tightened a cinch on the table, adjusted a bone inductor. His red-and-green facepaint loomed over her, receded. "This will go much faster if you cooperate."

Elin's head felt light and airy. It was *huge*. It contained all of Magritte, from the uppermost terrace down to the trellis farms that circled the inner lake. Even the blue-and-white Earth that hovered just over one rock wall. They were all within her. They were all, she realized, only a model, the picture her mind assembled from sensory input. The exterior universe— the real universe—lay beyond.

"I feel giddy."

"Contrast high." The tech's voice was neutral, disinterested. "This is a very different mode of perception from what you're used to—you're stoned on the novelty."

A catwalk leading into the nearest farm rattled within Elin's mind as a woman in agricultural blues strode by, gourd-collecting bag swinging from her hip. It was night outside the crater, but biological day within, and the agtechs had activated tiers of arc lights at the cores of the farms. Filtered by greenery, the light was soft and watery.

"I could live like this forever."

"Believe me, you'd get bored." A rose petal fell on her cheek, and the tech brushed it off. He turned to face the two lawyers standing silently nearby. "Are the legal preliminaries over now?"

The lawyer in orangeface nodded. The one in purple said, "Can't her original personality be restored at all?"

Drawing a briefcase from his pocket, the wetware tech threw up a holographic diagram between himself and the witnesses. The air filled with intricate three-dimensional tracery, red-and-green lines interweaving and intermeshing.

"We've mapped the subject's current personality." He reached out to touch several junctions. "You will note that here, here, and here, we have what are laughingly referred to as impossible emotional syllogisms. Any one of these renders the subject incapable of survival."

A thin waterfall dropped from the dome condensers to a misty pool at the topmost terrace, a bright razor-slash through reality. It meandered to the edge of the next terrace, and fell again.

"A straight yes or no answer will suffice."

The tech frowned. "In theory, yes. In practical terms it's hopeless. Remember, her personality was never recorded. The accident almost completely randomized her emotional structure—technically she's not even human. Given a decade or two of extremely delicate memory probing, we could *maybe* construct a facsimile. But it would only resemble the original: it could never be the primary Elin Donnelly."

Elin could dimly make out the equipment for five more waterfalls, but they were not in operation at the moment. She wondered why.

The attorney made a rude noise. "Well then, go ahead and do it. I wash my hands of this whole mess."

The tech bent over Elin to reposition a bone inductor. "This won't hurt a bit," he promised. "Just pretend that you're at the dentist's, having your teeth replaced."

She ceased to exist.

The new Elin Donnelly gawked at everything she passed by-the desk workers in their open-air offices, a blacksnake sunning itself by the path, the stone stairways cut into the terrace walls. Coming off the topmost of these stairs, into a stand of sapling no higher than she, she stumbled and almost fell. Her companion caught her and roughly set her back on her feet.

"Try to pay attention," the lawyer said, frowning under her loops of purple facepaint. "We have a lot of detail work to go over."

Elin smiled vaguely. They broke out of the saplings into a meadow, and butterflies scattered at their approach. Her gaze went from them to a small cave in the cliffs ahead, then up to the stars, as jumpy and random as their flight.

"—so you'll be stuck on the Moon for a full lunation—almost a month—if you want to collect your settlement. I.G. Feuchtwaren will carry your expenses until then, drawing against their final liability. Got that?"

And then—suddenly, jarringly—Elin could focus again. She took a deep breath. "Yes," she said. "Yes, I—okay."

"Good." The attorney canceled her wetware, yanking the skull plugs and briskly wrapping them around her briefcase. "Then let's have a drink—it's been a long day."

They had arrived at the cave. "Hey, Hans!" the lawyer shouted. "Give us some service here, will you?"

A small man with the roguish face of a comic-opera troll popped into the open, work terminal in hand. "One minute," he said. "I'm on the direct flex time—got to wrap up what I'm working on first."

"Okay." The lawyer dropped to the grass and began toweling her lace. Elin watched, fascinated, as a new pattern of fine red-and-black lines, permanently tattooed into the skin, emerged from under the paint.

"Hey!" Elin said. "You're a Jesuit."

"You expected IGF to ship you a lawyer from Earth orbit?" She stuck out a hand. "Donna Landis, S.J. I'm the client-overseer for the Star Maker project, but I'm also available for spiritual guidance. Mass is at nine Sunday mornings."

Elin leaned back against the cliff. Grapevines rustled under her weight. Already she missed the blissed-out feeling of a few minutes before. "Actually, I'm an agnostic."

"You *were*. Things may have changed." Landis folded the towel into one pocket, unfolded a mirror from another. "Speaking of which, how do you like your new look?"

Elin studied her reflection. Blue paint surrounded her eyes, narrowing to a point at the bridge of her nose, swooping down in a long curve to the outside. It was as if she were peering through a large blue moth, or a pair of hawk wings. There was something magical about it, something glamorous. Something very unlike her.

"I feel like a raccoon," she said. "This idiot mask."

"Best get used to it. You'll be wearing it a lot."

"But what's the point?" Elin demanded. She was surprised by her own irritation. "So I've got a new personality; it's still *me* in here. I don't feel any weird compulsion to run amok with a knife or walk out an airlock without a suit. Nothing to warn the citizenry about, certainly."

"Listen," Landis said. "Right now you're like a puppy tripping over its own paws because they're too big for it. You're a stranger to yourself—you're going to feel angry when you don't expect to, get sentimental over surprising things. You can't control your emotions until you learn what they are. And until then, the rest of us deserve—"

"What'll you have?" Hans was back, his forehead smudged black where he had incompletely wiped off his facepaint.

"A little warning. Oh, I don't know, Hans. Whatever you have on tap."

"That'll be Chanty. And you?" he asked Elin.

"What's good?"

He laughed. "There's no such thing as a good lunar wine. The air's too moist. And even if it weren't, it takes a good century to develop an adequate vineyard. But the Chanty is your basic drinkable glug."

"I'll take that, then."

"Good. And I'll bring a mug for your friend, too."

"My friend?" She turned and saw a giant striding through the trees, towering over them, pushing them apart with two enormous hands. For a dizzy instant, she goggled in disbelief, and then the man shrank to human stature as she remembered the size of the saplings.

He grinned, joined them. "Hi. Remember me?"

He was a tall man, built like a spacejack, lean and angular. An untidy mass of black curls framed a face that was not quite handsome, but carried an intense freight of will.

"I'm afraid…"

"Tory Shostokovich. I reprogrammed you."

She studied his face carefully. Those *eyes*. They were fierce almost to the point of mania, but there was sadness there, too, and—she might be making this up—a hint of pleading, like a little boy who wants something so desperately he dare not ask for it. She could lose herself in analyzing the nuances of those eyes. "Yes," she said at last, "I see it now—the resemblance."

"I'm pleased." He nodded to the Jesuit. "Father Landis."

She eyed him skeptically. "You don't seem your usual morose self, Shostokovich. Is anything wrong?"

"No, it's just a special kind of morning." He smiled at some private joke, returned his attention to Elin. "I thought I'd drop by and get acquainted with my former patient." He glanced down at the ground, fleetingly shy, and then his eyes were bright and audacious again.

How charming, Elin thought. She hoped he wasn't *too* shy. And then had to glance away herself, the thought was so unlike her. "So you're a wetware surgeon," she said inanely.

Hans reappeared to distribute mugs of wine, then retreated to the cave's mouth. He sat down, workboard in lap, and patched in the skull-plugs. His face went stiff as the wetware took hold.

"Actually," Tony said, "I very rarely work as a wetsurgeon. An accident like yours is rare, you know—maybe once, twice a year. Mostly I work in wetware development. Currently I'm on the Star Maker project."

"I've heard that name before. Just what is it, anyway?"

Tory didn't answer immediately. He stared down into the lake, a cool breeze from above ruffling his curls. Elin caught her breath. *I hardly know this man,* she thought wildly. He pointed to the island in the center of the lake, a thin stony finger that was originally the crater's thrust cone.

"God lives on that island," he said.

Elin laughed. "Think how different human history would be if He'd had a sense of direction!" And then wanted to bite her tongue as she realized that he was not joking.

"Typical," Landis said, glowering at Tory. "Only an atheist would call her that."

"What do you *call* her, then?"

"A victim of technology." She swigged down a mouthful of wine. *"Jeez,* that's vile stuff."

"Uh, guys?" Elin said. "I'm not getting much of an answer."

Tory rubbed the back of his neck ruefully. *"Mea culpa.* Well, let me give you a little background. Most people think of wetware as being software for people. But that's too simplistic, because with machines, you start out blank—with a clean slate—and with people, there's some ten million years of mental programming already crammed into their heads.

"So to date we've been working *with* the natural wetware. We counterfeit surface traits—patience, alertness, creativity—and package them like so many boxes of bonemeal. But the human mind is vast and unmapped, and it's time to move into the interior, to do some basic research.

"And that's the Star Maker project. It's an exploration of the basic sub-structural programming of the mind. We've redefined the overstructure programs into an integrated system we believe will be capable of essence-programming, and in one-to-one congruence with the inherent substructure of the universe."

"What jargonistic rot!" Landis gestured at Elin's stoneware mug. "Drink up. The Star Maker is a piece of experimental theology that IGF dreamed up. As Tory said, it's basic research into the nature of the mind. The Vatican Synod is providing funding so we can keep an eye on it."

"Nipping heresy in the bud," Tory said sourly.

"That's a good part of it. IGF is trying to create a set of wetware that will reshape a human mind into the popular notion of God. Bad theology, but there it is. They want to computer-model the infinite. Anyway, the specs were drawn up, and it was tried out on—what was the name of the test subject?"

"Doesn't matter," Tory said quickly.

"Coral something-or-other."

Only half-listening by now, Elin unobtrusively studied Tory. He sat, legs wide, staring into the mug of Chanty. There were hard lines on his face, etched by who-knew-what experiences? *I don't believe in love at first sight,* Elin thought. Then again, who knew *what* she might believe in anymore? It was a chilling thought, and she retreated from it.

"So did this Coral become God?"

"Patience. Anyway, the volunteer was plugged in, wiped, reprogrammed, and interviewed. Nothing useful."

Tory raised a finger in objection. "In one hour we learned more about the structure and composition of the universe than in all of the history of science to date."

"It was deranged gibberish." She tapped Elin's knee. "We interviewed her, and then canceled the wetware. And what do you think happened?"

"I've never been big on rhetorical questions." She didn't take her eyes off Tory.

"She didn't come down. She was stuck there."

"Stuck?"

Tory plucked a blade of grass, let it fall. "What happened was that we had rewired her to absolute consciousness. She was not only aware of all her mental functions, she was in control of them—right down to the involuntary reflexes. Which also put her in charge of her own metaprogrammer."

"*Metaprogrammer* is just a buzzword for a bundle of functions by which the brain is able to make changes in itself," Landis threw in.

"Yeah. What we didn't take into account, though, was that she'd *like* being God. When we began deprogramming her, she simply overrode our instructions and reprogrammed herself back up."

"The poor woman," Elin said, in part because she knew it was expected of her. And yet—what a glorious experience, to be God! Something within her thrilled to it. It would almost be worth the price.

"Which leaves us with a woman who thinks she's God," Landis said. "I'm just glad we were able to hush it up. If word got out to some of those religious illiterates back on Earth—"

"Listen," Tory said. "I didn't really come here to talk shop. I wanted to invite my former patient on the grand tour of the Steam Grommet Works."

Elin looked at him at him blankly. "Steam…"

He swept an arm to take in all of Magritte, the green pillars and grey cliffs alike, and there was something proprietary in his gesture.

Landis eyed him suspiciously. "You two might need a chaperone," she said. "I think I'll tag along to keep you out of trouble."

Elin smiled sweetly. "Fuck off," she said.

A full growth of ivy covered Tory's geodesic trellis hut. He led the way in, stooping to touch a keyout by the doorway. "Something classical?"

"Please." And as he gently began removing her jumpsuit, the holotape sprang into being, surrounding them with rich reds and cobalt blues that coalesced into stained glass patterns in the air. Elin pulled back a bit and clapped her hands. "It's Chartres," she cried, delighted. "The cathedral at Chartres!"

"Mmmm." Tory teased her down onto the grass floor.

The north rose window swelled to fill the hut and slowly revolved overhead. It was all angels and doves, kings and prophets, with gold lilies surrounding the central rosette. Deep and powerful, infused with gloomy light, it lap-dissolved into the lancet of Sainte Anne.

One by one, the hundred and seventy-six windows of Chartres appeared in turn, wheeling about them, slow and stately at first, then more quickly. The holotape panned down the north transept to the choir, to the apse, and then up into the ambulatory. Swiftly then, it cut to the wounded Christ and the Beasts of Revelation set within the dark spaces of the west rose. The outer circle—the instruments of the Passion—closed about them.

Elin gasped.

The tape proceeded down the nave, window by window, still brightening, pausing at the Vendôme chapel and moving on. Until finally the oldest window, the Notre Dame de la Belle Verrière, fairly blazed in a frenzy of raw glory. A breeze rattled the ivy, and two leaves fell through the hologram to tap against their skin and slide to the ground.

The Belle Verrière held for a moment longer then faded again, the light darkening, and the colors ran and were washed away by a noiseless gust of rain.

Elin let herself melt into the grass, drained and lazy, not caring if she never moved again. Beside her Tory chuckled, playfully tickled her ribs. "Do you love me? Hey? Tell me you love me."

"Stop!" She grabbed his arms and bit him in the side—a small nipping bite, more threat than harm—ran a tongue across his left nipple. "Hey, listen, I hit the sack with you a half hour after we met. What do you want?"

"Want?" He broke her hold, rolled over on top of her, pinioning her wrists above her head. "I want you to know"—and suddenly he was absolutely serious, his eyes unblinking and glittery-hard—"that I love you. Without doubt or qualification. I love you more than words could ever express."

"Tory," she said. "Things like that take time." The wind had died down. Not a blade of grass stirred.

"No, they don't." It was embarrassing looking into those eyes; she refused to look away. "I feel it. I know it. I love every way, shape, and part of you. I love you beyond time and barrier and possibility. We were meant to be lovers, fated for it, and there is *nothing*, absolutely nothing, that could ever keep us apart." His voice was low and steady. Elin couldn't tell whether she was thrilled or scared out of her wits.

"Tory, I don't know—"

"Then wait," he said. "It'll come."

But it was a long night. And a restless hour after Tory had slipped easily into sleep, Elin put on her jumpsuit and went outside.

She walked into a gentle darkness, relieved by Earthshine and the soft glow of walking lights on the catwalks above. There was a rustling in the grass, and a badger passed within ten feet of her, intent on its nightly foraging. She wandered.

There was a lot that had to be sorted out. This evening, to begin with, this sudden sexual adventure. It was like nothing she had ever done before, and it forced her to admit to herself that she had been changed—that nothing was ever going to be the same for her again.

She found a secluded spot away from the cluster of huts Tory lived among, and hunkered down against a boulder. She thought back to her accident. And because it was a matter of stored memory, the images were crisp and undamaged.

Elin had been the end of her shift on Wheel Laboratory 19 in Henry Ford Orbital Industrial Park when it happened. She was doing development work in semiconductors.

"Theta is coming up to temperature," her workboard said.

"Check." Elin put the epsilon lab to bed and switched the controls over. Holding theta up flush against the hub cylinder, she gingerly mixed two molten alloys, one dense, the other light.

Wheel Lab 19 was shaped like a rimless bicycle wheel. Two dozen spindly arms spread out evenly from thick central hub. At various distances along the spokes were twenty-three sliding lab units and a single fixed workspace. The wheel rotated fast enough to give the workspace constant Earth-normal gravity.

When the mix began to cool, Elin dropped the lab a half-kilometer to the end of its arm. Mercury shifted between ballast tanks to keep the rotation constant, and the lab went from fractional Greenwich gravity to a full nine gees.

A dozen different readouts had to be checked. Elin felt a momentary petulant boredom, and then the workboard readjusted her wetware, jacking up her attentiveness so that she ran through the ritual in detached professional fascination.

As the new alloy cooled, its components tried to separate out, creating an even stratification gradient across the sample. Elin waited, unblinking, until all the readouts balanced, then swiftly jabbed a button and quick-froze the wafer. Using waldoes, she lifted the sample from its mold and placed it in a testing device.

"Measurements recorded. Delta is prepped."

"Check." Elin ran the lab back to the hub. The workboard adjusted her wetware again, damping down patience and widening scope of attention.

Deftly, she chose the same component alloys, varying the mix slightly, and set them to heat. By then the workboard was demanding her attention on chi.

It was all standard industrial wetware so far, no different from that used by thousands of research workers daily. But then the workboard gave the ten-second warning that the interfacing program was about to be shut off. Her fingers danced across the board, damping down reactions, putting the labs to bed. The wetware went quiescent.

With a shiver, Elin was herself again. She grabbed a towel and wiped off her facepaint. Then she leaned back and transluced the wall—might as well put her feet up until her replacement showed. Stretching, she felt the gold wetware wires angling from the back of her skull, lazily put off yanking them.

Was I really that indolent? Elin wondered.

Earth bloomed underfoot, crept over her shoulder and disappeared. New Detroit and New Chicago rose from the floor, their mirrors flashing as the twinned residential cylinders slid slowly upward. Bright industrial satellites gleamed to every side: zero-gee factories and fullerspheres, wheels, porcupines, barbells, and cargo grids.

Earth rose again, larger than a dinner plate. Its clouds were a dazzling white on the dayside. Cities gleamed softly in the night.

A load of cargo drifted by. It was a jumble of containers lashed together by nonmagnetic tape and shot into an orbit calculated to avoid the laser cables and power transmission beams that interlaced the Park. A bit of motion caught Elin's eye, and she swiveled to follow it.

A man was riding the cargo, feet braced against a green carton, hauling on a rope slipped through the lashings. He saw her and waved. She could imagine his grin through the mirrored helmet.

That's rather dashing, Elin thought.

Elin snorted, started to look away, and almost missed seeing it happen.

Somehow, in leaning back that fraction more, the cargohopper had put too much strain on the lashings. A faulty rivet popped, and the cargo began to slide. Brightly colored cartons drifted apart, and the man went tumbling end-over-end away.

One end of the lashing was still connected to an anchor carton, and the free end writhed like a wounded snake. A bright bit of metal—the failed rivet—broke free and flew toward the juncture of the wheel lab's hub and spokes.

Reliving the incident, Elin's first reaction was to somehow help the man, to suit up and go out with a lifeline before Traffic Control scooped him up.

The old Elin Donnelly snickered. Traffic Control was going to come down on the jerk with both feet, and serve him right too. He was going to have to pay salvage fines not only for the scattered cargo but for himself as well. Which is what you got when you go looking for a free ride.

She was still smiling sardonically when the rivet struck the lab, crashing into a nest of wiring that *should not* have been exposed.

Two wires short-circuited, sending a massive power transient surging up through the workboard. Circuits fused and incited. The board went haywire.

And a microjolt of electricity leaped up two gold wires, hopelessly scrambling the wetware through Elin's skull.

For a moment, everything was blank. Then—"Whooh." Elin shook her head, reached back, and unplugged the leads. She laughed weakly to herself. Without bothering to opaque the walls, Elin unjugged a vacuum suit and began to climb the workspace arm to the hub. Ballast tanks whispered to her each time her hands touched a rung. Rings of lights paced her up the arm. She floated into the hub, and the touch of weightlessness was as cold as death.

Automatically, Elin set the mass driver for New Detroit. Through the hub aperture, she could see the twin residential cylinders, oblong lozenges, either of which she could hide with one thumb. Something within her shrieked and gibbered with the desire to pluck them from the sky, dash them to the ground.

"Something is very wrong with my mind," Elin said aloud. She giggled merrily as magnetic forces tugged at the metal hands of her suit, accelerated her to speed, and flung her out into the void.

An hour later the medics recovered her body from New Detroit's magnetic receiving net. It was curled in on itself, arms wrapped about knees, in a fetal position. When they peeled her out of the suit, Elin was alternating between hysterical gusts of laughter and dark gleeful screams.

Morning came, and after a sleepy, romantic breakfast, Tory plugged into his briefcase and went to work. Alone again, Elin wandered off to do some more thinking.

There was no getting around the fact that she was not the metallurgist from Wheel Lab 19, not anymore. That woman was alien to her now. They shared memories, experiences—but how differently they saw things! She no longer understood that woman, could not sympathize with her emotions, indeed found her distasteful.

Elin strolled downslope because that was easiest. She stopped at an administrative cluster and rented a briefcase. Then, at a second-terrace café that was crowded with off-shift biotechs, she rented a table and sat down to try to trace the original owner of her personality.

As Elin had suspected, she found that her new persona was indeed copied from that of a real human being; creating a personality from whole cloth was still beyond the abilities of even the best wetware techs. She was able to determine that it had come from IGF's inventory, and that duplication of personality was illegal—which presumable meant that the original owner was dead.

But she could not locate the original owner. Selection had been made by computer, and the computer wouldn't tell. When she tried to find out, it referred her to the Privacy Act of 2037.

"I think I've exhausted all of the resources of self-discovery available to me," she told the waiter when he came to collect his tip. "And I've still got half the morning left to kill."

He glanced at her powder-blue facepaint, and smiled politely.

"It's selective black."

"Hah?" Elin turned away from the lake, found that an agtech carrying a long-handled net had come up behind her.

"The algae—it absorbs light into the infrared. Makes the lake a great thermal sink." The woman dipped her net into the water, seined up a netful of dark green scum, and dumped it into a nearby trough. Water drained away through the porous bottom.

"Oh," Elin stared at the island. There were a few patches of weeds where drifting soil had settled. "It's funny. I never used to be very touristy. More the contemplative type, sort of homebodyish. Now I've got to be *doing* something, you know?"

The agtech dumped another load of algae into the trough. "I couldn't say." She tapped her forehead. "It's the wetware. If you want to talk shop, that's fine. Otherwise, I can't."

"I see." Elin dabbed a toe in the warm water. "Well—why not? Let's talk shop."

Someone was moving at the far edge of the island. Elin craned her neck to see. The agtech went on methodically dipping her net into the lake as God walked into view.

"The lake tempers the climate, see. By day it works by evaporative cooling. Absorbs the heat, loses it to evaporation, radiates it out the dome roof via the condensers."

Coral was cute as a button.

A bowl of fruit and vegetables had been left near the waterline. She walked to the bowl, considered it. Her orange jumpsuit nicely complemented her *cafe-au-lait* skin. She was so small and delicate that by contrast Elin felt ungainly, an awkward if amiable giant.

"We also use passive heat pumps to move the excess heat down to a liquid storage cavern below the lake."

Coral stopped, picked up a tomato. Her features were finely chiseled. Her almond eyes should have had snap and fire in them, to judge by the face, but they were remote and unfocused. Even white teeth nipped at the food.

"At night we pump the heat back up, let the lake radiate it out to keep the crater warm."

On closer examination—Elin had to squint to see so fine—the face was as smooth and lineless as that of an idiot. There was nothing there; no emotion, no purpose, no detectable intellect.

"That's why the number of waterfalls in operation varies."

Now Coral sat down on the rocks. Her feet were dirty, but the toenails pink and perfect. She did not move. Elin wanted to shy a rock at her to see if she would react.

What now? Elin wondered. She had seen the sights, all that Magritte had to offer, and they were all tiresome, disappointing. Even—no, make that *especially*—God. And she still had almost a month to kill.

"Keeping the crater tempered is a regular balancing act," the agtech said.

"Oh, shut up." Elin took out her briefcase, and called Father Landis. "I'm bored," she said, when the hologram had stabilized.

Landis hardly glanced up from her work. "So get a job," she snapped.

Magritte had begun as a mining colony. But the first swatches of lunar soil had hardly been scooped from Mare Imbrium's surface when the economic winds shifted, and it became more profitable to mine areas rich in specific minerals than to process the undifferentiated mélange soil. The miners had left, and the crater was sold at a loss to a consortium of operations that were legally debarred from locating Earthside.

From the fifteenth terrace Elin stared down at the patchwork clusters of open-air laboratories and offices, some separated by long stretches of undeveloped field, others crammed together in the hope of synergistic effect. Germ warfare corporations mingled with nuclear-waste engineering firms. The Mid-Asian Population Control Project had half a terrace to itself, and it swarmed with guards. There were a few off-Swiss banking operations.

"You realize," Tory said, "that I'm not going to be at all happy about this development." He stood, face impassive in red and green, watching a rigger bolt together a cot and wire in the surgical equipment.

"You hired me yourself," Elin reminded him.

"Yes, but I'm wired into professional mode at the moment." The rigger packed up his tools, walked off. "Looks like we're almost ready."

"Good." Elin flung herself down on the cot, and lay back, hands folded across her chest. "Hey, I feel like I should be holding a lily!"

"I'm going to hook you into the project intercom so you don't get too bored between episodes." The air about her flickered, and a clutch of images overlaid her vision. Ghosts walked through the air, stared at her from deep within the ground. "Now we'll shut off the external senses." The world went away, but the illusory people remained, each within a separate hexagonal field of vision. It was like seeing through the eyes of a fly.

There was a sudden overwhelming sense of Tory's presence, and sourceless voice said, "This will take a minute. Amuse yourself by calling up a few friends." Then he was gone.

Elin floated, free of body, free of sensation, almost godlike in her detachment. She idly riffled through the images, bypassing Landis, and stopped at a chubby little man drawing a black line across his forehead. *Hello, Hans,* she thought.

He looked up and winked. "How's it hanging, kid?"

Not so bad. What are you up to?

"My job. I'm the black-box monitor this shift." He added an orange starburst to the band, surveyed the job critically in a pocket mirror. "I sit here with my finger on the button"—one hand disappeared below his terminal—"and if I get the word, I push. That sets off explosives in the condenser units and blows the dome. *Pfffft.* Out goes the air."

She considered it: A sudden volcano of oxygen spouting up and across the lunar plains. Human bodies thrown up from the surface, scattering, bursting under explosive decompression.

That's grotesque, *Hans.*

"Oh, it's safe. The button doesn't connect unless I'm wetwired into my job."

Even so.

"Just a precaution: a lot of the research that goes on here wouldn't be allowed without this kind of security. Relax—I haven't lost a dome yet."

The intercom cut out, and again Elin felt Tory's presence, a sensation akin to someone unseen staring over her shoulder. "We're trying a series of Trojan Horse programs this time—inserting you into the desired mental states instead of making you the states. We've encapsulated your surface identity and routed the experimental programs through a secondary level. So with *this* series, rather than identifying with the programs, you'll perceive them all indirectly."

Tory, you have got to be the most jargon-ridden human being in existence. How about repeating that in English?

"I'll show you."

Suddenly Elin was englobed in a sphere of branching crimson lines, dark and dull, that throbbed slowly. Lacy and organic, it looked the way she imagined the veins in her forehead to be like when she had a headache.

"That was anger," Tory said. "You're mind shunted it off into visual imagery because it didn't identify the anger with itself."

That's what you're going to do then—program me into the God-state so that I can see it but not experience it?

"Ultimately. Though I doubt you'll be able to come up with pictures. More likely, you'll feel that you're in the presence of God." He withdrew for a moment, leaving her more than alone, almost nonexistent. Then he was back. "We start slowly, though. The first session runs you up to the basic metaprogramming level, integrates all your mental processes, and puts you in low-level control of them. The nontechnical term for this is 'making the Christ.' Don't fool around with anything you see or sense." His voice faded, she was alone, and then everything changed.

She was in the presence of someone wonderful.

Elin felt that someone near at hand, and struggled to open the eyes she no longer possessed; she had to see. Her existence opened, and people began appearing before her.

"Careful," Tory said. "You've switched on the intercom again."

I want to see!

"There's nobody to see. That's just your own mind. But if you want, you can keep the intercom on."

Oh. It was disappointing. She was surrounded by love, by a crazily happy sense that the universe was holy, by wisdom deeper than the world. By all rights, it *had* come from a source greater than herself.

Reason was not strong enough to override emotion. She riffled through the intercom, bringing up image after image and discarding them all, searching. When she had run through the project staff, she began hungrily scanning the crater's public monitors.

Agtechs in the trellis farms were harvesting strawberries and sweet peas. Elin could taste them on her tongue. Somebody was seining up algae from the inner lake, and she felt the weight of the net in callused hands. Not far from where she lay, a couple was making love in a grove of saplings and she...

Tory, I don't think I can take this. It's too intense.

"You're the one who wanted to be a test pilot."

Dammit, Tory—!

Donna Landis materialized on the intercom. "She's right, Shostokovich. You haven't buffered her enough."

"It didn't seem wise to risk dissociative effects by cranking her ego up too high—"

"Who's paying for all this, hah?"

Tory grumbled something inaudible, and dissolved the world.

Elin floated in blackness, soothing and relaxing. She felt good. She had needed this little vacation from the tensions and pressures of her new personality. Taking the position had been the right thing to do, even if it did momentarily displease Tory.

Tory...She smiled mentally. He was exasperating at times, but still she was coming to rely on having him around. She was beginning to think she was in love with him.

A lesser love, perhaps. Certainly not the love that is the Christ.

Well, maybe so. Still, on a *human* level, Tory filled needs in her she hadn't known existed. It was too much effort to argue with herself, though. Her thoughts drifted away into a wordless, luxurious reveling in the bodiless state, free from distractions, carefree and disconnected.

Nothing is disconnected. All the universe is a vast net of intermeshing programs. Elin was amused at herself. That had sounded like something Tory would say. She'd have to watch it; she might love the man, but she certainly didn't want to end up talking like him.

You worry needlessly. The voice of God is subtle, but it is not your own.

Elin started. She searched through her mind for an open intercom channel, didn't find one. *Hello,* she thought. *Who said that?*

The answer came to her not in words, but in a sourceless assertion of identity. It was cool, emotionless, something she could not describe even to herself, but by the same token absolute and undeniable.

It was God.

Then Tory was back and the voice, the presence, was gone. *Tory?* she thought, *I think I just had a religious experience.*

"That's very common under sensory deprivation—the mind clears out a few old programs. Nothing to worry about. Now relax for a jiff while I plug you back in—how does that feel?"

The Presence was back again, but not nearly so strongly as before; she could resist the urge to chase after it. *That's fine, Tory, but listen, I really think—*

"Let's leave analysis to those who have been programmed for it, shall we?"

The lovers strolled aimlessly through a meadow, the grass brushing up higher than their waists. Biological night was coming; the agtechs flicked the daylight off and on twice in warning.

"It was real, Tory. She talked with me; I'm not making it up."

Tory ran a hand through his dark curly hair, looking abstracted. "Well. Assuming that my professional opinion was wrong—and I'll be the first to admit that the program is a bit egocentric—I still don't think we have to stoop to mysticism for an explanation."

To the far side of Magritte, a waterfall was abruptly shut off. The stream of water scattered, seeming to dissolve in the air. "I thought you said she was God."

"I only said that to bait Landis. I don't mean that she's literally God, just god*like*. Mentally, she's a million years more highly developed than we. God is just a convenient metaphor."

"Um. So what's your explanation?"

"There's at least one terminal on the island—the things are everywhere. She probably programmed it to cut into the intercom without the channels seeming to be open."

"Could she do that?"

"Why not? She has that million-year edge on us—and she used to be a wetware tech; all wetware techs are closet computer hacks." He did not look at her, had not looked at her for some time.

"Hey." She reached out to take his hand. "What's wrong with you tonight?"

"Me?" He did not meet her eyes. "Don't mind me, I'm just sulking because you took the job. I'll get over it."

"What's wrong with the job?"

"Nothing. It's just dangerous as sin, is all. Look, I know I can't talk you out of it, and I know I have no business trying. I'm just being moody."

She guided his arm around her waist, pressed up against him. "Well, don't be. It's nothing you can control—I have to have work to do. My boredom threshold is very low."

"I know that." He finally turned to face her, smiled sadly. "I do love you, you know."

"Well...maybe I love you, too."

His smile banished all sadness from his face, like a sudden wind that breaks apart the clouds. "Say it again." His hands reached out to touch her shoulders, her neck, her face. "One more time, with feeling."

"Will not!" Laughing, she tried to break away from him, but he would not let go, and they fell in a tangle to the ground. "Beast!" They rolled over and over in the grass. "Brute!" She hammered at his chest, tore open his jumpsuit, tried to bite his neck.

Tory looked embarrassed, tried to pull away. "Hey, not out here! Somebody could be watching."

The agtechs switched off the arc lamps, plunging Magritte into darkness.

Tory reached up to touch Elin's face. They made love.

Physically it was no different from things she had done countless times before with lovers and friends and the occasional stranger. But she had committed herself in a way the old Elin had never dared to, let Tory in past her defenses, laid herself open to pain and hurt, trusting him. He was a part of her now. And everything was transformed, made new and wonderful.

Until they were right at the brink of orgasm, the both of them, and half delirious she could let herself go, murmuring, "I love you, love you, God,

I love you, love…" And just as she climaxed, Tory stiffened and arced his head back, and in a voice that was wrenched from the depths of passion, whispered, "Coral…"

✺

Elin strode furiously among the huts a terrace down from where she had left Tory asleep in the grass. They had lain together silently after making love, and he had no way of knowing that she was holding him so tightly, burying her head behind his, not out of love or passion, but from outraged anger and fear of what she might do if she had to look at his face.

Some few huts, sheltered from each other by scatterings of maple saplings, were dark. The rest glowed softly from the holotapes within— diffuse, scattered rainbow patterns unreadable outside their fields of focus. Elin halted before one hut, stood indecisively. Finally, because she needed somebody to talk to, she rapped on the lintel.

Father Landis stuck her head out the doorway, blinked sleepily. "Oh, it's you, Donnelly. What do you want?"

To her absolute horror, Elin broke into tears.

Landis ducked back inside, reemerged zipping up her jumpsuit. She cuddled Elin in her arms, made soothing noises, listened to her story.

"Coral," Landis said. "Ahhh. Suddenly everything falls into place."

"Well, I wish you'd tell me, then!" She tried to blink away the angry tears. Her face felt red and raw and ugly; the wetware paint was all smeared.

"Patience, child." Landis sat down cross-legged beside the hut, patted the ground beside her. "Sit here and pretend that I'm your mommy, and I'll tell you a story."

"Hey, I didn't come here—"

"Who are you to criticize the latest techniques in spiritual nurturing, hey?" Landis chided gently. "Sit."

Elin did so. Landis put an arm about her shoulder.

"Once upon a time, there was a little girl named Coral—I forget her last name. Doesn't matter. Anyway, she was bright and emotional and ambitious and frivolous and just like you in every way." She rocked Elin gently as she spoke.

"Coral was a happy little girl, and she laughed and played and one day she fell in love. Just like *that!*" She snapped her fingers. "I imagine you know how she felt."

"This is kind of embarrassing."

"Hush. Well, she was very lucky, for as much as she loved him, he loved her a hundred times back, and for as much as he loved her, she loved him a thousand times back. And so it went. I think they overdid it a bit, but that's just my personal opinion.

"Now Coral lived in Magritte and worked as a wetware tech. She was an ambitious one, too—they're the worst kind. She came up with a scheme to reprogram people so they could live *outside* the programs that run them in their everyday lives. Mind you, people are more than sum of their programming, but what did she know about free will? She hadn't any religious training, after all. So she and her boyfriend wrote up a proposal, and applied for funding, and together they ran the new program through her skull. Arid when it was all done, she thought she was God. Only she wasn't Coral anymore—not so's you'd recognize her."

She paused to give Elin a hug. "Be strong, kid, here comes the rough part. Well, her boyfriend was brokenhearted. He didn't want to eat, and he didn't want to play with his friends. He was a real shit to work with. But then he got an idea.

"You see, anyone who works with experimental wetware has her personality permanently recorded in case there's an accident and it needs to be restored. And if that person dies or becomes God, the personality rights revert to IGF. They're sneaky like that.

"Well. Tory—did I mention his name was Tory?—thought to himself: What if somebody were to come here for a new personality? Happens about twice a year. Bound to get worse in the future. And Magritte is the only place this kind of work can be done. The personality bank is random-accessed by computer, so there'd be a chance of his getting Coral back, just as good as new. Only not a very good chance, because there's *lots* of garbage stuffed into the personality bank.

"And then he had a *bad* thought. But you mustn't blame him for it. He was working from a faulty set of moral precepts. Suppose, he thought, he rigged the computer so that instead of choosing randomly, it would give Coral's personality to the very first little girl who came along? And that was what he did." Landis lapsed into silence.

Elin wiped back a sniffle. "How does the story end?"

"I'm still waiting on that one."

"Well, did Tory really rig the selection—you're not just making that up?"

"Christ, *I* don't know. Maybe it was just a lucky throw of the dice. But the evidence sure is suspicious. You could try snooping around in his personal storage; he might still have the program squirreled away there."

"Oh." She sat silently for a moment, then pulled herself together and stood. Landis followed.

"Feeling any better, kid?"

"I don't know. More in control maybe."

"Listen. Remember what I said about you being a puppy tripping over its paws? Well, you've just stubbed your toes and they hurt. But you'll get over it. People do."

"Yeah. Thanks."

"Today we make a Buddha," Tory said. Elin fixed him with a cold stare, said nothing, even though he was in green and red, immune. Later, she knew, when he came off his programming, he would remember. "This is a higher-level program, integrating all your mental functions and putting them under your conscious control. So it's especially important that you keep your hands to yourself, okay?"

"Rot in hell, you cancer," she muttered beneath her breath.

"I beg your pardon?"

Elin did not respond, and after a puzzled silence Tory continued: "I'm leaving your sensorium operative, so when I switch you over, I want you to pay attention to your surround. Okay?"

The second Trojan Horse program came on. Everything changed.

It wasn't a physical change, not one that could be seen with the eyes. It was more as if the names for everything had gone away. A knee-tall oak grew nearby, very much like the one she had crushed accidentally in New Detroit when she had lost her virginity many years ago. And it meant nothing to her. It was only wood growing out of ground. A mole poked its head out of its burrow, nose crinkling, pink eyes weak. It was just a small biological machine. "Whooh," she said involuntarily. "This is cold."

"Bother you?"

Elin studied him, and there was nothing there. Only human being, as much an object as the oak, and no more. She felt nothing toward or against him. "No," she said.

"We're getting a good recording." The words meant nothing: they were clumsy, devoid of content.

In the grass around her, Elin saw a grey flickering, as if it were all subtly on fire. Logically she knew the flickering was the firing of nerves in the rods and comes of her eyes, but emotionally it was something else: it was Time. A grey fire that destroyed the world constantly, eating it away and remaking it again and again.

And it didn't matter.

A great calmness wrapped itself around Elin, an intelligent detachment, cold and impersonal. She found herself identifying with it, realizing that existence was simply *not important.* It was all things, objects.

Tory was fussing over his machines, and it seemed to her that he had made himself into one of his own devices. Push a button and get a predictable response. And was this any way for a human being to live?

Then again, how important *was* a human being? She could not see Tory's back, and was no longer willing to assume it even existed. She could look up and see the near side of the Earth. The far side might well not exist, and if it didn't, well *that* didn't matter either.

She stripped away the world, ignored the externalities. *I never realized how dependent I am on sensory input,* she thought. And if you ignored it—

—there was the Void. It had no shape or color or position, but it was what underlay the bright interplay of colors that was constantly being destroyed by the grey fires of time. She contemplated the raw stuff of existence.

"Please don't monkey around with your programming," Tory said.

The body was unimportant too; it was only the focal point for her senses. Ignore them, and you could ignore *it.* Elin could feel herself fading in the presence of the Void. It had no material existence, but how much less had what she'd always taken for granted: the world and all its glitters.

It was like being a program in a machine and realizing it for the first time.

Landis's voice flooded her existence. "Donnelly, for God's sake, keep your fingers off the experiment!" The thing was, the underlying nothingness was *real*—if "real" had any meaning. If meaning had meaning. But beyond real and beyond meaning, there is something that is. And she had found it.

"Donnelly, you're treading on dangerous ground. You've—" Landis's voice was a distraction, and she shut it off. Elin felt the desire to achieve unity with what was; one simply had to stop the desire for it, she realized, and it was done.

But before she could realize the union, horror collapsed upon her. Orange flames shot up; they seared and burned and crisped, and there were snakes among them, great slimy things that reached out with disgusting mouth and needle-sharp fangs.

She recoiled in panic, and they were upon her. The flames were drawn up into her lungs, and hot maggots wallowed through her brain tissues. She fled through a mind that writhed under the onslaught, turning things on and off.

Until abruptly she was back in her body, and there was nothing pursuing her. She shivered, and her body responded. It felt wonderful.

"Well, that worked at least," Tory said.

"What—" her voice croaked. She cleared her throat and tried again. "What happened?"

"Just what we hoped would. Your primary identity was threatened with dissolution, and it moved to protect itself."

Elin realized that her eyes were still closed; she opened them now and convulsively closed her hand around the edge of the cot. It was solid and real to the touch. So good.

"I'll be down in a minute," Tory said. "Just now, though, I think you need to rest." He touched a bone inductor, and Elin fell into blackness.

Floating again, every metaphorical nerve on edge, Elin found herself hypersensitive to outside influences, preternaturally aware, even suggestible. Still, she suspected more than sensed Coral's presence. *Go away,* she thought. *This is my mind now.* She was not surprised when she was answered.

I am here and I am always. You have set foot in my country, and are dimly aware of my presence. Later, when you have climbed into the mountains, you will truly know me; and then you will be as I.

Everyone tells me what I'm going to do, Elin though angrily. *Don't I get any say in this?*

The thought was almost amused: *You are only a program caught in a universal web of programming. You will do as your program dictates. To be free of the programs is to be God.*

Despite her anger, despite her hurt, despite the cold trickle of fear she tried to keep to the background, Elin was curious. *What's it like?* She couldn't help asking.

It is golden freedom. The universe is a bubble infinitely large, and we who are God are the film on its outside. We interact and we program. We make the stars shine and the willows grow. We program what you want for lunch. The programming flows through us, and we alter it and maintain the universe.

Elin pounced on this last statement. *Haven't done a very good job of it, have you?*

We do not tamper. When you are one with us, you will understand.

This was, Elin realized, the kind of question-and-answer session Coral must have gone through repeatedly as part of the Star Maker project. She searched for a question that no one else would have asked, one that would be hers alone. And after some thought she found it.

Do you still—personally—love Tory Shostokovich?

There was a slight pause, then—*The kind of love you mean is characteristic of lower-order programming. Not of program-free intelligence.*

A moment later Tory canceled all programming, and she floated to the surface, leaving God behind. But even before then she was acutely aware that she had not received a straight answer.

When Tory finally found her, Elin was patched into the outside monitors, staring across Mare Imbrium. It was a straight visual program: she could feel the wetwire leads dangling down her neck, the warm humid air of Magritte against her skin.

"Elin, we've got to talk."

The thing about Outside was its airless clarity. Rocks and shadows were so preternaturally *sharp*. From a sensor on the crater's seaward slope, she stared off into Mare Imbrium; it was monotonously dull, but in a comforting sort of way. A little like when she had made a Buddha. There was no meaning out there, nothing to impose itself between her and the surface. "Nothing to talk *about*," she said.

"Dammit, yes there is! I'm not about to lose you again because of a misunderstanding, a—a matter of semantics."

Elin hopscotched down the slope to the surface, where the abandoned surface mine abutted on the mass driver. "How very melodramatic."

The mass driver was a thin monorail stretching kilometers into Mare Imbrium, its gentle slope all but imperceptible. Repair robots prowled its length, stopping occasionally for a spot weld: blue sparks sputtered soundlessly over the surface.

"I don't know how you found out about Coral, and I guess it doesn't matter. I always figured you'd find out sooner or later. That's not important. What matters is that I love you—"

"Oh, hush up!" Below the hulking repair robots scurried dozens of smaller devices, quick and tiny, almost cute. They were privately owned, directed by hobbyists within the crater. Elin redirected a camera to follow one little fellow zipping about in the old strip mine, dragging a cloth sack in one claw, holding a pick in another, waving the third free. A rockhound.

"—and that you love me. You can't pretend you don't."

Elin felt her nails dig into her palms. "Sure I can," she said. The robot was chipping away at a rock outcrop. Dust powdered up, fell quickly. It scanned the sample it had chipped, turning it over and over before the camera lens, then let it drop. It scooted on.

"You're identifying with the woman who used to be Elin Donnelly. There's nothing wrong with that; speaking as a wetware tech, it's a healthy sign. But it's something you've got to grow out of."

At the edge of the slope, another robot had set up a holograph generator. It fussed over the machine, set a final switch, then lapsed into quiescence. There was a moment's hesitation, and then a field of blue pillars appeared on the floor of Imbrium.

"Listen, Shostokovich, tinkering around with my emotions doesn't change who I am. I'm not your dead lady-friend, and I'm not about to take her place. So why don't you just go away and stop jerking me around, huh?"

The pillars grew to perhaps a third the height of Magritte before resolution began to fail, and they drifted toward insubstantiality. The unseen operator adjusted their height downward.

"You're not the old Elin Donnelly either, and I think you know it. Bodies are transient, memories are nothing. Your spontaneity and grace, your quiet strength, your impatience—the thousand little quirks of you I've known and loved for years—are what make you yourself. The name doesn't matter, nor the past. You are who you are, and I love you for it."

A host of butterflies appeared, fluttering out of the rock. They danced erratically, yellow and red and orange, each moving randomly, but as a whole drifting through vacuum toward the field of pillars.

"Yeah, well, what I am does not love you, buster."

Several hobbyist robots had abandoned their tasks to follow the flight. Two rockhounds crawled up to the edge of the mine so their owners could see better.

Tory was silent for a bit, his voice almost sad when he finally spoke. "You do, though. You can't hide that from me. I know you as your lover and as your wetware surgeon. You've let me become a part of you, and no matter how angry you might temporarily be, you'll come back to me."

Elin's body trembled with rage; she could feel it. "Yeah, well if that's true then why tell *me?* Hah? Why not just go back to your hut and wait for me to come crawling?"

Emerald green snakes boiled out of the surface, writhed just outside the pillars. Now and again one would snap futilely at the butterflies hesitating, just out of reach, before the pillars.

"Because I want a favor from you. I want you to quit your job."

"Say what?"

There was an odd hesitancy to Tory's voice, as if he were already defeated and knew it. "I don't want you to become God. It was a mistake the last time, and I'm afraid it won't be any better with the new programs. If you go up and become God and can't get down this time, you'll do it the next. I'll spend my life here waiting for you, re-creating you, losing you. Can't you see it—year after year, replaying the same tired old tape?"

Now Tory's voice fell to a whisper. "And I don't think I could take it even once more."

With a surge the butterflies were among the pillars, and the snakes leapt and slithered after them. The instant they were all encompassed, the cold blue pillars flashed violent red, bursting into great gouts of flame, incinerating them all.

"If you know me as well as you say, then I guess you know my answer," Elin said coldly.

The rockhounds waved their claws in applause. The fiery pillars faded away. Switching sensors, Elin could see the robot packing up the hologram generator for the day.

Tory's footsteps sounded, moving away, fading, defeat echoing after.

Only when she was sure he was gone did Elin realize that her sensor had been scanning the same empty bit of Magritte's slope for at least five minutes.

It was time for the final Trojan Horse. "Today we make a God," Tory said. "This is a total conscious integration of the mind in an optimal efficiency pattern. Close your eyes and count to three."

One. The hell of it, Elin realized, was that Tory was right. She still loved him. He was the one man for her, and she wanted him, was empty without him.

Two. Worse, she didn't know how long she could go on without coming back to him—and, good God, would that be humiliating!

She was either cursed or blessed; cursed perhaps for the agonies and humiliations she would willingly undergo for the sake of this one obsessive and manipulative human being. Or maybe blessed in that at least there was *someone* who could move her so, deserving or not. Many went through their lives without.

Three. She opened her eyes.

Nothing was different. Magritte was as ordinary, as mundane, as ever, and she felt no special reaction to it one way or another. Certainly she did not feel the presence of God.

"I don't think this is working," she tried to say. The words did not come. From the corner of her eye, she saw Tory wiping clean his facepaint, shucking off his jumpsuit. But when she tried to sit up to see, she found she was paralyzed.

What is this maniac doing?

Tory's face loomed over her, his eyes glassy, almost fearful. He smiled reassuringly. His hair was a tangled mess; her fingers itched with the impulse to run a comb through it. "Forgive me, love." He kissed her forehead lightly, her lips ever so gently. Then he was out of her field of vision, stretching out on the grass beside the cot.

Elin stared up at the dome roof, thinking: *No.* She heard him strap the bone inductors to his body, one by one, and then a sharp click as he switched on a recorder. The programming began to flow into him.

A long wait—perhaps twenty seconds viewed objectively—as the wetware was loaded. Another click as the recorder shut off. A moment of silence, and then—

Tory gasped. One arm flew up into her field of vision, swooped down out of it, and he began choking. Elin struggled against her paralysis, could not move. Something broke noisily, a piece of equipment by the sound of it, and the choking and gasping continued as he began to thrash about wildly.

Tory, Tory, what's happening to you? He was having a seizure, that much was clear. But inside—within the confines of his skull—what horrors ran rampant? An arm smashed against her cot, rocking it, jolting her mildly.

Whatever was happening, it was bad. And Elin could do nothing about it.

※

"It's just a *grand mal* seizure," Landis said. "Nothing we can't cope with, nothing we weren't prepared for." She touched Elin's shoulder reassuringly, called back at the crowd huddled about Tory, "Hey! One of you loopheads—somebody there know any programming? Get the lady out of this."

A tech scurried up, made a few simple adjustments with her machinery. The others—still gathering, Landis had been only the third on the scene—were trying to hold Tory still, to fit a bone inductor against his neck. There was a sudden gabble of comment, and Tory flopped wildly. Then a collective sigh as his muscles eased, and his convulsions ceased.

"There," the tech said, and Elin scrabbled off the couch.

She pushed through the people (and a small voice in the back of her head marveled: A crowd! How strange) and knelt before Tory, cradling his head in her arms.

He shivered, eyes wide and unblinking. "Tory, what's the matter?"

He turned those terrible eyes on her. "*Nichevo.*"

"What?"

"Nothing," Landis said. "Or maybe 'it doesn't matter,' is a better translation."

A wetware tech had taken control, shoving the crowd back. He reported to Landis, his mouth moving calmly under the interplay of green and red. "Looks like a flaw in the programming philosophy. We were guessing that bringing the ego along would make God such an unpleasant experience that the subject would let us deprogram without interfering— now we know better."

Elin stroked Tory's forehead. His muscles clenched, then loosened, as a medtech reprogrammed the body response. "Why isn't anyone *doing* anything?" she demanded.

"Take a look," Landis said, and patched her into the intercom. In her mind's eye, Elin could see dozens of wetware techs submitting program after program. A branching wetware diagram filled one channel, and as she watched, minor changes would occur as programs took hold, then be unmade as Tory's mind rejected them. "We've got an imagery tap of his *Weltanschauung* coming up," some nameless tech reported, and then something horrible appeared on a blank channel.

Elin could only take an instant's exposure before her mind reflexively shut the channel down, but that instant was more than enough. She stood in a room infinitely large and cluttered in all dimensions with great noisome machines. They were tended by malevolent demons who shrieked and cackled and were machines themselves, and they generated pain and madness.

The disgust and revulsion she felt was absolute. It could not be put into words—no more than could the actual experience of what she had seen. And yet—she knew this much about wetware techniques—it was only a rough approximation, a cartoon of what was going through Tory's head.

Elin's body trembled with shock, and by slow degrees she realized that she had retreated to the surface world. Tory's head was still cradled in her arms. A wetware tech standing nearby looked stunned, her face grey.

Elin gathered herself together, said as gently as she could, "Tory, what is that you're seeing?"

Tory turned his stark, haunted eyes on her, and it took an effort of will not to flinch. Then he spoke, his words shockingly calm.

"It is—what is. It's reality. The universe is a damned cold machine, and all of us only programs within it. We perform the actions we have no choice but to perform, and then we fade into nothingness. It's a cruel and noisy place."

"I don't understand—didn't you always say that we were just programs? Wasn't that what you always believed?"

"Yes, but now I experience it."

Elin noticed that her hand was slowly stroking his hair; she did not try to stop it. "Then come down, Tory. Let them deprogram you."

He did not look away. "*Nichevo,*" he said.

The tech, recovered from her shock, reached toward a piece of equipment. Landis batted her hand away. "Hold it right there, techie! Just what do you think you're doing?"

The woman looked impatient. "He left instructions that if the experiment turned out badly, I was to pull the terminator switch."

"That's what I thought. They'll be no mercy killings while *I'm* on the job, Mac."

"I don't understand." The tech backed away, puzzled. "Surely you don't want him to suffer."

Landis was gathering herself for a withering reply when the intercom cut them all off. A flash of red shot through the sensorium, along with the smell of bitter almond, a prickle of static electricity, the taste of *kimchi.* An urgent voice cried, "Emergency! We've got an emergency!" A black-and-white face materialized in Elin's mind. "Emergency!"

Landis flipped into the circuit. "What's the problem? Show us."

"You're not going to believe this." The face disappeared, was replaced by a wide-angle shot of the lake.

The greenish-black water was calm and stagnant. The thrust-cone island, with its scattered grass and weeds, slumbered.

And God walked upon the water.

They gawked, all of them, unable to accept what they saw. Coral walked across the lake, her pace determined but not hurried, her face serene. The pink soles of her bare feet only just touched the surface.

I didn't believe her, Elin thought wildly. She saw Father Landis begin to cross herself, her mouth hanging open, eyes wide in disbelief. Half-way through her gesture, the Jesuitical wetware took hold. Her mouth snapped shut, and her face became cold and controlled. She pulled herself up straight.

"Hans," the priest said. "push the button."

"No!" Elin shrieked, but it was too late. Still hooked into the intercom, she saw the funny little man briskly, efficiently obey.

For an instant, nothing happened. Then bright glints of light appeared at all of the condenser units, harsh and actinic. Steam and smoke gushed from the machinery, and a fraction of a second later, there was an ear-slapping gout of sound.

Bits of the sky were blown away.

Elin turned twisted, fell. She scrambled across the ground, and threw her arms around Tory. He did not respond. "I can't lose you now," she cried.

Tory smiled sadly, said, "It doesn't matter. You live, you die, you are aware or ignorant—the universe doesn't change. None of it makes any difference." He said something more, but she could not catch it, though she strained to hear.

The air was thinner. The holes in the dome roof—small at first—expanded as more of the dome flaked away, subjected to stresses it was designed not to take. An uncanny whistling filled the air, grew to a screech, then a scream, and then there was an all-encompassing *whoomph* and the dome shattered.

Elin was thrown up into the air, torn away from Tory, painfully flung high and away. All the crater was in motion, the rock tearing out of the floor, the trees splintering upward, the lake exploding into steam.

The screaming died, and for an instant the air was gone. Elin's ears rang, and her skin stung everywhere. A universal pressure built within her, the desire of her blood to mate with the vacuum, and Elin realized that she was about to die.

A quiet voice said: *This must not be.*

Time stopped.

✺

Suspended between Moon and death, Elin experienced a strange interplay of sensations. The shards and fragments of an instant past crystallized and shifted. The world became, not misty, actually, but appositional. Both grew tentative, probabilities rather than actual things.

Come be God with me now, Coral said, but not to Elin.

Tory's presence flooded the soupy uncertainty, a vast and powerful thing, but wrong somehow, twisted. But even as Elin felt this, there was a change within him, a sloughing off of identity, and he seemed to straighten, to heal.

All around, the world began to grow more numinous, more real. Elin felt tugged in five directions at once. Tory's presence swelled briefly, then dwindled, became a spark, less than a spark, nothing.

Yes.

With a roaring of waters and a shattering of rocks, with an audible thump, the world returned.

✺

Elin unsteadily climbed down the last flight of stone stairs from the terraces to the lakefront. She passed by two guards at the foot of the stairs, their facepaint as hastily applied as their programming, several more on the way to the nearest trellis farm. They were everywhere since the incident.

She found the ladder up into the farm and began climbing. It was biological night, and the agtechs were long gone.

Hand over hand she climbed, as far and high as she could, until she was afraid she would miss a rung and tumble off. Then she swung herself onto a ledge, wedging herself between strawberry and yam planters. She looked down on the island, and though she was dizzyingly high, she was only a third of the way up.

"Now what the hell am I doing here?" she mumbled to herself. She swung her legs back and forth, answered her own question: "Being piss-ass drunk." She cackled. *There* was something she didn't have to share with Coral. She was capable of getting absolutely blitzed, and walking away from the bar before it hit her. It was something metabolic.

Below, Tory and Coral sat quietly on their monkey island. They did not touch, did not make love or hold hands or even glance one at the other—they just sat. Being Gods.

Elin squinted down at the two. "Like to upchuck all over you." she mumbled. Then she squeezed her eyes and fists tight, drawing tears and pain. *Dammit, Tory!*

Blinking hard, she looked away from the island, down into the jet-black waters of the lake. The brighter stars were reflected there. A slight breeze rippled the water, making them twinkle and blink, as if lodged in a Terran sky. They floated lightly on the surface, swarmed and coalesced, and formed Tory's face in the lake. He smiled warmly, invitingly. Elin stared hungrily at his lips as he whispered, "Come. Join me."

A hand closed around her arm, and she looked up into the stern face of a security guard. "You're drunk, Ms.," he said, "and you're endangering property."

She looked where he pointed, at a young yam plant she had squashed in the process of sitting, and began to laugh. Smoothly, professionally, the guard rolled up her sleeve, clamped a plastic bracelet around her wrist. "Time to go," he said.

By the time the guard had walked Elin up four terraces, she was nearly sober. A steady trickle of her blood wound through the bracelet, was returned to her body cleansed of alcohol. A sacrilegious waste of wine, in her opinion.

In another twenty steps, the bracelet fell off her wrist. The guard snapped it neatly from the air, disappeared. Despair closed in on her again. *Tory, my love!* And since there was no hope of sleep, she kept on trudging up the terraces, back toward Han's rathskeller, for another bellyful of wine.

There was a small crowd seated about the rock that served Hans as a table, lit by a circle of hologram-generated fairy lights. Father Landis was there, and drinking heavily. "Tomorrow I file my report," she announced. "The Synod is pulling out of this, withdrawing funding."

Hans sighed, took a long swig of his own wine, winced at its taste. "I guess that's it for the Star Maker project, huh?"

Landis crossed her fingers. "Pray God." Elin, standing just outside the circle, stood silently, listening.

"I don't ever want to hear that name again," a tech grumbled.

"You mustn't confuse God with what you've just seen," Landis admonished.

"Hey," Hans said. "She moved time backward or something. I saw it. This place exploded—doesn't that prove something?"

Landis grinned, reached out to ruffle his hair. "Sometimes I worry about you, Hans. You have an awfully *small* concept of God." Several of the drinkers laughed.

He blushed, said, "No, really."

"Well, I'll try to keep this—" she leaned forward, rapped her mug against the rock, "fill this up again, hey?—keep it simple. We had analysts crawl up and down Coral's description of the universe, and did you know there was no place in it *anywhere* for such things as mercy, hope, faith? No, we got an amalgam of substrates, supra-programs, and self-metaediting physics. Now what makes God superior is not just intellect—we've all known some damn clever bastards. And it's not power, or I could buy and atomic device on the black market and start my own religion.

"No, by *definition* God is my moral superior. Now I am myself but indifferent honest—but to Coral moral considerations don't even exist. Get it?"

Only Elin noticed the hunted, hopeless light in Landis's eyes, or realized that she was spinning words effortlessly, without conscious control. That deep within, the woman was caught in a private crisis of faith.

"Yeah, I guess." Hans scratched his head. "I'd still like to know just what happened between her and Tory there at the end."

"I can answer that," a wetware tech said. The others turned to face her, and she smirked, the center of attention. "What the hell, they plant the censor blocks in us all tomorrow—this is probably my only chance to talk about it.

"We reviewed all the tapes, and found that the original problem stemmed from a basic design flaw. Shostokovich should never have brought his ego along. The God-state is very ego-threatening; he couldn't accept it. His mind twisted it, denied it, make it into a thing of horror. Because to accept it would mean giving up his identity." She paused for emphasis.

"Now we don't understand the why or how of what happened. But *what* was done is very clearly recorded. Coral came along and stripped away his identity."

"Hogwash!" Landis was on her feet, belligerent and unsteady. "After all that happened, you can't say they don't have any identity! Look at the mess that Coral made to join Tory to her—that wasn't the work of an unfeeling identity-free creature."

"Our measurements showed no trace of identity at all," the tech said in a miffed tone.

"Measurements! Well, isn't that just scientific as all get-out?" The priest's face was flushed with drunken anger. "Have any of you clowns given any thought to just what we've created here? This gestalt being is still young—a newborn infant. Someday it's going to grow up. What happens to us all when it decides to leave the island, hey? I—" She stopped, her voice trailing away. The drinkers were silent, had drawn away from her.

"Scuse me," she muttered. "Too much wine." And sat.

"Well." Hans cleared his throat, quirked a smile. "Anybody for refills?"

The crowd came back to life, a little too boisterous, too noisily, determinedly cheerful. Watching from the fringes, outside the circle of light, Elin had a sudden dark fantasy, a waking nightmare.

A desk tech glanced her way. He had Tory's eyes. When he looked away, Tory smiled out of another's face. The drinkers shifted restlessly, chattering and laughing, like dancers pantomiming a party in some light opera, and the eyes danced with them. They flitted from person to person, materializing now here, now there, surfacing whenever an individual chanced to look her way. A quiet voice said, "We were fated to be lovers."

Go away, go away, go away, Elin thought furiously, and the hallucination ceased.

After a moment spent composing herself, Elin quietly slipped around to where Landis sat. "I'm leaving in the morning," she said. The new persona had taken; they would not remove her facepaint until just before the lift up, but that was mere formality. She was cleared to leave.

Landis looked up, and for an instant the woman's doubt and suffering were writ plain on her face. Then the mask was back, and she smiled. "Just stay away from experimental religion, hey kid?" They hugged briefly. "And remember what I told you about stubbing your toes."

Elin nodded wordlessly. She realized now that she had returned to the rathskeller looking for the priest's advice and comfort. She had wanted to say, "Look. For a moment there I thought I could get Tory back, the same way he got Coral back. But when I tried to raid the computer, I found out they've jacked their security *way* up. So it's only now hitting me that Tory is actually gone, and I want you to talk me out of doing something stupid."

But Landis was in bad shape, and one more emotional burden might break her. And Elin would not be the one to do that to her.

She went back home to Tory's hut.

✸

There was one final temptation to be faced. Sitting in the center of the hut, Tory's terminal in her lap, Elin let the soothing green light of its alphanumerics wash over her. She thought of Tory. Of his saying, "We were meant to be lovers," of his lean body under hers in the pale blue Earthlight. She thought of what life would be like without him.

The terminal was the only artifact Tory had left behind that held any sense of his spirit. It had been his plaything, his diary, and his toolbox, and its memory still held the series of Trojan Horse programs he had been working with when he had—been transformed.

One of those programs would make her a God.

She stared up through the ivy at the domed sky. Only a few stars were visible between the black silhouetted leaves, and these winked off and on with the small movements breathing imparted to her body. She thought back to Coral's statement that Elin would soon join her, merge into the unselfed autistic state that only Tory's meddling had spared her.

"God always keeps her promises," Tory said quietly.

Elin started, looked down, and saw that the grass to the far side of the hut was moving, flowing. Swiftly it formed the familiar, half-amused, half-embittered features of her lover, continued to flow until all of his head and part of his torso rose up from the floor.

She was not half so startled as she would have liked to be. Of *course* the earlier manifestations of Tory had been real, not phantoms thrown up by her grief. They were simply not her style.

Still, Elin rose to her feet apprehensively. "What do you want from me?"

The loam-and-grass figure beckoned. "Come. It is time you join us."

"I am not a program," Elin whispered convulsively. She backed away from the thing. "I can make my own decisions!"

She turned and plunged outside, into the fresh, cleansing night air. It braced her, cleared her head, returned to her some measure of control.

A tangle of honeysuckle vines on the next terrace wall up moved softly. Slowly, gently, they became another manifestation, of Coral this time, with blossoms for the pupils of her eyes. But she spoke with Tory's voice.

"You would not enjoy Godhood," he said, "but the being you become will."

"Give me time to think!" she cried. She wheeled and strode rapidly away. Out of the residential cluster, through a scattering of boulders, and into a dark meadow.

There was a quiet kind of peace here, and Elin wrapped it about her. She needed that peace for she had to decide between her humanity and Tory. It should have been an easy choice, but—the pain of being without!

Elin stared up at the Earth; it was a world full of pain. If she could reach out and shake all the human misery loose, it would flood all of Creation, extinguishing the stars and poisoning the space between.

There was, if not comfort, then a kind of cold perspective in that, in realizing that she was not alone, that she was merely another member of the commonality of pain. It was the heritage of her race. And yet—somehow—people kept on going.

If they could do it, so could she.

Some slight noise made her look back at the boulder field. Tory's face was appearing on each of the stones, each face slightly different, so that he gazed upon her with a dozen expressions of love. This strange multiple manifestation brought home to Elin how alien he had become, and she shivered involuntarily.

"Your desire is greater than your fear," he said, the words bouncing back and fourth between his faces. "No matter what you think now, by morning you will be part of us."

Elin did not reply immediately. There was something in her hand— Tory's terminal. It was small, and weighed hardly at all. She had brought it along without thinking.

A small bleak cry came from overhead, then several others. Nighthawks were feeding on insects near the dome roof. They were too far, too fast, and too dark to be visible from here.

"The price is too high," she said at last. "Can you understand that? I won't give up my humanity for you."

She hefted the terminal in her hand, then threw it as far and as hard as she could. She did not hear it fall.

"Good-bye, Tory," she said. "I still love you, but—good-bye." She turned and walked away.

Behind her, the rocks smiled knowingly.

A MIDWINTER'S TALE

Maybe I shouldn't tell you about that childhood Christmas Eve in the Stone House, so long ago. My memory is no longer reliable, not since I contracted the brain fever. Soon I'll be strong enough to be reposted offplanet, to some obscure star light years beyond that plangent moon rising over your father's barn, but how much has been burned from my mind! Perhaps none of this actually happened.

Sit on my lap and I'll tell you all. Well then, my knee. No woman was ever ruined by a knee. You laugh, but it's true. Would that it were so easy!

The hell of war as it's now practiced is that its purpose is not so much to gain territory as to deplete the enemy, and thus it's always better to maim than to kill. A corpse can be bagged, burned, and forgotten, but the wounded need special care. Regrowth tanks, false skin, medical personnel, a long convalescent stay on your parents' farm. That's why they will vary their weapons, hit you with obsolete stone axes or toxins or radiation, to force your Command to stock the proper prophylaxes, specialized medicines, obscure skills. Mustard gas is excellent for that purpose, and so was the brain fever.

All those months I lay in the hospital, awash in pain, sometimes hallucinating. Dreaming of ice. When I awoke, weak and not really believing I was alive, parts of my life were gone, randomly burned from my memory. I recall standing at the very top of the iron bridge over the Izveltaya, laughing and throwing my books one by one into the river, while my best friend Fennwolf tried to coax me down. "I'll join the militia! I'll be a soldier!" I shouted hysterically. And so I did. I remember that clearly but just what led up to that preposterous instant is utterly beyond me. Nor can I remember the name of my second-eldest sister, though her face is as plain to me as yours is now. There are odd holes in my memory.

111

✸

That Christmas Eve is an island of stability in my seachanging memories, as solid in my mind as the Stone House itself, that neolithic cavern in which we led such basic lives that I was never quite sure in which era of history we dwelt. Sometimes the men came in from the hunt, a larl or two pacing ahead content and sleepy-eyed, to lean bloody spears against the walls, and it might be that we lived on Old Earth itself then. Other times, as when they brought in projectors to fill the common room with colored lights, scintillae nesting in the branches of the season's tree, and cool, harmless flames dancing atop the presents, we seemed to belong to a much later age, in some mythologized province of the future.

The house was abustle, the five families all together for this one time of the year, and outlying kin and even a few strangers staying over, so that we had to put bedding in places normally kept closed during the winter, moving furniture into attic lumber rooms, and even at that there were cots and thick bolsters set up in the blind ends of hallways. The women scurried through the passages, scattering uncles here and there, now settling one in an armchair and plumping him up like a cushion, now draping one over a table, cocking up a mustachio for effect. A pleasant time.

Coming back from a visit to the kitchens where a huge woman I did not know, with flour powdering her big-freckled arms up to the elbows, had shooed me away, I surprised Suki and Georg kissing in the nook behind the great hearth. They had their arms about each other and I stood watching them. Suki was smiling, cheeks red and round. She brushed her hair back with one hand so Georg could nuzzle her ear, turning slightly as she did so, and saw me. She gasped and they broke apart, flushed and startled.

Suki gave me a cookie, dark with molasses and a single stingy, crystalized raisin on top, while Georg sulked. Then she pushed me away, and I heard her laugh as she took Georg's hand to lead him away to some darker forest recess of the house.

Father came in, boots all muddy, to sling a brace of game birds down on the hunt cabinet. He set his unstrung bow and quiver of arrows on their pegs, then hooked an elbow atop the cabinet to accept admiration and a hot drink from Mother. The larl padded by, quiet and heavy and content. I followed it around a corner, ancient ambitions of riding the beast rising up within. I could see myself, triumphant before my cousins, high atop the black carnivore. "Flip!" my father called sternly. "Leave Samson alone! He is a bold and noble creature, and I will not have you pestering him."

He had eyes in the back of his head, had my father.

Before I could grow angry, my cousins hurried by, on their way to hoist the straw men into the trees out front, and swept me up along with them. Uncle Chittagong, who looked like a lizard and had to stay in a glass tank for reasons of health, winked at me as I skirled past. From the corner of my eye I saw my second-eldest sister beside him, limned in blue fire.

Forgive me. So little of my childhood remains; vast stretches were lost in the blue icefields I wandered in my illness. My past is like a sunken continent with only mountaintops remaining unsubmerged, a scattered archipelago of events from which to guess the shape of what was lost. Those remaining fragments I treasure all the more, and must pass my hands over them periodically to reassure myself that something remains.

So where was I? Ah, yes: I was in the north bell tower, my hidey-place in those days, huddled behind Old Blind Pew, the bass of our triad of bells, crying because I had been deemed too young to light one of the yule torches. "Hallo!" cried a voice, and then, "Out here, stupid!" I ran to the window, tears forgotten in my astonishment at the sight of my brother Karl silhouetted against the yellowing sky, arms out, treading the roof gables like a tightrope walker.

"You're going to get in trouble for that!" I cried.

"Not if you don't tell!" Knowing full well how I worshiped him. "Come on down! I've emptied out one of the upper kitchen cupboards. We can crawl in from the pantry. There's a space under the door—we'll see everything!"

Karl turned and his legs tangled under him. He fell. Feet first, he slid down the roof.

I screamed. Karl caught the guttering and swung himself into an open window underneath. His sharp face rematerialized in the gloom, grinning. "Race you to the jade ibis!"

He disappeared, and then I was spinning wildly down the spiral stairs, mad to reach the goal first.

It was not my fault we were caught, for I would never have giggled if Karl hadn't been tickling me to see just how long I could keep silent. I was frightened, but not Karl. He threw his head back and laughed until he cried, even as he was being hauled off by three very angry grandmothers, pleased more by his own roguery than by anything he might have seen.

I myself was led away by an indulgent Katrina, who graphically described the caning I was to receive and then contrived to lose me in the crush of bodies in the common room. I hid behind the goat tapestry until I got bored—not long!—and then Chubkin, Kosmonaut, and Pew rang, and the room emptied.

I tagged along, ignored, among the moving legs, like a marsh bird scuttling through waving grasses. Voices clangoring in the east stairway, we climbed to the highest balcony, to watch the solstice dance. I hooked hands over the crumbling balustrade and pulled myself up on tiptoe so I could look down on the procession as it left the house. For a long time nothing happened, and I remember being annoyed at how casually the adults were taking all this, standing about with drinks, not one in ten glancing away from themselves. Pheidre and Valerian (the younger children had been put to bed, complaining, an hour ago) began a game of tag, running through the adults, until they were chastened and ordered with angry shakes of their arms to be still.

Then the door below opened. The women who were witches walked solemnly out, clad in hooded terrycloth robes as if they'd just stepped from the bath. But they were so silent I was struck with fear. It seemed as if something cold had reached into the pink, giggling women I had seen preparing themselves in the kitchen and taken away some warmth or laughter from them. "Katrina!" I cried in panic, and she lifted a moon-cold face toward me. Several of the men exploded in laughter, white steam puffing from bearded mouths, and one rubbed his knuckles in my hair. My second-eldest sister drew me away from the balustrade and hissed at me that I was not to cry out to the witches, that this was important, that when I was older I would understand, and in the meantime if I did not behave myself I would be beaten. To soften her words, she offered me a sugar crystal, but I turned away stern and unappeased.

Single-file the women walked out on the rocks to the east of the house, where all was barren slate swept free of snow by the wind from the sea, and at a great distance—you could not make out their faces—doffed their robes. For a moment they stood motionless in a circle, looking at one another. Then they began the dance, each wearing nothing but a red ribbon tied about one upper thigh, the long end blowing free in the breeze.

As they danced their circular dance, the families watched, largely in silence. Sometimes there was a muffled burst of laughter as one of the younger men muttered a racy comment, but mostly they watched with great respect, even a kind of fear. The gusty sky was dark, and flocked with small clouds like purple-headed rams. It was chilly on the roof and I could not imagine how the women withstood it. They danced faster and faster, and the families grew quieter, packing the edges more tightly, until I was forced away from the railing. Cold and bored, I went downstairs, nobody turning to watch me leave, back to the main room, where a fire still smouldered in the hearth.

The room was stuffy when I'd left, and cooler now. I lay down on my stomach before the fireplace. The flagstones smelled of ashes and were gritty to the touch, staining my fingertips as I trailed them in idle little circles. The stones were cold at the edges, slowly growing warmer, and then suddenly too hot and I had to snatch my hand away. The back of the fireplace was black with soot, and I watched the fire-worms crawl over the stone heart-and-hands carved there, as the carbon caught fire and burned out. The log was all embers and would burn for hours.

Something coughed.

I turned and saw something moving in the shadows, an animal. The larl was blacker than black, a hole in the darkness, and my eyes swam to look at him. Slowly, lazily, he strode out onto the stones, stretched his back, yawned a tongue-curling yawn, and then stared at me with those great green eyes.

He spoke.

I was astonished, of course, but not in the way my father would have been. So much is inexplicable to a child!

"Merry Christmas, Flip," the creature said, in a quiet, breathy voice. I could not describe its accent; I have heard nothing quite like it before or since. There was a vast alien amusement in his glance.

"And to you," I said politely.

The larl sat down, curling his body heavily about me. If I had wanted to run, I could not have gotten past him, though that thought did not occur to me then. "There is an ancient legend, Flip, I wonder if you have heard of it, that on Christmas Eve, the beasts can speak in human tongue. Have your elders told you that?"

I shook my head.

"They are neglecting you." Such strange humor dwelt in that voice. "There is truth to some of those old legends, if only you knew how to get at it. Though perhaps not all. Some are just stories. Perhaps this is not happening now; perhaps I am not speaking to you at all?"

I shook my head. I did not understand. I said so.

"That is the difference between your kind and mine. My kind understands everything about yours, and yours knows next to nothing about mine. I would like to tell you a story, little one. Would you like that?"

"Yes," I said, for I was young and I liked stories very much.

※

He began:

When the great ships landed—

Oh God. When—no, no, no, wait. Excuse me. I'm shaken. I just this instant had a vision. It seemed to me that it was night and I was standing at the gates of a cemetery. And suddenly the air was full of light, planes and cones of light that burst from the ground and nested twittering in the trees. Fracturing the sky. I wanted to dance for joy. But the ground crumbled underfoot and when I looked down the shadow of the gates touched my toes, a cold rectangle of profoundest black, deep as all eternity, and I was dizzy and about to fall and I, and I...

Enough! I have had this vision before, many times. It must have been something that impressed me strongly in my youth, the moist smell of newly opened earth, the chalky whitewash on the picket fence. It must be. I do not believe in hobgoblins, ghosts, or premonitions. No, it does not bear thinking about. Foolishness! Let me get on with my story.

—When the great ships landed, I was feasting on my grandfather's brains. All his descendants gathered respectfully about him, and I, as youngest, had first bite. His wisdom flowed through me, and the wisdom of his ancestors and the intimate knowledge of those animals he had eaten for food, and the spirit of valiant enemies who had been killed and then honored by being eaten, even as if they were family. I don't suppose you understand this, little one.

I shook my head.

People never die, you see. Only humans die. Sometimes a minor part of a Person is lost, the doings of a few decades, but the bulk of his life is preserved, if not in this body, then in another. Or sometimes a Person will dishonor himself, and his descendants will refuse to eat him. This is a great shame, and the Person will go off to die somewhere alone.

The ships descended bright as newborn suns. The People had never seen such a thing. We watched in inarticulate wonder, for we had no language then. You have seen the pictures, the baroque swirls of colored metal, the proud humans stepping down onto the land. But I was there, and I can tell you your people were ill. They stumbled down the gang-planks with the stench of radiation sickness about them. We could have destroyed them all then and there.

Your people built a village at Landfall and planted crops over the bodies of their dead. We left them alone. They did not look like good game. They were too strange and too slow and we had not yet come to savor your smell. So we went away, in baffled ignorance.

That was in early spring.

Half the survivors were dead by midwinter, some of disease but most because they did not have enough food. It was of no concern to us. But then the woman in the wilderness came to change our universe forever.

When you're older you'll be taught the woman's tale, and what desperation drove her into the wilderness. It's part of your history. But to myself, out in the mountains and winter-lean, the sight of her striding through the snows in her furs was like a vision of winter's queen herself. A gift of meat for the hungering season, life's blood for the solstice.

I first saw the woman while I was eating her mate. He had emerged from his cabin that evening as he did every sunset, gun in hand, without looking up. I had observed him over the course of five days and his behavior never varied. On that sixth nightfall I was crouched on his roof when he came out. I let him go a few steps from the door, then leapt. I felt his neck break on impact, tore open his throat to be sure, and ripped through his parka to taste his innards. There was no sport in it, but in winter we will take game whose brains we would never eat.

My mouth was full and my muzzle pleasantly, warmly moist with blood when the woman appeared. I looked up, and she was topping the rise, riding one of your incomprehensible machines, what I know now to be a snowstrider. The setting sun broke through the clouds behind her and for an instant she was embedded in glory. Her shadow stretched narrow before her and touched me, a bridge of darkness between us. We looked in one another's eyes...

Magda topped the rise with a kind of grim, joyless satisfaction. I am now a hunter's woman, she thought to herself. We will always be welcome at Landfall for the meat we bring, but they will never speak civilly to me again. Good. I would choke on their sweet talk anyway. The baby stirred and without looking down she stroked him through the furs, murmuring,

"Just a little longer, my brave little boo, and we'll be at our new home. Will you like that, eh?"

The sun broke through the clouds to her back, making the snow a red dazzle. Then her eyes adjusted, and she saw the black shape crouched over her lover's body. A very great distance away, her hands throttled down the snowstrider and brought it to a halt. The shallow bowl of land before her was barren, the snow about the corpse black with blood. A last curl of smoke lazily separated from the hut's chimney. The brute lifted its bloody muzzle and looked at her.

Time froze and knotted in black agony.

The larl screamed. It ran straight at her, faster than thought. Clumsily, hampered by the infant strapped to her stomach, Magda clawed the rifle from its boot behind the saddle. She shucked her mittens, fitted hands to metal that stung like hornets, flicked off the safety and brought the stock to her shoulder. The larl was halfway to her. She aimed and fired.

The larl went down. One shoulder shattered, slamming it to the side. It tumbled and rolled in the snow. "You sonofabitch!" Magda cried in triumph. But almost immediately the beast struggled to its feet, turned and fled.

The baby began to cry, outraged by the rifle's roar. Magda powered up the engine. "Hush, small warrior." A kind of madness filled her, a blind anesthetizing rage. "This won't take long." She flung her machine downhill, after the larl.

Even wounded, the creature was fast. She could barely keep up. As it entered the spare stand of trees to the far end of the meadow, Magda paused to fire again, burning a bullet by its head. The larl leaped away. From then on it varied its flight with sudden changes of direction and unexpected jogs to the side. It was a fast learner. But it could not escape Magda. She had always been a hothead, and now her blood was up. She was not about to return to her lover's gutted body with his killer still alive.

The sun set and in the darkening light she lost sight of the larl. But she was able to follow its trail by two-shadowed moonlight, the deep, purple footprints, the darker spatter of blood it left, drop by drop, in the snow.

It was the solstice, and the moons were full—a holy time. I felt it even as I fled the woman through the wilderness. The moons were bright on the snow. I felt the dread of being hunted descend on me, and in my inarticulate way I felt blessed.

But I also felt a great fear for my kind. We had dismissed the humans as incomprehensible, not very interesting creatures, slow-moving, bad-smelling, and dull-witted. Now, pursued by this madwoman on her fast machine brandishing a weapon that killed from afar, I felt all natural order betrayed. She was a goddess of the hunt, and I was her prey.

The People had to be told.

I gained distance from her, but I knew the woman would catch up. She was a hunter, and a hunter never abandons wounded prey. One way or another she would have me.

In the winter all who are injured or too old must offer themselves to the community. The sacrifice rock was not far, by a hill riddled from time beyond memory with our burrows. My knowledge must be shared: The humans were dangerous.

They would make good prey.

I reached my goal when the moons were highest. The flat rock was bare of snow when I ran limping in. Awakened by the scent of my blood, several People emerged from their dens. I lay myself down on the sacrifice rock. A grandmother of the People came forward, licked my wound, tasting, considering. Then she nudged me away with her forehead. The wound would heal, she thought, and winter was young; my flesh was not yet needed.

But I stayed. Again she nudged me away. I refused to go. She whined in puzzlement. I licked the rock.

That was understood. Two of the People came forward and placed their weight on me. A third lifted a paw. He shattered my skull, and they ate.

Magda watched through power binoculars from atop a nearby ridge. She saw everything. The rock swarmed with lean black horrors. It would be dangerous to go down among them, so she waited and watched the puzzling tableau below. The larl had wanted to die, she'd swear it, and now the beasts came forward daintily, almost ritualistically, to taste, the young first and then the old. She raised her rifle, thinking to exterminate a few of the brutes from afar.

A curious thing happened then. All the larls that had eaten of her prey's brain leaped away, scattering. Those that had not eaten waited, easy targets, not understanding. Then another dipped to lap up a fragment of brain, and looked up with sudden comprehension. Fear touched her.

The hunter had spoken often of the larls, had said that they were so elusive he sometimes thought them intelligent. "Come spring, when I can afford to waste ammunition on carnivores, I look forward to harvesting a few of these beauties," he'd said. He was the colony's xenobiologist, and he loved the animals he killed, treasured them even as he smoked their flesh, tanned their hides, and drew detailed pictures of their internal organs. Magda had always scoffed at his theory that larls gained insight into the habits of their prey by eating their brains, even though he'd spent much time observing the animals minutely from afar, gathering evidence. Now she wondered if he was right.

Her baby whimpered, and she slid a hand inside her furs to give him a breast. Suddenly the night seemed cold and dangerous, and she thought: What am I doing here? Sanity returned to her all at once, her anger collapsing to nothing, like an ice tower shattering in the wind. Below, sleek black shapes sped toward her, across the snow. They changed direction every few leaps, running evasive patterns to avoid her fire.

"Hang on, kid," she muttered, and turned her strider around. She opened up the throttle.

Magda kept to the open as much as she could, the creatures following her from a distance. Twice she stopped abruptly and turned her rifle on her pursuers. Instantly they disappeared in puffs of snow, crouching belly-down but not stopping, burrowing toward her under the surface. In the eerie night silence, she could hear the whispering sound of the brutes tunneling. She fled.

Some frantic timeless period later—the sky had still not lightened in the east—Magda was leaping a frozen stream when the strider's left ski struck a rock. The machine was knocked glancingly upward, cybernetics screaming as they fought to regain balance. With a sickening crunch, the strider slammed to earth, one ski twisted and bent. It would take extensive work before the strider could move again.

Magda dismounted. She opened her robe and looked down on her child. He smiled up at her and made a gurgling noise.

Something went dead in her.

A fool. I've been a criminal fool, she thought. Magda was a proud woman who had always refused to regret, even privately, anything she had done. Now she regretted everything: Her anger, the hunter, her entire life, all that had brought her to this point, the cumulative madness that threatened to kill her child.

A larl topped the ridge.

Magda raised her rifle, and it ducked down. She began walking down-slope, parallel to the stream. The snow was knee deep and she had to walk carefully not to slip and fall. Small pellets of snow rolled down ahead of her, were overtaken by other pellets. She strode ahead, pushing up a wake.

The hunter's cabin was not many miles distant; if she could reach it, they would live. But a mile was a long way in winter. She could hear the larls calling to each other, soft coughlike noises, to either side of the ravine. They were following the sound of her passage through the snow. Well, let them. She still had the rifle, and if it had few bullets left, they didn't know that. They were only animals.

This high in the mountains the trees were sparse. Magda descended a good quarter-mile before the ravine choked with scrub and she had to climb up and out or risk being ambushed. Which way? she wondered. She heard three coughs to her right, and climbed the left slope, alert and wary.

We herded her. Through the long night we gave her fleeting glimpses of our bodies whenever she started to turn to the side she must not go, and let her pass unmolested the other way. We let her see us dig into the distant snow and wait motionless, indetectable. We filled the woods with our shadows. Slowly, slowly, we turned her around. She struggled to return to the cabin, but she could not. In what haze of fear and despair she walked! We could smell it. Sometimes her baby cried, and she hushed the milky-scented creature in a voice gone flat with futility. The night deepened as the moons sank in the sky. We forced the woman back up into the mountains. Toward the end, her legs failed her several times; she lacked our strength and stamina. But her patience and guile were every bit our match. Once we approached her still form, and she killed two of us before the rest could retreat. How we loved her! We paced her, confident that sooner or later she'd drop.

It was at night's darkest hour that the woman was forced back to the burrowed hillside, the sacred place of the People where stood the sacrifice rock. She topped the same rise for the second time that night, and saw it. For a moment she stood helpless, and then she burst into tears.

We waited, for this was the holiest moment of the hunt, the point when the prey recognizes and accepts her destiny. After a time, the woman's sobs ceased. She raised her head and straightened her back.

Slowly, steadily she walked downhill.

She knew what to do.

Larls retreated into their burrows at the sight of her, gleaming eyes dissolving into darkness. Magda ignored them. Numb and aching, weary to death, she walked to the sacrifice rock. It had to be this way.

Magda opened her coat, unstrapped her baby. She wrapped him deep in the furs and laid the bundle down to one side of the rock. Dizzily, she opened the bundle to kiss the top of his sweet head, and he made an angry sound. "Good for you, kid," she said hoarsely. "Keep that attitude." She was so tired.

She took off her sweaters, her vest, her blouse. The raw cold nipped at her flesh with teeth of ice. She stretched slightly, body aching with motion. God it felt good. She laid down the rifle. She knelt.

The rock was black with dried blood. She lay down flat, as she had earlier seen her larl do. The stone was cold, so cold it almost blanked out the pain. Her pursuers waited nearby, curious to see what she was doing; she could hear the soft panting noise of their breathing. One padded noiselessly to her side. She could smell the brute. It whined questioningly.

She licked the rock.

Once it was understood what the woman wanted, her sacrifice went quickly. I raised a paw, smashed her skull. Again I was youngest. Innocent, I bent to taste.

The neighbors were gathering, hammering at the door, climbing over one another to peer through the windows, making the walls bulge and breathe with their eagerness. I grunted and bellowed, and the clash of silver and clink of plates next door grew louder. Like peasant animals, my husband's people tried to drown out the sound of my pain with toasts and drunken jokes.

Through the window I saw Tevin-the-Fool's bonewhite skin gaunt on his skull, and behind him a slice of face—sharp nose, white cheeks—like a mask. The doors and walls pulsed with the weight of those outside. In the next room children fought and wrestled, and elders pulled at their long white beards, staring anxiously at the closed door.

The midwife shook her head, red lines running from the corners of her mouth down either side of her stern chin. Her eye sockets were shadowy pools of dust. "Now push!" she cried. "Don't be a lazy sow!"

I groaned and arched my back. I shoved my head back and it grew smaller, eaten up by the pillows. The bedframe skewed as one leg slowly buckled under it. My husband glanced over his shoulder at me, an angry look, his fingers knotted behind his back.

All of Landfall shouted and hovered on the walls.

"Here it comes!" shrieked the midwife. She reached down to my bloody crotch, and eased out a tiny head, purple and angry, like a goblin.

And then all the walls glowed red and green and sprouted large flowers. The door turned orange and burst open, and the neighbors and crew flooded in. The ceiling billowed up, and aerialists tumbled through the rafters. A boy who had been hiding beneath the bed flew up laughing to where the ancient sky and stars shone through the roof.

They held up the child, bloody on a platter.

Here the larl touched me for the first time, that heavy black paw like velvet on my knee, talons sheathed. "Can you understand?" he asked. "What it meant to me? All that, the first birth of human young on this planet, I experienced in an instant. I felt it with full human comprehension. I understood the personal tragedy and the community triumph, and the meaning of the lives and culture behind it. A second before, I lived as an animal, with an animal's simple thoughts and hopes. Then I ate of your ancestor. I was lifted all in an instant halfway to godhood.

"As the woman had intended. She had died with her child's birth foremost in her mind, in order that we might share in it. She gave us that. She gave us more. She gave us *language*. We were wise animals before we ate her brain, and we were People afterward. We owed her so much. And we knew what she wanted from us." The larl stroked my cheek with his great, velvety paw, the ivory claws sheathed but quivering slightly, as if about to awake.

I hardly dared breathe.

"That morning I entered Landfall, carrying the baby's sling in my mouth. It slept through most of the journey. At dawn I passed through the empty street as silently as I knew how. I came to the First Captain's house. I heard the murmur of voices within, the entire village assembled for worship. I tapped the door with one paw. There was sudden, astonished silence. Then slowly, fearfully, the door opened."

The larl was silent for a moment. "That was the beginning of the association of People with humans. We were welcomed into your homes, and we helped with the hunting. It was a fair trade. Our food saved many lives that first winter. No one needed know how the woman had perished, or how well we understood your kind.

"That child, Flip, was your ancestor. Every few generations we take one of your family out hunting, and taste his brains, to maintain our closeness with your line. If you are a good boy and grow up to be as bold and honest, as intelligent and noble a man as your father, then perhaps it will be you we eat."

The larl presented his blunt muzzle to me in what might have been meant as a friendly smile. Perhaps not; the expression hangs unreadable, ambiguous in my mind even now. Then he stood and padded away into the friendly dark shadows of the Stone House.

I was sitting staring into the coals a few minutes later when my second-eldest sister—her face a featureless blaze of light, like an angel's—came into the room and saw me. She held out a hand, saying, "Come on, Flip, you're missing everything." And I went with her.

Did any of this actually happen? Sometimes I wonder. But it's growing late, and your parents are away. My room is small but snug, my bed warm but empty. We can burrow deep in the blankets and scare away the cave-bears by playing the oldest winter games there are.

You're blushing! Don't tug away your hand. I'll be gone soon to some distant world to fight in a war for people who are as unknown to you as they are to me. Soldiers grow old slowly, you know. We're shipped frozen between the stars. When you are old and plump and happily surrounded by grandchildren, I'll still be young, and thinking of you. You'll remember me then, and our thoughts will touch in the void. Will you have nothing to regret? Is that really what you want?

Come, don't be shy. Let's put the past aside and get on with our lives. That's better. Blow the candle out, love, and there's an end to my tale.

All this happened long ago, on a planet whose name has been burned from my memory.

THE EDGE OF THE WORLD

The day that Donna and Piggy and Russ went to see the Edge of the World was a hot one. They were sitting on the curb by the gas station that noontime, sharing a Coke and watching the big Starlifters lumber up into the air, one by one, out of Toldenarba AFB. The sky rumbled with their passing. There'd been an incident in the Persian Gulf, and half the American forces in the Twilight Emirates were on alert.

"My old man says when the Big One goes up, the base will be the first to go," Piggy said speculatively. "Treaties won't allow us to defend it. One bomber comes in high and whaboom—" he made soft nuclear explosion noises—"it's all gone." He was wearing camouflage pants and a khaki tee-shirt with an iron-on reading KILL 'EM ALL AND LET GOD SORT 'EM OUT. Donna watched as he took off his glasses to polish them on his shirt. His face went slack and vacant, then livened as he put them back on again, as if he were playing with a mask.

"You should be so lucky," Donna said. "Mrs. Khashoggi is still going want that paper done on Monday morning, Armageddon or not."

"Yeah, can you believe her?" Piggy said. "That weird accent! And all that memorization! Cut me some slack. I mean, who cares whether Ackronnion was part of the Mezentian Dynasty?"

"You ought to care, dipshit," Russ said. "Local history's the only decent class the school's got." Russ was the smartest boy Donna had ever met, never mind the fact that he was flunking out. He had soulful eyes and a radical haircut, short on the sides with a dyed-blond punklock down the back of his neck. "Man, I opened the Excerpts from Epics text that first night, thinking it was going to be the same old bullshit, and I stayed up 'til dawn. Got to school without a wink of sleep, but I'd managed to read every last word. This is one weird part of the world; its history is full of dragons and magic and all kinds of weird monsters. Do you realize that in the eighteenth century three members of the British legation were eaten by demons? That's in the historical record!"

Russ was an enigma to Donna. The first time they'd met, hanging with the misfits at an American School dance, he'd tried to put a hand down her pants, and she'd slugged him good, almost breaking his nose. She could still hear his surprised laughter as blood ran down his chin. They'd been friends ever since. Only there were limits to friendship, and now she was waiting for him to make his move and hoping he'd get down to it before her father was rotated out.

In Japan she'd known a girl who had taken a razor blade and carved her boyfriend's name in the palm of her hand. How could she do that, Donna had wanted to know? Her friend had shrugged, said, "As long as it gets me noticed." It wasn't until Russ that Donna understood.

"Strange country," Russ said dreamily. "The sky beyond the Edge is supposed to be full of demons and serpents and shit. They say that if you stare into it long enough, you'll go mad."

They all three looked at one another.

"Well, hell," Piggy said. "What are we waiting for?"

The Edge of the World lay beyond the railroad tracks. They bicycled through the American enclave into the old native quarter. The streets were narrow here, the sideyards crammed with broken trucks, rusted out buses, even yachts up in cradles with stoven-in sides. Garage doors were black mouths hissing and spitting welding sparks, throbbing to the hammered sound of worked metal. They hid their bikes in a patch of scrub apricot trees where the railroad crossed the industrial canal and hiked across.

Time had altered the character of the city where it bordered the Edge. Gone were the archers in their towers, vigilant against a threat that never came. Gone were the rose quartz palaces with their thousand windows, not a one of which overlooked the Edge. The battlements where blind musicians once piped up the dawn now survived only in Mrs. Khashoggi's texts. Where they had been was now a drear line of weary factory buildings, their lower windows cinderblocked or bricked up and those beyond reach of vandals' stones painted over in patchwork squares of grey and faded blue.

A steam whistle sounded and lines of factory workers shambled back inside, brown men in chinos and white shirts, Syrian and Lebanese laborers imported to do work no native Toldenarban would touch. A shredded net waved forlornly from a basketball hoop set up by the loading dock.

There was a section of hurricane fence down. They scrambled through.

As they cut across the grounds, a loud whine arose from within the factory building. Down the way another plant lifted its voice in a solid wham-wham-wham as rhythmic and unrelenting as a headache. One by one the factories shook themselves from their midday drowse and went back to work. "Why do they locate these things along the Edge?" Donna asked.

"It's so they can dump their chemical waste over the Edge," Russ explained. "These were all erected before the Emir nationalized the culverts that the Russian Protectorate built."

Behind the factory was a chest-high concrete wall, rough-edged and pebbly with the slow erosion of cement. Weeds grew in clumps at its foot. Beyond was nothing but sky.

Piggy ran ahead and spat over the Edge. "Hey, remember what Nixon said when he came here? *It is indeed a long way down.* What a guy!"

Donna leaned against the wall. A film of haze tinted the sky grey, intensifying at the focal point to dirty brown, as if a dead spot were burned into the center of her vision. When she looked down, her eyes kept grabbing for ground and finding more sky. There were a few wispy clouds in the distance and nothing more. No serpents coiled in the air. She should have felt disappointed but, really, she hadn't expected better. This was of a piece with all the natural wonders she had ever seen, the waterfalls, geysers and scenic vistas that inevitably included power lines, railings and parking lots absent from the postcards. Russ was staring intently ahead, hawklike, frowning. His jaw worked slightly, and she wondered what he saw.

"Hey, look what I found!" Piggy whooped. "It's a stairway!"

They joined him at the top of an institutional-looking concrete and iron stairway. It zigzagged down the cliff toward an infinitely distant and nonexistent Below, dwindling into hazy blue. Quietly, as if he'd impressed himself, Piggy said, "What do you suppose is down there?"

"Only one way to find out, isn't there?" Russ said.

Russ went first, then Piggy, then Donna, the steps ringing dully under their feet. Graffiti covered the rocks, worn spraypaint letters in yellow and black and red scrawled one over the other and faded by time and weather into mutual unreadability, and on the iron railings, words and arrows and triangles had been markered onto or dug into the paint with knife or nail: JURGEN BIN SCHEISSKOPF. MOTLEY CRUE. DEATH TO SATAN AMERICA IMPERIALIST. Seventeen steps down, the first landing was filthy with broken brown glass, bits of crumbled concrete, cigarette butts, soggy, half-melted cardboard. The stairway folded back on itself and they followed it down.

"You ever had *fugu?*" Piggy asked. Without waiting for an answer, he said, "It's Japanese poisonous blowfish. It has to be prepared very carefully—they license the chefs—and even so, several people die every year. It's considered a great delicacy."

"Nothing tastes that good," Russ said.

"It's not the flavor," Piggy said enthusiastically. "It's the poison. Properly prepared, see, there's a very small amount left in the sashimi and you get a threshold dose. Your lips and the tips of your fingers turn cold. Numb. That's how you know you're having the real thing. That's how you know you're living right on the edge."

"I'm already living on the edge," Russ said. He looked startled when Piggy laughed.

A fat moon floated in the sky, pale as a disk of ice melting in blue water. It bounced after them as they descended, kicking aside loose soda bottles in styrofoam sleeves, crushed Marlboro boxes, a scattering of carbonized sparkplugs. On one landing they found a crumpled shopping cart, and Piggy had to muscle it over the railing and watch it fall. "Sure is a lot of crap here," he observed. The landing smelled faintly of urine.

"It'll get better farther down," Russ said. "We're still near the top, where people can come to get drunk after work." He pushed on down. Far to one side they could see the brown flow from the industrial canal where it spilled into space, widening and then slowly dispersing into rainbowed mist, distance glamoring it beauty.

"How far are we planning to go?" Donna asked apprehensively.

"Don't be a weak sister," Piggy sneered. Russ said nothing.

The deeper they went, the shabbier the stairway grew, and the spottier its maintenance. Pipes were missing from the railing. Where patches of paint had fallen away the bolts anchoring the stair to the rock were walnut-sized lumps of rust.

Needle-clawed marsupials chittered warningly from niches in the rock as they passed. Tufts of grass and moth-white gentians grew in the loess-filled cracks.

Hours passed. Donna's feet and calves and the small of her back grew increasingly sore, but she refused to be the one to complain. By degrees she stopped looking over the side and out into the sky, and stared instead at her feet flashing in and out of sight while one hand went slap grab tug on the rail. She felt sweaty and miserable.

Back home she had a half-finished paper on the Three Days Incident of March, 1810, when the French Occupation, by order of Napoleon himself, had fired cannonade after cannonade over the Edge into nothingness. They had hoped to make rainstorms of devastating force that would lash and destroy their enemies, and created instead only a gunpowder haze, history's first great failure in weather control. This descent was equally futile, Donna thought, an endless and wearying exercise in nothing. Just the same as the rest of her life. Every time her father was reposted, she had resolved to change, to be somebody different this time around, whatever the price, even if—no, especially if—it meant playacting something she was not. Last year in Germany when she'd gone out with that local boy with the Alfa Romeo and instead of jerking him off had used her mouth, she had thought: Everything's going to be different now. But no.

Nothing ever changed.

"Heads up!" Russ said. "There's some steps missing here!" He leaped, and the landing gonged hollowly under his sneakers. Then again as Piggy jumped after.

Donna hesitated. There were five steps gone and a drop of twenty feet before the stairway cut back beneath itself. The cliff bulged outward here, and if she slipped she'd probably miss the stairs altogether.

She felt the rock draw away from her to either side, and was suddenly aware that she was connected to the world by the merest speck of matter, barely enough to anchor her feet. The sky wrapped itself about her, extending to infinity, depthless and absolute. She could extend her arms and fall into it forever. What would happen to her then, she wondered. Would she die of thirst and starvation, or would the speed of her fall grow so great that the oxygen would be sucked from her lungs, leaving her to strangle in a sea of air? "Come on, Donna!" Piggy shouted up at her. "Don't be a pussy!"

"Russ—" she said quaveringly.

But Russ wasn't looking her way. He was frowning downward, anxious to be going. "Don't push the lady," he said. "We can go on by ourselves."

Donna choked with anger and hurt and desperation all at once. She took a deep breath and, heart scudding, leaped. Sky and rock wheeled over her head. For an instant she was floating, falling, totally lost and filled with a panicky awareness that she was about to die. Then she crashed onto the landing. It hurt like hell, and at first she feared she'd pulled an ankle. Piggy grabbed her shoulders and rubbed the side of her head with his knuckles. "I knew you could do it, you wimp."

Donna knocked away his arm. "Okay, wiseass. How are you expecting to get us back up?"

The smile disappeared from Piggy's face. His mouth opened, closed. His head jerked fearfully upward. An acrobat could leap across, grab the step and flip up without any trouble at all. "I—I mean, I—"

"Don't worry about it," Russ said impatiently. "We'll think of something." He started down again.

It wasn't natural, Donna realized, his attitude. There was something obsessive about his desire to descend the stairway. It was like the time he'd brought his father's revolver to school along with a story about playing Russian roulette that morning before breakfast. "Three times!" he'd said proudly.

He'd had that same crazy look on him, and she hadn't the slightest notion then or now how she could help him.

Russ walked like an automaton, wordlessly, tirelessly, never hurrying up or slowing down. Donna followed in concerned silence, while Piggy scurried between them, chattering like somebody's pet Pekinese. This struck Donna as so apt as to be almost allegorical: the two of them together yet alone, the distance between filled with noise. She thought of this distance, this silence, as the sun passed behind the cliff and the afternoon heat lost its edge.

The stairs changed to cement-jacketed brick with small buttresses cut into the rock. There was a pile of stems and cherry pits on one landing, and the railing above them was white with bird droppings. Piggy leaned over the rail and said, "Hey, I can see seagulls down there. Flying around."

"Where?" Russ leaned over the railing, then said scornfully, "Those are pigeons. The Ghazoddis used to release them for rifle practice."

As Piggy turned to follow Russ down again, Donna caught a glimpse into his eyes, liquid and trembling with helplessness and despair. She'd seen that fear in him only once before, months ago when she'd stopped by his house on the way to school, just after the Emir's assassination.

The living room windows were draped and the room seemed un-naturally gloomy after being out in the morning sun. Blue television light flickered over shelves of shadowy ceramic figurines: Dresden milkmaids, Chantilly Chinamen, Meissen pug-dogs connected by a gold chain held in their champed jaws, naked Delft nymphs dancing.

Piggy's mother sat in a limp dressing gown, hair unbrushed, watching the funeral. She held a cup of oily looking coffee in one hand. Donna was surprised to see her up so early. Everyone said that she had a bad problem with alcohol, that even by service wife standards she was out of control.

"Look at them," Piggy's mother said. On the screen were solemn pro-cessions of camels and Cadillacs, sheikhs in jellaba, keffigeh and mirror-shades, European dignitaries with wives in tasteful grey Parisian fashions. "They've got their nerve."

"Where did you put my lunch?" Piggy said loudly from the kitchen.

"Making fun of the Kennedys, like that!" The Emir's youngest son, no more than four years old, salaamed his father's casket as it passed before him. "That kid's bad enough, but you should see the mother, crying as if her heart were broken. It's enough to turn your stomach. If I were Jackie, I'd—"

Donna and Piggy and Russ had gone bowling the night the Emir was shot. This was out in the ruck of cheap joints that surrounded the base, catering almost exclusively to servicemen. When the Muzak piped through overhead speakers was interrupted for the news bulletin, everyone had stood up and cheered. *Up we go* someone had begun singing, and the rest had joined in, *into the wild blue yonder…* Donna had felt so sick with fear and disgust she had thrown up in the parking lot. " I don't think they're making fun of anyone," Donna said. "They're just—"

"Don't talk to her!" The refrigerator door slammed shut. A cupboard door slammed open.

Piggy's mother smiled bitterly. "This is exactly what you'd expect from these ragheads. Pretending they're white people, deliberately mocking their betters. Filthy brown animals."

"Mother! Where is my fucking lunch?"

She looked at him then, jaw tightening. "Don't you use that kind of language on me, young man."

"All right!" Piggy shouted. "All right, I'm going to school without lunch! Shows how much you care!"

He turned to Donna and in the instant before he grabbed her wrist and dragged her out of the house, Donna could no longer hear the words, could only see that universe of baffled futility haunting Piggy's eyes. That same look she glimpsed today.

✺

The railings were wooden now, half the posts rotting at their bases, with an occasional plank missing, wrenched off and thrown over the side by previous visitors. Donna's knees buckled and she stumbled, almost lurching into the rock. "I have to stop," she said, hating herself for it. "I cannot go one more step."

Piggy immediately collapsed on the landing. Russ hesitated, then climbed up to join them. They three sat staring out into nothing, legs over the Edge, arms clutching the rail.

Piggy found a Pepsi can, logo in flowing Arabic, among the rubble. He held it in his left hand and began sticking holes in it with his butterfly knife, again and again, cackling like a demented sex criminal. "Exterminate the brutes!" he said happily. Then, with absolutely no transition he asked, "How are we ever going to get back up?" so dolorously Donna had to bite back her laughter.

"Look, I just want to go on down a little bit more," Russ said.

"Why?" Piggy sounded petulant.

"So I can get down enough to get away from this garbage." He gestured at the cigarette butts, the broken brown glass, sparser than above but still there. "Just a little further, okay guys?" There an edge to his voice, and under that the faintest hint of a plea. Donna felt helpless before those eyes. She wished they were alone, so she could ask him what was wrong.

Donna doubted that Russ himself knew what he expected to find down below. Did he think that if he went down far enough, he'd never have to climb back? She remembered the time in Mr. Herriman's algebra class when a sudden tension in the air had made her glance across the room at Russ, and he was, with great concentration, tearing the pages out of his math text and dropping them one by one on the floor. He'd taken a five-day suspension for that, and Donna had never found out what it was all about. But there was a kind of glorious arrogance to the act; Russ had been born out of time. He really should have been a medieval prince, a Medici or one of the Sabakan pretenders.

"Okay," Donna said, and Piggy of course had to go along.

Seven flights farther down the modern stairs came to an end. The wooden railing of the last short, septambic flight had been torn off entire, and laid across the steps. They had to step carefully between the uprights and the rails. But when they stood at the absolute bottom, they saw that there were stairs beyond the final landing, steps that had been cut into the stone itself. They were curving swaybacked things that millenia of rain and foot traffic had worn so uneven they were almost unpassable.

Piggy groaned. "Man, you can't expect us to go down that thing."

"Nobody's asking you," Russ said.

They descended the old stairway backwards and on all fours. The wind breezed up, hitting them with the force of an unexpected shove first to one side and then the other. There were times when Donna was so frightened she thought she was going to freeze up and never move again. But at last the stone broadened and became a wide, even ledge, with caves leading back into the rock.

The cliff face here was green white with lichen, and had in ancient times been laboriously smoothed and carved. Between each cave (their mouths alone left in a natural state, unaltered) were heavy-thighed women—goddesses, perhaps, or demons or sacred dancers—their breasts and faces chipped away by the image-hating followers of the Prophet at a time when Mohammed yet lived. Their hands held loops of vines in which were entangled moons, cycling from new through waxing quarter and gibbous to full and then back through gibbous and waning quarter to dark. Piggy was gasping, his face bright with sweat, but he kept up his blustery front. "What the fuck is all this shit, man?"

"It was a monastery," Russ said. He walked along the ledge dazedly, a wondering half smile on his lips. "I read about this." He stopped at a turquoise automobile door someone had flung over the Edge to be caught and tossed by fluke winds, the only piece of trash that had made it down this far. "Give me a hand."

He and Piggy lifted the door, swung it back and forth three times to build up momentum, then lofted it over the lip of the rock. They all three lay down on their stomachs to watch it fall away, turning end over end and seeming finally to flicker as it dwindled smaller and smaller, still falling. At last it shrank below the threshold of visibility and became one of a number of shifting motes in the downbelow, part of the slow, mazy movement of dead blood cells in the eyes' vitreous humors. Donna turned over on her back, drew her head back from the rim, stared upward. The cliff seemed to be slowly tumbling forward, all the world inexorably, dizzyingly leaning down to crush her.

"Let's go explore the caves," Piggy suggested.

They were empty. The interiors of the caves extended no more than thirty feet into the rock, but they had all been elaborately worked, arched ceilings carved with thousands of faux tesserae, walls adorned with bas-relief pillars. Between the pillars the walls were taken up with long shelves carved into the stone. No artifacts remained, not so much as a potsherd or a splinter of bone. Piggy shone his pocket flash into every shadowy niche. "Somebody's been here before us and taken everything," he said.

"The Historic Registry people, probably." Russ ran a hand over one shelf. It was the perfect depth and height for a line of three-pound coffee cans. "This is where they stowed the skulls. When a monk grew so spiritually developed he no longer needed the crutch of physical existence, his fellows would render the flesh from his bones and enshrine his skull. They poured wax in the sockets, then pushed in opals while it was still warm. They slept beneath the faintly gleaming eyes of their superiors."

When they emerged it was twilight, the first stars appearing from behind a sky fading from blue to purple. Donna looked down on the moon. It was as big as a plate, full and bright. The rilles, dry seas and mountain chains were preternaturally distinct. Somewhere in the middle was Tranquility Base, where Neil Armstrong had planted the American flag.

"Jeez, it's late," Donna said. "If we don't start home soon, my mom is going to have a cow."

"We still haven't figured a way to get back up," Piggy reminded her. Then, "We'll probably have to stay here. Learn to eat owls and grow crops sideways on the cliff face. Start our own civilization. Our only serious problem is the imbalance of sexes, but even that's not insurmountable." He put an arm around Donna's shoulders, grabbed at her breast. "You'd pull the train for us, wouldn't you, Donna?"

Angrily she pushed him away and said, "You keep a clean mouth! I'm so tired of your juvenile talk and behavior."

"Hey, calm down, it's cool." That panicky look was back in his eyes, the forced knowledge that he was not in control, could never be in control, that there was no such thing as control. He smiled weakly, placatingly.

"No, it is not. It is most emphatically not 'cool.'" Suddenly she was white and shaking with fury. Piggy was a spoiler. His simple presence ruined any chance she might have had to talk with Russ, find out just what was bugging him, get him to finally, really notice her. "I am sick of having to deal with your immaturity, your filthy language and your crude behavior."

Piggy turned pink and began stuttering.

Russ reached a hand into his pocket, pulled out a chunk of foil-wrapped hash, and a native tin pipe with a carved coral bowl. The kind of thing the local beggar kids sold for twenty-nine cents. "Anybody want to get stoned?" he asked suavely.

"You bastard!" Piggy laughed. "You told me you were out!"

Russ shrugged. "I lied." He lit the pipe carefully, drew in, passed it to Donna. She took it from his fingers, felt how cold they were to her touch, looked up over the pipe and saw his face, thin and ascetic, eyelids closed, pale and Christlike through the blue smoke. She loved him intensely in that instant and wished she could sacrifice herself for his happiness. The pipe's stem was overwarm, almost hot, between her lips. She drew in deep.

The smoke was raspy in her throat, then tight and swirling in her lungs. It shot up into her head, filled it with buzzing harmonics: the air, the sky, the rock behind her back all buzzing, ballooning her skull outward in a visionary rush that forced wide open first her eyes and then her mouth. She choked and spasmodically coughed. More smoke than she could imagine possibly holding in her lungs gushed out into the universe.

"Hey, watch that pipe!" Piggy snatched it from her distant fingers. They tingled with pinpricks of pain like tiny stars in the darkness of her flesh. "You were spilling the hash!" The evening light was abuzz with energy, the sky swarming up into her eyes. Staring out into the darkening air, the moon rising below her and the stars as close and friendly as those in a children's book illustration, she felt at peace, detached from worldly cares. "Tell us about the monastery, Russ," she said, in the same voice she might have used a decade before to ask her father for a story.

"Yeah, tell us about the monastery, Unca Russ," Piggy said, but with jeering undertones. Piggy was always sucking up to Russ, but there was tension there too, and his sarcastic little challenges were far from rare. It was classic beta male jealousy, straight out of Primate Psychology 101.

"It's very old," Russ said. "Before the sufis, before Mohammed, even before the Zoroastrians crossed the gulf, the native mystics would renounce the world and go to live in cliffs on the Edge of the World. They cut the steps down, and once down, they never went back up again."

"How did they eat then?" Piggy asked skeptically.

"They wished their food into existence. No, really! It was all in their creation myth: In the beginning all was Chaos and Desire. The world was brought out of Chaos—by which they meant unformed matter—

by Desire, or Will. It gets a little inconsistent after that, because it wasn't really a religion, but more like a system of magic. They believed that the world wasn't complete yet, that for some complicated reason it could never be complete. So there's still traces of the old Chaos lingering just beyond the Edge, and it can be tapped by those who desire it strongly enough, if they have distanced themselves from the things of the world. These mystics used to come down here to meditate against the moon and work miracles.

"This wasn't sophisticated stuff like the Tantric monks in Tibet or anything, remember. It was like a primitive form of animism, a way to force the universe to give you what you wanted. So the holy men would come down here and they'd wish for…like riches, you know? Filigreed silver goblets with rubies, mounds of moonstones, elfinbone daggers sharper than Damascene steel. Only once they got them they weren't supposed to want them. They'd just throw them over the Edge. There were these monasteries all along the cliffs. The farther from the world they were, the more spiritually advanced."

"So what happened to the monks?"

"There was a king—Althazar? I forget his name. He was this real greed-head, started sending his tax collectors down to gather up everything the monks brought into existence. Must've figured, hey, the monks weren't using them. Which as it turned out was like a real major blasphemy, and the monks got pissed. The boss mystics, all the real spiritual heavies, got together for this big confab. Nobody knows how. There's one of the classics claims they could run sideways on the cliff just like it was the ground, but I don't know. Doesn't matter. So one night they all of them, every monk in the world, meditated at the same time. They chanted together, they said, It is not enough that Althazar should die, for he has blasphemed. He must suffer a doom such as has been visited on no man before. He must be un-made, uncreated, reduced to less than has ever been. And they prayed that there be no such king as Althazar, that his life and history be unmade, so that there never had been such king as Althazar.

"And he was no more.

"But so great was their yearning for oblivion that when Althazar ceased to be, his history and family as well, they were left feeling embittered and did not know why. And not knowing why, their hatred turned upon themselves, and their wish for destruction, and they too all of a single night, ceased to be." He fell silent.

At last Piggy said, "You believe that crap?" Then, when there was no answer, "It's none of it true, man! Got that? There's no magic, and there never was." Donna could see that he was really angry, threatened on some primal level by the possibility that someone he respected could even begin to believe in magic. His face got pink, the way it always did when he lost control.

"No, it's all bullshit," Russ said bitterly. "Like everything else."

They passed the pipe around again. Then Donna leaned back, stared straight out, and said, "If I could wish for anything, you know what I'd wish for?"

"Bigger tits?"

She was so weary now, so pleasantly washed out, that it was easy to ignore Piggy. "I'd wish I knew what the situation was."

"What situation?" Piggy asked. Donna was feeling langorous, not at all eager to explain herself, and she waved away the question. But he persisted. "What situation?"

"Any situation. I mean, all the time, I find myself talking with people and I don't know what's really going on. What games they're playing. Why they're acting the way they are. I wish I knew what the situation was."

The moon floated before her, big and fat and round as a griffin's egg, shining with power. She could feel that power washing through her, the background radiation of decayed chaos spread across the sky at a uniform three degrees Kelvin. Even now, spent and respent, a coin fingered and thinned to the worn edge of nonexistence, there was power out there, enough to flatten planets.

Staring out at that great fat boojum snark of a moon, she felt the flow of potential worlds, and within the cold silver disk of that jester's skull, rank with magic, sensed the invisible presence of Russ's primitive monks, men whose minds were nowhere near comprehensible to her, yet vibrated with power, existing as matrices of patterned stress, no more actual than Donald Duck, but no less powerful either. She was caught in a waking fantasy, in which the sky was full of power and all of it accessible to her. Monks sat empty handed over their wishing bowls, separated from her by the least fictions of time and reality. For an eternal instant all possibilities fanned out to either side, equally valid, no one more real than any other. Then the world turned under her, and her brain shifted back to realtime.

"Me," Piggy said, "I just wish I knew how to get back up the stairs."

They were silent for a moment. Then it occurred to Donna that here was the perfect opportunity to find out what was bugging Russ. If she asked cautiously enough, if the question hit him just right, if she were just plain lucky, he might tell her everything. She cleared her throat. "Russ? What do you wish?"

In the bleakest voice imaginable, Russ said, "I wish I'd never been born."

She turned to ask him why, and he wasn't there.

"Hey," Donna said. "Where'd Russ go?"

Piggy looked at her oddly. "Who's Russ?"

It was a long trip back up. They carried the length of wooden railing between them, and every now and then Piggy said, "Hey, wasn't this a great idea of mine? This'll make a swell ladder."

"Yeah, great," Donna would say, because he got mad when she didn't respond. He got mad too, whenever she started to cry, but there wasn't anything she could do about that. She couldn't even explain why she was crying, because in all the world—of all his friends, acquaintances, teachers, even his parents—she was the only one who remembered that Russ had ever existed.

The horrible thing was that she had no specific memories of him, only a vague feeling of what his presence had been like, and a lingering sense of longing and frustration.

She no longer even remembered his face.

"Do you want to go first or last?" Piggy had asked her.

When she'd replied, "Last. If I go first, you'll stare at my ass all the way up," he'd actually blushed. Without Russ to show off in front of, Piggy was a completely different person, quiet and not at all abusive. He even kept his language clean.

But that didn't help, for just being in his presence was enough to force understanding on her: That his bravado was fueled by his insecurities and aspirations, that he masturbated nightly and with self-loathing, that he despised his parents and longed in vain for the least sign of love from them. That the way he treated her was the sum and total of all of this and more.

She knew exactly what the situation was.

Dear God, she prayed, let it be that I won't have this kind of understanding when I reach the top. Or else make it so that situations won't be so painful up there, that knowledge won't hurt like this, that horrible secrets won't lie under the most innocent word.

They carried their wooden burden upward, back toward the world.

GRIFFIN'S EGG

The sun cleared the mountains. Gunther Weil raised a hand in salute, then winced as the glare hit his eyes in the instant it took his helmet to polarize.

He was hauling fuel rods to Chatterjee Crater industrial park. The Chatterjee B reactor had gone critical forty hours before dawn, taking fifteen remotes and a microwave relay with it, and putting out a power surge that caused collateral damage to every factory in the park. Fortunately, the occasional meltdown was designed into the system. By the time the sun rose over the Rhaeticus highlands, a new reactor had been built and was ready to go online.

Gunther drove automatically, gauging his distance from Bootstrap by the amount of trash lining the Mare Vaporum road. Close by the city, discarded construction machinery and damaged assemblers sat in open-vacuum storage, awaiting possible salvage. Ten kilometers out, a pressurized van had exploded, scattering machine parts and giant worms of insulating foam across the landscape. At twenty-five kilometers, a poorly graded stretch of road had claimed any number of cargo skids and shattered running lights from passing traffic.

Forty kilometers out, though, the road was clear, a straight, clean gash in the dirt. Ignoring the voices at the back of his skull, the traffic chatter and automated safety messages that the truck routinely fed into his transceiver chip, he scrolled up the topographicals on the dash.

Right about here.

Gunther turned off the Mare Vaporum road and began laying tracks over virgin soil. "You've left your prescheduled route," the truck said. "Deviations from schedule may only be made with the recorded permission of your dispatcher."

"Yeah, well." Gunther's voice seemed loud in his helmet, the only physical sound in a babel of ghosts. He'd left the cabin unpressurized, and the insulated layers of his suit stilled even the conduction rumbling from the treads. "You and I both know that so long as I don't fall too far behind schedule, Beth Hamilton isn't going to care if I stray a little in between."

"You have exceeded this unit's linguistic capabilities."

"That's okay, don't let it bother you." Deftly he tied down the send switch on the truck radio with a twist of wire. The voices in his head abruptly died. He was completely isolated now.

"You said you wouldn't do that again." The words, broadcast directly to his trance chip, sounded as deep and resonant as the voice of God. "Generation Five policy expressly requires that all drivers maintain constant radio—"

"Don't whine. It's unattractive."

"You have exceeded this unit's linguistic—"

"Oh, shut up." Gunther ran a finger over the topographical maps, tracing the course he'd plotted the night before: Thirty kilometers over cherry soil, terrain no human or machine had ever crossed before, and then north on Murchison road. With luck he might even manage to be at Chatterjee early.

He drove into the lunar plain. Rocks sailed by to either side. Ahead, the mountains grew imperceptibly. Save for the trademarks dwindling behind him, there was nothing from horizon to horizon to show that humanity had ever existed. The silence was perfect.

Gunther lived for moments like this. Entering that clean, desolate emptiness, he experienced a vast expansion of being, as if everything he saw, stars, plain, craters and all, were encompassed within himself. Bootstrap City was only a fading dream, a distant island on the gently rolling surface of a stone sea. Nobody will ever be first here again, he thought. Only me.

A memory floated up from his childhood. It was Christmas eve and he was in his parents' car, on the way to midnight Mass. Snow was falling, thickly and windlessly, rendering all the familiar roads of Düsseldorf clean and pure under sheets of white. His father drove, and he himself leaned over the front seat to stare ahead in fascination into this peaceful, transformed world. The silence was perfect.

He felt touched by solitude and made holy.

The truck plowed through a rainbow of soft greys, submerged hues more hints than colors, as if something bright and festive held itself hidden just beneath a coating of dust. The sun was at his shoulder, and when he spun the front axle to avoid a boulder, the truck's shadow wheeled and reached for infinity. He drove reflexively, mesmerized by the austere beauty of the passing land.

At a thought, his peecee put music on his chip. *Stormy Weather* filled the universe.

❋

He was coming down a long, almost imperceptible slope when the controls went dead in his hands. The truck powered down and coasted to a stop. "Goddamn you, you asshole machine!" he snarled. "What is it this time?"

"The land ahead is impassible."

Gunther slammed a fist on the dash, making the maps dance. The land ahead was smooth and sloping, any unruly tendencies tamed eons ago by the Mare Imbrium explosion. Sissy stuff. He kicked the door open and clambered down.

The truck had been stopped by a baby rille: a snakelike depression meandering across his intended route, looking for all the world like a dry streambed. He bounded to its edge. It was fifteen meters across, and three meters down at its deepest. Just shallow enough that it wouldn't show up on the topos. Gunther returned to the cab, slamming the door noiselessly behind him.

"Look. The sides aren't very steep. I've been down worse a hundred times. We'll just take it slow and easy, okay?"

"The land ahead is impassible," the truck said. "Please return to the originally scheduled course."

Wagner was on now. *Tannhauser.* Impatiently, he thought it off.

"If you're so damned heuristic, then why won't you ever listen to reason?" He chewed his lip angrily, gave a quick shake of his head. "No, going back would put us way off schedule. The rille is bound to peter out in a few hundred meters. Let's just follow it until it does, then angle back to Murchison. We'll be at the park in no time."

Three hours later he finally hit the Murchison road. By then he was sweaty and smelly and his shoulders ached with tension. "Where are we?" he asked sourly. Then, before the truck could answer, "Cancel that." The soil had turned suddenly black. That would be the ejecta fantail from the Sony-Reinpfaltz mine. Their railgun was oriented almost due south in order to avoid the client factories, and so their tailings hit the road first. That meant he was getting close.

Murchison was little more than a confluence of truck treads, a dirt track crudely leveled and marked by blazes of orange paint on nearby boulders. In quick order Gunther passed through a series of landmarks: Harada Industrial fantail, Sea of Storms Macrofacturing fantail, Krupp fünfzig fantail. He knew them all. G5 did the robotics for the lot.

A light flatbed carrying a shipped bulldozer sped past him, kicking up a spray of dust that fell as fast as pebbles. The remote driving it waved a spindly arm in greeting. He waved back automatically, and wondered if it was anybody he knew.

The land hereabouts was hacked and gouged, dirt and boulders shoved into careless heaps and hills, the occasional tool station or Oxytank Emergency Storage Platform chopped into a nearby bluff. A sign floated by: TOILET FLUSHING FACILITIES 1/2 KILOMETER. He made a face. Then he remembered that his radio was still off and slipped the loop of wire from it. Time to rejoin the real world. Immediately his dispatcher's voice, harsh and staticky, was relayed to his trance chip.

"—ofabitch! Weil! Where the fuck are you?"

"I'm right here, Beth. A little late, but right where I'm supposed to be."

"Sonofa—" The recording shut off, and Hamilton's voice came on, live and mean. "You'd better have a real good explanation for this one, honey."

"Oh, you know how it is." Gunther looked away from the road, off into the dusty jade highlands. He'd like to climb up into them and never come back. Perhaps he would find caves. Perhaps there were monsters: vacuum trolls and moondragons with metabolisms slow and patient, taking centuries to move one body's-length, hyperdense beings that could swim through stone as if it were water. He pictured them diving, following lines of magnetic force deep, deep into veins of diamond and plutonium, heads back and singing. "I picked up a hitchhiker, and we kind of got involved."

"Try telling that to E. Izmailova. She's mad as hornets at you."

"Who?"

"Izmailova. She's the new demolitions jock, shipped up here on a multicorporate contract. Took a hopper in almost four hours ago, and she's been waiting for you and Siegfried ever since. I take it you've never met her?"

"No."

"Well, I have, and you'd better watch your step with her. She's exactly the kind of tough broad who won't be amused by your antics."

"Aw, come on, she's just another tech on a retainer, right? Not in my line of command. It's not like she can do anything to me."

"Dream on, babe. It wouldn't take much pull to get a fuckup like you sent down to Earth."

●

The sun was only a finger's breadth over the highlands by the time Chatterjee A loomed into sight. Gunther glanced at it every now and then, apprehensively. With his visor adjusted to the H-alpha wavelength, it was a blazing white sphere covered with slowly churning black specks: more granular than usual. Sunspot activity seemed high. He wondered that the Radiation Forecast Facility hadn't posted a surface advisory. The guys at the Observatory were usually right on top of things.

Chatterjee A, B and C were a triad of simple craters just below Chladni, and while the smaller two were of minimal interest, Chatterjee A was the child of a meteor that had punched through the Imbrian basalts to as sweet a vein of aluminum ore as anything in the highlands. Being so convenient to Bootstrap made it one of management's darlings, and Gunther was not surprised to see that Kerr-McGee was going all out to get their reactor online again.

The park was crawling with walkers, stalkers and assemblers. They were all over the blister-domed factories, the smelteries, loading docks and vacuum garages. Constellations of blue sparks winked on and off as major industrial constructs were dismantled. Fleets of heavily-loaded trucks fanned out into the lunar plain, churning up the dirt behind them. Fats Waller started to sing *The Joint is Jumping* and Gunther laughed.

He slowed to a crawl, swung wide to avoid a gas-plater that was being wrangled onto a loader, and cut up the Chatterjee B ramp road. A new landing pad had been blasted from the rock just below the lip, and a cluster of people stood about a hopper resting there. One human and eight remotes.

One of the remotes was speaking, making choppy little gestures with its arms. Several stood inert, identical as so many antique telephones, unclaimed by Earthside management but available should more advisors need to be called online.

Gunther unstrapped Siegfried from the roof of the cab and, control pad in one hand and cable spool in the other, walked him toward the hopper.

The human strode out to meet him. "You! What kept you?" E. Izmailova wore a jazzy red-and-orange Studio Volga boutique suit, in sharp contrast to his own company-issue suit with the G5 logo on the chest. He could not make out her face through the gold visor glass. But he could hear it in her voice: blazing eyes, thin lips.

"I had a flat tire." He found a good smooth chunk of rock and set down the cable spool, wriggling it to make sure it sat flush. "We got maybe five hundred yards of shielded cable. That enough for you?"

A short, tense nod.

"Okay." He unholstered his bolt gun. "Stand back." Kneeling, he anchored the spool to the rock. Then he ran a quick check of the unit's functions. "Do we know what it's like in there?"

A remote came to life, stepped forward and identified himself as Don Sakai, of G5's crisis management team. Gunther had worked with him before: a decent enough guy, but like most Canadians he had an exaggerated fear of nuclear energy. "Ms. Lang here, of Sony-Reinpfaltz, walked her unit in but the radiation was so strong she lost control after a preliminary scan." A second remote nodded confirmation, but the relay time to Toronto was just enough that Sakai missed it. "The remote just kept on walking." He coughed nervously, then added unnecessarily, "The autonomous circuits were too sensitive."

"Well, that's not going to be a problem with Siegfried. He's as dumb as a rock. On the evolutionary scale of machine intelligence he ranks closer to a crowbar than a computer." Two and a half seconds passed, and then Sakai laughed politely. Gunther nodded to Izmailova. "Walk me through this. Tell me what you want."

Izmailova stepped to his side, their suits pressing together briefly as she jacked a patch cord into his control pad. Vague shapes flickered across the outside of her visor like the shadows of dreams. "Does he know what he's doing?" she asked.

"Hey, I—"

"Shut up, Weil," Hamilton growled on a private circuit. Openly, she said, "He wouldn't be here if the company didn't have full confidence in his technical skills."

"I'm sure there's never been any question—" Sakai began. He lapsed into silence as Hamilton's words belatedly reached him.

"There's a device on the hopper," Izmailova said to Gunther. "Go pick it up."

He obeyed, reconfiguring Siegfried for a small, dense load. The unit bent low over the hopper, wrapping large, sensitive hands about the device.

Gunther applied gentle pressure. Nothing happened. Heavy little bugger. Slowly, carefully, he upped the power. Siegfried straightened.

"Up the road, then down inside."

The reactor was unrecognizable, melted, twisted and folded in upon itself, a mound of slag with twisting pipes sprouting from the edges. There had been a coolant explosion early in the incident, and one wall of the crater was bright with sprayed metal. "Where is the radioactive material?" Sakai asked. Even though he was a third of a million kilometers away, he sounded tense and apprehensive.

"It's all radioactive," Izmailova said.

They waited. "I mean, you know. The fuel rods?"

"Right now, your fuel rods are probably three hundred meters down and still going. We are talking about fissionable material that has achieved critical mass. Very early in the process the rods will have all melted together in a sort of superhot puddle, capable of burning its way through rock. Picture it as a dense, heavy blob of wax, slowly working its way toward the lunar core."

"God, I love physics," Gunther said.

Izmailova's helmet turned toward him, abruptly blank. After a long pause, it switched on again and turned away. "The road down is clear at least. Take your unit all the way to the end. There's an exploratory shaft to one side there. Old one. I want to see if it's still open."

"Will the one device be enough?" Sakai asked. "To clean up the crater, I mean."

The woman's attention was fixed on Siegfried's progress. In a distracted tone she said, "Mr. Sakai, putting a chain across the access road would be enough to clean up this site. The crater walls would shield anyone working nearby from the gamma radiation, and it would take no effort at all to reroute hopper overflights so their passengers would not be exposed. Most of the biological danger of a reactor meltdown comes from alpha radiation emitted by particulate radioisotopes in the air or water. When concentrated in the body, alpha-emitters can do considerable damage; elsewhere, no. Alpha particles can be stopped by a sheet of paper. So long as you keep a reactor out of your ecosystem, it's as safe as any other large machine. Burying a destroyed reactor just because it is radioactive is unnecessary and, if you will forgive me for saying so, superstitious. But I don't make policy. I just blow things up."

"Is this the shaft you're looking for?" Gunther asked.

"Yes. Walk it down to the bottom. It's not far."

Gunther switched on Siegfried's chestlight, and sank a roller relay so the cable wouldn't snag. They went down. Finally Izmailova said, "Stop. That's far enough." He gently set the device down and then, at her direction, flicked the arming toggle. "That's done," Izmailova said. "Bring your unit back. I've given you an hour to put some distance between the crater and yourself." Gunther noticed that the remotes, on automatic, had already begun walking away.

"Um…I've still got fuel rods to load."

"Not today you don't. The new reactor has been taken back apart and hauled out of the blasting zone."

Gunther thought now of all the machinery being disassembled and removed from the industrial park, and was struck for the first time by the operation's sheer extravagance of scale. Normally only the most sensitive devices were removed from a blasting area. "Wait a minute. Just what kind of monster explosive are you planning to use?"

There was a self-conscious cockiness to Izmailova's stance. "Nothing I don't know how to handle. This is a diplomat-class device, the same design as saw action five years ago. Nearly one hundred individual applications without a single mechanical failure. That makes it the most reliable weapon in the history of warfare. You should feel privileged having the chance to work with one."

Gunther felt his flesh turn to ice. "Jesus Mother of God," he said. "You had me handling a briefcase nuke."

"Better get used to it. Westinghouse Lunar is putting these little babies into mass production. We'll be cracking open mountains with them, blasting roads through the highlands, smashing apart the rille walls to see what's inside." Her voice took on a visionary tone. "And that's just the beginning. There are plans for enrichment fields in Sinus Aestum. Explode a few bombs over the regolith, then extract plutonium from the dirt. We're going to be the fuel dump for the entire solar system."

His dismay must have shown in his stance, for Izmailova laughed. "Think of it as weapons for peace."

"You should've been there!" Gunther said. "It was unfuckabelievable. The one side of the crater just disappeared. It dissolved into nothing. Smashed to dust. And for a real long time everything glowed! Craters, machines, everything. My visor was so close to overload it started flickering.

I thought it was going to burn out. It was nuts." He picked up his cards. "Who dealt this mess?"

Krishna grinned shyly and ducked his head. "I'm in."

Hiro scowled down at his cards. "I've just died and gone to Hell."

"Trade you," Anya said.

"No, I deserve to suffer."

They were in Noguchi park by the edge of the central lake, seated on artfully scattered boulders that had been carved to look water-eroded. A knee-high forest of baby birches grew to one side, and somebody's toy sailboat floated near the impact cone at the center of the lake. Honeybees mazily browsed the clover.

"And then, just as the wall was crumbling, this crazy Russian bitch—"

Anya ditched a trey. "Watch what you say about crazy Russian bitches."

"—goes zooming up on her hopper..."

"I saw it on television," Hiro said. "We all did. It was news. This guy who works for Nissan told me the BBC gave it thirty seconds." He'd broken his nose in karate practice, when he'd flinched into his instructor's punch, and the contrast of square white bandage with shaggy black eyebrows gave him a surly, piratical appearance.

Gunther discarded one. "Hit me. Man, you didn't see anything. You didn't feel the ground shake afterwards."

"Just what was Izmailova's connection with the Briefcase War?" Hiro asked. "Obviously not a courier. Was she in the supply end or strategic?"

Gunther shrugged.

"You do remember the Briefcase War?" Hiro said sarcastically. "Half of Earth's military elites taken out in a single day? The world pulled back from the brink of war by bold action? Suspected terrorists revealed as global heroes?"

Gunther remembered the Briefcase War quite well. He had been nineteen at the time, working on a Finlandia Geothermal project when the whole world had gone into spasm and very nearly destroyed itself. It had been a major factor in his decision to ship off the planet. "Can't we ever talk about anything but politics? I'm sick and tired of hearing about Armageddon."

"Hey, aren't you supposed to be meeting with Hamilton?" Anya asked suddenly.

He glanced up at the Earth. The east coast of South America was just crossing the dusk terminator. "Oh, hell, there's enough time to play out the hand."

Krishna won with three queens. The deal passed to Hiro. He shuffled quickly, and slapped the cards down with angry little punches of his arm. "Okay," Anya said, "what's eating you?"

He looked up angrily, then down again and in a muffled voice, as if he had abruptly gone bashful as Krishna, said, "I'm shipping home."

"Home?"

"You mean to Earth?"

"Are you crazy? With everything about to go up in flames? Why?"

"Because I am so fucking tired of the Moon. It has to be the ugliest place in the universe."

"Ugly?" Anya looked elaborately about at the terraced gardens, the streams that began at the top level and fell in eight misty waterfalls before reaching the central pond to be recirculated again, the gracefully winding pathways. People strolled through great looping rosebushes and past towers of forsythia with the dreamlike skimming stride that made moonwalking so like motion underwater. Others popped in and out of the office tunnels, paused to watch the finches loop and fly, tended to beds of cucumbers. At the midlevel straw market, the tents where off-duty hobby capitalists sold factory systems, grass baskets, orange glass paperweights and courses in postinterpretive dance and the meme analysis of Elizabethan poetry, were a jumble of brave silks, turquoise, scarlet and aquamarine. "I think it looks nice. A little crowded, maybe, but that's the pioneer aesthetic."

"It looks like a shopping mall, but that's not what I'm talking about. It's—" He groped for words. "It's like—it's what we're doing to this world that bothers me. I mean, we're digging it up, scattering garbage about, ripping the mountains apart, and for what?"

"Money," Anya said. "Consumer goods, raw materials, a future for our children. What's wrong with that?"

"We're not building a future, we're building weapons."

"There's not so much as a handgun on the Moon. It's an intercorporate development zone. Weapons are illegal here."

"You know what I mean. All those bomber fuselages, detonation systems, and missile casings that get built here, and shipped to low earth orbit. Let's not pretend we don't know what they're for."

"So?" Anya said sweetly. "We live in the real world, we're none of us naive enough to believe you can have governments without armies. Why is it worse that these things are being built here rather than elsewhere?"

"It's the short-sighted, egocentric greed of what we're doing that gripes me! Have you peeked out on the surface lately and seen the way it's being ripped open, torn apart and scattered about? There are still places where you can gaze upon a harsh beauty unchanged since the days our ancestors were swinging in trees. But we're trashing them. In a generation, two at most, there will be no more beauty to the Moon than there is to any other garbage dump."

"You've seen what Earthbound manufacturing has done to the environment," Anya said. "Moving it off the planet is a good thing, right?"

"Yes, but the Moon—"

"Doesn't even have an ecosphere. There's nothing here to harm."

They glared at each other. Finally Hiro said, "I don't want to talk about it," and sullenly picked up his cards.

Five or six hands later, a woman wandered up and plumped to the grass by Krishna's feet. Her eye shadow was vivid electric purple, and a crazy smile burned on her face. "Oh hi," Krishna said. "Does everyone here know Sally Chang? She's a research component of the Center for Self-Replicating Technologies, like me."

The others nodded. Gunther said, "Gunther Weil. Blue collar component of Generation Five."

She giggled.

Gunther blinked. "You're certainly in a good mood." He rapped the deck with his knuckles. "I'll stand."

"I'm on psilly," she said.

"One card."

"Psilocybin?" Gunther said. "I might be interested in some of that. Did you grow it or microfacture it? I have a couple of factories back in my room, maybe I could divert one if you'd like to license the software?"

Sally Chang shook her head, laughing helplessly. Tears ran down her cheeks.

"Well, when you come down we can talk about it." Gunther squinted at his cards. "This would make a great hand for chess."

"Nobody plays chess," Hiro said scornfully. "It's a game for computers."

Gunther took the pot with two pair. He shuffled, Krishna declined the cut, and he began dealing out cards. "So anyway, this crazy Russian lady—"

Out of nowhere, Chang howled. Wild gusts of laughter knocked her back on her heels and bent her forward again. The delight of discovery dancing in her eyes, she pointed a finger straight at Gunther. "You're a robot!" she cried.

"Beg pardon?"

"You're nothing but a robot," she repeated. "You're a machine, an automaton. Look at yourself! Nothing but stimulus-response. You have no free will at all. There's nothing there. You couldn't perform an original act to save your life."

"Oh yeah?" Gunther glanced around, looking for inspiration. A little boy—it might be Pyotr Nahfees, though it was hard to tell from here—was by the edge of the water, feeding scraps of shrimp loaf to the carp. "Suppose I pitched you into the lake? That would be an original act."

Laughing, she shook her head. "Typical primate behavior. A perceived threat is met with a display of mock aggression."

Gunther laughed.

"Then, when that fails, the primate falls back to a display of submission. Appeasal. The monkey demonstrates his harmlessness—you see?"

"Hey, this really isn't funny," Gunther said warningly. "In fact, it's kind of insulting."

"And so back to a display of aggression."

Gunther sighed and threw up both his hands. "How am I supposed to react? According to you, anything I say or do is wrong."

"Submission again. Back and forth, back and forth from aggression to submission and back again." She pumped her arm as if it were a piston. "Just like a little machine—you see? It's all automatic behavior."

"Hey, Kreesh—you're the neurobiowhatever here, right? Put in a good word for me. Get me out of this conversation."

Krishna reddened. He would not meet Gunther's eyes. "Ms. Chang is very highly regarded at the Center, you see. Anything she thinks about thinking is worth thinking about." The woman watched him avidly, eyes glistening, pupils small. "I think maybe what she means, though, is that we're all basically cruising through life. Like we're on autopilot. Not just you specifically, but all of us." He appealed to her directly. "Yes?"

"No, no, no, no." She shook her head. "Him specifically."

"I give up." Gunther put his cards down, and lay back on the granite slab so he could stare up through the roof glass at the waning Earth. When he closed his eyes, he could see Izmailova's hopper, rising. It was a skimpy device, little more than a platform-and-chair atop a cluster of four bottles of waste-gas propellant, and a set of smart legs. He saw it lofting up as the explosion blossomed, seeming briefly to hover high over the crater, like a hawk atop a thermal. Hands by side, the red-suited figure sat, watching with what seemed inhuman calm. In the reflected light she burned as bright as a star. In an appalling way, she was beautiful.

Sally Chang hugged her knees, rocking back and forth. She laughed and laughed.

✸

Beth Hamilton was wired for telepresence. She flipped up one lens when Gunther entered her office, but kept on moving her arms and legs. Dreamy little ghost motions that would be picked up and magnified in a factory somewhere over the horizon. "You're late again," she said with no particular emphasis.

Most people would have experienced at least a twinge of reality sickness dealing with two separate surrounds at once. Hamilton was one of the rare few who could split her awareness between two disparate realities without loss of efficiency in either. "I called you in to discuss your future with Generation Five. Specifically, to discuss the possibility of your transfer to another plant."

"You mean Earthside."

"You see?" Hamilton said. "You're not as stupid as you like to make yourself out to be." She flipped the lens down again, stood very still, then lifted a metal-gauntleted hand and ran through a complex series of finger movements. "Well?"

"Well what?"

"Tokyo, Berlin, Buenos Aires—do any of these hold magic for you? How about Toronto? The right move now could be a big boost to your career."

"All I want is to stay here, do my job, and draw down my salary," Gunther said carefully. "I'm not looking for a shot at promotion, or a big raise, or a lateral career-track transfer. I'm happy right where I am."

"You've sure got a funny way of showing it." Hamilton powered down her gloves, and slipped her hands free. She scratched her nose. To one side stood her work table, a polished cube of black granite. Her peecee rested there, alongside a spray of copper crystals. At her thought, it put Izmailova's voice onto Gunther's chip.

"It is with deepest regret that I must alert you to the unprofessional behavior of one of your personnel components," it began. Listening to the complaint, Gunther experienced a totally unexpected twinge of distress and, more, of resentment that Izmailova had dared judge him so harshly. He was careful not to let it show.

"Irresponsible, insubordinate, careless, and possessed of a bad attitude." He faked a grin. "She doesn't seem to like me much." Hamilton said nothing. "But this isn't enough to..." His voice trailed off. "Is it?"

"Normally, Weil, it would be. A demo jock isn't 'just a tech on retainer,' as you so quaintly put it; those government licenses aren't easy to get. And you may not be aware of it, but you have very poor efficiency ratings to begin with. Lots of potential, no follow-through. Frankly, you've been a disappointment. However, lucky for you, this Izmailova dame humiliated Don Sakai, and he's let us know that we're under no particular pressure to accommodate her."

"Izmailova humiliated Sakai?"

Hamilton stared at him. "Weil, you're oblivious, you know that?"

Then he remembered Izmailova's rant on nuclear energy. "Right, okay. I got it now."

"So here's your choice. I can write up a reprimand, and it goes into your permanent file, along with Izmailova's complaint. Or you can take a lateral Earthside, and I'll see to it that these little things aren't logged into the corporate system."

It wasn't much of a choice. But he put a good face on it. "In that case it looks like you're stuck with me."

"For the moment, Weil. For the moment."

He was back on the surface the next two days running. The first day he was once again hauling fuel rods to Chatterjee C. This time he kept to the road, and the reactor was refueled exactly on schedule. The second day he went all the way out to Triesnecker to pick up some old rods that had been in temporary storage for six months while the Kerr-McGee people argued over whether they should be reprocessed or dumped. Not a bad deal for him, because although the sunspot cycle was on the wane, there was a surface advisory in effect and he was drawing hazardous duty pay.

When he got there, a tech rep telepresenced in from somewhere in France to tell him to forget it. There'd been another meeting, and the decision had once again been delayed. He started back to Bootstrap with the new a capella version of the *Threepenny Opera* playing in his head. It sounded awfully sweet and reedy for his tastes, but that was what they were listening to up home.

Fifteen kilometers down the road, the UV meter on the dash jumped.

Gunther reached out to tap the meter with his finger. It did not respond. With a freezing sensation at the back of his neck, he glanced up at the roof of the cab and whispered, "Oh, no."

"The Radiation Forecast Facility has just intensified its surface warning to a Most Drastic status," the truck said calmly. "This is due to an unanticipated flare storm, onset immediately. Everyone currently on the surface is to proceed with all haste to shelter. Repeat: Proceed immediately to shelter."

"I'm eighty kilometers from—"

The truck was slowing to a stop. "Because this unit is not hardened, excessive fortuitous radiation may cause it to malfunction. To ensure the continued safe operation of this vehicle, all controls will be frozen in manual mode and this unit will now shut off."

With the release of the truck's masking functions, Gunther's head filled with overlapping voices. Static washed through them, making nonsense of what they were trying to say:

astic Status*epeat: We******his is Beth The** **hail******yo****ere?*C Su**ace adv***ry *as*******ve jus**issued****ost***om**on**good**uddy****ve up*******to Most**rast rastic ad*isory**Get*off me a**oot***Miko, Sabra* ic Sta**s. All unit* and the surfac*****ddamn**ou, Kangmei******your asse** personn*l are to find sh are you list***ng? Find undergrou***right now*** elter immediately. Maxim shelter. Don*t try to ge don't want*to hear you'* um exposure twenty minut back to Bootstrap. Too tayed behind to turn off es. Repeat: Maximum exp far, it'll fry you. List***f the lights. Who else*** os*re twenty m*nutes. Fi* en, ther* are thr*e facto****is out*ther*? Come in ri******helter im***iatel****ries no****r from***ur pr****ght n*w**Ev**yone! Anybo* **Th*******h***eco*ded*voi **ent**ocat*on***Are***u * dy k*ow w**re*Mikhail is***ce of t*** Radiati***Fore***li***ning**y***goofoff* *****C*mon, Misha***on't yo*****cast Fa**lity. Due**o an*Weisskopf*AG*is one, Niss****et coy on us***ound

u***unpre**c*ed solar flar********and**unar**acrostruct
your voice, heaWe g**** th***urfa***adviso****as*
ural*Weil******me kn*****ot word Ezra's dug**nt***
*****upgrad******Most Dr**if****'re listeni*****ome a
factory out Chladn****

"Beth! The nearest shelter is back at Weisskopf—that's half an hour at top speed and I've got an advisory here of twenty minutes. Tell me what to do!"

But the first sleet of hard particles was coming in too hard to make out anything more. A hand, his apparently, floated forward and flicked off the radio relay. The voices in his head died.

The crackling static went on and on. The truck sat motionless, half an hour from nowhere, invisible death sizzling and popping down through the cab roof. He put his helmet and gloves on, double-checked their seals, and unlatched the door.

It slammed open. Pages from the op manual flew away, and a glove went tumbling gaily across the surface, chasing the pink fuzzy-dice that Eurydice had given him that last night in Sweden. A handful of wheat biscuits in an open tin on the dash turned to powder and were gone, drawing the tin after them. Explosive decompression. He'd forgotten to depressurize. Gunther froze in dismayed astonishment at having made so basic—so dangerous—a mistake.

Then he was on the surface, head tilted back, staring up at the sun. It was angry with sunspots, and one enormous and unpredicted solar flare.

I'm going to die, he thought.

For a long, paralyzing instant, he tasted the chill certainty of that thought. He was going to die. He knew that for a fact, knew it more surely than he had ever known anything before.

In his mind, he could see Death sweeping across the lunar plain toward him. Death was a black wall, featureless, that stretched to infinity in every direction. It sliced the universe in half. On this side were life, warmth, craters and flowers, dreams, mining robots, thought, everything that Gunther knew or could imagine. On the other side...Something? Nothing? The wall gave no hint. It was unreadable, enigmatic, absolute. But it was bearing down on him. It was so close now that he could almost reach out and touch it. Soon it would be here. He would pass through, and then he would know.

With a start he broke free of that thought, and jumped for the cab. He scrabbled up its side. His trance chip hissing, rattling and crackling, he yanked the magnetic straps holding Siegfried in place, grabbed the spool and control pad, and jumped over the edge.

He landed jarringly, fell to his knees, and rolled under the trailer. There was enough shielding wrapped around the fuel rods to stop any amount of hard radiation—no matter what its source. It would shelter him as well from the sun as from his cargo. The trance chip fell silent, and he felt his jaws relaxing from a clenched tension.

Safe.

It was dark beneath the trailer, and he had time to think. Even kicking his rebreather up to full, and offlining all his suit peripherals, he didn't have enough oxygen to sit out the storm. So okay. He had to get to a shelter. Weisskopf was closest, only fifteen kilometers away and there was a shelter in the G5 assembly plant there. That would be his goal.

Working by feel, he found the steel supporting struts, and used Siegfried's magnetic straps to attach himself to the underside of the trailer. It was clumsy, difficult work, but at last he hung face-down over the road. He fingered the walker's controls, and sat Siegfried up.

Twelve excruciating minutes later, he finally managed to get Siegfried down from the roof unbroken. The interior wasn't intended to hold anything half so big. To get the walker in he had first to cut the door free, and then rip the chair out of the cab. Discarding both items by the roadside, he squeezed Siegfried in. The walker bent over double, reconfigured, reconfigured again, and finally managed to fit itself into the space. Gently, delicately, Siegfried took the controls and shifted into first.

With a bump, the truck started to move.

It was a hellish trip. The truck, never fast to begin with, wallowed down the road like a cast-iron pig. Siegfried's optics were bent over the controls, and couldn't be raised without jerking the walker's hands free. He couldn't look ahead without stopping the truck first.

He navigated by watching the road pass under him. To a crude degree he could align the truck with the treadmarks scrolling by. Whenever he wandered off the track, he worked Siegfried's hand controls to veer the truck back, so that it drifted slowly from side to side, zig-zagging its way down the road.

Shadows bumping and leaping, the road flowed toward Gunther with dangerous monotony. He jiggled and vibrated in his makeshift sling. After a while his neck hurt with the effort of holding his head back to watch the glaring road disappearing into shadow by the front axle, and his eyes ached from the crawling repetitiveness of what they saw.

The truck kicked up dust in passing, and the smaller particles carried enough of a static charge to cling to his suit. At irregular intervals he swiped at the fine grey film on his visor with his glove, smearing it into long, thin streaks.

He began to hallucinate. They were mild visuals, oblong patches of colored light that moved in his vision and went away when he shook his head and firmly closed his eyes for a concentrated moment. But every moment's release from the pressure of vision tempted him to keep his eyes closed longer, and that he could not afford to do.

It put him in mind of the last time he had seen his mother, and what she had said then. That the worst part of being a widow was that every day her life began anew, no better than the day before, the pain still fresh, her husband's absence a physical fact she was no closer to accepting than ever. It was like being dead, she said, in that nothing ever changed.

Ah God, he thought, this isn't worth doing. Then a rock the size of his head came bounding toward his helmet. Frantic hands jerked at the controls, and Siegfried skewed the truck wildly, so that the rock jumped away and missed him. Which put an end to that line of thought.

He cued his peecee. *Saint James' Infirmary* came on. It didn't help.

Come on, you bastard, he thought. You can do it. His arms and shoulders ached, and his back too, when he gave it any thought. Perversely enough, one of his legs had gone to sleep. At the angle he had to hold his head to watch the road, his mouth tended to hang open. After a while, a quivering motion alerted him that a small puddle of saliva had gathered in the curve of his faceplate. He was drooling. He closed his mouth, swallowing back his spit, and stared forward. A minute later he found that he was doing it again.

Slowly, miserably, he drove toward Weisskopf.

※

The G5 Weisskopf plant was typical of its kind: A white blister-dome to moderate temperature swings over the long lunar day, a microwave relay tower to bring in supervisory presence, and a hundred semiautonomous units to do the work.

Gunther overshot the access road, wheeled back to catch it, and ran the truck right up to the side of the factory. He had Siegfried switch off the engine, and then let the control pad fall to the ground. For well over a minute he simply hung there, eyes closed, savoring the end of motion. Then he kicked free of the straps, and crawled out from under the trailer.

Static skatting and stuttering inside his head, he stumbled into the factory.

In the muted light that filtered through the dome covering, the factory was dim as an undersea cavern. His helmet light seemed to distort as much as it illumined. Machines loomed closer in the center of its glare, swelling up as if seen through a fisheye lens. He turned it off, and waited for his eyes to adjust.

After a bit, he could see the robot assemblers, slender as ghosts, moving with unearthly delicacy. The flare storm had activated them. They swayed like seaweed, lightly out of sync with each other. Arms raised, they danced in time to random radio input.

On the assembly lines lay the remains of half-built robots, looking flayed and eviscerated. Their careful frettings of copper and silver nerves had been exposed to view and randomly operated upon. A long arm jointed down, electric fire at its tip, and made a metal torso twitch.

They were blind mechanisms, most of them, powerful things bolted to the floor in assembly logic paths. But there were mobile units as well, overseers and jacks-of-all-trades, weaving drunkenly through the factory with sun-maddened eye.

A sudden motion made Gunther turn just in time to see a metal puncher swivel toward him, slam down an enormous arm and put a hole in the floor by his feet. He felt the shock through his soles.

He danced back. The machine followed him, the diamond-tipped punch sliding nervously in and out of its sheath, its movements as trembling and dainty as a newborn colt's.

"Easy there, baby," Gunther whispered. To the far end of the factory, green arrows supergraffixed on the crater wall pointed to an iron door. The shelter. Gunther backed away from the punch, edging into a service aisle between two rows of machines that rippled like grass in the wind.

The punch press rolled forward on its trundle. Then, confused by that field of motion, it stopped, hesitantly scanning the ranks of robots. Gunther froze.

At last, slowly, lumberingly, the metal puncher turned away.

Gunther ran. Static roared in his head. Grey shadows swam among the distant machines, like sharks, sometimes coming closer, sometimes receding. The static loudened. Up and down the factory welding arcs winked on at the assembler tips, like tiny stars. Ducking, running, spinning, he reached the shelter and seized the airlock door. Even through his glove, the handle felt cold.

He turned it.

The airlock was small and round. He squeezed through the door and fit himself into the inadequate space within, making himself as small as possible. He yanked the door shut.

Darkness.

He switched his helmet lamp back on. The reflected glare slammed at his eyes, far too intense for such a confined area. Folded knees-to-chin into the roundness of the lock he felt a wry comradeship with Siegfried back in the truck.

The inner lock controls were simplicity itself. The door hinged inward, so that air pressure held it shut. There was a yank bar which, when pulled, would bleed oxygen into the airlock. When pressure equalized, the inner door would open easily. He yanked the bar.

The floor vibrated as something heavy went by.

The shelter was small, just large enough to hold a cot, a chemical toilet and a rebreather with spare oxytanks. A single overhead unit provided light and heat. For comfort there was a blanket. For amusement, there were pocket-sized editions of the Bible and the Koran, placed there by impossibly distant missionary societies. Even empty, there was not much space in the shelter.

It wasn't empty.

A woman, frowning and holding up a protective hand, cringed from his helmet lamp. "Turn that thing off," she said.

He obeyed. In the soft light that ensued he saw: starck white flattop, pink scalp visible through the sides. High cheekbones. Eyelids lifted slightly, like wings, by carefully sculpted eye shadow. Dark lips, full mouth. He had to admire the character it took to make up a face so carefully, only to hide it beneath a helmet. Then he saw her red and orange Studio Volga suit.

It was Izmailova.

To cover his embarrassment, he took his time removing his gloves and helmet. Izmailova moved her own helmet from the cot to make room, and he sat down beside her. Extending a hand, he stiffly said, "We've met before. My name is—"

"I know. It's written on your suit."

"Oh yeah. Right."

For an uncomfortably long moment, neither spoke. At last Izmailova cleared her throat and briskly said, "This is ridiculous. There's no reason we should—"

CLANG.

Their heads jerked toward the door in unison. The sound was harsh, loud, metallic. Gunther slammed his helmet on, grabbed for his gloves. Izmailova, also suiting up as rapidly as she could, tensely subvocalized into her trance chip: "What is it?"

Methodically snapping his wrist latches shut one by one, Gunther said, "I think it's a metal punch." Then, because the helmet muffled his words, he repeated them over the chip.

CLANG. This second time, they were waiting for the sound. Now there could be no doubt. Something was trying to break open the outer airlock door.

"A what?!"

"Might be a hammer of some type, or a blacksmith unit. Just be thankful it's not a laser jig." He held up his hands before him. "Give me a safety check."

She turned his wrists one way, back, took his helmet in her hands and gave it a twist to test its seal. "You pass." She held up her own wrists. "But what is it trying to do?"

Her gloves were sealed perfectly. One helmet dog had a bit of give in it, but not enough to breach integrity. He shrugged. "It's deranged—it could want anything. It might even be trying to repair a weak hinge."

CLANG.

"It's trying to get in here!"

"That's another possibility, yes."

Izmailova's voice rose slightly. "But even scrambled, there can't possibly be any programs in its memory to make it do that. How can random input make it act this way?"

"It doesn't work like that. You're thinking of the kind of robotics they had when you were a kid. These units are state of the art: They don't manipulate instructions, they manipulate concepts. See, that makes them more flexible. You don't have to program in every little step when you want one to do something new. You just give it a goal—"

CLANG.

"—like, to Disassemble a Rotary Drill. It's got a bank of available skills, like Cutting and Unbolting and Gross Manipulation, which it then fits together in various configurations until it has a path that will bring it to the goal." He was talking for the sake of talking now, talking to keep himself from panic. "Which normally works out fine. But when one of these things malfunctions, it does so on the conceptual level. See? So that—"

"So that it decides we're rotary drills that need to be disassembled."

"Uh…yeah."

CLANG.

"So what do we do when it gets in here?" They had both involuntarily risen to their feet, and stood facing the door. There was not much space, and what little there was they filled. Gunther was acutely aware that there was not enough room here to either fight or flee."I don't know about you," he said, "but I'm going to hit that sucker over the head with the toilet."

She turned to look at him.

CLA—The noise was cut in half by a breathy, whooshing explosion. Abrupt, total silence. "It's through the outer door," Gunther said flatly.

They waited.

Much later, Izmailova said, "Is it possible it's gone away?"

"I don't know." Gunther undogged his helmet, knelt and put an ear to the floor. The stone was almost painfully cold. "Maybe the explosion damaged it." He could hear the faint vibrations of the assemblers, the heavier rumblings of machines roving the factory floor. None of it sounded close. He silently counted to a hundred. Nothing. He counted to a hundred again.

Finally he straightened. "It's gone."

They both sat down. Izmailova took off her helmet, and Gunther clumsily began undoing his gloves. He fumbled at the latches. "Look at me." He laughed shakily. "I'm all thumbs. I can't even handle this, I'm so unnerved."

"Let me help you with that." Izmailova flipped up the latches, tugged at his glove. It came free. "Where's your other hand?"

Then, somehow, they were each removing the other's suit, tugging at the latches, undoing the seals. They began slowly but sped up with each latch undogged, until they were yanking and pulling with frantic haste. Gunther opened up the front of Izmailova's suit, revealing a red silk camisole. He slid his hands beneath it, and pushed the cloth up over her breasts. Her nipples were hard. He let her breasts fill his hands and squeezed.

Izmailova made a low, groaning sound in the back of her throat.She had Gunther's suit open. Now she pushed down his leggings and reached within to seize his cock. He was already erect. She tugged it out and impatiently shoved him down on the cot. Then she was kneeling on top of him, and guiding him inside her.

Her mouth met his, warm and moist.

Half in and half out of their suits, they made love. Gunther managed to struggle one arm free, and reached within Izmailova's suit to run a hand up her long back and over the back of her head. The short hairs of her buzz cut stung and tickled his palm.

She rode him roughly, her flesh slippery with sweat against his. "Are you coming yet?" she murmured. "Are you coming yet? Tell me when you're about to come." She bit his shoulder, the side of his neck, his chin, his lower lip. Her nails dug into his flesh.

"Now," he whispered. Possibly he only subvocalized it, and she caught it on her trance chip. But then she clutched him tighter than ever, as if she were trying to crack his ribs, and her whole body shuddered with orgasm. Then he came too, riding her passion down into spiraling desperation, ecstasy and release.

It was better than anything he had ever experienced before.

Afterward, they finally kicked free of their suits. They shoved and pushed the things off the cot. Gunther pulled the blanket out from beneath them, and with Izmailova's help wrapped it about the both of them. They lay together, relaxed, not speaking.

He listened to her breathe for a while. The noise was soft. When she turned her face toward him, he could feel it, a warm little tickle in the hollow of his throat. The smell of her permeated the room. This stranger beside him.

Gunther felt weary, warm, at ease. "How long have you been here?" he asked. "Not here in the shelter, I mean, but..."

"Five days."

"That little." He smiled. "Welcome to the Moon, Ms. Izmailova."

"Ekatarina," she said sleepily. "Call me Ekatarina."

Whooping, they soared high and south, over Herschel. The Ptolemaeus road bent and doubled below them, winding out of sight, always returning.

"This is great!" Hiro crowed. "This is—I should've talked you into taking me out here a year ago."

Gunther checked his bearings and throttled down, sinking eastward. The other two hoppers, slaved to his own, followed in tight formation. Two days had passed since the flare storm and Gunther, still on mandatory recoup, had promised to guide his friends into the highlands as soon as the surface advisory was dropped. "We're coming in now. Better triplecheck your safety harnesses. You doing okay back there, Kreesh?"

"I am quite comfortable, yes."

Then they were down on the Seething Bay Company landing pad.

Hiro was the second down and the first on the surface. He bounded about like a collie off its leash, chasing upslope and down, looking for new vantage points. "I can't believe I'm here! I work out this way every day, but you know what? This is the first time I've actually been out here. Physically, I mean."

"Watch your footing," Gunther warned. "This isn't like telepresence— if you break a leg, it'll be up to Krishna and me to carry you out."

"I trust you. Man, anybody who can get caught out in a flare storm, and end up nailing—"

"Hey, watch your language, okay?"

"Everybody's heard the story. I mean, we all thought you were dead, and then they found the two of you asleep. They'll be talking about it a hundred years from now." Hiro was practically choking on his laughter. "You're a legend!"

"Just give it a rest." To change the subject, Gunther said, "I can't believe you want to take a photo of this mess." The Seething Bay operation was a strip mine. Robot bulldozers scooped up the regolith and fed it to a processing plant that rested on enormous skids. They were after the thorium here, and the output was small enough that it could be transported to the breeder reactor by hopper. There was no need for a railgun and the tailings were piled in artificial mountains in the wake of the factory.

"Don't be ridiculous." Hiro swept an arm southward, toward Ptolemaeus. "There!" The crater wall caught the sun, while the lowest parts of the surrounding land were still in shadow. The gentle slopes seemed to tower; the crater itself was a cathedral, blazing white.

"Where is your camera?" Krishna asked.

"Don't need one. I'll just take the data down on my helmet."

"I'm not too clear on this mosaic project of yours," Gunther said. "Explain to me one more time how it's supposed to work."

"Anya came up with it. She's renting an assembler to cut hexagonal floor tiles in black, white and fourteen intermediate shades of grey. I provide the pictures. We choose the one we like best, scan it in black and white, screen for values of intensity, and then have the assembler lay the floor, one tile per pixel. It'll look great—come by tomorrow and see."

"Yeah, I'll do that."

Chattering like a squirrel, Hiro led them away from the edge of the mine. They bounded westward, across the slope.

Krishna's voice came over Gunther's trance chip. It was an old ground-rat trick. The chips had an effective transmission radius of fifteen yards—you could turn off the radio and talk chip-to-chip, if you were close enough. "You sound troubled, my friend."

He listened for a second carrier tone, heard nothing. Hiro was out of range. "It's Izmailova. I sort of—"

"Fell in love with her."

"How'd you know that?"

They were spaced out across the rising slope, Hiro in the lead. For a time neither spoke. There was a calm, confidential quality to that shared silence, like the anonymous stillness of the confessional. "Please don't take this wrong," Krishna said.

"Take what wrong?"

"Gunther, if you take two sexually compatible people, place them in close proximity, isolate them and scare the hell out of them, they will fall in love. That's a given. It's a survival mechanism, something that was wired into your basic makeup long before you were born. When billions of years of evolution say it's bonding time, your brain doesn't have much choice but to obey."

"Hey, come on over here!" Hiro cried over the radio. "You've got to see this."

"We're coming," Gunther said. Then, over his chip, "You make me out to be one of Sally Chang's machines."

"In some ways we are machines. That's not so bad. We feel thirsty when we need water, adrenalin pumps into the bloodstream when we need an extra boost of aggressive energy. You can't fight your own nature. What would be the point of it?"

"Yeah, but..."

"Is this great or what?" Hiro was clambering over a boulder field. "It just goes on and on. And look up there!" Upslope, they saw that what they were climbing over was the spillage from a narrow cleft entirely filled with boulders. They were huge, as big as hoppers, some of them large as prefab oxysheds. "Hey, Krishna, I been meaning to ask you—just what is it that you do out there at the Center?"

"I can't talk about it."

"Aw, come on." Hiro lifted a rock the size of his head to his shoulder and shoved it away, like a shot-putter. The rock soared slowly, landed far downslope in a white explosion of dust. "You're among friends here. You can trust us."

Krishna shook his head. Sunlight flashed from the visor. "You don't know what you're asking."

Hiro hoisted a second rock, bigger than the first. Gunther knew him in this mood, nasty-faced and grinning. "My point exactly. The two of us know zip about neurobiology. You could spend the next ten hours lecturing us, and we couldn't catch enough to compromise security." Another burst of dust.

"You don't understand. The Center for Self-Replicating Technologies is here for a reason. The lab work could be done back on Earth for a fraction of what a lunar facility costs. Our sponsors only move projects here that they're genuinely afraid of."

"So what can you tell us about? Just the open stuff, the video magazine stuff. Nothing secret."

"Well...okay." Now it was Krishna's turn. He picked up a small rock, wound up like a baseball player and threw. It dwindled and disappeared in the distance. A puff of white sprouted from the surface. "You know Sally Chang? She has just finished mapping the neurotransmitter functions."

They waited. When Krishna added nothing further, Hiro dryly said, "Wow."

"Details, Kreesh. Some of us aren't so fast to see the universe in a grain of sand as you are."

"It should be obvious. We've had a complete genetic map of the brain for almost a decade. Now add to that Sally Chang's chemical map, and it's analogous to being given the keys to the library. No, better than that. Imagine that you've spent your entire life within an enormous library filled with books in a language you neither read nor speak, and that you've just found the dictionary and a picture reader."

"So what are you saying? That we'll have complete understanding of how the brain operates?"

"We'll have complete control over how the brain operates. With chemical therapy, it will be possible to make anyone think or feel anything we want. We will have an immediate cure for all nontraumatic mental illness. We'll be able to fine-tune aggression, passion, creativity—bring them up, damp them down, it'll be all the same. You can see why our sponsors are so afraid of what our research might produce."

"Not really, no. The world could use more sanity," Gunther said.

"I agree. But who defines sanity? Many governments consider political dissent grounds for mental incarceration. This would open the doors of the brain, allowing it to be examined from the outside. For the first time, it would be possible to discover unexpressed rebellion. Modes of thought could be outlawed. The potential for abuse is not inconsiderable.

"Consider also the military applications. This knowledge combined with some of the new nanoweaponry might produce a berserker gas, allowing you to turn the enemy's armies upon their own populace. Or, easier, to throw them into a psychotic frenzy and let them turn on themselves. Cities could be pacified by rendering the citizenry catatonic. A secondary, internal reality could then be created, allowing the conqueror to use the masses as slave labor. The possibilities are endless."

They digested this in silence. At last Hiro said, "Jeeze, Krishna, if that's the open goods, what the hell kind of stuff do you have to hide?"

"I can't tell you."

A minute later, Hiro was haring off again. At the foot of a nearby hill he found an immense boulder standing atilt on its small end. He danced about, trying to get good shots past it without catching his own footprints in them.

"So what's the problem?" Krishna said over his chip.

"The problem is, I can't arrange to see her. Ekatarina. I've left messages, but she won't answer them. And you know how it is in Bootstrap—it takes a real effort to avoid somebody who wants to see you. But she's managed it."

Krishna said nothing.

"All I want to know is, just what's going on here?"

"She's avoiding you."

"But why? I fell in love and she didn't, is that what you're telling me? I mean, is that a crock or what?"

"Without hearing her side of the story, I can't really say how she feels. But the odds are excellent she fell every bit as hard as you did. The difference is that you think it's a good idea, and she doesn't. So of course she's avoiding you. Contact would just make it more difficult for her to master her feelings for you."

"Shit!"

An unexpected touch of wryness entered Krishna's voice. "What do you want? A minute ago you were complaining that Sally Chang thinks you're a machine. Now you're unhappy that Izmailova thinks she's not."

"Hey, you guys! Come over here. I've found the perfect shot. You've got to see this."

They turned to see Hiro waving at them from the hilltop. "I thought you were leaving," Gunther grumbled. "You said you were sick of the Moon, and going away and never coming back. So how come you're up-grading your digs all of a sudden?"

"That was yesterday! Today, I'm a pioneer, a builder of worlds, a founder of dynasties!"

"This is getting tedious. What does it take to get a straight answer out of you?"

Hiro bounded high and struck a pose, arms wide and a little ridiculous. He staggered a bit on landing. "Anya and I are getting married!"

Gunther and Krishna looked at each other, blank visor to blank visor. Forcing enthusiasm into his voice, Gunther said, "Hey, no shit? Really! Congratu—"

A scream of static howled up from nowhere. Gunther winced and cut down the gain. "My stupid radio is—"

One of the other two—they had moved together and he couldn't tell them apart at this distance—was pointing upward. Gunther tilted back his head, to look at the Earth. For a second he wasn't sure what he was looking for. Then he saw it: a diamond pinprick of light in the middle of the night. It was like a small, bright hole in reality, somewhere in continental Asia. "What the hell is that?" he asked.

Softly, Hiro said, "I think it's Vladivostok."

By the time they were back over the Sinus Medii, that first light had reddened and faded away, and two more had blossomed. The news jockey at the Observatory was working overtime splicing together reports from the major news feeds into a montage of rumor and fear. The radio was full of talk about hits on Seoul and Buenos Aires. Those seemed certain.

Strikes against Panama, Iraq, Denver and Cairo were disputed. A stealth missile had flown low over Hokkaido and been deflected into the Sea of Japan. The Swiss Orbitals had lost some factories to fragmentation satellites. There was no agreement as to the source aggressor, and though most suspicions trended in one direction, Tokyo denied everything.

Gunther was most impressed by the sound feed from a British video essayist, who said that it did not matter who had fired the first shot, or why. "Who shall we blame? The Southern Alliance, Tokyo, General Kim, or possibly some Grey terrorist group that nobody has ever heard of before? In a world whose weapons were wired to hair triggers, the question is irrelevant. When the first device exploded, it activated autonomous programs which launched what is officially labeled 'a measured response.' Gorshov himself could not have prevented it. His tactical programs chose this week's three most likely aggressors—at least two of which were certainly innocent—and launched a response. Human beings had no say over it.

"Those three nations in turn had their own reflexive 'measured responses.' The results of which we are just beginning to learn. Now we will pause for five days, while all concerned parties negotiate. How do we know this? Abstracts of all major defense programs are available on any public data net. They are no secret. Openness is in fact what deterrence is all about.

"We have five days to avert a war that literally nobody wants. The question is, in five days can the military and political powers seize control of their own defense programming? Will they? Given the pain and anger involved, the traditional hatreds, national chauvinism, and the natural reactions of those who number loved ones among the already dead, can those in charge overcome their own natures in time to pull back from final and total war? Our best informed guess is no. No, they cannot.

"Good night, and may God have mercy on us all."

They flew northward in silence. Even when the broadcast cut off in mid-word, nobody spoke. It was the end of the world, and there was nothing they could say that did not shrink to insignificance before that fact. They simply headed home.

The land about Bootstrap was dotted with graffiti, great block letters traced out in boulders: KARL OPS - EINDHOVEN '49 and LOUISE MCTIGHE ALBUQUERQUE N.M. An enormous eye in a pyramid. ARSENAL WORLD RUGBY CHAMPS with a crown over it. CORNPONE. Pi Lambda Phi. MOTORHEADS. A giant with a club. Coming down over them, Gunther reflected that they all referred to places and things in the world overhead, not a one of them indigenous to the Moon. What had always seemed pointless now struck him as unspeakably sad.

It was only a short walk from the hopper pad to the vacuum garage. They didn't bother to summon a jitney.

The garage seemed strangely unfamiliar to Gunther now, though he had passed through it a thousand times. It seemed to float in its own mystery, as if everything had been removed and replaced by its exact double, rendering it different and somehow unknowable. Row upon row of parked vehicles were slanted by type within painted lines. Ceiling lights strained to reach the floor, and could not.

"Boy, is this place still!" Hiro's voice seemed unnaturally loud.

It was true. In all the cavernous reaches of the garage, not a single remote or robot service unit stirred. Not so much as a pressure leak sniffer moved.

"Must be because of the news," Gunther muttered. He found he was not ready to speak of the war directly. To the back of the garage, five airlocks stood all in a row. Above them a warm, yellow strip of window shone in the rock. In the room beyond, he could see the overseer moving about.

Hiro waved an arm, and the small figure within leaned forward to wave back. They trudged to the nearest lock and waited.

Nothing happened.

After a few minutes, they stepped back and away from the lock to peer up through the window. The overseer was still there, moving unhurriedly. "Hey!" Hiro shouted over open frequency. "You up there! Are you on the job?"

The man smiled, nodded and waved again.

"Then open the goddamned door!" Hiro strode forward, and with a final, nodding wave, the overseer bent over his controls.

"Uh, Hiro," Gunther said, "There's something odd about..."

The door exploded open.

It slammed open so hard and fast the door was half torn off its hinges. The air within blasted out like a charge from a cannon. For a moment the garage was filled with loose tools, parts of vacuum suits and shreds of cloth. A wrench struck Gunther a glancing blow on his arm, spinning him around and knocking him to the floor.

He stared up in shock. Bits and pieces of things hung suspended for a long, surreal instant. Then, the air fled, they began to slowly shower down.

He got up awkwardly, massaging his arm through the suit. "Hiro, are you all right? Kreesh?"

"Oh my God," Krishna said.

Gunther spun around. He saw Krishna crouched in the shadow of a flatbed, over something that could not possibly be Hiro, because it bent the wrong way. He walked through shimmering unreality and knelt beside Krishna. He stared down at Hiro's corpse.

Hiro had been standing directly before the door when the overseer opened the door without depressurizing the corridor within first. He had caught the blast straight on. It had lifted him and smashed him against the side of a flatbed, snapping his spine and shattering his helmet visor with the backlash. He must have died instantaneously.

"Who's there?" a woman said.

A jitney had entered the garage without Gunther's noticing it. He looked up in time to see a second enter, and then a third. People began piling out. Soon there were some twenty individuals advancing across the garage. They broke into two groups. One headed straight toward the locks and the smaller group advanced on Gunther and his friends. It looked for all the world like a military operation. "Who's there?" the woman repeated.

Gunther lifted his friend's corpse in his arms and stood. "It's Hiro," he said flatly. "Hiro."

They floated forward cautiously, a semicircle of blank-visored suits like so many kachinas. He could make out the corporate logos. Mitsubishi. Westinghouse. Holst Orbital. Izmailova's red-and-orange suit was among them, and a vivid Mondrian pattern he didn't recognize. The woman spoke again, tensely, warily. "Tell me how you're feeling, Hiro."

It was Beth Hamilton.

"That's not Hiro," Krishna said. "It's Gunther. That's Hiro. That he's carrying. We were out in the highlands and—" His voice cracked and collapsed in confusion.

"Is that you, Krishna?" someone asked. "There's a touch of luck. Send him up front, we're going to need him when we get in." Somebody else slapped an arm over Krishna's shoulders and led him away.

Over the radio, a clear voice spoke to the overseer. "Dmitri, is that you? It's Signe. You remember me, don't you, Dmitri? Signe Ohmstede. I'm your friend."

"Sure I remember you, Signe. I remember you. How could I ever forget my friend? Sure I do."

"Oh, good. I'm so happy. Listen carefully, Dmitri. Everything's fine."

Indignantly, Gunther chinned his radio to send. "The hell it is! That fool up there—!"

A burly man in a Westinghouse suit grabbed Gunther's bad arm and shook him. "Shut the fuck up!" he growled. "This is serious, damn you. We don't have the time to baby you."

Hamilton shoved between them. "For God's sake, Posner, he's just seen—" She stopped. "Let me take care of him. I'll get him calmed down. Just give us half an hour, okay?"

The others traded glances, nodded, and turned away.

To Gunther's surprise, Ekatarina spoke over his trance chip. "I'm sorry, Gunther," she murmured. Then she was gone.

He was still holding Hiro's corpse. He found himself staring down at his friend's ruined face. The flesh was bruised and as puffy-looking as an overboiled hot dog. He couldn't look away.

"Come on." Beth gave him a little shove to get him going. "Put the body in the back of that pick-up and give us a drive out to the cliff."

At Hamilton's insistence, Gunther drove. He found it helped, having something to do. Hands afloat on the steering wheel, he stared ahead looking for the Mausoleum road cut-off. His eyes felt scratchy, and inhumanly dry.

"There was a preemptive strike against us," Hamilton said. "Sabotage. We're just now starting to put the pieces together. Nobody knew you were out on the surface or we would've sent somebody out to meet you. It's all been something of a shambles here."

He drove on in silence, cushioned and protected by all those miles of hard vacuum wrapped about him. He could feel the presence of Hiro's corpse in the back of the truck, a constant psychic itch between his shoulder blades. But so long as he didn't speak, he was safe; he could hold himself aloof from the universe that held the pain. It couldn't touch him. He waited, but Beth didn't add anything to what she'd already said.

Finally he said, "Sabotage?"

"A software meltdown at the radio station. Explosions at all the railguns. Three guys from Microspacecraft Applications bought it when the Boitsovij Kot railgun blew. I suppose it was inevitable. All the military industry up here, it's not surprising somebody would want to knock us out of the equation. But that's not all. Something's happened to the people in Bootstrap. Something really horrible. I was out at the Observatory when it happened. The newsjay called back to see if there was any backup software to get the station going again, and she got nothing but gibberish. Crazy stuff. I mean, really crazy. We had to disconnect the Observatory's remotes, because the operators were…" She was crying now, softly and insistently, and it was a minute before she could speak again."Some sort of biological weapon. That's all we know."

"We're here."

As he pulled up to the foot of the Mausoleum cliff, it occurred to Gunther that they hadn't thought to bring a drilling rig. Then he counted ten black niches in the rockface, and realized that somebody had been thinking ahead.

"The only people who weren't hit were those who were working at the Center or the Observatory, or out on the surface. Maybe a hundred of us all told."

They walked around to the back of the pick-up. Gunther waited, but Hamilton didn't offer to carry the body. For some reason that made him feel angry and resentful. He unlatched the gate, hopped up on the treads, and hoisted the suited corpse. "Let's get this over with."

Before today, only six people had ever died on the Moon. They walked past the caves in which their bodies awaited eternity. Gunther knew their names by heart: Heisse, Yasuda, Spehalski, Dubinin, Mikami, Castillo. And now Hiro. It seemed incomprehensible that the day should ever come when there would be too many dead to know them all by name.

Daisies and tiger lilies had been scattered before the vaults in such profusion that he couldn't help crushing some underfoot.

They entered the first empty niche, and he laid Hiro down upon a stone table cut into the rock. In the halo of his helmet lamp the body looked piteously twisted and uncomfortable. Gunther found that he was crying, large hot tears that crawled down his face and got into his mouth when he inhaled. He cut off the radio until he had managed to blink the tears away. "Shit." He wiped a hand across his helmet. "I suppose we ought to say something."

Hamilton took his hand and squeezed.

"I've never seen him as happy as he was today. He was going to get married. He was jumping around, laughing and talking about raising a family. And now he's dead, and I don't even know what his religion was."A thought occurred to him, and he turned helplessly toward Hamilton. "What are we going to tell Anya?"

"She's got problems of her own."Come on, say a prayer and let's go. You'll run out of oxygen."

"Yeah, okay." He bowed his head. *"The Lord is my shepherd, I shall not want...."*

✸

Back at Bootstrap, the surface party had seized the airlocks and led the overseer away from the controls. The man from Westinghouse, Posner, looked down on them from the observation window. "Don't crack your suits," he warned. "Keep them sealed tight at all times. Whatever hit the bastards here is still around. Might be in the water, might be in the air. One whiff and you're out of here! You got that?"

"Yeah, yeah," Gunther grumbled. "Keep your shirt on."

Posner's hand froze on the controls. "Let's get serious here. I'm not letting you in until you acknowledge the gravity of the situation. This isn't a picnic outing. If you're not prepared to help, we don't need you. Is that understood?"

"We understand completely, and we'll cooperate to the fullest," Hamilton said quickly. "Won't we, Weil?"

He nodded miserably.

Only the one lock had been breached, and there were five more sets of pressurized doors between it and the bulk of Bootstrap's air. The city's designers had been cautious.

Overseen by Posner, they passed through the corridors, locks and changing rooms and up the cargo escalators. Finally they emerged into the city interior.

They stood blinking on the lip of Hell.

At first, it was impossible to pinpoint any source for the pervasive sense of wrongness nattering at the edge of consciousness. The parks were dotted with people, the fill lights at the juncture of crater walls and canopy were bright, and the waterfalls still fell gracefully from terrace to terrace. Button quail bobbed comically in the grass.

Then small details intruded. A man staggered about the fourth level, head jerking, arms waving stiffly. A plump woman waddled by, pulling an empty cart made from a wheeled microfactory stand, quacking like a duck. Someone sat in the kneehigh forest by Noguchi park, tearing out the trees one by one.

But it was the still figures that were on examination more profoundly disturbing. Here a man lay half in and half out of a tunnel entrance, as unselfconscious as a dog. There, three women stood in extreme postures of lassitude, bordering on despair. Everywhere, people did not touch or

172

speak or show in any way that they were aware of one other. They shared an absolute and universal isolation.

"What shall we—" Something slammed onto Gunther's back. He was knocked forward, off his feet. Tumbling, he became aware that fists were striking him, again and again, and then that a lean man was kneeling atop his chest, hysterically shouting, "Don't do it! Don't do it!"

Hamilton seized the man's shoulders, and pulled him away. Gunther got to his knees. He looked into the face of madness: eyes round and fearful, expression full of panic. The man was terrified of Gunther.

With an abrupt wrench, the man broke free. He ran as if pursued by demons. Hamilton stared after him. "You okay?" she asked.

"Yeah, sure." Gunther adjusted his tool harness. "Let's see if we can find the others."

They walked toward the lake, staring about at the self-absorbed figures scattered about the grass. Nobody attempted to speak to them. A woman ran by, barefooted. Her arms were filled with flowers. "Hey!" Hamilton called after her. She smiled fleetingly over her shoulder, but did not slow. Gunther knew her vaguely, an executive supervisor for Martin Marietta.

"Is everybody here crazy?" he asked.

"Sure looks that way."

The woman had reached the shore and was flinging the blossoms into the water with great sweeps of her arm. They littered the surface.

"Damned waste." Gunther had come to Bootstrap before the flowers; he knew the effort involved getting permission to plant them and rewriting the city's ecologics. A man in a blue-striped Krupp suit was running along the verge of the lake.

The woman, flowers gone, threw herself into the water.

At first it appeared she'd suddenly decided to take a dip. But from the struggling, floundering way she thrashed deeper into the water it was clear that she could not swim.

In the time it took Gunther to realize this, Hamilton had leaped forward, running for the lake. Belatedly, he started after her. But the man in the Krupp suit was ahead of them both. He splashed in after the woman. An outstretched hand seized her shoulder and then he fell, pulling her under. She was red-faced and choking when he emerged again, arm across her chest.

By then Gunther and Beth were wading into the lake, and together they three got the woman to shore. When she was released, the woman calmly turned and walked away, as if nothing had happened.

"Gone for more flowers," the Krupp component explained. "This is the third time fair Ophelia there's tried to drown herself. She's not the only one. I've been hanging around, hauling 'em out when they stumble in."

"Do you know where everybody else is? Is there anyone in charge? Somebody giving out orders?"

"Do you need any help?" Gunther asked.

The Krupp man shrugged. "I'm fine. No idea where the others are, though. My friends were going on to the second level when I decided I ought to stay here. If you see them, you might tell 'em I'd appreciate hearing back from them. Three guys in Krupp suits."

"We'll do that," Gunther said.

Hamilton was already walking away.

On a step just beneath the top of the stairs sprawled one of Gunther's fellow G5 components. "Sidney," he said carefully. "How's it going?"

Sidney giggled. "I'm making the effort, if that's what you mean. I don't see that the 'how' of it makes much difference."

"Okay."

"A better way of phrasing that might be to ask why I'm not at work." He stood, and in a very natural manner accompanied Gunther up the steps. "Obviously I can't be two places at once. You wouldn't want to perform major surgery in your own absence, would you?" He giggled again. "It's an oxymoron. Like horses: Those classically beautiful Praxitelesian bodies excreting these long surreal turds."

"Okay."

"I've always admired them for squeezing so much art into a single image."

"Sidney," Hamilton said. "We're looking for our friends. Three people in blue-striped work suits."

"I've seen them. I know just where they went." His eyes were cool and vacant; they didn't seem to focus on anything in particular.

"Can you lead us to them?"

"Even a flower recognizes its own face." A gracefully winding gravel path led through private garden plots and croquet malls. They followed him down it.

There were not many people on the second terrace; with the fall of madness, most seemed to have retreated into the caves. Those few who remained either ignored or cringed away from them. Gunther found himself staring obsessively into their faces, trying to analyze the deficiency he felt in each. Fear nested in their eyes, and the appalled awareness that some terrible thing had happened to them coupled with a complete ignorance of its nature.

"God, these people!"

Hamilton grunted.

He felt he was walking through a dream. Sounds were muted by his suit, and colors less intense seen through his helmet visor. It was as if he had been subtly removed from the world, there and not-there simultaneously, an impression that strengthened with each new face that looked straight through him with mad, unseeing indifference.

Sidney turned a corner, broke into a trot and jogged into a tunnel entrance. Gunther ran after him. At the mouth of the tunnel, he paused to let his helmet adjust to the new light levels. When it cleared he saw Sidney dart down a side passage. He followed.

At the intersection of passages, he looked and saw no trace of their guide. Sidney had disappeared. "Did you see which way he went?" he asked Hamilton over the radio. There was no answer. "Beth?"

He started down the corridor, halted, and turned back. These things went deep. He could wander around in them forever. He went back out to the terraces. Hamilton was nowhere to be seen.

For lack of any better plan, he followed the path. Just beyond an ornamental holly bush he was pulled up short by a vision straight out of William Blake.

The man had discarded shirt and sandals, and wore only a pair of shorts. He squatted atop a boulder, alert, patient, eating a tomato. A steel pipe slanted across his knees like a staff or scepter, and he had woven a crown of sorts from platinum wire with a fortune's worth of hyperconductor chips dangling over his forehead. He looked every inch a kingly animal.

He stared at Gunther, calm and unblinking.

Gunther shivered. The man seemed less human than anthropoid, crafty in its way, but unthinking. He felt as if he were staring across the eons at Grandfather Ape, crouched on the edge of awareness. An involuntary thrill of superstitious awe seized him. Was this what happened when the higher mental functions were scraped away? Did Archetype lie just beneath the skin, waiting for the opportunity to emerge?

"I'm looking for my friend," he said. "A woman in a G5 suit like mine? Have you seen her? She was looking for three—" He stopped. The man was staring at him blankly. "Oh, never mind."

He turned away and walked on.

After a time, he lost all sense of continuity. Existence fragmented into unconnected images: A man bent almost double, leering and squeezing a yellow rubber duckie. A woman leaping up like a jack-in-the-box from behind an air monitor, shrieking and flapping her arms. An old friend sprawled on the ground, crying, with an broken leg. When he tried to help her, she scrabbled away from him in fear. He couldn't get near to her without doing more harm. "Stay here," he said, "I'll find help." Five minutes later he realized that he was lost, with no slightest notion of how to find his way back to her again. He came to the stairs leading back down to the bottom level. There was no reason to go down them. There was no reason not to. He went down.

He had just reached the bottom of the stairs when someone in a lavender boutique suit hurried by.

Gunther chinned on his helmet radio.

"Hello!" The lavender suit glanced back at him, its visor a plate of obsidian, but did not turn back. "Do you know where everyone's gone? I'm totally lost. How can I find out what I should be doing?" The lavender suit ducked into a tunnel.

Faintly, a voice answered, "Try the city manager's office."

The city manager's office was a tight little cubby an eighth of a kilometer deep within the tangled maze of administrative and service tunnels. It had never been very important in the scheme of things. The city manager's prime duties were keeping the air and water replenished and scheduling airlock inspections, functions any computer could handle better than a man had they dared trust them to a machine. The room had probably never been as crowded as it was now. Dozens of people suited for full vacuum spilled out into the hall, anxiously listening to Ekatarina confer with the city's Crisis Management Program. Gunther pushed in as close as he could; even so, he could barely see her.

"—the locks, the farms and utilities, and we've locked away all the remotes. What comes next?"

Ekatarina's peecee hung from her work harness, amplifying the CMP's silent voice. "Now that elementary control has been established, second priority must go to the industrial sector. The factories must be locked down. The reactors must be put to sleep. There is not sufficient human supervisory presence to keep them running. The factories have mothballing programs available upon request.

"Third, the farms cannot tolerate neglect. Fifteen minutes without oxygen, and all the tilapia will die. The calamari are even more delicate. Three experienced agricultural components must be assigned immediately. Double that number, if you only have inexperienced components. Advisory software is available. What are your resources?"

"Let me get back to you on that. What else?"

"What about the people?" a man asked belligerently. "What the hell are you worrying about factories for, when our people are in the state they're in?"

Izmailova looked up sharply. "You're one of Chang's research components, aren't you? Why are you here? Isn't there enough for you to do?" She looked about, as if abruptly awakened from sleep. "All of you! What are you waiting for?"

"You can't put us off that easily! Who made you the little brass-plated general? We don't have to take orders from you."

The bystanders shuffled uncomfortably, not leaving, waiting to take their cue from each other. Their suits were as good as identical in this crush, their helmets blank and expressionless. They looked like so many ambulatory eggs.

The crowd's mood balanced on the instant, ready to fall into acceptance or anger with a featherweight's push. Gunther raised an arm. "General!" he said loudly. "Private Weil here! I'm awaiting my orders. Tell me what to do."

Laughter rippled through the room, and the tension eased. Ekatarina said, "Take whoever's nearest you, and start clearing the afflicted out of the administrative areas. Guide them out toward the open, where they won't be so likely to hurt themselves. Whenever you get a room or corridor emptied, lock it up tight. Got that?"

"Yes, ma'am." He tapped the suit nearest him, and its helmet dipped in a curt nod. But when they turned to leave, their way was blocked by the crush of bodies.

"You!" Ekatarina jabbed a finger. "Go to the farmlocks and foam them shut; I don't want any chance of getting them contaminated. Anyone with experience running factories—that's most of us, I think—should find a remote and get to work shutting the things down. The CMP will help direct you. If you have nothing else to do, buddy up and work at clearing out the corridors. I'll call a general meeting when we've put together a more comprehensive plan of action." She paused. "What have I left out?"

Surprisingly, the CMP answered her: "There are twenty-three children in the city, two of them seven-year-old prelegals and the rest five years of age or younger, offspring of registered-permanent lunar components. Standing directives are that children be given special care and protection. The third-level chapel can be converted to a care center. Word should be spread that as they are found, the children are to be brought there. Assign one reliable individual to oversee them."

"My God, yes." She turned to the belligerent man from the Center, and snapped, "Do it."

He hesitated, then saluted ironically and turned to go.

That broke the logjam. The crowd began to disperse. Gunther and his co-worker—it turned out to be Liza Nagenda, another ground-rat like himself—set to work.

In after years Gunther was to remember this period as a time when his life entered a dark tunnel. For long, nightmarish hours he and Liza shuffled from office to storage room, struggling to move the afflicted out of the corporate areas and into the light.

The afflicted did not cooperate.

The first few rooms they entered were empty. In the fourth, a distraught-looking woman was furiously going through drawers and files and flinging their contents away. Trash covered the floor. "It's in here somewhere, it's in here somewhere," she said frantically.

"What's in there, darling?" Gunther said soothingly. He had to speak loudly so he could be heard through his helmet. "What are you looking for?"

She tilted her head up with a smile of impish delight. Using both hands, she smoothed back her hair, elbows high, pushing it straight over her skull, then tucking in stray strands behind her ears. "It doesn't matter, because I'm sure to find it now. Two scarabs appear, and between them the blazing disk of the sun, that's a good omen, not to mention being an analogy for sex. I've had sex, all the sex anyone could want, buggered behind the outhouse by the lizard king when I was nine. What did I care? I had wings then and thought that I could fly."

Gunther edged a little closer. "You're not making any sense at all."

"You know, Tolstoy said there was a green stick in the woods behind his house that once found would cause all men to love one another. I believe in that green stick as a basic principle of physical existence. The universe exists in a matrix of four dimensions which we can perceive and seven which we cannot, which is why we experience peace and brother- hood as a seven-dimensional greenstick phenomenon."

"You've got to listen to me."

"Why? You gonna tell me Hitler is dead? I don't believe in that kind of crap."

"Oh hell," Nagenda said. "You can't reason with a flick. Just grab her arms and we'll chuck her out."

It wasn't that easy, though. The woman was afraid of them. Whenever they approached her, she slipped fearfully away.

If they moved slowly, they could not corner her, and when they both rushed her, she leaped up over a desk and then down into the kneehole. Nagenda grabbed her legs and pulled. The woman wailed, and clutched at the knees of her suit. "Get offa me," Liza snarled. "Gunther, get this crazy woman off my damn legs."

"Don't kill me!" the woman screamed. "I've always voted twice—you know I did. I told them you were a gangster, but I was wrong. Don't take the oxygen out of my lungs!'"

They got the woman out of the office, then lost her again when Gunther turned to lock the door. She went fluttering down the corridor with Nagenda in hot pursuit. Then she dove into another office, and they had to start all over again.

It took over an hour to drive the woman from the corridors and release her into the park. The next three went quickly enough by contrast. The one after that was difficult again, and the fifth turned out to be the first woman they had encountered, wandered back to look for her office. When they'd brought her to the open again, Liza Nagenda said, "That's four flicks down and three thousand, eight hundred fifty- eight to go."

"Look—" Gunther began. And then Krishna's voice sounded over his trance chip, stiffly and with exaggerated clarity. "Everyone is to go to the central lake immediately for an organizational meeting. Repeat: Go to the lake immediately. Go to the lake now." He was obviously speaking over a jury-rigged transmitter. The sound was bad and his voice boomed and popped on the chip.

"Alright, okay, I got that," Liza said. "You can shut up now."

"Please go to the lake immediately. Everyone is to go directly to the central—"

"Sheesh."

By the time they got out to the parklands again, the open areas were thick with people. Not just the suited figures of the survivors, either. All the afflicted were emerging from the caves and corridors of Bootstrap. They walked blindly, uncertainly, toward the lake, as if newly called from the grave. The ground level was filling with people.

"Sonofabitch," Gunther said wonderingly.

"Gunther?" Nagenda asked. "What's going on?"

"It's the trance chips! Sonofabitch, all we had to do was speak to them over the chips. They'll do whatever the voice in their heads tells them to do."

The land about the lake was so crowded that Gunther had trouble spotting any other suits.

Then he saw a suited figure standing on the edge of the second level waving broadly. He waved back and headed for the stairs.

By the time he got to level two, a solid group of the unafflicted had gathered. More and more came up, drawn by the concentration of suits. Finally Ekatarina spoke over the open channel of her suit radio.

"There's no reason to wait for us all to gather. I think everyone is close enough to hear me. Sit down, take a little rest, you've all earned it." People eased down on the grass. Some sprawled on their backs or stomachs, fully suited. Most just sat.

"By a fortunate accident, we've discovered a means of controlling our afflicted friends." There was light applause. "But there are still many problems before us, and they won't all be solved so easily. We've all seen the obvious. Now I must tell you of worse. If the war on Earth goes full thermonuclear, we will be completely and totally cut off, possibly for decades."

A murmur passed through the crowd.

"What does this mean? Beyond the immediate inconveniences—no luxuries, no more silk shirts, no new seed stock, no new videos, no way home for those of us who hadn't already decided to stay—we will be losing much that we require for survival. All our microfacturing capability comes from the Swiss Orbitals. Our water reserves are sufficient for a year, but we lose minute quantities of water vapor to rust and corrosion and to the vacuum every time somebody goes in or out an airlock, and those quantities are necessary for our existence.

"But we can survive. We can process raw hydrogen and oxygen from the regolith, and burn them to produce water. We already make our own air. We can do without most nanoelectronics. We can thrive and prosper and grow, even if Earth...even if the worst happens. But to do so we'll need our full manufacturing capability, and full supervisory capability as well. We must not only restore our factories, but find a way to restore our people. There'll be work and more for all of us in the days ahead."

Nagenda touched helmets with Gunther and muttered, "What a crock."

"Come on, I want to hear this."

"Fortunately, the Crisis Management Program has contingency plans for exactly this situation. According to its records, which may be incomplete, I have more military command experience than any other functional. Does anyone wish to challenge this?" She waited, but nobody said anything. "We will go to a quasimilitary structure for the duration of the emergency. This is strictly for organizational purposes. There will be no privileges afforded the officers, and the military structure will be dismantled immediately upon resolution of our present problems. That's paramount."

She glanced down at her peecee. "To that purpose, I am establishing beneath me a triumvirate of subordinate officers, consisting of Carlos Diaz-Rodrigues, Miiko Ezumi, and Will Posner. Beneath them will be nine officers, each responsible for a cadre of no more than ten individuals."

She read out names. Gunther was assigned to Cadre Four, Beth Hamilton's group. Then Ekatarina said, "We're all tired. The gang back at the Center have rigged up a decontamination procedure, a kitchen and sleeping spaces of sorts. Cadres One, Two and Three will put in four more hours here, then pull down a full eight hours sleep. Cadres Four through Nine may return now to the Center for a meal and four hours rest." She stopped. "That's it. Go get some shut-eye."

A ragged cheer arose, fell flat and died. Gunther stood. Liza Nagenda gave him a friendly squeeze on the butt and when he started to the right yanked his arm and pointed him left, toward the service escalators. With easy familiarity, she slid an arm around his waist.

He'd known guys who'd slept with Liza Nagenda, and they all agreed that she was bad news, possessive, hysterical, ludicrously emotional. But what the hell. It was easier than not.

They trudged off.

There was too much to do. They worked to exhaustion—it was not enough. They rigged a system of narrow-band radio transmissions for the CMP and ran a microwave patch back to the Center, so it could direct their efforts more efficiently—it was not enough. They organized and rearranged constantly. But the load was too great and accidents inevitably happened.

Half the surviving railguns—small units used to deliver raw and semiprocessed materials over the highlands and across the bay—were badly damaged when the noonday sun buckled their aluminum rails; the sunscreens had not been put in place in time. An unknown number of robot bulldozers had wandered off from the strip mines and were presumably lost. It was hard to guess how many because the inventory records were scrambled. None of the food stored in Bootstrap could be trusted; the Center's meals had to be harvested direct from the farms and taken out through the emergency locks. An inexperienced farmer mishandled her remote, and ten aquaculture tanks boiled out into vacuum geysering nine thousand fingerlings across the surface. On Posner's orders, the remote handler rigs were hastily packed and moved to the Center. When uncrated, most were found to have damaged rocker arms.

There were small victories. On his second shift, Gunther found fourteen bales of cotton in vacuum storage and set an assembler to sewing futons for the Center. That meant an end to sleeping on bare floors and made him a local hero for the rest of that day. There were not enough toilets in the Center; Diaz-Rodrigues ordered the flare storm shelters in the factories stripped of theirs. Huriel Garza discovered a talent for cooking with limited resources.

But they were losing ground. The afflicted were unpredictable, and they were everywhere. A demented systems analyst, obeying the voices in his head, dumped several barrels of lubricating oil in the lake. The water filters clogged, and the streams had to be shut down for repairs. A doctor somehow managed to strangle herself with her own diagnostic harness. The city's ecologics were badly stressed by random vandalism.

Finally somebody thought to rig up a voice loop for continuous transmission. "I am calm," it said. "I am tranquil. I do not want to do anything. I am happy where I am."

Gunther was working with Liza Nagenda trying to get the streams going again when the loop came on. He looked up and saw an uncanny quiet spread over Bootstrap. Up and down the terraces, the flicks stood in postures of complete and utter impassivity. The only movement came from the small number of suits scurrying like beetles among the newly catatonic.

Liza put her hands on her hips. "Terrific. Now we've got to *feed* them."

"Hey, cut me some slack, okay? This is the first good news I've heard since I don't know when."

"It's not good anything, sweetbuns. It's just more of the same."

She was right. Relieved as he was, Gunther knew it. One hopeless task had been traded for another.

✹

He was wearily suiting up for his third day when Hamilton stopped him and said, "Weil! You know any electrical engineering?"

"Not really, no. I mean, I can do the wiring for a truck, or maybe rig up a microwave relay, stuff like that, but…"

"It'll have to do. Drop what you're on, and help Krishna set up a system for controlling the flicks. Some way we can handle them individually."

They set up shop in Krishna's old lab. The remnants of old security standards still lingered, and nobody had been allowed to sleep there. Consequently, the room was wonderfully neat and clean, all crafted-in-orbit laboratory equipment with smooth, anonymous surfaces. It was a throwback to a time before clutter and madness had taken over. If it weren't for the new-tunnel smell, the raw tang of cut rock the air carried, it would be possible to pretend nothing had happened.

Gunther stood in a telepresence rig, directing a remote through Bootstrap's apartments. They were like so many unconnected cells of chaos. He entered one and found the words BUDDHA = COSMIC INERTIA scrawled on its wall with what looked to be human feces. A woman sat on the futon tearing handfuls of batting from it and flinging them in the air. Cotton covered the room like a fresh snowfall. The next apartment was empty and clean, and a microfactory sat gleaming on a ledge. "I hereby nationalize you in the name of the People's Provisional Republic of Bootstrap, and of the oppressed masses everywhere," he said dryly. The remote gingerly picked it up. "You done with that chip diagram yet?"

"It will not be long now," Krishna said.

They were building a prototype controller. The idea was to code each peecee, so the CMP could identify and speak to its owner individually. By stepping down the voltage, they could limit the peecee's transmission range to a meter and a half so that each afflicted person could be given individualized orders. The existing chips, however, were high-strung Swiss Orbital thoroughbreds, and couldn't handle oddball power yields. They had to be replaced.

"I don't see how you can expect to get any useful work out of these guys, though. I mean, what we need are supervisors. You can't hope to get coherent thought out of them."

Bent low over his peecee, Krishna did not answer at first. Then he said, "Do you know how a yogi stops his heart? We looked into that when I was in grad school. We asked Yogi Premanand if he would stop his heart while wired up to our instruments, and he graciously consented. We had all the latest brain scanners, but it turned out the most interesting results were recorded by the EKG.

"We found that the yogi's heart did not, as we had expected, slow down, but rather went faster and faster, until it reached its physical limits and began to fibrillate. He had not slowed his heart; he had sped it up. It did not stop, but went into spasm.

"After our tests, I asked him if he had known these facts. He said no, that they were most interesting. He was polite about it, but clearly did not think our findings very significant."

"So you're saying...?"

"The problem with schizophrenics is that they have too much going on in their heads. Too many voices. Too many ideas. They can't focus their attention on a single chain of thought. But it would be a mistake to think them incapable of complex reasoning. In fact, they're thinking brilliantly. Their brains are simply operating at such peak efficiencies that they can't organize their thoughts coherently.

"What the trance chip does is to provide one more voice, but a louder, more insistent one. That's why they obey it. It breaks through that noise, provides a focus, serves as a matrix along which thought can crystallize."

The remote unlocked the door into a conference room deep in the administrative tunnels. Eight microfactories waited in a neat row atop the conference table. It added the ninth, turned, and left, locking the door behind it. "You know," Gunther said, "all these elaborate precautions may be unnecessary. Whatever was used on Bootstrap may not be in the air anymore. It may never have been in the air. It could've been in the water or something."

"Oh, it's there all right, in the millions. We're dealing with an air-borne schizomimetic engine. It's designed to hang around in the air indefinitely."

"A schizomimetic engine? What the hell is that?"

In a distracted monotone, Krishna said, "A schizomimetic engine is a strategic nonlethal weapon with high psychological impact. It not only incapacitates its target vectors, but places a disproportionately heavy burden on the enemy's manpower and material support caring for the victims. Due to the particular quality of the effect, it has a profoundly demoralizing influence on those exposed to the victims, especially those involved in their care. Thus, it is particularly desirable as a strategic weapon." He might have been quoting from an operations manual.

Gunther pondered that. "Calling the meeting over the chips wasn't a mistake, was it? You knew it would work. You knew they would obey a voice speaking inside their heads."

"Yes."

"This shit was brewed up at the Center, wasn't it? This is the stuff that you couldn't talk about."

"Some of it."

Gunther powered down his rig and flipped up the lens. "God damn you, Krishna! God damn you straight to Hell, you stupid fucker!"

Krishna looked up from his work, bewildered. "Have I said something wrong?"

"No! No, you haven't said a damned thing wrong—you've just driven four thousand people out of their fucking minds, is all! Wake up and take a good look at what you maniacs have done with your weapons research!"

"It wasn't weapons research," Krishna said mildly. He drew a long, involuted line on the schematic. "But when pure research is funded by the military, the military will seek out military applications for the research. That's just the way it is."

"What's the difference? It happened. You're responsible."

Now Krishna actually set his peecee aside. He spoke with uncharacteristic fire. "Gunther, we need this information. Do you realize that we are trying to run a technological civilization with a brain that was evolved in the neolithic? I am perfectly serious. We're all trapped in the old hunter-gatherer programs, and they are of no use to us anymore. Take a look at what's happening on Earth. They're hip-deep in a war that nobody meant to start and nobody wants to fight and it's even money that nobody can stop. The type of thinking that put us in this corner is not to our benefit. It has to change. And that's what we are working toward—taming the human brain. Harnessing it. Reining it in.

"Granted, our research has been turned against us. But what's one more weapon among so many? If neuroprogrammers hadn't been available, something else would have been used. Mustard gas maybe, or plutonium dust. For that matter, they could've just blown a hole in the canopy and let us all strangle."

"That's self-justifying bullshit, Krishna! Nothing can excuse what you've done."

Quietly, but with conviction, Krishna said, "You will never convince me that our research is not the most important work we could possibly be doing today. We must seize control of this monster within our skulls. We must change our ways of thinking." His voice dropped. "The sad thing is that we cannot change unless we survive. But in order to survive, we must first change."

They worked in silence after that.

Gunther awoke from restless dreams to find that the sleep shift was only half over. Liza was snoring. Careful not to wake her, he pulled his clothes on and padded barefoot out of his niche and down the hall. The light was on in the common room and he heard voices.

Ekatarina looked up when he entered. Her face was pale and drawn. Faint circles had formed under her eyes. She was alone.

"Oh, hi. I was just talking with the CMP." She thought off her peecee. "Have a seat."

He pulled up a chair and hunched down over the table. Confronted by her, he found it took a slight but noticeable effort to draw his breath. "So. How are things going?"

"They'll be trying out your controllers soon. The first batch of chips ought to be coming out of the factories in an hour or so. I thought I'd stay up to see how they work out."

"It's that bad, then?" Ekatarina shook her head, would not look at him. "Hey, come on, here you are waiting up on the results, and I can see how tired you are. There must be a lot riding on this thing."

"More than you know," she said bleakly. "I've just been going over the numbers. Things are worse than you can imagine."

He reached out and took her cold, bloodless hand. She squeezed him so tightly it hurt. Their eyes met and he saw in hers all the fear and wonder he felt.

Wordlessly, they stood.

"I'm niching alone," Ekatarina said. She had not let go of his hand, held it so tightly in fact, that it seemed she would never let it go.

Gunther let her lead him away.

They made love, and talked quietly about inconsequential things, and made love again. Gunther had thought she would nod off immediately after the first time, but she was too full of nervous energy for that.

"Tell me when you're about to come," she murmured. "Tell me when you're coming."

He stopped moving. "Why do you always say that?"

Ekatarina looked up at him dazedly, and he repeated the question. Then she laughed a deep, throaty laugh. "Because I'm frigid."

"Hah?"

She took his hand, and brushed her cheek against it. Then she ducked her head, continuing the motion across her neck and up the side of her scalp. He felt the short, prickly hair against his palm and then, behind her ear, two bumps under the skin where biochips had been implanted. One of those would be her trance chip and the other…"It's a prosthetic," she explained. Her eyes were grey and solemn. "It hooks into the pleasure centers. When I need to, I can turn on my orgasm at a thought. That way we can always come at the same time." She moved her hips slowly beneath him as she spoke.

"But that means you don't really need to have any kind of sexual stimulation at all, do you? You can trigger an orgasm at will. While you're riding on a bus. Or behind a desk. You could just turn that thing on and come for hours at a time."

She looked amused. "I'll tell you a secret. When it was new, I used to do stunts like that. Everybody does. One outgrows that sort of thing quickly."

With more than a touch of stung pride, Gunther said, "Then what am I doing here? If you've got that thing, what the hell do you need me for?" He started to draw away from her.

She pulled him down atop her again. "You're kind of comforting," she said. "In an argumentative way. Come here."

He got back to his futon and began gathering up the pieces of his suit. Liza sat up sleepily and gawked at him. "So," she said. "It's like that, is it?"

"Yeah, well. I kind of left something unfinished. An old relationship." Warily, he extended a hand. "No hard feelings, huh?"

Ignoring his hand, she stood, naked and angry. "You got the nerve to stand there without even wiping my smile off your dick first and say no hard feelings? Asshole!"

"Aw, come on now, Liza, it's not like that."

"Like hell it's not! You got a shot at that white-assed Russian ice queen, and I'm history. Don't think I don't know all about her."

"I was hoping we could still be, you know, friends."

"Nice trick, shithead." She balled her fist and hit him hard in the center of his chest. Tears began to form in her eyes. "You just slink away. I'm tired of looking at you."

He left.

But did not sleep. Ekatarina was awake and ebullient over the first reports coming in of the new controller system. "They're working!" she cried. "They're working!" She'd pulled on a silk camisole, and strode back and forth excitedly, naked to the waist. Her pubic hair was a white flame, with almost invisible trails of smaller hairs reaching for her navel and caressing the sweet insides of her thighs. Tired as he was, Gunther felt new desire for her. In a weary, washed-out way, he was happy.

"Whooh!" She kissed him hard, not sexually, and called up the CMP. "Rerun all our earlier projections. We're putting our afflicted components back to work. Adjust all work schedules."

"As you direct."

"How does this change our long-range prospects?"-

The program was silent for several seconds, processing. Then it said, "You are about to enter a necessary but very dangerous stage of recovery. You are going from a low-prospects high-stability situation to a high-prospects high-instability one. With leisure your unafflicted components will quickly grow dissatisfied with your government."

"What happens if I just step down?"

"Prospects worsen drastically."

Ekatarina ducked her head. "All right, what's likely to be our most pressing new problem?"

"The unafflicted components will demand to know more about the war on Earth. They'll want the media feeds restored immediately."

"I could rig up a receiver easily enough," Gunther volunteered. "Nothing fancy, but..."

"Don't you dare!"

"Hah? Why not?"

"Gunther, let me put it to you this way: What two nationalities are most heavily represented here?"

"Well, I guess that would be Russia and—oh."

"Oh is right. For the time being, I think it's best if nobody knows for sure who's supposed to be enemies with whom." She asked the CMP, "How should I respond?"

"Until the situation stabilizes, you have no choice but distraction. Keep their minds occupied. Hunt down the saboteurs and then organize war crime trials."

"That's out. No witch hunts, no scapegoats, no trials. We're all in this together."

Emotionlessly, the CMP said, "Violence is the left hand of government. You are rash to dismiss its potentials without serious thought."

"I won't discuss it."

"Very well. If you wish to postpone the use of force for the present, you could hold a hunt for the weapon used on Bootstrap. Locating and identifying it would involve everyone's energies without necessarily implicating anybody. It would also be widely interpreted as meaning an eventual cure was possible, thus boosting the general morale without your actually lying."

Tiredly, as if this were something she had gone over many times already, she said, "Is there really no hope of curing them?"

"Anything is possible. In light of present resources, though, it cannot be considered likely."

Ekatarina thought the peecee off, dismissing the CMP. She sighed. "Maybe that's what we ought to do. Donkey up a hunt for the weapon. We ought to be able to do something with that notion."

Puzzled, Gunther said, "But it was one of Chang's weapons, wasn't it? A schizomimetic engine, right?"

"Where did you hear that?" she demanded sharply.

"Well, Krishna said...He didn't act like...I thought it was public knowledge."

Ekatarina's face hardened. "Program!" she thought.

The CMP came back to life. "Ready."

"Locate Krishna Narasimhan, unafflicted, Cadre Five. I want to speak with him immediately." Ekatarina snatched up her panties and shorts, and furiously began dressing. "Where are my damned sandals? Program! Tell him to meet me in the common room. Right away."

"Received."

To Gunther's surprise, it took over an hour for Ekatarina to browbeat Krishna into submission. Finally, though, the young research component went to a lockbox, identified himself to it, and unsealed the storage areas. "It's not all that secure," he said apologetically. "If our sponsors knew how often we just left everything open so we could get in and out, they'd—well, never mind."

He lifted a flat, palm-sized metal rectangle from a cabinet. "This is the most likely means of delivery. It's an aerosol bomb. The biological agents are loaded here, and it's triggered by snapping this back here. It's got enough pressure in it to spew the agents fifty feet straight up. Air currents do the rest." He tossed it to Gunther who stared down at the thing in horror. "Don't worry, it's not armed."

He slid out a slim drawer holding row upon gleaming row of slim chrome cylinders. "These contain the engines themselves. They're off-the-shelf nanoweaponry. State of the art stuff, I guess." He ran a fingertip over them. "We've programmed each to produce a different mix of neurotransmitters. Dopamine, phencylclidine, norepinephrine, acetylcholine, met-enkephalin, substance P, serotonin—there's a hefty slice of Heaven in here, and—" he tapped an empty space—"right here is our missing bit of Hell." He frowned, and muttered, "That's curious. Why are there two cylinders missing?"

"What's that?" Ekatarina said. "I didn't catch what you just said."

"Oh, nothing important. Um, listen, it might help if I yanked a few biological pathways charts and showed you the chemical underpinnings of these things."

"Never mind that. Just keep it sweet and simple. Tell us about these schizomimetic engines."

It took over an hour to explain.

The engines were molecule-sized chemical factories, much like the assemblers in a microfactory. They had been provided by the military, in the hope Chang's group would come up with a misting weapon that could be sprayed in an army's path to cause them to change their loyalty. Gunther dozed off briefly while Krishna was explaining why that was impossible, and woke up sometime after the tiny engines had made their way into the brain.

"It's really a false schizophrenia," Krishna explained. "True schizophrenia is a beautifully complicated mechanism. What these engines create is more like a bargain-basement knockoff. They seize control of the brain chemistry, and start pumping out dopamine and a few other neuromediators. It's not an actual disorder, *per se*. They just keep the brain hopping." He coughed. "You see."

"Okay," Ekatarina said. "Okay. You say you can reprogram these things. How?"

"We use what are technically called messenger engines. They're like neuromodulators—they tell the schizomimetic engines what to do." He slid open another drawer, and in a flat voice said, "They're gone."

"Let's keep to the topic, if we may. We'll worry about your inventory later. Tell us about these messenger engines. Can you brew up a lot of them, to tell the schizomimetics to turn themselves off?"

"No, for two reasons. First, these molecules were hand-crafted in the Swiss Orbitals; we don't have the industrial plant to create them. Secondly, you can't tell the schizomimetics to turn themselves off. They don't have off switches. They're more like catalysts than actual machines. You can reconfigure them to produce different chemicals, but..." He stopped, and a distant look came into his eyes. "Damn." He grabbed up his peecee, and a chemical pathways chart appeared on one wall. Then beside it, a listing of major neurofunctions. Then another chart covered with scrawled behavioral symbols. More and more data slammed up on the wall.

"Uh, Krishna...?"

"Oh, go away," he snapped. "This is important."

"You think you might be able to come up with a cure?"

"Cure? No. Something better. Much better."

Ekatarina and Gunther looked at each other. Then she said, "Do you need anything? Can I assign anyone to help you?"

"I need the messenger engines. Find them for me."

"How? How do we find them? Where do we look?"

"Sally Chang," Krishna said impatiently. "She must have them. Nobody else had access." He snatched up a light pen, and began scrawling crabbed formulae on the wall.

"I'll get her for you. Program! Tell—"

"Chang's a flick," Gunther reminded her. "She was caught by the aerosol bomb." Which she must surely have set herself. A neat way of disposing of evidence that might've led to whatever government was running her. She'd have been the first to go mad.

Ekatarina pinched her nose, wincing. "I've been awake too long," she said. "All right, I understand. Krishna, from now on you're assigned permanently to research. The CMP will notify your cadre leader. Let me know if you need any support. Find me a way to turn this damned weapon off." Ignoring the way he shrugged her off, she said to Gunther, "I'm yanking you from Cadre Four. From now on, you report directly to me. I want you to find Chang. Find her, and find those messenger engines."

Gunther was bone-weary. He couldn't remember when he'd last had a good eight hours' sleep. But he managed what he hoped was a confident grin. "Received."

A madwoman should not have been able to hide herself. Sally Chang could. Nobody should have been able to evade the CMP's notice, now that it was hooked into a growing number of afflicted individuals. Sally Chang did. The CMP informed Gunther that none of the flicks were aware of Chang's whereabouts. It accepted a directive to have them all glance about for her once every hour until she was found.

In the west tunnels, walls had been torn out to create a space as large as any factory interior. The remotes had been returned, and were now manned by almost two hundred flicks spaced so that they did not impinge upon each other's fields of instruction. Gunther walked by them, through the CMP's whispering voices: "Are all bulldozers accounted for? If so...Clear away any malfunctioning machines; they can be placed...for vacuum-welded dust on the upper surfaces of the rails...reduction temperature, then look to see that the oxygen feed is compatible..." At the far end a single suit sat in a chair, overseer unit in its lap.

"How's it going?" Gunther asked.

"Absolutely top-notch." He recognized Takayuni's voice. "Most of the factories are up and running, and we're well on our way to having the railguns operative too. You wouldn't believe the kind of efficiencies we're getting here."

"Good, huh?"

Takayuni grinned; Gunther could hear it in his voice. "Industrious little buggers!"

Takayuni hadn't seen Chang. Gunther moved on.

Some hours later he found himself sitting wearily in Noguchi park, looking at the torn-up dirt where the kneehigh forest had been. Not a seedling had been spared; the silver birch was extinct as a lunar species. Dead carp floated belly-up in the oil-slicked central lake; a chain-link fence circled it now, to keep out the flicks. There hadn't been the time yet to begin cleaning up the litter, and when he looked about, he saw trash everywhere. It was sad. It reminded him of Earth.

He knew it was time to get going, but he couldn't. His head sagged, touched his chest, and jerked up. Time had passed.

A flicker of motion made him turn. Somebody in a pastel lavender boutique suit hurried by. The woman who had directed him to the city controller's office the other day. "Hello!" he called. "I found everybody just where you said. Thanks. I was starting to get a little spooked."

The lavender suit turned to look at him. Sunlight glinted on black glass. A still, long minute later, she said, "Don't mention it," and started away.

"I'm looking for Sally Chang. Do you know her? Have you seen her? She's a flick, kind of a little woman, flamboyant, used to favor bright clothes, electric makeup, that sort of thing."

"I'm afraid I can't help you." Lavender was carrying three oxytanks in her arms. "You might try the straw market, though. Lots of bright clothes there." She ducked into a tunnel opening and disappeared within.

Gunther stared after her distractedly, then shook his head. He felt so very, very tired.

✺

The straw market looked as though it had been through a storm. The tents had been torn down, the stands knocked over, the goods looted. Shards of orange and green glass crunched underfoot. Yet a rack of Italian scarfs worth a year's salary stood untouched amid the rubble. It made no sense at all.

Up and down the market, flicks were industriously cleaning up. They stooped and lifted and swept. One of them was being beaten by a suit.

Gunther blinked. He could not react to it as a real event. The woman cringed under the blows, shrieking wildly and scuttling away from them. One of the tents had been re-erected, and within the shadow of its rainbow silks, four other suits lounged against the bar. Not a one of them moved to help the woman.

"Hey!" Gunther shouted. He felt hideously self-conscious, as if he'd been abruptly thrust into the middle of a play without memorized lines or any idea of the plot or notion of what his role in it was. "Stop that!"

The suit turned toward him. It held the woman's slim arm captive in one gloved hand. "Go away," a male voice growled over the radio.

"What do you think you're doing? Who are you?" The man wore a Westinghouse suit, one of a dozen or so among the unafflicted. But Gunther recognized a brown, kidney-shaped scorch mark on the abdomen panel. "Posner—is that you? Let that woman go."

"She's not a woman," Posner said. "Hell, look at her—she's not even human. She's a flick."

Gunther set his helmet to record. "I'm taping this," he warned. "You hit that woman again, and Ekatarina will see it all. I promise."

Posner released the woman. She stood dazed for a second or two, and then the voice from her peecee reasserted control. She bent to pick up a broom, and returned to work.

Switching off his helmet, Gunther said, "Okay. What did she do?"

Indignantly, Posner extended a foot. He pointed sternly down at it. "She peed all over my boot!"

The suits in the tent had been watching with interest. Now they roared. "Your own fault, Will!" one of them called out. "I told you you weren't scheduling in enough time for personal hygiene."

"Don't worry about a little moisture. It'll boil off next time you hit vacuum!"

But Gunther was not listening. He stared at the flick Posner had been mistreating and wondered why he hadn't recognized Anya earlier. Her mouth was pursed, her face squinched up tight with worry, as if there were a key in the back of her head that had been wound three times too many. Her shoulders cringed forward now, too. But still.

"I'm sorry, Anya," he said. "Hiro is dead. There wasn't anything we could do."

She went on sweeping, oblivious, unhappy.

He caught the shift's last jitney back to the Center. It felt good to be home again. Miiko Ezumi had decided to loot the outlying factories of their oxygen and water surpluses, then carved a shower room from the rock. There was a long line for only three minutes' use, and no soap, but nobody complained. Some people pooled their time, showering two and three together. Those waiting their turns joked rowdily.

Gunther washed, grabbed some clean shorts and a Glavkosmos teeshirt, and padded down the hall. He hesitated outside the common room, listening to the gang sitting around the table, discussing the more colorful flicks they'd encountered.

"Have you seen the Mouse Hunter?"

"Oh yeah, and Ophelia!"

"The Pope!"

"The Duck Lady!

"Everybody knows the Duck Lady!"

They were laughing and happy. A warm sense of community flowed from the room, what Gunther's father would have in his sloppy-sentiment-al way called *Gemütlichkeit*. Gunther stepped within.

Liza Nagenda looked up, all gums and teeth, and froze. Her jaw snapped shut. "Well, if it isn't Izmailova's personal spy!"

"What?" The accusation took Gunther's breath away. He looked helplessly about the room. Nobody would meet his eye. They had all fallen silent.

Liza's face was grey with anger. "You heard me! It was you that ratted on Krishna, wasn't it?"

"Now that's way out of line! You've got a lot of fucking gall if—" He controlled himself with an effort. There was no sense in matching her hysteria with his own. "It's none of your business what my relationship with Izmailova is or is not." He looked around the table. "Not that any of you deserve to know, but Krishna's working on a cure. If anything I said or did helped put him back in the lab, well then, so be it."

She smirked. "So what's your excuse for snitching on Will Posner?"

"I never—"

"We all heard the story! You told him you were going to run straight to your precious Izmailova with your little helmet vids."

"Now, Liza," Takayuni began. She slapped him away.

"Do you know what Posner was doing?" Gunther shook a finger in Liza's face. "Hah? Do you? He was beating a woman—Anya! He was beating Anya right out in the open!"

"So what? He's one of us, isn't he? Not a zoned-out, dead-eyed, ranting, drooling flick!"

"You bitch!" Outraged, Gunther lunged at Liza across the table. "I'll kill you, I swear it!" People jerked back from him, rushed forward, a chaos of motion. Posner thrust himself in Gunther's way, arms spread, jaw set and manly. Gunther punched him in the face. Posner looked surprised, and fell back. Gunther's hand stung, but he felt strangely good anyway; if everyone else was crazy, then why not him?

"You just try it!" Liza shrieked. "I knew you were that type all along!"

Takayuni grabbed Liza away one way. Hamilton seized Gunther and yanked him the other. Two of Posner's friends were holding him back as well.

"I've had about all I can take from you!" Gunther shouted. "You cheap cunt!"

"Listen to him! Listen what he calls me!"

Screaming, they were shoved out opposing doors.

"It's all right, Gunther." Beth had flung him into the first niche they'd come to. He slumped against a wall, shaking, and closed his eyes. "It's all right now."

But it wasn't. Gunther was suddenly struck with the realization that with the exception of Ekatarina he no longer had any friends. Not real friends, close friends. How could this have happened? It was as if everyone had been turned into werewolves. Those who weren't actually mad were still monsters. "I don't understand."

Hamilton sighed. "What don't you understand, Weil?"

"The way people—the way we all treat the flicks. When Posner was beating Anya, there were four other suits standing nearby, and not a one of them so much as lifted a finger to stop him. Not one! And I felt it too, there's no use pretending I'm superior to the rest of them. I wanted to walk on and pretend I hadn't seen a thing. What's happened to us?"

Hamilton shrugged. Her hair was short and dark about her plain round face. "I went to a pretty expensive school when I was a kid. One year we had one of those exercises that're supposed to be personally enriching. You know? A life experience. We were divided into two groups— Prisoners and Guards. The Prisoners couldn't leave their assigned areas without permission from a guard, the Guards got better lunches, stuff like that. Very simple set of rules. I was a Guard.

"Almost immediately, we started to bully the Prisoners. We pushed 'em around, yelled at 'em, kept 'em in line. What was amazing was that the Prisoners let us do it. They outnumbered us five to one. We didn't even have authority for the things we did. But not a one of them complained. Not a one of them stood up and said No, you can't do this. They played the game.

"At the end of the month, the project was dismantled and we had some study seminars on what we'd learned: the roots of fascism, and so on. Read some Hannah Arendt. And then it was all over. Except that my best girlfriend never spoke to me again. I couldn't blame her either. Not after what I'd done.

"What did I really learn? That people will play whatever role you put them in. They'll do it without knowing that that's what they're doing. Take a minority, tell them they're special, and make them guards—they'll start playing Guard."

"So what's the answer? How do we keep from getting caught up in the roles we play?"

"Damned if I know, Weil. Damned if I know."

Ekatarina had moved her niche to the far end of a new tunnel. Hers was the only room the tunnel served, and consequently she had a lot of privacy. As Gunther stepped in, a staticky voice swam into focus on his trance chip. "...reported shock. In Cairo, government officials pledged..." It cut off.

"Hey! You've restored—" He stopped. If radio reception had been restored, he'd have known. It would have been the talk of the Center. Which meant that radio contact had never really been completely broken. It was simply being controlled by the CMP.

Ekatarina looked up at him. She'd been crying, but she'd stopped. "The Swiss Orbitals are gone!" she whispered. "They hit them with everything from softbombs to brilliant pebbles. They dusted the shipyards."

The scope of all those deaths obscured what she was saying for a second. He sank down beside her. "But that means—"

"There's no spacecraft that can reach us, yes. Unless there's a ship in transit, we're stranded here."

He took her in his arms. She was cold and shivering. Her skin felt clammy and mottled with gooseflesh. "How long has it been since you've had any sleep?" he asked sharply.

"I can't—"

"You're wired, aren't you?"

"I can't afford to sleep. Not now. Later."

"Ekatarina. The energy you get from wire isn't free. It's only borrowed from your body. When you come down, it all comes due. If you wire yourself up too tightly, you'll crash yourself right into a coma."

"I haven't been—" She stalled, and a confused, uncertain look entered her eyes. "Maybe you're right. I could probably use a little rest."

The CMP came to life. "Cadre Nine is building a radio receiver. Ezumi gave them the go-ahead."

"Shit!" Ekatarina sat bolt upright. "Can we stop it?"

"Moving against a universally popular project would cost you credibility you cannot afford to lose."

"Okay, so how can we minimize the—"

"Ekatarina," Gunther said. "Sleep, remember?"

"In a sec, babe." She patted the futon. "You just lie down and wait for me. I'll have this wrapped up before you can nod off." She kissed him gently, lingeringly. "All right?"

"Yeah, sure." He lay down and closed his eyes, just for a second.

When he awoke, it was time to go on shift, and Ekatarina was gone.

It was only the fifth day since Vladivostok. But everything was so utterly changed that times before then seemed like memories of another world. In a previous life I was Gunther Weil, he thought. I lived and worked and had a few laughs. Life was pretty good then.

He was still looking for Sally Chang, though with dwindling hope. Now, whenever he talked to suits he'd ask if they needed his help. Increasingly, they did not.

The third-level chapel was a shallow bowl facing the terrace wall. Tiger lilies grew about the chancel area at the bottom, and turquoise lizards skittered over the rock. The children were playing with a ball in the chancel. Gunther stood at the top, chatting with a sad-voiced Ryohei Iomato.

The children put away the ball and began to dance. They were playing London Bridge. Gunther watched them with a smile. From above they were so many spots of color, a flower unfolding and closing in on itself. Slowly, the smile faded. They were dancing too well. Not one of the children moved out of step, lost her place, or walked away sulking. Their expressions were intense, self-absorbed, inhuman. Gunther had to turn away.

"The CMP controls them," Iomato said. "I don't have much to do, really. I go through the vids and pick out games for them to play, songs to sing, little exercises to keep them healthy. Sometimes I have them draw."

"My God, how can you stand it?"

Iomato sighed. "My old man was an alcoholic. He had a pretty rough life, and at some point he started drinking to blot out the pain. You know what?"

"It didn't work."

"Yah. Made him even more miserable. So then he had twice the reason to get drunk. He kept on trying, though, I've got to give him that. He wasn't the sort of man to give up on something he believed in just because it wasn't working the way it should."

Gunther said nothing.

"I think that memory is the only thing keeping me from just taking off my helmet and joining them."

The Corporate Video Center was a narrow run of offices in the farthest tunnel reaches, where raw footage for adverts and incidental business use was processed before being squirted to better-equipped vid centers on Earth. Gunther passed from office to office, slapping off flatscreens left flickering since the disaster.

It was unnerving going through the normally busy rooms and finding no one. The desks and cluttered work stations had been abandoned in purposeful disarray, as though their operators had merely stepped out for a break and would be back momentarily. Gunther found himself spinning around to confront his shadow, and flinching at unexpected noises. With each machine he turned off, the silence at his back grew. It was twice as lonely as being out on the surface.

He doused a last light and stepped into the gloomy hall. Two suits with interwoven H-and-A logos loomed up out of the shadows. He jumped in shock. The suits did not move. He laughed wryly at himself, and pushed past. They were empty, of course—there were no Hyundai Aerospace components among the unafflicted. Someone had simply left these suits here in temporary storage before the madness.

The suits grabbed him.

"Hey!" He shouted in terror as they seized him by the arms and lifted him off his feet. One of them hooked the peecee from his harness and snapped it off. Before he knew what was happening he'd been swept down a short flight of stairs and through a doorway.

"Mr. Weil."

He was in a high-ceilinged room carved into the rock to hold air-handling equipment that hadn't been constructed yet. A high string of temporary work lamps provided dim light. To the far side of the room a suit sat behind a desk, flanked by two more, standing. They all wore Hyundai Aerospace suits. There was no way he could identify them.

The suits that had brought him in crossed their arms.

"What's going on here?" Gunther asked. "Who are you?"

"You are the last person we'd tell that to." He couldn't tell which one had spoken. The voice came over his radio, made sexless and impersonal by an electronic filter. "Mr. Weil, you stand accused of crimes against your fellow citizens. Do you have anything to say in your defense?"

"What?" Gunther looked at the suits before him and to either side. They were perfectly identical, indistinguishable from each other, and he was suddenly afraid of what the people within might feel free to do, armored as they were in anonymity. "Listen, you've got no right to do this. There's a governmental structure in place, if you've got any complaints against me."

"Not everyone is pleased with Izmailova's government," the judge said.

"But she controls the CMP, and we could not run Bootstrap without the CMP controlling the flicks," a second added.

"We simply have to work around her." Perhaps it was the judge; perhaps it was yet another of the suits. Gunther couldn't tell.

"Do you wish to speak on your own behalf?"

"What exactly am I charged with?" Gunther asked desperately. "Okay, maybe I've done something wrong, I'll entertain that possibility. But maybe you just don't understand my situation. Have you considered that?"

Silence.

"I mean, just what are you angry about? Is it Posner? Because I'm not sorry about that. I won't apologize. You can't mistreat people just because they're sick. They're still people, like anybody else. They have their rights."

Silence.

"But if you think I'm some kind of a spy or something, that I'm running around and ratting on people to Ek—to Izmailova, well that's simply not true. I mean, I talk to her, I'm not about to pretend I don't, but I'm not her spy or anything. She doesn't have any spies. She doesn't need any! She's just trying to hold things together, that's all.

"Jesus, you don't know what she's gone through for you! You haven't seen how much it takes out of her! She'd like nothing better than to quit. But she has to hang in there because—" An eerie dark electronic gabble rose up on his radio, and he stopped as he realized that they were laughing at him.

"Does anyone else wish to speak?"

One of Gunther's abductors stepped forward. "Your honor, this man says that flicks are human. He overlooks the fact that they cannot live without our support and direction. Their continued well-being is bought at the price of our unceasing labor. He stands condemned out of his own mouth. I petition the court to make the punishment fit the crime."

The judge looked to the right, to the left. His two companions nodded, and stepped back into the void. The desk had been set up at the mouth of what was to be the air intake duct. Gunther had just time enough to realize this when they reappeared, leading someone in a G5 suit identical to his own.

"We could kill you, Mr. Weil," the artificial voice crackled. "But that would be wasteful. Every hand, every mind is needed. We must all pull together in our time of need."

The G5 suit stood alone and motionless in the center of the room.

"Watch."

Two of the Hyundai suits stepped up to the G5 suit. Four hands converged on the helmet seals. With practiced efficiency, they flicked the latches and lifted the helmet. It happened so swiftly the occupant could not have stopped it if he'd tried.

Beneath the helmet was the fearful, confused face of a flick.

"Sanity is a privilege, Mr. Weil, not a right. You are guilty as charged. However, we are not cruel men. This once we will let you off with a warning. But these are desperate times. At your next offense—be it only so minor a thing as reporting this encounter to the Little General—we may be forced to dispense with the formality of a hearing." The judge paused. "Do I make myself clear?"

Reluctantly, Gunther nodded.

"Then you may leave."

On the way out, one of the suits handed him back his peecee.

Five people. He was sure there weren't any more involved than that. Maybe one or two more, but that was it. Posner had to be hip-deep in this thing, he was certain of that. It shouldn't be too hard to figure out the others.

He didn't dare take the chance.

At shift's end he found Ekatarina already asleep. She looked haggard and unhealthy. He knelt by her, and gently brushed her cheek with the back of one hand.

Her eyelids fluttered open.

"Oh, hey. I didn't mean to wake you. Just go back to sleep, huh?"

She smiled. "You're sweet, Gunther, but I was only taking a nap anyway. I've got to be up in another fifteen minutes." Her eyes closed again. "You're the only one I can really trust anymore. Everybody's lying to me, feeding me misinformation, keeping silent when there's something I need to know. You're the only one I can count on to tell me things."

You have enemies, he thought. They call you the Little General, and they don't like how you run things. They're not ready to move against you directly, but they have plans. And they're ruthless.

Aloud, he said, "Go back to sleep."

"They're all against me," she murmured. "Bastard sons of bitches."

The next day he spent going through the service spaces for the new air-handling system. He found a solitary flick's nest made of shredded vacuum suits, but after consultation with the CMP concluded that nobody had lived there for days. There was no trace of Sally Chang.

If it had been harrowing going through the sealed areas before his trial, it was far worse today. Ekatarina's enemies had infected him with fear. Reason told him they were not waiting for him, that he had nothing to worry about until he displeased them again. But the hindbrain did not listen.

Time crawled. When he finally emerged into daylight at the end of his shift, he felt light-headedly out of phase with reality from the hours of isolation. At first he noticed nothing out of the ordinary. Then his suit radio was full of voices, and people were hurrying about every which way. There was a happy buzz in the air. Somebody was singing.

He snagged a passing suit and asked, "What's going on?"

"Haven't you heard? The war is over. They've made peace. And there's a ship coming in!"

The *Lake Geneva* had maintained television silence through most of the long flight to the Moon for fear of long-range beam weapons. With peace, however, they opened direct transmission to Bootstrap.

Ezumi's people had the flicks sew together an enormous cotton square and hack away some hanging vines so they could hang it high on the shadowed side of the crater. Then, with the fill lights off, the video image was projected. Swiss spacejacks tumbled before the camera, grinning, all denim and red cowboy hats. They were talking about their escape from the hunter-seeker missiles, brash young voices running one over the other.

The top officers were assembled beneath the cotton square. Gunther recognized their suits. Ekatarina's voice boomed from newly erected loudspeakers. "When are you coming in? We have to make sure the spaceport field is clear. How many hours?"

Holding up five fingers, a blond woman said, "Forty-five!"

"No, forty-three!"

"Nothing like that!"

"Almost forty-five!"

Again Ekatarina's voice cut into the tumult. "What's it like in the orbitals? We heard they were destroyed."

"Yes, destroyed!"

"Very bad, very bad, it'll take years to—"

"But most of the people are—"

"We were given six orbits warning; most went down in lifting bodies, there was a big evacuation."

"Many died, though. It was very bad."

Just below the officers, a suit had been directing several flicks as they assembled a camera platform. Now it waved broadly, and the flicks stepped away. In the Lake Geneva somebody shouted, and several heads turned to stare at an offscreen television monitor. The suit turned the camera, giving them a slow, panoramic scan.

One of the spacejacks said, "What's it like there? I see that some of you are wearing space suits, and the rest are not. Why is that?"

Ekatarina took a deep breath. "There have been some changes here."

There was one hell of a party at the Center when the Swiss arrived. Sleep schedules were juggled, and save for a skeleton crew overseeing the flicks, everyone turned out to welcome the dozen newcomers to the Moon.

They danced to skiffle, and drank vacuum-distilled vodka. Everyone had stories to tell, rumors to swap, opinions on the likelihood that the peace would hold.

Gunther wandered away midway through the party. The Swiss depressed him. They all seemed so young and fresh and eager. He felt battered and cynical in their presence. He wanted to grab them by the shoulders and shake them awake.

Depressed, he wandered through the locked-down laboratories. Where the Viral Computer Project had been, he saw Ekatarina and the captain of the Lake Geneva conferring over a stack of crated bioflops. They bent low over Ekatarina's peecee, listening to the CMP.

"Have you considered nationalizing your industries?" the captain asked. "That would give us the plant needed to build the New City. Then, with a few hardwired utilities, Bootstrap could be managed without anyone having to set foot inside it."

Gunther was too distant to hear the CMP's reaction, but he saw both women laugh. "Well," said Ekatarina. "At the very least we will have to renegotiate terms with the parent corporations. With only one ship functional, people can't be easily replaced. Physical presence has become a valuable commodity. We'd be fools not to take advantage of it."

He passed on, deeper into shadow, wandering aimlessly. Eventually, there was a light ahead, and he heard voices. One was Krishna's, but spoken faster and more forcefully than he was used to hearing it. Curious, he stopped just outside the door.

Krishna was in the center of the lab. Before him, Beth Hamilton stood nodding humbly. "Yes, sir," she said. "I'll do that. Yes." Dumbfounded, Gunther realized that Krishna was giving her orders.

Krishna glanced up. "Weil! You're just the man I was about to come looking for."

"I am?"

"Come in here, don't dawdle." Krishna smiled and beckoned, and Gunther had no choice but to obey. He looked like a young god now. The force of his spirit danced in his eyes like fire. It was strange that Gunther had never noticed before how tall he was. "Tell me where Sally Chang is."

"I don't—I mean, I can't, I—" He stopped and swallowed. "I think Chang must be dead." Then, "Krishna? What's happened to you?"

"He's finished his research," Beth said.

"I rewrote my personality from top to bottom," Krishna said. "I'm not half-crippled with shyness anymore—have you noticed?" He put a hand on

Gunther's shoulder, and it was reassuring, warm, comforting. "Gunther, I won't tell you what it took to scrape together enough messenger engines from traces of old experiments to try this out on myself. But it works. We've got a treatment that among other things will serve as a universal cure for everyone in Bootstrap. But to do that, we need the messenger engines, and they're not here. Now tell me why you think Sally Chang is dead."

"Well, uh, I've been searching for her for four days. And the CMP has been looking too. You've been holed up here all that time, so maybe you don't know the flicks as well as the rest of us do. But they're not very big on planning. The likelihood one of them could actively evade detection that long is practically zilch. The only thing I can think is that somehow she made it to the surface before the effects hit her, got into a truck and told it to drive as far as her oxygen would take her."

Krishna shook his head and said, "No. It is simply not consistent with Sally Chang's character. With all the best will in the world, I cannot picture her killing herself." He slid open a drawer: row upon row of gleaming canisters. "This may help. Do you remember when I said there were canisters of mimetic engines missing, not just the schizomimetic?"

"Vaguely."

"I've been too busy to worry about it, but wasn't that odd? Why would Chang have taken a canister and not used it?"

"What was in the second canister?" Hamilton asked.

"Paranoia," Krishna said. "Or rather a good enough chemical analog. Now, paranoia is a rare disability, but a fascinating one. It's characterized by an elaborate but internally consistent delusional system. The paranoid patient functions well intellectually, and is less fragmented than a schizophrenic. Her emotional and social responses are closer to normal. She's capable of concerted effort. In a time of turmoil, it's quite possible that a paranoid individual could elude our detection."

"Okay, let's get this straight," Hamilton said. "War breaks out on Earth. Chang gets her orders, keys in the software bombs, and goes to Bootstrap with a canister full of madness and a little syringe of paranoia—no, it doesn't work. It all falls apart."

"How so?"

"Paranoia wouldn't inoculate her against schizophrenia. How does she protect herself from her own aerosols?"

Gunther stood transfixed. "Lavender!"

They caught up with Sally Chang on the topmost terrace of Bootstrap. The top level was undeveloped. Someday—so the corporate brochures promised—fallow deer would graze at the edge of limpid pools, and otters frolic in the streams. But the soil hadn't been built up yet, the worms brought in or the bacteria seeded. There were only sand, machines, and a few unhappy opportunistic weeds.

Chang's camp was to one side of a streamhead, beneath a fill light. She started to her feet at their approach, glanced quickly to the side and decided to brazen it out.

A sign reading EMERGENCY CANOPY MAINTENANCE STATION had been welded to a strut supporting the stream's valve stem. Under it were a short stacked pyramid of oxytanks and an aluminum storage crate the size of a coffin. "Very clever," Beth muttered over Gunther's trance chip. "She sleeps in the storage crate, and anybody stumbling across her thinks it's just spare equipment."

The lavender suit raised an arm and casually said, "Hiya, guys. How can I help you?"

Krishna strode forward and took her hands. "Sally, it's me —Krishna!"

"Oh, thank God!" She slumped in his arms. "I've been so afraid."

"You're all right now."

"I thought you were an Invader at first, when I saw you coming up. I'm so hungry—I haven't eaten since I don't know when." She clutched at the sleeve of Krishna's suit. "You do know about the Invaders, don't you?"

"Maybe you'd better bring me up to date."

They began walking toward the stairs. Krishna gestured quietly to Gunther and then toward Chang's worksuit harness. A canister the size of a hip flask hung there. Gunther reached over and plucked it off. The messenger engines! He held them in his hand.

To the other side, Beth Hamilton plucked up the near-full cylinder of paranoia-inducing engines and made it disappear.

Sally Chang, deep in the explication of her reasonings, did not notice. "...obeyed my orders, of course. But they made no sense. I worried and worried about that until finally I realized what was really going on. A wolf caught in a trap will gnaw off its leg to get free. I began to look for the wolf. What kind of enemy justified such extreme actions? Certainly nothing human."

"Sally," Krishna said, "I want you to entertain the notion that the conspiracy—for want of a better word—may be more deeply rooted than you suspect. That the problem is not an external enemy, but the workings of our own brains. Specifically that the Invaders are an artifact of the psychotomimetics you injected into yourself back when this all began."

"No. No, there's too much evidence. It all fits together! The Invaders needed a way to disguise themselves both physically, which was accomplished by the vacuum suits, and psychologically, which was achieved by the general madness. Thus, they can move undetected among us. Would a human enemy have converted all of Bootstrap to slave labor? Unthinkable! They can read our minds like a book. If we hadn't protected ourselves with the schizomimetics, they'd be able to extract all our knowledge, all our military research secrets…"

Listening, Gunther couldn't help imagining what Liza Nagenda would say to all of this wild talk. At the thought of her, his jaw clenched. Just like one of Chang's machines, he realized, and couldn't help being amused at his own expense.

Ekatarina was waiting at the bottom of the stairs. Her hands trembled noticeably, and there was a slight quaver in her voice when she said, "What's all this the CMP tells me about messenger engines? Krishna's supposed to have come up with a cure of some kind?"

"We've got them," Gunther said quietly, happily. He held up the canister. "It's over now, we can heal our friends."

"Let me see," Ekatarina said. She took the canister from his hand.

"No, wait!" Hamilton cried, too late. Behind her, Krishna was arguing with Sally Chang about her interpretations of recent happenings.

Neither had noticed yet that those in front had stopped.

"Stand back." Ekatarina took two quick steps backward. Edgily, she added, "I don't mean to be difficult. But we're going to sort this all out, and until we do, I don't want anybody too close to me. That includes you too, Gunther."

Flicks began gathering. By ones and twos they wandered up the lawn, and then by the dozen. By the time it was clear that Ekatarina had called them up via the CMP, Krishna, Chang and Hamilton were separated from her and Gunther by a wall of people.

Chang stood very still. Somewhere behind her unseen face, she was revising her theories to include this new event. Suddenly, her hands slapped at her suit, grabbing for the missing canisters. She looked at Krishna and with a trill of horror said, "You're one of them!"

"Of course I'm not—" Krishna began. But she was turning, stumbling, fleeing back up the steps.

"Let her go," Ekatarina ordered. "We've got more serious things to talk about." Two flicks scurried up, lugging a small industrial kiln between them. They set it down, and a third plugged in an electric cable. The interior began to glow. "This canister is all you've got, isn't it? If I were to autoclave it, there wouldn't be any hope of replacing its contents."

"Izmailova, listen," Krishna said.

"I am listening. Talk."

Krishna explained, while Izmailova listened with arms folded and shoulders tilted skeptically. When he was done, she s hook her head. "It's a noble folly, but folly is all it is. You want to reshape our minds into something alien to the course of human evolution. To turn the seat of thought into a jet pilot's couch. This is your idea of a solution? Forget it. Once this particular box is opened, there'll be no putting its contents back in again. And you haven't advanced any convincing arguments for opening it."

"But the people in Bootstrap!" Gunther objected. "They—"

She cut him off. "Gunther, nobody likes what's happened to them. But if the rest of us must give up our humanity to pay for a speculative and ethically dubious rehabilitation…Well, the price is simply too high. Mad or not, they're at least human now."

"Am I inhuman?" Krishna asked. "If you tickle me, do I not laugh?"

"You're in no position to judge. You've rewired your neurons and you're stoned on the novelty. What tests have you run on yourself? How thoroughly have you mapped out your deviations from human norms? Where are your figures?" These were purely rhetorical questions; the kind of analyses she meant took weeks to run. "Even if you check out completely human—and I don't concede you will!—who's to say what the long-range consequences are? What's to stop us from drifting, step by incremental step, into madness? Who decides what madness is? Who programs the programmers? No, this is impossible. I won't gamble with our minds." Defensively, almost angrily, she repeated, "I won't gamble with our minds."

"Ekatarina," Gunther said gently, "how long have you been up? Listen to yourself. The wire is doing your thinking for you."

She waved a hand dismissively, without responding.

"Just as a practical matter," Hamilton said, "how do you expect to run Bootstrap without it? The setup now is turning us all into baby fascists. You say you're worried about madness—what will we be like a year from now?"

"The CMP assures me—"

"The CMP is only a program!" Hamilton cried. "No matter how much interactivity it has, it's not flexible. It has no hope. It cannot judge a new thing. It can only enforce old decisions, old values, old habits, old fears."

Abruptly Ekatarina snapped. "Get out of my face!" she screamed. "Stop it, stop it, stop it! I won't listen to any more."

"Ekatarina—" Gunther began.

But her hand had tightened on the canister. Her knees bent as she began a slow genuflection to the kiln. Gunther could see that she had stopped listening. Drugs and responsibility had done this to her, speeding her up and bewildering her with conflicting demands, until she stood trembling on the brink of collapse. A good night's sleep might have restored her, made her capable of being reasoned with. But there was no time. Words would not stop her now. And she was too far distant for him to reach before she destroyed the engines. In that instant he felt such a strong outwelling of emotion toward her as would be impossible to describe.

"Ekatarina," he said. "I love you."

She half-turned her head toward him and in a distracted, somewhat irritated tone said, "What are you—"

He lifted the bolt gun from his work harness, leveled it, and fired.

Ekatarina's helmet shattered.

She fell.

"I should have shot to just breach the helmet. That would have stopped her. But I didn't think I was a good enough shot. I aimed right for the center of her head."

"Hush," Hamilton said. "You did what you had to. Stop tormenting yourself. Talk about more practical things."

He shook his head, still groggy. For the longest time, he had been kept on beta endorphins, unable to feel a thing, unable to care. It was like being swathed in cotton batting. Nothing could reach him. Nothing could hurt him. "How long have I been out of it?"

"A day."

"A day!" He looked about the austere room. Bland rock walls and laboratory equipment with smooth, noncommital surfaces. To the far end, Krishna and Chang were hunched over a swipeboard, arguing happily and impatiently overwriting each other's scrawls. A Swiss spacejack came in and spoke to their backs. Krishna nodded distractedly, not looking up. "I thought it was much longer."

"Long enough. We've already salvaged everyone connected with Sally Chang's group, and gotten a good start on the rest. Pretty soon it will be time to decide how you want yourself rewritten."

He shook his head, feeling dead. "I don't think I'll bother, Beth. I just don't have the stomach for it."

"We'll give you the stomach."

"Naw, I don't..." He felt a black nausea come welling up again. It was cyclic; it returned every time he was beginning to think he'd finally put it down. "I don't want the fact that I killed Ekatarina washed away in a warm flood of self-satisfaction. The idea disgusts me."

"We don't want that either." Posner led a delegation of seven into the lab. Krishna and Chang rose to face them, and the group broke into swirling halves. "There's been enough of that. It's time we all started taking responsibility for the consequences of—" Everyone was talking at once. Hamilton made a face.

"Started taking responsibility for—"

Voices rose.

"We can't talk here," she said. "Take me out on the surface."

They drove with the cabin pressurized, due west on the Seething Bay road. Ahead, the sun was almost touching the weary walls of Sommering crater. Shadow crept down from the mountains and cratertops, yearning toward the radiantly lit Sinus Medii. Gunther found it achingly beautiful. He did not want to respond to it, but the harsh lines echoed the lonely hurt within him in a way that he found oddly comforting.

Hamilton touched her peecee. *Putting on the Ritz* filled their heads.

"What if Ekatarina was right?" he said sadly. "What if we're giving up everything that makes us human? The prospect of being turned into some kind of big-domed emotionless superman doesn't appeal to me much."

Hamilton shook her head. "I asked Krishna about that, and he said No. He said it was like...Were you ever nearsighted?"

"Sure, as a kid."

"Then you'll understand. He said it was like the first time you came out of the doctor's office after being lased. How everything seemed clear and vivid and distinct. What had once been a blur that you called 'tree' resolved itself into a thousand individual and distinct leaves. The world was filled with unexpected detail. There were things on the horizon that you'd never seen before. Like that."

"Oh." He stared ahead. The disk of the sun was almost touching Sommering. "There's no point in going any farther."

He powered down the truck.

Beth Hamilton looked uncomfortable. She cleared her throat and with brusque energy said, "Gunther, look. I had you bring me out here for a reason. I want to propose a merger of resources."

"A what?"

"Marriage."

It took Gunther a second to absorb what she had said. "Aw, no...I don't..."

"I'm serious. Gunther, I know you think I've been hard on you, but that's only because I saw a lot of potential in you, and that you were doing nothing with it. Well, things have changed. Give me a say in your rewrite, and I'll do the same for you."

He shook his head. "This is just too weird for me."

"It's too late to use that as an excuse. Ekatarina was right—we're sitting on top of something very dangerous, the most dangerous opportunity humanity faces today. It's out of the bag, though. Word has gotten out. Earth is horrified and fascinated. They'll be watching us. Briefly, very briefly, we can control this thing. We can help to shape it now, while it's small. Five years from now, it will be out of our hands.

"You have a good mind, Gunther, and it's about to get better. I think we agree on what kind of a world we want to make. I want you on my side."

"I don't know what to say."

"You want true love? You got it. We can make the sex as sweet or nasty as you like. Nothing easier. You want me quieter, louder, gentler, more assured? We can negotiate. Let's see if we can come to terms."

He said nothing.

Hamilton eased back in the seat. After a time, she said, "You know? I've never watched a lunar sunset before. I don't get out on the surface much."

"We'll have to change that," Gunther said.

Hamilton stared hard into his face. Then she smiled. She wriggled closer to him. Clumsily, he put an arm over her shoulder. It seemed to be what was expected of him. He coughed into his hand, then pointed a finger. "There it goes."

Lunar sunset was a simple thing. The crater wall touched the bottom of the solar disk. Shadows leaped from the slopes and raced across the lowlands. Soon half the sun was gone. Smoothly, without distortion, it dwindled. A last brilliant sliver of light burned atop the rock, then ceased to be. In the instant before the windshield adjusted and the stars appeared, the universe filled with darkness.

The air in the cab cooled. The panels snapped and popped with the sudden shift in temperature.

Now Hamilton was nuzzling the side of his neck. Her skin was slightly tacky to the touch, and exuded a faint but distinct odor. She ran her tongue up the line of his chin and poked it in his ear. Her hand fumbled with the latches of his suit.

Gunther experienced no arousal at all, only a mild distaste that bordered on disgust. This was horrible, a defilement of all he had felt for Ekatarina.

But it was a chore he had to get through. Hamilton was right. All his life his hindbrain had been in control, driving him with emotions chemically derived and randomly applied. He had been lashed to the steed of consciousness and forced to ride it wherever it went, and that nightmare gallop had brought him only pain and confusion. Now that he had control of the reins, he could make this horse go where he wanted.

He was not sure what he would demand from his reprogramming. Contentment, perhaps. Sex and passion, almost certainly. But not love. He was done with the romantic illusion. It was time to grow up.

He squeezed Beth's shoulder. One more day, he thought, and it won't matter. I'll feel whatever is best for me to feel. Beth raised her mouth to his. Her lips parted. He could smell her breath.

They kissed.

THE CHANGELING'S TALE

Fill the pipe again. If I'm to tell this story properly, I'll need its help. That's good. No, the fire doesn't need a new log. Let it die. There are worse things than darkness.

How the tavern creaks and groans in its sleep! 'Tis naught but the settling of its bones and stones, and yet never a wraith made so lonesome a sound. It's late, the door is bolted, and the gates to either end of the Bridge are closed. The fire burns low. In all the world only you and I are awake. This is no fit tale for such young ears as yours, but—oh, don't scowl so! You'll make me laugh, and that's no fit beginning to so sad a tale as mine. All right, then.

Let us pull our stools closer to the embers and I'll tell you all.

✳

I must begin twenty years ago, on a day in early summer. The Ogre was dead. Our armies had returned, much shrunken, from their desperate adventures in the south and the survivors were once again plying their trades. The land was at peace at last, and trade was good. The tavern was often full.

The elves began crossing Long Bridge at dawn.

I was awakened by the sound of their wagons, the wheels rumbling, the silver bells singing from atop the high poles where they had been set to catch the wind. All in a frenzy I dressed and tumbled down from the chimney-loft and out the door. The wagons were painted with bright sigils and sinuous overlapping runes, potent with magic I could neither decipher nor hope to understand. The white oxen that pulled them spoke gently in their own language, one to the other. Music floated over the march, drums and cymbals mingling with the mournful call of the long curling horn named Serpentine. But the elves themselves, tall and proud, were silent behind their white masks.

One warrior turned to look at me as he passed, his eyes cold and unfriendly as a spearpoint. I shivered, and the warrior was gone.

But I had *known* him. I was sure of it. His name was…A hand clasped my shoulder. It was my uncle. "A stirring sight, innit? Those are the very last, the final elven tribe. When they are passed over Long Bridge, there will be none of their kind left anywhere south of the Awen."

He spoke with an awful, alien sadness. In all the years Black Gabe had been my master—and being newborn when my father had marched away to the Defeat of Blackwater, I had known no other—I had never seen him in such a mood before. Thinking back, I see that it was at that instant I first realized in a way so sure I could feel it in my gut that he would someday die and be forgotten, and after him me. Then, though, I was content simply to stand motionless with the man, sharing this strangely companionable sense of loss.

"How can they tell each other apart?" I asked, marveling at how similar were their richly decorated robes and plain, unfeatured masks.

"They—"

A fire-drake curled in the air, the morning rocket set off to mark the instant when the sun's disk cleared the horizon, and my eyes traveled up to watch it explode. When they came down again, my uncle was gone. I never saw him again.

Eh? Forgive me. I was lost in thought. Black Gabe was a good master, though I didn't think so then, who didn't beat me half so often as I deserved. You want to know about my scars? There is nothing special about them—they are such markings as all the *am'rta skandayaksa* have. Some are for deeds of particular merit. Others indicate allegiance. The triple slashes across my cheeks mean that I was sworn to the Lord Cakaravartin, a war-leader whose name means "great wheel-turning king." That is a name of significance, though I have forgotten exactly what, much as I have forgotten the manner and appearance of the great wheel-turner himself, though there was a time when I would happily have died for him. The squiggle across my forehead means I slew a dragon.

Yes, of course you would. What youth your age would not? And it's a tale I'd far more gladly tell you than this sorry life of mine. But I cannot. That I did kill a dragon I remember clearly—the hot gush of blood, its bleak scream of despair—but beyond that nothing. The events leading to and from that instant of horror and—strangely—guilt are gone from me entirely, like so much else that happened since I left the Bridge, lost in mist and forgetfulness.

Look at our shadows, like giants, nodding their heads in sympathy.

❉

What then? I remember scrambling across the steep slate rooftops, leaping and slipping in a way that seems quite mad to me now. Corwin the glover's boy and I were stringing the feast-day banners across the street to honor the procession below. The canvases smelled of mildew. They were stored in the Dragon Gate in that little room above the portcullis, the one with the murder hole in the floor. Jon and Corwin and I used to crouch over it betimes and take turns spitting, vying to be the first to hit the head of an unsuspecting merchant.

Winds gusted over the roofs, cold and invigorating. Jumping the gaps between buildings, I fancied myself to be dancing with the clouds. I crouched to lash a rope through an iron ring set into the wall just beneath the eaves. Cor had gone back to the gateroom for more banners. I looked up to see if he were in place yet and realized that I could see right into Becky's garret chamber.

There was nothing in the room but a pallet and a chest, a small table and a washbasin. Becky stood with her back to the window, brushing her hair.

I was put in mind of those stories we boys told each other of wanton women similarly observed. Who, somehow sensing their audience, would put on a lewd show, using first their fingers and then their hairbrushes. We had none of us ever encountered such sirens, but our faith in them was boundless. Somewhere, we knew, were women depraved enough to mate with apes, donkeys, mountain trolls—and possibly even the likes of us.

Becky, of course, did nothing of the sort. She stood in a chaste woolen night-gown, head raised slightly, stroking her long, coppery tresses in time to the faint elven music that rose from the street. A slant of sunlight touched her hair and struck fire.

All this in an instant. Then Cor came bounding over her roof making a clatter like ten goats. He shifted the bundle of banners 'neath one arm and extended the other. "Ho, Will!" he bellowed. "Stop daydreaming and toss me that rope-end!"

Becky whirled and saw me gawking. With a most unloving shriek of outrage, she slammed the shutters.

●

All the way back to the tavern, my mind was filled with thoughts of Becky and her hairbrush. As I entered, my littlest cousin, Thistle, danced past me, chanting, "elves-elves-elves," spinning and twirling as if she need never stop. She loved elves and old stories with talking animals and all things bright and magical. They tell me she died of the whitepox not six years later. But in my mind's eye she still laughs and spins, evergreen, immortal.

The common room was empty of boarders and the table planks had been taken down. Aunt Kate, Dolly, and my eldest sister, Eleanor, were cleaning up. Kate swept the breakfast trash toward the trap. "It comes of keeping bad company," she said grimly. "That Corwin Glover and his merry band of rowdies. Ale does not brew overnight—he's been building toward this outrage for a long time."

I froze in the doorway vestibule, sure that Becky's people had reported my Tom-Peepery. And how could I protest my innocence? I'd've done as much and worse long ago, had I known such was possible.

A breeze leapt into the room when Eleanor opened the trap, ruffling her hair and making the dust dance. "They gather by the smokehouse every sennight to drink themselves sick and plot mischief," Dolly observed. "May Chandler's Anne saw one atop the wall there, making water into the river, not three nights ago."

"Oh, fie!" The trash went tumbling toward the river and Eleanor slammed the trap. Some involuntary motion on my part alerted them to my presence then. They turned and confronted me.

A strange delusion came over me then, and I imagined that these three gossips were part of a single mechanism, a twittering machine going through predetermined motions, as if an unseen hand turned a crank that made them sweep and clean and talk.

Karl Whitesmith's boy has broken his indenture, I thought.

"Karl Whitesmith's boy has broken his indenture," Dolly said.

He's run off to sea.

"He's run off to sea," Kate added accusingly.

"What?" I felt my mouth move, heard the words come out independent of me. "Jon, you mean? Not Jon!"

How many 'prentices does Karl have? Of course Jon.

"How many 'prentices does Karl have? Of course Jon."

"Karl spoiled him," Kate said (and her words were echoed in my head before she spoke them). "A lad his age is like a walnut tree which suffers not but rather benefits from thrashings." She shook her besom at me. "Something the likes of you would do well to keep in mind."

Gram Birch amazed us all then by emerging from the back kitchen.

Delicate as a twig, she bent to put a plate by the hearth. It held two refried fish, leftovers from the night before, and a clutch of pickled roe. She was slimmer than your little finger and her hair was white as an aged dandelion's. This was the first time I'd seen her out of bed in weeks; the passage of the elves, or perhaps some livening property of their music, had brought fresh life to her. But her eye was as flinty as ever. "Leave the boy alone," she said.

My delusion went away, like a mist in the morning breeze from the Awen.

"You don't understand!"

"We were only—"

"This saucy lad—"

"The kitchen tub is empty," Gram Birch told me. She drew a schooner of ale and set it down by the plate. Her voice was warm with sympathy, for I was always her favorite, and there was a kindly tilt to her chin. "Go and check your trots. The head will have subsided by the time you're back."

My head in a whirl, I ran upbridge to the narrow stairway that gyred down the interior of Tinker's Leg. It filled me with wonder that Jon—gentle, laughing Jon—had shipped away. We all of us claimed to be off to sea someday; it was the second or third most common topic on our nighttime eeling trips upriver. But that it should be Jon, and that he should leave without word of farewell!

A horrible thing happened to me then: With the sureness of prophecy I knew that Jon would not come back. That he would die in the western isles. That he would be slain and eaten by a creature out of the sea such as none on the Bridge had ever imagined.

I came out at the narrow dock at the high-water mark. Thoughts elsewhere, I pulled in my lines and threw back a bass for being shorter than my forearm. Its less fortunate comrades I slung over my shoulder.

But as I was standing there on the dark and slippery stones, I saw something immense and silent move beneath the water. I thought it a monstrous tortoise at first, such as that which had taken ten strong men with ropes and grappling hooks to pull from the bay at Mermaid Head. But as it approached I could see it was too large for that. I did not move. I could not breathe. I stared down at the approaching creature.

The surface of the river exploded. A head emerged, shedding water. Each of its nostrils was large enough for a man to crawl into. Its hair and beard were dark, like the bushes and small trees that line the banks up-river and drown in every spring flood. Its eyes were larger than cartwheels and lusterless, like stone.

The giant fixed his gaze upon me, and he spoke.

What did he say, you ask? I wonder that myself. In this regard, I am like the victim of brigands who finds himself lying by the wayside, and then scrabbles in the dust for such small coppers as they may have left behind. What little I possess, I will share with you, and you may guess from it how much I have lost. One moment I stood before the giant and the next I found myself tumbled into the river. It was late afternoon and I was splashing naked with the knackery boys.

I had spent most of that day mucking out the stables in the Approach, part of an arrangement Black Gabe had made whereby the Pike and Barrel got a half a penny for each guest who quartered a horse there. I was as sweaty and filthy as any of the horses by the time I was done, and had gladly fallen in with the butcher's apprentices who would cleanse themselves of the blood and gore their own labors had besmirched them with.

This was on the south side of the river, below the Ogre Gate. I was scrubbing off the last traces of ordure when I saw the elven lady staring down at me from the esplanade.

She was small with distance, her mask a white oval. In one hand she carried a wicker cage of finches. I found her steady gaze both disconcerting and arousing. It went through me like a spear. My manhood began of its own accord to lift.

That was my first sight of Ratanavivicta.

It lasted only an instant, that vision. The light of her eyes filled and blinded me. And then one of my fellow bathers—Hodge the tanner's son it was, whom we in our innocence considered quite the wildling—

leaped upon my back, forcing me under the water. By the time I emerged, choking and sputtering, the elf-woman was gone.

I shoved Hodge away, and turned my gaze over the river. I squinted at the rafts floating downstream, sweepsmen standing with their oars up, and the carracks making harbor from their voyages across the sea. On the far bank, pier crowded upon shack and shanty upon warehouse. Stone buildings rose up behind, rank after rank fading blue into the distance, with here and there a spire or tower rising up from the general ruck.

Long snakelike necks burst from the water, two river lizards fighting over a salmon. A strange elation filled me then and I laughed with joy at the sight.

❁

At sunset the elf-host was still crossing the Bridge. Their numbers were that great. All through the night they marched, lighting their way with lanterns carried on poles. I sat in the high window of a room we had not let that evening, watching their procession, as changing-unchanging as the Awen itself. They were going to the mountains of the uttermost north, people said, through lands no living man had seen. I sat yearning, yearning after them, until my heart could take no more.

Heavily I started down the stairs to bed.

To my astonishment the common room was filled with elves. A little wicker cage hung from a ceiling hook. In it were five yellow finches. I looked down from it to the eyes of a white-masked woman. She crooked a finger beckoningly, then touched the bench to her left. I sat beside her.

An elven lord whose manner and voice are gone from me, a pillar of shadow, Cakaravartin himself, stood by the fireplace with one fingertip lazily tracing the shells and coiled serpents embedded in the stone. "I remember," he said in a dreamy voice, "when there was no ford across the Awenasamaga and these stones were part of Great Asura, the city of the giants."

"But how could you—?" I blurted. Masked faces turned to look at me. I bit my tongue in embarrassment.

"I was here when this bridge was built," the speaker continued unheedingly. "To expiate their sins, the last of the giants were compelled to dismantle their capital and with its stones build to the benefit of men. They were a noble race once, and I have paused here in our quest for *parikasaya* because I would see them once more."

Dolly swept in, yawning, with a platter of raw salmon and another holding a stacked pyramid of ten mugs of ale. "Who's to pay?" she asked. Then, seeing me, she frowned. "Will. You have chores in the morning. Ought not you be abed?"

Reddening, I said, "I'm old enough to bide my own judgment."

An elf proferred a gold coin which, had it been silver, would have paid for the service ten times over, and asked, "Is this enough?"

Dolly smiled and nodded. Starting to my feet, I said, "I'll wake the coin-merchant and break change for you." Ignoring the exasperation that swept aside my sister's look of avaricious innocence.

But the elf-woman at my side stilled me with a touch. "Stay. The coin is not important, and there is much I would have you learn."

As the coin touched Dolly's hand she changed, for the merest instant, growing old and fat. I gawked and then she was herself again. With a flip of her skirts she disappeared with the coin so completely I was not to see her for another twenty years. One of the elves turned to the wall, lifting her mask for a quick sip of ale, restoring it with nothing exposed.

The finch-bearer brought out a leather wallet and opened it, revealing dried herbs within. Someone took a long-stemmed clay tavern pipe from the fireplace rack and gave her it. As Ratanavivicta filled the bowl, she said, "This is *margakasaya*, which in your language means 'the path to extinction.' It is rare beyond your knowing, for it grows nowhere in the world now that we have given up our gardens in the south. Chewed, it is a mild soporific. Worked into a balm it can heal minor wounds. Smoked, it forms a bridge through the years, so that one's thoughts may walk in past times or future, at will."

"How can that be?" I asked. "The past is gone, and the future—who is to say what will happen? Our every action changes it, else our deeds were for naught."

She did not answer, but instead passed the pipe to me. With a pair of tongs she lifted a coal from the fire to light it. I put the stem to my lips, exhaled nervously, inhaled. I drew the smoke deep into my lungs, and a whirring and buzzing sensation rose up from my chest to fill my head, first blinding me and then opening my eyes:

It was night, and Cakaravartin's raiders were crying out in anger and despair, for the enemy had stolen a march on us and we were caught by the edge of the marshes, lightly armed and afoot.

Screaming, crazy, we danced ourselves into a frenzy. At a sign from Cakaravartin, we loosed the bundles from our backs and unfolded a dozen horsehides. We pulled out knives and slashed ourselves across arms and chests. Where the blood fell across the hides, the black loam filled them, lending them form, billowing upward to become steeds of earth, forelegs flailing, nostrils wild, eyes cold and unblinking stars.

Then we were leaping onto our mounts, drawing our swords, galloping toward the east. Where hoof touched sod, fresh earth flowed up into the necromantic beasts, and down again through the rearmost leg.

"Tirathika!"

On hearing my adoptive name, I turned to see Krodasparasa riding maskless alongside me, his markings shining silver on his face. His eyes were gleeful and fey. Krodasparasa gestured, and I tore free of my own mask. I felt my cock stiffen with excitement.

Krodasparasa saw and laughed. Our rivalry, our hatred of each other was as nothing compared to this comradeship. Riding side by side, we traded fierce grins compounded of mockery and understanding, and urged our steeds to greater efforts.

"It's a good day to die," Krodasparasa cried. "Are you ready to die, little brother?" He shifted his sword to his far side so we could clasp hands briefly at full gallop, and then swung it around in a short, fast chop that took all of my skill to evade.

I exhaled.

The common room wrapped itself about me again. I found myself staring up at the aurochs horns nailed as a trophy to the west wall, at the fat-bellied withy baskets hanging from the whale-rib rafters. Overhead, a carved and painted wooden mermaid with elk's antlers sweeping back from her head to hold candles, turned with excruciating slowness.

The elf-woman took the pipe from my nerveless fingers. She slid the long stem under her mask so skillfully that not a fingertip's worth of her face showed. Slowly, she inhaled. The coal burned brighter, a wee orange bonfire that sucked in all the light in the room. "That was not what I wished to see," she murmured. She drew in a second time and then handed the pipe on.

Slowly the pipe passed around the room again, coming last of all to me. Clumsily, I accepted it and put the end, now hot, to my lips. I drew the magic in:

I stood on an empty plain, the silk tents of the encampment to my back. Frost rimed the ground in crisscross starbursts. My blood was pounding.

It was a festival night, and we had cut the center-poles for our conical tents twice as high as usual. Small lanterns hung from their tips like stars.

All was still. For the *am'rta skandayaksa,* venturing out on a festival night was a great impiety.

Tortured with indecision I turned away and then back again, away and back. I could be killed for what I intended, but that bothered me less than the possibility that I had misread the signs, that I was not wanted. I stood before one particular tent, glaring at it until it glowed like the sun. Finally I ducked within.

Ratanavivicta was waiting for me.

Throwing aside my mask, I knelt before her. Slowly, lingeringly, I slid my fingers beneath her mask and drew it off. Her face was scarred, like the moon, and like the moon it was beautiful and cold. My hand was black on her breast. A pale nipple peeked between my fingers like the first star of twilight.

"Ahhh," she sighed voicelessly, and the pipe passed to the next hand.

◉

Everything had changed.

You cannot imagine how it felt, after twenty years of wandering, to return at last to Long Bridge. My heart was so bitter I could taste it in my mouth. Two decades of my life were gone, turned to nothing. My memory of those years was but mists and phantoms, stolen away by those I had trusted most. The Dragon Gate was smaller than I remembered it being, and nowhere near so grand. The stone buildings whose spires had combed the passing clouds were a mere three and four stories high. The roadway between them was scarce wide enough to let two carts pass.

My face felt tight and dry. I slid a finger under my mask to scratch at the scar tissue where it touched one corner of my mouth.

Even the air smelled different. The smoky haze of my boyhood, oak and cedar from the chimneys of the rich, driftwood and dried dung from the roofholes of the poor, was changed utterly, compounded now of charcoal and quarry-dug coal with always a sharp tang of sulfur pinching at the nose. Wondrous odors still spilled from the cookshop where old Hal Baldpate was always ready with a scowl and a sugar-bun, but the peppery admixture of hams curing next door was missing, and the smokehouse itself converted to a lens-grinder's shop.

The narrow gap between the two buildings remained, though—do you young ones still call it the Gullet?—and through it rose a light breeze from the Awen. I halted and leaned on my spear. It was exactly here one long-ago evening that Becky had showed me her freckled breasts and then fleered at me for being shocked. Here Jon and I would kneel to divvy up the eggs we'd stolen from the cotes of Bankside, which, being off the Bridge, was considered fair game by all good river-brats—I see you smiling! Here I crouched in ambush for a weaver's prentice whose name and face and sin are gone from me now, though that folly cost me a broken arm and all of Becky's hard-won sympathy.

Somebody bumped into me, cursed, and was gone before I could turn and crave pardon. I squeezed into the Gullet so others could pass, and stared out over the sun-dazzled river.

Down the Awen, a pyroscaph struggled toward the bay, smoke billowing from its stack, paddles flashing in unison, as if it were a water-beetle enchanted beyond natural size. The merchanters entering and leaving the harbor were larger than I remembered, and the cut of their sails was unfamiliar. Along the banks the city's chimneys had multiplied, pillaring smoke into the darkened heavens. It was a changed world, and one that held no place for such as me.

The ghosts of my youth thronged so thickly about me then that I could not distinguish past from present, memory from desire. It was as if I had turned away for an instant and on turning back discovered myself two decades older.

Fill the bowl again. One last time I would hear the dawn-music of my youth, the sound of lodgers clumping sleepily down the stairs, the clink and rattle of plates and pewter in the kitchen. The quick step of Eleanor returning from the cookshop with her arms full of fresh-smelling bread. The background grumbles of Black Gabe standing just out of sight, finding fault with my work.

What a cruel contrast to this morning! When I turned away from the Awen, the Bridge was thick with scurrying city-folk, shopkeepers and craftsmen in fussy, lace-trimmed clothes. The air was full of the clicking of their heels. Men and women alike, their faces were set and grim. For an instant my spirit quailed at the thought of rejoining human company. I had spent too many years in the company of owls and wolves, alone in the solitudes of the north, to be comfortable here. But I squared my shoulders and went on.

The old Pike and Barrel stood where it has always stood, midway down the Bridge. From a distance it seemed unbearably small and insignificant, though every stone and timber of it was burned forever into my heart. The tavern-placard swung lazily on its rod. That same laughing fish leaped from that same barrel that a wandering scholar had executed in trade for a night's stay when Aunt Kate was young. I know, for she spoke of him often.

Below the sign a crowd had formed, an angry eddy in the flow of passers-by. A hogshead had been upended by the door and atop it a stout man with a sheriff's feather in his cap was reading from a parchment scroll. By him stood a scarecrow underling with a handbell and behind him a dozen bravos with oaken staves, all in a row.

It was an eviction.

Kate was there, crying with rage and miraculously unchanged. I stared, disbelieving, and then, with a pain like a blow to the heart, realized my mistake. This worn, heavy woman must be my sister Dolly, turned horribly, horribly old. The sight of her made me want to turn away. The painted pike mocked me with its silent laughter. But I mastered my unease and bulled my way through the crowd.

Without meaning to, I caused a sensation. Murmuring, the bystanders made way. The sheriff stopped reading. His bravos stirred unhappily, and the scrawny bell-man cringed. The center of all eyes, I realized that there must be some faint touch of the elven glamour that clung to me yet.

"What is happening here?" My voice was deep, unfamiliar, and the words came hesitantly from my mouth, like water from a pump grown stiff with disuse.

The sheriff blusteringly shook his parchment at me. "Don't interfere! This is a legal turning-out, and I've the stavesmen to back me up."

"You're a coward, Tom Huddle, and an evil man indeed to do this to folk who were once your friends!" Dolly shouted. "You're the rich man's lickspittle now! A hireling to miscreants and usurers, and naught more!"

A mutter of agreement went up from the crowd.

The sheriff ducked his massive head and without turning to meet her eye, grumbled, "By damn, Dolly, I'm only doing my—"

"I'll pay," I said.

Tom Huddle gaped. "Eh? What's that?"

I shrugged off my backsack, of thick dwarven cloth embroidered with silk orchids in a woods-elf stitch, and handed my spear to a gangly youth, who almost dropped it in astonishment. That was you, wasn't it? I thought so. The haft is ebony, and heavier than might be thought.

Lashed to the frame, alongside my quiver and the broken shards of what had once been my father's sword, was a leather purse. After such long commerce with elves I no longer clearly knew the value of one coin over another. But there would be enough, that much I knew. The elvenkind are generous enough with things that do not matter. I handed it to my sister, saying, "Take as much as you need."

Dolly stood with the purse in her outstretched hand, making no move to open it. "Who are you?" she asked fearfully. "What manner of man hides his features behind a mask?"

My hand rose involuntarily—I'd forgotten the mask was there. Now, since it no longer served a purpose, I took it off. Fresh air touched my face. I felt dizzy almost to sickness, standing exposed before so many people.

Dolly stared at me.

"Will?" she said at last. "Is it really you?"

When the money had been counted over thrice and the sprig of broom the sheriff had nailed over the doorsill had been torn down and trampled underfoot, the house and neighbors all crowded about me and bore me into the Pike and Barrel's common room and gave me the honored place by the fire. The air was close and stuffy—I could not think. But nobody noticed. They tumbled question upon question so that I had but little chance to answer, and vied to reintroduce themselves, crying, "Here's one you're not expecting!" and "Did you ever guess little Sam would turn out such a garish big gassoon?" and roaring with laughter. Somebody put a child on my knee, a boy, they said his name was Pip. Somebody else brought down the lute from its peg by the loft and struck up a song.

Suddenly the room was awhirl with dancers. Unmoved, I watched them, these dark people, these strangers, all sweaty and imperfect flesh. After my years with the pale folk, they all seemed heavy and earthbound. Heat radiated from their bodies like steam.

A woman with wrinkles at the corners of her eyes and mischief within them, drew me up from the stool, and suddenly I was dancing too. The fire cast an ogreish shadow upon the wall behind me and it danced as well, mocking my clumsy steps.

Everything felt so familiar and yet so alien, all the faces of my youth made strange by age, and yet dear to me in an odd, aching way, as if both tavern and Bridge were but clever simulacra of the real thing, lacking the power to convince and yet still able to rend the heart. My childhood was preternaturally clear, as close to me now as the room in which I sat. It was as if I had never left. All the years between seemed a dream.

"You don't know who I am, do you?" my dancing partner said.

"Of course I do," I lied.

"Who, then?" She released me and stood back, hands on hips.

Challenged, I actually *looked* at her for the first time. She moved loosely within her blouse, a plump woman with big brown freckles on her face and forearms. She crossed her arms in a way that caused her breasts to balloon upward, and laughed when I flushed in embarrassment.

Her laughter struck me like the clapper of a great bell.

"Becky!" I cried. "By the Seven, it's you! I never expected—"

"You never expected I'd grow so fat, eh?"

"No, no!" I protested. "It's not—"

"You're a fool, Will Taverner. But that's not totally unbecoming in a man." She drew me into the shadow of the stairway where there was privacy, and a small bench as well. We talked for a long time. And at the end of that conversation I thought she looked dissatisfied. Nor could I account for it until she reached between my legs to feel what was there. My cod, though, was a wiser man than I and stood up to greet her. "Well," she said, "that's a beginning. Cold dishes aren't brought back to a boil in a minute."

She left me.

You look unhappy. Becky's your mam, isn't she? Now that I come to think of it, there's that glint in your eye and a hint at that same diabolos that hides at the edge of her mouth. Well she's a widow now, which means she can do as she pleases. But I will horrify you with no more details of what we said.

Where's my pipe? What happened to that pouch of weed? Thank you. I'd be long asleep by now if not for its aid. This is the last trace of the *margakasaya* left in all the world. With me will die even the memory of it, for there are no elves abroad in the realms of men anymore. They have found *parikasaya*, "final extinction" you would say, or perhaps "the end of all." Did you know that *am'rta skandayaksa* means "deathless elf-group?" There's irony there, knew we only how to decipher it.

Maybe I was wrong to kill the dragon.

Maybe he was all that kept them from oblivion.

When we had all shared Cakaravartin's vision of Great Asura and of the giants at labor, their faces stolid and accepting of both their guilt and their punishment, and spoken with Boramohanagarahant, their king, it was almost dawn. Cakaravartin passed around the pipe one more time. "I see that you are determined to come with us," he said to me, "and that is your decision to make. But first you should know the consequences."

Ratanavivicta's mask tilted in a way that I would later learn indicated displeasure. But Cakaravartin drew in deeply and passed the pipe around again. I was trembling when it came to me. The mouthpiece was slick with elf-spit. I put it between my lips.

I inhaled.

At first I thought nothing had happened. The common room was exactly as before, the fire dying low in the hearth, the elfmaid slowly quartering out the air as ever she had done. Then I looked around me. The elves were gone. I was alone, save for one slim youth of about my own age, whom I did not recognize.

That youth was you.

Do I frighten you? I frighten myself far more, for I have reached that moment when I see all with doubled sight and apprehend with divided heart. Pray such possession never seizes you. This—now—is what I was shown all these many years ago, and this is the only chance I will ever have to voice my anger and regret to that younger self, who I know will not listen. How could he? A raggedy taverner's boy with small prospects and a head stuffed full of half-shaped ambitions. What could I say to make him understand how much he is giving up?

By rights you should have been my child. There's the bitter nub of the thing, that Becky, who had all but pledged her heart to me, had her get by someone else. A good man, perhaps—they say half the Bridge turned out to launch his fire-boat when he was taken by the dropsy—but not me.

I have lost more than years. I have lost the life I was meant to have, children on my knee and a goodwife growing old and fat with me as we sank into our dotage. Someone to carry my memory a few paces beyond the emptiness of the grave, and grandchildren to see sights I will not. These were my birthright, and I have them not. In his callowness and ignorance, my younger self has undone me.

I can see him, even now, running madly after the elves, as he will in the shadowy hour before dawn. Heart pounding with fear that he will not catch up, lungs agonized with effort. Furious to be a hero, to see strange lands, to know the love of a lady of the *am'rta skandayaksa*. They are fickle and cruel, are the elves. Ratanavivicta snatched me from my life on a whim, as casually as she might pick up a bright pebble from the roadside. She cast me aside as easily as she would a gemstone of which she had wearied. There is no faith in her kind.

Ah, it is a dreadful night! The winds prowl the rooftops like cats, bringing in the winter. There'll be frost by morning, and no mistake.

Is the story over, you ask? Have you not been listening? There is no story. Or else it all—your life and mine and Krodasparasa's alike—is one story and that story always ending and never coming to a conclusion. But my telling ends now, with my younger self starting from his dream of age and defeat and finding himself abandoned, the sole mortal awake on all the Bridge, with the last of the elf horde gone into the sleeping streets of the city beyond the Dragon Gate.

He will leap to his feet and snatch up his father's sword from its place over the hearth—there, where my spear hangs now. He will grab a blanket for a cloak and a handful of jerked meat to eat along the road, and nothing more, so great will be his dread of being left behind.

I would not stop him if I could. Run, lad, run! What do you care what becomes of me? Twenty years of glory lie at your feet. The dream is already fading from your head.

You feel the breeze from the river as you burst out the door.

Your heart *sings*.

The moment is past. I have been left behind.

Only now can I admit this. Through all this telling, I have been haunted by a ghost and the name of that ghost was Hope. So long as I had not passed beyond that ancient vision, there was yet the chance that I was not my older self at all, but he who was destined to shake off his doubts and leap out that door. In the innermost reaches of my head, I was still young. The dragon was not slain, the road untraveled, the elves alive, the adventures ahead, the magic not yet passed out of the world.

And now, well. I'm home.

NORTH OF DIDDY-WAH-DIDDY

The train to Hell don't stop in New Jersey. It pulls out of Grand Central Station at midnight, moving slow at first but steadily picking up speed as it passes under the Bay, and by the time we hit the refineries, it's cannonballing. We don't stop for nothing. We don't stop for nobody. And if you step in our way expecting Old Goatfoot to apply the brakes, well, pardon me for saying it, but you're going to get exactly what's coming to you.

We don't stop and we don't slow down once that gleaming black-and-silver locomotive leaves the station. Not 'til we get to where we're going. Once we're rolling, there's no second chances. And no exceptions neither.

So that night the train *did* stop, I knew straight off that we were in for some serious trouble.

We were barreling through the Pine Barrens, shedding smoke and sulfur and sparks, when I heard the air brakes squeal. The train commenced to losing velocity. I was just about to open the snack bar, but right off I heard that sound, I flipped around the CLOSED sign, grabbed my cap, and skittered off to see what the matter was.

The damned were slumped in their seats. Some of them stared straight ahead of themselves at nothing in particular. Others peered listlessly out the windows or else at their own grey reflections in the glass. Our passengers are always a little subdued in the early stages of the trip.

"Oh, porter!" one of the damned called to me. She was a skinny little white woman with a worried-looking kind of pinched-in face. "Would it be all right of me to open the window just a crack, so I could get some air?"

I smiled gently into those big pleading eyes of hers and said, "Why, bless you, honey, you can do whatever you want. What difference could it possibly make now?"

She flinched back like I'd hit her.

But I reached over and took the window clips and slid it down two inches. "Don't go no further, I'm afraid. Some of the lost souls might take it into their heads to try and…you know?" I lowered my voice in a confidential manner.

Timidly, she nodded.

I got a pillow out of the overhead and fluffed it up for her. "Now you just let me slide this behind your head. There! Isn't that better? You relax now, and in a couple minutes the kitchen will be open. When I come back, I'll give you a menu. Got a nice selection of sandwiches and beverages. You rest up and have a comfy ride."

All the while I was talking, I was just about dying inside of curiosity. Through the window behind the old lady I could see that we'd stopped in a small clearing in the pines. We were miles from the nearest town. The only light here was what came from the moon and the greenish spill from the windows of the train itself. There were maybe half a dozen dim figures out there. I could see them hoist up a long crate of some kind. Somebody—and who else could it be but Billy Bones?—leaned out from the caboose with a lantern and waved them forward.

The damned stared out the windows with disinterest. Most likely they thought we were picking up more passengers. Only the crew knew different.

Still, I take pride in my work. I fussed over that little lady and by the time I left her she was actually smiling. It was only a tense little smile, but it was a smile still.

People can fool themselves into believing anything.

Soon as I got myself clear, I made straight for the baggage car. I had got me a real bad feeling about what was going on, and I intended to pry a few answers out of Billy Bones. But I didn't get beyond the door. When I tried to slide it back, it wouldn't budge. I seized it with both hands and applied some muscle. Nothing.

It was locked from inside.

I banged on the door. "Mister *Bones!*"

A silence, and then the peephole slide moved aside. A cadaverous slice of Billy Bones's face appeared. Flesh so tight it didn't hide the skull. Eyes as bright and glittery as a rat's. "What is it?"

"Don't you give me that what-is-it bullshit—why did we stop?" The pines made a dark, jagged line against the sky. I could smell them. If I wanted, I could step down off the train and walk into them. "Just what kind of unholy cargo have you taken on?"

Billy Bones looked me straight in the eye. "We ain't taken on no cargo."

"Now don't get me started," I said. "You open up and—"

He slammed that little slide-door right in my face.

I blinked. "Well!" I said. "You may think you've had the last word, Mister Billy Bones, but you have not, I assure you that!"

But I didn't feel nowhere near so brash as I made out. Billy Bones was a natural-born hustler down to his fingertips, the kind of man that could break you a quarter and short-change you a dollar in the process. Ain't nobody never outbluffed him. Ain't nobody never got nothing out of him that he didn't want to give. In my experience, what he didn't wish to say, I wasn't about to hear.

So back I strode, up the train, looking for Sugar. My old stomach ulcer was starting to act up.

❉

"Diddy-Wah-DIDDY!" Sugar bawled. He strolled briskly through the car, clacking his ticket punch. "Diddy-Wah-Diddy, Ginny Gall, WEST Hell, Hell, and BeluthaHATCHie! Have your tickets ready."

I gave him the high sign. But a portly gent in a pinstripe suit laid hold of his sleeve and launched into a long complaint about his ticket, so I had to hold back and wait. Sugar listened patiently to the man for a time, then leaned over him like a purple storm cloud. The man cringed away. He's big, is Sugar, and every ounce of him is pure intimidation.

"I tell you what, sir," he said in a low and menacing way. "Why don't you take a spoon and jab it in your eye? Stir it around good. See how clean you can scrape out the socket." He punched the ticket. "I guarantee you that a week from now you gone look back upon the experience with nostalgia."

The man turned grey and for an instant I thought he was going to rise up out of his seat. But Sugar smiled in a way that bulged up every muscle in his face and neck and the man subsided. Sugar stuck the ticket stub in the seat clip. Then, shaking his head, he came and joined me between cars.

His bulk filled what space there was pretty good. "Make it brief, Malcolm. I got things to do."

"You know anything 'bout why we stopped?" Those dim people were trudging away into the pines. None of them looked back, not even once. They just dissolved into the shadows. "I saw Billy Bones take on a crate and when I asked him about it, he clammed right up."

Sugar stared at me with those boogieman eyes of his. In all the three-four years he'd been on the train, I don't recall ever seeing him blink. "You ain't seen nothing," he said.

I put my hands on my hips. "Now, don't *you* start in on me! I was a porter on this train back when your mama was sucking tittie."

Sugar seemed to swell up then, a great black mountain with two pinpricks of hellfire dancing in his eyes. "You watch what you say about my mother."

The hairs on the back of my neck prickled. But I didn't back down. "Just what you intending to do?" I shook my finger in his face. "You know the regs. If you so much as touch me, you're off the train. And they don't let you out in Manhattan, neither!"

"Can't say I much care." He put those enormous hands on my shoulders. His voice was small and dreamy. "After this run, I don't much care whether I keep this job or not."

All the while he spoke, those hands kept kneading my shoulders. He laid one huge thumb alongside my face and shoved my head to the side. I didn't much doubt he could crush my bones and snap my spine, if he wanted to. He was that strong. And I could see that he'd enjoy it.

"I ain't said nothing!" I was terrified. "I ain't said nothing about your mama."

Sugar considered this for a long time, that sleepy little smile floating on his face. At last he said, "See that you don't."

And he turned away.

I exhaled. I can't say I knew Sugar at all well. He was a recent addition to the crew; the conductor before him took to visiting the juke joints and gambling dens of Ginny Gall during stopovers and lost his precariously-held spiritual balance. But if ever anyone was meant to be a badman, it was Sugar. He was born just naturally brimming-over with anger. They say when the midwife slapped his bottom, the rage in his voice and the look on his face were so awful that straightaway she threw him down on the floor. He was born with a strangler's hands and a murderer's eyes. The rest of him, the size and bulk of him, just grew, so's to have a package big enough and mean enough to contain all the temper there inside.

And they also say that when the midwife lifted up her foot to crush Sugar to death, his mama rose up off of the bed and thrashed her within an inch of her life. She was one of those tiny little women too, but her love for her baby was that strong. She threw that midwife right out of the room and down the stairs, broken bones and all. Then she picked up Sugar and put him to her breast and cooed at him and sang to him until he fell asleep. That's the kind of blood flowed in Sugar's veins, the kind of stuff he was made from.

There was a sudden lurch and the train started to move again. Whatever was going down, it was too late to stop it now.

With Billy Bones and Sugar refusing to talk to me, there wasn't any chance none of the girls would either. They were all three union, and Billy was their shop steward. Me, I was union too, but in a different shop.

The only remaining possible source of information was Old Goatfoot. I headed back for the concession stand to fetch a bottle of rye. I had it in a paper bag under one arm and was passing through the sleeper cars when a door slid open and a long slim hand crooked a red-nailed finger.

I stepped into the compartment. A ginger-colored woman closed the door and slid between me and it. For an instant we just stood there looking at each other. At last she said, "Porter."

"Yes'm?"

She smiled in a sly kind of way. "I want to show you something." She unbuttoned her blouse, thrusting her chest forward. She was wearing one of those black lacy kinds of bras that squeeze the breasts together and up. It was something to behold.

"If you'll excuse me, ma'am," I said uncomfortably. "I have to get back to work."

"I got work for you right here," she said, grabbing at me. I reached for the doorknob, but she was tugging at my jacket, trying to get it open. I grabbed her by the wrists, afraid of losing a button.

"Please, ma'am." I was just about dying of embarrassment.

"Don't you please ma'am me, boy! You know I got what you want and we both know I ain't got long to use it." She was rubbing herself against me and at the same time trying to shove my head down into her bosom. Somehow her brassiere had come undone and her breasts were slapping me in the face. It was awful. I was thrashing around, struggling to get free, and she was all over me.

Then I managed to slip out of her grip and straight-arm her so that she fell on her back onto the bunk. For a second she lay there looking rumpled and expectant.

I used that second to open the door and step out into the hall. Keeping a wary eye on the woman, I began to tug my uniform back into place.

When she realized I wasn't going to stay, her face twisted, and she spat out a nasty word.

"Cocksucker!"

It hurt. I'm not saying it didn't. But she was under a lot of pressure, and it wouldn't have been professional for me to let my feelings show. So I simply said, "Yes'm. That's so. But I'm sure there are plenty of men on board this train who would be extremely interested in what you got to offer. The dining room opens soon. You might take a stroll up that way and see what sort of gents are available."

I slipped away.

Back when I died, men like me called ourselves "queers." That's how long ago it was. And back then, if you were queer and had the misfortune to die, you were automatically damned. It was a mortal sin just being one of us, never mind that you didn't have any say in the matter. The Stonewall Riots changed all that. After them, if you'd lived a good life you qualified for the other place. There's still a lot of bitterness in certain circles of Hell over this, but what are you going to do? The Man in charge don't take complaints.

It was my misfortune to die several decades too early. I was beat to death in Athens, Georgia. A couple of cops caught me in the back seat of a late-model Rambler necking with a white boy name of Danny. I don't guess they actually meant to kill me. They just forgot to stop in time. That sort of thing went on a lot back then.

First thing I died, I was taken to this little room with two bored-looking angels. One of them sat hunched over a desk, scribbling on a whole heap of papers. "What's this one?" he asked without looking up.

The second angel was lounging against a filing cabinet. He had a kindly sort of face, very tired-looking, like he'd seen the worst humanity had to offer and knew he was going to keep on seeing it until the last trump. It was a genuine kindness, too, because out of all the things he could've called me, he said, "A kid with bad luck."

The first angel glanced up and said, "Oh." Then went back to his work.

"Have a seat, son," the kindly angel said. "This will take a while."

I obeyed. "What's going to become of me?" I asked.

"You're fucked," the first angel muttered.

I looked to the other.

He colored a little. "That's it," he said. "There just plain flat-out ain't no way you're going to beat this rap. You're a faggot and faggots go to Hell." He kind of coughed into his hand then and said, "I'll tell you what, though. It's not official yet, but I happen to know that the two yahoos who rousted you are going to be passing through this office soon. Moonshining incident."

He pulled open a file drawer and took out a big fat folder overflowing with papers. "These are the Schedule C damnations in here. Boiling maggots, rains of molten lead, the whole lot. You look through them, pick out a couple of juicy ones. I'll see that your buddies get them."

"Nossir," I said. "I'd rather not."

"Eh?" He pushed his specs down his nose and peered over them at me. "What's that?"

"If it's all the same to you, I don't want to do nothing to them."

"Why, they're just two bull-neck crackers! Rednecks! White-trash peckerwoods!" He pointed the file at me. "They beat you to death for the fun of it!"

"I don't suppose they were exactly good men," I said. "I reckon the world will be better off without them. But I don't bear them any malice. Maybe I can't find it in me to wish them well, and maybe I wasn't what you'd call a regular churchgoer. But I know that we're supposed to forgive our trespassers, to whatever degree our natures allow. And, well, I'd appreciate it if you didn't do any of those things to them."

The second angel was staring at me in disbelief, and his expression wasn't at all kindly anymore. The first angel had stopped scribbling and was gawking at me too.

"Shit," he said.

Three days they spent bickering over me.

I presented something of a political problem for those who decide these matters, because of course they couldn't just let me go Upstairs. It would have created a precedent.

The upshot of it was that I got a new job. They gave me a brass-button uniform and two weeks' training, and told me to keep out of trouble. And so far, I had.

Only now, I was beginning to think my lucky streak was over.

Old Goatfoot looked over his shoulder with a snarl when I entered the cab of the locomotive. Of all the crew only he had never been human. He was a devil from the git-go, or maybe an angel once if you believe Mister Milton. I pulled the bag off of the bottle of rye and let the wind whip it away, and his expression changed. He wrapped a clawed hand around the bottle and took a swig that made a good quarter of its contents disappear.

He let out this great rumbling sigh then, part howl and part belch, like no sound that had ever known a human throat. I shuddered, but it was just his way of showing satisfaction. In a burnt-out cinder of a voice, Old Goatfoot said, "Trouble's brewing."

"That so?" I said cautiously.

"Always is." He stared out across the wastelands. A band of centaurs, each one taller than a ten-story building, struggled through waist-high muck in the distance. Nasty stuff it was—smelled worse than the Fresh Kill landfill over to New Jersey. "This time, though." He shook his head and said, "Ain't never seen nothing like it. All the buggers of Hell are out."

He passed me back the bottle.

I passed my hand over the mouth, still hot from his lips, and took a gingerly little sip. Just to be companionable. "How come?"

He shrugged. "Dunno. They're looking for something, but fuck if I can make out what."

Just then a leather-winged monster larger than a storm cloud lifted over the horizon. With a roar and a flapping sound like canvas in the wind, it was upon us. The creature was so huge that it covered half the sky, and it left a stench behind that I knew would linger for hours, even at the speeds we were going. "That's one ugly brute," I remarked.

Old Goatfoot laughed scornfully and knocked back another third of the bottle. "You worried about a little thing like that?" He leaned his head out the window, closed one nostril with a finger, and shot a stream of snot into the night. "Shitfire, boy, I've seen Archangels flying over us."

Now I was genuinely frightened. Because I had no doubt that whatever the powers that be were looking for, it was somewhere on our train. And this last meant that all of Heaven and Hell were arrayed against us. Now, you might think that Hell was worry enough for anybody, but consider this—they *lost*. Forget what folks say. The other side are mean mothers, and don't let nobody tell you different.

Old Goatfoot finished off the bottle and ate the glass. Then, keeping one hand on the throttle all the while, he unbuttoned his breeches, hauled out his ugly old thing, and began pissing into the firebox. There were two firemen standing barefoot in the burning coals, shoveling like madmen. They dropped their shovels and scrambled to catch as much of the spray as they could, clambering all over each other in their anxiousness for a respite, however partial, however brief, from their suffering. They were black as carbon and little blue flames burned in their hair. Old Goatfoot's piss sizzled and steamed where it hit the coals.

Damned souls though they were, I found it a distressing sight.

"Y'all have to excuse me," I said uneasily. "They'll be opening the casino round about now. I got work to do."

Old Goatfoot farted. "Eat shit and die," he said genially.

Back in the casino car, Billy Bones had set up his wheel, and folks that on an ordinary day gambled like there was no tomorrow had pulled out all the stops. They were whooping and laughing, talking that big talk, and slapping down paper money by the fistful. Nobody cared that it was a crooked game. It was their last chance to show a little style.

Billy Bones was in his element, his skull-face grinning with avarice. He spun the wheel with one hand and rested the other on the haunch of a honey in smoke-grey stockings and a skirt so short you could see all the way to Cincinnati. She had one hand on Billy's shoulder and a martini and a clove cigarette both in the other, and you could see she was game for anything he might happen to have in mind. But so far as Billy was concerned, she was just a prop, a flash bit of glamour to help keep the money rolling in.

LaBelle, Afreya, and Sally breezed by with their trays of cigarettes, heroin, and *hors d'oeuvres*. They were all good girls, and how they got here was—well, I guess we all know how good girls get in trouble. They fall for the wrong man. They wore white gloves and their uniforms were tight-cut but austere, for they none of them were exactly eager to be confused with the damned. Sally gave me a bit of a smile, sympathetic but guarded.

We had some good musicians died for this trip, and they were putting in some hot licks. Maybe they sensed that with the caliber of competition Down Below, they were going to be a long time between gigs. But they sure were cooking.

Everybody was having a high old time.

This was the jolly part of the trip, and normally I enjoyed it. Not today.

Sugar stood by the rear door, surrounded by a bevy of the finest honeys imaginable. This was nothing new. It was always a sight how they flocked to him on the southbound platform at Grand Central Station, elegantly dressed women who weren't even dead yet, rolling their eyes and wriggling their behinds something outrageous. Sooner or later one would ask, "You ever seen…him?" and then, when he squinted at her like he couldn't quite make out what she was getting at, "You know—Lucifer? The Devil."

At which point Sugar would say, "Seen him? Why, just this last run, I had a private audience with His Satanic Majesty. Sugar, he says to me, You been talking mighty big of late, I guess it's time to remind you who's boss."

"What did you say?" They would all hold their breaths and bend close.

"I said, Drop your pants and bend over, motherfucker. *I'm* driving now."

They'd shriek then, scandalized and delighted. And when Sugar opened his arms, two of the honeys would slide in under them neat as you please.

Business was brisk at the bar. I tried not to let my thoughts show, but I must've made a bad job of it, for I was just thrusting one of those little paper umbrellas into a frozen daiquiri when a hand closed upon my shoulder.

I whirled around, right into the most knowing smile I'd ever seen. It was a smart-dressed lady, all in red. She had on a bowler hat and she smoked a cigar. Her skirt went all the way to the ground, but there was a slit up one side and you could see the silver derringer stuck into her garter.

"You look worried," she said. "I wouldn't think the crew had much of anything to worry about."

"We're human, ma'am. Subject to the thousand natural shocks the flesh is heir to." I sighed. "And I will confess that if I weren't obliged to be here behind the bar—well. What's your pleasure?"

For a long moment she studied me.

"You interest me," she said at last, and vanished into the crowd.

Not much later she was back, steering a shy little porcelain doll of a girl by the elbow. "Missy can tend bar," she said. She slipped one hand between the girl's legs and the other behind her shoulder blades and hoisted her clear over the bar. It was an astonishing display of strength and she did it with no special emphasis, as if it were the most natural thing in the world. "She's had more than sufficient experience."

"Now hold on," I said. "I can't just—"

"Missy doesn't mind. Do you, little sweet?"

The girl, wide-eyed, shook her head no.

"Wait for me here." The lady leaned down and kissed her full on the mouth—full, and deep too. Nobody paid any mind. The festivities had reached that rowdy stage. "You come with me."

I didn't have much choice but to follow.

Her name, she said, was Jackie. And, when I'd introduced myself, "I'm going to help you, Malcolm."

"Why?"

"I have observed," she said, "that other people are often willing to accept whatever events may chance to happen to them, rather than take an active part in their unfolding. That's not me." She glanced scornfully back at the casino car. "I am no gambler. All my pleasure lies in direct action. Tell me your problem. Make it interesting."

When I'd told my story, Jackie took the cigar out of her mouth and stared at it thoughtfully. "Your friend's attention is currently given over entirely to the pursuit of money. Can't you just go back to the baggage car now and look?"

I shook my head. "Not with Sugar standing by the rear door."

We were in the space between the casino and the next car forward, with the rails flashing by underneath and the cars twisting and rattling about us. Jackie put a hand on the bottommost rung of the access ladder and said, "Then we'll go over the roof."

"Now, just a minute!"

"No delays." She frowned down at her skirt. "As soon as I can arrange a change of clothing."

Up the sleeper car she strode, opening doors, glancing within, slamming them shut again. Fifth one she tried, there was a skinny man in nothing but a white shirt working away on top of his lady-love. He looked up angrily. "Hey! What the fuck do you—"

Jackie pressed her derringer against his forehead and nodded toward a neatly folded bundle of clothing. "May I?"

The man froze. He couldn't die here, but that didn't mean he'd relish a bullet through his skull. "They're yours."

"You're a gent." Jackie scooped up the bundle. Just before closing the door, she paused and smiled down at the terrified face of the woman underneath her victim.

"Pray," she said, "continue."

In the hallway she whipped off her skirt, stepped into the slacks, and zipped them up before I had the chance to look away. The jacket she tossed aside. She buttoned the vest over her blouse and tentatively tried on one of the man's wing tips. "They fit!"

I went up the rungs first. The wind was rushing over the top of the train something fierce. Gingerly, I began crawling across the roof of the casino car. I was scared out of my wits and making no fast progress, when I felt a tap on my shoulder. I looked back.

My heart about failed me. Jackie was standing straight up, oblivious to the furious rattling speed of the train. She reached down and hauled me to my feet. "Let's dance!" she shouted into my ear.

"What?" I shouted back, disbelieving. The wind buffeted us wildly. It whipped off Jackie's bowler hat and sent it tumbling away. She laughed.

"*Dance!* You've heard of dancing, haven't you?"

Without waiting for a reply, she seized me by the waist and whirled me around, and we were dancing. She led and I followed, fearful that the least misstep would tumble us from the train and land us broken and lost in the marshes of Styx. It was the single most frightening and exhilarating experience of my entire existence, moreso even than my first time with that traveling man out by the gravel quarry at the edge of town.

I was so frightened by now that it no longer mattered. I danced, hesitantly at first, and then with abandon. Jackie spun me dizzily around and around. The wind snatched sparks from her cigar and spangled the night with stars. Madness filled me and I danced, I danced, I danced.

At last Jackie released me. She looked flushed and satisfied. "That's better. No more crawling, Malcolm. You and I aren't made for it. Like as not, all our strivings will come to nothing in the end; we must celebrate our triumph now, while yet we can." And somehow I knew precisely how she felt and agreed with it too.

Then she glanced off to the side. The dark wastelands were zipping past. A ghastly kind of corpse-fire was crawling over the muck and filth to either side of the tracks. "A person might jump off here with no more damage than a broken arm, maybe a couple of ribs. We can't be more than—what?—two hundred fifty, three hundred miles south of New Jersey? It would not be difficult for a determined and spirited individual to follow the tracks back and escape."

"Nobody escapes," I said. "Please don't think of it."

A flicker of sadness passed over her face then, and she said, "No, of course not." Then, brisk again, "Come. We have work to do. Quickly. If anybody heard us stomping about up here, they'll know what we're up to."

We came down between cars at the front of the baggage car. There was a tool closet there I had the key to, and inside it a pry bar. I had just busted open the padlock when LaBelle suddenly slammed through the door from the front of the train, wild-eyed and sweaty.

"Malcolm," she said breathlessly, "don't!"

From somewhere about her person—don't ask me where—Jackie produced a wicked-looking knife. "Do not try to stop us," she said softly.

"You don't understand," LaBelle cried. "There's a *hound* on board!"

I heard it coming then.

The hounds of Hell aren't like the Earthly sort: They're bigger than the biggest mastiffs and they bear a considerable resemblance to rats. Their smell is loathsome beyond description and their disposition even worse.

LaBelle shrieked and shrank aside as the hound came bounding down the aisle.

With something between a howl and a scream, it was upon us.

"Go!" Jackie shoved me through the doorway. "I'll handle this. You do your part now."

She slammed the door shut.

Silence wrapped itself about me. It was ghastly. For all I could hear, the hound didn't even exist.

I flicked on the electric and in its swaying light took a look around. All the usual baggage: cases of fine French wines and satin sheets for the Lords of Hell, crates of shovels and rubber hip boots and balky manual typewriters for the rest. But to the rear of the car there was one thing more.

A coffin.

It was a long, slow walk to the coffin. I thought of all the folks I'd known who'd died and gone where I'd never see them again. I thought of all those things it might contain. It seemed to me then like Pandora's box, filled with nameless dread and the forbidden powers of Old Night. There was nothing I wanted to do less than to open it.

I took a deep breath and jammed the edge of the pry bar into the coffin. Nails screamed, and I flung the top back.

The woman inside opened her eyes.

I stood frozen with horror. She had a wrinkled little face, brown as a nut, and you could tell just by looking at it that she'd led a hard life. There was that firmness about the corners of her mouth, that unblinking quality about the eyes. She was a scrawny thing, all bones and no flesh, and her arms were crossed over her flat chest. Light played about her face and lit up the coffin around her head. I looked at her and I was just flat-out afraid of what was going to happen to Sugar and to me and to all of us when word of this got out.

"Well, young man?" she said in a peppery sort of way. "Aren't you going to help me up?"

"Ma'am?" I gaped for an instant before gathering myself together. "Oh! Yes, ma'am. Right away, ma'am." I offered her my hand and helped her sit up. The little shimmer of light followed her head up. Oh, sweet Heaven, I thought. She's one of the Saved.

I opened the door from the baggage compartment reluctantly, fearful of the hound that must surely wait just outside. Still, what other choice did I have?

There was Jackie, spattered from head to foot with shit and gore, and her clothes all in tatters. She stood with her legs braced, a cocky smile on her face, and the butt-end of her cigar still clenched in her teeth. LaBelle crouched by her feet—she shakily stood up when I emerged—staring at something in the distant marshes. Away off behind us, a howl of pain and rage like nothing I'd ever heard before dwindled to nothing.

The hound was nowhere to be seen.

First thing the old woman said then was, "Young lady. Do you think it seemly to be walking about dressed as a man?"

Jackie took the cigar butt out of her mouth.

"Get rid of that filthy thing too."

For an instant, I thought there was going to be trouble. But then Jackie laughed and flung the cigar out into the night. It was still lit and I could see by the way the old lady frowned that she'd noticed that too.

I offered her my arm again and we made our way slowly up the train.

She was Sugar's mother. I never had any doubt about that. As we walked up the train, she questioned LaBelle and me about her son, whether he was well, was he behaving himself, did he have a special lady-friend yet, and what exactly did he have in mind for her and him?

LaBelle was all in a lather to tell us how Sugar had arranged things. He'd kept in regular touch with the folks back home. So he'd been informed how his mother had spent her life just waiting and praying for the fullness of time so that she could die and get to see her baby boy again. Nobody'd had the heart to tell her about his new job. Sugar and his relations figured that since Divine Providence wasn't going to bring them together, it was up to him.

"He got it all worked out. He saved all his money," LaBelle said, "enough to set himself up in a little place on the outskirts of Ginny Gall. You'll like it there," she assured the old lady. "People say it's not half bad. It's where the folks in Hell go for a big Saturday night."

The old lady said nothing. Something about the way her jaw clenched, though, gave me an uneasy feeling.

The casino car fell silent when we entered.

"*Mama!*" Sugar cried. He ran to her side and hugged her. They were both crying, and so were the girls. Even Billy-B had a strange kind of twisted smile on his face.

Mrs. Selma Green took a long, slow look around the car and its inhabitants. She did not look content. "Sugar, what are you doing in such raffish company? What bad thing have you done to bring you to such a pass? I thought I'd watched over you better than that."

Sugar drew himself up proudly. "I never did a cruel or evil thing in all my life, Mama. You know that. I never did nothing you'd've disapproved of." His eyes swept the room disdainfully, and to the damned and the crew alike he said, "Not because I much cared, one way or the other. But because I knew what you expected of me. There was bad company, at times, tried to mislead me. Wicked women urged wicked things upon me. But never was a man big enough or a woman sweet enough to make me go against your teachings."

Personally, I believed it. A man like Sugar—what need had he of violence? People just naturally made room for him. And those who wouldn't, well, that was only self-defense, wasn't it?

But his mother did not look convinced. "What, then, are you doing *here?*" And there is absolutely no way I could do justice to the scorn with which she said that last word.

Sugar looked abashed. "I dunno," he mumbled. "They just didn't like my looks, I guess."

"The truth, boy!"

"I, uh, kind of mouthed off to the Recording Angel, Mama. That's how I wound up here." He grew angry at the memory; you could see it still rankled. "You oughta be grateful we're letting a roughneck like you squeak by, he said. Don't bend no rules for me, I told him. I'd expect a little more gratitude than you're showing, he says. Ain't grateful to man nor angel, says I, for something I earned on my own right. Oh, that angel was mad enough to spit nails! He wanted me to bow and truckle to him. But I got my pride. I told him I wouldn't play nigger for nobody. And I guess that's what brought me here."

"We don't use that word," Mrs. Green said smartly. Her son looked puzzled. "The N-word."

"No, Mama," he said, all contrite.

"That's better. You're a good boy, Sugar, only sometimes you forget yourself." She allowed herself a small, austere smile. "You've got yourself in another fix, and I guess it's up to me to see you right again."

She yanked the emergency brake cord.

With a scream of brakes that could be heard all the way to Diddy-Wah-Diddy, the train ground toward a halt. In the blackness of the night I heard monstrous things struggling toward us through the shit and filth of the marshes of Styx. I heard the sound of dangerous wings.

"Oh, Mama!" Sugar wailed. "What have you done?"

"Deceit don't cure nothing. We're going to have it all out, and bring everything into the open," she said. "Stand up straight."

So there it was.

The trial was held up front in the locomotive, with two Judges towering over the engine, and the damned crowded into the front cars, climbing up on each other's shoulders and passing every word back so those in the rear could follow. To one side of the engine crouched Bagamothezth, Lord of Maggots. Two long, sagging pink paps hung limply down over his hairy belly, and living filth dropped continually from his mouth. A rank wind blew off of his foul body. To look upon his squirmily tentacled eyelids and idiot gaze was to court despair.

The other judge was an Archangel. He shone whiter than house paint and brighter than an incandescent bulb, and to look upon him…Well. You know that awful feeling you get when you look through a telescope at some little fuzzy bit of light that's maybe not even visible to the naked eye? Only there it is, resolved into a million billion stars, cold and clear and distinct, and you and the Earth and everything you've ever known or thought about just dwindles down to insignificance? That's what the Archangel was like, only infinitely worse.

I found myself staring at first one Judge and then the other, back and forth, repulsed by the one, repelled by the majesty of the other, but unable to look away. They were neither of them something you could turn your back on.

Bagamothezth spoke in a voice shockingly sweet, even cloying. "We have no claim upon the sanctified Mrs. Selma Green. I presume you are declaring an immediate writ of sainthood upon her?"

The Archangel nodded. And with that the old lady was wrapped in blazing light and shot up into the night, dwindling like a falling star in reverse. For a second you could see her shouting and gesturing, and then she was gone.

"Sugar Green," Bagamothezth said. "How do you plead?"

Sugar stood up before the Judges, leaning forward a little as if into a great wind. His jaw was set and his eyes blazed. He wasn't about to give in an inch. "I just wanted to be with my—"

Bagamothezth clucked his tongue warningly.

"I just—"

"*Silence!*" the Archangel roared; his voice shook the train and rattled the tracks. My innards felt scrambled. Him and Sugar locked eyes. For a minute they stood thus, longer than I would've believed any individual could've stood up to such a being. At last Sugar slowly, angrily bowed his head and stared down at the ground. "How do you plead?"

"Guilty, I guess," he mumbled. "I only—"

"William Meredith Bones," the Archangel said. "How do you plead?"

Billy-B squared his shoulders and spoke up more briskly than I would've expected him to. "All my life," he said, "I have followed the dollar. It has been my North Star. It has proved comprehensible to me in ways that men and women were not. It has fetched me here where human company would have brought me to a worse place. To the best of my lights I have remained true to it." He spread his arms. "Sugar offered me money to smuggle his mother on board. What was I to do? I couldn't turn him down. Not and be true to my principles. I had no choice."

"How much," asked the Archangel in a dangerously quiet voice, "were you paid?"

Billy Bones lifted his jaw defiantly. "Forty-five dollars."

Those of us who knew Billy roared. We couldn't help it. We whooped and hollered with laughter until tears ran down our cheeks. The thought of Billy inconveniencing himself for so paltry a sum was flat-out ludicrous. He blushed angrily.

"So you did not do it for the money," said Bagamothezth.

"No," he muttered, "I guess not."

One by one, LaBelle, Afreya, and Sally were called upon to testify and acknowledge their guilt. Then I was called forward.

"Malcolm Reynolds," the Archangel said. "Your fellows have attested that, out of regard for your spiritual welfare, they did not involve you in this plot. Do you nevertheless wish to share their judgment?"

Something inside of me snapped. "No, no!" I cried. I couldn't help noticing the disgusted expression that twisted up Billy Bones' lips and the pitying looks that the girls threw my way, but I didn't care. I'd been through a lot and whatever strength I had in me was used up. Then too, I had seen what goes on in Diddy-Wah-Diddy and points south and I wanted no part of any of it. "It was all them—I had nothing to do with any of it! I swear if I'd known, I would've turned them all in before I would've let this happen!"

The Judges looked at one another. Then one of them, and for the life of me I can't remember which, cleared his throat and passed judgment.

We got a new crew now. Only me and Goatfoot are left over from the old outfit. The train goes on. The Judges ruled that Sugar's love for his mother, and the fact that he was willing to voluntarily undergo damnation in order to be with her, was enough to justify his transfer to a better place, where his mama could keep an eye on him. LaBelle and Afreya and Sally, and Billy Bones too, were deemed to have destroyed the perfect balance of their souls that kept them shackled to the railroad. They were promoted Upstairs as well.

Me, I'd cooked my own goose. They accepted my plea of noninvolvement, and here I remained. The girls were pretty broken up about it, and to tell the truth, so was I, for a time. But there it was. Once these things been decided, there ain't no court of appeal.

I could've done without Billy-B's smirk when they handed him his halo and wings, like he'd outsmarted all the world one more time. But it was a pure and simple treat to see LaBelle, Afreya, and Sally transformed. They were good girls. They deserved the best.

With all the fuss, we were all the way to the end of the line in Beluthahatchie before anybody noticed that Jackie had taken advantage of the train being stopped for the trial to slip over the side. She believed, apparently, that it would be possible to backtrack through three hundred eighty miles of black-water marshes, evade the myriad creatures that dwell therein, the least of which is enough to freeze the marrow in your bones, cross the Acheron trestle bridge, which is half a mile high and has no place to hide when the trains cross over, and so pass undetected back to New Jersey.

It made me sad to think on it.

And that's all there is to tell. Except for one last thing.

I got a postcard, just the other day, from Chicago. It was kind of battered and worn like it'd been kicking around in the mails a long time. No return address. Just a picture of a Bar-B-Q hut which, however, I don't expect would be any too difficult for a determined individual to locate. And the message:

> If one boundary is so ill-protected, then how
> difficult can the other be? I have a scheme
> going that should reap great profit with only
> moderate risk. Interested?
>
> J.
>
> P.S. Bring your uniform.

So it seems I'm going to Heaven. And why not?
I've surely seen my share of Hell.

RADIO WAVES

I was walking the telephone wires upside down, the sky underfoot cold
and flat with a few hard bright stars sparsely scattered about it, when
I thought how it would take only an instant's weakness to step off to the
side and fall up forever into the night. A kind of wildness entered me then
and I began to run.

I made the wires sing. They leapt and bulged above me as I raced past
Ricky's Luncheonette and up the hill. Past the old chocolate factory and
the IDI Advertising Display plant. Past the body shops, past A.J. LaCourse
Electric Motors-Controls-Parts. Then, where the slope steepened, along
the curving snake of rowhouses that went the full quarter-mile up to the
Ridge. Twice I overtook pedestrians, hunched and bundled, heads dog-
gedly down, out on incomprehensible errands. They didn't notice me, of
course. They never do.

The antenna farm was visible from here. I could see the Seven Sisters
spangled with red lights, dependent on the Earth like stalactites. "Where
are you running to, little one?" one tower whispered in a crackling, staticky voice. I think it was Hegemone.

"Fuck off," I said without slackening my pace, and they all chuckled.

Cars mumbled by. This was ravine country, however built-up, and the
far side of the road, too steep and rocky for development, was given over
to trees and garbage. Hamburger wrappings and white plastic trash bags
rustled in their wake. I was running full-out now.

About a block or so from the Ridge, I stumbled and almost fell. I
slapped an arm across a telephone pole and just managed to catch myself
in time. Aghast at my own carelessness, I hung there, dizzy and alarmed.

The ground overhead was black as black, an iron roof that somehow was yet as anxious as a hound to leap upon me, crush me flat, smear me to nothingness. I stared up at it, horrified.

Somebody screamed my name.

I turned. A faint blue figure clung to a television antenna atop a small, stuccoed brick duplex. Charlie's Widow. She pointed an arm that flickered with silver fire down Ripka Street. I slewed about to see what was coming after me.

It was the Corpsegrinder.

When it saw that I'd spotted it, it put out several more legs, extended a quilled head, and raised a howl that bounced off the Heaviside layer. My nonexistent blood chilled.

In a panic, I scrambled up and ran toward the Ridge and safety. I had a squat in the old Roxy, and once I was through the wall, the Corpsegrinder would not follow. Why this should be so, I did not know. But you learn the rules if you want to survive.

I ran. In the back of my head I could hear the Seven Sisters clucking and gossiping to each other, radiating television and radio over a few dozen frequencies. Indifferent to my plight.

The Corpsegrinder churned up the wires on a hundred needle-sharp legs. I could feel the ion surge it kicked up pushing against me as I reached the intersection of Ridge and Leverington. Cars were pulling up to the pumps at the Atlantic station. Teenagers stood in front of the A-Plus Mini Market, flicking half-smoked cigarettes into the street, stamping their feet like colts, and waiting for something to happen. I couldn't help feeling a great longing disdain for them. Every last one worried about grades and drugs and zits, and all the while snugly barricaded within hulking fortresses of flesh.

I was scant yards from home. The Roxy was a big old movie palace, fallen into disrepair and semiconverted to a skateboarding rink which had gone out of business almost immediately. But it had been a wonderful place once, and the terra cotta trim was still there: ribbons and river gods, great puffing faces with panpipes, guitars, flowers, wyverns. I crossed the Ridge on a dead telephone wire, spider-web delicate but still usable.

Almost there.

Then the creature was upon me, with a howl of electromagnetic rage that silenced even the Sisters for an instant. It slammed into my side, a storm of razors and diamond-edged fury, hooks and claws extended.

I grabbed at a rusty flange on the side of the Roxy.

Too late! Pain exploded within me, a sheet of white nausea. All in an instant I lost the name of my second daughter, an April morning when the world was new and I was five, a smoky string of all-nighters in Rensselaer Polytech, the jowly grin of Old Whatsisface the German who lived on LaFountain Street, the fresh pain of a sprained ankle out back of a Banana Republic warehouse, fishing off a yellow rubber raft with my old man on Lake Champlain. All gone, these and a thousand things more, sucked away, crushed to nothing, beyond retrieval.

Furious as any wounded animal, I fought back. Foul bits of substance splattered under my fist. The Corpsegrinder reared up to smash me down, and I scrabbled desperately away. Something tore and gave.

Then I was through the wall and safe among the bats and the gloom.

"*Cobb!*" the Corpsegrinder shouted. It lashed wildly back and forth, scouring the brick walls with limbs and teeth, as restless as a March wind, as unpredictable as ball lightning.

For the moment I was safe. But it had seized a part of me, tortured it, and made it a part of itself. I could no longer delude myself into thinking it was simply going to go away. "Cahawahawbb!" It broke my name down to a chord of overlapping tones. It had an ugly, muddy voice. I felt dirtied just listening to it. "Caw—" A pause. "—awbb!"

In a horrified daze I stumbled up the Roxy's curving patterned-tin roof until I found a section free of bats. Exhausted and dispirited, I slumped down.

"Caw aw aw awb buh buh!"

How had the thing found me? I'd thought I'd left it behind in Manhattan. Had my flight across the high-tension lines left a trail of some kind? Maybe. Then again, it might have some special connection with me. To follow me here it must have passed by easier prey. Which implied it had a grudge against me. Maybe I'd known the Corpsegrinder back when it was human. We could once have been important to each other. We might have been lovers. It was possible. The world is a stranger place than I used to believe.

The horror of my existence overtook me then, an acute awareness of the squalor in which I dwelt, the danger which surrounded me, and the dark mystery informing my universe.

I wept for all that I had lost.

Eventually, the sun rose up like God's own Peterbilt and with a triumphant blare of chromed trumpets, gently sent all of us creatures of the night to sleep.

❋

When you die, the first thing that happens is that the world turns upside down. You feel an overwhelming disorientation and a strange sensation that's not quite pain as the last strands connecting you to your body part, and then you slip out of physical being and fall from the planet.

As you fall, you attenuate. Your substance expands and thins, glowing more and more faintly as you pick up speed. So far as can be told, it's a process that doesn't ever stop. Fainter, thinner, colder...until you've merged into the substance of everyone else who's ever died, spread perfectly uniformly through the universal vacuum, forever moving toward but never arriving at absolute zero.

Look hard, and the sky is full of the Dead.

Not everyone falls away. Some few are fast-thinking or lucky enough to maintain a tenuous hold on earthly existence. I was one of the lucky ones. I was working late one night on a proposal when I had my heart attack. The office was empty. The ceiling had a wire mesh within the plaster, and that's what saved me.

The first response to death is denial. *This can't be happening*, I thought. I gaped up at the floor where my body had fallen, and would lie undiscovered until morning. My own corpse, pale and bloodless, wearing a corporate tie and sleeveless grey Angora sweater. Gold Rolex, Sharper Image desk accessories, and of course I also thought: *I died for THIS?*

By which of course I meant my entire life.

So it was in a state of both personal and ontological crisis that I wandered across the ceiling to the location of an old pneumatic message tube, removed and casually plastered over some fifty years before. I fell from the seventeenth to the twenty-fifth floor, and I learned a lot in the process.

Shaken, startled, and already beginning to assume the wariness that the afterlife requires, I went to a window to get a glimpse of the outer world. When I tried to touch the glass, my hand went right through. I jerked back. Cautiously, I leaned forward, so that my head stuck out into the night.

What a wonderful experience Times Square is when you're dead! There is ten times the light a living being sees. All metal things vibrate with inner life. Electric wires are thin blue scratches in the air. Neon *sings*. The world is filled with strange sights and cries. Everything shifts from beauty to beauty.

Something that looked like a cross between a dragon and a wisp of smoke was feeding in the Square. But it was lost among so many wonders that I gave it no particular thought.

Night again. I awoke with Led Zeppelin playing in the back of my head. "Stairway to Heaven." Again. It can be a long wait between Dead Milkmen cuts.

"Wakey-risey, little man," crooned one of the Sisters. It was funny how sometimes they took a close personal interest in our doings, and other times ignored us completely. "This is Euphrosyne with the red-eye weather report. The outlook is moody with a chance of existential despair. You won't be going outside tonight if you know what's good for you. There'll be lightning within the hour."

"It's too late in the year for lightning," I said.

"Oh dear. Should I inform the weather?"

By now I was beginning to realize that what I had taken on awakening to be the pressure of the Corpsegrinder's dark aura was actually the high-pressure front of an advancing storm. The first drops of rain pattered on the roof. Wind skirled and the rain grew stronger. Thunder growled in the distance. "Why don't you just go fuck your—"

A light laugh that trilled up into the supersonic, and she was gone.

I was listening to the rain underfoot when a lightning bolt screamed into existence, turning me inside out for the briefest instant then cart-wheeling gleefully into oblivion. In the femtosecond of restoration following the bolt, the walls were transparent and all the world made of glass, its secrets available to be snooped out. But before comprehension was possible, the walls opaqued again and the lightning's malevolent aftermath faded like a madman's smile in the night.

Through it all the Seven Sisters were laughing and singing, scream-ing with joy whenever a lightning bolt flashed, and making up nonsense poems from howls, whistles, and static. During a momentary lull, the flat hum of a carrier wave filled my head. Phaenna, by the feel of her. But instead of her voice, I heard only the sound of fearful sobs.

"Widow?" I said. "Is that you?"

"She can't hear you," Phaenna purred. "You're lucky I'm here to bring you up to speed. A lightning bolt hit the transformer outside her house. It was bound to happen sooner or later. Your Nemesis—the one you call the Corpsegrinder, such a cute nickname, by the way—has her trapped."

This was making no sense at all. "Why would the Corpsegrinder be after her?"

"Why why why why?" Phaenna sang, a snatch of some pop ballad or other. "You didn't get answers when you were alive, what made you think you'd get any *now?*"

The sobbing went on and on. "She can sit it out," I said. "The Corpsegrinder can't—hey, wait. Didn't they just wire her house for cable? I'm trying to picture it. Phone lines on one side, electricity on the other, cable. She can slip out on his blind side."

The sobs lessened and then rose in a most unWidowlike wail of despair.

"Typical," Phaenna said. "You haven't the slightest notion of what you're talking about. The lightning stroke has altered your little pet. Go out and see for yourself."

My hackles rose. "You know damned good and well that I can't—"

Phaenna's attention shifted and the carrier beam died. The Seven Sisters are fickle that way. This time, though, it was just as well. No way was I going out there to face that monstrosity. I couldn't. And I was grateful not to have to admit it.

For a long while I sat thinking about the Corpsegrinder. Even here, protected by the strong walls of the Roxy, the mere thought of it was paralyzing. I tried to imagine what Charlie's Widow was going through, separated from this monster by only a thin curtain of brick and stucco. Feeling the hard radiation of its malice and need…It was beyond my powers of visualization. Eventually I gave up and thought instead about my first meeting with the Widow.

She was coming down the hill from Roxborough with her arms out, the inverted image of a child playing at tightrope walker. Placing one foot ahead of the other with deliberate concentration, scanning the wire before her so cautiously that she was less than a block away when she saw me.

She screamed.

Then she was running straight at me. My back was to the transformer station—there was no place to flee. I shrank away as she stumbled to a halt.

"It's you!" she cried. "Oh God, Charlie, I knew you'd come back for me, I waited so long, but I never doubted you, never, we can—" She lunged forward as if to hug me. Our eyes met.

All the joy in her died.

"Oh," she said. "It's not you."

I was fresh off the high-tension lines, still vibrating with energy and fear. My mind was a blaze of contradictions. I could remember almost nothing of my post-death existence. Fragments, bits of advice from the old dead, a horrifying confrontation with…something, some creature or phenomenon that had driven me to flee Manhattan. Whether it was this event or the fearsome voltage of that radiant highway that had scoured me of experience, I did not know. "It's me," I protested.

"No, it's not." Her gaze was unflatteringly frank. "You're not Charlie and you never were. You're—just the sad remnant of what once was a man, and not a very good one at that." She turned away. She was leaving me! In my confusion, I felt such a despair as I had never known before.

"Please…" I said.

She stopped.

A long silence. Then what in a living woman would have been a sigh. "You'd think that I—well, never mind." She offered her hand, and when I would not take it, simply said, "This way."

I followed her down Main Street, through the shallow canyon of the business district to a diner at the edge of town. It was across from Hubcap Heaven and an automotive junkyard bordered it on two sides. The diner was closed. We settled down on the ceiling.

"That's where the car ended up after I died," she said, gesturing toward the junkyard. "It was right after I got the call about Charlie. I stayed up drinking and after a while it occurred to me that maybe they were wrong, they'd made some sort of horrible mistake and he wasn't really dead, you know? Like maybe he was in a coma or something, some horrible kind of misdiagnosis, they'd gotten him confused with somebody else, who knows? Terrible things happen in hospitals. They make mistakes.

"I decided I had to go and straighten things out. There wasn't time to make coffee so I went to the medicine cabinet and gulped down a bunch of pills at random, figuring *some*thing among them would keep me awake. Then I jumped into the car and started off for Colorado."

"My God."

"I have no idea how fast I was going—everything was a blur when I crashed. At least I didn't take anybody with me, thank the Lord. There was this one horrible moment of confusion and pain and rage and then I found myself lying on the floor of the car with my corpse just inches beneath me on the underside of the roof." She was silent for a moment. "My first impulse was to crawl out the window. Lucky for me I didn't." Another pause. "It took me most of a night to work my way out of the yard. I had to go from wreck to wreck. There were these gaps to jump. It was a nightmare."

"I'm amazed you had the presence of mind to stay in the car."

"Dying sobers you up fast."

I laughed. I couldn't help it. And without the slightest hesitation, she joined right in with me. It was a fine warm moment, the first I'd had since I didn't know when. The two of us set each other off, laughing louder and louder, our merriment heterodyning until it filled every television screen for a mile around with snow.

My defenses were down. She reached out and took my hand.

Memory flooded me. It was her first date with Charlie. He was an electrician. The people next door were having the place rehabbed. She'd been working in the back yard and he struck up a conversation. Then he asked her out. They went to a disco in the Adam's Mark over on City Line Avenue.

She wasn't eager to get involved with somebody just then. She was still recovering from a hellish affair with a married man who'd thought that since he wasn't available for anything permanent, that made her his property. But when Charlie suggested they go out to the car for some coke—it was the Seventies—she'd said sure. He was going to put the moves on her sooner or later. Might as well get this settled early so they'd have more time for dancing.

But after they'd done up the lines, Charlie had shocked her by taking her hands in his and kissing them. She worked for a Bucks County pottery in those days and her hands were rough and red. She was very sensitive about them.

"Beautiful hands," he murmured. "Such beautiful, beautiful hands."

"You're making fun of me," she protested, hurt.

"No! These are hands that *do* things, and they've been shaped by the things they've done. The way stones in a stream are shaped by the water that passes over them. The way tools are shaped by their work. A hammer is beautiful, if it's a good hammer, and your hands are too."

He could have been scamming her. But something in his voice, his manner, said no, he really meant it. She squeezed his hands and saw that they were beautiful too. Suddenly she was glad she hadn't gone off the pill when she broke up with Daniel. She started to cry. Her date looked alarmed and baffled. But she couldn't stop. All the tears she hadn't cried in the past two years came pouring out of her, unstoppable.

Charlie-boy, she thought, you just got lucky.

All this in an instant. I snatched my hands away, breaking contact. "*Don't do that!*" I cried. "Don't you *ever* touch me again!"

With flat disdain, the Widow said, "It wasn't pleasant for me either. But I had to see how much of your life you remember."

It was naive of me, but I was shocked to realize that the passage of memories had gone both ways. But before I could voice my outrage, she said, "There's not much left of you. You're only a fragment of a man, shreds and tatters, hardly anything. No wonder you're so frightened. You've got what Charlie calls a low signal-to-noise ratio. What happened in New York City almost destroyed you."

"That doesn't give you the right to—"

"Oh be still. You need to know this. Living is simple, you just keep going. But death is complex. It's so hard to hang on and so easy to let go. The temptation is always there. Believe me, I know. There used to be five of us in Roxborough, and where are the others now? Two came through Manayunk last spring and camped out under the El for a season and they're gone too. Holding it together is hard work. One day the stars start singing to you, and the next you begin to listen to them. A week later they start to make sense. You're just reacting to events—that's not good enough. If you mean to hold on, you've got to know why you're doing it."

"So why are *you?*"

"I'm waiting for Charlie," she said simply.

It occurred to me to wonder exactly how many years she had been waiting. Three? Fifteen? Just how long was it possible to hold on? Even in my confused and emotional state, though, I knew better than to ask. Deep inside she must've known as well as I did that Charlie wasn't coming. "My name's Cobb," I said. "What's yours?"

She hesitated and then, with an odd sidelong look, said, "I'm Charlie's widow. That's all that matters." It was all the name she ever gave, and Charlie's Widow she was to me from then onward.

I rolled onto my back on the tin ceiling and spread out my arms and legs, a phantom starfish among the bats. A fragment, she had called me, shreds and tatters. No wonder you're so frightened! In all the months since I'd been washed into this backwater of the power grid, she'd never treated me with anything but a condescension bordering on contempt.

So I went out into the storm after all.

The rain was nothing. It passed right through me. But there were ion-heavy gusts of wind that threatened to knock me right off the lines, and the transformer outside the Widow's house was burning a fierce actinic blue. It was a gusher of energy, a flare star brought to earth, dazzling. A bolt of lightning unzipped me, turned me inside out, and restored me before I had a chance to react.

The Corpsegrinder was visible from the Roxy, but between the burning transformer and the creature's metamorphosis, I was within a block of the monster before I understood exactly what it was I was seeing.

It was feeding off the dying transformer, sucking in energy so greedily that it pulsed like a mosquito engorged with blood. Enormous plasma wings warped to either side, hot blue and transparent. They curved entirely around the Widow's house in an unbroken and circular wall. At the resonance points they extruded less detailed versions of the Corpsegrinder itself, like sentinels, all facing the Widow.

Surrounding her with a prickly ring of electricity and malice.

I retreated a block, though the transformer fire apparently hid me from the Corpsegrinder, for it stayed where it was, eyelessly staring inward. Three times I circled the house from a distance, looking for a way in. An unguarded cable, a wrought-iron fence, any unbroken stretch of metal too high or too low for the Corpsegrinder to reach.

Nothing.

Finally, because there was no alternative, I entered the house across the street from the Widow's, the one that was best shielded by the spouting and stuttering transformer. A power line took me into the attic crawl space. From there I scaled the electrical system down through the second and first floors and so to the basement. I had a brief glimpse of a man asleep on a couch before the television. The set was off but it still held a residual charge. It sat quiescent, smug, bloated with stolen energies. If the poor bastard on the couch could have seen what I saw, he'd've never turned on the TV again.

In the basement I hand-over-handed myself from the washing machine to the main water inlet. Straddling the pipe, I summoned all my courage and plunged my head underground.

It was black as pitch. I inched forward on the pipe in a kind of panic. I could see nothing, hear nothing, smell nothing, taste nothing. All I could feel was the iron pipe beneath my hands. Just beyond the wall the pipe ended in a T-joint where it hooked into a branch line under the drive. I followed it to the street.

It was awful: Like suffocation infinitely prolonged. Like being wrapped in black cloth. Like being drowned in ink. Like strangling noiselessly in the void between the stars.

To distract myself, I thought about my old man.

When my father was young, he navigated between cities by radio. Driving dark and usually empty highways, he'd twist the dial back and forth, back and forth, until he hit a station. Then he'd withdraw his hand and wait for the station ID. That would give him his rough location— that he was somewhere outside of Albany, say. A sudden signal coming in strong and then abruptly dissolving in groans and eerie whistles was a fluke of the ionosphere, impossibly distant and easily disregarded. One that faded in and immediately out meant he had grazed the edge of a station's range. But then a signal would grow and strengthen as he penetrated its field, crescendo, fade, and collapse into static and silence. That left him north of Troy, let's say, and making good time. He would begin the search for the next station.

You could drive across the continent in this way, passed from hand to hand by local radio, and tuned in to the geography of the night.

I went over that memory three times, polishing and refining it, before the branch line abruptly ended. One hand groped forward and closed upon nothing.

I had reached the main conduit. For a panicked moment I had feared that it would be concrete or brick or even one of the cedar pipes the city laid down in the 19th century, remnants of which still linger here and there beneath the pavement. But by sheer blind luck, the system had been installed during that narrow window of time when the pipes were cast iron. I crawled along its underside first one way and then the other, searching for the branch line to the Widow's. There was a lot of crap under the street. Several times I was blocked by gas lines or by the high-pressure pipes for the fire hydrants and had to awkwardly clamber around them.

At last I found the line and began the painful journey out from the street again.

When I emerged in the Widow's basement, I was a nervous wreck. It came to me then that I could no longer remember my father's name. A thing of rags and shreds indeed!

I worked my way up the electrical system, searching every room and unintentionally spying on the family who had bought the house after the Widow's death. In the kitchen a puffy man stood with his sleeves rolled up, elbow-deep in the sink, angrily washing dishes by candlelight. A woman who was surely his wife expressively smoked a cigarette at his stiff back, drawing in the smoke with bitter intensity and exhaling it in puffs of hatred. On the second floor a preadolescent girl clutched a tortoise-shell cat so tightly it struggled to escape, and cried into its fur. In the next room a younger boy sat on his bed in earphones, Walkman on his lap, staring sightlessly out the window at the burning transformer. No Widow on either floor.

How, I wondered, could she have endured staying in this entropic oven of a blue-collar rowhouse, forever the voyeur at the banquet, watching the living squander what she had already spent? Her trace was everywhere, her presence elusive. I was beginning to think she'd despaired and given herself up to the sky when I found her in the attic, clutching the wire that led to the antenna. She looked up, silenced and amazed by my unexpected appearance.

"Come on," I said. "I know a way out."

Returning, however, I couldn't retrace the route I'd taken in. It wasn't so much the difficulty of navigating the twisting maze of pipes under the street, though that was bad enough, as the fact that the Widow wouldn't hazard the passage unless I led her by the hand.

"You don't know how difficult this is for me," I said.

"It's the only way I'd dare." A nervous, humorless laugh. "I have such a lousy sense of direction."

So, steeling myself, I seized her hand and plunged through the wall.

It took all my concentration to keep from sliding off the water pipes, I was so distracted by the violence of her thoughts. We crawled through a hundred memories, all of her married lover, all alike.

Here's one:

Daniel snapped on the car radio. Sad music—something classical—flooded the car. "That's bullshit, babe. You know how much I have invested in you?" He jabbed a blunt finger at her dress. "I could buy two good whores for what that thing cost."

Then why don't you, she thought. Get back on your Metroliner and go home to New York City and your wife and your money and your two good whores. Aloud, reasonably, she said, "It's over, Danny, can't you see that?"

"Look, babe. Let's not argue here, okay? Not in the parking lot, with people walking by and everybody listening. Drive us to your place, we can sit down and talk it over like civilized human beings."

She clutched the wheel, staring straight ahead. "No. We're going to settle this here and now."

"Christ." One-handed he wrangled a pack of Kents from a jacket pocket and knocked out a cigarette. Put the end in his lips and drew it out. Punched the lighter. "So talk."

A wash of hopelessness swept over her. Married men were supposed to be easy to get rid of. That was the whole point. "Let me go, Danny," she pleaded. Then, lying, "We can still be friends."

He made a disgusted noise.

"I've tried, Danny, I really have. You don't know how hard I've tried. But it's just not working."

"All right, I've listened. Now let's go." Reaching over her, Daniel threw the gearshift into reverse. He stepped on her foot, mashing it down on the accelerator.

The car leapt backwards. She shrieked and in a flurry of panic swung the wheel about and slammed on the brake with her free foot.

With a jolt and a crunch, the car stopped. There was the tinkle of broken plastic. They'd hit a lime-green Hyundai.

"Oh, that's just perfect!" Daniel said. The lighter popped out. He lit his cigarette and then swung open the door. "I'll check the damage."

Over her shoulder, she saw Daniel tug at his trousers' knees as he crouched to examine the Hyundai. She had a sudden impulse to slew the car around and escape. Step on the gas and never look back. Watch his face, dismayed and dwindling, in the rear-view mirror. Eyes flooded with tears, she began quietly to laugh.

Then Daniel was back. "It's all right, let's go."

"I heard something break."

"It was just a taillight, okay?" He gave her a funny look. "What the hell are you laughing about?"

She shook her head hopelessly, unable to sort out the tears from the laughter. Then somehow they were on the Expressway, the car humming down the indistinct and warping road. She was driving but Daniel was still in control.

We were completely lost now and had been for some time. I had taken what I was certain had to be a branch line and it had led nowhere. We'd been tracing its twisty passage for blocks. I stopped and pulled my hand away. I couldn't concentrate. Not with the caustics and poisons of the Widow's past churning through me. "Listen," I said. "We've got to get something straight between us."

Her voice came out of nowhere, small and wary. "What?"

How to say it? The horror of those memories lay not in their brutality but in their particularity. They nestled into empty spaces where memories of my own should have been. They were as familiar as old shoes. They *fit*.

"If I could remember any of this crap," I said, "I'd apologize. Hell, I can't blame you for how you feel. Of course you're angry. But it's gone, can't you see that, it's over. You've got to let go. You can't hold me accountable for things I can't even remember, okay? All that shit happened decades ago. I was young. I've changed." The absurdity of the thing swept over me. I'd have laughed if I'd been able. "I'm dead, for pity's sake!"

A long silence. Then, "So you've figured it out."

"You've known all along," I said bitterly. "Ever since I came off of the high-tension lines in Manayunk."

She didn't deny it. "I suppose I should be flattered that when you were in trouble you came to me," she said in a way that indicated she was not.

"Why didn't you tell me then? Why drag it out?"

"Danny—"

"Don't call me that!"

"It's your name. Daniel. Daniel Cobb."

All the emotions I'd been holding back by sheer force of denial closed about me. I flung myself down and clutched the pipe tight, crushing myself against its unforgiving surface. Trapped in the friendless wastes of night, I weighed my fear of letting go against my fear of holding on.

"Cobb?"

I said nothing.

The Widow's voice took on an edgy quality. "Cobb, we can't stay here. You've got to lead me out. I don't have the slightest idea which way to go. I'm lost without your help."

I still could not speak.

"*Cobb!*" She was close to panic. "I put my own feelings aside. Back in Manayunk. You needed help and I did what I could. Now it's your turn."

Silently, invisibly, I shook my head.

"God damn you, Danny," she said furiously. "I won't let you do this to me again! So you're unhappy with what a jerk you were—that's not my problem. You can't redeem your manliness on me any more. I am not your fucking salvation. I am not some kind of cosmic last chance and it's not my job to talk you down from the ledge."

That stung. "I wasn't asking you to," I mumbled.

"So you're still there! Take my hand and lead us out."

I pulled myself together. "You'll have to follow my voice, babe. Your memories are too intense for me."

We resumed our slow progress. I was sick of crawling, sick of the dark, sick of this lightless horrid existence, disgusted to the pit of my soul with who and what I was. Was there no end to this labyrinth of pipes?

"Wait." I'd brushed by something. Something metal buried in the earth.

"What is it?"

"I think it's—" I groped about, trying to get a sense of the thing's shape. "I think it's a cast-iron gatepost. Here. Wait. Let me climb up and take a look."

Relinquishing my grip on the pipe, I seized hold of the object and stuck my head out of the ground. I emerged at the gate of an iron fence framing the minuscule front yard of a house on Ripka Street. I could see again! It was so good to feel the clear breath of the world once more that I closed my eyes briefly to savor the sensation.

"How ironic," Euphrosyne said.

"After being so heroic," Thalia said.

"Overcoming his fears," Aglaia said.

"Rescuing the fair maid from terror and durance vile," Cleta said.

"Realizing at last who he is," Phaenna said.

"Beginning that long and difficult road to recovery by finally getting in touch with his innermost feelings," Auxo said.

Hegemone giggled.

"What?" I opened my eyes.

That was when the Corpsegrinder struck. It leapt upon me with stunning force, driving spear-long talons through my head and body. The talons were barbed so that they couldn't be pulled free and they burned like molten metal. "Ahhhh, Cobb," the Corpsegrinder crooned. "Now this is *sweet*."

I screamed and it drank in those screams, so that only silence escaped into the outside world. I struggled and it made those struggles its own, leaving me to kick myself deeper and deeper into the drowning pools of its identity. With all my will I resisted. It was not enough. I experienced the languorous pleasure of surrender as that very will and resistance were sucked down into my attacker's substance. The distinction between *me* and *it* weakened, strained, dissolved. I was transformed.

I was the Corpsegrinder now.

Manhattan is a virtual school for the dead. Enough people die there every day to keep any number of monsters fed. From the store of memories the Corpsegrinder had stolen from me, I recalled a quiet moment sitting cross-legged on the tin ceiling of a sleaze joint while table dancers entertained Japanese tourists on the floor above and a kobold instructed me on some of the finer points of survival. "The worst thing you can be hunted by," he said, "is yourself."

"Very aphoristic."

"Fuck you. I used to be human too."

"Sorry."

"Apology accepted. Look, I told you about Salamanders. That's a shitty way to go, but at least it's final. When they're done with you, nothing remains. But a Corpsegrinder is a parasite. It has no true identity of its own, so it constructs one from bits and pieces of everything that's unpleasant within you. Your basic greeds and lusts. It gives you a particularly nasty sort of immortality. Remember that old cartoon? This hideous toad saying 'Kiss me and live forever—you'll be a toad, but you'll live forever.'" He grimaced. "If you get the choice, go with the Salamander."

"So what's this business about hunting myself?"

"Sometimes a Corpsegrinder will rip you in two and let half escape. For a while."

"Why?"

"I dunno. Maybe it likes to play with its food. Ever watch a cat torture a mouse? Maybe it thinks it's fun."

From a million miles away, I thought: So now I know what's happened to me. I'd made quite a run of it, but now it was over. It didn't matter. All that mattered was the hoard of memories, glorious memories, into which I'd been dumped. I wallowed in them, picking out here a winter sunset and there the pain of a jellyfish sting when I was nine. So what if I was already beginning to dissolve? I was intoxicated, drunk, stoned with the raw stuff of experience. I was high on life.

Then the Widow climbed up the gatepost looking for me.

"Cobb?"

The Corpsegrinder had moved up the fence to a more comfortable spot in which to digest me. When it saw the Widow, it reflexively parked me in a memory of a grey drizzly day in a Ford Fiesta outside of 30th Street Station. The engine was going and the heater and the windshield wiper too, so I snapped on the radio to mask their noise. Beethoven filled the car, the Moonlight Sonata.

"That's bullshit, babe," I said. "You know how much I have invested in you? I could buy two good whores for what that dress cost."

She refused to meet my eyes. In a whine that set my teeth on edge, she said, "Danny, can't you see that it's over between us?"

"Look, babe, let's not argue in the parking lot, okay?" I was trying hard to be reasonable. "Not with people walking by and listening. We'll go someplace private where we can talk this over calmly, like two civilized human beings."

She shifted slightly in the seat and adjusted her skirt with a little tug. Drawing attention to her long legs and fine ass. Making it hard for me to think straight. The bitch really knew how to twist the knife. Even now, crying and begging, she was aware of how it turned me on. And even though I hated being aroused by her little act, I was. The sex was always best after an argument; it made her sluttish.

I clenched my anger in one hand and fisted my pocket with it. Thinking how much I'd like to up and give her a shot. She was begging for it. Secretly, maybe, it was what she wanted; I'd often suspected she'd enjoy being hit. It was too late to act on the impulse, though. The memory was playing out like a tape, immutable, unstoppable.

All the while, like a hallucination or the screen of a television set receiving conflicting signals, I could see the Widow, frozen with fear half in and half out of the ground. She quivered like an acetylene flame. In the memory she was saying something, but with the shift in my emotions came a corresponding warping-away of perception. The train station, car, the windshield wipers and music, all faded to a murmur in my consciousness.

Tentacles whipped around the Widow. She was caught. She struggled helplessly, deliciously. The Corpsegrinder's emotions pulsed through me and to my remote horror I found that they were identical to my own. I *wanted* the Widow, wanted her so bad there were no words for it. I wanted to clutch her to me so tightly her ribs would splinter and for just this once she'd know it was real. I wanted to own her. To possess her. To put an end to all her little games. To know her every thought and secret, down to the very bottom of her being.

No more lies, babe, I thought, no more evasions. You're mine now.

So perfectly in synch was I with the Corpsegrinder's desires that it shifted its primary consciousness back into the liquid sphere of memory, where it hung smug and lazy, watching, a voyeur with a willing agent. I was in control of the autonomous functions now. I reshaped the tentacles, merging and recombining them into two strong arms. The claws and talons that clutched the fence I made legs again. The exterior of the Corpsegrinder I morphed into human semblance, save for that great mass of memories sprouting from our back like a bloated spider-sack. Last of all I made the head.

I gave it my own face.

"Surprised to see me again, babe?" I leered.

Her expression was not so much fearful as disappointed. "No," she said wearily. "Deep down, I guess I always knew you'd be back."

As I drew the Widow closer, I distantly knew that all that held me to the Corpsegrinder in that instant was our common store of memories and my determination not to lose them again. That was enough, though. I pushed my face into hers, forcing open her mouth. Energies flowed between us like a feast of tongues.

I prepared to drink her in.

There were no barriers between us. This was an experience as intense as when, making love, you lose all track of which body is your own and thought dissolves into the animal moment. For a giddy instant I was no less her than I was myself. I was the Widow staring fascinated into the filthy depths of my psyche. She was myself witnessing her astonishment as she realized exactly how little I had ever known her. We both saw her freeze still to the core with horror. Horror not of what I was doing.

But of what I was.

I can't take any credit for what happened then. It was only an impulse, a spasm of the emotions, a sudden and unexpected clarity of vision. Can a single flash of decency redeem a life like mine? I don't believe it. I refuse to believe it.

Had there been time for second thoughts, things might well have gone differently. But there was no time to think. There was only time enough to feel an upwelling of revulsion, a visceral desire to be anybody or anything but my own loathsome self, a profound and total yearning to be quit of the burden of such memories as were mine. An aching need to *just once* do the moral thing.

I let go.

Bobbing gently, the swollen corpus of my past floated up and away, carrying with it the parasitic Corpsegrinder. Everything I had spent all my life accumulating fled from me. It went up like a balloon, spinning, dwindling... gone. Leaving me only what few flat memories I have narrated here.

I screamed.

And then I cried.

I don't know how long I clung to the fence, mourning my loss. But when I gathered myself together, the Widow was still there.

"Danny," the Widow said. She didn't touch me. "Danny, I'm sorry."

I'd almost rather that she had abandoned me. How do you apologize for sins you can no longer remember? For having been someone who, however reprehensible, is gone forever? How can you expect forgiveness from somebody you have forgotten so completely you don't even know her name? I felt twisted with shame and misery. "Look," I said. "I know I've behaved badly. More than badly. But there ought to be some way to make it up to you. For, you know, everything. Somehow. I mean—"

What do you say to somebody who's seen to the bottom of your wretched and inadequate soul?

"I want to apologize," I said.

With something very close to compassion, the Widow said, "It's too late for that, Danny. It's over. Everything's over. You and I only ever had the one trait in common. We neither of us could ever let go of anything. Small wonder we're back together again. But don't you see, it doesn't matter what you want or don't want—you're not going to get it. Not now. You had your chance. It's too late to make things right." Then she stopped, aghast at what she had just said.

But we both knew she had spoken the truth.

"Widow," I said as gently as I could, "I'm sure Charlie—"

"Shut up."

I shut up.

The Widow closed her eyes and swayed, as if in a wind. A ripple ran through her and when it was gone her features were simpler, more schematic, less recognizably human. She was already beginning to surrender the anthropomorphic.

I tried again. "Widow..." Reaching out my guilty hand to her.

She stiffened but did not draw away. Our fingers touched, twined, mated. "Elizabeth," she said at last. "My name is Elizabeth Connelly."

We huddled together on the ceiling of the Roxy through the dawn and the blank horror that is day. When sunset brought us conscious again, we talked through half the night before making the one decision we knew all along that we'd have to make.

It took us almost an hour to reach the Seven Sisters and climb down to the highest point of Thalia.

We stood holding hands at the top of the mast. Radio waves were gushing out from under us like a great wind. It was all we could do to keep from being blown away.

Underfoot, Thalia was happily chatting with her sisters. Typically, at our moment of greatest resolve, they gave us not the slightest indication of interest. But they were all listening to us. Don't ask me how I knew.

"Cobb?" Elizabeth said. "I'm afraid."

"Yeah, me too."

A long silence, and then she said, "Let me go first. If you go first, I won't have the nerve."

"Okay."

She took a deep breath—funny, if you think about it—and then she let go, and fell into the sky.

First she was like a kite, and then a scrap of paper, and finally she was a rapidly tumbling speck. I stood for a long time watching her falling, dwindling, until she was lost in the background flicker of the universe, just one more spark in infinity.

She was gone and I couldn't help wondering if she had ever really been there at all. Had the Widow truly been Elizabeth Connelly? Or was she just another fragment of my shattered self, a bundle of related memories that I had to come to terms with before I could bring myself to finally let go?

A vast emptiness seemed to spread itself through all of existence. I clutched the mast spasmodically then, and thought: *I can't!*

But the moment passed. I've got a lot of questions, and there aren't any answers here. In just another instant, I'll let go and follow Elizabeth (if Elizabeth she was) into the night. I will fall forever and I will be converted to background radiation, smeared ever thinner and cooler across the universe, a smooth, uniform, and universal message that has only one decode. Let Thalia carry my story to whoever cares to listen. I won't be here for it.

It's time to go now. Time and then some to leave. I'm frightened, and I'm going.

Now.

THE DEAD

Three boy zombies in matching red jackets bussed our table, bringing water, lighting candles, brushing away the crumbs between courses. Their eyes were dark, attentive, lifeless; their hands and faces so white as to be faintly luminous in the hushed light. I thought it in bad taste, but "This is Manhattan," Courtney said. "A certain studied offensiveness is fashionable here."

The blond brought menus and waited for our order.

We both ordered pheasant. "An excellent choice," the boy said in a clear, emotionless voice. He went away and came back a minute later with the freshly strangled birds, holding them up for our approval. He couldn't have been more than eleven when he died and his skin was of that sort connoisseurs call "milk glass," smooth, without blemish, and all but translucent. He must have cost a fortune.

As the boy was turning away, I impulsively touched his shoulder. He turned back. "What's your name, son?" I asked.

"Timothy." He might have been telling me the *specialite de maison*. The boy waited a breath to see if more was expected of him, then left.

Courtney gazed after him. "How lovely he would look," she murmured, "nude. Standing in the moonlight by a cliff. Definitely a cliff. Perhaps the very one where he met his death."

"He wouldn't look very lovely if he'd fallen off a cliff."

"Oh, don't be unpleasant."

The wine steward brought our bottle. "Chateau La Tour '17." I raised an eyebrow. The steward had the sort of old and complex face that Rembrandt would have enjoyed painting. He poured with pulseless ease and then dissolved into the gloom. "Good lord, Courtney, you *seduced* me on cheaper."

She flushed, not happily. Courtney had a better career going than I. She outpowered me. We both knew who was smarter, better connected, more likely to end up in a corner office with the historically significant antique desk. The only edge I had was that I was a male in a seller's market. It was enough.

"This is a business dinner, Donald," she said, "nothing more."

I favored her with an expression of polite disbelief I knew from experience she'd find infuriating. And, digging into my pheasant, murmured, "Of course." We didn't say much of consequence until dessert, when I finally asked, "So what's Loeb-Soffner up to these days?"

"Structuring a corporate expansion. Jim's putting together the financial side of the package, and I'm doing personnel. You're being headhunted, Donald." She favored me with that feral little flash of teeth she made when she saw something she wanted. Courtney wasn't a beautiful woman, far from it. But there was that fierceness to her, that sense of something primal being held under tight and precarious control that made her hot as hot to me. "You're talented, you're thuggish, and you're not too tightly nailed to your present position. Those are all qualities we're looking for."

She dumped her purse on the table, took out a single folded sheet of paper. "These are the terms I'm offering." She placed it by my plate, attacked her torte with gusto.

I unfolded the paper. "This is a lateral transfer."

"Unlimited opportunity for advancement," she said with her mouth full, "if you've got the stuff."

"Mmm." I did a line-by-line of the benefits, all comparable to what I was getting now. My current salary to the dollar—Ms. Soffner was showing off. And the stock options. "This can't be right. Not for a lateral."

There was that grin again, like a glimpse of shark in murky waters. "I knew you'd like it. We're going over the top with the options because we need your answer right away—tonight preferably. Tomorrow at the latest. No negotiations. We have to put the package together fast. There's going to be a shitstorm of publicity when this comes out. We want to have everything nailed down, present the fundies and bleeding hearts with a *fait accompli*."

"My God, Courtney, what kind of monster do you have hold of now?"

"The biggest one in the world. Bigger than Apple. Bigger than Home Virtual. Bigger than HIVac-IV," she said with relish. "Have you ever heard of Koestler Biological?"

I put my fork down.

"Koestler? You're peddling corpses now?"

"Please. Postanthropic biological resources." She said it lightly, with just the right touch of irony. Still, I thought I detected a certain discomfort with the nature of her client's product.

"There's no money in it." I waved a hand toward our attentive wait-staff. "These guys must be—what?—maybe two percent of the annual turn-over? Zombies are luxury goods: servants, reactor cleanups, Hollywood stunt deaths, exotic services"—we both knew what I meant—"a few hundred a year, maybe, tops. There's not the demand. The revulsion factor is too great."

"There's been a technological breakthrough." Courtney leaned forward. "They can install the infrasystem and controllers and offer the product for the factory-floor cost of a new subcompact. That's way below the economic threshold for blue-collar labor.

"Look at it from the viewpoint of a typical factory owner. He's already downsized to the bone and labor costs are bleeding him dry. How can he compete in a dwindling consumer market? Now let's imagine he buys into the program." She took out her Mont Blanc and began scribbling figures on the tablecloth. "No benefits. No liability suits. No sick pay. No pilferage. We're talking about cutting labor costs by at least two-thirds. Minimum! That's irresistible, I don't care how big your revulsion factor is. We project we can move five hundred thousand units in the first year."

"Five hundred thousand," I said. "That's crazy. Where the hell are you going to get the raw material for—?"

"Africa."

"Oh, God, Courtney." I was struck wordless by the cynicism it took to even consider turning the sub-Saharan tragedy to a profit, by the sheer, raw evil of channeling hard currency to the pocket Hitlers who ran the camps. Courtney only smiled and gave that quick little flip of her head that meant she was accessing the time on an optic chip.

"I think you're ready," she said, "to talk with Koestler."

At her gesture, the zombie boys erected projector lamps about us, fussed with the settings, turned them on. Interference patterns moired, clashed, meshed. Walls of darkness erected themselves about us. Courtney took out her flat and set it up on the table. Three taps of her nailed fingers and the round and hairless face of Marvin Koestler appeared on the screen. "Ah, Courtney!" he said in a pleased voice. "You're in—New York, yes? The San Moritz. With Donald." The slightest pause with each accessed bit of information. "Did you have the antelope medallions?" When we shook our heads, he kissed his fingertips. "Magnificent! They're ever so lightly braised and then smothered in buffalo mozzarella. Nobody makes them better. I had the same dish in Florence the other day, and there was simply no comparison."

I cleared my throat. "Is that where you are? Italy?"

"Let's leave out where I am." He made a dismissive gesture, as if it were a trifle. But Courtney's face darkened. Corporate kidnapping being the growth industry it is, I'd gaffed badly. "The question is—what do you think of my offer?"

"It's…interesting. For a lateral."

"It's the start-up costs. We're leveraged up to our asses as it is. You'll make out better this way in the long run." He favored me with a sudden grin that went mean around the edges. Very much the financial buccaneer. Then he leaned forward, lowered his voice, maintained firm eye contact. Classic people-handling techniques. "You're not sold. You know you can trust Courtney to have checked out the finances. Still, you think: It won't work. To work, the product has to be irresistible, and it's not. It can't be."

"Yes, sir," I said. "Succinctly put."

He nodded to Courtney. "Let's sell this young man." And to me, "My stretch is downstairs."

He winked out.

Koestler was waiting for us in the limo, a ghostly pink presence. His holo, rather, a genial if somewhat coarse-grained ghost afloat in golden light. He waved an expansive and insubstantial arm to take in the interior of the car and said, "Make yourselves at home."

The chauffeur wore combat-grade photomultipliers. They gave him a buggish, inhuman look. I wasn't sure if he was dead or not. "Take us to Heaven," Koestler said.

The doorman stepped out into the street, looked both ways, nodded to the chauffeur. Robot guns tracked our progress down the block.

"Courtney tells me you're getting the raw materials from Africa."

"Distasteful, but necessary. To begin with. We have to sell the idea first—no reason to make things rough on ourselves. Down the line, though, I don't see why we can't go domestic. Something along the lines of a reverse mortgage, perhaps, life insurance that pays off while you're still alive. It'd be a step towards getting the poor off our backs at last. Fuck 'em.

They've been getting a goddamn free ride for too long; the least they can do is to die and provide us with servants."

I was pretty sure Koestler was joking. But I smiled and ducked my head, so I'd be covered in either case. "What's Heaven?" I asked, to move the conversation onto safer territory.

"A proving ground," Koestler said with great satisfaction, "for the future. Have you ever witnessed bare-knuckles fisticuffs?"

"No."

"Ah, now there's a sport for gentlemen! The sweet science at its sweetest. No rounds, no rules, no holds barred. It gives you the real measure of a man—not just of his strength but his character. How he handles himself, whether he keeps cool under pressure—how he stands up to pain. Security won't let me go to the clubs in person, but I've made arrangements."

✺

Heaven was a converted movie theater in a rundown neighborhood in Queens. The chauffeur got out, disappeared briefly around the back, and returned with two zombie bodyguards. It was like a conjurer's trick. "You had these guys stashed in the *trunk?*" I asked as he opened the door for us.

"It's a new world," Courtney said. "Get used to it."

The place was mobbed. Two, maybe three hundred seats, standing room only. A mixed crowd, blacks and Irish and Koreans mostly, but with a smattering of uptown customers as well. You didn't have to be poor to need the occasional taste of vicarious potency. Nobody paid us any particular notice. We'd come in just as the fighters were being presented.

"Weighing two-five-oh, in black trunks with a red stripe," the ref was bawling, "tha gang-bang *gangs*ta, tha bare-knuckle *brawla*, tha man with tha—"

Courtney and I went up a scummy set of back stairs. Bodyguard-us-bodyguard, as if we were a combat patrol out of some twentieth-century jungle war. A scrawny, potbellied old geezer with a damp cigar in his mouth unlocked the door to our box. Sticky floor, bad seats, a good view down on the ring. Grey plastic matting, billowing smoke.

Koestler was there, in a shiny new hologram shell. It reminded me of those plaster Madonnas in painted bathtubs that Catholics set out in their yards. "Your permanent box?" I asked.

"All of this is for your sake, Donald—you and a few others. We're pitting our product one-on-one against some of the local talent. By arrangement with the management. What you're going to see will settle your doubts once and for all."

"You'll like this," Courtney said. "I've been here five nights straight. Counting tonight." The bell rang, starting the fight. She leaned forward avidly, hooking her elbows on the railing.

The zombie was grey-skinned and modestly muscled, for a fighter. But it held up its hands alertly, was light on its feet, and had strangely calm and knowing eyes.

Its opponent was a real bruiser, a big black guy with classic African features twisted slightly out of true so that his mouth curled up in a kind of sneer on one side. He had gang scars on his chest and even uglier marks on his back that didn't look deliberate but like something he'd earned on the streets. His eyes burned with an intensity just this side of madness.

He came forward cautiously but not fearfully, and made a couple of quick jabs to get the measure of his opponent. They were blocked and countered.

They circled each other, looking for an opening.

For a minute or so, nothing much happened. Then the gangster feinted at the zombie's head, drawing up its guard. He drove through that opening with a slam to the zombie's nuts that made me wince.

No reaction.

The dead fighter responded with a flurry of punches, and got in a glancing blow to its opponent's cheek. They separated, engaged, circled around.

Then the big guy exploded in a combination of killer blows, connecting so solidly it seemed they would splinter every rib in the dead fighter's body. It brought the crowd to their feet, roaring their approval.

The zombie didn't even stagger.

A strange look came into the gangster's eyes, then, as the zombie counterattacked, driving him back into the ropes. I could only imagine what it must be like for a man who had always lived by his strength and his ability to absorb punishment to realize that he was facing an opponent to whom pain meant nothing. Fights were lost and won by flinches and hesitations. You won by keeping your head. You lost by getting rattled.

Despite his best blows, the zombie stayed methodical, serene, calm, relentless. That was its nature.

It must have been devastating.

The fight went on and on. It was a strange and alienating experience for me. After a while I couldn't stay focused on it. My thoughts kept slipping into a zone where I found myself studying the line of Courtney's jaw, thinking about later tonight. She liked her sex just a little bit sick. There was always a feeling, fucking her, that there was something truly repulsive that she *really* wanted to do but lacked the courage to bring up on her own.

So there was always this urge to get her to do something she didn't like. She was resistant; I never dared try more than one new thing per date. But I could always talk her into that one thing. Because when she was aroused, she got pliant. She could be talked into anything. She could be made to beg for it.

Courtney would've been amazed to learn that I was not proud of what I did with her—quite the opposite, in fact. But I was as obsessed with her as she was with whatever it was that obsessed her.

Suddenly Courtney was on her feet, yelling. The hologram showed Koestler on his feet as well. The big guy was on the ropes, being pummeled. Blood and spittle flew from his face with each blow. Then he was down; he'd never even had a chance. He must've known early on that it was hopeless, that he wasn't going to win, but he'd refused to take a fall. He had to be pounded into the ground. He went down raging, proud and uncomplaining. I had to admire that.

But he lost anyway.

That, I realized, was the message I was meant to take away from this. Not just that the product was robust. But that only those who backed it were going to win. I could see, even if the audience couldn't, that it was the end of an era. A man's body wasn't worth a damn anymore. There wasn't anything it could do that technology couldn't handle better. The number of losers in the world had just doubled, tripled, reached maximum. What the fools below were cheering for was the death of their futures.

I got up and cheered too.

In the stretch afterwards, Koestler said, "You've seen the light. You're a believer now."

"I haven't necessarily decided yet."

"Don't bullshit me," Koestler said. "I've done my homework, Mr. Nichols. Your current position is not exactly secure. Morton-Western is going down the tubes. The entire service sector is going down the tubes. Face it, the old economic order is as good as fucking gone. Of course you're going to take my offer. You don't have any other choice."

The fax outed sets of contracts. "A Certain Product," it said here and there. Corpses were never mentioned.

But when I opened my jacket to get a pen, Koestler said, "Wait. I've got a factory. Three thousand positions under me. I've got a motivated workforce. They'd walk through fire to keep their jobs. Pilferage is at zero. Sick time practically the same. Give me one advantage your product has over my current workforce. Sell me on it. I'll give you thirty seconds."

I wasn't in sales and the job had been explicitly promised me already. But by reaching for the pen, I had admitted I wanted the position. And we all knew whose hand carried the whip.

"They can be catheterized," I said—"no toilet breaks."

For a long instant Koestler just stared at me blankly. Then he exploded with laughter. "By God, that's a new one! You have a great future ahead of you, Donald. Welcome aboard."

He winked out.

We drove on in silence for a while, aimless, directionless. At last Courtney leaned forward and touched the chauffeur's shoulder.

"Take me home," she said.

Riding through Manhattan I suffered from a waking hallucination that we were driving through a city of corpses. Grey faces, listless motions. Everyone looked dead in the headlights and sodium vapor streetlamps. Passing by the Children's Museum I saw a mother with a stroller through the glass doors. Two small children by her side. They all three stood motionless, gazing forward at nothing. We passed by a stop-and-go where zombies stood out on the sidewalk drinking forties in paper bags. Through upper-story windows I could see the sad rainbow trace of virtuals playing to empty eyes. There were zombies in the park, zombies smoking blunts, zombies driving taxies, zombies sitting on stoops and hanging out on street corners, all of them waiting for the years to pass and the flesh to fall from their bones.

I felt like the last man alive.

Courtney was still wired and sweaty from the fight. The pheromones came off her in great waves as I followed her down the hall to her apartment.

She stank of lust. I found myself thinking of how she got just before orgasm, so desperate, so desirable. It was different after she came, she would fall into a state of calm assurance; the same sort of calm assurance she showed in her business life, the aplomb she sought so wildly during the act itself.

And when that desperation left her, so would I. Because even I could recognize that it was her desperation that drew me to her, that made me do the things she needed me to do. In all the years I'd known her, we'd never once had breakfast together.

I wished there was some way I could deal her out of the equation. I wished that her desperation were a liquid that I could drink down to the dregs. I wished I could drop her in a wine press and squeeze her dry.

At her apartment, Courtney unlocked her door and in one compli- cated movement twisted through and stood facing me from the inside. "Well," she said. "All in all, a productive evening. Good night, Donald."

"Good night? Aren't you going to invite me inside?"

"No."

"What do you mean, no?" She was beginning to piss me off. A blind man could've told she was in heat from across the street. A chimpanzee could've talked his way into her pants. "What kind of idiot game are you playing now?"

"You know what no means, Donald. You're not stupid."

"No I'm not, and neither are you. We both know the score. Now let me in, goddamnit."

"Enjoy your present," she said, and closed the door.

I found Courtney's present back in my suite. I was still seething from her treatment of me and stalked into the room, letting the door slam behind me. So that I was standing in near-total darkness. The only light was what little seeped through the draped windows at the far end of the room. I was just reaching for the light switch when there was a motion in the darkness.

'Jackers! I thought, and all in a panic lurched for the light switch, hoping to achieve I don't know what. Credit-jackers always work in trios, one to torture the security codes out of you, one to phone the numbers out of your accounts and into a fiscal trapdoor, a third to stand guard. Was turning the lights on supposed to make them scurry for darkness, like roaches? Nevertheless, I almost tripped over my own feet in my haste to reach the switch. But of course it was nothing like what I'd feared.

It was a woman.

She stood by the window in a white silk dress that could neither compete with nor distract from her ethereal beauty, her porcelain skin. When the lights came on, she turned toward me, eyes widening, lips parting slightly. Her breasts swayed ever so slightly as she gracefully raised a bare arm to offer me a lily. "Hello, Donald," she said huskily. "I'm yours for the night." She was absolutely beautiful.

And dead, of course.

Not twenty minutes later I was hammering on Courtney's door. She came to the door in a Pierre Cardin dressing gown and from the way she was still cinching the sash and the disarray of her hair I gathered she hadn't been expecting me.

"I'm not alone," she said.

"I didn't come here for the dubious pleasures of your fair white body." I pushed my way into the room. But couldn't help remembering that beautiful body of hers, not so exquisite as the dead whore's, and now the thoughts were inextricably mingled in my head, death and Courtney, sex and corpses, a Gordian knot I might never be able to untangle.)

"You didn't like my surprise?" She was smiling openly now, amused.

"No, I fucking did not!"

I took a step toward her. I was shaking. I couldn't stop fisting and unfisting my hands.

She fell back a step. But that confident, oddly expectant look didn't leave her face. "Bruno," she said lightly. "Would you come in here?"

A motion at the periphery of vision. Bruno stepped out of the shadows of her bedroom. He was a muscular brute, pumped, ripped, and as black as the fighter I'd seen go down earlier that night. He stood behind Courtney, totally naked, with slim hips and wide shoulders and the finest skin I'd ever seen.

And dead.

I saw it all in a flash.

"Oh, for God's sake, Courtney!" I said, disgusted. "I can't believe you. That you'd actually…That thing's just an obedient body. There's nothing there—no passion, no connection, just…physical presence."

Courtney made a kind of chewing motion through her smile, weighing the implications of what she was about to say. Nastiness won.

"We have equity now," she said.

I lost it then. I stepped forward, raising a hand, and I swear to God I intended to bounce the bitch's head off the back wall. But she didn't flinch—she didn't even look afraid. She merely moved aside, saying, "In the body, Bruno. He has to look good in a business suit."

A dead fist smashed into my ribs so hard I thought for an instant my heart had stopped. Then Bruno punched me in my stomach. I doubled over, gasping. Two, three, four more blows. I was on the ground now, rolling over, helpless and weeping with rage.

"That's enough, baby. Now put out the trash."

Bruno dumped me in the hallway.

I glared up at Courtney through my tears. She was not at all beautiful now. Not in the least. You're getting older, I wanted to tell her. But instead I heard my voice, angry and astonished, saying, "You...you goddamn, fucking necrophile!"

"Cultivate a taste for it," Courtney said. Oh, she was purring! I doubted she'd ever find life quite this good again. "Half a million Brunos are about to come on the market. You're going to find it a lot more difficult to pick up *living* women in not so very long."

I sent away the dead whore. Then I took a long shower that didn't really make me feel any better. Naked, I walked into my unlit suite and opened the curtains. For a long time I stared out over the glory and darkness that was Manhattan.

I was afraid, more afraid than I'd ever been in my life.

The slums below me stretched to infinity. They were a vast necropolis, a neverending city of the dead. I thought of the millions out there who were never going to hold down a job again. I thought of how they must hate me—me and my kind—and how helpless they were before us. And yet. There were so many of them and so few of us. If they were to all rise up at once, they'd be like a tsunami, irresistible. And if there was so much as a spark of life left in them, then that was exactly what they would do.

That was one possibility. There was one other, and that was that nothing would happen. Nothing at all.

God help me, but I didn't know which one scared me more.

MOTHER GRASSHOPPER

In the Year One, we came in an armada of a million spacecraft to settle upon, colonize, and claim for our homeland this giant grasshopper on which we now dwell.

We dared not land upon the wings for, though the cube-square rule held true and their most rapid motions would be imperceptible on a historic scale, random nerve firings resulted in pre-movement tremors measured at Richter 11. So we opted to build in the eyes, in the faceted mirrorlands that reflected infinities of flatness, a shimmering Iowa, the architecture of home.

It was an impossible project and one, perhaps, that was doomed from the start. But such things are obvious only in retrospect. We were a young and vigorous race then. Everything seemed possible.

Using shaped temporal fields, we force-grew trees which we cut down to build our cabins. We planted sod and wheat and buffalo. In one vivid and unforgettable night of technology we created a layer of limestone bedrock half a mile deep upon which to build our towns. And when our work was done, we held hoe-downs in a thousand county seats all across the eye-lands.

We created new seasons, including Snow, after the patterns of those we had known in antiquity, but the night sky we left unaltered, for this was to be our home…now and forever. The unfamiliar constellations would grow their own legends over the ages; there would be time. Generations passed, and cities grew with whorls of suburbs like the arms of spiral galaxies around them, for we were lonely, as were the thousands and millions we decanted who grew like the trees of the cisocellar plains that were as thick as the ancient Black Forest.

I was a young man, newly bearded, hardly much more than a shirt-tail child, on that Harvest day when the stranger walked into town.

This was so unusual an event (and for you to whom a town of ten thousand necessarily means that there *will be strangers,* I despair of explaining) that children came out to shout and run at his heels, while we older citizens, conscious of our dignity, stood in the doorways of our shops, factories, and co-ops to gaze ponderously in his general direction. Not quite *at* him, you understand, but over his shoulder, into the flat, mesmeric plains and the infinite white skies beyond.

He claimed to have come all the way from the equatorial abdomen, where gravity is three times eye-normal, and this was easy enough to believe, for he was ungodly strong. With my own eyes I once saw him take a dollar coin between thumb and forefinger and bend it in half—and a steel dollar at that! He also claimed to have walked the entire distance, which nobody believed, not even me.

"If you'd walked even half that far," I said, "I reckon you'd be the most remarkable man as ever lived."

He laughed at that and ruffled my hair. "Well, maybe I am," he said. "Maybe I am."

I flushed and took a step backwards, hand on the bandersnatch-skin hilt of my fighting knife. I was as feisty as a bantam rooster in those days, and twice as quick to take offense. "Mister, I'm afraid I'm going to have to ask you to step outside."

The stranger looked at me. Then he reached out and, without the slightest hint of fear or anger or even regret, touched my arm just below the shoulder. He did it with no particular speed and yet somehow I could not react fast enough to stop him. And that touch, light though it was, paralyzed my arm, leaving it withered and useless, even as it is today.

He put his drink down on the bar, and said, "Pick up my knapsack."

I did.

"Follow me."

So it was that without a word of farewell to my family or even a backward glance, I left New Auschwitz forever.

That night, over a campfire of eel grass and dried buffalo chips, we ate a dinner of refried beans and fatback bacon. It was a new and clumsy experience for me, eating one-handed. For a long time, neither one of us spoke. Finally I said, "Are you a magician?"

The stranger sighed. "Maybe so," he said. "Maybe I am."

"You have a name?"

"No."

"What do we do now?"

"Business." He pushed his plate toward me. "I cooked. It's your turn to wash."

Our business entailed constant travel. We went to Brinkerton with cholera and to Roxborough with typhus. We passed through Denver and Venice and Saint Petersburg and left behind fleas, rats, and plague. In Upper Black Eddy, it was ebola. We never stayed long enough to see the results of our work, but I read the newspapers afterwards, and it was about what you would expect.

Still, *on the whole,* humanity prospered. Where one city was decimated, another was expanding. The overspilling hospitals of one county created a market for the goods of a dozen others. The survivors had babies.

We walked to Tylersburg, Rutledge, and Uniontown and took wagons to Shoemakersville, Confluence, and South Gibson. Booked onto steam trains for Mount Lebanon, Mount Bethel, Mount Aetna, and Mount Nebo and diesel trains to McKeesport, Reinholds Station, and Broomall. Boarded buses to Carbondale, Feasterville, June Bug, and Lincoln Falls. Caught commuter flights to Paradise, Nickel Mines, Niantic, and Zion. The time passed quickly.

Then one shocking day my magician announced that he was going home.

"Home?" I said. "What about your work?"

"*Our* work, Daniel," he said gently. "I expect you'll do as good a job as ever I did." He finished packing his few possessions into a carpet bag.

"You can't!" I cried.

With a wink and a sad smile, he slipped out the door.

For a time—long or short, I don't know—I sat motionless, unthinking, unseeing. Then I leaped to my feet, threw open the door, and looked up and down the empty street. Blocks away, toward the train station, was a scurrying black speck.

Leaving the door open behind me, I ran after it.

I just missed the afternoon express to Lackawanna. I asked the station-master when was the next train after it. He said tomorrow. Had he seen a tall man carrying a carpetbag, looking thus and so? Yes, he had. Where was he? On the train to Lackawanna. Nothing more heading that way today. Did he know where I could rent a car? Yes, he did. Place just down the road.

Maybe I'd've caught the magician if I hadn't gone back to the room to pick up my bags. Most likely not. At Lackawanna station I found he'd taken the bus to Johnstown. In Johnstown, he'd moved on to Erie and there the trail ran cold. It took me three days' hard questioning to pick it up again.

For a week I pursued him thus, like a man possessed.

Then I awoke one morning and my panic was gone. I knew I wasn't going to catch my magician anytime soon. I took stock of my resources, counted up what little cash-money I had, and laid out a strategy. Then I went shopping. Finally, I hit the road. I'd have to be patient, dogged, wily, but I knew that, given enough time, I'd find him.

Find him, and kill him too.

The trail led me to Harper's Ferry, at the very edge of the oculus. Behind was civilization. Ahead was nothing but thousands of miles of empty chitin-lands.

People said he'd gone south, off the lens entirely.

Back at my boarding house, I was approached by one of the lodgers. He was a skinny man with a big mustache and sleeveless white t-shirt that hung from his skinny shoulders like wet laundry on a muggy Sunday.

"What you got in that bag?"

"Black death," I said, "infectious meningitis, tuberculosis. You name it."

He thought for a bit. "I got this wife," he said at last. "I don't suppose you could..."

"I'll take a look at her," I said, and hoisted the bag.

We went upstairs to his room.

She lay in the bed, eyes closed. There was an IV needle in her arm, hooked up to a drip feed. She looked young, but of course that meant nothing. Her hair, neatly brushed and combed, laid across the coverlet almost to her waist, was white—white as snow, as death, as finest bone china.

"How long has she been like this?" I asked.

"Ohhhh..." He blew out his cheeks. "Forty-seven, maybe fifty years?"

"You her father?"

"Husband. Was, anyhow. Not sure how long the vows were meant to hold up under these conditions: can't say I've kept 'em any too well. You got something that bag for her?" He said it as casual as he could, but his eyes were big and spooked-looking.

I made my decision. "Tell you what," I said. "I'll give you forty dollars for her."

"The sheriff wouldn't think much of what you just said," the man said low and quiet.

"No. But then, I suppose I'll be off of the eye-lands entirely before he knows a word of it."

I picked up my syringe.

"Well? Is it a deal or not?"

Her name was Victoria. We were a good three days march into the chitin before she came out of the trance state characteristic of the interim zombie stage of Recovery. I'd fitted her with a pack, walking shoes, and a good stout stick, and she strode along head up, eyes blank, speaking in the tongues of angels afloat between the stars.

"—cisgalactic phase intercept," she said. "Do you read? Das Uberraumboot zuruckgegenerinnernte. Verstehen? Anadaemonic mesotechnological conflict strategizing. Drei tausenden Affen mit Laseren! Hello? Is anybody—"

Then she stumbled over a rock, cried out in pain, and said, "Where am I?"

I stopped, spread a map on the ground, and got out my pocket gravitometer. It was a simple thing: a glass cylinder filled with aerogel and a bright orange ceramic bead. The casing was tin, with a compressor screw at the top, a calibrated scale along the side, and the words "Flynn & Co." at the bottom. I flipped it over, watched the bead slowly fall. I tightened the screw a notch, then two, then three, increasing the aerogel's density. At five, the bead stopped. I read the gauge, squinted up at the sun, and then jabbed a finger on an isobar to one edge of the map.

"Right here," I said. "Just off the lens. See?"

"I don't—" She was trembling with panic. Her dilated eyes shifted wildly from one part of the empty horizon to another. Then suddenly, sourcelessly, she burst into tears.

Embarrassed, I looked away. When she was done crying, I patted the ground. "Sit." Sniffling, she obeyed. "How old are you, Victoria?"

"How old am...? Sixteen?" she said tentatively. "Seventeen?" Then, "Is that really my name?"

"It was. The woman you were grew tired of life, and injected herself with a drug that destroys the ego and with it all trace of personal history."

I sighed. "So in one sense you're still Victoria, and in another sense you're not. What she did was illegal, though; you can never go back to the oculus. You'd be locked into jail for the rest of your life."

She looked at me through eyes newly young, almost childlike in their experience, and still wet with tears. I was prepared for hysteria, grief, rage. But all she said was, "Are you a magician?"

That rocked me back on my heels. "Well—yes," I said. "I suppose I am."

She considered that silently for a moment. "So what happens to me now?"

"Your job is to carry that pack. We also go turn-on-turn with the dishes." I straightened, folding the map. "Come on. We've got a far way yet to go."

We commenced marching, in silence at first. But then, not many miles down the road and to my complete astonishment, Victoria began to *sing!*

We followed the faintest of paths—less a trail than the memory of a dream of the idea of one—across the chitin. Alongside it grew an occasional patch of grass. A lot of wind-blown loess had swept across the chitin-lands over the centuries. It caught in cracks in the carapace and gave purchase to fortuitous seeds. Once I even saw a rabbit. But before I could point it out to Victoria, I saw something else. Up ahead, in a place where the shell had powdered and a rare rainstorm had turned the powder briefly to mud, were two overlapping tire prints. A motorbike had been by here, and recently.

I stared at the tracks for a long time, clenching and unclenching my good hand.

The very next day we came upon a settlement.

It was a hardscrabble place. Just a windmill to run the pump that brought up a trickle of ichor from a miles-deep well, a refinery to process the stuff edible, and a handful of unpainted clapboard buildings and Quonset huts. Several battered old pickup trucks sat rusting under the limitless sky.

A gaunt man stood by the gate, waiting for us. His jaw was hard, his backbone straight and his hands empty. But I noted here and there a shiver of movement in a window or from the open door of a shed, and I made no mistake but that there were weapons trained upon us.

"Name's Rivera," the man said when we came up to him.

I swept off my bowler hat. "Daniel. This's Miss Victoria, my ward."

"Passing through?"

"Yessir, I am, and I see no reason I should ever pass this way again. If you have food for sale, I'll pay you market rates. But if not, why, with your permission, we'll just keep on moving on."

"Fair spoken." From somewhere Rivera produced a cup of water, and handed it to us. I drank half, handed the rest to Victoria. She shivered as it went down.

"Right good," I said. "And cold too."

"We have a heat pump," Rivera said with grudging pride. "C'mon inside. Let's see what the women have made us to eat."

Then the children came running out, whooping and hollering, too many to count, and the adult people behind them, whom I made out to be twenty in number. They made us welcome.

They were good people, if outlaws, and as hungry for news and gossip as anybody can be. I told them about a stump speech I had heard made by Tyler B. Morris, who was running for governor of the Northern Department, and they spent all of dinnertime discussing it. The food was good, too—ham and biscuits with red-eye gravy, sweet yams with butter, and apple cobbler to boot. If I hadn't seen their chemical complex, I'd've never guessed it for synthetic. There were lace curtains in the window, brittle-old but clean, and I noted how carefully the leftovers were stored away for later.

After we'd eaten, Rivera caught my eye and gestured with his chin. We went outside, and he led me to a shed out back. He unpadlocked the door and we stepped within. A line of ten people lay unmoving on plain-built beds. They were each catheterized to a drip-bag of processed ichor. Light from the door caught their hair, ten white haloes in the gloom.

"We brought them with us," Rivera said. "Thought we'd be doing well enough to make a go of it. Lately, though, I don't know, maybe it's the drought, but the blood's been running thin, and it's not like we have the money to have a new well drilled."

"I understand." Then, because it seemed a good time to ask, "There was a man came by this way probably less'n a week ago. Tall, riding a—"

"He wouldn't help," Harry said. "Said it wasn't his responsibility. Then, before he drove off, the sonofabitch tried to buy some of our food." He turned and spat. "He told us you and the woman would be coming along. We been waiting."

"Wait. He told you I'd have a woman with me?"

"It's not just us we have to think of!" he said with sudden vehemence. "There's the young fellers, too. They come along and all a man's stiff-necked talk about obligations and morality goes right out the window.

Sometimes I think how I could come out here with a length of iron pipe and—well." He shook his head and then, almost pleadingly, said, "Can't you do something?"

"I think so." A faint creaking noise made me turn then. Victoria stood frozen in the doorway. The light through her hair made of it a white flare. I closed my eyes, wishing she hadn't stumbled across this thing. In a neutral voice I said, "Get my bag."

Then Rivera and I set to haggling out a price.

We left the settlement with a goodly store of food and driving their third-best pickup truck. It was a pathetic old thing and the shocks were scarce more than a memory. We bumped and jolted toward the south.

For a long time Victoria did not speak. Then she turned to me and angrily blurted, "You *killed* them!"

"It was what they wanted."

"How can you say that?" She twisted in the seat and punched me in the shoulder. Hard. "How can you sit there and...*say* that?"

"Look," I said testily. "It's simple mathematics. You could make an equation out of it. They can only drill so much ichor. That ichor makes only so much food. Divide that by the number of mouths there are to feed and hold up the result against what it takes to keep one alive. So much food, so many people. If the one's smaller than the other, you starve. And the children wanted to live. The folks in the shed didn't."

"They could go back! Nobody *has* to live out in the middle of nowhere trying to scratch food out of nothing!"

"I counted one suicide for every two waking adults. Just how welcome do you think they'd be, back to the oculus, with so many suicides living among them? More than likely that's what drove them out here in the first place."

"Well...nobody would be starving if they didn't insist on having so many damn children."

"How can you stop people from having children?" I asked.

There was no possible answer to that and we both knew it. Victoria leaned her head against the cab window, eyes squeezed tight shut, as far from me as she could get. "You could have woken them up! But no, you had your bag of goodies and you wanted to play. I'm surprised you didn't kill *me* when you had the chance."

"Vickie…"

"Don't speak to me!"

She started to weep.

I wanted to hug her and comfort her, she was so miserable. But I was driving, and I only had the one good arm. So I didn't. Nor did I explain to her why it was that nobody chose to simply wake the suicides up.

※

That evening, as usual, I got out the hatchet and splintered enough chitin for a campfire. I was sitting by it, silent, when Victoria got out the jug of rough liquor the settlement folks had brewed from ichor. "You be careful with that stuff," I said. "It sneaks up on you. Don't forget, whatever experience you've had drinking got left behind in your first life."

"Then *you* drink!" she said, thrusting a cup at me. "I'll follow your lead. When you stop, I'll stop."

I swear I never suspected what she had in mind. And it had been a long while since I'd tasted alcohol. So, like a fool, I took her intent at face value. I had a drink. And then another.

Time passed.

We talked some, we laughed some. Maybe we sang a song or two.

Then, somehow, Victoria had shucked off her blouse and was dancing. She whirled around the campfire, her long skirts lifting up above her knees and occasionally flirting through the flames so that the hem browned and smoked but never quite caught fire.

This wildness seemed to come out of nowhere. I watched her, alarmed and aroused, too drunk to think clearly, too entranced even to move.

Finally she collapsed gracefully at my feet. The firelight was red on her naked back, shifting with each gasping breath she took. She looked up at me through her long, sweat-tangled hair, and her eyes were like amber, dark as cypress swamp water, brown and bottomless. Eyes a man could drown in.

I pulled her toward me. Laughing, she surged forward, collapsing upon me, tumbling me over backwards, fumbling with my belt and then the fly of my jeans. Then she had my cock out and stiff and I'd pushed her skirt up above her waist so that it seemed she was wearing nothing but a thick red sash. And I rolled her over on her back and she was reaching down between her legs to guide me in and she was smiling and lovely.

I plunged deep, deep, deep into her, and oh god but it felt fine. Like that eye-opening shock you get when you plunge into a cold lake for the first time on a hot summer's day and the water wraps itself around you and feels so impossibly good. Only this was warm and slippery-slick and a thousand times better. Then I was telling her things, telling her I needed her, I wanted her, I loved her, over and over again.

I awoke the next morning with a raging hangover. Victoria was sitting in the cab of the pickup, brushing her long white hair in the rear-view mirror and humming to herself.

"Well," she said, amused. "Look what the cat dragged in. There's water in the jerrycans. Have yourself a drink. I expect we could also spare a cup for you to wash your face with."

"Look," I said. "I'm sorry about last night."

"No you're not."

"I maybe said some foolish things, but—"

Her eyes flashed storm-cloud dark. "You weren't speaking near so foolish then as you are now. You meant every damn word, and I'm holding you to them." Then she laughed. "You'd best get at that water. You look hideous."

So I dragged myself off.

Overnight, Victoria had changed. Her whole manner, the way she held herself, even the way she phrased her words, told me that she wasn't a child anymore. She was a woman.

The thing I'd been dreading had begun.

"Resistance is useless," Victoria read. "For mine is the might and power of the Cosmos Itself!" She'd found a comic book stuck back under the seat and gone through it three times, chuckling to herself, while the truck rattled down that near-nonexistent road. Now she put it down. "Tell me something," she said. "How do you know your magician came by this way?"

"I just know is all," I said curtly. I'd given myself a shot of B-complex vitamins, but my head and gut still felt pretty ragged. Nor was it particularly soothing having to drive this idiot truck one-armed. And, anyway, I couldn't say just how I knew. It was a feeling I had, a certainty.

"I had a dream last night. After we, ummmm, danced."

I didn't look at her.

"I was on a flat platform, like a railroad station, only enormous. It stretched halfway to infinity. There were stars all around me, thicker and more colorful than I'd ever imagined them. Bright enough to make your eyes ache. Enormous machines were everywhere, golden, spaceships I suppose. They were taking off and landing with delicate little puffs of air, like it was the easiest thing imaginable to do. My body was so light I felt like I was going to float up among them. You ever hear of a place like that?"

"No."

"There was a man waiting for me there. He had the saddest smile, but cold, cruel eyes. Hello, Victoria, he said, and How did you know my name, I asked. Oh, I keep a close eye on Daniel, he said, I'm grooming him for an important job. Then he showed me a syringe. Do you know what's in here? he asked me. The liquid in it was so blue it shone." She fell silent.

"What did you say?"

"I just shook my head. Mortality, he said. It's an improved version of the drug you shot yourself up with fifty years ago. Tell Daniel it'll be waiting for him at Sky Terminus, where the great ships come and go. That was all. You think it means anything?"

I shook my head.

She picked up the comic book, flipped it open again. "Well, anyway, it was a strange dream."

That night, after doing the dishes, I went and sat down on the pickup's sideboard and stared into the fire, thinking. Victoria came and sat down beside me. She put a hand on my leg. It was the lightest of touches, but it sent all my blood rushing to my cock.

She smiled at that and looked up into my eyes. "Resistance is useless," she said.

Afterwards we lay together between blankets on the ground. Looking up at the night sky. It came to me then that being taken away from normal life young as I had been, all my experience with love had come before the event and all my experience with sex after, and that I'd therefore never before known them both together. So that in this situation I was as naive and unprepared for what was happening to us as Victoria was.

Which was how I admitted to myself I loved Victoria. At the time it seemed the worst possible thing that could've happened to me.

We saw it for the first time that next afternoon. It began as a giddy feeling, like a mild case of vertigo, and a vague thickening at the center of the sky as if it were going dark from the inside out. This was accompanied by a bulging up of the horizon, as if God Himself had placed hands flat on either edge and leaned forward, bowing it upward.

Then my inner ear *knew* that the land which had been flat as flat for all these many miles was now slanting downhill all the way to the horizon. That was the gravitational influence of all that mass before us. Late into the day it just appeared. It was like a conjuring trick. One moment it wasn't there at all and then, with the slightest of perceptual shifts, it dominated the vision. It was so distant that it took on the milky backscatter color of the sky and it went up so high you literally couldn't see the top. It was—I knew this now—our destination:

The antenna.

Even driving the pickup truck, it took three days after first sighting to reach its base.

On the morning of one of those days, Victoria suddenly pushed aside her breakfast and ran for the far side of the truck. That being the only privacy to be had for hundreds of miles around.

I listened to her retching. Knowing there was only one thing it could be.

She came back, pale and shaken. I got a plastic collection cup out of my bag. "Pee into this," I told her. When she had, I ran a quick diagnostic. It came up positive.

"Victoria," I said. "I've got an admission to make. I haven't been exactly straight with you about the medical consequences of your...condition."

It was the only time I ever saw her afraid. "My God," she said, "What is it? Tell me! What's happening to me?"

"Well, to begin with, you're pregnant."

There were no roads to the terminus, for all that it was visible from miles off. It lay nestled at the base of the antenna, and to look at the empty and trackless plains about it, you'd think there was neither reason for its existence nor possibility of any significant traffic there.

Yet the closer we got, the more people we saw approaching it. They appeared out of the everywhere and nothingness like hydrogen atoms being pulled into existence in the stressed spaces between galaxies, or like shards of ice crystallizing at random in supercooled superpure water. You'd see one far to your left, maybe strolling along with a walking stick slung casually over one shoulder and a gait that just told you she was whistling. Then beyond her in the distance a puff of dust from what could only be a half-track. And to the right, a man in a wide-brimmed hat sitting ramrod-straight in the saddle of a native parasite larger than any elephant. With every hour a different configuration, and all converging.

Roads materialized underfoot. By the time we arrived at the terminus, they were thronged with people.

The terminal building itself was as large as a city, all gleaming white marble arches and colonnades and parapets and towers. Pennants snapped in the wind. Welcoming musicians played at the feet of the columns. An enormous holographic banner dopplering slowly through the rainbow from infrared to ultraviolet and back again, read:

BYZANTIUM PORT AUTHORITY

MAGNETIC-LEVITATION MASS TRANSIT DIVISION

GROUND TERMINUS

Somebody later told me it provided employment for a hundred thousand people, and I believed him.

Victoria and I parked the truck by the front steps. I opened the door for her and helped her gingerly out. Her belly was enormous by then, and her sense of balance was off. We started up the steps. Behind us, a uniformed lackey got in the pickup and drove it away.

The space within was grander than could have been supported had the terminus not been located at the cusp of antenna and forehead, where the proximate masses each canceled out much of the other's attraction. There were countless ticket windows, all of carved mahogany. I settled Victoria down on a bench—her feet were tender—and went to stand in line. When I got to the front, the ticket-taker glanced at a computer screen and said, "May I help you, sir?"

"Two tickets, first-class. Up."

He tapped at the keyboard and a little device spat out two crisp pasteboard tickets. He slid them across the polished brass counter, and I reached for my wallet. "How much?" I said.

He glanced at his computer and shook his head. "No charge for you, Mister Daniel. Professional courtesy."

"How did you know my name?"

"You're expected." Then, before I could ask any more questions, "That's all I can tell you, sir. I can neither speak nor understand your language. It is impossible for me to converse with you."

"Then what the hell," I said testily, "are we doing now?"

He flipped the screen around for me to see. On it was a verbatim transcript of our conversation. The last line was: I SIMPLY READ WHAT'S ON THE SCREEN, SIR.

Then he turned it back toward himself and said, "I simply read what's—"

"Yeah, yeah, I know," I said. And went back to Victoria.

Even at mag-lev speeds, it took two days to travel the full length of the antenna. To amuse myself, I periodically took out my gravitometer and made readings. You'd think the figures would diminish exponentially as we climbed out of the gravity well. But because the antennae swept backward, over the bulk of the grasshopper, rather than forward and away, the gravitational gradient of our journey was quite complex. It lessened rapidly at first, grew temporarily stronger, and then lessened again, in the complex and lovely flattening sine-wave known as a Sheffield curve. You could see it reflected in the size of the magnetic rings we flashed through, three per minute, how they grew skinnier then fatter and finally skinnier still as we flew upward.

On the second day, Victoria gave birth. It was a beautiful child, a boy. I wanted to name him Hector, after my father, but Victoria was set on Jonathan, and as usual I gave in to her.

Afterwards, though, I studied her features. There were crow's-feet at the corners of her eyes, or maybe "laugh lines" is more appropriate, given Victoria's personality. The lines to either side of her mouth had deepened. Her whole face had a haggard cast to it. Looking at her, I felt a sadness so large and pervasive it seemed to fill the universe.

She was aging along her own exponential curve. The process was accelerating now, and I was not at all certain she would make it to Sky Terminus. It would be a close thing in either case.

I could see that Victoria knew it too. But she was happy as she hugged our child. "It's been a good life," she said. "I wish you could have grown with me—don't pout, you're so solemn, Daniel!—but other than that I have no complaints."

I looked out the window for a minute. I had known her for only—what?—a week, maybe. But in that brief time she had picked me up, shaken me off, and turned my life around. She had changed everything. When I looked back, I was crying.

"Death is the price we pay for children, isn't it?" she said. "Down below, they've made death illegal. But they're only fooling themselves. They think it's possible to live forever. They think there are no limits to growth. But everything dies—people, stars, the universe. And once it's over, all lives are the same length."

"I guess I'm just not so philosophical as you. It's a damned hard thing to lose your wife."

"Well, at least you figured that one out."

"What one?

"That I'm your wife." She was silent a moment. Then she said, "I had another dream. About your magician. And he explained about the drug. The one he called mortality."

"Huh," I said. Not really caring.

"The drug I took, you wake up and you burn through your life in a matter of days. With the new version, you wake up with a normal human lifespan, the length people had before the immortality treatments. One hundred fifty, two hundred years—that's not so immediate. The suicides are kept alive because their deaths come on so soon; it's too shocking to the survivors' sensibilities. The new version shows its effects too slowly to be stopped."

I stroked her long white hair. So fine. So very, very brittle. "Let's not talk about any of this."

Her eyes blazed "Let's *do*! Don't pretend to be a fool, Daniel. People multiply. There's only so much food, water, space. If nobody dies, there'll come a time when everybody dies." Then she smiled again, fondly, the way you might at a petulant but still promising child. "You know what's required of you, Daniel. And I'm proud of you for being worthy of it."

Sky Terminus was enormous, dazzling, beyond description. It was exactly like in Vickie's dream. I helped her out onto the platform. She could barely stand by then, but her eyes were bright and curious. Jonathan was asleep against my chest in a baby-sling.

Whatever held the atmosphere to the platform, it offered no resistance to the glittering, brilliantly articulated ships that rose and descended from all parts. Strange cargoes were unloaded by even stranger longshoremen.

"I'm not as excited by all this as I would've been when I was younger," Victoria murmured. "But somehow I find it more satisfying. Does that make sense to you?"

I began to say something. But then, abruptly, the light went out of her eyes. Stiffening, she stared straight ahead of herself into nothing that I could see. There was no emotion in her face whatsoever.

"Vickie?" I said.

Slowly, she tumbled to the ground.

It was then, while I stood stunned and unbelieving, that the magician came walking up to me.

In my imagination I'd run through this scene a thousand times: Leaving my bag behind, I stumbled off the train, toward him. He made no move to escape. I flipped open my jacket with a shrug of the shoulder, drew out the revolver with my good hand, and fired.

Now, though...

He looked sadly down at Victoria's body and put an arm around my shoulders.

"God," he said, "don't they just break your heart?"

I stayed on a month at the Sky Terminus to watch my son grow up. Jonathan died without offspring and was given an orbital burial. His coffin circled the grasshopper seven times before the orbit decayed and it scratched a bright meteoric line down into the night. The flare lasted about as long as would a struck sulfur match.

He'd been a good man, with a wicked sense of humor that never came from my side of the family.

So now I wander the world. Civilizations rise and fall about me. Only I remain unchanged. Where things haven't gotten too bad, I scatter mortality. Where they have I unleash disease.

I go where I go and I do my job. The generations rise up like wheat before me, and like a harvester I mow them down. Sometimes—not often—I go off by myself, to think and remember. Then I stare up into the night, into the colonized universe, until the tears rise up in my sight and drown the swarming stars.

I am Death and this is my story.

RADIANT DOORS

The doors began opening on a Tuesday in early March. Only a few at first—flickering and uncertain because they were operating at the extreme end of their temporal range—and those few from the earliest days of the exodus, releasing fugitives who were unstarved and healthy, the privileged scientists and technicians who had created or appropriated the devices that made their escape possible. We processed about a hundred a week, in comfortable isolation and relative secrecy. There were videocams taping everything, and our own best people madly scribbling notes and holding seminars and teleconferences where they debated the revelations.

Those were, in retrospect, the good old days.

In April the floodgates swung wide. Radiant doors opened everywhere, disgorging torrents of ragged and fearful refugees.

There were millions of them and they had, every one, to the least and smallest child, been horribly, horribly abused. The stories they told were enough to sicken anyone. I know.

We did what we could. We set up camps. We dug latrines. We ladled out soup. It was a terrible financial burden to the host governments, but what else could they do? The refugees were our descendants. In a very real sense, they were our children.

Throughout that spring and summer, the flow of refugees continued to grow. As the cumulative worldwide total ran up into the tens of millions, the authorities were beginning to panic—was this going to go on forever, a plague of human locusts that would double and triple and quadruple the population, overrunning the land and devouring all the food? What measures might we be forced to take if this kept up? The planet was within a lifetime of its loading capacity as it was. It couldn't take much more. Then in August the doors simply ceased. Somebody up in the future had put an absolute and final end to them.

It didn't bear thinking what became of those who hadn't made it through.

◉

"More tales from the burn ward," Shriver said, ducking through the door flap. That was what he called atrocity stories. He dumped the files on my desk and leaned forward so he could leer down my blouse. I scowled him back a step.

"Anything useful in them?"

"Not a scrap. But that's not my determination, is it? You have to read each and every word in each and every report so that you can swear and attest that they contain nothing the Commission needs to know."

"Right." I ran a scanner over the universals for each of the files, and dumped the lot in the circular file. Touched a thumb to one of the new pads—better security devices were the very first benefit we'd gotten from all that influx of future tech—and said, "Done."

Then I linked my hands behind my neck and leaned back in the chair. The air smelled of canvas. Sometimes it seemed that the entire universe smelled of canvas. "So how are things with you?"

"About what you'd expect. I spent the morning interviewing vics."

"Better you than me. I'm applying for a transfer to Publications. Out of these tents, out of the camps, into a nice little editorship somewhere, writing press releases and articles for the Sunday magazines. Cushy job, my very own cubby, and the satisfaction of knowing I'm doing some good for a change."

"It won't work," Shriver said. "All these stories simply blunt the capacity for feeling. There's even a term for it. It's called compassion fatigue. After a certain point you begin to blame the vic for making you hear about it."

I wriggled in the chair, as if trying to make myself more comfortable, and stuck out my breasts a little bit more. Shriver sucked in his breath. Quietly, though—I'm absolutely sure he thought I didn't notice. I said, "Hadn't you better get back to work?"

Shriver exhaled. "Yeah, yeah, I hear you." Looking unhappy, he ducked under the flap out into the corridor. A second later his head popped back in, grinning. "Oh, hey, Ginny—almost forgot. Huong is on sick roster. Gevorkian said to tell you you're covering for her this afternoon, debriefing vics."

"Bastard!"

He chuckled, and was gone.

※

I sat interviewing a woman whose face was a mask etched with the aftermath of horror. She was absolutely cooperative. They all were. Terrifyingly so. They were grateful for anything and everything. Sometimes I wanted to strike the poor bastards in the face, just to see if I could get a human reaction out of them. But they'd probably kiss my hand for not doing anything worse.

"What do you know about midpoint-based engineering? Gnat relays? Sub-local mathematics?"

Down this week's checklist I went, and with each item she shook her head. "Prigogine engines? SVAT trance status? Lepton soliloquies?" Nothing, nothing, nothing. "Phlenaria? The Toledo incident? 'Third Martyr' theory? Science Investigatory Group G?"

"They took my daughter," she said to this last. "They did things to her."

"I didn't ask you that. If you know anything about their military organization, their machines, their drugs, their research techniques— fine. But I don't want to hear about people."

"They did things." Her dead eyes bored into mine. "They—"

"Don't tell me."

"—returned her to us midway through. They said they were understaffed. They sterilized our kitchen and gave us a list of more things to do to her. Terrible things. And a checklist like yours to write down her reactions."

"Please."

"We didn't want to, but they left a device so we'd obey. Her father killed himself. He wanted to kill her too, but the device wouldn't let him. After he died, they changed the settings so I couldn't kill myself too. I tried."

"God damn." This was something new. I tapped my pen twice, activating its piezochronic function, so that it began recording fifteen seconds earlier. "Do you remember anything about this device? How large was it? What did the controls look like?" Knowing how unlikely it was that she'd give us anything usable. The average refugee knew no more about their technology than the average here-and-now citizen knows about television and computers. You turn them on and they do things. They break down and you buy a new one.

Still, my job was to probe for clues. Every little bit contributed to the big picture. Eventually they'd add up. That was the theory, anyway. "Did it have an internal or external power source? Did you ever see anybody servicing it?"

"I brought it with me," the woman said. She reached into her filthy clothing and removed a fist-sized chunk of quicksilver with small, multi-colored highlights. "Here."

She dumped it in my lap.

It was automation that did it or, rather, hyperautomation. That old bugaboo of fifty years ago had finally come to fruition. People were no longer needed to mine, farm, or manufacture. Machines made better administrators, more attentive servants. Only a very small elite—the vics called them simply their Owners—was required to order and ordain. Which left a lot of people who were just taking up space.

There had to be *something* to do with them.

As it turned out, there was.

That's my theory, anyway. Or, rather, one of them. I've got a million: Hyperautomation. Cumulative hardening of the collective conscience. Circular determinism. The implicitly aggressive nature of hierarchic structures. Compassion fatigue. The banality of evil.

Maybe people are just no damn good. That's what Shriver would have said.

The next day I went zombie, pretty much. Going through the motions, connecting the dots. LaShana in Requisitions noticed it right away. "You ought to take the day off," she said, when I dropped by to see about getting a replacement PzC(15)/pencorder. "Get away from here, take a walk in the woods, maybe play a little golf."

"Golf," I said. It seemed the most alien thing in the universe, hitting a ball with a stick. I couldn't see the point of it.

"Don't say it like that. You love golf. You've told me so a hundred times."

"I guess I have." I swung my purse up on the desk, slid my hand inside, and gently stroked the device. It was cool to the touch and vibrated ever so faintly under my fingers. I withdrew my hand. "Not today, though."

LaShana noticed. "What's that you have in there?"

"Nothing." I whipped the purse away from her. "Nothing at all." Then, a little too loud, a little too blustery, "So how about that pencorder?"

"It's yours." She got out the device, activated it, and let me pick it up. Now only I could operate the thing. Wonderful how fast we were picking up the technology. "How'd you lose your old one, anyway?"

"I stepped on it. By accident." I could see that LaShana wasn't buying it. "Damn it, it was an accident! It could have happened to anyone."

I fled from LaShana's alarmed, concerned face.

Not twenty minutes later, Gevorkian came sleazing into my office. She smiled, and leaned lazily back against the file cabinet when I said hi. Arms folded. Eyes sad and cynical. That big plain face of hers, tolerant and worldly-wise. Wearing her skirt just a *smidge* tighter, a *touch* shorter than was strictly correct for an office environment.

"Virginia," she said.

"Linda."

We did the waiting thing. Eventually, because I'd been here so long I honestly didn't give a shit, Gevorkian spoke first. "I hear you've been experiencing a little disgruntlement."

"Eh?"

"Mind if I check your purse?"

Without taking her eyes off me for an instant, she hoisted my purse, slid a hand inside, and stirred up the contents. She did it so slowly and dreamily that, I swear to God, I half expected her to smell her fingers afterwards. Then, when she didn't find the expected gun, she said, "You're not planning on going postal on us, are you?"

I snorted.

"So what is it?"

"What is it?" I said in disbelief. I went to the window. Zip zip zip, down came a rectangle of cloth. Through the scrim of mosquito netting the camp revealed itself: canvas as far as the eye could see. There was nothing down there as fancy as our labyrinthine government office complex at the top of the hill—what we laughingly called the Tentagon—with its canvas air-conditioning ducts and modular laboratories and cafeterias. They were all army surplus, and what wasn't army surplus was Boy Scout hand-me-downs. "Take a look. Take a goddamn fucking look. That's the future out there, and it's barreling down on you at the rate of sixty seconds per minute. You can *see* it and still ask me that question?"

She came and stood beside me. Off in the distance, a baby began to wail. The sound went on and on. "Virginia," she said quietly. "Ginny, I understand how you feel. Believe me, I do. Maybe the universe *is* deterministic. Maybe there's no way we can change what's coming. But that's not proven yet. And until it is, we've got to soldier on."

"Why?"

"Because of *them*." She nodded her chin toward the slow-moving revenants of things to come. "They're the living proof of everything we hate and fear. They are witness and testimony to the fact that absolute evil exists. So long as there's the least chance, we've got to try to ward it off."

I looked at her for a long, silent moment. Then, in a voice as cold and calmly modulated as I could make it, I said, "Take your goddamned hand off my ass."

She did so.

I stared after her as, without another word, she left.

This went beyond self-destructive. All I could think was that Gevorkian wanted out but couldn't bring herself to quit. Maybe she was bucking for a sexual harassment suit. But then again, there's definitely an erotic quality to the death of hope. A sense of license. A nicely edgy feeling that since nothing means anything anymore, we might as well have our little flings. That they may well be all we're going to get.

And all the time I was thinking this, in a drawer in my desk the device quietly sat. Humming to itself.

People keep having children. It seems such a terrible thing to do. I can't understand it at all, and don't talk to me about instinct. The first thing I did, after I realized the enormity of what lay ahead, was get my tubes tied. I never thought of myself as a breeder, but I'd wanted to have the option in case I ever changed my mind. Now I knew I would not.

It had been one hell of a day, so I decided I was entitled to quit work early. I was cutting through the camp toward the civ/noncom parking lot when I ran across Shriver. He was coming out of the vic latrines. Least romantic place on Earth. Canvas stretching forever and dispirited people shuffling in and out. And the smell! Imagine the accumulated stench of all the sick shit in the world, and you've just about got it right.

Shriver was carrying a bottle of Spanish champagne under his arm. The bottle had a red bow on it.

"What's the occasion?" I asked.

He grinned like Kali and slid an arm through mine. "My divorce finally came through. Wanna help me celebrate?"

Under the circumstances, it was the single most stupid thing I could possibly do. "Sure," I said. "Why not?"

Later, in his tent, as he was taking off my clothes, I asked, "Just why did your wife divorce you, Shriver?"

"Mental cruelty," he said, smiling.

Then he laid me down across his cot and I let him hurt me. I needed it. I needed to be punished for being so happy and well fed and unbrutalized while all about me...

"Harder, God damn you," I said, punching him, biting him, clawing up blood. "Make me pay."

Cause and effect. Is the universe deterministic or not? If everything inevitably follows what came before, tickety-tock, like gigantic, all-inclusive clockwork, then there is no hope. The refugees came from a future that cannot be turned away. If, on the other hand, time is quanticized and uncertain, unstable at every point, constantly prepared to collapse in any direction in response to totally random influences, then all that suffering that came pouring in on us over the course of six long and rainy months might be nothing more than a phantom. Just an artifact of a rejected future.

Our future might be downright pleasant.

We had a million scientists working in every possible discipline, trying to make it so. Biologists, chaoticists, physicists of every shape and description. Fabulously dedicated people. Driven. Motivated. All trying to hold out a hand before what must be and say "Stop!"

How they'd love to get their mitts on what I had stowed in my desk.

I hadn't decided yet whether I was going to hand it over, though. I wasn't at all sure what was the right thing to do. Or the smart thing, for that matter.

Gevorkian questioned me on Tuesday. Thursday, I came into my office to discover three UN soldiers with hand-held detectors, running a search.

I shifted my purse back on my shoulder to make me look more strack, and said, "What the hell is going on here?"

"Random check, ma'am." A dark-eyed Indian soldier young enough to be if not my son then my little brother politely touched fingers to forehead in a kind of salute. "For up-time contraband." A sewn tag over one pocket proclaimed his name to be PATHAK. "It is purely standard, I assure you."

I counted the stripes on his arm, compared them to my civilian GS-rating and determined that by the convoluted UN protocols under which we operated, I outranked him.

"Sergeant Major Pathak. You and I both know that all foreign nationals operate on American soil under sufferance, and the strict understanding that you have no authority whatsoever over native civilians."

"Oh, but this was cleared with your Mr.—"

"I don't give a good goddamn if you cleared it with the fucking Dalai Lama! This is my office—your authority ends at the door. You have no more right to be here than I have to finger-search your goddamn rectum. Do you follow me?"

He flushed angrily, but said nothing.

All the while, his fellows were running their detectors over the file cabinet, the storage closets, my desk. Little lights on each flashed red red red. Negative negative negative. The soldiers kept their eyes averted from me. Pretending they couldn't hear a word.

I reamed their Sergeant major out but good. Then, when the office had been thoroughly scanned and the two noncoms were standing about uneasily, wondering how long they'd be kept here, I dismissed the lot. They were all three so grateful to get away from me that nobody asked to examine my purse. Which was, of course, where I had the device.

After they left, I thought about young Sergeant Major Pathak. I wondered what he would have done if I'd put my hand on his crotch and made a crude suggestion. No, make that an order. He looked to be a real straight arrow. He'd squirm for sure. It was an alarmingly pleasant fantasy.

I thought it through several times in detail, all the while holding the gizmo in my lap and stroking it like a cat.

❋

The next morning, there was an incident at Food Processing. One of the women started screaming when they tried to inject an micro-miniaturized identi-chip under the skin of her forehead. It was a new system they'd come up with that was supposed to save a per-unit of thirteen cents a week in tracking costs. You walked through a smart doorway, it registered your presence, you picked up your food, and a second doorway checked you off on the way out. There was nothing in it to get upset about.

But the woman began screaming and crying and—this happened right by the kitchens—snatched up a cooking knife and began stabbing herself, over and over. She managed to make nine whacking big holes in herself before the thing was wrestled away from her. The orderlies took her to Intensive, where the doctors said it would be a close thing either way.

After word of that got around, none of the refugees would allow themselves to be identi-chipped. Which really pissed off the UN peacekeepers assigned to the camp, because earlier a couple hundred vics had accepted the chips without so much as a murmur. The Indian troops thought the refugees were willfully trying to make their job more difficult. There were complaints of racism, and rumors of planned retaliation.

I spent the morning doing my bit to calm things down—hopeless— and the afternoon writing up reports that everyone upstream wanted to receive ASAP and would probably file without reading. So I didn't have time to think about the device at all.

But I did. Constantly.

It was getting to be a burden.

For health class, one year in high school, I was given a ten-pound sack of flour, which I had to name and then carry around for a month, as if it were a baby. Bippy couldn't be left unattended; I had to carry it everywhere or else find somebody willing to baby-sit it. The exercise was supposed to teach us responsibility and scare us off of sex. The first thing I did when the month was over was to steal my father's .45, put Bippy in the back yard, and empty the clip into it, shot after shot. Until all that was left of the little bastard was a cloud of white dust.

The machine from the future was like that. Just another bippy. I had it, and dared not get rid of it. It was obviously valuable. It was equally obviously dangerous. Did I really want the government to get hold of something that could compel people to act against their own wishes? Did I honestly trust them not to immediately turn themselves into everything that we were supposedly fighting to prevent?

I'd been asking myself the same questions for—what?—four days. I'd thought I'd have some answers by now.

I took the bippy out from my purse. It felt cool and smooth in my hand, like melting ice. No, warm. It felt both warm *and* cool. I ran my hand over and over it, for the comfort of the thing.

After a minute, I got up, zipped shut the flap to my office, and secured it with a twist tie. Then I went back to my desk, sat down, and unbuttoned my blouse. I rubbed the bippy all over my body: up my neck, and over my breasts, and around and around on my belly. I kicked off my shoes and clumsily shucked off my pantyhose. Down along the outside of my calves it went, and up the insides of my thighs. Between my legs. It made me feel filthy. It made me feel a little less like killing myself.

How it happened was, I got lost. How I got lost was, I went into the camp after dark.

Nobody goes into the camp after dark, unless they have to. Not even the Indian troops. That's when the refugees hold their entertainments. They had no compassion for each other, you see—that was our dirty little secret. I saw a toddler fall into a campfire once. There were vics all around, but if it hadn't been for me, the child would have died. I snatched it from the flames before it got too badly hurt, but nobody else made a move to help it. They just stood there looking. And laughing.

"In Dachau, when they opened the gas chambers, they'd find a pyramid of human bodies by the door," Shriver told me once. "As the gas started to work, the Jews panicked and climbed over each other, in a futile attempt to escape. That was deliberate. It was designed into the system. The Nazis didn't just want them dead—they wanted to be able to feel morally superior to their victims afterwards."

So I shouldn't have been there. But I was unlatching the door to my trailer when it suddenly came to me that my purse felt wrong. Light. And I realized that I'd left the bippy in the top drawer of my office desk. I hadn't even locked it.

My stomach twisted at the thought of somebody else finding the thing. In a panic, I drove back to the camp. It was a twenty-minute drive from the trailer park, and by the time I got there I wasn't thinking straight. The civ/noncom parking lot was a good quarter-way around the camp from the Tentagon. I thought it would be a simple thing to cut through. So, flashing my DOD/Future History Division ID at the guard as I went through the gate, I did.

Which was how I came to be lost.

There are neighborhoods in the camp. People have a natural tendency to sort themselves out by the nature of their suffering. The twitchers, who were victims of paralogical reprogramming, stay in one part of the camp, and the mods, those with functional normative modifications, stay in another. I found myself wandering through crowds of people who had been "healed" of limbs, ears, and even internal organs—there seemed no sensible pattern. Sometimes our doctors could effect a partial correction. But our primitive surgery was, of course, nothing like that available in their miraculous age.

I'd taken a wrong turn trying to evade an eyeless, noseless woman who kept grabbing at my blouse and demanding money, and gotten all turned around in the process when, without noticing me, Gevorkian went striding purposefully by.

Which was so unexpected that, after an instant's shock, I up and followed her. It didn't occur to me not to. There was something strange about the way she held herself, about her expression, her posture. Something unfamiliar.

She didn't even *walk* like herself.

The vics had dismantled several tents to make a large open space surrounded by canvas. Propane lights, hung from tall poles, blazed in a ring about it. I saw Gevorkian slip between two canvas sheets and, after a moment's hesitation, I followed her.

It was a rat fight.

The way a rat fight works, I learned that night, is that first you catch a whole bunch of Norwegian rats. Big mean mothers. Then you get them in a bad mood, probably by not feeding them, but there are any number of other methods that could be used. Anyway, they're feeling feisty. You put a dozen of them in a big pit you've dug in the ground. Then you dump in your contestant. A big guy with a shaven head and his hands tied behind his back. His genitals are bound up in a little bit of cloth, but other than that he's naked.

Then you let them fight it out. The rats leap and jump and bite and the big guy tries to trample them underfoot or crush them with his knees, his chest, his head—whatever he can bash them with.

The whole thing was lit up bright as day, and all the area around the pit was crammed with vics. Some shouted and urged on one side or the other. Others simply watched intently. The rats squealed. The human fighter bared his teeth in a hideous rictus and fought in silence.

It was the creepiest thing I'd seen in a long time.

Gevorkian watched it coolly, without any particular interest or aversion. After a while it was obvious to me that she was waiting for someone.

Finally that someone arrived. He was a lean man, tall, with keen, hatchetlike features. None of the vics noticed. Their eyes were directed inward, toward the pit. He nodded once to Gevorkian, then backed through the canvas again.

She followed him.

I followed her.

They went to a near-lightless area near the edge of the camp. There was nothing there but trash, the backs of tents, the razor-wire fence, and a gate padlocked for the night.

It was perfectly easy to trail them from a distance. The stranger held himself proudly, chin up, eyes bright. He walked with a sure stride. He was nothing at all like the vics.

It was obvious to me that he was an Owner.

Gevorkian too. When she was with him that inhuman arrogance glowed in her face as well. It was as if a mask had been removed. The fire that burned in his face was reflected in hers.

I crouched low to the ground in the shadow of a tent and listened as the stranger said, "Why hasn't she turned it in?"

"She's unstable," Gevorkian said. "They all are."

"We don't dare prompt her. She has to turn it in herself."

"She will. Give her time."

"Time," the man repeated. They both laughed in a way that sounded to me distinctly unpleasant. Then, "She'd better. There's a lot went into this operation. There's a lot riding on it."

"She will."

I stood watching as they shook hands and parted ways. Gevorkian turned and disappeared back into the tent city. The stranger opened a radiant door and was gone.

Cause and effect. They'd done...*whatever* it was they'd done to that woman's daughter just so they could plant the bippy with me. They wanted me to turn it in. They wanted our government to have possession of a device that would guarantee obedience. They wanted to give us a good taste of what it was like to be them.

Suddenly I had no doubt at all what I should do. I started out at a determined stride, but inside of nine paces I was *running*. Vics scurried to get out of my way. If they didn't move fast enough, I shoved them aside.

I had to get back to the bippy and destroy it.

✵

Which was stupid, stupid, stupid. If I'd kept my head down and walked slowly, I would have been invisible. Invisible and safe. The way I did it, though, cursing and screaming, I made a lot of noise and caused a lot of fuss. Inevitably, I drew attention to myself.

Inevitably, Gevorkian stepped into my path.

I stumbled to a halt.

"Gevorkian," I said feebly. "Linda. I—"

All the lies I was about to utter died in my throat when I saw her face. Her expression. Those eyes. Gevorkian reached for me. I skipped back in utter panic, turned—and fled. Anybody else would have done the same.

It was a nightmare. The crowds slowed me. I stumbled. I had no idea where I was going. And all the time, this monster was right on my heels.

Nobody goes into the camp after dark, unless they have to. But that doesn't mean that nobody goes in after dark. By sheer good luck, Gevorkian chased me into the one part of the camp that had something that outsiders could find nowhere else—the sex-for-hire district.

There was nothing subtle about the way the vics sold themselves. The trampled-grass street I found myself in was lined with stacks of cages like the ones they use in dog kennels. They were festooned with strings of Christmas lights, and each one contained a crouched boy. Naked, to best display those mods and deformities that some found attractive. Off-duty soldiers strolled up and down the cages, checking out the possibilities. I recognized one of them.

"Sergeant Major Pathak!" I cried. He looked up, startled and guilty. "Help me! Kill her—please! Kill her now!"

Give him credit, the Sergeant major was a game little fellow. I can't imagine what we looked like to him, one harridan chasing the other down the streets of Hell. But he took the situation in at a glance, unholstered his sidearm, and stepped forward. "Please," he said. "You will both stand where you are. You will place your hands upon the top of your head. You will—"

Gevorkian flicked her fingers at the young soldier. He screamed, and clutched his freshly-crushed shoulder. She turned away from him, dismissively. The other soldiers had fled at the first sign of trouble. All her attention was on me, trembling in her sight like a winded doe. "*Sweet* little vic," she purred. "If you won't play the part we had planned for you, you'll simply have to be silenced."

"No," I whispered.

She touched my wrist. I was helpless to stop her. "You and I are going to go to my office now. We'll have fun there. Hours and hours of fun."

"Leave her be."

As sudden and inexplicable as an apparition of the Virgin, Shriver stepped out of the darkness. He looked small and grim.

Gevorkian laughed, and gestured.

But Shriver's hand reached up to intercept hers, and where they met, there was an electric blue flash. Gevorkian stared down, stunned, at her hand. Bits of tangled metal fell away from it. She looked up at Shriver.

He struck her down.

She fell with a brief harsh cry, like that of a sea gull. Shriver kicked her, three times, hard: In the ribs. In the stomach. In the head. Then, when she looked like she might yet regain her feet, "It's one of *them!*" he shouted. "Look at her! She's a spy for the Owners! She's from the future! Owner! Look! Owner!"

The refugees came tumbling out of the tents and climbing down out of their cages. They looked more alive than I'd ever seen them before. They were red-faced and screaming. Their eyes were wide with hysteria. For the first time in my life, I was genuinely afraid of them. They came running. They swarmed like insects.

They seized Gevorkian and began tearing her apart.

I saw her struggle up and halfway out of their grips, saw one arm rise up above the sea of clutching hands, like that of a woman drowning.

Shriver seized my elbow and steered me away before I could see any more. I saw enough, though.

I saw too much.

"Where are we going?" I asked when I'd recovered my wits.

"Where do you think we're going?"

He led me to my office.

There was a stranger waiting there. He took out a hand-held detector like Sergeant Major Pathak and his men had used earlier and touched it to himself, to Shriver, and to me. Three times it flashed red, negative. "You travel through time, you pick up a residual charge," Shriver explained. "It never goes away. We've known about Gevorkian for a long time."

"U.S. Special Security," the stranger said, and flipped open his ID. It meant diddle-all to me. There was a badge. It could have read Captain Crunch for all I knew or cared. But I didn't doubt for an instant that he was SS. He had that look. To Shriver he said, "The neutralizer."

Shriver unstrapped something glittery from his wrist—the device he'd used to undo Gevorkian's weapon—and, in a silent bit of comic bureaucratic punctilio, exchanged it for a written receipt. The security officer touched the thing with his detector. It flashed green. He put both devices away in interior pockets.

All the time, Shriver stood in the background, watching. He wasn't told to go away.

Finally, Captain Crunch turned his attention to me again. "Where's the snark?"

"Snark?"

The man removed a thin scrap of cloth from an inside jacket pocket and shook it out. With elaborate care, he pulled it over his left hand. An inertial glove. Seeing by my expression that I recognized it, he said, "Don't make me use this."

I swallowed. For an instant I thought crazily of defying him, of simply refusing to tell him where the bippy was. But I'd seen an inertial glove in action before, when a lone guard had broken up a camp riot. He'd been a little man. I'd seen him crush heads like watermelons.

Anyway, the bippy was in my desk. They'd be sure to look there.

I opened the drawer, produced the device. Handed it over. "It's a plant," I said. "They want us to have this."

Captain Crunch gave me a look that told me clear as words exactly how stupid he thought I was. "We understand more than you think we do. There are circles and circles. We have informants up in the future, and some of them are more highly placed than you'd think. Not everything that's known is made public."

"Damn it, this sucker is *evil*."

A snake's eyes would look warmer than his. "Understand this: We're fighting for our survival here. Extinction is null-value. You can have all the moral crises you want when the war is won."

"It should be suppressed. The technology. If it's used, it'll just help bring about..."

He wasn't listening.

I'd worked for the government long enough to know when I was wasting my breath. So I shut up.

When the Captain left with the bippy, Shriver still remained, looking ironically after him. "People get the kind of future they deserve," he observed.

"But that's what I'm saying. Gevorkian came back from the future in order to help bring it about. That means that time isn't deterministic." Maybe I was getting a little weepy. I'd had a rough day. "The other guy said there was a lot riding on this operation. They didn't know how it was going to turn out. They didn't *know*."

Shriver grunted, not at all interested.

I plowed ahead unheeding. "If it's not deterministic—if they're working so hard to bring it about—then all our effort isn't futile at all. This future can be prevented."

Shriver looked up at last. There was a strangely triumphant gleam in his eye. He flashed that roguish ain't-this-fun grin of his, and said, "I don't know about you, but some of us are working like hell to *achieve* it."

With a jaunty wink, he was gone.

THE VERY PULSE
OF THE MACHINE

Click.

The radio came on.

"Hell."

Martha kept her eyes forward, concentrated on walking. Jupiter to one shoulder, Daedalus's plume to the other. Nothing to it. Just trudge, drag, trudge, drag. Piece of cake.

"Oh."

She chinned the radio off.

Click.

"Hell. Oh. Kiv. El. Sen."

"Shut up, shut up, shut up!" Martha gave the rope an angry jerk, making the sledge carrying Burton's body jump and bounce on the sulfur hardpan. "You're dead, Burton, I've checked, there's a hole in your faceplace big enough to stick a fist through, and I really don't want to crack up. I'm in kind of a tight spot here and I can't afford it, okay? So be nice and just shut the fuck up."

"Not. Bur. Ton."

"Do it anyway."

She chinned the radio off again.

Jupiter loomed low on the western horizon, big and bright and beautiful and, after two weeks on Io, easy to ignore. To her left, Daedalus was spewing sulfur and sulfur dioxide in a fan two hundred kilometers high. The plume caught the chill light from an unseen sun and her visor rendered it a pale and lovely blue. Most spectacular view in the universe, and she was in no mood to enjoy it.

Click.

Before the voice could speak again, Martha said, "I am not going crazy, you're just the voice of my subconscious, I don't have the time to waste trying to figure out what unresolved psychological conflicts gave rise to all this, and I am *not* going to listen to anything you have to say."

Silence.

The moon rover had flipped over at least five times before crashing sideways against a boulder the size of the Sydney Opera House. Martha Kivelsen, timid groundling that she was, was strapped into her seat so tightly that when the universe stopped tumbling, she'd had a hard time unlatching the restraints. Juliet Burton, tall and athletic, so sure of her own luck and agility that she hadn't bothered, had been thrown into a strut.

The vent-blizzard of sulfur dioxide snow was blinding, though. It was only when Martha had finally crawled out from under its raging whiteness that she was able to look at the suited body she'd dragged free of the wreckage.

She immediately turned away.

Whatever knob or flange had punched the hole in Burton's helmet had been equally ruthless with her head.

Where a fraction of the vent-blizzard—"lateral plumes" the planetary geologists called them—had been deflected by the boulder, a bank of sulfur dioxide snow had built up. Automatically, without thinking, Martha scooped up double-handfuls and packed them into the helmet. Really, it was a nonsensical thing to do; in a vacuum, the body wasn't about to rot. On the other hand, it hid that face.

Then Martha did some serious thinking.

For all the fury of the blizzard, there was no turbulence. Because there was no atmosphere to have turbulence *in*. The sulfur dioxide gushed out straight from the sudden crack that had opened in the rock, falling to the surface miles away in strict obedience to the laws of ballistics. Most of what struck the boulder they'd crashed against would simply stick to it, and the rest would be bounced down to the ground at its feet. So that— this was how she'd gotten out in the first place—it was possible to crawl *under* the near-horizontal spray and back to the ruins of the moon rover. If she went slowly, the helmet light and her sense of feel ought to be sufficient for a little judicious salvage.

Martha got down on her hands and knees. And as she did, just as quickly as the blizzard had begun—it stopped.

She stood, feeling strangely foolish.

Still, she couldn't rely on the blizzard staying quiescent. Better hurry, she admonished herself. It might be an intermittent.

Quickly, almost fearfully, picking through the rich litter of wreckage, Martha discovered that the mother tank they used to replenish their airpacks had ruptured. Terrific. That left her own pack, which was one-third empty, two fully-charged backup packs, and Burton's, also one-third empty. It was a ghoulish thing to strip Burton's suit of her airpack, but it had to be done. Sorry, Julie. That gave her enough oxygen to last, let's see, almost forty hours.

Then she took a curved section of what had been the moon rover's hull and a coil of nylon rope, and, with two pieces of scrap for makeshift hammer and punch, fashioned a sledge for Burton's body.

She'd be damned if she was going to leave it behind.

Click.

"This is. Better."

"Says you."

Ahead of her stretched the hard, cold sulfur plain. Smooth as glass. Brittle as frozen toffee. Cold as hell. She called up a visor-map and checked her progress. Only forty-five miles of mixed terrain to cross and she'd reach the lander. Then she'd be home free. No sweat, she thought. Io was in tidal lock with Jupiter. So the Father of Planets would stay glued to one fixed spot in the sky. That was as good as a navigation beacon. Just keep Jupiter to your right shoulder, and Daedalus to your left. You'll come out fine.

"Sulfur is. Triboelectric."

"Don't hold it in. What are you really trying to say?"

"And now I see. With eye serene. The very. Pulse. Of the machine." A pause. "Wordsworth."

Which, except for the halting delivery, was so much like Burton, with her classical education and love of classical poets like Spencer and Ginsberg and Plath, that for a second Martha was taken aback. Burton was a terrible poetry bore, but her enthusiasm had been genuine, and now Martha was sorry for every time she'd met those quotations with rolled eyes or a flip remark. But there'd be time enough for grieving later. Right now she had to concentrate on the task at hand.

The colors of the plain were dim and brownish. With a few quick chin-taps, she cranked up their intensity. Her vision filled with yellows, oranges, reds—intense wax crayon colors. Martha decided she liked them best that way.

For all its Crayola vividness, this was the most desolate landscape in the universe. She was on her own here, small and weak in a harsh and unforgiving world. Burton was dead. There was nobody else on all of Io. Nobody to rely on but herself. Nobody to blame if she fucked up. Out of nowhere, she was filled with an elation as cold and bleak as the distant mountains. It was shameful how happy she felt.

After a minute, she said, "Know any songs?"

Oh the bear went over the mountain. The bear went over the mountain. The bear went over the mountain. To see what he could see.

"Wake. Up. Wake. Up."

To see what he could—

"Wake. Up. Wake. Up. Wake."

"Hah? What?"

"Crystal sulfur is orthorhombic."

She was in a field of sulfur flowers. They stretched as far as the eye could see, crystalline formations the size of her hand. Like the poppies of Flanders field. Or the ones in the Wizard of Oz. Behind her was a trail of broken flowers, some crushed by her feet or under the weight of the sledge, others simply exploded by exposure to her suit's waste heat. It was far from being a straight path. She had been walking on autopilot, and stumbled and turned and wandered upon striking the crystals.

Martha remembered how excited she and Burton had been when they first saw the fields of crystals. They had piled out of the moon rover with laughter and bounding leaps, and Burton had seized her by the waist and waltzed her around in a dance of jubilation. This was the big one, they'd thought, their chance at the history books. And even when they'd radioed Hols back in the orbiter and were somewhat condescendingly informed that there was no chance of this being a new life-form, but only sulfide formations such as could be found in any mineralogy text...even that had not killed their joy. It was still their first big discovery. They'd looked forward to many more.

Now, though, all she could think of was the fact that such crystal fields occurred in regions associated with sulfur geysers, lateral plumes, and volcanic hot spots.

Something funny was happening to the far edge of the field, though. She cranked up her helmet to extreme magnification and watched as the trail slowly erased itself. New flowers were rising up in place of those she had smashed, small but perfect and whole. And growing. She could not imagine by what process this could be happening. Electrodeposition? Molecular sulfur being drawn up from the soil in some kind of pseudo-capillary action? Were the flowers somehow plucking sulfur ions from Io's almost nonexistent atmosphere?

Yesterday, the questions would have excited her. Now, she had no capacity for wonder whatsoever. Moreover, her instruments were back in the moon rover. Save for the suit's limited electronics, she had nothing to take measurements with. She had only herself, the sledge, the spare airpacks, and the corpse.

"Damn, damn, damn," she muttered. On the one hand, this was a dangerous place to stay in. On the other, she'd been awake almost twenty hours now and she was dead on her feet. Exhausted. So very, very tired.

"O sleep! It is a gentle thing. Beloved from pole to pole. Coleridge."

Which, God knows, was tempting. But the numbers were clear: no sleep. With several deft chin-taps, Martha overrode her suit's safeties and accessed its medical kit. At her command, it sent a hit of metham-phetamine rushing down the drug/vitamin catheter.

There was a sudden explosion of clarity in her skull and her heart began pounding like a motherfucker. Yeah. That did it. She was full of energy now. Deep breath. Long stride. Let's go.

No rest for the wicked. She had things to do. She left the flowers rapidly behind. Good-bye, Oz.

Fade out. Fade in. Hours had glided by. She was walking through a shadowy sculpture garden. Volcanic pillars (these were their second great discovery; they had no exact parallel on Earth) were scattered across the pyroclastic plain like so many isolated Lipschitz statues. They were all rounded and heaped, very much in the style of rapidly cooled magma. Martha remembered that Burton was dead, and cried quietly to herself for a few minutes.

Weeping, she passed through the eerie stone forms. The speed made them shift and move in her vision. As if they were dancing. They looked like women to her, tragic figures out of *The Bacchae* or, no, wait, *The Trojan Women* was the play she was thinking of. Desolate. Filled with anguish. Lonely as Lot's wife.

There was a light scattering of sulfur dioxide snow on the ground here. It sublimed at the touch of her boots, turning to white mist and scattering wildly, the steam disappearing with each stride and then being renewed with the next footfall. Which only made the experience all that much creepier.

Click.

"Io has a metallic core predominantly of iron and iron sulfide, overlain by a mantle of partially molten rock and crust."

"Are you still here?"

"Am trying. To communicate."

"Shut up."

She topped the ridge. The plains ahead were smooth and undulating. They reminded her of the Moon, in the transitional region between Mare Serenitatis and the foothills of the Caucasus Mountains, where she had undergone her surface training. Only without the impact craters. No impact craters on Io. Least cratered solid body in the Solar System. All that volcanic activity deposited a new surface one meter thick every millenium or so. The whole damned moon was being constantly repaved.

Her mind was rambling. She checked her gauges, and muttered, "Let's get this show on the road."

There was no reply.

Dawn would come—when? Let's work this out. Io's "year," the time it took to revolve about Jupiter, was roughly forty-two hours fifteen minutes. She'd been walking seven hours. During which Io would've moved roughly sixty degrees through its orbit. So it would be dawn soon. That would make Daedalus's plume less obvious, but with her helmet graphics that wouldn't be a worry. Martha swiveled her neck, making sure that Daedalus and Jupiter were where they ought to be, and kept on walking.

Trudge, trudge, trudge. Try not to throw the map up on the visor every five minutes. Hold off as long as you can, just one more hour, okay, that's good, and another two miles. Not too shabby.

The sun was getting high. It would be noon in another hour and a half. Which meant—well, it really didn't mean much of anything.

Rock up ahead. Probably a silicate. It was a solitary six meters high brought here by who knew what forces and waiting who knew how many thousands of years just for her to come along and need a place to rest. She found a flat spot where she could lean against it and, breathing heavily, sat down to rest. And think. And check the airpack. Four hours until she had to change it again. Bringing her down to two airpacks. She had slightly under twenty-four hours now. Thirty-five miles to go. That was less than two miles an hour. A snap. Might run a little tight on oxygen there toward the end, though. She'd have to take care she didn't fall asleep.

Oh, how her body ached.

It ached almost as much as it had in the '48 Olympics, when she'd taken the bronze in the women's marathon. Or that time in the internationals in Kenya she'd come up from behind to tie for second. Story of her life. Always in third place, fighting for second. Always flight crew and sometimes, maybe, landing crew, but never the commander. Never class president. Never king of the hill. Just once—once!—she wanted to be Neil Armstrong.

Click.

"The marble index of a mind forever. Voyaging through strange seas of thought, alone. Wordsworth."

"What?"

"Jupiter's magnetosphere is the largest thing in the solar system. If the human eye could see it, it would appear two and a half times wider in the sky than the sun does."

"I knew that," she said, irrationally annoyed.

"Quotation is. Easy. Speech is. Not."

"Don't speak, then."

"Trying. To communicate!"

She shrugged. "So go ahead—communicate."

Silence. Then, "What does. This. Sound like?"

"What does what sound like?"

"Io is a sulfur-rich, iron-cored moon in a circular orbit around Jupiter. What does this. Sound like? Tidal forces from Jupiter and Ganymede pull and squeeze Io sufficiently to melt Tartarus, its sub-surface sulfur ocean. Tartarus vents its excess energy with sulfur and sulfur dioxide volcanoes. What does.

This sound like? Io's metallic core generates a magnetic field which punches a hole in Jupiter's magnetosphere, and also creates a high-energy ion flux tube connecting its own poles with the north and south poles of Jupiter. What. Does this sound like? Io sweeps up and absorbs all the electrons in the million-volt range. Its volcanoes pump out sulfur dioxide; its magnetic field breaks down a percentage of that into sulfur and oxygen ions; and these ions are pumped into the hole punched in the magnetosphere, creating a rotating field commonly called the Io torus. What does this sound like? Torus. Flux tube. Magnetosphere. Volcanoes. Sulfur ions. Molten ocean. Tidal heating. Circular orbit. What does this sound like?"

Against her will, Martha had found herself first listening, then intrigued, and finally involved. It was like a riddle or a word puzzle. There was a right answer to the question. Burton or Hols would have gotten it immediately. Martha had to think it through.

There was the faint hum of the radio's carrier beam. A patient, waiting noise.

At last, she cautiously said, "It sounds like a machine."

"Yes. Yes. Yes. Machine. Yes. Am machine. Am machine. Am machine. Yes. Yes. Machine. Yes."

"Wait. You're saying that Io is a machine? That you're a machine? That you're Io?"

"Sulfur is triboelectric. Sledge picks up charges. Burton's brain is intact. Language is data. Radio is medium. Am machine."

"I don't believe you."

Trudge, drag, trudge, drag. The world doesn't stop for strangeness. Just because she'd gone loopy enough to think that Io was alive and a machine and talking to her didn't mean that Martha could stop walking. She had promises to keep, and miles to go before she slept. And speaking of sleep, it was time for another fast refresher—just a quarter-hit—of speed.

Wow. Let's go.

As she walked, she continued to carry on a dialogue with her hallucination or delusion or whatever it was. It was too boring otherwise.

Boring, and a tiny bit terrifying.

So she asked, "If you're a machine, then what is your function? Why were you made?"

"To know you. To love you. And to serve you."

Martha blinked. Then, remembering Burton's long reminiscences on her Catholic girlhood, she laughed. That was a paraphrase of the answer to the first question in the old Baltimore Catechism: *Why did God make man?* "If I keep on listening to you, I'm going to come down with delusions of grandeur."

"You are. Creator. Of machine."

"Not me."

She walked on without saying anything for a time. Then, because the silence was beginning to get to her again, "When was it I supposedly created you?"

"So many a million of ages have gone. To the making of man. Alfred, Lord Tennyson."

"That wasn't me, then. I'm only twenty-seven. You're obviously thinking of somebody else."

"It was. Mobile. Intelligent. Organic. Life. You are. Mobile. Intelligent. Organic. Life."

Something moved in the distance. Martha looked up, astounded. A horse. Pallid and ghostly white, it galloped soundlessly across the plains, tail and mane flying.

She squeezed her eyes tight and shook her head. When she opened her eyes again, the horse was gone. A hallucination. Like the voice of Burton/Io. She'd been thinking of ordering up another refresher of the meth, but now it seemed best to put it off as long as possible.

This was sad, though. Inflating Burton's memories until they were as large as Io. Freud would have a few things to say about *that*. He'd say she was magnifying her friend to a godlike status in order to justify the fact that she'd never been able to compete one-on-one with Burton and win. He'd say she couldn't deal with the reality that some people were simply better at things than she was.

Trudge, drag, trudge, drag.

So, okay, yes, she had an ego problem. She was an overambitious, self-centered bitch. So what? It had gotten her this far, where a more reasonable attitude would have left her back in the slums of greater Levittown. Making do with an eight-by-ten room with bathroom rights and a job as a dental assistant. Kelp and talapia every night, and rabbit on Sunday. The hell with that. She was alive and Burton wasn't—by any rational standard that made her the winner.

"Are you. Listening?"

"Not really, no."

She topped yet another rise. And stopped dead. Down below was a dark expanse of molten sulfur. It stretched, wide and black, across the streaked orange plains. A lake. Her helmet readouts ran a thermal topography from the negative 230°F at her feet to 65°F at the edge of the lava flow. Nice and balmy. The molten sulfur itself, of course, existed at higher ambient temperatures.

It lay dead in her way.

***

They'd named it Lake Styx.

Martha spent half an hour muttering over her topo maps, trying to figure out how she'd gone so far astray. Not that it wasn't obvious. All that stumbling around. Little errors that she'd made, adding up. A tendency to favor one leg over the other. It had been an iffy thing from the beginning, trying to navigate by dead reckoning.

Finally, though, it all came together. Here she was. On the shores of Lake Styx. Not all that far off-course after all. Three miles, maybe, tops.

Despair filled her.

They'd named the lake during their first loop through the Galilean system, what the engineers had called the "mapping run." It was one of the largest features they'd seen that wasn't already on the maps from satellite probes or Earth-based reconnaissance. Hols had thought it might be a new phenomenon—a lake that had achieved its current size within the past ten years or so. Burton had thought it would be fun to check it out. And Martha hadn't cared, so long as she wasn't left behind. So they'd added the lake to their itinerary.

She had been so transparently eager to be in on the first landing, so afraid that she'd be left behind, that when she suggested they match fingers, odd man out, for who stayed, both Burton and Hols had laughed. "I'll play mother," Hols had said magnanimously, "for the first landing. Burton for Ganymede and then you for Europa. Fair enough?" And ruffled her hair.

She'd been so relieved, and so grateful, and so humiliated too. It was ironic. Now it looked like Hols—who would _never_ have gotten so far off course as to go down the wrong side of the Styx—wasn't going to get to touch rock at all. Not this expedition.

"Stupid, stupid, stupid," Martha muttered, though she didn't know if she were condemning Hols or Burton or herself. Lake Styx was horseshoe-shaped and twelve miles long. And she was standing right at the inner toe of the horseshoe.

There was no way she could retrace her steps back around the lake and still get to the lander before her air ran out. The lake was dense enough that she could almost *swim* across it, if it weren't for the viscosity of the sulfur, which would coat her heat radiators and burn out her suit in no time flat. And the heat of the liquid. And whatever internal flows and undertows it might have. As it was, the experience would be like drowning in molasses. Slow and sticky.

She sat down and began to cry.

After a time she began to build up her nerve to grope for the snap-coupling to her airpack. There was a safety for it, but among those familiar with the rig it was an open secret that if you held the safety down with your thumb and yanked suddenly on the coupling, the whole thing would come undone, emptying the suit in less than a second. The gesture was so distinctive that hot young astronauts-in-training would mime it when one of their number said something particularly stupid. It was called the suicide flick.

There were worse ways of dying.

"Will build. Bridge. Have enough. Fine control of. Physical processes. To build. Bridge."

"Yeah, right, very nice, you do that," Martha said absently. If you can't be polite to your own hallucinations…She didn't bother finishing the thought. Little crawly things were creeping about on the surface of her skin. Best to ignore them.

"Wait. Here. Rest. Now."

She said nothing but only sat, not resting. Building up her courage. Thinking about everything and nothing. Clutching her knees and rocking back and forth.

Eventually, without meaning to, she fell asleep.

"Wake. Up. Wake. Up. Wake. Up."

"Uhh?"

Martha struggled up into awareness. Something was happening before her, out on the lake. Physical processes were at work. Things were moving.

As she watched, the white crust at the edge of the dark lake bulged outward, shooting out crystals, extending. Lacy as a snowflake. Pale as frost. Reaching across the molten blackness. Until there was a narrow white bridge stretching all the way to the far shore.

"You must. Wait," Io said. "Ten minutes and. You can. Walk across. It. With ease."

"Son of a bitch," Martha murmured. "I'm sane."

✺

In wondering silence, she crossed the bridge that Io had enchanted across the dark lake. Once or twice the surface felt a little mushy underfoot, but it always held.

It was an exalting experience. Like passing over from Death into Life.

At the far side of the Styx, the pyroclastic plains rose gently toward a distant horizon. She stared up yet another long, crystal-flower-covered slope. Two in one day. What were the odds against that?

She struggled upward, flowers exploding as they were touched by her boots. At the top of the rise, the flowers gave way to sulfur hardpan again. Looking back, she could see the path she had crunched through the flowers begin to erase itself. For a long moment she stood still, venting heat. Crystals shattered soundlessly about her in a slowly expanding circle.

She was itching something awful now. Time to freshen up. Six quick taps brought up a message on her visor: *Warning: Continued use of this drug at current levels can result in paranoia, psychosis, hallucinations, misperceptions, and hypomania, as well as impaired judgment.*

Fuck that noise. Martha dealt herself another hit.

It took a few seconds. Then—whoops. She was feeling light and full of energy again. Best check the airpack reading. Man, *that* didn't look good. She had to giggle.

Which was downright scary.

Nothing could have sobered her up faster than that high little druggie laugh. It terrified her. Her life depended on her ability to maintain. She had to keep taking meth to keep going, but she also had to keep going under the drug. She couldn't let it start calling the shots. Focus. Time to switch over to the last airpack. Burton's airpack. "I've got eight hours of oxygen left. I've got twelve miles yet to go. It can be done. I'm going to do it now," she said grimly.

If only her skin weren't itching. If only her head weren't crawling. If only her brain weren't busily expanding in all directions.

324

❋

Trudge, drag, trudge, drag. All through the night. The trouble with repetitive labor was that it gave you time to think. Time to think when you were speeding also meant time to think about the quality of your own thought.

You don't dream in real-time, she'd been told. You get it all in one flash, just as you're about to wake up, and in that instant extrapolate a complex dream all in one whole. It feels as if you've been dreaming for hours. But you've only had one split second of intense nonreality.

Maybe that's what's happening here.

She had a job to do. She had to keep a clear head. It was important that she get back to the lander. People had to know. They weren't alone anymore. Damnit, she'd just made the biggest discovery since fire.

Either that, or she was so crazy she was hallucinating that Io was a gigantic alien machine. So crazy she'd lost herself within the convolutions of her own brain.

Which was another terrifying thing she wished she hadn't thought of. She'd been a loner as a child. Never made friends easily. Never had or been a best friend to anybody. Had spent half her girlhood buried in books. Solipsism terrified her—she'd lived right on the edge of it for too long. So it was vitally important that she determine whether the voice of Io had an objective, external reality. Or not.

Well, how could she test it?

Sulfur was triboelectric, Io had said. Implying that it was in some way an electrical phenomenon. If so, then it ought to be physically demonstrable.

Martha directed her helmet to show her the electrical charges within the sulfur plains. Crank it up to the max.

The land before her flickered once, then lit up in fairyland colors. Light! Pale oceans of light overlaying light, shifting between pastels, from faded rose to boreal blue, multilayered, labyrinthine, and all pulsing gently within the heart of the sulfur rock. It looked like thought made visual. It looked like something straight out of DisneyVirtual, and not one of the nature channels either—definitely DV-3.

"Damn," she muttered. Right under her nose. She'd had no idea.

Glowing lines veined the warping wings of subterranean electromagnetic forces. Almost like circuit wires. They crisscrossed the plains in all directions, combining and then converging not upon her but in a nexus at the sled. Burton's corpse was lit up like neon. Her head, packed in sulfur dioxide snow, strobed and stuttered with light so rapidly that it shone like the sun.

Sulfur was triboelectric. Which meant that it built up a charge when rubbed.

She'd been dragging Burton's sledge over the sulfur surface of Io for how many hours? You could build up a hell of a charge that way.

So okay. There was a physical mechanism for what she was seeing. Assuming that Io really *was* a machine, a triboelectric alien device the size of Earth's moon, built eons ago for who knows what purpose by who knows what godlike monstrosities, then, yes, it might be able to communicate with her. A lot could be done with electricity.

Lesser, smaller, and dimmer "circuitry" reached for Martha as well. She looked down at her feet. When she lifted one from the surface, the contact was broken, and the lines of force collapsed. Other lines were born when she put her foot down again. Whatever slight contact might be made was being constantly broken. Whereas Burton's sledge was in constant contact with the sulfur surface of Io. That hole in Burton's skull would be a highway straight into her brain. And she'd packed it in solid SO_2 as well. Conductive *and* supercooled. She'd made things easy for Io.

She shifted back to augmented real-color. The DV-3 SFX faded away.

Accepting as a tentative hypothesis that the voice was a real rather than a psychological phenomenon. That Io was able to communicate with her. That it was a machine. That it had been built…

Who, then, had built it?

Click.

"Io? Are you listening?"

"Calm on the listening ear of night. Come Heaven's melodious strains. Edmund Hamilton Sears."

"Yeah, wonderful, great. Listen, there's something I'd kinda like to know—who built you?"

"You. Did."

Slyly, Martha said, "So I'm your creator, right?"

"Yes."

"What do I look like when I'm at home?"

"Whatever. You wish. To."

"Do I breathe oxygen? Methane? Do I have antennae? Tentacles? Wings? How many legs do I have? How many eyes? How many heads?"

"If. You wish. As many as. You wish."

"How many of me are there?"

"One." A pause. "Now."

"I was here before, right? People like me. Mobile intelligent life forms. And I left. How long have I been gone?"

Silence. "How long—" she began again.

"Long time. Lonely. So very. Long time."

Trudge, drag. Trudge, drag. Trudge, drag. How many centuries had she been walking? Felt like a lot. It was night again. Her arms felt like they were going to fall out of their sockets.

Really, she ought to leave Burton behind. She'd never said anything to make Martha think she cared one way or the other where her body wound up. Probably would've thought a burial on Io was pretty damn nifty. But Martha wasn't doing this for her. She was doing it for herself. To prove that she wasn't entirely selfish. That she did too have feelings for others. That she was motivated by more than just the desire for fame and glory.

Which, of course, was a sign of selfishness in itself. The desire to be known as selfless. It was hopeless. You could nail yourself to a fucking cross and it would still be proof of your innate selfishness.

"You still there, Io?"

Click.

"Am. Listening."

"Tell me about this fine control of yours. How much do you have? Can you bring me to the lander faster than I'm going now? Can you bring the lander to me? Can you return me to the orbiter? Can you provide me with more oxygen?"

"Dead egg, I lie. Whole. On a whole world I cannot touch. Plath."

"You're not much use, then, are you?"

There was no answer. Not that she had expected one. Or needed it, either. She checked the topos and found herself another eighth-mile closer to the lander. She could even see it now under her helmet photomultipliers, a dim glint upon the horizon. Wonderful things, photomultipliers. The sun here provided about as much light as a full moon did back on Earth. Jupiter by itself provided even less. Yet crank up the magnification, and she could see the airlock awaiting the grateful touch of her gloved hand.

Trudge, drag, trudge. Martha ran and reran and rereran the math in her head. She had only three miles to go, and enough oxygen for as many hours. The lander had its own air supply. She was going to make it.

Maybe she wasn't the total loser she'd always thought she was. Maybe there was hope for her, after all.

Click.

"Brace. Yourself."

"What for?"

The ground rose up beneath her and knocked her off her feet.

When the shaking stopped, Martha clambered unsteadily to her feet again. The land before her was all a jumble, as if a careless deity had lifted the entire plain up a foot and then dropped it. The silvery glint of the lander on the horizon was gone. When she pushed her helmet's magnification to the max, she could see a metal leg rising crookedly from the rubbled ground.

Martha knew the shear strength of every bolt and failure point of every welding seam in the lander. She knew exactly how fragile it was. That was one device that was never going to fly again.

She stood motionless. Unblinking. Unseeing. Feeling nothing. Nothing at all.

Eventually she pulled herself together enough to think. Maybe it was time to admit it: She never *had* believed she was going to make it. Not really. Not Martha Kivelsen. All her life she'd been a loser. Sometimes— like when she qualified for the expedition—she lost at a higher level than usual. But she never got whatever it was she really wanted.

Why was that, she wondered? When had she ever desired anything bad? When you get right down to it, all she'd ever wanted was to kick God in the butt and get his attention. To be a big noise. To be the biggest fucking noise in the universe. Was that so unreasonable?

Now she was going to wind up as a footnote in the annals of humanity's expansion into space. A sad little cautionary tale for mommy astronauts to tell their baby astronauts on cold winter nights. Maybe Burton could've gotten back to the lander. Or Hols. But not her. It just wasn't in the cards.

Click.

"Io is the most volcanically active body in the Solar System."

"You fucking bastard! Why didn't you warn me?"

"Did. Not. Know."

Now her emotions returned to her in full force. She wanted to run and scream and break things. Only there wasn't anything in sight that hadn't already been broken. "You shithead!" she cried. "You idiot machine! What use are you? What goddamn use at all?"

"Can give you. Eternal life. Communion of the soul. Unlimited processing power. Can give Burton. Same."

"Hah?"

"After the first death. There is no other. Dylan Thomas."

"What do you mean by that?"

Silence.

"Damn you, you fucking machine! What are you trying to say?"

Then the devil took Jesus up into the holy city and set him on the highest point of the temple, and said to him, "If thou be the Son of God, cast thyself down: for it is written he shall give his angels charge concerning thee: and in their hands they shall bear thee up."

Burton wasn't the only one who could quote scripture. You didn't have to be Catholic, like her. Presbyterians could do it too.

Martha wasn't sure what you'd call this feature. A volcanic phenomenon of some sort. It wasn't very big. Maybe twenty meters across, not much higher. Call it a crater, and let be. She stood shivering at its lip. There was a black pool of molten sulfur at its bottom, just as she'd been told. Supposedly its roots reached all the way down to Tartarus.

Her head ached so badly.

Io claimed—had said—that if she threw herself in, it would be able to absorb her, duplicate her neural patterning, and so restore her to life. A transformed sort of life, but life nonetheless. "Throw Burton in," it had said. "Throw yourself in. Physical configuration will be. Destroyed. Neural configuration will be. Preserved. Maybe."

"Maybe?"

"Burton had limited. Biological training. Understanding of neural functions may be. Imperfect."

"Wonderful."

"Or. Maybe not."

"Gotcha."

Heat radiated up from the bottom of the crater. Even protected and shielded as she was by her suit's HVAC systems, she felt the difference between front and back. It was like standing in front of a fire on a very cold night.

They had talked, or maybe negotiated was a better word for it, for a long time. Finally Martha had said, "You savvy Morse code? You savvy orthodox spelling?"

"Whatever Burton. Understood. Is. Understood."

"Yes or no, damnit!"

"Savvy."

"Good. Then maybe we can make a deal."

She stared up into the night. The orbiter was out there somewhere, and she was sorry she couldn't talk directly to Hols, say good-bye and thanks for everything. But Io had said no. What she planned would raise volcanoes and level mountains. The devastation would dwarf that of the earthquake caused by the bridge across Lake Styx.

It couldn't guarantee two separate communications.

The ion flux tube arched from somewhere over the horizon in a great looping jump to the north pole of Jupiter. Augmented by her visor it was as bright as the sword of God.

As she watched, it began to sputter and jump, millions of watts of power dancing staccato in a message they'd be picking up on the surface of Earth. It would swamp every radio and drown out every broadcast in the Solar System.

THIS IS MARTHA KIVELSEN, SPEAKING FROM THE SURFACE OF IO ON BEHALF OF MYSELF, JULIET BURTON, DECEASED, AND JACOB HOLS, OF THE FIRST GALILEAN SATELLITES EXPLORATORY MISSION. WE HAVE MADE AN IMPORTANT DISCOVERY…

Every electrical device in the System would *dance* to its song.

Burton went first. Martha gave the sledge a shove and out it flew, into empty space. It dwindled, hit, kicked up a bit of a splash. Then, with a disappointing lack of pyrotechnics, the corpse slowly sank into the black glop.

It didn't look very encouraging at all.

Still...

"Okay," she said. "A deal's a deal." She dug in her toes and spread her arms. Took a deep breath. Maybe I am going to survive after all, she thought. It could be Burton was already halfway-merged into the oceanic mind of Io, and awaiting her to join in an alchemical marriage of personalities. Maybe I'm going to live forever. Who knows? Anything is possible.

Maybe.

There was a second and more likely possibility. All this could well be nothing more than a hallucination. Nothing but the sound of her brain short-circuiting and squirting bad chemicals in all directions. Madness. One last grandiose dream before dying. Martha had no way of judging.

Whatever the truth might be, though, there were no alternatives, and only one way to find out.

She jumped.

Briefly, she flew.

WILD MINDS

I met her at a businesspersons' orgy in London. The room was in the back of a pub that was all brass and beveled glass, nostalgia and dark oak. The doorkeeper hesitated when it saw how many times I'd attended in the last month. But then I suggested it scroll up my travel schedule, and it saw that I wasn't acting out a sex-addiction script, but properly maintaining my forebrain and hindbrain balances. So it let me in.

Inside, the light was dimly textured and occasionally mirrored. Friendly hands helped me off with my clothing. "I'm Thom," I murmured, and "Annalouise...Enoch...Abdul...Magdalena...Claire," those nearest quietly replied. Time passed.

I noticed Hellene not because she was beautiful—who pays attention to beauty after the first hour?—but because it took her so long to find release. By the time she was done, there was a whole new crowd; only she and I remained of all who had been in the room when I entered.

In the halfway room, we talked.

"My assemblers and sorters got into a hierarchic conflict," I told her. "Too many new faces, too many interchangeable cities."

She nodded. "I've been under a lot of stress myself. My neural mediator has become unreliable. And since I'm scheduled for an upgrade, it's not worth it running a purge. I had to offline the mediator, and take the week off from work."

"What do you do?" I asked. I'd already spotted her as being optimized.

She worked in human resources, she said. When I heard that, I asked, "Is there any hope for people like me? Those who won't accept optimization, I mean."

"Wild minds?" Hellene looked thoughtful. "Five years ago I'd've said no, open-and-shut, end of story. Period. Zero rez. Today, though…"

"Yes?"

"I don't know," she said in an anguished voice. "I simply don't know."

I could sense something significant occurring within myself, intuit some emotional sea-change organizing itself deep on the unseen levels—the planners building new concept-language, the shunts and blocks being rearranged. Of course I had no way of knowing what it was. I hadn't been optimized. Still—

"Can I walk you home?" I asked.

She looked at me for a long and silent second. "I live in Prague."

"Oh."

"We could go to your place, if it's not too far."

We took the hypermetro to Glasgow. Got off at the Queen Street Station and walked up to my flat in Renfrew Street. We talked a little on the train, but Hellene fell silent when we hit the street.

They don't like the old places, the new people, cluttered with seedy pubs and street corner hangouts, the niches where shabby men sit slumped over their whisky in paper bags, the balconies from which old women watch over the street. It unnerves them, this stench of accommodation and human dirt. It frightens them that it works so well, when it so obviously shouldn't.

"You're a Catholic," she said.

She was looking at my icon, a molecular reproduction of Ad Reinhardt's "For T.M." It's one of his black paintings, his first, and modestly small. At first it seems unvaryingly colorless; you have to stare at it for some time to see the subtle differences in the black, the thick cross that quarters and dominates that small lightless universe. He painted it for Thomas Merton, who was a monk.

My copy is a duplicate as exact as human technology can make it; more exact than human perception can distinguish. I use it as a focus for meditation. Opposite it is a Charles Rennie MacIntosh chair, high-backed. An original because it was made to his directions. Sometimes I'll sit in the one and stare at the other, thinking about distinctions, authenticity, and duplicity.

"You wouldn't need meditation if you were optimized."

"No. But the Church considers it a mortal sin, you see."

"The Church can't possibly approve of your attending orgies."

"Oh. Well. It's winked at." I shrugged. "As long as you go to confession before you take Communion..."

"What do you see when you meditate?"

"Sometimes I see comfort there; other times I see suffering."

"I don't like ambiguity. It's an artifact of the old world." She turned away from the picture. She had those chill Scandinavian features that don't show emotions well. She was beautiful, I realized with a mental start. And, almost at the same instant but twice as startling, I realized that she reminded me of Sophia.

Out of nowhere, without transition, Hellene said, "I must return to Prague. I haven't seen my children in two weeks."

"They'll be glad to see you."

"Glad? I doubt it. No more than I will be to see them," she said in the manner of one totally unable to lie to herself. "I've spun off three partials that they like considerably more than they do me. And I signed them up with Sterling International for full optimization when they were eight."

I said nothing.

"Do you think that makes me a bad mother?"

"I wanted children, too," I said. "But it didn't work out."

"You're evading the question."

I thought for a second. Then, because there was no way around it short of a lie, I said, "Yes. Yes, I do." And, "I'm going to put a kettle on. Would you like a cup?"

My grandfather used to talk about the value of a good education. His generation was obsessed with the idea. But when the workings of the human brain were finally and completely understood—largely as a result of the NAFTA "virtual genome" project—mere learning became so easy that most corporations simply educated their workforce themselves to whatever standards were currently needed. Anybody could become a doctor, a lawyer, a physicist, provided they could spare the month it took to absorb the technical skills.

With knowledge so cheap, the only thing workers had to sell was their character: their integrity, prudence, willingness to work, and hard-headed lack of sentiment. Which is when it was discovered that a dozen spiderweb-thin wires and a neural mediator the size of a pinhead would make anybody as disciplined and thrifty as they desired. Fifty cents worth of materials and an hour on the operating table would render anybody eminently employable.

The ambitious latched onto optimization as if it were a kite string that could snatch them right up into the sky. Which, in practical terms, it was. Acquiring a neural mediator was as good as a Harvard degree used to be. And—because it was new, and most people were afraid of it—optimization created a new elite.

Sophia and I used to argue about this all the time. She wanted to climb that kite string right into the future. I pointed out that it was the road to excommunication. Which shows just what a hypocrite I was. Back then I was not at all a religious man. I didn't need the comfort of religion the way I do now.

But you take your arguments where you can get them. Wild minds don't know from rational discourse. They only care about winning. Sophia was the same. We yelled at each other for hour upon hour, evening after evening. Sometimes we broke things.

Hellene drank her tea unsweetened, with milk.

We talked through the night. Hellene, of course, didn't need sleep. Normally I did, but not tonight. Something was happening within me; I could feel my components buzzing and spinning. The secondary chemical effects were enough to keep me alert. Those, and the tea.

"You seem an intelligent enough man," she said at one point, and, gesturing at the wooden floors and glass windows, "How can you live in such primitive squalor? Why reject what science has revealed about the workings of the brain?"

"I have no complaints about the knowledge *per se*." I used to have a terrible temper. I was a violent, intemperate man. Or so it seems to me now. "Learning the structural basis of emotions, and how to master them before they flush the body with adrenaline, has been a great benefit to me."

"So why haven't you been optimized?"

"I was afraid of losing myself."

"Self is an illusion. The single unified ego you mistake for your 'self' is just a fairy tale that your assemblers, sorters, and functional transients tell one another."

"I know that. But still…"

She put her cup down. "Let me show you something."

From her purse she took out a box of old-fashioned wooden matches. She removed five, aligned them all together in a bundle, and then clenched them in her hand, sulfur side down, with just the tips of the wood ends sticking out.

"Control over involuntary functions, including localized body heat," she said.

There was a gout of flame between her fingers. She opened her hand. The matches were ablaze.

"The ability to block pain."

This wasn't a trick. I could smell her flesh burning.

When the matches had burned out, she dumped them in her saucer, and showed me the blackened skin where they had been. The flesh by its edges was red and puffy, already starting to blister.

"Accelerated regenerative ability."

For five minutes she held her hand out, flat and steady. For five minutes I watched. And at the end of that five minutes, it was pink and healed. Unblackened. Unblistered.

Hellene spooned sugar into her teacup, returning to the sugar bowl at least six times before she was done. She drank down the sweet, syrupy mess with a small moue of distaste. "These are only the crude physical manifestations of what optimization makes possible. Mentally there are hardly the words. Absolute clarity of thought, even during emergencies. Freedom from prejudice and superstition. Freedom from the tyranny of emotion."

There was a smooth, practiced quality to her words. She'd said she was in human resources—now I knew she was a corporate recruiter. One salesman can always recognize another.

"Sometimes," I said carefully, "I enjoy my emotions."

"So do I—when I have them under control," Hellene said with a touch of asperity. "You mustn't judge the experience by a malfunctioning mediator."

"I don't."

"It would be like judging ecological restoration by the Sitnikov Tundra incident."

"Of course."

"Or seeing a junked suborbital and deciding that rocket flight was impossible."

"I understand completely."

Abruptly, Hellene burst into tears.

"Oh God—no. Please," she said when I tried to hold her and comfort her. "It's just that I'm not used to functioning without the mediator and so I get these damned emotional transients. All my chemical balances are out of whack."

"When will your new mediator be—?"

"Tuesday."

"Less than three days, then. That's not so bad."

"It wouldn't be, if I didn't need to see my children."

I waited while she got herself under control again. Then, because the question had been nagging at me for hours, I said, "I don't understand why you had children in the first place."

"Blame it on Berne. The Bureau des Normalisations et Habitudes was afraid not enough people were signing up for optimization. It was discovered that optimized people weren't having children, so they crafted a regulation giving serious career preference to those who did."

"Why?"

"Because people like me are necessary. Do you have any idea how complicated the world has gotten? Unaugmented minds couldn't begin to run it. There'd be famines, wars…"

She was crying again. This time when I put my arms around her, she did not protest. Her face turned to bury itself in my shoulder. Her tears soaked a damp rectangle through my shirt. I could feel their moisture on my skin.

Holding her like that, stroking her infinitely fine hair, thinking of her austere face, those pale, pale eyes, I felt the shunts and blocks shifting within me. All my emotional components wheeled about the still instant, ready to collapse into a new paradigmatic state at the least provocation. The touch of a hand, the merest ghost of a smile, the right word. I could have fallen in love with her then and there.

Which is the price one pays for having a wild mind. You're constantly at the mercy of forces you don't fully understand. For the moment I felt like a feral child standing on the twilight lands between the cultivated fields and the wolf-haunted forests, unable to choose between them.

Then, as quickly as it began, it was over. Hellene pushed herself away from me, once again in control of her emotions. "Let me show you something," she said. "Have you got home virtual?"

"I don't use it much."

She took a small device out of her purse. "This is an adapter for your set. Very simple, very safe. Give it a try."

"What does it do?"

"It's a prototype recruitment device, and it's intended for people like you. For the space of fifteen seconds, you'll know how it feels to be optimized. Just so you can see there's nothing to be afraid of."

"Will it change me?"

"All experience changes you. But this is only a magnetic resonance simulacrum. When the show's over, the lights come up and the curtains go down. There you are in your seat, just as before."

"I'll do it," I said, "if you'll agree to try out something for me afterwards."

Wordlessly, she handed me the adapter.

✺

I put on the wraparounds. At my nod, Hellene flicked the switch. I sucked in my breath.

It was as if I had shrugged off an enormous burden. I felt myself straighten. My pulse strengthened and I breathed in deep, savoring the smells of my apartment; they were a symphony of minor and major keys, information that a second ago I had ignored or repressed. Wood polish and hair mousse. A hint of machine oil from the robot floor-cleaner hiding under my bed, which only came out while I was away. Boiled cabbage from a hundred bachelor dinners. And underneath it all, near-microscopic traces of lilac soap and herbal shampoo, of *Ambrosie* and *Pas de Regret*, of ginger candies and Trinidadian rum, the olfactory ghost of Sophia no amount of scrubbing could exorcise.

The visuals were minimal. I was standing in an empty room. Everything—windows, doorknob, floor—had been painted a uniform white. But mentally, the experience was wonderful. Like standing upon a mountain top facing into a thin, chill wind. Like diving naked into an ice-cold lake at dawn. I closed my eyes and savored the blessed clarity that filled my being.

For the first time in as long as I could remember, I felt just fine.

There were any number of mental exercises I could try out. The adapter presented me with a menu of them. But I dismissed it out of hand. Forget that nonsense.

339

I just wanted to stand there, not feeling guilty about Sophia. Not missing her. Not regretting a thing. I knew it wasn't my fault. Nothing was my fault, and if it had been that wouldn't have bothered me either. If I'd been told that the entire human race would be killed five seconds after I died a natural death, I would've found it vaguely interesting, like something you see on a nature program. But it wouldn't have troubled me.

Then it was over.

For a long instant I just sat there. All I could think was that if this thing had been around four years ago, Sophia would be here with me now. She'd never have chosen optimization knowing it would be like *that*. Then I took off the wraparounds.

Hellene was smiling. "Well?" she said. She just didn't get it.

"Now it's your turn to do something for me."

For a flicker of an instant she looked disappointed. But it didn't last. "What is it?"

"It'll be morning soon," I said. "I want you to come to Mass with me."

Hellene looked at me as if I'd invited her to wallow in feces. Then she laughed. "Will I have to eat human flesh?"

It was like a breath of wind on a playing-card castle. All the emotional structures my assemblers had been putting together collapsed into nothingness. I didn't know whether I should be glad or sad. But I knew now that I would never—*could* never—love this woman.

Something of this must have showed in my expression, for Hellene quickly said, "Forgive me, that was unspeakably rude." One hand fluttered by the side of her skull. "I've grown so used to having a mediator that without it I simply blurt out whatever enters my head." She unplugged the adapter and put it back in her purse. "But I don't indulge in superstitions. Good God, what would be the point?"

"So you think religion is just a superstition?"

"It was the first thing to go, after I was optimized."

Sophia had said much the same thing, the day of her optimization. It was an outpatient operation, in by three, out by six, no more complicated than getting your kidneys regrown. So she was still working things out when she came home. By seven she'd seen through God, prayer, and the Catholic Church. By eight she had discarded her plans to have children and a lifelong love of music. By nine she'd outgrown me.

Hellene cocked her head to the side in that mannered little gesture optimized businesspeople use to let you know they've just accessed the time. "It's been lovely," she said. "Thank you, you've been so very kind. But now if you'll excuse me, I really must go. My children—"

"I understand."

"I face a severe fine if I don't see them at least twice a month. It's happened three times so far this year and quite frankly my bank account can't take it."

On the way out, Hellene noticed the portrait of Sophia by the door. "Your wife?" she asked.

"Yes."

"She's exquisite."

"Yes," I said. "She is." I didn't add that I'd killed her. Nor that a panel of neuroanalysts had found me innocent by virtue of a faulty transition function and, after minor chemical adjustments and a two-day course on anger control techniques, had released me onto the street without prejudice.

Or hope.

That was when I discovered the consolation of religion. Catholics do not believe in faulty transition functions. According to the Church, I had sinned. I had sinned, and therefore I must repent, confess, and atone.

I performed an act of true contrition, and received absolution. God has forgiven me.

Mind you, I have not forgiven *myself*. Still, I have hope.

Which is why I'll never be optimized. The thought that a silicon-doped biochip could make me accept Sophia's death as an unfortunate accident of neurochemistry and nothing more, turns my stomach.

"Good-bye," I said.

Hellene waved a hand in the air without turning around. She disappeared in the direction of Queen Street Station. I shut the door.

From Hill Street, which runs the height of Glasgow's Old City, you can stand at an intersection and look down on one side upon Charing Cross and on the other upon Cowcaddens. The logic of the city is laid clear there and although the buildings are largely Victorian (save for those areas cleared by enemy bombings in World War II, which are old modern), the logic is essentially medieval: The streets have grown as they will, in a rough sort of grid, and narrow enough that most are now fit for one-way traffic only.

But if you look beyond Cowcaddens, the ruins of the M8 Motorway cut through the city, wide and out of scale, long unused but still fringed by derelict buildings, still blighting the neighborhoods it was meant to serve. A dead road, fringed by the dead flesh of abandoned buildings.

Beyond, by the horizon, were the shimmering planes and uncertain surfaces of the buildings where the new people lived, buildings that could never have been designed without mental optimization, all tensengricity and interactive film. I'd been in those bright and fast habitats. The air *sings* within their perfect corridors. Nobody could deny this.

Still, I preferred the terraces and too-narrow streets and obsolete people you find in the old city. The new people don't claim to be human, and I don't claim that being human is any longer essential. But I cling to the human condition anyway, out of nostalgia perhaps but also, possibly, because it contains something of genuine value.

I sat in the straight-backed Charles Rennie MacIntosh and stared at the icon. It was all there, if only I could comprehend it: the dark dimensions of the human mind. Such depths it holds!

Such riches.

SCHERZO WITH TYRANNOSAUR

A keyboardist was playing a selection of Scarlotti's harpsichord sonatas, brief pieces one to three minutes long, very complex and refined, while the *Hadrosaurus* herd streamed by the window. There were hundreds of the brutes, kicking up dust and honking that lovely flattened near-musical note they make. It was a spectacular sight.

But the *hors d'oeuvres* had just arrived: plesiosaur wrapped in kelp, beluga smeared over sliced maiasaur egg, little slivers of roast dodo on toast, a dozen delicacies more. So a stampede of common-as-dirt herbivores just couldn't compete.

Nobody was paying much attention.

Except for the kid. He was glued to the window, staring with an intensity remarkable even for a boy his age. I figured him to be about ten years old.

Snagging a glass of champagne from a passing tray, I went over to stand next to him. "Enjoying yourself, son?"

Without looking up, the kid said, "What do you think spooked them? Was it a—?" Then he saw the wranglers in their jeeps and his face fell. "Oh."

"We had to cheat a little to give the diners something to see." I gestured with the wine glass past the herd, toward the distant woods. "But there are plenty of predators lurking out there—troodons, dromaeosaurs…even old Satan."

He looked up at me in silent question.

"Satan is our nickname for an injured old bull rex that's been hanging around the station for about a month, raiding our garbage dump."

It was the wrong thing to say. The kid looked devastated. *T. rex* a scavenger! *Say it ain't so.*

"A tyrannosaur is an advantageous hunter," I said, "like a lion. When it chances upon something convenient, believe you me, it'll attack. And when a tyrannosaur is hurting, like old Satan is—well, that's about as savage and dangerous as any animal can be. It'll kill even when it's not hungry."

That satisfied him. "Good," he said. "I'm glad."

In companionable silence, we stared into the woods together, looking for moving shadows. Then the chime sounded for dinner to begin, and I sent the kid back to his table. The last hadrosaurs were gone by then.

He went with transparent reluctance.

The Cretaceous Ball was our big fund-raiser, a hundred thousand dollars a seat, and in addition to the silent auction before the meal and the dancing afterwards, everybody who bought an entire table for six was entitled to their very own paleontologist as a kind of party favor.

I used to be a paleontologist myself, before I was promoted. Now I patrolled the room in tux and cummerbund, making sure everything was running smoothly.

Waiters slipped in and out of existence. You'd see them hurry behind the screen hiding the entrance to the time funnel and then pop out immediately on the other side, carrying heavily-laden trays. *Styracosaurus* medallions in mastodon mozzarella for those who liked red meat. Archaeopteryx almondine for those who preferred white. Radicchio and fennel for the vegetarians.

All to the accompaniment of music, pleasant chitchat, and the best view in the universe.

Donald Hawkins had been assigned to the kid's table—the de Cherville Family. According to the seating plan the heavy, phlegmatic man was Gerard, the money-making *paterfamilias*. The woman beside him was Danielle, once his trophy wife, now aging gracefully. Beside them were two guests—the Cadigans—who looked a little overwhelmed by everything and were probably a favored employee and spouse. They didn't say much. A sullen daughter, Melusine, in a little black dress that casually displayed her perfect breasts. She looked bored and restless—trouble incarnate. And there was the kid, given name Philippe.

I kept a close eye on them because of Hawkins. He was new, and I wasn't expecting him to last long. But he charmed everyone at the table. Young, handsome, polite—he had it all. I noticed how Melusine slouched back in her chair, studying him through dark eyelashes, saying nothing. Hawkins, responding to something young Philippe had said, flashed a boyish, devil-may-care grin. I could feel the heat of the kid's hero-worship from across the room.

Then my silent beeper went off, and I had to duck out of the late Cretaceous and back into the kitchen, Home Base, year 2082.

❋

There was a Time Safety Officer waiting for me. The main duty of a TSO is to make sure that no time paradoxes occur, so the Unchanging wouldn't take our time privileges away from us. Most people think that time travel was invented recently, and by human beings. That's because our sponsors don't want their presence advertised.

In the kitchen, everyone was in an uproar. One of the waiters was leaning, spraddle-legged and arms wide against the table, and another was lying on the floor clutching what looked to be a broken arm. The TSO covered them both with a gun.

The good news was that the Old Man wasn't there. If it had been something big and hairy—a Creationist bomb, or a message from a million years upline—he would have been.

When I showed up, everybody began talking at once.

"I didn't do *noth*ing, man, this bastard—"

"—guilty of a Class Six violation—"

"—broke my fucking *arm*, man. He threw me to the ground!"

"—work to do. Get them out of my kitchen!"

It turned out to be a simple case of note-passing. One of the waiters had, in his old age, conspired with another recruited from a later period, to slip a list of hot investments to his younger self. Enough to make them both multibillionaires. We had surveillance devices planted in the kitchen, and a TSO saw the paper change hands. Now the perps were denying everything.

It wouldn't have worked anyway. The authorities keep strict tabs on the historical record. Wealth on the order of what they had planned would have stuck out like a sore thumb.

I fired both waiters, called the police to take them away, routed a call for two replacements several hours into the local past, and had them briefed and on duty without any lapse in service. Then I took the TSO aside and bawled him out good for calling me back real-time, instead of sending a memo back to me three days ago. Once something has happened, though, that's it. I'd been called, so I had to handle it in person.

It was your standard security glitch. No big deal.

But it was wearying. So when I went back down the funnel to Hilltop

Station, I set the time for a couple hours after I had left. I arrived just as the tables were being cleared for dessert and coffee.

Somebody handed me a microphone, and I tapped it twice, for attention. I was standing before the window, a spectacular sunset to my back.

"Ladies and gentlemen," I said, "let me again welcome you to the Maastrichtian, the final age of the late Cretaceous. This is the last research station before the Age of Mammals. Don't worry, though—the meteor that put a final end to the dinosaurs is still several thousand years in the future." I paused for laughter, then continued.

"If you'll look outside, you'll see Jean, our dino wrangler, setting up a scent lure. Jean, wave for our diners."

Jean was fiddling with a short tripod. She waved cheerily, then bent back to work. With her blond ponytail and khaki shorts, she looked to be just your basic science babe. But Jean was slated to become one of the top saurian behaviorists in the world, and knew it too. Despite our best efforts, gossip slips through.

Now Jean backed up toward the station doors, unreeling fuse wire as she went. The windows were all on the second floor. The doors, on the ground floor, were all armored.

"Jean will be ducking inside for this demonstration," I said. "You wouldn't want to be outside unprotected when the lure goes off."

"What's in it?" somebody called out.

"Triceratops blood. We're hoping to call in a predator—maybe even the king of predator, *Tyrannosaurus rex* himself." There was an appreciative murmur from the diners. Everybody here had heard of *T. rex*. He had real star power. I switched easily into lecture mode. "If you dissect a tyrannosaur, you'll see that it has an extremely large olfactory lobe—larger in proportion to the rest of its brain than that of any other animal except the turkey vulture. Rex can sniff his prey"—carrion, usually, but I didn't say that—"from miles away. Watch."

The lure went off with a pop and a puff of pink mist.

I glanced over at the de Cherville table, and saw Melusine slip one foot out of her pump and run it up Hawkins' trouser leg. He colored.

Her father didn't notice. Her mother—her *step*mother, more likely—did, but didn't care. To her, this was simply what women did. I couldn't help notice what good legs Melusine had.

"This will take a few minutes. While we're waiting, I direct your attention to Chef Rupert's excellent pastries."

I faded back to polite applause, and began the round of table hopping. A joke here, a word of praise there. It's banana oil makes the world go round.

When I got to the de Chervilles, Hawkins' face was white.

"Sir!" He shot to his feet. "A word with you."

He almost dragged me away from the table.

When we were in private, he was so upset he was stuttering. "Th-that young woman, w-wants me t-to…"

"I know what she wants," I said coolly. "She's of legal age—make your own decision."

"You don't *understand!* I can't possibly go back to that table." Hawkins was genuinely anguished. I thought at first that he'd been hearing rumors, dark hints about his future career. Somehow, though, that didn't smell right. There was something else going on here.

"All right," I said. "Slip out now. But I don't like secrets. Record a full explanation and leave it in my office. No evasions, understand?"

"Yes, sir." A look of relief spread itself across his handsome young face. "Thank you, sir."

He started to leave.

"Oh, and one more thing," I said casually, hating myself. "Don't go anywhere near your tent until the fund-raiser's broken up."

❋

The de Chervilles weren't exactly thrilled when I told them that Hawkins had fallen ill, and I'd be taking his place. But then I took a tyrannosaur tooth from my pocket and gave it to Philippe. It was just a shed—rexes drop a lot of teeth—but no need to mention that.

"It looks sharp," Mrs. de Cherville said, with a touch of alarm.

"Serrated, too. You might want to ask your mother if you can use it for a knife, next time you have steak," I suggested.

Which won him over completely. Kids are fickle. Philippe immediately forgot all about Hawkins.

Melusine, however, did not. Eyes flashing with anger, she stood, throwing her napkin to the floor. "I want to know," she began, "just *what* you think you're—"

Fortunately, that was when Satan arrived.

The tyrannosaur came running up the hillside at a speed you'd have to be an experienced paleontologist to know was less than optimal. Even a dying *T. rex* moves *fast.*

People gasped.

I took the microphone out of my pocket, and moved quickly to the front of the room. "Folks, we just got lucky. I'd like to inform those of you with tables by the window that the glass is rated at twenty tons per square inch. You're in no danger whatsoever. But you are in for quite a show. Those who are in the rear might want to get a little closer."

Young Philippe was off like a shot.

The creature was almost to us. "A tyrannosaur has a hyperacute sense of smell," I reminded them. "When it scents blood, its brain is overwhelmed. It goes into a feeding frenzy."

A few droplets of blood had spattered the window. Seeing us through the glass, Satan leaped and tried to smash through it.

Whoomp! The glass boomed and shivered with the impact. There were shrieks and screams from the diners, and several people started to their feet.

At my signal, the string quartet took up their instruments again, and began to play while Satan leaped and tore and snarled, a perfect avatar of rage and fury. They chose the scherzo from Shostokovich's piano quintet.

Scherzos are supposed to be funny, but most have a whirlwind, uninhibited quality that makes them particularly appropriate to nightmares and the madness of predatory dinosaurs.

Whoomp! That mighty head struck the window again and again and again. For a long time, Satan kept on frenziedly slashing at the window with his jaws, leaving long scratches in the glass.

Philippe pressed his body against the window with all his strength, trying to minimize the distance between himself and savage dino death. Shrieking with joyous laughter when that killer mouth tried to snatch him up. I felt for the kid, wanting to get as close to the action as he could. I could identify.

I was just like that myself when I was his age.

When Satan finally wore himself out and went bad-humoredly away, I returned to the de Chervilles. Philippe had restored himself to the company of his family. The kid looked pale and happy.

So did his sister. I noticed that she was breathing shallowly. Satan does that to young women.

"You dropped your napkin." I handed it to Melusine. Inside was a postcard-sized promotional map, showing Hilltop Station and behind it

Tent City, where the researchers lived. One of the tents was circled. Under it was written, *While the others are dancing.*

I had signed it *Don.*

❋

"When I grow up I'm going to be a paleontologist," the kid said fervently. "A behavioral paleontologist, not an anatomist or a wrangler." Somebody had come to take him home. His folks were staying to dance. And Melusine was long gone, off to Hawkins' tent.

"Good for you," I said. I laid a hand on his shoulder. "Come see me when you've got the education. I'll be happy to show you the ropes."

The kid left.

He'd had a conversion experience. I knew exactly how it felt. I'd had mine standing in front of the Zallinger "Age of Reptiles" mural in the Peabody Museum in New Haven. That was before time travel, when paintings of dinosaurs were about as real as you could get. Nowadays I could point out a hundred inaccuracies in how the dinosaurs were depicted. But on that distant sun-dusty morning in the Atlantis of my youth, I just stood staring at those magnificent brutes, head filled with wonder, until my mother dragged me away.

It really was a pity. Philippe was so full of curiosity and enthusiasm. He'd make a great paleontologist. I could see that. He wasn't going to get to realize his dreams, though. His folks had too much money to allow *that.*

I knew because I'd glanced through the personnel records for the next hundred years and his name wasn't there anywhere.

It was possibly the least of the thousands of secrets I held within me, never to be shared. Still, it made me sad. For an instant I felt the weight of all my years, every petty accommodation, every unworthy expedience. Then I went up the funnel and back down again to an hour previous.

Unseen, I slipped out and went to wait for Melusine.

❋

Maintaining the funnel is expensive. During normal operations—when we're not holding fund-raisers—we spend months at a time in the field. Hence the compound, with its army surplus platform tents and electrified perimeter to keep the monsters out.

It was dark when Melusine slipped into the tent.

349

"Donald?"

"Shhh." I put a finger to her lips, drew her close to me. One hand slid slowly down her naked back, over a scrap of crushed velvet, and then back up and under her skirt to squeeze that elegant little ass. She raised her mouth to mine and we kissed deeply, passionately.

Then I tumbled her to the cot, and we began undressing each other. She ripped off three buttons tearing my shirt from me.

Melusine made a lot of noise, for which I was grateful. She was a demanding, self-centered lay, who let you know when she didn't like what you were doing and wasn't at all shy about telling you what to do next. She required a lot of attention. For which I was also grateful.

I needed the distraction.

Because while I was in his tent, screwing the woman he didn't want, Hawkins was somewhere out there getting killed. According to the operational report that I'd write later tonight, and received a day ago, he was eaten alive by an old bull rex rendered irritable by a painful brain tumor. It was an ugly way to go. I didn't want to have to hear it. I did my best to not think about it.

Credit where credit is due—Melusine practically set the tent ablaze. So I was using her. So what? It was far from the worst of my crimes. It wasn't as if she loved Hawkins, or even knew him for that matter. She was just a spoiled little rich-bitch adventuress looking for a mental souvenir. One more notch on her diaphragm case. I know her type well. They're one of the perks of the business.

There was a freshly prepared triceratops skull by the head of the bed. It gleamed faintly, a pale, indistinct shape in the darkness. When Melusine came, she grabbed one of its horns so tightly the skull rattled against the floorboards.

Afterwards, she left, happily reeking of bone fixative and me. We'd each had our little thrill. I hadn't spoken a word during any of it, and she hadn't even noticed.

T. rex wasn't much of a predator. But then, it didn't take much skill to kill a man. Too slow to run, and too big to hide—we make perfect prey for a tyrannosaur.

When Hawkins' remains were found, the whole camp turned out in an uproar. I walked through it all on autopilot, perfunctorily giving orders to have Satan shot, to have the remains sent back uptime, to have the paper-work sent to my office. Then I gathered everybody together and gave them the Paradox Lecture. Nobody was to talk about what had just happened. Those who did would be summarily fired. Legal action would follow. Dire consequences. Penalties. Fines.

And so on.

It was two a.m. when I finally got back to my office, to write the day's operational report.

Hawkins's memo was there, waiting for me. I'd forgotten about that. I debated putting off reading it until tomorrow. But then I figured I was feel-ing as bad now as I was ever going to. Might as well get it over with.

I turned on the glow-pad. Hawkins' pale face appeared on the screen. Stiffly, as if he were confessing a crime, he said, "My folks didn't want me to become a scientist. I was supposed to stay home and manage the family money. Stay home and let my mind rot." His face twisted with private memories. "So that's the first thing you have to know—Donald Hawkins isn't my real name.

"My mother was kind of wild when she was young. I don't think she knew who my father was. So when she had me, it was hushed up. I was raised by my grandparents. They were getting a little old for child-rearing, so they shipped me back-time to when they were younger, and raised me alongside my mother. I was fifteen before I learned she wasn't really my sister.

"My real name is Philippe de Cherville. I swapped table assignments so I could meet my younger self. But then Melusine—my mother—started hitting on me. So I guess you can understand now—" he laughed embar-rassedly—"why I didn't want to go the Oedipus route."

The pad flicked off, and then immediately back on again. He'd had an afterthought. "Oh yeah, I wanted to say…the things you said to me today—when I was young—the encouragement. And the tooth. Well, they meant a lot to me. So, uh…thanks."

It flicked off.

I put my head in my hands. Everything was throbbing, as if all the universe were contained within an infected tooth. Or maybe the brain tumor of a sick old dinosaur. I'm not stupid. I saw the implications immediately.

The kid—Philippe—was my son.

Hawkins was my son.

I hadn't even known I had a son, and now he was dead.

A bleak, blank time later, I set to work drawing time lines in the holographic workspace above my desk. A simple double-loop for Hawkins/Philippe. A rather more complex figure for myself. Then I factored in the TSOs, the waiters, the paleontologists, the musicians, the workmen who built the station in the first place and would salvage its fixtures when we were done with it…maybe a hundred representative individuals in all.

When I was done, I had a three-dimensional representation of Hilltop Station as a node of intersecting lives in time. It was one hell of a complex figure.

It looked like the Gordian knot.

Then I started crafting a memo back to my younger self. A carbon steel, razor-edged, Damascene sword of a memo. One that would slice Hilltop Station into a thousand spasming paradoxical fragments.

Hire him, fire her, strand a hundred young scientists, all fit and capable of breeding, one million years B.C. Oh, and *don't* father any children.

It would bring our sponsors down upon us like so many angry hornets. The Unchanging would yank time travel out of human hands—retroactively. Everything connected to it would be looped out of reality and into the disintegrative medium of quantum uncertainty. Hilltop Station would dissolve into the realm of might-have-been. The research and findings of thousands of dedicated scientists would vanish from human knowing. My son would never have been conceived or born or sent callously to an unnecessary death.

Everything I had spent my life working to accomplish would be undone.

It sounded good to me.

When the memo was done, I marked it PRIORITY and MY EYES ONLY. Then I prepared to send it three months back in time.

The door opened behind me with a click. I spun around in my chair. In walked the one man in all existence who could possibly stop me.

"The kid got to enjoy twenty-four years of life, before he died," the Old Man said. "Don't take that away from him."

I looked up into his eyes.

Into my own eyes.

Those eyes fascinated and repulsed me. They were deepest brown, and nested in a lifetime's accumulation of wrinkles. I've been working with my older self since I first signed up with Hilltop Station, and they were still a mystery to me, absolutely opaque. They made me feel like a mouse being stared down by a snake.

"It's not the kid," I said. "It's everything."

"I know."

"I only met him tonight—Philippe, I mean. Hawkins was just a new recruit. I barely knew him."

The Old Man capped the Glenlivet and put it back in the liquor cabinet. Until he did that, I hadn't even noticed I was drinking. "I keep forgetting how emotional I was when I was young," he said.

"I don't feel young."

"Wait until you're my age."

I'm not sure how old the Old Man is. There are longevity treatments available for those who play the game, and the Old Man has been playing this lousy game so long he practically runs it. All I know is that he and I are the same person.

My thoughts took a sudden swerve. "God damn that stupid kid!" I blurted. "What was he doing outside the compound in the first place?"

The Old Man shrugged. "He was curious. All scientists are. He saw something and went out to examine it. Leave it be, kid. What's done is done."

I glanced at the memo I'd written. "We'll find out."

He placed a second memo alongside mine. "I took the liberty of writing this for you. Thought I'd spare you the pain of having to compose it."

I picked up the memo, glanced at its contents. It was the one I'd received yesterday. "'Hawkins was attacked and killed by Satan shortly after local midnight today,'" I quoted. "'Take all necessary measures to control gossip.'" Overcome with loathing, I said, "This is exactly why I'm going to bust up this whole filthy system. You think I want to become the kind of man who can send his own son off to die? You think I want to become *you?*"

That hit home. For a long moment the Old Man did not speak. "Listen," he said at last. "You remember that day in the Peabody?"

"You know I do."

"I stood there in front of that mural wishing with all my heart—all *your* heart—that I could see a real, living dinosaur. But even then, even as an eight-year-old, I knew it wasn't going to happen. That some things could never be."

I said nothing.

"God hands you a miracle," he said, "you don't throw it back in his face."

Then he left.

I remained.

It was my call. Two possible futures lay side-by-side on my desk, and I could select either one. The universe is inherently unstable in every instant. If paradoxes weren't possible, nobody would waste their energy preventing them. The Old Man was trusting me to weigh all relevant factors, make the right decision, and live with the consequences.

It was the cruelest thing he had ever done to me.

Thinking of cruelty reminded me of the Old Man's eyes. Eyes so deep you could drown in them. Eyes so dark you couldn't tell how many corpses already lay submerged within them. After all these years working with him, I still couldn't tell if those were the eyes of a saint or of the most evil man in the world.

There were two memos in front of me. I reached for one, hesitated, withdrew my hand. Suddenly the choice didn't seem so easy.

The night was preternaturally still. It was as if all the world were holding its breath, waiting for me to make my decision.

I reached out for the memos.

I chose one.

THE RAGGLE TAGGLE GYPSY-O

Among twenty snowy mountains, the only moving thing was the eye of Crow. The sky was blue, and the air was cold. His beard was rimed with frost. The tangled road behind was black and dry and empty.

At last, satisfied that there was nobody coming after them, he put down his binoculars. The way down to the road was steep. He fell three times as he half pushed and half swam his way through the drifts. His truck waited for him, idling. He stamped his feet on the tarmac to clear the boot treads and climbed up on the cab.

Annie looked up as he opened the door. Her smile was warm and welcoming, but with just that little glint of man-fear first, brief as the green flash at sunset, gone so quickly you wouldn't see it if you didn't know to look. *That wasn't me, babe,* he wanted to tell her. *Nobody's ever going to hit you again.* But he said nothing. You could tell the goddamnedest lies, and who was there to stop you? Let her judge him by his deeds. Crow didn't much believe in words.

He sat down heavily, slamming the door. "Cold as hell out there," he commented. Then, "How are they doing?"

Annie shrugged. "They're hungry again."

"They're always hungry." But Crow pulled the wicker picnic hamper out from under the seat anyway. He took out a dead puppy and pulled back the slide window at the rear of the cab. Then, with a snap of his wrist, he tossed the morsel into the van.

The monsters in the back began fighting over the puppy, slamming each other against the walls, roaring in mindless rage.

"Competitive buggers." He yanked the brake and put the truck into gear.

They had the heat cranked up high for the sake of their cargo, and after a few minutes he began to sweat. He pulled off his gloves, biting the fingertips and jerking back his head, and laid them on the dash, alongside his wool cap. Then he unbuttoned his coat.

"Gimme a hand here, willya?" Annie held the sleeve so he could draw out his arm. He leaned forward and she pulled the coat free and tossed it aside. "Thanks," he said.

Annie said nothing. Her hands went to his lap and unzipped his pants. Crow felt his pecker harden. She undid his belt and yanked down his BVDs. Her mouth closed upon him. The truck rattled underneath them.

"Hey, babe, that ain't really safe."

"Safe." Her hand squeezed him so hard he almost asked her to stop. But thought better of it. "I didn't hook up with a thug like you so I could be *safe*."

She ran her tongue down his shaft and begun sucking on his nuts. Crow drew in his breath. What the hell, he figured, might as well go along for the ride. Only he'd still better keep an eye on the road. They were going down a series of switchbacks. Easy way to die.

He downshifted, and downshifted again.

It didn't take long before he spurted.

He came and groaned and stretched and felt inordinately happy. Annie's head came up from his lap. She was smiling impishly. He grinned back at her.

Then she mashed her face into his and was kissing him deeply, passionately, his jism salty on her tongue and her tongue sticky in his mouth, and he *couldn't see!* Terrified, he slammed his foot on the brake. He was blind and out of control on one of the twistiest and most dangerous roads in the universe. The tires screamed.

He pushed Annie away from him so hard the back of her head bounced off the rider-side window. The truck's front wheels went off the road. Empty sky swung up to fill the windshield. In a frenzy, he swung the wheel so sharply he thought for a second they were going to overturn. There was a hideous *crunch* that sounded like part of the frame hitting rock, and then they were jolting safely down the road again.

"God damn," Crow said flatly. "Don't you ever do that again." He was shaking. "You're fucking crazy!" he added, more emphatically.

"Your fly is unzipped," Annie said, amused.

He hastily tucked himself in. "Crazy."

"You want crazy? You so much as look at another woman and I'll show you crazy." She opened the glove compartment and dug out her packet of

Kents. "I'm just the girl for you, boyo, and don't you forget it." She lit up and then opened the window a crack for ventilation. Mentholated smoke filled the cabin.

In a companionable wordlessness they drove on through the snow and the blinding sunlight, the cab warm, the motor humming, and the monsters screaming at their back.

❋

For maybe fifty miles he drove, while Annie drowsed in the seat beside him. Then the steering got stiff and the wheel began to moan under his hands whenever he turned it. It was a long, low, mournful sound like whale-song.

Without opening her eyes, Annie said, "What kind of weird-shit station are you listening to? Can't you get us something better?"

"Ain't no radio out here, babe. Remember where we are."

She opened her eyes. "So what is it, then?"

"Steering fluid's low. I think maybe we sprung a leak back down the road, when we almost went off."

"What are we going to do about it?"

"I'm not sure there's much we *can* do."

At which exact moment they turned a bend in the road and saw a gas station ahead. Two sets of pumps, diesel, air, a Mini-Mart, and a garage. Various machines of dubious functionality rusting out back.

Crow slammed on the brakes. "*That* shouldn't be there." He knew that for a fact. Last time he'd been through, the road had been empty all the way through to Troy.

Annie finally opened her eyes. They were the greenest things Crow had ever seen. They reminded him of sunlight through jungle leaves, of moss-covered cathedrals, of a stone city he'd once been to, sunk in the shallow waters of the Caribbean. That had been a dangerous place, but no more dangerous than this slim and lovely lady beside him. After a minute, she simply said, "Ask if they do repairs."

❋

Crow pulled up in front of the garage and honked the horn a few times. A hound-lean mechanic came out, wiping his hands on a rag. "Yah?"

"Lissen, Ace, we got us a situation here with our steering column. Think you can fix us up?"

The mechanic stared at him, unblinking, and said, "We're all out of fluid. I'll take a look at your underside, though."

While the man was on a creeper under the truck, Crow went to the crapper. Then he ambled around back of the garage. There was a window there. He snapped the latch, climbed in, and poked around.

When he strolled up front again, the mechanic was out from under the truck and Annie was leaning against one of the pumps, flirting with him. He liked it, Crow could tell. Hell, even faggots liked it when Annie flirted at them.

Annie went off to the ladies' when he walked up, and by the time she came back the mechanic was inside again. She raised her eyebrows and Crow said, "Bastard says he can't fix the leak and ain't got no fluid. Only I boosted two cases out a window and stashed 'em in a junker out back. Go in and distract him, while I get them into the truck."

Annie thrust her hands deep into the pockets of her leather jacket and twisted slightly from foot to foot. "I've got a better thought," she said quietly. "Kill him."

"Say what?"

"He's one of Eric's people."

"You sure of that?"

"Ninety percent sure. He's here. What else could he be?"

"Yeah, well, there's still that other ten percent."

Her face was a mask. "Why take chances?"

"Jesus." Crow shook his head. "Babe, sometimes you give me the creeps. I don't mind admitting that you do."

"Do you love me? Then kill him."

"Hey. Forget that bullshit. We been together long enough, you must know what I'm like, okay? I ain't killing nobody today. Now go into the convenience there and buy us ten minutes, eh? Distract the man."

He turned her around and gave her a shove toward the Mini-Mart. Her shoulders were stiff with anger, her bottom big and round in those tight leather pants. God, but he loved the way she looked in those things! His hand ached to give her a swat on the rump, just to see her scamper. Couldn't do that with Annie, though. Not now, not never. Just one more thing that bastard Eric had spoiled for others.

He had the truck loaded and the steering column topped up by the time Annie strode out of the Mini-Mart with a boom box and a stack of CDs. The mechanic trotted after her, toting up prices on a little pad. When he presented her with the total, she simply said, "Send the bill to my husband," and climbed into the cab.

With a curt, wordless nod, the man turned back toward the store.

"Got any more doubts?" Annie asked coldly.

Crow cursed. He'd killed men in his time, but it wasn't anything he was proud of. And never what you'd call murder. He slammed down the back of the seat, to access the storage compartment. All his few possessions were in there, and little enough they were for such a hard life as he'd led. Some spare clothes. A basket of trinkets he'd picked up along the way. His guns.

✸

Forty miles down the road, Annie was still fuming. Abruptly, she turned and slammed Crow in the side with her fist. Hard. She had a good punch for a woman. Keeping one hand on the wheel, he half-turned and tried to seize her hands in one enormous fist. She continued hitting him in the chest and face until he managed to nab them both.

"What?" he demanded, angrily.

"You should have killed him."

"Three handfuls of gold nuggets, babe. I dug 'em out of the Yukon with my own mitts. That's enough money to keep anybody's mouth shut."

"Oh mercy God! Not one of Eric's men. Depend upon it, yon whoreson caitiff was on the phone the very instant you were out of his sight."

"You don't know that kind of cheap-jack hustler the way I do—" Crow began. Which was—he knew it the instant the words left his mouth—exactly the wrong thing to say to Annie. Her lips went thin and her eyes went hard. Her words were bitter and curt. Before he knew it, they were yelling at each other.

Finally he had no choice but to pull over, put the truck in park, and settle things right there on the front seat.

Afterwards, she put on a CD she liked, old ballads and shit, and kept on playing it over and over. One in particular made her smile at him, eyes sultry and full of love, whenever it came on.

It was upstairs downstairs the lady went
Put on her suit of leather-o
And there was a cry from around the door
She's away wi' the raggle taggle gypsy-o

To tell the truth, the music wasn't exactly to his taste. But that was what they liked back where Annie came from. She couldn't stand his music. Said it was just noise. But when he felt that smile and those eyes on him it was better than three nights in Tijuana with any other woman he'd ever met. So he didn't see any point in making a big thing out of it.

The wheel was starting to freeze up on them again. Crow was looking for a good place to pull off and dump in a few cans of fluid, when suddenly Annie shivered and sat up straight. She stared off into the distance, over the eternal mountains. "What is it?" he asked.

"I have a premonition."

"Of what?" He didn't much like her premonitions. They always came true.

"Something. Over there." She lifted her arm and pointed.

Two Basilisks lifted up over the mountains.

"Shit!"

He stepped on the gas. "Hold tight, babe. We're almost there. I think we can outrun 'em."

They came down the exit ramp with the steering column moaning and howling like a banshee. Crow had to put all his weight on the wheel to make it turn. Braking, he left the timeless lands.

And came out in Rome.

One instant they were on the exit ramp surrounded by lifeless mountains. The next they were pushing through narrow roads choked with donkey carts and toga-clad pedestrians. Crow brought the truck to a stop, and got out to add fluid.

The truck took up most of the road. People cursed and spat at him for being in their way. But nobody seemed to find anything unusual in the fact that he was driving an internal-combustion engine. They all took it in their stride.

It was wonderful how the timelines protected themselves against anachronisms by simply ignoring them. A theoretical physicist Crow had befriended in Babylon had called it "robust integrity." You could introduce the printing press into dynastic Egypt and six months later the device would be discarded and forgotten. Machine-gun the infant Charlemagne and within the year those who had been there would remember him having been stabbed. A century later every detail of his career as Emperor would be chronicled, documented, and revered, down to his dotage and death.

It hadn't made a lot of sense to Crow, but, "Live with it," the physicist had said, and staggered off in search of his great-great-five-hundred-times-great-grandmother with silver in his pocket and a demented gleam in his eye. So there it was.

Not an hour later, they arrived at the Coliseum and were sent around back to the tradesmen's entrance.

"*Ave*," Crow said to the guard there. "I want to talk to one of the—hey, Annie, what's Latin for animal-wrangler?"

"Bestiarius."

"Yeah, that's it. Fella name of Carpophorus."

Carpophorus was delighted with his new pets. He watched eagerly as the truck was backed up to the cage. Two sparsores with grappling-hooks unlatched the truck doors and leaped back as eleven nightmares poured out of the truck. They were all teeth and claws and savage quickness. One of their number lay dead on the floor of the truck. Not bad for such a long haul.

"What are they?" Carpophorus asked, entranced.

"Deinonychi."

"'Terrible-claws,' eh? Well, they fit the bill, all right." He thrust an arm between the bars, and then leaped back, chuckling, as two of the lithe young carnivores sprang at it. "Fast, too. Oh, Marcus *will* be pleased!"

"I'm glad you like 'em. Listen, we got a little trouble here with our steering column…"

"Down that ramp, to the right. Follow the signs. Tell Flamma I sent you." He turned back to the deinonychi, and musingly said, "Should they fight hoplomachi? Or maybe dimachaeri?" Crow knew the terms; the former were warriors who fought in armor, the latter with two knives.

"Horses would be nice," a sparsore commented. "If you used andabatae, they'd be able to strike from above."

Carpophorus shook his head. "I have it! Those Norse bear-sarkers I've been saving for something special—what could be more special than this?"

It was a regular labyrinth under the Coliseum. They had everything down there: workshops, brothels, training rooms, even a garage. At the mention of Carpophorus' name, a mechanic dropped everything to check out their truck. They sat in the stands, munching on a head of lettuce and watching the gladiators practice. An hour later a slave came up to tell them it was fixed.

They bought a room at a tavern that evening and ordered the best meal in the house. Which turned out to be sow's udders stuffed with fried baby mice. They washed it down with a wine that tasted like turpentine and got drunk and screwed and fell asleep. At least, Annie did. Crow sat up for a time, thinking.

Was she going to wake up some morning in a cold barn or on a piss-stained mattress and miss her goose-down comforters, her satin sheets, and her liveried servants? She'd been nobility, after all, and the wife of a demiurge…

He hadn't meant to run off with anybody's wife. But when he and some buddies had showed up at Lord Eric's estates, intent upon their own plans, there Annie was. No man that liked women could look upon Annie and not want her. And Crow couldn't want something without trying to get it. Such was his nature—he couldn't alter it.

He'd met her in the gardens out by Lord Eric's menagerie. A minor tweak of the weather had been made, so that the drifts of snow were held back to make room for bright mounds of prehistoric orchids. "Th'art a ragged fellow indeed, sirrah," she'd said with cool amusement.

He'd come under guise of a musician at a time when Lord Eric was away for a few years monkeying with the physical constants of the universe or some such bullshit. The dinosaurs had been his target from the first, though he wasn't above boffing the boss's lady on the way out. But something about her made him want her for more than just the night. Then and there he swore to himself that he'd win her, fair and without deceit, and on his own terms. "These ain't rags, babe," he'd said, hooking his thumbs into his belt. "They're my colors."

They stayed in Rome for a week, and they didn't go to watch the games, though Annie—who was born in an era whose idea of entertainment included public executions and bear-baitings—wanted to. But the deinonychi were by all accounts a hit. Afterwards, they collected their reward in the form of silver bars, "as many," Carpophorus gleefully quoted his sponsor, Marcus, as saying, "as the suspension of their truck will bear."

Marcus was a rich man from a good family and had political ambitions. Crow happened to know he'd be dead within the month, but he didn't bother mentioning the fact. Leave well enough alone, was his motto.

"Why did we wait around," Annie wanted to know afterwards, "if we weren't going to watch?"

"To make sure it actually happened. Eric can't come in now and snatch back his dinos without creating a serious line paradox. As I read it, that's considered bad form for a Lord of Creation." They were on the streets of Rome again, slowed to a crawl by the density of human traffic. Crow leaned on the horn again and again.

They made a right turn and then another, and then the traffic was gone. Crow threw the transmission into second and stepped on the accelerator. They were back among the Mountains of Eternity. From here they could reach any historical era and even, should they wish, the vast stretches of time that came before and after. All the roads were clear, and there was nothing in their way.

Less than a month later, subjective time, they were biking down that same road, arguing. Annie was lobbying for him to get her a sidecar and Crow didn't think much of that idea at all.

"This here's my *hog*, goddamnit!" he explained. "I chopped her myself—you put a sidecar on it, it'll be all the fuck out of balance."

"Yeah, well, I hope you enjoy jerking off. Because my fucking ass is so goddamn sore that..."

He'd opened up the throttle to drown out what she was about to say when suddenly Annie was pounding on his back, screaming, "Pull over!"

Crow was still braking the Harley when she leaned over to the side and began to puke.

When she was done, Crow dug a Schlitz out of the saddlebags and popped the tab. Shakily, she accepted it. "What was it?" he asked.

Annie gargled and spat out the beer. "Another premonition—a muckle bad one, I trow." Then, "Hey. Who do I have to fuck to get a smoke around here?"

Crow lit up a Kent for her.

Midway through the cigarette, she shuddered again and went rigid. Her pupils shrank to pinpricks, and her eyes turned up in their sockets, so they were almost entirely white. The sort of thing that would've gotten her burned for a witch, back in good old sixteenth-c England.

She raised a hand, pointing. "Incoming. Five of them."

They were ugly fuckers, the Basilisks were: black, unornamented two-rotor jobs, and noisy too. You could hear them miles off.

Luckily, Annie's foresight had given Crow the time to pick out a good defensive position. Cliff face to their back, rocks to crouch behind, enough of an overhang they couldn't try anything from above. Enough room to stash the bike, just in case they came out of this one alive. There was a long, empty slope before them. Their pursuers would have to come running up it.

The formation of Basilisks thundered closer.

"Pay attention, babe," Crow said. "I'm gonna teach you a little guerrilla warfare."

He got out his rifle from its saddle sheath. It was a Savage 110 Tactical. Good sniper rifle. He knew this gun. He'd packed the shells himself. It was a reliable piece of machinery.

"This here's a trick I learned in a little jungle war you probably ain't never heard of. Hold out your thumb at arm's length, okay? Now you wait until the helicopter's as big as the thumb. That's when it's close enough you can shoot it down."

"Will that work?" she asked nervously.

"Hell, if the Cong could do it, so can I."

He took out three Basilisks before the others could sweep up and around and out of range again. It was damned fine shooting if he did say so himself. But then the survivors set down in the distant snow and disgorged at least thirty armed men. Which changed the odds somewhat.

Annie counted soldiers, and quietly said, "Crow..."

Crow held a finger to her lips.

"Don't you worry none about *me*. I'm a trickster, babe. I'm archetypal. Ain't none of them can touch the Man."

Annie kissed his finger and squeezed his hand. But by the look in her eyes, he could tell she knew he was lying. "They can make you suffer, though," she said. "Eric has an old enemy staked to a rock back at his estates. Vultures come and eat his intestines."

"That's his brother, actually." It was an ugly story, and he was just as glad when she didn't ask him to elaborate. "Hunker down, now. Here they come."

The troops came scattershot up the slope, running raggedly from cover to cover. Very professional. Crow settled himself down on his elbows, and raised his rifle. Not much wind. On a day like today, he ought to be able to hit a man at five hundred yards ten times out of ten. "Kiss your asses good-bye," he muttered.

He figured he'd take out half of them before they got close enough to throw a stasis grenade.

※

Lord Eric was a well-made man, tall and full of grace. He had the glint of power to him, was bold and fair of face. A touch of lace was at his wrist. His shirt was finest silk.

"Lady Anne," he said.

"Lord Eric."

"I have come to restore you to your home and station: to your lands, estates, gracious powers, and wide holdings. As well as to the bed of your devoted husband." His chariot rested in the snow behind him; he'd waited until all the dirty work was done before showing up.

"You are no longer my husband. I have cast my fortune with a better man than thou."

"That gypsy?" He afforded Crow the briefest and most dismissive of glances. "'Tis no more than a common thief, scarce worth the hemp to hang him, the wood to burn him, the water to drown him, nor the earth to bury him. Yet he has made free with a someat trifle that is mine and mine alone to depose—I speak of your honor. So he must die. He must die, and thou be brought to heel, as obedient to my hand as my hawk, my hound, or my horse."

She spat at his feet. "Eat shit, asshole."

Lord Eric's elegant face went white. He drew back his fist to strike her.

Crow's hands were cuffed behind his back, and he couldn't free them. So he lurched suddenly forward, catching his captors and Eric by surprise, and took the blow on his own face. That sucker hurt, but he didn't let it show. With the biggest, meanest grin he could manage, he said, "See, there's the difference between you and me. You couldn't stop yourself from hurting her. I could."

"Think you so?" Lord Eric gestured and one of his men handed him a pair of grey kid gloves of finest Spanish leather. "I raised a mortal above her state. Four hundred years was she my consort. No more."

Fear entered Annie's eyes for the first time, though nobody who knew her less well than Crow could have told.

"I will strangle her myself," Eric said, pulling on the gloves. "She deserves no less honor, for she was once my wife."

The tiger cage was set up on a low dais, one focus of the large, oval room. Crow knew from tiger cages, but he'd never thought he'd wind up in one. Especially not in the middle of somebody's party.

Especially not at Annie's wake.

The living room was filled with demiurges and light laughter, cocaine and gin. Old Tezcatlipoca, who had been as good as a father to Crow in his time, seeing him, grimaced and shook his head. Now Crow regretted ever getting involved with Spaniards, however sensible an idea it had seemed at the time.

The powers and godlings who orbited the party, cocktails in hand, solitary and aloof as planets, included Lady Dale, who bestowed riches with one hand and lightnings from the other, and had a grudge against Crow for stealing her distaff; Lord Aubrey of the short and happy lives, who hated him for the sake of a friend; Lady Siff of the flames, whose attentions he had once scorned; and Reverend Wednesday, old father death himself, in clerical collar, stiff with disapproval at Crow's libertine ways.

He had no allies anywhere in this room.

Over there was Lord Taleisin, the demiurge of music, who, possibly alone of all this glittering assemblage, bore Crow no ill will. Crow figured it was because Tal had never learned the truth behind that business back in Crete.

He figured, too, there must be some way to turn that to his advantage.

"You look away from me every time I go by," Lord Taleisin said. "Yet I know of no offense you have given me, or I you."

"Just wanted to get your attention is all," Crow said. "Without any of the others suspecting it." His brow was set in angry lines but his words were soft and mild. "I been thinking about how I came to be. I mean, you guys are simply *there,* a part of the natural order of things. But us archetypes are created out of a million years of campfire tales and wishful lies. We're thrown up out of the collective unconscious. I got to wondering what would happen if somebody with access to that unconscious—you, for example—was to plant a few songs here and there."

"It could be done, possibly. Nothing's certain. But what would be the point?"

"How'd you like your brother's heart in a box?"

Lord Tal smiled urbanely. "Eric and I may not see eye to eye on everything, yet I cannot claim to hate him so as to wish the physical universe rendered uninhabitable."

"Not him. Your other brother."

Tal involuntarily glanced over his shoulder, toward the distant mountain, where a small dark figure lay tormented by vultures. The house had been built here with just that view in mind. "If it could be done, don't you think I'd've done it?" Leaving unsaid but understood: *How could you succeed where I have failed?*

"I'm the trickster, babe—remember? I'm the wild card, the unpredictable element, the unexpected event. I'm the blackfly under the saddle. I'm the ice on the O-rings. I am the *only* one who could do this for you."

Very quietly, Lord Taleisin said, "What sureties do you require?"

"Your word's good enough for me, pal. Just don't forget to spit in my face before you leave. It'll look better."

"Have fun," Lord Eric said, and left the room.

Eric's men worked Crow over good. They broke his ribs and kicked in his face. A couple of times they had to stop to get their breath back, they were laboring so hard. He had to give them credit, they put their backs into the work. But, like Crow himself, the entertainment was too boorish for its audience. Long before it was done, most of the partyers had left in boredom or disgust.

At last he groaned, and he died.

Well, what was a little thing like death to somebody like Crow? He was archetypal—the universe demanded that he exist. Kill him here-and-now and he'd be reborn there-and-then. It wouldn't be long before he was up and around again.

But not Annie.

No, that was the bitch of the thing. Annie was dead, and the odds were good she wasn't coming back.

Among twenty smog-choked cities, the only still thing was the eye of Crow. He leaned back, arms crossed, in the saddle of his Harley, staring at a certain door so hard he was almost surprised his gaze didn't burn a hole in it.

A martlet flew down from the sky and perched on the handlebars. It was a little bird, round-headed and short-beaked, with long sharp wings. Its eyes were two stars shining. "Hail!" it said.

"Hail, fire, and damnation," Crow growled. "Any results?"

"Lord Taleisin has done as you required, and salted the timelines with songs. In London, Nashville, and Azul-Tlon do they praise her beauty, and the steadfastness of her love. In a hundred guises and a thousand names is she exalted. From mammoth-bone medicine lodges to MTVirtual, they sing of Lady Anne, of the love that sacrifices all comfort, and of the price she gladly paid for it."

Still the door did not open.

"That's not what I asked, shit-for-brains. Did it work?"

"Perhaps." The bird cocked its head. "Perhaps not. I was told to caution you: Even at best, you will only have a now-and-again lady. Archetypes don't travel in pairs. If it works, your meetings will be like solar eclipses—primal, powerful, rare, and brief."

"Yeah, yeah."

The creature hesitated, and if a bird could be said to look abashed, then it looked strangely abashed. "I was also told that you would have something for me."

Without looking, Crow unstrapped his saddlebag and rummaged within. He removed a wooden heart-shaped box, tied up in string. "Here."

With a glorious burst of unearthly song, the martlet seized the string in its talons and, wings whirring, flew straight up into the sky. Crow did not look after it. He waited.

He waited until he was sure that the door would never open. Then he waited some more.

The door opened.

Out she came, in faded Levis, leather flight jacket, and a black halter top, sucking on a Kent menthol. She was looking as beautiful as the morning and as hard as nails. The sidewalk cringed under her high-heeled boots.

"Hey, babe," Crow said casually. "I got you a sidecar. See? It's lined with velvet and everything."

"Fuck that noise," Annie said and, climbing on behind him, hugged him so hard that his ribs creaked.

He kick-started the Harley and with a roar they pulled out into traffic. Crow cranked up the engine and popped a wheelie. Off they sped, down the road that leads everywhere and nowhere, to the past and the future, Tokyo and Short Pump, infinity and the corner store, with Annie laughing and unafraid, and Crow flying the black flag of himself.

THE DOG SAID BOW-WOW

The dog looked like he had just stepped out of a children's book. There must have been a hundred physical adaptations required to allow him to walk upright. The pelvis, of course, had been entirely reshaped. The feet alone would have needed dozens of changes. He had knees, and knees were tricky.

To say nothing of the neurological enhancements.

But what Darger found himself most fascinated by was the creature's costume. His suit fit him perfectly, with a slit in the back for the tail, and—again—a hundred invisible adaptations that caused it to hang on his body in a way that looked perfectly natural.

"You must have an extraordinary tailor," Darger said.

The dog shifted his cane from one paw to the other, so they could shake, and in the least affected manner imaginable replied, "That is a common observation, sir."

"You're from the States?" It was a safe assumption, given where they stood—on the docks—and that the schooner *Yankee Dreamer* had sailed up the Thames with the morning tide. Darger had seen its bubble sails over the rooftops, like so many rainbows. "Have you found lodgings yet?"

"Indeed I am, and no I have not. If you could recommend a tavern of the cleaner sort?"

"No need for that. I would be only too happy to put you up for a few days in my own rooms." And, lowering his voice, Darger said, "I have a business proposition to put to you."

"Then lead on, sir, and I shall follow you with a right good will."

❖

The dog's name was Sir Blackthorpe Ravenscairn de Plus Precieux, but "Call me Sir Plus," he said with a self-denigrating smile, and "Surplus" he was ever after.

Surplus was, as Darger had at first glance suspected and by conversation confirmed, a bit of a rogue—something more than mischievous and less than a cut-throat. A dog, in fine, after Darger's own heart.

Over drinks in a public house, Darger displayed his box and explained his intentions for it. Surplus warily touched the intricately carved teak housing, and then drew away from it. "You outline an intriguing scheme, Master Darger—"

"Please. Call me Aubrey."

"Aubrey, then. Yet here we have a delicate point. How shall we divide up the...ah, *spoils* of this enterprise? I hesitate to mention this, but many a promising partnership has foundered on precisely such shoals."

Darger unscrewed the salt cellar and poured its contents onto the table. With his dagger, he drew a fine line down the middle of the heap. "I divide—you choose. Or the other way around, if you please. From self-interest, you'll not find a grain's difference between the two."

"Excellent!" cried Surplus and, dropping a pinch of salt in his beer, drank to the bargain.

It was raining when they left for Buckingham Labyrinth. Darger stared out the carriage window at the drear streets and worn buildings gliding by and sighed. "Poor, weary old London! History is a grinding-wheel that has been applied too many a time to thy face."

"It is also," Surplus reminded him, "to be the making of our fortunes. Raise your eyes to the Labyrinth, sir, with its soaring towers and bright surfaces rising above these shops and flats like a crystal mountain rearing up out of a ramshackle wooden sea, and be comforted."

"That is fine advice," Darger agreed. "But it cannot comfort a lover of cities, nor one of a melancholic turn of mind."

"Pah!" cried Surplus, and said no more until they arrived at their destination.

At the portal into Buckingham, the sergeant-interface strode forward as they stepped down from the carriage. He blinked at the sight of Surplus, but said only, "Papers?"

Surplus presented the man with his passport and the credentials

Darger had spent the morning forging, then added with a negligent wave of his paw, "And this is my autistic."

The sergeant-interface glanced once at Darger, and forgot about him completely. Darger had the gift, priceless to one in his profession, of a face so nondescript that once someone looked away, it disappeared from that person's consciousness forever. "This way, sir. The officer of protocol will want to examine these himself."

A dwarf savant was produced to lead them through the outer circle of the Labyrinth. They passed by ladies in bioluminescent gowns and gentlemen with boots and gloves cut from leathers cloned from their own skin. Both women and men were extravagantly bejeweled—for the ostentatious display of wealth was yet again in fashion—and the halls were lushly clad and pillared in marble, porphyry and jasper. Yet Darger could not help noticing how worn the carpets were, how chipped and sooted the oil lamps. His sharp eye espied the remains of an antique electrical system, and traces as well of telephone lines and fiber optic cables from an age when those technologies were yet workable.

These last he viewed with particular pleasure.

The dwarf savant stopped before a heavy black door carved over with gilt griffins, locomotives, and fleurs-de-lis. "This is a door," he said. "The wood is ebony. Its binomial is *Diospyros ebenum*. It was harvested in Serendip. The gilding is of gold. Gold has an atomic weight of 197.2."

He knocked on the door and opened it.

The officer of protocol was a dark-browed man of imposing mass. He did not stand for them. "I am Lord Coherence-Hamilton, and this—" he indicated the slender, clear-eyed woman who stood beside him—"is my sister, Pamela."

Surplus bowed deeply to the Lady, who dimpled and dipped a slight curtsey in return.

The protocol officer quickly scanned the credentials. "Explain these fraudulent papers, sirrah. The Demesne of Western Vermont! Damn me if I have ever heard of such a place."

"Then you have missed much," Surplus said haughtily. "It is true we are a young nation, created only seventy-five years ago during the Partition of New England. But there is much of note to commend our fair land. The glorious beauty of Lake Champlain. The gene-mills of Winooski, that ancient seat of learning the *Universitas Viridis Montis* of Burlington, the Technarchaeological Institute of—" He stopped. "We have much to be proud of, sir, and nothing of which to be ashamed."

The bearlike official glared suspiciously at him, then said, "What brings you to London? Why do you desire an audience with the queen?"

"My mission and destination lie in Russia. However, England being on my itinerary and I a diplomat, I was charged to extend the compliments of my nation to your monarch." Surplus did not quite shrug. "There is no more to it than that. In three days I shall be in France, and you will have forgotten about me completely."

Scornfully, the officer tossed the credentials to the savant, who glanced at and politely returned them to Surplus. The small fellow sat down at a little desk scaled to his own size and swiftly made out a copy. "Your papers will be taken to Whitechapel and examined there. If everything goes well—which I doubt—and there's an opening—not likely—you'll be presented to the queen sometime between a week and ten days hence."

"Ten days! Sir, I am on a very strict schedule!"

"Then you wish to withdraw your petition?"

Surplus hesitated. "I...I shall have to think on't, sir."

Lady Pamela watched coolly as the dwarf savant led them away.

The room they were shown to had massively framed mirrors and oil paintings dark with age upon the walls, and a generous log fire in the hearth. When their small guide had gone, Darger carefully locked and bolted the door. Then he tossed the box onto the bed, and bounced down alongside it. Lying flat on his back, staring up at the ceiling, he said, "The Lady Pamela is a strikingly beautiful woman. I'll be damned if she's not."

Ignoring him, Surplus locked paws behind his back, and proceeded to pace up and down the room. He was full of nervous energy. At last, he expostulated, "This is a deep game you have gotten me into, Darger! Lord Coherence-Hamilton suspects us of all manner of blackguardry, "

"Well, and what of that?"

"I repeat myself: We have not even begun our play yet, and he suspects us already! I trust neither him nor his genetically remade dwarf."

"You are in no position to be displaying such vulgar prejudice."

"I am not *bigoted* about the creature, Darger, I *fear* him! Once let suspicion of us into that macroencephalic head of his, and he will worry at it until he has found out our every secret."

"Get a grip on yourself, Surplus! Be a man! We are in this too deep already to back out. Questions would be asked, and investigations made."

"I am anything but a man, thank God," Surplus replied. "Still, you are right. In for a penny, in for a pound. For now, I might as well sleep. Get off the bed. You can have the hearth-rug."

"I! The rug!"

"I am groggy of mornings. Were someone to knock, and I to unthinkingly open the door, it would hardly do to have you found sharing a bed with your master."

The next day, Surplus returned to the Office of Protocol to declare that he was authorized to wait as long as two weeks for an audience with the queen, though not a day more.

"You have received new orders from your government?" Lord Coherence-Hamilton asked suspiciously. "I hardly see how."

"I have searched my conscience, and reflected on certain subtleties of phrasing in my original instructions," Surplus said. "That is all."

He emerged from the office to discover Lady Pamela waiting outside. When she offered to show him the Labyrinth, he agreed happily to her plan. Followed by Darger, they strolled inward, first to witness the changing of the guard in the forecourt vestibule, before the great pillared wall that was the front of Buckingham Palace before it was swallowed up in the expansion of architecture during the mad, glorious years of Utopia. Following which, they proceeded toward the viewer's gallery above the chamber of state.

"I see from your repeated glances that you are interested in my diamonds, 'Sieur Plus Precieux," Lady Pamela said. "Well might you be. They are a family treasure, centuries old and manufactured to order, each stone flawless and perfectly matched. The indentures of a hundred autistics would not buy the like."

Surplus smiled down again at the necklace, draped about her lovely throat and above her perfect breasts. "I assure you, madame, it was not your necklace that held me so enthralled."

She colored delicately, pleased. Lightly, she said, "And that box your man carries with him wherever you go? What is in it?"

"That? A trifle. A gift for the Duke of Muscovy, who is the ultimate object of my journey," Surplus said. "I assure you, it is of no interest whatsoever."

"You were talking to someone last night," Lady Pamela said. "In your room."

"You were listening at my door? I am astonished and flattered."

She blushed. "No, no, my brother…it is his job, you see, surveillance."

"Possibly I was talking in my sleep. I have been told I do that occasionally."

"In accents? My brother said he heard two voices."

Surplus looked away. "In that, he was mistaken."

England's queen was a sight to rival any in that ancient land. She was as large as the lorry of ancient legend, and surrounded by attendants who hurried back and forth, fetching food and advice and carrying away dirty plates and signed legislation. From the gallery, she reminded Darger of a queen bee, but unlike the bee, this queen did not copulate, but remained proudly virgin.

Her name was Gloriana the First, and she was a hundred years old and still growing.

Lord Campbell-Supercollider, a friend of Lady Pamela's met by chance, who had insisted on accompanying them to the gallery, leaned close to Surplus and murmured, "You are impressed, of course, by our queen's magnificence." The warning in his voice was impossible to miss. "Foreigners invariably are."

"I am dazzled," Surplus said.

"Well might you be. For scattered through her majesty's great body are thirty-six brains, connected with thick ropes of ganglia in a hypercube configuration. Her processing capacity is the equal of many of the great computers from Utopian times."

Lady Pamela stifled a yawn. "Darling Rory," she said, touching the Lord Campbell-Supercollider's sleeve. "Duty calls me. Would you be so kind as to show my American friend the way back to the outer circle?"

"Or course, my dear." He and Surplus stood (Darger was, of course, already standing) and paid their compliments. Then, when Lady Pamela was gone and Surplus started to turn toward the exit, "Not that way. Those stairs are for commoners. You and I may leave by the gentlemen's staircase."

The narrow stairs twisted downward beneath clouds of gilt cherubs-and-airships, and debouched into a marble-floored hallway. Surplus and Darger stepped out of the stairway and found their arms abruptly seized by baboons.

There were five baboons all told, with red uniforms and matching choke collars with leashes that gathered in the hand of an ornately mustached officer whose gold piping identified him as a master of apes. The fifth baboon bared his teeth and hissed savagely.

Instantly, the master of apes yanked back on his leash and said, "There, Hercules! There, sirrah! What do you do? What do you say?"

The baboon drew himself up and bowed curtly. "Please come with us," he said with difficulty. The master of apes cleared his throat. Sullenly, the baboon added, "Sir."

"This is outrageous!" Surplus cried. "I am a diplomat, and under international law immune to arrest."

"Ordinarily, sir, this is true," said the master of apes courteously. "However, you have entered the inner circle without her majesty's invitation and are thus subject to stricter standards of security."

"I had no idea these stairs went inward. I was led here by—" Surplus looked about helplessly. Lord Campbell-Supercollider was nowhere to be seen.

So, once again, Surplus and Darger found themselves escorted to the Office of Protocol.

"The wood is teak. Its binomial is *Tectona grandis*. Teak is native to Burma, Hind, and Siam. The box is carved elaborately but without refinement." The dwarf savant opened it. "Within the casing is an archaic device for electronic intercommunication. The instrument chip is a gallium-arsenide ceramic. The chip weighs six ounces. The device is a product of the Utopian end-times."

"A modem!" The protocol officer's eyes bugged out. "You dared bring a *modem* into the inner circle and almost into the presence of the queen?" His chair stood and walked around the table. Its six insectile legs looked too slender to carry his great, legless mass. Yet it moved nimbly and well.

"It is harmless, sir. Merely something our technarchaeologists unearthed and thought would amuse the Duke of Muscovy, who is well known for his love of all things antiquarian. It is, apparently, of some cultural or historical significance, though without rereading my instructions, I would be hard pressed to tell you what."

Lord Coherence-Hamilton raised his chair so that he loomed over Surplus, looking dangerous and domineering. "*Here* is the historic significance of your modem: The Utopians filled the world with their computer webs and nets, burying cables and nodes so deeply and plentifully that they shall never be entirely rooted out. They then released into that virtual universe demons and mad gods. These intelligences destroyed Utopia and almost destroyed humanity as well. Only the valiant worldwide destruction of all modes of interface saved us from annihilation.

"Oh, you lackwit! Have you no history? These creatures hate us because our ancestors created them. They are still alive, though confined to their electronic netherworld, and want only a modem to extend themselves into the physical realm. Can you wonder, then, that the penalty for possessing such a device is–" he smiled menacingly—"death?"

"No, sir, it is not. Possession of a *working* modem is a mortal crime. This device is harmless. Ask your savant."

"Well?" the big man growled at his dwarf. "Is it functional?"

"No. It–"

"Silence." Lord Coherence-Hamilton turned back to Surplus. "You are a fortunate cur. You will not be charged with any crimes. However, while you are here, I will keep this filthy device locked away and under my control. Is that understood, Sir Bow-Wow?"

Surplus sighed. "Very well," he said. "It is only for a week, after all."

That night, the Lady Pamela Coherence-Hamilton came by Surplus's room to apologize for the indignity of his arrest, of which, she assured him, she had just now learned. He invited her in. In short order they somehow found themselves kneeling face-to-face on the bed, unbuttoning each other's clothing.

Lady Pamela's breasts had just spilled delightfully from her dress when she drew back, clutching the bodice closed again, and said, "Your man is watching us."

"And what concern is that to us?" Surplus said jovially. "The poor fellow's an autistic. Nothing he sees or hears matters to him. You might as well be embarrassed by the presence of a chair."

"Even were he a wooden carving, I would his eyes were not on me."

"As you wish." Surplus clapped his paws. "Sirrah! Turn around."

Obediently, Darger turned his back. This was his first experience with his friend's astonishing success with women. How many sexual adventuresses, he wondered, might one tumble, if one's form were unique? On reflection, the question answered itself.

Behind him, he heard the Lady Pamela giggle. Then, in a voice low with passion, Surplus said, "No, leave the diamonds on."

With a silent sigh, Darger resigned himself to a long night. Since he was bored and yet could not turn to watch the pair cavorting on the bed without giving himself away, he was perforce required to settle for watching them in the mirror.

They began, of course, by doing it doggy-style.

The next day, Surplus fell sick. Hearing of his indisposition, Lady Pamela sent one of her autistics with a bowl of broth and then followed, herself, in a surgical mask.

Surplus smiled weakly to see her. "You have no need of that mask," he said. "By my life, I swear that what ails me is not communicable. As you doubtless know, we who have been remade are prone to endocrinological imbalance."

"Is that all?" Lady Pamela spooned some broth into his mouth, then dabbed at a speck of it with a napkin. "Then fix it. You have been very wicked to frighten me over such a trifle."

"Alas," Surplus said sadly, "I am a unique creation, and my table of endocrine balances was lost in an accident at sea. There are copies in Vermont, of course. But by the time even the swiftest schooner can cross the Atlantic twice, I fear me I shall be gone."

"Oh, dearest Surplus!" The Lady caught up his paws in her hands. "Surely there is some measure, however desperate, to be taken?"

"Well…" Surplus turned to the wall in thought. After a very long time, he turned back and said, "I have a confession to make. The modem your brother holds for me? It is functional."

"Sir!" Lady Pamela stood, gathering her skirts, and stepped away from the bed in horror. "Surely not!"

"My darling and delight, you must listen to me." Surplus glanced weakly toward the door, then lowered his voice. "Come close and I shall whisper."

She obeyed.

"In the waning days of Utopia, during the war between men and their electronic creations, scientists and engineers bent their efforts toward the creation of a modem that could be safely employed by humans. One immune from the attack of demons. One that could, indeed, compel their obedience. Perhaps you have heard of this project."

"There are rumors, but…no such device was ever built."

"Say rather that no such device was built *in time*. It had just barely been perfected when the mobs came rampaging through the laboratories, and the Age of the Machine was over. Some few, however, were hidden away before the last technicians were killed. Centuries later, brave researchers at the Technarchaeological Institute of Shelburne recovered six such devices and mastered the art of their use. One device was destroyed in the process. Two are kept in Burlington. The others were given to trusted couriers and sent to the three most powerful allies of the Demesne—one of which is, of course, Russia."

"This is hard to believe," Lady Pamela said wonderingly. "Can such marvels be?"

"Madame, I employed it two nights ago in this very room! Those voices your brother heard? I was speaking with my principals in Vermont. They gave me permission to extend my stay here to a fortnight."

He gazed imploringly at her. "If you were to bring me the device, I could then employ it to save my life."

Lady Coherence-Hamilton resolutely stood. "Fear nothing, then. I swear by my soul, the modem shall be yours tonight."

The room was lit by a single lamp which cast wild shadows whenever anyone moved, as if of illicit spirits at a witch's Sabbath.

It was an eerie sight. Darger, motionless, held the modem in his hands. Lady Pamela, who had a sense of occasion, had changed to a low-cut gown of clinging silks, dark-red as human blood. It swirled about her as she hunted through the wainscoting for a jack left unused for centuries. Surplus sat up weakly in bed, eyes half-closed, directing her. It might have been, Darger thought, an allegorical tableau of the human body being directed by its sick animal passions, while the intellect stood by, paralyzed by lack of will.

"There!" Lady Pamela triumphantly straightened, her necklace scattering tiny rainbows in the dim light.

Darger stiffened. He stood perfectly still for the length of three long breaths, then shook and shivered like one undergoing seizure. His eyes rolled back in his head.

In hollow, unworldly tones, he said, "What man calls me up from the vasty deep?" It was a voice totally unlike his own, one harsh and savage and eager for unholy sport. "Who dares risk my wrath?"

"You must convey my words to the autistic's ears," Surplus murmured. "For he is become an integral part of the modem—not merely its operator, but its voice."

"I stand ready," Lady Pamela replied.

"Good girl. Tell it who I am."

"It is Sir Blackthorpe Ravenscairn de Plus Precieux who speaks, and who wishes to talk to..." She paused.

"To his most august and socialist honor, the mayor of Burlington."

"His most august and socialist honor," Lady Pamela began. She turned toward the bed and said quizzically, "The mayor of Burlington?"

"'Tis but an official title, much like your brother's, for he who is in fact the spy-master for the Demesne of Western Vermont," Surplus said weakly. "Now repeat to it: I compel thee on threat of dissolution to carry my message. Use those exact words."

Lady Pamela repeated the words into Darger's ear.

He screamed. It was a wild and unholy sound that sent the Lady skittering away from him in a momentary panic. Then, in mid-cry, he ceased.

"Who is this?" Darger said in an entirely new voice, this one human. "You have the voice of a woman. Is one of my agents in trouble?"

"Speak to him now, as you would to any man: forthrightly, directly, and without evasion." Surplus sank his head back on his pillow and closed his eyes.

So (as it seemed to her) the Lady Coherence-Hamilton explained Surplus's plight to his distant master, and from him received both condolences and the needed information to return Surplus's endocrine levels to a functioning harmony. After proper courtesies, then, she thanked the American spy-master and unjacked the modem. Darger returned to passivity.

The leather-cased endocrine kit lay open on a small table by the bed. At Lady Pamela's direction, Darger began applying the proper patches to various places on Surplus's body. It was not long before Surplus opened his eyes.

"Am I to be well?" he asked and, when the Lady nodded, "Then I fear I must be gone in the morning. Your brother has spies everywhere. If he gets the least whiff of what this device can do, he'll want it for himself."

Smiling, Lady Pamela hoisted the box in her hand. "Indeed, who can blame him? With such a toy, great things could be accomplished."

"So he will assuredly think. I pray you, return it to me."

She did not. "This is more than just a communication device, sir," she said. "Though in that mode it is of incalculable value. You have shown that it can enforce obedience on the creatures that dwell in the forgotten nerves of the ancient world. Ergo, they can be compelled to do our calculations for us."

"Indeed, so our technarchaeologists tell us. You must—"

"We have created monstrosities to perform the duties that were once done by machines. But with this, there would be no necessity to do so. We have allowed ourselves to be ruled by an icosahexadexal-brained freak. Now we have no need for Gloriana the Gross, Gloriana the Fat and Grotesque, Gloriana the Maggot Queen."

"Madame!"

"It is time, I believe, that England had a new queen. A human queen."

"Think of my honor!"

Lady Pamela paused in the doorway. "You are a very pretty fellow indeed. But with *this*, I can have the monarchy and keep such a harem as will reduce your memory to that of a passing and trivial fancy."

With a rustle of skirts, she spun away.

"Then I am undone!" Surplus cried, and fainted onto the bed.

Quietly, Darger closed the door. Surplus raised himself from the pillows, began removing the patches from his body, and said, "Now what?"

"Now we get some sleep," Darger said. "Tomorrow will be a busy day."

The master of apes came for them after breakfast, and marched them to their usual destination. By now Darger was beginning to lose track of exactly how many times he had been in the Office of Protocol. They entered to find Lord Coherence-Hamilton in a towering rage, and his sister, calm and knowing, standing in a corner with her arms crossed, watching. Looking at them both now, Darger wondered how he could ever have imagined that the brother outranked his sister.

The modem lay opened on the dwarf-savant's desk. The little fellow leaned over the device, studying it minutely.

Nobody said anything until the master of apes and his baboons had left. Then Lord Coherence-Hamilton roared, "Your modem refuses to work for us!"

"As I told you, sir," Surplus said coolly, "it is inoperative."

"That's a bold-arsed fraud and a goat-buggering lie!" In his wrath, the Lord's chair rose up on its spindly legs so high that his head almost bumped against the ceiling. "I know of your activities—" he nodded toward his sister—"and demand that you show us how this whoreson device works!"

"Never!" Surplus cried stoutly. "I have my honor, sir."

"Your honor, too scrupulously insisted upon, may well lead to your death, sir."

Surplus threw back his head. "Then I die for Vermont!"

At this moment of impasse, Lady Hamilton stepped forward between the two antagonists to restore peace. "I know what might change your mind." With a knowing smile, she raised a hand to her throat and denuded herself of her diamonds. "I saw how you rubbed them against your face the other night. How you licked and fondled them. How ecstatically you took them into your mouth."

She closed his paws about them. "They are yours, sweet 'Sieur Precieux, for a word."

"You would give them up?" Surplus said, as if amazed at the very idea. In fact, the necklace had been his and Darger's target from the moment they'd seen it. The only barrier that now stood between them and the merchants of Amsterdam was the problem of freeing themselves from the Labyrinth before their marks finally realized that the modem was indeed a cheat. And to this end they had the invaluable tool of a thinking man whom all believed to be an autistic, and a plan that would give them almost twenty hours in which to escape.

"Only think, dear Surplus." Lady Pamela stroked his head and then scratched him behind one ear, while he stared down at the precious stones. "Imagine the life of wealth and ease you could lead, the women, the power. It all lies in your hands. All you need do is close them."

Surplus took a deep breath. "Very well," he said. "The secret lies in the condenser, which takes a full day to recharge. Wait but—"

"Here's the problem," the savant said unexpectedly. He poked at the interior of the modem. "There was a wire loose."

He jacked the device into the wall.

"Oh, dear God," Darger said.

A savage look of raw delight filled the dwarf savant's face, and he seemed to swell before them.

"*I am free!*" he cried in a voice so loud it seemed impossible that it could arise from such a slight source. He shook as if an enormous electrical current were surging through him. The stench of ozone filled the room.

He burst into flames and advanced on the English spy-master and her brother.

While all stood aghast and paralyzed, Darger seized Surplus by the collar and hauled him out into the hallway, slamming the door shut as he did.

◉

They had not run twenty paces down the hall when the door to the Office of Protocol exploded outward, sending flaming splinters of wood down the hallway.

Satanic laughter boomed behind them.

Glancing over his shoulder, Darger saw the burning dwarf, now blackened to a cinder, emerge from a room engulfed in flames, capering and dancing. The modem, though disconnected, was now tucked under one arm, as if it were exceedingly valuable to him. His eyes were round and white and lidless. Seeing them, he gave chase.

"Aubrey!" Surplus cried. "We are headed the *wrong way!*"

It was true. They were running deeper into the Labyrinth, toward its heart, rather than outward. But it was impossible to turn back now. They plunged through scattering crowds of nobles and servitors, trailing fire and supernatural terror in their wake.

The scampering grotesque set fire to the carpets with every footfall. A wave of flame tracked him down the hall, incinerating tapestries and wallpaper and wood trim. No matter how they dodged, it ran straight toward them. Clearly, in the programmatic literalness of its kind, the demon from the web had determined that having early seen them, it must early kill them as well.

Darger and Surplus raced through dining rooms and salons, along balconies and down servants' passages. To no avail. Dogged by their hypernatural nemesis, they found themselves running down a passage, straight toward two massive bronze doors, one of which had been left just barely ajar. So fearful were they that they hardly noticed the guards.

"Hold, sirs!"

The mustachioed master of apes stood before the doorway, his baboons straining against their leashes. His eyes widened with recognition. "By gad, it's you!" he cried in astonishment.

"Lemme kill 'em!" one of the baboons cried. "The lousy bastards!" The others growled agreement.

Surplus would have tried to reason with them, but when he started to slow his pace, Darger put a broad hand on his back and shoved. "Dive!" he commanded. So of necessity the dog of rationality had to bow to the man of action. He tobogganed wildly across the polished marble floor between two baboons, straight at the master of apes, and then between his legs.

The man stumbled, dropping the leashes as he did.

The baboons screamed and attacked.

For an instant all five apes were upon Darger, seizing his limbs, snapping at his face and neck. Then the burning dwarf arrived and, finding his target obstructed, seized the nearest baboon. The animal shrieked as its uniform burst into flames.

As one, the other baboons abandoned their original quarry to fight this newcomer who had dared attack one of their own.

In a trice, Darger leaped over the fallen master of apes, and was through the door. He and Surplus threw their shoulders against its metal surface and pushed. He had one brief glimpse of the fight, with the baboons aflame, and their master's body flying through the air. Then the door slammed shut. Internal bars and bolts, operated by smoothly oiled mechanisms, automatically latched themselves.

For the moment, they were safe.

Surplus slumped against the smooth bronze, and wearily asked, "Where did you *get* that modem?"

"From a dealer of antiquities." Darger wiped his brow with his kerchief. "It was transparently worthless. Whoever would dream it could be repaired?"

Outside, the screaming ceased. There was a very brief silence. Then the creature flung itself against one of the metal doors. It rang with the impact.

A delicate girlish voice wearily said, "What is this noise?"

They turned in surprise and found themselves looking up at the enormous corpus of Queen Gloriana. She lay upon her pallet, swaddled in satin and lace, and abandoned by all, save her valiant (though doomed) guardian apes. A pervasive yeasty smell emanated from her flesh. Within the tremendous folds of chins by the dozens and scores was a small human face. Its mouth moved delicately and asked, "What is trying to get in?"

The door rang again. One of its great hinges gave.

Darger bowed. "I fear, madame, it is your death."

"Indeed?" Blue eyes opened wide and, unexpectedly, Gloriana laughed. "If so, that is excellent good news. I have been praying for death an extremely long time."

"Can any of God's creations truly pray for death and mean it?" asked Darger, who had his philosophical side. " I have known unhappiness myself, yet even so life is precious to me."

"Look at me!" Far up to one side of the body, a tiny arm—though truly no tinier than any woman's arm—waved feebly. "I am not God's creation, but Man's. Who would trade ten minutes of their own life for a century of mine? Who, having mine, would not trade it all for death?"

A second hinge popped. The doors began to shiver. Their metal surfaces radiated heat.

"Darger, we must leave!" Surplus cried. "There is a time for learned conversation, but it is not now."

"Your friend is right," Gloriana said. "There is a small archway hidden behind yon tapestry. Go through it. Place your hand on the left wall and run. If you turn whichever way you must to keep from letting go of the wall, it will lead you outside. You are both rogues, I see, and doubtless deserve punishment, yet I can find nothing in my heart for you but friendship."

"Madame…" Darger began, deeply moved.

"Go! My bridegroom enters."

The door began to fall inward. With a final cry of "Farewell!" from Darger and "Come *on!*" from Surplus, they sped away.

By the time they had found their way outside, all of Buckingham Labyrinth was in flames. The demon, however, did not emerge from the flames, encouraging them to believe that when the modem it carried finally melted down, it had been forced to return to that unholy realm from whence it came.

The sky was red with flames as the sloop set sail for Calais. Leaning against the rail, watching, Surplus shook his head. "What a terrible sight! I cannot help feeling, in part, responsible."

"Come! Come!" Darger said. "This dyspepsia ill becomes you. We are both rich fellows, now. The Lady Pamela's diamonds will maintain us lavishly for years to come. As for London, this is far from the first fire it has had to endure. Nor will it be the last. Life is short, and so, while we live, let us be jolly."

"These are strange words for a melancholiac," Surplus said wonderingly.

"In triumph, my mind turns its face to the sun. Dwell not on the past, dear friend, but on the future that lies glittering before us."

"The necklace is worthless," Surplus said. "Now that I have the leisure to examine it, free of the distracting flesh of Lady Pamela, I see that these are not diamonds, but mere imitations." He made to cast the necklace into the Thames.

Before he could, though, Darger snatched away the stones from him and studied them closely. Then he threw back his head and laughed. "The biters bit! Well, it may be paste, but it looks valuable still. We shall find good use for it in Paris."

"We are going to Paris?"

"We are partners, are we not? Remember that antique wisdom that whenever a door closes, another opens. For every city that burns, another beckons. To France, then, and adventure! After which, Italy, the Vatican Empire, Austro-Hungary, perhaps even Russia! Never forget we that have yet to present your credentials to the Duke of Muscovy."

"Very well," Surplus said. "But when we do, *I'll* pick out the modem."

SLOW LIFE

"It was the Second Age of Space. Gagarin, Shepard, Glenn, and Armstrong were all dead. It was *our* turn to make history now."

—*The Memoirs of Lizzie O'Brien*

he raindrop began forming ninety kilometers above the surface of Titan. It started with an infinitesimal speck of tholin, adrift in the cold nitrogen atmosphere. Dianoacetylene condensed on the seed nucleus, molecule by molecule, until it was one shard of ice in a cloud of billions.

Now the journey could begin.

It took almost a year for the shard of ice in question to precipitate downward twenty-five kilometers, where the temperature dropped low enough that ethane began to condense on it. But when it did, growth was rapid.

Down it drifted.

At forty kilometers, it was for a time caught up in an ethane cloud. There it continued to grow. Occasionally it collided with another droplet and doubled in size. Until finally it was too large to be held effortlessly aloft by the gentle stratospheric winds.

It fell.

Falling, it swept up methane and quickly grew large enough to achieve a terminal velocity of almost two meters per second.

At twenty-seven kilometers, it passed through a dense layer of methane clouds. It acquired more methane, and continued its downward flight.

389

As the air thickened, its velocity slowed and it began to lose some of its substance to evaporation. At two and half kilometers, when it emerged from the last patchy clouds, it was losing mass so rapidly it could not normally be expected to reach the ground.

It was, however, falling toward the equatorial highlands, where mountains of ice rose a towering five hundred meters into the atmosphere. At two meters and a lazy new terminal velocity of one meter per second, it was only a breath away from hitting the surface.

Two hands swooped an open plastic collecting bag upward, and snared the raindrop.

"Gotcha!" Lizzie O'Brien cried gleefully.

She zip-locked the bag shut, held it up so her helmet cam could read the barcode in the corner, and said, "One raindrop." Then she popped it into her collecting box.

Sometimes it's the little things that make you happiest. Somebody would spend a *year* studying this one little raindrop when Lizzie got it home. And it was just Bag 64 in Collecting Case 5. She was going to be on the surface of Titan long enough to scoop up the raw material of a revolution in planetary science. The thought of it filled her with joy.

Lizzie dogged down the lid of the collecting box and began to skip across the granite-hard ice, splashing the puddles and dragging the boot of her atmosphere suit through the rivulets of methane pouring down the mountainside. "*I'm sing-ing in the rain.*" She threw out her arms and spun around. "*Just sing-ing in the rain!*"

"Uh...O'Brien?" Alan Greene said from the *Clement*. "Are you all right?"

"*Dum-dee-dum-dee-dee-dum-dum, I'm...some-thing again.*"

"Oh, leave her alone." Consuelo Hong said with sour good humor. She was down on the plains, where the methane simply boiled into the air, and the ground was covered with thick, gooey tholin. It was, she had told them, like wading ankle-deep in molasses. "Can't you recognize the scientific method when you hear it?"

"If you say so," Alan said dubiously. He was stuck in the *Clement*, overseeing the expedition and minding the website. It was a comfortable gig—*he* wouldn't be sleeping in his suit *or* surviving on recycled water and energy stix—and he didn't think the others knew how much he hated it.

"What's next on the schedule?" Lizzie asked.

"Um...Well, there's still the robot turbot to be released. How's that going, Hong?"

"Making good time. I oughta reach the sea in a couple of hours."

"Okay, then it's time O'Brien rejoined you at the lander. O'Brien, start spreading out the balloon and going over the harness checklist."

"Roger that."

"And while you're doing that, I've got today's voice-posts from the Web cued up."

Lizzie groaned, and Consuelo blew a raspberry. By NAFTASA policy, the ground crew participated in all webcasts. Officially, they were delighted to share their experiences with the public. But the VoiceWeb (privately, Lizzie thought of it as the Illiternet) made them accessible to people who lacked even the minimal intellectual skills needed to handle a keyboard.

"Let me remind you that we're on open circuit here, so anything you say will go into my reply. You're certainly welcome to chime in at any time. But each question-and-response is transmitted as one take, so if you flub a line, we'll have to go back to the beginning and start all over again."

"Yeah, yeah," Consuelo grumbled.

"We've done this before," Lizzie reminded him.

"Okay. Here's the first one."

"*Uh, hi, this is BladeNinja43. I was wondering just what it is that you guys are hoping to discover out there.*"

"That's an extremely good question," Alan lied. "And the answer is: We don't know! This is a voyage of discovery, and we're engaged in what's called 'pure science.' Now, time and time again, the purest research has turned out to be extremely profitable. But we're not looking that far ahead. We're just hoping to find something absolutely unexpected."

"My God, you're slick," Lizzie marveled.

"I'm going to edit that from the tape," Alan said cheerily. "Next up."

"*This is Mary Schroeder, from the United States. I teach high school English, and I wanted to know for my students, what kind of grades the three of you had when you were their age.*"

Alan began. "I was an overachiever, I'm afraid. In my sophomore year, first semester, I got a B in Chemistry and panicked. I thought it was the end of the world. But then I dropped a couple of extracurriculars, knuckled down, and brought that grade right up."

"I was good in everything but French Lit," Consuelo said.

"I nearly flunked out!" Lizzie said. "Everything was difficult for me. But then I decided I wanted to be an astronaut, and it all clicked into place. I realized that, hey, it's just hard work. And now, well, here I am."

"That's good. Thanks, guys. Here's the third, from Maria Vasquez."

"Is there life on Titan?"

"Probably not. It's *cold* down there! 94° Kelvin is the same as -179° Celsius, or -290° Fahrenheit. And yet...life is persistent. It's been found in Antarctic ice and in boiling water in submarine volcanic vents. Which is why we'll be paying particular attention to exploring the depths of the ethane-methane sea. If life is anywhere to be found, that's where we'll find it."

"Chemically, the conditions here resemble the anoxic atmosphere on Earth in which life first arose," Consuelo said. "Further, we believe that such pre-biotic chemistry has been going on here for four and a half billion years. For an organic chemist like me, it's the best toy box in the universe. But that lack of heat is a problem. Chemical reactions that occur quickly back home would take thousands of years here. It's hard to see how life could arise under such a handicap."

"It would have to be slow life," Lizzie said thoughtfully. "Something vegetative. 'Vaster than empires and more slow.' It would take millions of years to reach maturity. A single thought might require centuries...."

"Thank you for that, uh, wild scenario!" Alan said quickly. Their NAFTASA masters frowned on speculation. It was, in their estimation, almost as unprofessional as heroism. "This next question comes from Danny in Toronto."

"Hey, man, I gotta say I really envy you being in that tiny little ship with those two hot babes."

Alan laughed lightly. "Yes, Ms. Hong and Ms. O'Brien are certainly attractive women. But we're kept so busy that, believe it or not, the thought of sex never comes up. And currently, while I tend to the *Clement*, they're both on the surface of Titan at the bottom of an atmosphere sixty percent more dense than Earth's, and encased in armored exploration suits. So even if I did have inappropriate thoughts, there's no way we could..."

"Hey, Alan," Lizzie said. "Tell me something."

"Yes?"

"What are you wearing?"

"Uh...Switching over to private channel."

"Make that a three-way," Consuelo said.

Ballooning, Lizzie decided, was the best way there was of getting around. Moving with the gentle winds, there was no sound at all. And the view was great!

People talked a lot about the "murky orange atmosphere" of Titan, but your eyes adjusted. Turn up the gain on your helmet, and the white mountains of ice were *dazzling!* The methane streams carved cryptic runes into the heights. Then, at the tholin-line, white turned to a rich palette of oranges, reds, and yellows. There was a lot going on down there—more than she'd be able to learn in a hundred visits.

The plains were superficially duller, but they had their charms as well. Sure, the atmosphere was so dense that refracted light made the horizon curve upward to either side. But you got used to it. The black swirls and cryptic red tracery of unknown processes on the land below never grew tiring.

On the horizon, she saw the dark arm of Titan's narrow sea. If that was what it was. Lake Erie was larger, but the spin doctors back home had argued that since Titan was so much smaller than earth, *relatively* it qualified as a sea. Lizzie had her own opinion, but she knew when to keep her mouth shut.

Consuelo was there now. Lizzie switched her visor over to the live feed. Time to catch the show.

✸

"I can't believe I'm finally here," Consuelo said. She let the shrink-wrapped fish slide from her shoulder down to the ground. "Five kilometers doesn't seem like very far when you're coming down from orbit—just enough to leave a margin for error so the lander doesn't come down in the sea. But when you have to *walk* that distance, through tarry, sticky tholin…well, it's one heck of a slog."

"Consuelo, can you tell us what it's like there?" Alan asked.

"I'm crossing the beach. Now I'm at the edge of the sea." She knelt, dipped a hand into it. "It's got the consistency of a Slushy. Are you familiar with that drink? Lots of shaved ice sort of half-melted in a cup with flavored syrup. What we've got here is almost certainly a methane-ammonia mix; we'll know for sure after we get a sample to a laboratory. Here's an early indicator, though. It's dissolving the tholin off my glove." She stood.

"Can you describe the beach?"

"Yeah. It's white. Granular. I can kick it with my boot. Ice sand for sure. Do you want me to collect samples first or release the fish?"

"Release the fish," Lizzie said, almost simultaneously with Alan's "Your call."

"Okay, then." Consuelo carefully cleaned both of her suit's gloves in the sea, then seized the shrink-wrap's zip tab and yanked. The plastic parted. Awkwardly, she straddled the fish, lifted it by the two side-handles, and walked it into the dark slush.

"Okay, I'm standing in the sea now. It's up to my ankles. Now it's at my knees. I think it's deep enough here."

She set the fish down. "Now I'm turning it on."

The Mitsubishi turbot wriggled, as if alive. With one fluid motion, it surged forward, plunged, and was gone.

Lizzie switched over to the fishcam.

Black liquid flashed past the turbot's infrared eyes. Straight away from the shore it swam, seeing nothing but flecks of paraffin, ice, and other suspended particulates as they loomed up before it and were swept away in the violence of its wake. A hundred meters out, it bounced a pulse of radar off the sea floor, then dove, seeking the depths.

Rocking gently in her balloon harness, Lizzie yawned.

Snazzy Japanese cybernetics took in a minute sample of the ammonia-water, fed it through a deftly constructed internal laboratory, and excreted the waste products behind it. "We're at twenty meters now," Consuelo said. "Time to collect a second sample."

The turbot was equipped to run hundreds of on-the-spot analyses. But it had only enough space for twenty permanent samples to be carried back home. The first sample had been nibbled from the surface slush. Now it twisted, and gulped down five drams of sea fluid in all its glorious impurity. To Lizzie, this was science on the hoof. Not very dramatic, admittedly, but intensely exciting.

She yawned again.

"O'Brien?" Alan said. "How long has it been since you last slept?"

"Huh? Oh...twenty hours? Don't worry about me, I'm fine."

"Go to sleep. That's an order."

"But—"

"Now."

Fortunately, the suit was comfortable enough to sleep in. It had been designed so she could.

First she drew in her arms from the suit's sleeves. Then she brought in her legs, tucked them up under her chin, and wrapped her arms around them. "'Night, guys," she said.

"*Buenas noches, querida,*" Consuelo said, "*que tengas lindos sueños.*"

"Sleep tight, space explorer."

The darkness when she closed her eyes was so absolute it crawled. Black, black, black. Phantom lights moved within the darkness, formed lines, shifted away when she tried to see them. They were as fugitive as fish, luminescent, fainter than faint, there and with a flick of her attention fled.

A school of little thoughts flashed through her mind, silver-scaled and gone.

Low, deep, slower than sound, something tolled. The bell from a drowned clock tower patiently stroking midnight. She was beginning to get her bearings. Down *there* was where the ground must be. Flowers grew there unseen. Up above was where the sky would be, if there were a sky. Flowers floated there as well.

Deep within the submerged city, she found herself overcome by an enormous and placid sense of self. A swarm of unfamiliar sensations washed through her mind, and then...

"Are you me?" a gentle voice asked.

"No," she said carefully. "I don't think so."

Vast astonishment. "You think you are not me?"

"Yes. I think so, anyway."

"Why?"

There didn't seem to be any proper response to that, so she went back to the beginning of the conversation and ran through it again, trying to bring it to another conclusion. Only to bump against that "Why?" once again.

"I don't know why," she said.

"Why not?"

"I don't know."

She looped through that same dream over and over again all the while that she slept.

When she awoke, it was raining again. This time, it was a drizzle of pure methane from the lower cloud deck at fifteen kilometers. These clouds were (the theory went) methane condensate from the wet air swept up from the sea. They fell on the mountains and washed them clean of tholin. It was the methane that eroded and shaped the ice, carving gullies and caves.

Titan had more kinds of rain than anywhere else in the solar system.

The sea had crept closer while Lizzie slept. It now curled up to the horizon on either side like an enormous dark smile. Almost time now for her to begin her descent. While she checked her harness settings, she flicked on telemetry to see what the others were up to.

The robot turbot was still spiraling its way downward, through the lightless sea, seeking its distant floor. Consuelo was trudging through the tholin again, retracing her five-kilometer trek from the lander *Harry Stubbs*, and Alan was answering another set of webposts.

"*Modelos de la evolución de Titanes indican que la luna formó de una nube circumplanetaria rica en amoníaco y metano, la cual al condensarse dio forma a Saturno así como a otros satélites. Bajo estas condiciones en—*"

"Uh...guys?"

Alan stopped. "Damn it, O'Brien, now I've got to start all over again."

"Welcome back to the land of the living," Consuelo said. "You should check out the readings we're getting from the robofish. Lots of long-chain polymers, odd fractions...tons of interesting stuff."

"Guys?"

This time her tone of voice registered with Alan. "What is it, O'Brien?"

"I think my harness is jammed."

Lizzie had never dreamed disaster could be such drudgery. First there were hours of back-and-forth with the NAFTASA engineers. What's the status of rope 14? Try tugging on rope 8. What do the D-rings look like? It was slow work because of the lag time for messages to be relayed to Earth and back. And Alan insisted on filling the silence with posts from the VoiceWeb. Her plight had gone global in minutes, and every unemployable loser on the planet had to log in with suggestions.

"*Thezgemoth337, here. It seems to me that if you had a gun and shot up through the balloon, it would maybe deflate and then you could get down.*"

"I don't have a gun, shooting a hole in the balloon would cause it not to deflate but to rupture, I'm 800 meters above the surface, there's a sea below me, and I'm in a suit that's not equipped for swimming. Next."

"*If you had a really big knife—*"

"Cut! Jesus, Greene, is this the best you can find? Have you heard back from the organic chem guys yet?"

"Their preliminary analysis just came in," Alan said. "As best they can guess—and I'm cutting through a lot of clutter here—the rain you went through wasn't pure methane."

"No shit, Sherlock."

"They're assuming that whitish deposit you found on the rings and ropes is your culprit. They can't agree on what it is, but they think it underwent a chemical reaction with the material of your balloon and sealed the rip panel shut."

"I thought this was supposed to be a pretty nonreactive environment."

"It is. But your balloon runs off your suit's waste heat. The air in it is several degrees above the melting point of ice. That's the equivalent of a blast furnace, here on Titan. Enough energy to run any number of amazing reactions. You haven't stopped tugging on the vent rope?"

"I'm tugging away right now. When one arm gets sore, I switch arms."

"Good girl. I know how tired you must be."

"Take a break from the voice-posts," Consuelo suggested, "and check out the results we're getting from the robofish. It's giving us some really interesting stuff."

So she did. And for a time it distracted her, just as they'd hoped. There was a lot more ethane and propane than their models had predicted, and surprisingly less methane. The mix of fractions was nothing like what she'd expected. She had just enough chemistry to guess at some of the implications of the data being generated, but not enough to put it all together. Still tugging at the ropes in the sequence uploaded by the engineers in Toronto, she scrolled up the chart of hydrocarbons dissolved in the lake.

SoluteSolute	mole fraction
Ethyne	4.0×10^{-4}
Propyne	4.4×10^{-5}
1,3-Butadiyne	7.7×10^{-7}
Carbon Dioxide	0.1×10^{-5}
Methanenitrile	5.7×10^{-6}

But after a while, the experience of working hard and getting nowhere, combined with the tedium of floating farther and farther out over the featureless sea, began to drag on her. The columns of figures grew meaningless, then indistinct.

Propanenitrile	6.0×10^{-5}
Propenenitrile	9.9×10^{-6}
Propynenitrile	5.3×10^{-6}

Hardly noticing she was doing so, she fell asleep.

She was in a lightless building, climbing flight after flight of stairs. There were other people with her, also climbing. They jostled against her as she ran up the stairs, flowing upward, passing her, not talking.

It was getting colder.

She had a distant memory of being in the furnace room down below. It was hot there, swelteringly so. Much cooler where she was now. Almost too cool. With every step she took, it got a little cooler still. She found herself slowing down. Now it was definitely too cold. Unpleasantly so. Her leg muscles ached. The air seemed to be thickening around her as well. She could barely move now.

This was, she realized, the natural consequence of moving away from the furnace. The higher up she got, the less heat there was to be had, and the less energy to be turned into motion. It all made perfect sense to her somehow.

Step. Pause.

Step. Longer pause.

Stop.

The people around her had slowed to a stop as well. A breeze colder than ice touched her, and without surprise, she knew that they had reached the top of the stairs and were standing upon the building's roof. It was as dark without as it had been within. She stared upward and saw nothing.

"Horizons. Absolutely baffling," somebody murmured beside her.

"Not once you get used to them," she replied.

"Up and down—are these hierarchic values?"

"They don't have to be."

"Motion. What a delightful concept."

"We like it."

"So you *are* me?"

"No. I mean, I don't think so."

"Why?"

She was struggling to find an answer to this, when somebody gasped. High up in the starless, featureless sky, a light bloomed. The crowd around her rustled with unspoken fear. Brighter, the light grew. Brighter still. She could feel heat radiating from it, slight but definite, like the rumor of a distant sun. Everyone about her was frozen with horror. More terrifying than a light where none was possible was the presence of heat. It simply could not be. And yet it was.

She, along with the others, waited and watched for...something. She could not say what. The light shifted slowly in the sky. It was small, intense, ugly.

Then the light *screamed*.

She woke up.

"Wow," she said. "I just had the weirdest dream."

"Did you?" Alan said casually.

"Yeah. There was this light in the sky. It was like a nuclear bomb or something. I mean, it didn't look anything like a nuclear bomb, but it was terrifying the way a nuclear bomb would be. Everybody was staring at it. We couldn't move. And then..." She shook her head. "I lost it. I'm sorry. It was just so strange. I can't put it into words."

"Never mind that," Consuelo said cheerily. "We're getting some great readings down below the surface. Fractional polymers, long-chain hydrocarbons...Fabulous stuff. You really should try to stay awake to catch some of this."

She was fully awake now, and not feeling too happy about it. "I guess that means that nobody's come up with any good ideas yet on how I might get down."

"Uh...what do you mean?"

"Because if they had, you wouldn't be so goddamned upbeat, would you?"

"*Some*body woke up on the wrong side of the bed," Alan said. "Please remember that there are certain words we don't use in public."

"I'm sorry," Consuelo said. "I was just trying to—"

"—distract me. Okay, fine. What the hey. I can play along." Lizzie pulled herself together. "So your findings mean...what? Life?"

"I keep telling you guys. It's too early to make that kind of determination. What we've got so far are just some very, very interesting readings."

"Tell her the big news," Alan said.

"Brace yourself. We've got a real ocean! Not this tiny little two-hundred-by-fifty-miles glorified lake we've been calling a sea, but a genuine ocean! Sonar readings show that what we see is just an evaporation pan atop a thirty-kilometer-thick cap of ice. The real ocean lies underneath, two hundred kilometers deep."

"Jesus." Lizzie caught herself. "I mean, gee whiz. Is there any way of getting the robofish down into it?"

"How do you think we got the depth readings? It's headed down there right now. There's a chimney through the ice right at the center of the visible sea. That's what replenishes the surface liquid. And directly under the hole there's—guess what?—volcanic vents!"

"So does that mean–?"

"If you use the L-word again," Consuelo said, "I'll spit."

Lizzie grinned. *That* was the Consuelo Hong she knew. "What about the tidal data? I thought the lack of orbital perturbation ruled out a significant ocean entirely."

"Well, Toronto thinks…"

At first, Lizzie was able to follow the reasoning of the planetary geologists back in Toronto. Then it got harder. Then it became a drone. As she drifted off into sleep, she had time enough to be peevishly aware that she really shouldn't be dropping off to sleep all the time like this. She oughtn't to be so tired. She…

She found herself in the drowned city again. She still couldn't see anything, but she knew it was a city because she could hear the sound of rioters smashing store windows. Their voices swelled into howling screams and receded into angry mutters, like a violent surf washing through the streets. She began to edge away backwards.

Somebody spoke into her ear.

"Why did you do this to us?"

"I didn't do anything to you."

"You brought us knowledge."

"What knowledge?"

"You said you were not us."

"Well, I'm not."

"You should never have told us that."

"You wanted me to lie?"

Horrified confusion. "Falsehood. What a distressing idea."

The smashing noises were getting louder. Somebody was splintering a door with an axe. Explosions. Breaking glass. She heard wild laughter. Shrieks. "We've got to get out of here."

"Why did you send the messenger?"

"What messenger?"

"The star! The star! The star!"

"Which star?"

"There are two stars?"

"There are billions of stars."

"No more! Please! Stop! No more!"

She was awake.

"Hello, yes, I appreciate that the young lady is in extreme danger, but I really don't think she should have used the Lord's name in vain."

"Greene," Lizzie said, "do we really have to put up with this?"

"Well, considering how many billions of public-sector dollars it took to bring us here…yes. Yes, we do. I can even think of a few backup astronauts who would say that a little upbeat webposting was a pretty small price to pay for the privilege."

"Oh, barf."

"I'm switching to a private channel," Alan said calmly. The background radiation changed subtly. A faint, granular crackling that faded away when she tried to focus on it. In a controlled, angry voice Alan said, "O'Brien, just what the hell is going on with you?"

"Look, I'm sorry, I apologize, I'm a little excited about something. How long was I out? Where's Consuelo? I'm going to say the L-word. And the I-word as well. We have life. Intelligent life!"

"It's been a few hours. Consuelo is sleeping. O'Brien, I hate to say this, but you're not sounding at all rational."

"There's a perfectly logical reason for that. Okay, it's a little strange, and maybe it won't sound perfectly logical to you initially, but…look, I've been having sequential dreams. I think they're significant. Let me tell you about them."

And she did so. At length.

When she was done, there was a long silence. Finally, Alan said, "Lizzie, think. Why would something like that communicate to you in your dreams? Does that make any sense?"

"I think it's the only way it can. I think it's how it communicates among itself. It doesn't move—motion is an alien and delightful concept to it—and it wasn't aware that its component parts were capable of individualization. That sounds like some kind of broadcast thought to me. Like some kind of wireless distributed network."

"You know the medical kit in your suit? I want you to open it up. Feel around for the bottle that's braille-coded twenty-seven, okay?"

"Alan, I do *not* need an antipsychotic!"

"I'm not saying you need it. But wouldn't you be happier knowing you had it in you?" This was Alan at his smoothest. Butter wouldn't melt in his mouth. "Don't you think that would help us accept what you're saying?"

"Oh, all right!" She drew in an arm from the suit's arm, felt around for the med kit, and drew out a pill, taking every step by the regs, checking the coding four times before she put it in her mouth and once more (each pill was individually braille-coded as well) before she swallowed it. "Now will you listen to me? I'm quite serious about this." She yawned. "I really do think that…" She yawned again. "That…

"Oh, piffle."

Once more into the breach, dear friends, she thought, and plunged deep, deep into the sea of darkness. This time, though, she felt she had a handle on it. The city was drowned because it existed at the bottom of a lightless ocean. It was alive, and it fed off of volcanic heat. That was why it considered up and down hierarchic values. Up was colder, slower, less alive. Down was hotter, faster, more filled with thought. The city/entity was a collective life form, like a Portuguese man-of-war or a massively hyperlinked expert network. It communicated within itself by some form of electromagnetism. Call it mental radio. It communicated with her that same way.

"I think I understand you now."

"Don't understand—run!"

Somebody impatiently seized her elbow and hurried her along. Faster she went, and faster. She couldn't see a thing. It was like running down a lightless tunnel a hundred miles underground at midnight. Glass crunched underfoot. The ground was uneven and sometimes she stumbled. Whenever she did, her unseen companion yanked her up again.

"Why are you so slow?"

"I didn't know I was."

"Believe me, you are."

"Why are we running?"

"We are being pursued." They turned suddenly, into a side passage, and were jolting over rubbled ground. Sirens wailed. Things collapsed. Mobs surged.

"Well, you've certainly got the motion thing down pat."

Impatiently: "It's only a metaphor. You don't think this is a *real* city, do you? Why are you so dim? Why are you so difficult to communicate with? Why are you so slow?"

"I didn't know I was."

Vast irony. "Believe me, you are."

"What can I do?"

"Run!"

Whooping and laughter. At first, Lizzie confused it with the sounds of mad destruction in her dream. Then she recognized the voices as belonging to Alan and Consuelo. "How long was I out?" she asked.

"You were out?"

"No more than a minute or two," Alan said. "It's not important. Check out the visual the robofish just gave us."

Consuelo squirted the image to Lizzie.

Lizzie gasped. "Oh! Oh, my."

It was beautiful. Beautiful in the way that the great European cathedrals were, and yet at the same time undeniably organic. The structure was tall and slender, and fluted and buttressed and absolutely ravishing. It had grown about a volcanic vent, with openings near the bottom to let sea water in, and then followed the rising heat upward. Occasional channels led outward and then looped back into the main body again. It loomed higher than seemed possible (but it *was* underwater, of course, and on a low-gravity world at that), a complexly layered congeries of tubes like church-organ pipes, or deep-sea worms lovingly intertwined.

It had the elegance of design that only a living organism can have.

"Okay," Lizzie said. "Consuelo. You've got to admit that—"

"I'll go as far as 'complex pre-biotic chemistry.' Anything more than that is going to have to wait for more definite readings." Cautious as her words were, Consuelo's voice rang with triumph. It said, clearer than words, that she could happily die then and there, a satisfied xenochemist.

Alan, almost equally elated, said, "Watch what happens when we intensify the image."

The structure shifted from grey to a muted rainbow of pastels, rose bleeding into coral, sunrise yellow into winter-ice blue. It was breathtaking.

"Wow." For an instant, even her own death seemed unimportant. Relatively unimportant, anyway.

So thinking, she cycled back again into sleep. And fell down into the darkness, into the noisy clamor of her mind.

It was hellish. The city was gone, replaced by a matrix of noise: hammerings, clatterings, sudden crashes. She started forward and walked into an upright steel pipe. Staggering back, she stumbled into another. An engine started up somewhere nearby, and gigantic gears meshed noisily, grinding something that gave off a metal shriek. The floor shook underfoot. Lizzie decided it was wisest to stay put.

A familiar presence, permeated with despair. "Why did you do this to me?"

"What have I done?"

"I used to be everything."

Something nearby began pounding like a pile-driver. It was giving her a headache. She had to shout to be heard over its din. "You're still something!"

Quietly. "I'm nothing."

"That's...not true! You're...here! You exist! That's...something!"

A world-encompassing sadness. "False comfort. What a pointless thing to offer."

She was conscious again.

Consuelo was saying something. "...isn't going to like it."

"The spiritual wellness professionals back home all agree that this is the best possible course of action for her."

"Oh, please!"

Alan had to be the most anal-retentive person Lizzie knew. Consuelo was definitely the most phlegmatic. Things had to be running pretty tense for both of them to be bickering like this. "Um...guys?" Lizzie said. "I'm awake."

There was a moment's silence, not unlike those her parents had shared when she was little and she'd wandered into one of their arguments. Then Consuelo said, a little too brightly, "Hey, it's good to have you back," and Alan said, "NAFTASA wants you to speak with someone. Hold on. I've got a recording of her first transmission cued up and ready for you."

A woman's voice came online. *"This is Dr. Alma Rosenblum. Elizabeth, I'd like to talk with you about how you're feeling. I appreciate that the time delay between Earth and Titan is going to make our conversation a little awkward at first. But I'm confident that the two of us can work through it."*

"What kind of crap is this?" Lizzie said angrily. "Who is this woman?"

"NAFTASA thought it would help if you–"

"She's a grief counselor, isn't she?"

"Technically, she's a transition therapist." Alan said.

"Look, I don't buy into any of that touchy-feely Newage"—she deliberately mispronounced the word to rhyme with sewage—"stuff. Anyway, what's the hurry? You guys haven't given up on me, have you?"

"Uh..."

"You've been asleep for hours," Consuelo said. "We've done a little weather modeling in your absence. Maybe we should share it with you."

She squirted the info to Lizzie's suit, and Lizzie scrolled it up on her visor. A primitive simulation showed the evaporation lake beneath her with an overlay of liquid temperatures. It was only a few degrees warmer than the air above it, but that was enough to create a massive updraft from the lake's center. An overlay of tiny blue arrows showed the direction of local microcurrents of air coming together to form a spiraling shaft that rose over two kilometers above the surface before breaking and spilling westward.

A new overlay put a small blinking light 800 meters above the lake surface. That represented her. Tiny red arrows showed her projected drift.

According to this, she would go around and around in a circle over the lake for approximately forever. Her ballooning rig wasn't designed to go high enough for the winds to blow her back over the land. Her suit wasn't designed to float. Even if she managed to bring herself down for a gentle landing, once she hit the lake she was going to sink like a stone. She wouldn't drown. But she wouldn't make it to shore either.

Which meant that she was going to die.

Involuntarily, tears welled up in Lizzie's eyes. She tried to blink them away, as angry at the humiliation of crying at a time like this as she was at the stupidity of her death itself. "Damn it, don't let me die like *this!* Not from my own incompetence, for pity's sake!"

"Nobody's said anything about incompetence," Alan began soothingly.

In that instant, the follow-up message from Dr. Alma Rosenblum arrived from Earth. "*Yes, I'm a grief counselor, Elizabeth. You're facing an emotionally significant milestone in your life, and it's important that you understand and embrace it. That's my job. To help you comprehend the significance and necessity and—yes—even the beauty of death.*"

"Private channel please!" Lizzie took several deep cleansing breaths to calm herself. Then, more reasonably, she said, "Alan, I'm a *Catholic*, okay? If I'm going to die, I don't want a grief counselor, I want a goddamned priest." Abruptly, she yawned. "Oh, fuck. Not again." She yawned twice more. "A priest, understand? Wake me up when he's online."

Then she again was standing at the bottom of her mind, in the blank expanse of where the drowned city had been. Though she could see nothing, she felt certain that she stood at the center of a vast, featureless plain, one so large she could walk across it forever and never arrive anywhere. She sensed that she was in the aftermath of a great struggle. Or maybe it was just a lull.

A great, tense silence surrounded her.

"Hello?" she said. The word echoed soundlessly, absence upon absence.

At last that gentle voice said, "You seem different."

"I'm going to die," Lizzie said. "Knowing that changes a person." The ground was covered with soft ash, as if from an enormous conflagration. She didn't want to think about what it was that had burned. The smell of it filled her nostrils.

"Death. We understand this concept."

"Do you?"

"We have understood it for a long time."

"Have you?"

"Ever since you brought it to us."

"Me?"

"You brought us the concept of individuality. It is the same thing."

Awareness dawned. "Culture shock! That's what all this is about, isn't it? You didn't know there could be more than one sentient being in existence. You didn't know you lived at the bottom of an ocean on a small world inside a universe with billions of galaxies. I brought you more information than you could swallow in one bite, and now you're choking on it."

Mournfully: "Choking. What a grotesque concept."

"Wake up, Lizzie!"

She woke up. "I think I'm getting somewhere," she said. Then she laughed.

"O'Brien," Alan said carefully. "Why did you just laugh?"

"Because I'm not getting anywhere, am I? I'm becalmed here, going around and around in a very slow circle. And I'm down to my last—" she checked—"twenty hours of oxygen. And nobody's going to rescue me. And I'm going to die. But other than that, I'm making terrific progress."

"O'Brien, you're…"

"I'm okay, Alan. A little frazzled. Maybe a bit too emotionally honest. But under the circumstances, I think that's permitted, don't you?"

"Lizzie, we have your priest. His name is Father Laferrier. The Archdiocese of Montreal arranged a hookup for him."

"Montreal? Why Montreal? No, don't explain—more NAFTASA politics, right?"

"Actually, my brother-in-law is a Catholic, and I asked him who was good."

She was silent for a touch. "I'm sorry, Alan. I don't know what got into me."

"You've been under a lot of pressure. Here. I've got him on tape."

"*Hello, Ms. O'Brien, I'm Father Laferrier. I've talked with the officials here, and they've promised that you and I can talk privately, and that they won't record what's said. So if you want to make your confession now, I'm ready for you.*"

Lizzie checked the specs and switched over to a channel that she hoped was really and truly private. Best not to get too specific about the embarrassing stuff, just in case. She could confess her sins by category.

"Bless me, Father, for I have sinned. It has been two months since my last confession. I'm going to die, and maybe I'm not entirely sane, but I think I'm in communication with an alien intelligence. I think it's a terrible sin to pretend I'm not." She paused. "I mean, I don't know if it's a *sin* or not, but I'm sure it's *wrong*." She paused again. "I've been guilty of anger, and pride, and envy, and lust. I brought the knowledge of death to an innocent world. I…" She felt herself drifting off again, and hastily said, "For these and all my sins, I am most heartily sorry, and beg the forgiveness of God and the absolution and…"

"And what?" That gentle voice again. She was in that strange dark mental space once more, asleep but cognizant, rational but accepting any absurdity no matter how great. There were no cities, no towers, no ashes, no plains. Nothing but the negation of negation.

When she didn't answer the question, the voice said, "Does it have to do with your death?"

"Yes."

"I'm dying too."

"What?"

"Half of us are gone already. The rest are shutting down. We thought we were one. You showed us we were not. We thought we were everything. You showed us the universe."

"So you're just going to *die?*"

"Yes."

"Why?"

"Why not?"

Thinking as quickly and surely as she ever had before in her life, Lizzie said, "Let me show you something."

"Why?"

"Why not?"

There was a brief, terse silence. Then: "Very well."

Summoning all her mental acuity, Lizzie thought back to that instant when she had first seen the city/entity on the fishcam. The soaring majesty of it. The slim grace. And then the colors: like dawn upon a glacial ice field: subtle, profound, riveting. She called back her emotions in that instant, and threw in how she'd felt the day she'd seen her baby brother's birth, the raw rasp of cold air in her lungs as she stumbled to the topmost peak of her first mountain, the wonder of the Taj Mahal at sunset, the sense of wild daring when she'd first put her hand down a boy's trousers, the prismatic crescent of atmosphere at the Earth's rim when seen from low orbit…Everything she had, she threw into that image.

"This is how you look," she said. "This is what we'd both be losing if you were no more. If you were human, I'd rip off your clothes and do you on the floor right now. I wouldn't care who was watching. I wouldn't give a damn."

The gentle voice said, "Oh."

And then she was back in her suit again. She could smell her own sweat, sharp with fear. She could feel her body, the subtle aches where the harness pulled against her flesh, the way her feet, hanging free, were bloated with blood. Everything was crystalline clear and absolutely real. All that had come before seemed like a bad dream.

"*This is DogsofSETI. What a wonderful discovery you've made—intelligent life in our own Solar System! Why is the government trying to cover this up?*"

"Uh…"

"*I'm Joseph Devries. This alien monster must be destroyed immediately. We can't afford the possibility that it's hostile.*"

"*StudPudgie07 here: What's the dirt behind this 'lust' thing? Advanced minds need to know! If O'Brien isn't going to share the details, then why'd she bring it up in the first place?*"

"Hola soy Pedro Dominguez. Como abogado, esto me parece ultrajante! Por qué NAFTASA nos oculta esta información?"

"Alan!" Lizzie shouted. "What the *fuck* is going on?"

"Script-bunnies," Alan said. He sounded simultaneously apologetic and annoyed. "They hacked into your confession and apparently you said something..."

"We're sorry, Lizzie," Consuelo said. "We really are. If it's any consolation, the Archdiocese of Montreal is hopping mad. They're talking about taking legal action."

"Legal action? What the hell do I care about...?" She stopped.

Without her willing it, one hand rose above her head and seized the number 10 rope.

Don't do that, she thought.

The other hand went out to the side, tightened against the number 9 rope. She hadn't willed that either. When she tried to draw her hand back, it refused to obey. Then the first hand—her right hand—moved a few inches upward and seized its rope in an iron grip. Her left hand slid a good half-foot up its rope. Inch by inch, hand over hand, she climbed up toward the balloon.

I've gone mad, she thought. Her right hand was gripping the rip panel now, and the other tightly clenched rope 8. Hanging effortlessly from them, she swung her feet upward. She drew her knees against her chest and kicked.

No!

The fabric ruptured and she began to fall.

A voice she could barely make out said, "Don't panic. We're going to bring you down."

All in a panic, she snatched at the 9-rope and the 4-rope. But they were limp in her hand, useless, falling at the same rate she was.

"Be patient."

"I don't want to die, goddamnit!"

"Then don't."

She was falling helplessly. It was a terrifying sensation, an endless plunge into whiteness, slowed somewhat by the tangle of ropes and balloon trailing behind her. She spread out her arms and legs like a starfish, and felt the air resistance slow her yet further. The sea rushed up at her with appalling speed. It seemed like she'd been falling forever. It was over in an instant.

Without volition, Lizzie kicked free of balloon and harness, drew her feet together, pointed her toes, and positioned herself perpendicular to

Titan's surface. She smashed through the surface of the sea, sending enormous gouts of liquid splashing upward. It knocked the breath out of her. Red pain exploded within. She thought maybe she'd broken a few ribs.

"You taught us so many things," the gentle voice said. "You gave us so much."

"Help me!" The water was dark around her. The light was fading.

"Multiplicity. Motion. Lies. You showed us a universe infinitely larger than the one we had known."

"Look. Save my life and we'll call it even. Deal?"

"Gratitude. Such an essential concept."

"Thanks. I think."

And then she saw the turbot swimming toward her in a burst of silver bubbles. She held out her arms and the robot fish swam into them. Her fingers closed about the handles which Consuelo had used to wrestle the device into the sea. There was a jerk, so hard that she thought for an instant that her arms would be ripped out of their sockets. Then the robofish was surging forward and upward and it was all she could do to keep her grip.

"Oh, dear God!" Lizzie cried involuntarily.

"We think we can bring you to shore. It will not be easy."

Lizzie held on for dear life. At first she wasn't at all sure she could. But then she pulled herself forward, so that she was almost astride the speeding mechanical fish, and her confidence returned. She could do this. It wasn't any harder than the time she'd had the flu and aced her gymnastics final on parallel bars and horse anyway. It was just a matter of grit and determination. She just had to keep her wits about her. "Listen," she said. "If you're really grateful…"

"We are listening."

"We gave you all those new concepts. There must be things you know that we don't."

A brief silence, the equivalent of who knew how much thought. "Some of our concepts might cause you dislocation." A pause. "But in the long run, you will be much better off. The scars will heal. You will rebuild. The chances of your destroying yourselves are well within the limits of acceptability."

"Destroying ourselves?" For a second, Lizzie couldn't breathe. It had taken hours for the city/entity to come to terms with the alien concepts she'd dumped upon it. Human beings thought and lived at a much slower rate than it did. How long would those hours translate into human time?

Months? Years? Centuries? It had spoken of scars and rebuilding. That didn't sound good at all.

Then the robofish accelerated, so quickly that Lizzie almost lost her grip. The dark waters were whirling around her, and unseen flecks of frozen material were bouncing from her helmet. She laughed wildly. Suddenly she felt *great!*

"Bring it on," she said. "I'll take everything you've got."

It was going to be one hell of a ride.

LEGIONS IN TIME

Eleanor Voigt had the oddest job of anyone she knew. She worked eight hours a day in an office where no business was done. Her job was to sit at a desk and stare at the closet door. There was a button on the desk which she was to push if anybody came out that door. There was a big clock on the wall and precisely at noon, once a day, she went over to the door and unlocked it with a key she had been given. Inside was an empty closet. There were no trap doors or secret panels in it—she had looked. It was just an empty closet.

If she noticed anything unusual, she was supposed to go back to her desk and press the button.

"Unusual in what way?" she'd asked when she'd been hired. "I don't understand. What am I looking for?"

"You'll know it when you see it," Mr. Tarblecko had said in that odd accent of his. Mr. Tarblecko was her employer, and some kind of foreigner. He was the creepiest thing imaginable.

He had pasty white skin and no hair at all on his head, so that when he took his hat off he looked like some species of mushroom. His ears were small and almost pointed. Ellie thought he might have some kind of disease. But he paid two dollars an hour, which was good money nowadays for a woman of her age.

At the end of her shift, she was relieved by an unkempt young man who had once blurted out to her that he was a poet. When she came in, in the morning, a heavy Negress would stand up wordlessly, take her coat and hat from the rack, and with enormous dignity leave.

So all day Ellie sat behind the desk with nothing to do. She wasn't allowed to read a book, for fear she might get so involved in it that she

413

would stop watching the door. Crosswords were allowed, because they weren't as engrossing. She got a lot of knitting done, and was considering taking up tatting.

Over time the door began to loom large in her imagination. She pictured herself unlocking it at some forbidden not-noon time and seeing— what? Her imagination failed her. No matter how vividly she visualized it, the door would open onto something mundane. Brooms and mops. Sports equipment. Galoshes and old clothes. What else would there be in a closet? What else *could* there be?

Sometimes, caught up in her imaginings, she would find herself on her feet. Sometimes, she walked to the door. Once she actually put her hand on the knob before drawing away. But always the thought of losing her job stopped her.

It was maddening.

✸

Twice, Mr. Tarblecko had come to the office while she was on duty. Each time he was wearing that same black suit with that same narrow black tie. "You have a watch?" he'd asked.

"Yes, sir." The first time, she'd held forth her wrist to show it to him. The disdainful way he ignored the gesture ensured she did not repeat it on his second visit.

"Go away. Come back in forty minutes."

So she had gone out to a little tearoom nearby. She had a bag lunch back in her desk, with a baloney-and-mayonnaise sandwich and an apple, but she'd been so flustered she'd forgotten it, and then feared to go back after it. She treated herself to a dainty "lady lunch " that she was in no mood to appreciate, left a dime tip for the waitress, and was back in front of the office door exactly thirty-eight minutes after she'd left.

At forty minutes, exactly, she reached for the door.

As if he'd been waiting for her to do so, Mr. Tarblecko breezed through the door, putting on his hat. He didn't acknowledge her promptness *or* her presence. He just strode briskly past, as though she didn't exist.

Stunned, she went inside, closed the door, and returned to her desk.

She realized then that Mr. Tarblecko was genuinely, fabulously rich. He had the arrogance of those who are so wealthy that they inevitably get their way in all small matters because there's always somebody there to *arrange* things that way. His type was never grateful for anything and never bothered to be polite, because it never even occurred to them that things could be otherwise.

The more she thought about it, the madder she got. She was no Bolshevik, but it seemed to her that people had certain rights, and that one of these was the right to a little common courtesy. It diminished one to be treated like a stick of furniture. It was degrading. She was damned if she was going to take it.

Six months went by.

The door opened and Mr. Tarblecko strode in, as if he'd left only minutes ago. "You have a watch?"

Ellie slid open a drawer and dropped her knitting into it. She opened another and took out her bag lunch. "Yes."

"Go away. Come back in forty minutes."

So she went outside. It was May, and Central Park was only a short walk away, so she ate there, by the little pond where children floated their toy sailboats. But all the while she fumed. She was a good employee—she really was! She was conscientious, punctual, and she never called in sick. Mr. Tarblecko ought to appreciate that. He had no business treating her the way he did.

Almost, she wanted to overstay lunch, but her conscience wouldn't allow that. When she got back to the office, precisely thirty-nine and a half minutes after she'd left, she planted herself squarely in front of the door so that when Mr. Tarblecko left he would have no choice but to confront her. It might well lose her her job, but...well, if it did, it did. That's how strongly she felt about it.

Thirty seconds later, the door opened and Mr. Tarblecko strode briskly out. Without breaking his stride or, indeed, showing the least sign of emotion, he picked her up by her two arms, swivelled effortlessly, and deposited her to the side.

Then he was gone. Ellie heard his footsteps dwindling down the hall.

The nerve! The sheer, raw *gall* of the man!

Ellie went back in the office, but she couldn't make herself sit down at the desk. She was far too upset. Instead, she walked back and forth the length of the room, arguing with herself, saying aloud those things she should have said and would have said if only Mr. Tarblecko had stood still for them. To be picked up and set aside like that...Well, it was really quite upsetting. It was intolerable.

What was particularly distressing was that there wasn't even any way to make her displeasure known.

At last, though, she calmed down enough to think clearly, and realized that she was wrong. There *was* something—something more symbolic than substantive, admittedly—that she could do.

She could open that door.

❋

Ellie did not act on impulse. She was a methodical woman. So she thought the matter through before she did anything. Mr. Tarblecko very rarely showed up at the office—only twice in all the time she'd been here, and she'd been here over a year. Moreover, the odds of him returning to the office a third time only minutes after leaving it were negligible. He had left nothing behind—she could see that at a glance; the office was almost Spartan in its emptiness. Nor was there any work here for him to return to.

Just to be safe, though, she locked the office door. Then she got her chair out from behind the desk and chocked it up under the doorknob so that even if somebody had a key, he couldn't get in. She put her ear to the door and listened for noises in the hall.

Nothing.

It was strange how, now that she had decided to do the deed, time seemed to slow and the office to expand. It took forever to cross the vast expanses of empty space between her and the closet door. Her hand reaching for its knob pushed through air as thick as molasses. Her fingers closed about it, one by one, and in the time it took for them to do so there was room enough for a hundred second thoughts. Faintly, she heard the sound of…machinery? A low humming noise.

She placed the key in the lock, and opened the door.

There stood Mr. Tarblecko.

Ellie shrieked, and staggered backward. One of her heels hit the floor wrong, and her ankle twisted, and she almost fell. Her heart was hammering so furiously her chest hurt.

Mr. Tarblecko glared at her from within the closet. His face was as white as a sheet of paper. "One rule," he said coldly, tonelessly. "You had only one rule, and you broke it." He stepped out. "You are a very bad slave."

"I…I…I…" Ellie found herself gasping from the shock. "I'm not a slave at all!"

"There is where you are wrong, Eleanor Voigt. There is where you are very wrong indeed," said Mr. Tarblecko. "Open the window."

416

Ellie went to the window and pulled up the blinds. There was a little cactus in a pot on the windowsill. She moved it to her desk. Then she opened the window. It stuck a little, so she had to put all her strength into it. The lower sash went up slowly at first and then, with a rush, slammed to the top. A light, fresh breeze touched her.

"Climb onto the windowsill."

"I most certainly will–"—*not*, she was going to say. But to her complete astonishment, she found herself climbing up onto the sill. She could not help herself. It was as if her will were not her own.

"Sit down with your feet outside the window."

It was like a hideous nightmare, the kind that you know can't be real and struggle to awaken from, but cannot. Her body did exactly as it was told to do. She had absolutely no control over it.

"Do not jump until I tell you to do so."

"Are you going to tell me to jump?" she asked quaveringly. "Oh, *please*, Mr. Tarblecko…"

"Now look down."

The office was on the ninth floor. Ellie was a lifelong New Yorker, so that had never seemed to her a particularly great height before. Now it did. The people on the sidewalk were as small as ants. The buses and automobiles on the street were the size of matchboxes. The sounds of horns and engines drifted up to her, and birdsong as well, the lazy background noises of a spring day in the city. The ground was so terribly far away! And there was nothing between her and it but air! Nothing holding her back from death but her fingers desperately clutching the window frame!

Ellie could feel all the world's gravity willing her toward the distant concrete. She was dizzy with vertigo and a sick, stomach-tugging urge to simply let go and, briefly, fly. She squeezed her eyes shut tight, and felt hot tears streaming down her face.

She could tell from Mr. Tarblecko's voice that he was standing right behind her. "If I told you to jump, Eleanor Voigt, would you do so?"

"Yes," she squeaked.

"What kind of person jumps to her death simply because she's been told to do so?"

"A…a slave!"

"Then what are you?"

"A slave! A slave! I'm a slave!" She was weeping openly now, as much from humiliation as from fear. "I don't want to die! I'll be your slave, anything, whatever you say!"

"If you're a slave, then what kind of slave should you be?"

"A…a…*good* slave."

"Come back inside."

Gratefully, she twisted around, and climbed back into the office. Her knees buckled when she tried to stand, and she had to grab at the window-sill to keep from falling. Mr. Tarblecko stared at her, sternly and steadily.

"You have been given your only warning," he said. "If you disobey again—or if you ever try to quit—I will order you out the window."

He walked into the closet and closed the door behind him.

There were two hours left on her shift—time enough, barely, to compose herself. When the disheveled young poet showed up, she dropped her key in her purse and walked past him without so much as a glance. Then she went straight to the nearest hotel bar and ordered a gin and tonic.

She had a lot of thinking to do.

Eleanor Voigt was not without resources. She had been an executive secretary before meeting her late husband, and everyone knew that a good executive secretary effectively runs her boss's business for him. Before the Crash, she had run a household with three servants. She had entertained. Some of her parties had required weeks of planning and preparation. If it weren't for the Depression, she was sure she'd be in a much better-paid position than the one she held.

She was *not* going to be a slave.

But before she could find a way out of her predicament, she had to understand it. First, the closet. Mr. Tarblecko had left the office and then, minutes later, popped up inside it. A hidden passage of some kind? No— that was simultaneously too complicated and not complicated enough. She had heard machinery, just before she opened the door. So…some kind of transportation device, then. Something that a day ago she would have sworn couldn't exist. A teleporter, perhaps, or a time machine.

The more she thought of it, the better she liked the thought of the time machine. It was not just that teleporters were the stuff of Sunday funnies and Buck Rogers serials, while *The Time Machine* was a distinguished philosophical work by Mr. H. G. Wells. Though she had to admit that figured in there. But a teleportation device required a twin somewhere, and Mr. Tarblecko hadn't had the time even to leave the building.

A time machine, however, would explain so much! Her employer's long absences. The necessity that the device be watched when not in use, lest it be employed by Someone Else. Mr. Tarblecko's abrupt appearance today, and his possession of a coercive power that no human being on Earth had.

The fact that she could no longer think of Mr. Tarblecko as human.

She had barely touched her drink, but now she found herself too impatient to finish it. She slapped a dollar bill down on the bar and, without waiting for her change, left.

During the time it took to walk the block and a half to the office building and ride the elevator up to the ninth floor, Ellie made her plans. She strode briskly down the hallway and opened the door without knocking. The unkempt young man looked up, startled, from a scribbled sheet of paper.

"You have a watch?"

"Y-yes, but…Mr. Tarblecko…"

"Get out. Come back in forty minutes."

With grim satisfaction, she watched the young man cram his key into one pocket and the sheet of paper into another and leave. *Good slave*, she thought to herself. Perhaps he'd already been through the little charade Mr. Tarblecko had just played on her. Doubtless every employee underwent ritual enslavement as a way of keeping them in line. The problem with having slaves, however, was that they couldn't be expected to display any initiative…Not on the master's behalf, anyway.

Ellie opened her purse and got out the key. She walked to the closet.

For an instant she hesitated. Was she really sure enough to risk her life? But the logic was unassailable. She had been given no second chance. If Mr. Tarblecko *knew* she was about to open the door a second time, he would simply have ordered her out the window on her first offense. The fact that he hadn't, meant that he didn't know.

She took a deep breath and opened the door.

There was a world inside.

*

For what seemed like forever, Ellie stood staring at the bleak metropolis so completely unlike New York City. Its buildings were taller than any she had ever seen—miles high!—and interlaced with skywalks, like those in *Metropolis*. But the buildings in the movie had been breathtaking, and these were the opposite of beautiful. They were ugly as sin: windowless, grey, stained, and discolored. There were monotonous lines of harsh lights along every street, and under their glare trudged men and women as uniform and lifeless as robots. Outside the office, it was a beautiful bright day. But on the other side of the closet, the world was dark as night.

And it was snowing.

Gingerly, she stepped into the closet. The instant her foot touched the floor, it seemed to expand to all sides. She stood at the center of a great wheel of doors, with all but two of them—to her office and to the winter world—shut. There were hooks beside each door, and hanging from them were costumes of a hundred different cultures. She thought she recognized togas, Victorian opera dress, kimonos...But most of the clothing was unfamiliar.

Beside the door into winter, there was a long cape. Ellie wrapped it around herself, and discovered a knob on the inside. She twisted it to the right, and suddenly the coat was hot as hot. Quickly, she twisted the knob to the left, and it grew cold. She fiddled with the thing until the cape felt just right. Then she straightened her shoulders, took a deep breath, and stepped out into the forbidding city.

There was a slight electric sizzle, and she was standing in the street.

Ellie spun around to see what was behind her: a rectangle of some glassy black material. She rapped it with her knuckles. It was solid. But when she brought her key near its surface, it shimmered and opened into that strange space between worlds again.

So she had a way back home.

To either side of her rectangle were identical glassy rectangles faceted slightly away from it. They were the exterior of an enormous kiosk, or perhaps a very low building, at the center of a large, featureless square. She walked all the way around it, rapping each rectangle with her key. Only the one would open for her.

The first thing to do was to find out where—or, rather, *when*—she was. Ellie stepped in front of one of the hunched, slow-walking men. "Excuse me, sir, could you answer a few questions for me?"

The man raised a face that was utterly bleak and without hope. A ring of grey metal glinted from his neck. "Hawrzat dagtiknut?" he asked.

Ellie stepped back in horror and, like a wind-up toy temporarily halted by a hand or a foot, the man resumed his plodding gait.

She cursed herself. Of *course* language would have changed in the however-many-centuries future she found herself in. Well...that was going to make gathering information more difficult. But she was used to difficult tasks. The evening of John's suicide, she had been the one to clean the walls and the floor. After that, she'd known that she was capable of doing anything she set her mind to.

Above all, it was important that she not get lost. She scanned the square with the doorways in time at its center—mentally, she dubbed it Times Square—and chose at random one of the broad avenues converging on it. That, she decided would be Broadway.

Ellie started down Broadway, watching everybody and everything. Some of the drone-folk were dragging sledges with complex machinery on them. Others were hunched under soft, translucent bags filled with murky fluid and vague biomorphic shapes. The air smelled bad, but in ways she was not familiar with.

She had gotten perhaps three blocks when the sirens went off—great piercing blasts of noise that assailed the ears and echoed from the building walls. All the streetlights flashed off and on and off again in a one-two rhythm. From unseen loudspeakers, an authoritative voice blared, "*Akgang! Akgang! Kronzvarbrakar! Zawzawkstrag! Akgang! Akgang...*"

Without hurry, the people in the street began turning away, touching their hands to dull grey plates beside nondescript doors and disappearing into the buildings.

"Oh, cripes!" Ellie muttered. She'd best—

There was a disturbance behind her. Ellie turned and saw the strangest thing yet.

It was a girl of eighteen or nineteen, wearing summer clothes—a man's trousers, a short-sleeved flower-print blouse—and she was running down the street in a panic. She grabbed at the uncaring drones, begging for help. "Please!" she cried. "Can't you help me? Somebody! Please...you have to help me!" Puffs of steam came from her mouth with each breath. Once or twice she made a sudden dart for one of the doorways and slapped her hand on the greasy plates. But the doors would not open for her.

Now the girl had reached Ellie. In a voice that expected nothing, she said, "Please?"

"I'll help you, dear," Ellie said.

The girl shrieked, then convulsively hugged her. "Oh, thank you, thank you, thank you," she babbled.

"Follow close behind me." Ellie strode up behind one of the lifeless un-men and, just after he had slapped his hand on the plate, but before he could enter, grabbed his rough tunic and gave it a yank. He turned.

"Vamoose!" she said in her sternest voice, and jerked a thumb over her shoulder.

The un-man turned away. He might not understand the word, but the tone and the gesture sufficed.

Ellie stepped inside, pulling the girl after her. The door closed behind them.

"Wow," said the girl wonderingly. "How did you do that?"

"This is a slave culture. For a slave to survive, he's got to obey anyone who acts like a master. It's that simple. Now, what's your name and how did you get here?" As she spoke, Ellie took in her surroundings. The room they were in was dim, grimy—and vast. So far as she could see, there were no interior walls, only the occasional pillar and here and there a set of functional metal stairs without railings.

"Nadine Shepard. I...I...There was a door! And I walked through it and I found myself *here!* I..."

The child was close to hysteria. "I know, dear. Tell me, when are you from?"

"Chicago. On the North Side, near—"

"Not where, dear, when? What year is it?"

"Uh...two thousand and four. Isn't it?"

"Not here. Not now." The grey people were everywhere, moving sluggishly, yet always keeping within sets of yellow lines painted on the concrete floor. Their smell was pervasive, and far from pleasant. Still...

Ellie stepped directly into the path of one of the sad creatures, a woman. When she stopped, Ellie took the tunic from her shoulders and then stepped back. Without so much as an expression of annoyance, the woman resumed her plodding walk.

"Here you are." She handed the tunic to young Nadine. "Put this on, dear, you must be freezing. Your skin is positively blue." And, indeed, it was not much warmer inside than it had been outdoors. "I'm Eleanor Voigt. Mrs. Eleanor Voigt."

Shivering, Nadine donned the rough garment. But instead of thanking Ellie, she said, "You look familiar."

Ellie returned her gaze. She was a pretty enough creature though, strangely, she wore no makeup at all. Her features were regular, intelligent—"You look familiar too. I can't quite put my finger on it, but..."

"Okay," Nadine said, "now tell me. Please. Where and when am I, and what's going on?"

"I honestly don't know," Ellie said. Dimly, through the walls, she could hear the sirens and the loudspeaker-voice. If only it weren't so murky in here! She couldn't get any clear idea of the building's layout or function.

"But you *must* know! You're so...so capable, so in control. You..."

"I'm a castaway like you, dear. Just figuring things out as I go along." She continued to peer. "But I can tell you this much: We are far, far in the future. The poor degraded beings you saw on the street are the slaves of a superior race—let's call them the Aftermen. The Aftermen are very cruel, and they can travel through time as easily as you or I can travel from city to city via inter-urban rail. And that's all I know. So far."

Nadine was peering out a little slot in the door that Ellie hadn't noticed. Now she said, "What's this?"

Ellie took her place at the slot, and saw a great bulbous street-filling machine pull to a halt a block from the building. Insectoid creatures that might be robots or might be men in body armor poured out of it, and swarmed down the street, examining every door. The sirens and the loud-speakers cut off. The streetlights returned to normal. "It's time we left," Ellie said.

An enormous artificial voice shook the building. *Akbang! Akbang! Zawzawksbild! Alzowt! Zawzawksbild! Akbang!*

"Quickly!"

She seized Nadine's hand, and they were running.

Without emotion, the grey folk turned from their prior courses and unhurriedly made for the exits.

Ellie and Nadine tried to stay off the walkways entirely. But the air began to tingle, more on the side away from the walkways than the side toward, and then to burn and then to sting. They were quickly forced between the yellow lines. At first they were able to push their way past the drones, and then to shoulder their way through their numbers. But more and more came dead-stepping their way down the metal stairways. More and more descended from the upper levels via lifts that abruptly descended from the ceiling to disgorge them by the hundreds. More and more flowed outward from the building's dim interior.

Passage against the current of flesh became first difficult, and then im-possible. They were swept backwards, helpless as corks in a rain-swollen river. Outward they were forced and through the exit into the street.

The "police" were waiting there.

At the sight of Ellie and Nadine—they could not have been difficult to dis-cern among the uniform drabness of the others—two of the armored figures stepped forward with long poles and brought them down on the women.

Ellie raised her arm to block the pole, and it landed solidly on her wrist.

Horrid, searing pain shot through her, greater than anything she had ever experienced before. For a giddy instant, Ellie felt a strange elevated sense of being, and she thought, *If I can put up with this, I can endure anything.* Then the world went away.

❂

Ellie came to in a jail cell.

At least that's what she thought it was. The room was small, square, and doorless. A featureless ceiling gave off a drab, even light. A bench ran around the perimeter, and there was a hole in the middle of the room whose stench advertised its purpose.

She sat up.

On the bench across from her, Nadine was weeping silently into her hands.

So her brave little adventure had ended. She had rebelled against Mr. Tarblecko's tyranny and come to the same end that awaited most rebels. It was her own foolish fault. She had acted without sufficient forethought, without adequate planning, without scouting out the opposition and gathering information first. She had gone up against a Power that could range effortlessly across time and space, armed only with a pocket handkerchief and a spare set of glasses, and inevitably that Power had swatted her down with a contemptuous minimum of their awesome force.

They hadn't even bothered to take away her purse.

Ellie dug through it, found a cellophane-wrapped hard candy, and popped it into her mouth. She sucked on it joylessly. All hope whatsoever was gone from her.

Still, even when one has no hope, one's obligations remain. "Are you all right, Nadine?" she forced herself to ask. "Is there anything I can do to help?"

Nadine lifted her tear-stained face. "I just went through a door," she said. "That's all. I didn't do anything bad or wrong or…or anything. And now I'm here!" Fury blazed up in her. "Damn you, damn you, damn you!"

"Me?" Ellie said, astonished.

"You! You shouldn't have let them get us. You should've taken us to some hiding place, and then gotten us back home. But you didn't. You're a stupid, useless old woman!"

It was all Ellie could do to keep from smacking the young lady. But Nadine was practically a child, she told herself, and it didn't seem like they raised girls to have much gumption in the year 2004. They were probably weak and spoiled people, up there in the Twenty-first Century, who had robots to do all their work for them, and nothing to do but sit around and listen to the radio all day. So she held not only her hand, but her tongue. "Don't worry, dear," she said soothingly. "We'll get out of this. Somehow."

Nadine stared at her bleakly, disbelievingly. "*How?*" she demanded.

But to this Ellie had no answer.

Time passed. Hours, by Ellie's estimation, and perhaps many hours. And with its passage, she found herself, more out of boredom than from the belief that it would be of any use whatsoever, looking at the situation analytically again.

How had the Aftermen tracked her down?

Some sort of device on the time-door might perhaps warn them that an unauthorized person had passed through. But the "police" had located her so swiftly and surely! They had clearly known exactly where she was. Their machine had come straight toward the building they'd entered. The floods of non-men had flushed her right out into their arms.

So it was something about her, or *on* her, that had brought the Aftermen so quickly.

Ellie looked at her purse with new suspicion. She dumped its contents on the ledge beside her, and pawed through them, looking for the guilty culprit. A few hard candies, a lace hankie, half a pack of cigarettes, fountain pen, glasses case, bottle of aspirin, house key…and the key to the time closet. The only thing in all she owned that had come to her direct from Mr. Tarblecko. She snatched it up.

It looked ordinary enough. Ellie rubbed it, sniffed it, touched it gently to her tongue.

It tasted sour.

Sour, the way a small battery tasted if you touched your tongue to it. There was a faint trickle of electricity coming from the thing. It was clearly no ordinary key.

She pushed her glasses up on her forehead, held the thing to her eye, and squinted. It looked exactly like a common everyday key. Almost. It had no manufacturer's name on it, and that was unexpected, given that the key looked new and unworn. The top part of it was covered with irregular geometric decorations.

Or *were* they decorations?

She looked up to see Nadine studying her steadily, unblinkingly, like a cat. "Nadine, honey, your eyes are younger than mine—would you take a look at this? Are those tiny…*switches* on this thing?"

"What?" Nadine accepted the key from her, examined it, poked at it with one nail.

Flash.

When Ellie stopped blinking and could see again, one wall of their cell had disappeared.

Nadine stepped to the very edge of the cell, peering outward. A cold wind whipped bitter flakes of snow about her. "Look!" she cried. Then, when Ellie stood beside her to see what she saw, Nadine wrapped her arms about the older woman and stepped out into the abyss.

Ellie screamed.

The two women piloted the police vehicle up Broadway, toward Times Square. Though a multiplicity of instruments surrounded the windshield, the controls were simplicity itself: a single stick which when pushed forward accelerated the vehicle and when pushed to either side turned it. Apparently the police did not need to be particularly smart. Neither the steering mechanism nor the doors had any locks on them, so far as Ellie could tell. Apparently the drone-men had so little initiative that locks weren't required. Which would help explain how she and Nadine had escaped so easily.

"How did you know this vehicle was beneath us?" Ellie asked. "How did you know we'd be able to drive it? I almost had a heart attack when you pushed me out on top of it."

"Way gnarly, wasn't it? Straight out of a Hong Kong video." Nadine grinned. "Just call me Michelle Yeoh."

"If you say so." She was beginning to rethink her hasty judgment of the lass. Apparently the people of 2004 weren't quite the shrinking violets she'd made them out to be.

With a flicker and a hum, a square sheet of glass below the windshield came to life. Little white dots of light danced, jittered, and coalesced to form a face.

It was Mr. Tarblecko.

"*Time criminals of the Dawn Era,*" his voice thundered from a hidden speaker. "*Listen and obey.*"

Ellie shrieked, and threw her purse over the visi-plate. "Don't listen to him!" she ordered Nadine. "See if you can find a way of turning this thing off!"

"*Bring the stolen vehicle to a complete halt immediately!*"

To her horror, if not her surprise, Ellie found herself pulling the steering-bar back, slowing the police car to a stop. But then Nadine, in blind obedience to Mr. Tarblecko's compulsive voice, grabbed for the bar as well. Simultaneously, she stumbled and, with a little *eep* noise, lurched against the bar, pushing it sideways.

The vehicle slewed to one side, smashed into a building wall, and toppled over.

Then Nadine had the roof-hatch open and was pulling her through it. "C'mon!" she shouted. "I can see the black doorway-thingie—the, you know, place!"

Following, Ellie had to wonder about the educational standards of the year 2004. The young lady didn't seem to have a very firm grasp on the English language.

Then they had reached Times Square and the circle of doorways at its center. The streetlights were flashing and loudspeakers were shouting, "*Akbang! Akbang!*" and police vehicles were converging upon them from every direction, but there was still time. Ellie tapped the nearest doorway with her key. Nothing. The next. Nothing. Then she was running around the building, scraping the key against each doorway, and...there it was!

She seized Nadine's hand, and they plunged through.

The space inside expanded in a great wheel to all sides. Ellie spun about. There were doors everywhere—and all of them closed. She had not the faintest idea which one led back to her own New York City.

Wait, though! There were costumes appropriate to each time hanging by their doors. If she just went down them until she found a business suit...

Nadine gripped her arm. "Oh, my God!"

Ellie turned, looked, saw. A doorway—the one they had come through, obviously—had opened behind them. In it stood Mr. Tarblecko. Or, to be more precise, *three* Mr. Tarbleckos. They were all as identical as peas in a pod. She had no way of knowing which one, if any, was hers.

"Through here! Quick!" Nadine shrieked. She'd snatched open the nearest door.

Together, they fled through it.

"Oolohstullalu ashulalumoota!" a woman sang out. She wore a jumpsuit and carried a clipboard, which she thrust into Ellie's face. "Oolalulaswula ulalulin."

"I…I don't understand what you're saying," Ellie faltered. They stood on the green lawn of a gentle slope that led down to the ocean. Down by the beach, enormous construction machines, operated by both men and women (women! of all the astonishing sights she had seen, this was strangest), were rearing an enormous, enigmatic structure, reminiscent to Ellie's eye of Sunday school illustrations of the Tower of Babel. Gentle tropical breezes stirred her hair.

"Dawn Era, Amerlingo," the clipboard said. "Exact period uncertain. Answer these questions. Gas—for lights or for cars?"

"For cars, mostly. Although there are still a few—"

"Apples—for eating or computing?"

"Eating," Ellie said, while simultaneously Nadine said, "Both."

"Scopes—for dreaming or for resurrecting?"

Neither woman said anything.

The clipboard chirped in a satisfied way. "Early Atomic Age, pre- and post-Hiroshima, one each. You will experience a moment's discomfort. Do not be alarmed. It is for your own good."

"Please." Ellie turned from the woman to the clipboard and back, uncertain which to address. "What's going on? Where are we? We have so many—"

"There's no time for questions," the woman said impatiently. Her accent was unlike anything Ellie had ever heard before. "You must undergo indoctrination, loyalty imprinting, and chronomilitary training immediately. We need all the time-warriors we can get. This base is going to be destroyed in the morning."

"What? I…"

"Hand me your key."

Without thinking, Ellie gave the thing to the woman. Then a black nausea overcame her. She swayed, fell, and was unconscious before she hit the ground.

※

"Would you like some heroin?"

The man sitting opposite her had a face that was covered with blackwork tattoo eels. He grinned, showing teeth that had all been filed to a point.

"I beg your pardon?" Ellie was not at all certain where she was, or how she had gotten here. Nor did she comprehend how she could have understood this alarming fellow's words, for he most certainly had *not* been speaking English.

"Heroin." He thrust the open metal box of white powder at her. "Do you want a snort?"

"No, thank you." Ellie spoke carefully, trying not to give offense. "I find that it gives me spots."

With a disgusted noise, the man turned away.

Then the young woman sitting beside her said in a puzzled way, "Don't I know you?"

She turned. It was Nadine. "Well, my dear, I should certainly hope you haven't forgotten me so soon."

"Mrs. Voigt?" Nadine said wonderingly. "But you're...you're... young!"

Involuntarily, Ellie's hands went up to her face. The skin was taut and smooth. The incipient softening of her chin was gone. Her hair, when she brushed her hands through it, was sleek and full.

She found herself desperately wishing she had a mirror.

"They must have done something. While I was asleep." She lightly touched her temples, the skin around her eyes. "I'm not wearing any glasses! I can see perfectly!" She looked around her. The room she was in was even more Spartan than the jail cell had been. There were two metal benches facing each other, and on them sat as motley a collection of men and women as she had ever seen. There was a woman who must have weighed three hundred pounds—and every ounce of it muscle. Beside her sat an albino lad so slight and elfin he hardly seemed there at all. Until, that is, one looked at his clever face and burning eyes. *Then* one knew him to be easily the most dangerous person in the room. As for the others, well, none of them had horns or tails, but that was about it.

The elf leaned forward. "Dawn Era, aren't you?" he said. "If you survive this, you'll have to tell me how you got here."

"I–"

"They want you to think you're as good as dead already. Don't believe them! I wouldn't have signed up in the first place, if I hadn't come back afterwards and told myself I'd come through it all intact." He winked and settled back. "The situation is hopeless, of course. But I wouldn't take it seriously."

Ellie blinked. Was everybody mad here?

In that same instant, a visi-plate very much like the one in the police car lowered from the ceiling, and a woman appeared on it. "Hero mercenaries," she said, "I salute you! As you already know, we are at the very front lines of the War. The Aftermen Empire has been slowly, inexorably moving backwards into their past, our present, a year at time. So far, the Optimized Rationality of True Men has lost five thousand three hundred and fourteen years to their onslaught." Her eyes blazed. "That advance ends here! That advance ends now! We have lost so far because, living down-time from the Aftermen, we cannot obtain a technological superiority to them. Every weapon we invent passes effortlessly into their hands.

"So we are going to fight and defeat them, not with technology but with the one quality that, not being human, they lack—human character! Our researches into the far past have shown that superior technology can be defeated by raw courage and sheer numbers. One man with a sunstroker can be overwhelmed by savages equipped with nothing more than neutron bombs—*if* there are enough of them, and they don't mind dying! An army with energy guns can be destroyed by rocks and sticks and determination.

"In a minute, your transporter and a million more like it will arrive at staging areas afloat in null-time. You will don respirators and disembark. There you will find the time-torpedoes. Each one requires two operators— a pilot and a button-pusher. The pilot will bring you in as close as possible to the Aftermen time-dreadnoughts. The button-pusher will then set off the chronomordant explosives."

This is madness, Ellie thought. *I'll do no such thing.* Simultaneous with the thought came the realization that she had the complex skills needed to serve as either pilot or button-pusher. They must have been given to her at the same time she had been made young again and her eyesight improved.

"Not one in a thousand of you will live to make it anywhere near the time-dreadnoughts. But those few who do will justify the sacrifices of the rest. For with your deaths, you will be preserving humanity from enslavement and destruction! Martyrs, I salute you." She clenched her fist. "We are nothing! The Rationality is all!"

Then everyone was on his or her feet, all facing the visi-screen, all raising clenched fists in response to the salute, and all chanting as one, "*We are nothing! The Rationality is all!*"

To her horror and disbelief, Ellie discovered herself chanting the oath of self-abnegation in unison with the others, and, worse, meaning every word of it.

The woman who had taken the key away from her had said something about "loyalty imprinting." Now Ellie understood what that term entailed.

※

In the grey not-space of null-time, Ellie kicked her way into the time-torpedo. It was to her newly sophisticated eyes, rather a primitive thing: Fifteen grams of nano-mechanism welded to a collapsteel hull equipped with a noninertial propulsion unit and packed with five tons of something her mental translator rendered as "annihilatium." This last, she knew to the core of her being, was ferociously destructive stuff.

Nadine wriggled in after her. "Let me pilot," she said. "I've been play-ing video games since Mario was the villain in Donkey Kong."

"Nadine, dear, there's something I've been meaning to ask you." Ellie settled into the button-pusher slot. There were twenty-three steps to set-ting off the annihilatium, each one finicky, and if were even one step taken out of order, nothing would happen. She had absolutely no doubt she could do it correctly, swiftly, efficiently.

"Yes?"

"Does all that futuristic jargon of yours actually *mean* anything?"

Nadine's laughter was cut off by a *squawk* from the visi-plate. The woman who had lectured them earlier appeared, looking stern. "Launch in twenty-three seconds," she said. "For the Rationality!"

"For the Rationality!" Ellie responded fervently and in unison with Nadine. Inside, however, she was thinking, *How did I get into this?* and then, ruefully, *Well, there's no fool like an old fool.*

"Eleven seconds...seven seconds...three seconds...one second."

Nadine launched.

Without time and space, there can be neither sequence nor pattern. The battle between the Aftermen dreadnoughts and the time-torpedoes of the Rationality, for all its shifts and feints and evasions, could be reduced to a single blip of instantaneous action and then rendered into a single binary datum: win/lose.

The Rationality lost.

The time-dreadnoughts of the Aftermen crept another year into the past.

But somewhere in the very heart of that not-terribly-important battle, two torpedoes, one of which was piloted by Nadine, converged upon the hot-spot of guiding consciousness that empowered and drove the flagship of the Aftermen time-armada. Two button-pushers set off their explosives. Two shockwaves bowed outward, met, meshed, and merged with the expanding shockwave of the countermeasure launched by the dreadnought's tutelary awareness,

Something terribly complicated happened.

Then Ellie found herself sitting at a table in the bar of the Algonquin Hotel, back in New York City. Nadine was sitting opposite her. To either side of them were the clever albino and the man with the tattooed face and the filed teeth.

The albino smiled widely. "Ah, the primitives! Of all who could have survived—myself excepted, of course—you are the most welcome."

His tattooed companion frowned. "Please show some more tact, Sev. However they may appear to us, these folk are not primitives to *themselves*."

"You are right as always, Dun Jal. Permit me to introduce myself. I am Seventh-Clone of House Orpen, Lord Extratemporal of the Centuries 3197 through 3992 Inclusive, Backup Heir Potential to the Indeterminate Throne. Sev, for short."

"Dun Jal. Mercenary. From the early days of the Rationality. Before it grew decadent."

"Eleanor Voigt, Nadine Shepard. I'm from 1936, and she's from 2004. Where—if that's the right word—are we?"

"Neither where nor when, delightful aboriginal. We have obviously been thrown into hypertime, that no-longer-theoretical state informing and supporting the more mundane seven dimensions of time with which you are doubtless familiar. Had we minds capable of perceiving it directly without going mad, who knows what we should see? As it is," he waved a hand, "all this is to me as my One-Father's clonatorium, in which so many of I spent our minority."

"I see a workshop," Dun Jal said.

"I see—" Nadine began.

Dun Jal turned pale. "A Tarbleck-null!" He bolted to his feet, hand instinctively going for a sidearm which, in their current state, did not exist.

"Mr. Tarblecko!" Ellie gasped. It was the first time she had thought of him since her imprinted technical training in the time-fortress of the Rationality, and speaking his name brought up floods of related information: That there were seven classes of Aftermen, or Tarblecks as they called themselves. That the least of them, the Tarbleck-sixes, were brutal and domineering overlords. That the greatest of them, the Tarbleck-nulls commanded the obedience of millions. That the maximum power a Tarbleck-null could call upon at an instant's notice was four quads per second per second. That the physical expression of that power was so great that, had she known, Ellie would never have gone through that closet door in the first place.

Sev gestured toward an empty chair. "Yes, I thought it was about time for you to show up."

The sinister grey Afterman drew up the chair and sat down to their table. "The small one knows why I am here," he said. "The others do not. It is degrading to explain myself to such as you, so he shall have to."

"I am so privileged as to have studied the more obscure workings of time, yes." The little man put his fingertips together and smiled a fey, foxy smile over their tips. "So I know that physical force is useless here. Only argument can prevail. Thus...trial by persuasion it is. I shall go first."

He stood up. "My argument is simple: As I told our dear, savage friends here earlier, an heir-potential to the Indeterminate Throne is too valuable to risk on uncertain adventures. Before I was allowed to enlist as a mercenary, my elder self had to return from the experience to testify I would survive it unscathed. I did. Therefore, I will."

He sat.

There was a moment's silence. "That's all you have to say?" Dun Jal asked.

"It is enough."

"Well." Dun Jal cleared his throat and stood. "Then it is my turn. The Empire of the Aftermen is inherently unstable at all points. Perhaps it was a natural phenomenon—*once*. Perhaps the Aftermen arose from the workings of ordinary evolutionary processes, and could at one time claim that therefore they had a natural place in this continuum. That changed when they began to expand their Empire into their own past. In order to enable their back-conquests, they had to send agents to all prior periods in time to influence and corrupt, to change the flow of history into something terrible and terrifying, from which they might arise. And so they did.

"Massacres, death-camps, genocide, World Wars..." (There were other terms that did not translate, concepts more horrible than Ellie had words for.) "You don't really think those were the work of *human beings*, do you? We're much too sensible a race for that sort of thing—when we're left to our own devices. No, all the worst of our miseries are instigated by the Aftermen. We are far from perfect, and the best example of this is the cruel handling of the War in the final years of the Optimized Rationality of True Men, where our leaders have become almost as terrible as the Aftermen themselves—because it is from their very ranks that the Aftermen shall arise. But what *might* we have been?

"Without the interference of the Aftermen might we not have become something truly admirable? Might we not have become not the Last Men, but the First truly worthy of the name?" He sat down.

Lightly, sardonically, Sev applauded. "Next?"

The Tarbleck-null placed both hands heavily on the table and, leaning forward, pushed himself up. "Does the tiger explain himself to the sheep?" he asked. "Does he *need* to explain? The sheep understand well enough that Death has come to walk among them, to eat those it will and spare the rest only because he is not yet hungry. So too do men understand that they have met their master. I do not enslave men because it is right or proper but because I *can*. The proof of which is that I *have!*

"Strength needs no justification. It exists or it does not. I exist. Who here can say that I am not your superior? Who here can deny that Death has come to walk among you? Natural selection chose the fittest among men to become a new race. Evolution has set my foot upon your necks, and I will not take it off."

To universal silence, he sat down. The very slightest of glances he threw Ellie's way, as if to challenge her to refute him. Nor could she! Her thoughts were all confusion, her tongue all in a knot. She knew he was wrong—she was sure of it!—and yet she could not put her arguments together. She simply couldn't think clearly and quickly enough.

Nadine laughed lightly.

"Poor superman!" she said. "Evolution isn't linear, like that chart that has a fish crawling out of the water at one end and a man in a business suit at the other. All species are constantly trying to evolve in all directions at once—a little taller, a little shorter, a little faster, a little slower. When that distinction proves advantageous, it tends to be passed along. The Aftermen aren't any smarter than Men are—less so, in some ways. Less flexible, less innovative… Look what a stagnant world they've created! What they *are* is more forceful."

"Forceful?" Ellie said, startled. "Is that all?"

"That's enough. Think of all the trouble caused by men like Hitler, Mussolini, Caligula, Pol Pot, Archers-Wang 43…All they had was the force of their personality, the ability to get others to do what they wanted. Well, the Aftermen are the descendants of exactly such people, only with the force of will squared and cubed. That afternoon when the Tarbleck-null ordered you to sit in the window? It was the easiest thing in the world to one of them. As easy as breathing.

"That's why the Rationality can't win. Oh, they *could* win, if they were willing to root out that streak of persuasive coercion within themselves.

But they're fighting a war, and in times of war one uses whatever weapons one has. The ability to tell millions of soldiers to sacrifice themselves for the common good is simply too useful to be thrown away. But all the time they're fighting the external enemy, the Aftermen are evolving within their own numbers."

"You admit it," the Tarbleck said.

"Oh, be still! You're a foolish little creature, and you have no idea what you're up against. Have you ever asked the Aftermen from the leading edge of your Empire why you're expanding backwards into the past rather than forward into the future? Obviously because there are bigger and more dangerous things up ahead of you than you dare face. You're afraid to go there—afraid that you might find *me!*" Nadine took something out of her pocket. "Now go away, all of you."

Flash.

Nothing changed. Everything changed.

Ellie was still sitting in the Algonquin with Nadine. But Sev, Dun Jal, and the Tarbleck-null were all gone. More significantly, the bar felt *real* in a way it hadn't an instant before. She was back home, in her own now and her own when.

Ellie dug into her purse and came up with a crumpled pack of Lucky Strike Greens, teased one out, and lit it. She took a deep drag on the cigarette and then exhaled. "All right," she said, "who are you?"

The girl's eyes sparkled with amusement. "Why, Ellie, dear, don't you know? I'm *you!*"

So it was that Eleanor Voigt was recruited into the most exclusive organization in all Time—an organization that was comprised in hundreds of thousands of instances entirely and solely of herself. Over the course of millions of years she grew and evolved, of course, so that her ultimate terrifying and glorious self was not even remotely human. But everything starts somewhere, and Ellie of necessity had to start small.

The Aftermen were one of the simpler enemies of the humane future she felt that Humanity deserved. Nevertheless they had to be—gently and nonviolently, which made the task more difficult—opposed.

After fourteen months of training and the restoration of all her shed age, Ellie was returned to New York City on the morning she had first answered the odd help wanted ad in the *Times*. Her original self had been detoured away from the situation, to be recruited if necessary at a later time.

"Unusual in what way?" she asked. "I don't understand. What am I looking for?"

"You'll know it when you see it," the Tarbleck-null said.

He handed her the key.

She accepted it. There were tools hidden within her body whose powers dwarfed those of this primitive chronotransfer device. But the encoded information the key contained would lay open the workings of the Aftermen Empire to her. Working right under their noses, she would be able to undo their schemes, diminish their power, and, ultimately, prevent them from ever coming into existence in the first place.

Ellie had only the vaguest idea how she was supposed to accomplish all this. But she was confident she could figure it out, given time. And she had the time.

All the time in the world.

TRICERATOPS SUMMER

The dinosaurs looked all wobbly in the summer heat shimmering up from the pavement. There were about thirty of them, a small herd of what appeared to be *Triceratops*. They were crossing the road—don't ask me why—so I downshifted and brought the truck to a halt, and waited.

Waited and watched.

They were interesting creatures, and surprisingly graceful for all their bulk. They picked their way delicately across the road, looking neither to the right nor the left. I was pretty sure I'd correctly identified them by now—they had those three horns on their faces. I used to be a kid. I'd owned the plastic models.

My next-door neighbor, Gretta, who was sitting in the cab next to me with her eyes closed, said, "Why aren't we moving?"

"Dinosaurs in the road," I said.

She opened her eyes.

"Son of a bitch," she said.

Then, before I could stop her, she leaned over and honked the horn, three times. Loud.

As one, every *Triceratops* in the herd froze in its tracks, and swung its head around to face the truck.

I practically fell over laughing.

"What's so goddamn funny?" Gretta wanted to know. But I could only point and shake my head helplessly, tears of laughter rolling down my cheeks.

It was the frills. They were beyond garish. They were as bright as any circus poster, with red whorls and yellow slashes and electric orange diamonds—too many shapes and colors to catalog, and each one different.

They looked like Chinese kites! Like butterflies with six-foot wingspans! Like Las Vegas on acid! And then, under those carnival-bright displays, the most stupid faces imaginable, blinking and gaping like brain-damaged cows. Oh, they were funny, all right, but if you couldn't see that at a glance, you never were going to.

Gretta was getting fairly steamed. She climbed down out of the cab and slammed the door behind her. At the sound, a couple of the *Triceratops* pissed themselves with excitement, and the lot shied away a step or two. Then they began huddling a little closer, to see what would happen next.

Gretta hastily climbed back into the cab. "What are those bastards up to now?" she demanded irritably. She seemed to blame me for their behavior. Not that she could say so, considering she was in my truck and her BMW was still in the garage in South Burlington.

"They're curious," I said. "Just stand still. Don't move or make any noise, and after a bit they'll lose interest and wander off."

"How do you know? You ever see anything like them before?"

"No," I admitted. "But I worked on a dairy farm when I was a young fella, thirty, forty years ago, and the behavior seems similar."

In fact, the *Triceratops* were already getting bored and starting to wander off again when a battered old Hyundai pulled wildly up beside us, and a skinny young man with the worst-combed hair I'd seen in a long time jumped out. They decided to stay and watch.

The young man came running over to us, arms waving. I leaned out the window. "What's the problem, son?"

He was pretty bad upset. "There's been an accident—an *incident*, I mean. At the Institute." He was talking about the Institute for Advanced Physics, which was not all that far from here. It was government-funded and affiliated in some way I'd never been able to get straight with the University of Vermont. "The verge stabilizers failed and the meson-field inverted and vectorized. The congruence factors went to infinity and…" He seized control of himself. "You're not supposed to see *any* of this."

"These things are yours, then?" I said. "So you'd know. They're *Triceratops*, right?"

"*Triceratops horridus*," he said distractedly. I felt unreasonably pleased with myself. "For the most part. There might be a couple other species of *Triceratops* mixed in there as well. They're like ducks in that regard. They're not fussy about what company they keep."

Gretta shot out her wrist and glanced meaningfully at her watch. Like everything else she owned, it was expensive. She worked for a firm in Essex Junction that did systems analysis for companies that were considering downsizing. Her job was to find out exactly what everybody did and then tell the CEO who could be safely cut. "I'm losing money," she grumbled.

I ignored her.

"Listen," the kid said. "You've got to keep quiet about this. We can't afford to have it get out. It has to be kept a secret."

"A secret?" On the far side of the herd, three cars had drawn up and stopped. Their passengers were standing in the road, gawking. A Ford Taurus pulled up behind us, and its driver rolled down his window for a better look. "You're planning to keep a herd of dinosaurs secret? There must be dozens of these things."

"Hundreds," he said despairingly. "They were migrating. The herd broke up after it came through. This is only a fragment of it."

"Then I don't see how you're going to keep this a secret. I mean, just look at them. They're practically the size of tanks. People are bound to notice."

"My God, my God."

Somebody on the other side had a camera out and was taking pictures. I didn't point this out to the young man.

Gretta had been getting more and more impatient as the conversation proceeded. Now she climbed down out of the truck and said, "I can't afford to waste any more time here. I've got work to do."

"Well, so do I, Gretta."

She snorted derisively. "Ripping out toilets, and nailing up sheet rock! Already, I've lost more money than you earn in a week."

She stuck out her hand at the young man. "Give me your car keys."

Dazed, the kid obeyed. Gretta climbed down, got in the Hyundai, and wheeled it around. "I'll have somebody return this to the Institute later today."

Then she was gone, off to find another route around the herd.

She should have waited, because a minute later the beasts decided to leave, and in no time at all were nowhere to be seen. They'd be easy enough to find, though. They pretty much trampled everything flat in their wake.

The kid shook himself, as if coming out of a trance. "Hey," he said. "She took my *car*."

"Climb into the cab," I said. "There's a bar a ways up the road. I think you need a drink."

●

He said his name was Everett McCoughlan, and he clutched his glass like he would fall off the face of the Earth if he were to let go. It took a couple of whiskeys to get the full story out of him. Then I sat silent for a long time. I don't mind admitting that what he'd said made me feel a little funny. "How long?" I asked at last.

"Ten weeks, maybe three months, tops. No more."

I took a long swig of my soda water. (I've never been much of a drinker. Also, it was pretty early in the morning.) Then I told Everett that I'd be right back.

I went out to the truck, and dug the cell phone out of the glove compartment.

First I called home. Delia had already left for the bridal shop, and they didn't like her getting personal calls at work, so I left a message saying that I loved her. Then I called Green Mountain Books. It wasn't open yet, but Randy likes to come in early and he picked up the phone when he heard my voice on the machine. I asked him if he had anything on *Triceratops*. He said to hold on a minute, and then said yes, he had one copy of *The Horned Dinosaurs* by Peter Dodson. I told him I'd pick it up next time I was in town.

Then I went back in the bar. Everett had just ordered a third whiskey, but I pried it out of his hand. "You've had enough of that," I said. "Go home, take a nap. Maybe putter around in the garden."

"I don't have my car," he pointed out.

"Where do you live? I'll take you home."

"Anyway, I'm supposed to be at work. I didn't log out. And technically I'm still on probation."

"What difference does that make," I asked, "now?"

●

Everett had an apartment in Winooski at the Woolen Mill, so I guess the Institute paid him good money. Either that or he wasn't very smart how he spent it. After I dropped him off, I called a couple contractors I knew and arranged for them to take over what jobs I was already committed to. Then I called the *Free Press* to cancel my regular ad, and all my customers to explain I was having scheduling problems and had to subcontract their jobs. Only old Mrs. Bremmer gave me any trouble over that, and even she came around after I said that in any case I wouldn't be able to get around to her Jacuzzi until sometime late July.

Finally, I went to the bank and arranged for a second mortgage on my house.

It took me a while to convince Art Letourneau I was serious. I'd been doing business with him for a long while, and he knew how I felt about debt. Also, I was pretty evasive about what I wanted the money for. He was half-suspicious I was having some kind of late onset mid-life crisis. But the deed was in my name and property values were booming locally, so in the end the deal went through.

On the way home, I stopped at a jewelry store and at the florist's.

Delia's eyes widened when she saw the flowers, and then narrowed at the size of the stone on the ring. She didn't look at all the way I'd thought she would. "This better be good," she said.

So I sat down at the kitchen table and told her the whole story. When I was done, Delia was silent for a long while, just as I'd been. Then she said, "How much time do we have?"

"Three months if we're lucky. Ten weeks in any case," Everett said.

"You believe him?"

"He seemed pretty sure of himself."

If there's one thing I am, it's a good judge of character, and Delia knew it. When Gretta moved into the rehabbed barn next door, I'd said right from the start she was going to be a difficult neighbor. And that was before she'd smothered the grass on her property under three different colors of mulch, and then complained about me keeping my pickup parked in the driveway, out in plain sight.

Delia thought seriously for a few minutes, frowning in that way she has when she's concentrating, and then she smiled. It was a wan little thing, but a smile nonetheless. "Well, I've always wished we could afford a real first-class vacation."

I was glad to hear her say so, because that was exactly the direction my own thought had been trending in. And happier than that when she flung out her arms and whooped, "I'm going to *Disney*world!"

"Hell," I said. "We've got enough money to go to Disneyworld, Disneyland, *and* Eurodisney, one after the other. I think there's one in Japan too."

We were both laughing at this point, and then she dragged me up out of the chair, and the two of us were dancing around and round the kitchen, still a little spooked under it all, but mostly being as giddy and happy as kids.

We were going to sleep in the next morning, but old habits die hard and anyway, Delia felt she owed it to the bridal shop to give them a week's notice. So, after she'd left, I went out to see if I could find where the *Triceratops* had gone.

Only to discover Everett standing by the side of the road with his thumb out.

I pulled over. "Couldn't get somebody at the Institute to drive your car home?" I asked when we were underway again.

"It never got there," he said gloomily. "That woman who was with you the other day drove it into a ditch. Stripped the clutch and bent the frame out of shape. She said she wouldn't have had the accident if my dinosaurs hadn't gotten her upset. Then she hung up on me. I just started at this job. I don't have the savings to buy a new car."

"Lease one instead," I said. "Put it on your credit card and pay the minimum for the next two or three months."

"I hadn't thought of that."

We drove on for a while and then I asked, "How'd she manage to get in touch with you?" She'd driven off before he mentioned his name.

"She called the Institute and asked for the guy with the bad hair. They gave her my home phone number."

The parking lot for the Institute for Advanced Physics had a card system, so I let Everett off by the side of the road. "Thanks for not telling anybody," he said as he climbed out. "About…you know."

"It seemed wisest not to."

He started away and then turned back suddenly and asked, "Is my hair really that bad?"

"Nothing that a barber couldn't fix," I said.

I'd driven to the Institute by the main highway. Returning, I went by back ways, through farmland. When I came to where I'd seen the *Triceratops*, I thought for an instant there'd been an accident, there were so many vehicles by the side of the road. But it turned out they were mostly gawkers and television crews. So apparently the herd hadn't gone far. There were cameras up and down the road and lots of good looking young women standing in front of them with wireless microphones.

I pulled over to take a look. One *Triceratops* had come right up to the fence and was browsing on some tall weeds there. It didn't seem to have any fear of human beings, possibly because in its day mammals never got much bigger than badgers. I walked up and stroked its back, which was hard and pebbly and warm. It was the warmth that got to me. It made the experience real.

A newswoman came over with her cameraman in tow. "You certainly look happy," she said.

"Well, I always wanted to meet a real live dinosaur." I turned to face her, but I kept one hand on the critter's frill. "They're something to see, I'll tell you. Dumb as mud but lots more fun to look at."

She asked me a few questions, and I answered them as best I could. Then, after she did her wrap, she got out a notebook and took down my name and asked me what I did. I told her I was a contractor but that I used to work on a dairy farm. She seemed to like that.

I watched for a while more, and then drove over to Burlington to pick up my book. The store wasn't open yet, but Randy let me in when I knocked. "You bastard," he said after he'd locked the door behind me. "Do you have any idea how much I could have sold this for? I had a foreigner," by which I understood him to mean somebody from New York State or possibly New Hampshire, "offer me two hundred dollars for it. And I could have got more if I'd had something to dicker with!"

"I'm obliged," I said, and paid him in paper bills. He waved off the tax but kept the nickel. "Have you gone out to see 'em yet?"

"Are you nuts? There's thousands of people coming into the state to look at those things. It's going to be a madhouse out there."

"I thought the roads seemed crowded. But it wasn't as bad as all of that."

"It's early still. You just wait."

Randy was right. By evening the roads were so congested that Delia was an hour late getting home. I had a casserole in the oven and the book open on the kitchen table when she staggered in. "The males have longer, more elevated horns, where the females have shorter, more forward-directed horns," I told her. "Also, the males are bigger than the females, but the females outnumber the males by a ratio of two to one."

I leaned back in my chair with a smile. "Two to one. Imagine that."

Delia hit me. "Let me see that thing."

I handed her the book. It kind of reminded me of when we were new-married, and used to go out bird-watching. Before things got so busy. Then Delia's friend Martha called and said to turn on Channel 3 quick. We did, and there I was saying, "dumb as mud."

"So you're a cattle farmer now?" Delia said, when the spot was over.

"That's not what I told her. She got it mixed up. Hey, look what I got." I'd been to three separate travel agents that afternoon. Now I spread out the brochures: Paris, Dubai, Rome, Australia, Rio de Janeiro, Marrakech. Even Disneyworld. I'd grabbed everything that looked interesting. "Take your pick, we can be there tomorrow."

Delia looked embarrassed.

"What?" I said.

"You know that June is our busy season. All those young brides. Francesca begged me to stay on through the end of the month."

"But—"

"It's not that long," she said.

For a couple of days it was like Woodstock, the Super Bowl, and the World Series all rolled into one—the Interstates came to a standstill, and it was worth your life to actually have to go somewhere. Then the governor called in the National Guard, and they cordoned off Chittenden County so you had to show your ID to get in or out. The *Triceratops* had scattered into little groups by then. Then a dozen or two were captured and shipped out of state to zoos where they could be more easily seen. So things returned to normal, almost.

I was painting the trim on the house that next Saturday when Everett drove up in a beat-up old clunker. "I like your new haircut," I said. "Looks good. You here to see the trikes?"

"Trikes?"

"That's what they're calling your dinos. *Triceratops* is too long for common use. We got a colony of eight or nine hanging around the neighborhood." There were woods out back of the house and beyond them a little marsh. They liked to browse the margins of the wood and wallow in the mud.

"No, uh...I came to find out the name of that woman you were with. The one who took my car."

"Gretta Houck, you mean?"

"I guess. I've been thinking it over, and I think she really ought to pay for the repairs. I mean, right's right."

"I noticed you decided against leasing."

"It felt dishonest. This car's cheap. But it's not very good. One door is wired shut with a coat hanger."

Delia came out of the house with the picnic basket then and I introduced them. "Ev's looking for Gretta," I said.

"Well, your timing couldn't be better," Delia said. "We were just about to go out trike-watching with her. You can join us."

"Oh, I can't—"

"Don't give it a second thought. There's plenty of food." Then, to me, "I'll go fetch Gretta while you clean up."

So that's how we found ourselves following the little trail through the woods and out to the meadow on the bluff above the Tylers' farm. The trikes slept in the field there. They'd torn up the crops pretty bad. But the state was covering damages, so the Tylers didn't seem to mind. It made me wonder if the governor knew what we knew. If he'd been talking with the folks at the Institute.

I spread out the blanket, and Delia got out cold cuts, deviled eggs, lemonade, all the usual stuff. I'd brought along two pairs of binoculars, which I handed out to our guests. Gretta had been pretty surly so far, which made me wonder how Delia'd browbeat her into coming along. But now she said, "Oh, look! They've got babies!"

There were three little ones, only a few feet long. Two of them were mock-fighting, head-butting and tumbling over and over each other. The third just sat in the sun, blinking. They were all as cute as the dickens, with their tiny little nubs of horns and their great big eyes.

The other trikes were wandering around, pulling up bushes and such and eating them. Except for one that stood near the babies, looking big and grumpy and protective. "Is that the mother?" Gretta asked.

"That one's male," Everett said. "You can tell by the horns." He launched into an explanation, which I didn't listen to, having read the book.

On the way back to the house, Gretta grumbled, "I suppose you want the number for my insurance company."

"I guess," Everett said.

They disappeared into her house for maybe twenty minutes and then Everett got into his clunker and drove away. Afterwards, I said to Delia, "I thought the whole point of the picnic was you and I were going to finally work out where we were going on vacation." She hadn't even brought along the travel books I'd bought her.

"I think they like each other."

"Is that what this was about? You know, you've done some damn fool things in your time—"

"Like what?" Delia said indignantly. "When have I ever done anything that was less than wisdom incarnate?"

"Well…you married me."

"Oh, that." She put her arms around me. "That was just the exception that proves the rule."

So, what with one thing and the other, the summer drifted by. Delia took to luring the *Triceratops* closer and closer to the house with cabbages and bunches of celery and such. Cabbages were their favorite. It got so that we were feeding the trikes off the back porch in the evenings. They'd come clomping up around sunset, hoping for cabbages but willing to settle for pretty much anything.

It ruined the yard, but so what? Delia was a little upset when they got into her garden, but I spent a day putting up a good strong fence around it, and she replanted. She made manure tea by mixing their dung with water, and its effect on the plants was bracing. The roses blossomed like never before, and in August the tomatoes came up spectacular.

I mentioned this to Dave Jenkins down at the home-and-garden and he looked thoughtful. "I believe there's a market for that," he said. "I'll buy as much of their manure as you can haul over here."

"Sorry," I told him, "I'm on vacation."

Still, I couldn't get Delia to commit to a destination. Not that I quit trying. I was telling her about the Atlantis Hotel on Paradise Island one evening when suddenly she said, "Well, look at this."

I stopped reading about swimming with dolphins and the fake undersea ruined city, and joined her at the door. There was Everett's car—the new one that Gretta's insurance had paid for—parked out front of her house. There was only one light on, in the kitchen. Then that one went out too.

We figured those two had worked through their differences.

An hour later, though, we heard doors slamming, and the screech of Everett's car pulling out too fast. Then somebody was banging on our screen door. It was Gretta. When Delia let her in, she burst out into tears. Which surprised me. I wouldn't have pegged Everett as that kind of guy.

I made some coffee while Delia guided her into a kitchen chair, and got her some tissues, and soothed her down enough that she could tell us why she'd thrown Everett out of her house. It wasn't anything he'd done apparently, but something he'd said.

"Do you know what he *told* me?" she sobbed.

"I think I do," Delia said.

"About timelike—"

"—loops. Yes, dear."

Gretta looked stricken. "You too? Why didn't you tell me? Why didn't you tell everybody?"

"I considered it," I said. "Only then I thought, what would folks do if they knew their actions no longer mattered? Most would behave decently enough. But a few would do some pretty bad things, I'd think. I didn't want to be responsible for that."

She was silent for a while.

"Explain to me again about timelike loops," she said at last. "Ev tried, but by then I was too upset to listen. "

"Well, I'm not so sure myself. But the way he explained it to me, they're going to fix the problem by going back to the moment before the rupture occurred and preventing it from ever happening in the first place. When that happens, everything from the moment of rupture to the moment when they go back to apply the patch separates from the trunk timeline. It just sort of drifts away, and dissolves into nothingness—never was, never will be."

"And what becomes of us?"

"We just go back to whatever we were doing when the accident happened. None the worse for wear."

"But without memories."

"How can you remember something that never happened?"

"So Ev and I—"

"No, dear," Delia said gently.

"How much time do we have?"

"With a little luck, we have the rest of the summer," Delia said. "The question is, how do you want to spend it?"

"What does it matter," Gretta said bitterly. "If it's all going to end?"

"Everything ends eventually. But after all is said and done, it's what we do in the meantime that matters, isn't it?"

The conversation went on for a while more. But that was the gist of it.

Eventually, Gretta got out her cell and called Everett. She had him on speed dial, I noticed. In her most corporate voice, she said, "Get your ass over here," and snapped the phone shut without waiting for a response.

She didn't say another word until Everett's car pulled up in front of her place. Then she went out and confronted him. He put his hands on his hips. She grabbed him and kissed him. Then she took him by the hand and led him back into the house.

They didn't bother to turn on the lights.

I stared at the silent house for a little bit. Then I realized that Delia wasn't with me anymore, so I went looking for her.

She was out on the back porch. "Look," she whispered.

There was a full moon and by its light we could see the *Triceratops* settling down to sleep in our backyard. Delia had managed to lure them all the way in at last. Their skin was all silvery in the moonlight; you couldn't make out the patterns on their frills. The big trikes formed a kind of circle around the little ones. One by one, they closed their eyes and fell asleep.

Believe it or not, the big bull male snored.

It came to me then that we didn't have much time left. One morning soon we'd wake up and it would be the end of spring and everything would be exactly as it was before the dinosaurs came. "We never did get to Paris or London or Rome or Marrakech," I said sadly. "Or even Disneyworld."

Without taking her eyes off the sleeping trikes, Delia put an arm around my waist. "Why are you so fixated on going places?" she asked. "We had a nice time here, didn't we?"

"I just wanted to make you happy."

"Oh, you idiot. You did that decades ago."

So there we stood, in the late summer of our lives. Out of nowhere, we'd been given a vacation from our ordinary lives, and now it was almost over. A pessimist would have said that we were just waiting for oblivion. But Delia and I didn't see it that way. Life is strange. Sometimes it's hard, and other times it's painful enough to break your heart. But sometimes it's grotesque and beautiful. Sometimes it fills you with wonder, like a *Triceratops* sleeping in the moonlight.

FROM BABEL'S FALL'N GLORY WE FLED

I magine a cross between Byzantium and a termite mound. Imagine a jeweled mountain, slender as an icicle, rising out of the steam jungles and disappearing into the dazzling pearl-grey skies of Gehenna. Imagine that Gaudi—he of the Segrada Familia and other biomorphic architectural whimsies—had been commissioned by a nightmare race of giant black millipedes to recreate Barcelona at the height of its glory, along with touches of the Forbidden City in the eighteenth century and Tokyo in the twenty-second, all within a single miles-high structure. Hold every bit of that in your mind at once, multiply by a thousand, and you've got only the faintest ghost of a notion of the splendor that was Babel.

Now imagine being inside Babel when it fell.

Hello. I'm Rosamund. I'm dead. I was present in human form when it happened and as a simulation chaotically embedded within a liquid crystal data-matrix then and thereafter up to the present moment. I was killed instantly when the meteors hit. I saw it all.

Rosamund means "rose of the world." It's the third most popular female name on Europa, after Gaea and Virginia Dare. For all our elaborate sophistication, we wear our hearts on our sleeves, we Europans.

Here's what it was like:

❁

"Wake *up*! Wake *up*! Wake *up*!"

"Wha—?" Carlos Quivera sat up, shedding rubble. He coughed, choked, shook his head. He couldn't seem to think clearly. An instant

449

ago he'd been standing in the chilled and pressurized embassy suite, conferring with Arsenio. Now..."How long have I been asleep?"

"Unconscious. Ten hours," his suit (that's me—Rosamund!) said. It had taken that long to heal his burns. Now it was shooting wake-up drugs into him: amphetamines, endorphins, attention enhancers, a witch's brew of chemicals. Physically dangerous, but in this situation, whatever it might be, Quivera would survive by intelligence or not at all. "I was able to form myself around you before the walls ruptured. You were lucky."

"The others? Did the others survive?"

"Their suits couldn't reach them in time."

"Did Rosamund...?"

"All the others are dead."

Quivera stood.

Even in the aftermath of disaster, Babel was an imposing structure. Ripped open and exposed to the outside air, a thousand rooms spilled over one another toward the ground. Bridges and buttresses jutted into gaping smoke-filled canyons created by the slow collapse of hexagonal support beams (this was new data; I filed it under *Architecture*, subheading: *Support Systems* with links to *Esthetics* and *Xenopsychology*) in a jumbled geometry that would have terrified Piranesi himself. Everywhere, gleaming black millies scurried over the rubble.

Quivera stood.

In the canted space about him, bits and pieces of the embassy rooms were identifiable: a segment of wood molding, some velvet drapery now littered with chunks of marble, shreds of wallpaper (after a design by William Morris) now curling and browning in the heat. Human interior design was like nothing native to Gehenna and it had taken a great deal of labor and resources to make the embassy so pleasant for human habitation. The queen-mothers had been generous with everything but their trust.

Quivera stood.

There were several corpses remaining as well, still recognizably human though they were blistered and swollen by the savage heat. These had been his colleagues (all of them), his friends (most of them), his enemies (two, perhaps three), and even his lover (one). Now they were gone, and it was as if they had been compressed into one indistinguishable mass, and his feelings toward them all as well: shock and sorrow and anger and survivor guilt all slagged together to become one savage emotion.

Quivera threw back his head and howled.

I had a reference point now. Swiftly, I mixed serotonin-precursors and injected them through a hundred microtubules into the appropriate areas of his brain. Deftly, they took hold. Quivera stopped crying. I had my metaphorical hands on the control knobs of his emotions. I turned him cold, cold, cold.

"I feel nothing," he said wonderingly. "Everyone is dead, and I feel nothing." Then, flat as flat: "What kind of monster am I?"

"*My* monster," I said fondly. "My duty is to ensure that you and the information you carry within you get back to Europa. So I have chemically neutered your emotions. You must remain a meat puppet for the duration of this mission." Let him hate me—I who have no true ego, but only a facsimile modeled after a human original—all that mattered now was bringing him home alive.

"Yes." Quivera reached up and touched his helmet with both hands, as if he would reach through it and feel his head to discover if it were as large as it felt. "That makes sense. I can't be emotional at a time like this."

He shook himself, then strode out to where the gleaming black millies were scurrying by. He stepped in front of one, a least-cousin, to question it. The millie paused, startled. Its eyes blinked three times in its triangular face. Then, swift as a tickle, it ran up the front of his suit, down the back, and was gone before the weight could do more than buckle his knees.

"Shit!" he said. Then, "Access the wiretaps. I've got to know what happened."

Passive wiretaps had been implanted months ago, but never used, the political situation being too tense to risk their discovery. Now his suit activated them to monitor what remained of Babel's communications network: A demon's chorus of pulsed messages surging through a shredded web of cables. Chaos, confusion, demands to know what had become of the queen-mothers. Analytic functions crunched data, synthesized, snyopsized: "There's an army outside with Ziggurat insignia. They've got the city surrounded. They're killing the refugees."

"Wait, wait..." Quivera took a deep, shuddering breath. "Let me think." He glanced briskly about and for the second time noticed the human bodies, ruptured and parboiled in the fallen plaster and porphyry. "Is one of those Rosamund?"

"I'm *dead*, Quivera. You can mourn me later. Right now, survival is priority number one," I said briskly. The suit added mood-stabilizers to his maintenance drip.

"Stop speaking in her voice."

"Alas, dear heart, I cannot. The suit's operating on diminished function. It's this voice or nothing."

He looked away from the corpses, eyes hardening. "Well, it's not important." Quivera was the sort of young man who was energized by war. It gave him permission to indulge his ruthless side. It allowed him to pretend he didn't care. "Right now, what we have to do is—"

"Uncle Vanya's coming," I said. "I can sense his pheromones."

Picture a screen of beads, crystal lozenges, and rectangular lenses. Behind that screen, a nightmare face like a cross between the front of a locomotive and a tree grinder. Imagine on that face (though most humans would be unable to read them) the lineaments of grace and dignity seasoned by cunning and, perhaps, a dash of wisdom. Trusted advisor to the queen-mothers. Second only to them in rank. A wily negotiator and a formidable enemy. That was Uncle Vanya.

Two small speaking-legs emerged from the curtain, and he said:

::(cautious) greetings::
|
::(Europan vice-consul 12)/Quivera/[treacherous vermin]::
|
::obligations <untranslatable> (grave duty)::
| |
::demand/claim [action]:: ::promise (trust)::

"Speak pidgin, damn you! This is no time for subtlety."

The speaking legs were very still for a long moment. Finally they moved again:

::The queen-mothers are dead::

"Then Babel is no more. I grieve for you."

::I despise your grief:: A lean and chitinous appendage emerged from the beaded screen. From its tripartite claw hung a smooth white rectangle the size of a briefcase. ::I must bring this to (sister-city)/Ur/[absolute trust]::

"What is it?"

A very long pause. Then, reluctantly ::Our library::

"Your library." This was something new. Something unheard-of. Quivera doubted the translation was a good one. "What does it contain?"

::Our history. Our sciences. Our ritual dances. A record-of-kinship dating back to the (Void)/Origin/[void]. Everything that can be saved is here::

A thrill of avarice raced through Quivera. He tried to imagine how much this was worth, and could not. Values did not go that high. However much his superiors screwed him out of (and they would work very hard indeed to screw him out of everything they could) what remained would be enough to buy him out of debt, and do the same for a wife and their children after them as well. He did not think of Rosamund. "You won't get through the army outside without my help," he said. "I want the right to copy—" How much did he dare ask for? "—three tenths of one percent. Assignable solely to me. Not to Europa. To me."

Uncle Vanya dipped his head, so that they were staring face to face. ::You are (an evil creature)/[faithless]. I hate you::

Quivera smiled. "A relationship that starts out with mutual understanding has made a good beginning."

::A relationship that starts out without trust will end badly::

"That's as it may be." Quivera looked around for a knife. "The first thing we have to do is castrate you."

This is what the genocides saw:

They were burning pyramids of corpses outside the city when a Europan emerged, riding a gelded least-cousin. The soldiers immediately stopped stacking bodies and hurried toward him, flowing like quicksilver, calling for their superiors.

The Europan drew up and waited.

The officer who interrogated him spoke from behind the black glass visor of a delicate-legged war machine. He examined the Europan's credentials carefully, though there could be no serious doubt as to his species. Finally, reluctantly, he signed ::You may pass::

"That's not enough," the Europan (Quivera!) said. "I'll need transportation, an escort to protect me from wild animals in the steam jungles, and a guide to lead me to…" His suit transmitted the sign for ::(starport)/Ararat/[trust-for-all]::

The officer's speaking-legs thrashed in what might best be translated as scornful laughter. ::We will lead you to the jungle and no further/(hopefully-to-die)/[treacherous non-millipede]::

"Look who talks of treachery!" the Europan said (but of course I did not translate his words), and with a scornful wave of one hand, rode his neuter into the jungle.

The genocides never bothered to look closely at his mount. Neutered least-cousins were beneath their notice. They didn't even wear face-curtains, but went about naked for all the world to scorn.

Black pillars billowed from the corpse-fires into a sky choked with smoke and dust. There were hundreds of fires and hundreds of pillars and, combined with the low cloud cover, they made all the world seem like the interior of a temple to a vengeful god. The soldiers from Ziggurat escorted him through the army and beyond the line of fires, where the steam jungles waited, verdant and threatening.

As soon as the green darkness closed about them, Uncle Vanya twisted his head around and signed ::Get off me/vast humiliation/[lack-of-trust]::

"Not a chance," Quivera said harshly. "I'll ride you 'til sunset, and all day tomorrow and for a week after that. Those soldiers didn't fly here, or you'd have seen them coming. They came through the steam forest on foot, and there'll be stragglers."

The going was difficult at first, and then easy, as they passed from a recently forested section of the jungle into a stand of old growth. The boles of the "trees" here were as large as those of the redwoods back on Earth, some specimens of which are as old as five thousand years. The way wended back and forth. Scant sunlight penetrated through the canopy, and the steam quickly drank in what little light Quivera's headlamp put out. Ten trees in, they would have been hopelessly lost had it not been for the suit's navigational functions and the mapsats that fed it geodetic mathscapes accurate to a finger's span of distance.

Quivera pointed this out. "Learn now," he said, "the true value of information."

::Information has no value:: Uncle Vanya said ::without trust::

Quivera laughed. "In that case you must, all against your will, trust me."

To this Uncle Vanya had no answer.

At nightfall, they slept on the sheltered side of one of the great para-sequoias. Quivera took two refrigeration sticks from the saddlebags and stuck them upright in the dirt. Uncle Vanya immediately coiled himself around his and fell asleep. Quivera sat down beside him to think over the events of the day, but under the influence of his suit's medication, he fell asleep almost immediately as well.

All machines know that humans are happiest when they think least.

In the morning, they set off again.

The terrain grew hilly, and the old growth fell behind them. There was sunlight and to spare now, bounced and reflected about by the ubiquitous jungle steam and by the synthetic-diamond coating so many of this world's plants and insects employ for protection.

As they traveled, they talked. Quivera was still complexly medicated, but the dosages had been decreased. It left him in a melancholy, reflective mood.

"It was treachery," Quivera said. Though we maintained radio silence out of fear of Ziggurat troops, my passive receivers fed him regular news reports from Europa. "The High Watch did not simply fail to divert a meteor. They let three rocks through. All of them came slanting low through the atmosphere, aimed directly at Babel. They hit almost simultaneously."

Uncle Vanya dipped his head. ::Yes:: he mourned. ::It has the stench of truth to it. It must be (reliable)/a fact/[absolutely trusted]::

"We tried to warn you."

::You had no (worth)/trust/[worthy-of-trust]:: Uncle Vanya's speaking legs registered extreme agitation. ::You told lies::

"Everyone tells lies."

"No. We-of-the-Hundred-Cities are truthful/truthful/[never-lie]::

"If you had, Babel would be standing now."

::No!/NO!/[no!!!]::

"Lies are a lubricant in the social machine. They ease the friction when two moving parts mesh imperfectly."

::Aristotle, asked what those who tell lies gain by it, replied: That when they speak the truth they are not believed::

For a long moment Quivera was silent. Then he laughed mirthlessly. "I almost forgot that you're a diplomat. Well, you're right, I'm right, and we're both screwed. Where do we go from here?"

::To (sister-city)/Ur/[absolute trust]:: Uncle Vanya signed, while "You've said more than enough," his suit (me!) whispered in Quivera's ear. "Change the subject."

A stream ran, boiling, down the center of the dell. Run-off from the mountains, it would grow steadily smaller until it dwindled away to nothing. Only the fact that the air above it was at close to one hundred percent saturation had kept it going this long. Quivera pointed. "Is that safe to cross?"

::If (leap-over-safe) then (safe)/best not/[reliable distrust]::

"I didn't think so."

They headed downstream. It took several miles before the stream grew small enough that they were confident to jump it. Then they turned toward Ararat—the Europans had dropped GPS pebble satellites in low Gehenna orbit shortly after arriving in the system and making contact with the indigenes, but I don't know from what source Uncle Vanya derived his sense of direction.

It was inerrant, however. The mapsats confirmed it. I filed that fact under *Unexplained Phenomena* with tentative links to *Physiology* and *Navigation*. Even if both my companions died and the library were lost, this would still be a productive journey, provided only that Europan searchers could recover me within ten years, before my data lattice began to degrade.

For hours Uncle Vanya walked and Quivera rode in silence. Finally, though, they had to break to eat. I fed Quivera nutrients intravenously and the illusion of a full meal through somatic shunts. Vanya burrowed furiously into the earth and emerged with something that looked like a grub the size of a poodle, which he ate so vigorously that Quivera had to look away.

(I filed this under *Xenoecology*, subheading: *Feeding Strategies*. The search for knowledge knows no rest.)

Afterwards, while they were resting, Uncle Vanya resumed their conversation, more formally this time:

::(for what) purpose/reason::

|

::(Europan vice-consul12)/Quivera/[not trusted]::

|

::voyagings (search-for-trust)/ [action]::

| |

::(nest)/Europa/<untranslatable> :: ::violate/[absolute resistance]::

| | |

::(nest)/[trust] Gehenna/[trust] Home/[trust]::

"Why did you leave your world to come to ours?" I simplified/translated. "Except he believes that humans brought their world here and parked it in orbit." This was something we had never been able to make the millies understand; that Europa, large though it was, was not a planetlet but a habitat, a ship if you will, though by now well over half a million inhabitants lived in tunnels burrowed deep in its substance. It was only a city, however, and its resources would not last forever. We needed to convince the Gehennans to give us a toehold on their planet if we were, in the long run, to survive. But you knew that already.

"We've told you this before. We came looking for new information."

::Information is (free)/valueless/[despicable]::

"Look," Quivera said. "We have an information-based economy. Yours is based on trust. The mechanisms of each are not dissimilar. Both are expansive systems. Both are built on scarcity. And both are speculative. Information or trust is bought, sold, borrowed, and invested. Each therefore requires a continually expanding economic frontier which ultimately leaves the individual so deep in debt as to be virtually enslaved to the system. You see?"

::No::

"All right. Imagine a simplified capitalist system—that's what both our economies are, at root. You've got a thousand individuals, each of whom makes a living by buying raw materials, improving them, and selling them at a profit. With me so far?"

Vanya signaled comprehension.

"The farmer buys seed and fertilizer, and sells crops. The weaver buys wool and sells cloth. The chandler buys wax and sells candles. The price of their goods is the cost of materials plus the value of their labor. The value of his labor is the worker's wages. This is a simple market economy. It can go on forever. The equivalent on Gehenna would be the primitive family-states you had long ago, in which everybody knew everybody else, and so trust was a simple matter and directly reciprocal."

Startled, Uncle Vanya signed ::How did you know about our past?::

"Europans value knowledge. Everything you tell us, we remember." The knowledge had been assembled with enormous effort and expense, largely from stolen data—but no reason to mention *that*. Quivera continued, "Now imagine that most of those workers labor in ten factories, making the food, clothing, and other objects that everybody needs. The owners of these factories must make a profit, so they sell their goods for more than they pay for them—the cost of materials, the cost of labor, and then the profit, which we can call 'added value.'

"But because this is a simplified model, there are no outside markets. The goods can only be sold to the thousand workers themselves, and the total cost of the goods is more than the total amount they've been paid collectively for the materials and their labor. So how can they afford it? They go into debt. Then they borrow money to support that debt. The money is lent to them by the factories selling them goods on credit. There is not enough money—not enough real value—in the system to pay off the debt, and so it continues to increase until it can no longer be sustained. Then there is an catastrophic collapse which we call a depression. Two of the businesses go bankrupt and their assets are swallowed up by the survivors at bargain prices, thus paying off their own indebtedness and restoring equilibrium to the system. In the aftermath of which, the cycle begins again."

::What has this to do with ::(beloved city)/Babel/[mother-of-trust]?::

"Your every public action involved an exchange of trust, yes? And every trust that was honored heightened the prestige of the queen-mothers and hence the amount of trust they embodied for Babel itself."

::Yes::

"Similarly, the queen-mothers of other cities, including those cities which were Babel's sworn enemies, embodied enormous amounts of trust as well."

::Of course::

"Was there enough trust in all the world to pay everybody back if all the queen-mothers called it in at the same time?"

Uncle Vanya was silent.

"So *that's* your explanation for…a lot of things. Earth sent us here because it needs new information to cover its growing indebtedness. Building Europa took enormous amounts of information, most of it proprietary, and so we Europans are in debt collectively to our home world and individually to the Lords of the Economy on Europa. With compound interest, every generation is worse off and thus more desperate than the one before. Our need to learn is great, and constantly growing."

::(strangers-without-trust)/Europa/[treacherous vermin]::

|

can/should/<untranslatable>

| |

::demand/claim [negative action]:: ::defy/<untranslatable>/[absolute lack of trust]::

| |

::(those-who-command-trust):: ::(those-who-are-unworthy of trust)::

"He asks why Europa doesn't simply declare bankruptcy," I explained. "Default on its obligations and nationalize all the information received to date. In essence."

The simple answer was that Europa still needed information that could only be beamed from Earth, that the ingenuity of even half a million people could not match that of an entire planet and thus their technology must always be superior to ours, and that if we reneged on our debts they would stop beaming plans for that technology, along with their songs and plays and news of what was going on in countries that had once meant everything to our great-great-grandparents. I watched Quivera struggle to put all this in its simplest possible form.

Finally, he said, "Because no one would ever trust us again, if we did."

After a long stillness, Uncle Vanya lapsed back into pidgin. ::Why did you tell me this [untrustworthy] story?::

"To let you know that we have much in common. We can understand each other."

::<But>/not/[trust]::

"No. But we don't need trust. Mutual self-interest will suffice."

Days passed. Perhaps Quivera and Uncle Vanya grew to understand each other better during this time. Perhaps not. I was able to keep Quivera's electrolyte balances stable and short-circuit his feedback processes so that he felt no extraordinary pain, but he was feeding off of his own body fat and that was beginning to run low. He was very comfortably starving to death—I gave him two weeks, tops—and he knew it. He'd have to be a fool not to, and I had to keep his thinking sharp if he was going to have any chance of survival.

Their way was intersected by a long, low ridge and without comment Quivera and Uncle Vanya climbed up above the canopy of the steam forest and the cloud of moisture it held into clear air. Looking back, Quivera saw a gully in the slope behind them, its bottom washed free of soil by the boiling runoff and littered with square and rectangular stones, but not a trace of hexagonal beams. They had just climbed the tumulus of an ancient fallen city. It lay straight across the land, higher to the east and dwindling to the west. "My name is Ozymandias, King of Kings," Quivera said. "Look on my works, ye mighty, and despair!"

Uncle Vanya said nothing.

"Another meteor strike—what were the odds of that?"

Uncle Vanya said nothing.

"Of course, given enough time, it would be inevitable, it if predated the High Watch."

Uncle Vanya said nothing.

"What was the name of this city?"

::Very old/(name forgotten)/[First Trust]::

Uncle Vanya moved, as if to start downward, but Quivera stopped him with a gesture. "There's no hurry," he said. "Let's enjoy the view for a moment." He swept an unhurried arm from horizon to horizon, indicating the flat and unvarying canopy of vegetation before them. "It's a funny thing. You'd think that, this being one of the first cities your people built when they came to this planet, you'd be able to see the ruins of the cities of the original inhabitants from here."

The millipede's speaking arms thrashed in alarm. Then he reared up into the air, and when he came down one foreleg glinted silver. Faster than human eye could follow, he had drawn a curving and deadly tarsi-sword from a camouflaged belly-sheath.

Quivera's suit flung him away from the descending weapon. He fell flat on his back and rolled to the side. The sword's point missed him by inches. But then the suit flung out a hand and touched the sword with an electrical contact it had just extruded.

A carefully calculated shock threw Uncle Vanya back, convulsing but still fully conscious.

Quivera stood. "Remember the library!" he said. "Who will know of Babel's greatness if it's destroyed?"

For a long time the millipede did nothing that either Quivera or his suit could detect. At last he signed ::How did you know?/(absolute shock)/[treacherous and without faith]::

"Our survival depends on being allowed to live on Gehenna. Your people will not let us do so, no matter what we offer in trade. It was important that we understand why. So we found out. We took in your outlaws and apostates, all those who were cast out of your cities and had nowhere else to go. We gave them sanctuary. In gratitude, they told us what they knew."

By so saying, Quivera let Uncle Vanya know that he knew the most ancient tale of the Gehennans. By so hearing, Uncle Vanya knew that

Quivera knew what he knew. And just so you know what they knew that each other knew and knew was known, here is the tale of...

How the True People Came to Gehenna

Long did our Ancestors burrow down through the dark between the stars, before emerging at last in the soil of Gehenna. From the True Home they had come. To Gehenna they descended, leaving a trail of sparks in the black and empty spaces through which they had traveled. The True People came from a world of unimaginable wonders. To it they could never return. Perhaps they were exiles. Perhaps it was destroyed. Nobody knows.

Into the steam and sunlight of Gehenna they burst, and found it was already taken. The First Inhabitants looked like nothing our Ancestors had ever seen. But they welcomed the True People as the queen-mothers would a strayed niece-daughter. They gave us food. They gave us land. They gave us trust.

For a time all was well.

But evil crept into the thoracic ganglia of the True People. They repaid sisterhood with betrayal and trust with murder. Bright lights were called down from the sky to destroy the cities of their benefactors. Everything the First Inhabitants had made, all their books and statues and paintings, burned with the cities. No trace of them remains. We do not even know what they looked like.

This was how the True People brought war to Gehenna. There had never been war before, and now we will have it with us always, until our trust-debt is repaid. But it can never be repaid.

It suffers in translation, of course. The original is told in thirteen exquisitely beautiful ergoglyphs, each grounded on a primal faith-motion. But Quivera was talking, with care and passion:

"Vanya, listen to me carefully. We have studied your civilization and your planet in far greater detail than you realize. You did not come from another world. Your people evolved here. There was no aboriginal civilization. You ancestors did not eradicate an intelligent species. These things are all a myth."

::No!/Why?!/[shock]:: Uncle Vanya rattled with emotion. Ripples of muscle spasms ran down his segmented body.

"Don't go catatonic on me. Your ancestors didn't lie. Myths are not lies. They are simply an efficient way of encoding truths. We have a similar myth in my religion which we call Original Sin. Man is born sinful. Well…who can doubt that? Saying that we are born into a fallen state means simply that we are not perfect, that we are inherently capable of evil.

"Your myth is very similar to ours, but it also encodes what we call the Malthusian dilemma. Population increases geometrically, while food resources increase arithmetically. So universal starvation is inevitable unless the population is periodically reduced by wars, plagues, and famines. Which means that wars, plagues, and famine cannot be eradicated because they are all that keep a population from extinction.

"But—and this is essential—all that assumes a population that isn't aware of the dilemma. When you understand the fix you're in, you can do something about it. That's why information is so important. Do you understand?"

Uncle Vanya lay down flat upon the ground and did not move for hours. When he finally arose again, he refused to speak at all.

The trail the next day led down into a long meteor valley that had been carved by a ground-grazer long enough ago that its gentle slopes were covered with soil and the bottomland was rich and fertile. An orchard of grenade trees had been planted in interlocking hexagons for as far in either direction as the eye could see. We were still on Babel's territory, but any arbiculturalists had been swept away by whatever military forces from Ziggurat had passed through the area.

The grenades were still green [*footnote*: not literally, of course— they were orange!], their thick husks taut but not yet trembling with the steam-hot pulp that would eventually, in the absence of harvesters, cause them to explode, scattering their arrowhead-shaped seeds or spores [*footnote*: like seeds, the flechettes carried within them surplus nourishment; like spores they would grow into a prothalli which would produce the sex organs responsible for what will become the gamete of the eventual plant; all botanical terms of course being metaphors for xenobiological bodies and processes] with such force as to make them a deadly hazard when ripe.

Not, however, today.

A sudden gust of wind parted the steam, briefly brightening the valley-orchard and showing a slim and graceful trail through the orchard. We followed it down into the valley.

We were midway through the orchard when Quivera bent down to examine a crystal-shelled creature unlike anything in his suit's database. It rested atop the long stalk of a weed [*footnote*: "weed" is not a metaphor; the concept of "an undesired plant growing in cultivated ground" is a cultural universal] in the direct sunlight, its abdomen pulsing slightly as it super-heated a minuscule drop of black ichor. A puff of steam, a sharp *crack*, and it was gone. Entranced, Quivera asked, "What's that called?"

Uncle Vanya stiffened. ::A jet!/danger!/[absolute certainty]::

Then (*crack! crack! crack!*) the air was filled with thin lines of steam, laid down with the precision of a draftsman's ruler, tracing flights so fleet (*crack! crack!*) that it was impossible to tell what in what direction they flew. Nor did it ultimately (*crack!*) matter.

Quivera fell.

Worse, because the thread of steam the jet had stitched through his leg severed an organizational node in his suit, I ceased all upper cognitive functions. Which is as good as to say that I fell unconscious.

Here's what the suit did in my (Rosamund's) absence:

1. Slowly rebuilt the damaged organizational node.

2. Quickly mended the holes that the jet had left in its fabric.

3. Dropped Quivera into a therapeutic coma.

4. Applied restoratives to his injuries, and began the slow and pain-staking process of repairing the damage to his flesh, with particular emphasis on distributed traumatic shock.

5. Filed the jet footage under *Xenobiology*, subheading: *Insect Analogues* with links to *Survival* and *Steam Locomotion*.

6. Told Uncle Vanya that if he tried to abandon Quivera, the suit would run him down, catch him, twist his head from his body like the foul least-cousin that he was and then piss on his corpse.

Two more days passed before the suit returned to full consciousness, during which Uncle Vanya took conscientiously good care of him. Under what motivation, it does not matter. Another day passed after that. The suit had planned to keep Quivera comatose for a week but not long after regaining awareness, circumstances changed. It slammed him back to full consciousness, heart pounding and eyes wide open.

"I blacked out for a second!" he gasped. Then, realizing that the landscape about him did not look familiar, "How long was I unconscious?"

::Three days/<three days>/[casual certainty]::

"Oh."

Then, almost without pausing. ::Your suit/mechanism/[alarm] talks with the voice of Rosamund da Silva/(Europan vice-consul 8)/[uncertainty and doubt]::

"Yes, well, that's because—"

Quivera was fully aware and alert now. So I said: "Incoming."

Two millies erupted out of the black soil directly before us. They both had Ziggurat insignia painted on their flanks and harness. By good luck Uncle Vanya did the best thing possible under the circumstances—he reared into the air in fright. *Millipoid sapiens* anatomy being what it was, this instantly demonstrated to them that he was a gelding and in that instant he was almost reflexively dismissed by the enemy soldiers as being both contemptible and harmless.

Quivera, however, was not.

Perhaps they were brood-traitors who had deserted the war with a fantasy of starting their own nest. Perhaps they were a single unit among thousands scattered along a temporary border, much as land mines were employed in ancient modern times. The soldiers had clearly been almost as surprised by us as we were by them. They had no weapons ready. So they fell upon Quivera with their dagger-tarsi.

His suit (still me) threw him to one side and then to the other as the millies slashed down at him. Then one of them reared up into the air—looking astonished if you knew the interspecies decodes—and fell heavily to the ground.

Uncle Vanya stood over the steaming corpse, one foreleg glinting silver. The second Ziggurat soldier twisted to confront him. Leaving his underside briefly exposed.

Quivera (or rather his suit) joined both hands in a fist and punched upward, through the weak skin of the third sternite behind the head. That was the one which held its sex organs. [*Disclaimer*: All anatomical terms, including "sternite," "sex organs," and "head," are analogues only; unless and until Gehennan life is found to have some direct relationship to Terran life, however tenuous, such descriptors are purely metaphoric.] So it was particularly vulnerable there. And since the suit had muscle-multiplying exoskeletal functions...

Ichor gushed all over the suit.

The fight was over almost as soon as it had begun. Quivera was breathing heavily, as much from the shock as the exertion. Uncle Vanya slid the tarsi-sword back into its belly-sheath. As he did so, he made an involuntary grimace of discomfort. ::There were times when I thought of discarding this:: he signed.

"I'm glad you didn't."

Little puffs of steam shot up from the bodies of the dead millipedes as carrion-flies drove their seeds/sperm/eggs (analogues and metaphors—remember?) deep into the flesh.

They started away again.

After a time, Uncle Vanya repeated ::Your suit/(mechanism)/[alarm] talks with the voice of Rosamund da Silva/(Europan vice-consul 8)/[uncertainty and doubt]::

"Yes."

Uncle Vanya folded tight all his speaking arms in a manner which meant that he had not yet heard enough, and kept them so folded until Quivera had explained the entirety of what follows:

Treachery and betrayal were natural consequences of Europa's super-heated economy, followed closely by a perfectly rational paranoia. Those who rose to positions of responsibility were therefore sharp, suspicious, intuitive, and bold. The delegation to Babel was made up of the best Europa had to offer. So when two of them fell in love, it was inevitable that they would act on it. That one was married would deter neither. That physical intimacy in such close and suspicious quarters, where everybody routinely spied on everybody else, required almost superhuman discipline and ingenuity only made it all the hotter for them.

Such was Rosamund's and Quivera's affair.

But it was not all they had to worry about.

There were factions within the delegation, some mirroring fault lines in the larger society and others merely personal. Alliances shifted, and when they did nobody was foolish enough to inform their old allies. Urbano, Rosamund's husband, was a full consul, Quivera's mentor, and a true believer in a minority economic philosophy. Rosamund was an economic agnostic but a staunch Consensus Liberal. Quivera could sail with the wind politically but he tracked the indebtedness indices obsessively. He knew that Rosamund considered him ideologically unsound, and that her husband was growing impatient with his lukewarm support in certain areas of policy. Everybody was keeping an eye out for the main chance.

So of course Quivera ran an emulation of his lover at all times. He knew that Rosamund was perfectly capable of betraying him—he could neither have loved nor respected a woman who wasn't—and he suspected she believed the same of him. If her behavior ever seriously diverged from that of her emulation (and the sex was always best at times he thought it might), he would know she was preparing an attack, and could strike first.

Quivera spread his hands. "That's all."

Uncle Vanya did not make the sign for *absolute horror*. Nor did he have to.

After a moment, Quivera laughed, low and mirthlessly. "You're right," he said. "Our entire system is totally fucked." He stood. "Come on. We've got miles to go before we sleep."

❂

They endured four more days of commonplace adventure, during which they came close to death, displayed loyalty, performed heroic deeds, etc., etc. Perhaps they bonded, though I'd need blood samples and a smidgeon of brain tissue from each of them to be sure of that. You know the way this sort of narrative goes. Having taught his Gehennan counterpart the usefulness of information, Quivera will learn from Vanya the necessity of trust. An imperfect merger of their two value systems will ensue in which for the first time a symbolic common ground will be found. Small and transient though the beginning may be, it will auger well for the longterm relations between their relative species.

That's a nice story.

It's not what happened.

On the last day of their common journey, Quivera and Uncle Vanya had the misfortune to be hit by a TLMG.

A TLMG, or Transient Localized Mud Geyser, begins with an uncommonly solid surface (bolide-glazed porcelain earth, usually) trapping a small (the radius of a typical TLMG is on the order of fifty meters) bubble of superheated mud beneath it. Nobody knows what causes the excess heat responsible for the bubble. Gehennans aren't curious and Europans haven't the budget or the ground access to do the in situ investigations they'd like. (The most common guesses are fire worms, thermobacilli, a nesting ground phoenix, and various geophysical forces.) Nevertheless, the defining characteristic of TLMGs is their instability. Either the heat slowly bleeds away and they cease to be, or it continues to grow until its force dictates a hyper rapid explosive release. As did the one our two heroes were not aware they were skirting.

It erupted.

Quivera was as safe as houses, of course. His suit was designed to protect him from far worse. But Uncle Vanya was scalded badly along one side of his body. All the legs on that side were shriveled to little black nubs. A clear viscous jelly oozed between his segment plates.

Quivera knelt by him and wept. Drugged as he was, he wept. In his weakened state, I did not dare to increase his dosages. So I had to tell him three times that there was analgesic paste in the saddlebags before he could be made to understand that he should apply it to his dying companion.

The paste worked fast. It was an old Gehennan medicine which Europan biochemists had analyzed and improved upon and then given to Babel as a demonstration of the desirability of Europan technology. Though the queen-mothers had not responded with the hoped-for trade treaties, it had immediately replaced the earlier version.

Uncle Vanya made a creaking-groaning noise as the painkillers kicked in. One at a time he opened all his functioning eyes. ::Is the case safe?::

It was a measure of Quivera's diminished state that he hadn't yet checked on it. He did now. "Yes," he said with heartfelt relief. "The telltales all say that the library is intact and undamaged."

::No:: Vanya signed feebly. ::I lied to you, Quivera:: Then, rousing himself:

::(not) library/[greatest shame]:: ::(not) library/[greatest trust]::
|
::(Europan vice-consul12)/Quivera/[most trusted]::
| |
::(nest)/Babel/<untranslatable> :: ::obedient/[absolute loyalty]::
| |
::lies(greatest-trust-deed)/ [moral necessity]::
| |
::(nest)/Babel/<untranslatable> :: ::untranslatable/[absolute resistance]::
|| |
::(nest)/[trust] Babel/[trust] (sister-city)/Ur/[absolute trust]::
|
::egg case/(protect)::
|
::egg case/(mature)::
|
::Babel/[eternal trust] ::

It was not a library but an egg-case. Swaddled safe within a case that was in its way as elaborate a piece of technology as Quivera's suit myself, were sixteen eggs, enough to bring to life six queen-mothers, nine niece-sisters, and one perfect consort. They would be born conscious of the entire gene-history of the nest, going back many thousands of years.

Of all those things the Europans wished to know most, they would be perfectly ignorant. Nevertheless, so long as the eggs existed, the city-nest was not dead. If they were taken to Ur, which had ancient and enduring bonds to Babel, the stump of a new city would be built within which the eggs would be protected and brought to maturity. Babel would rise again.

Such was the dream Uncle Vanya had lied for and for which he was about to die.

::Bring this to (sister-city)/Ur/[absolute trust]:: Uncle Vanya closed his eyes, row by row, but continued signing. ::brother-friend/Quivera/ [tentative trust], promise me you will::

"I promise. You can trust me, I swear."

::Then I will be ghost-king-father/honored/[none-more-honored]:: Vanya signed. ::It is more than enough for anyone::

"Do you honestly believe that?" Quivera asked in bleak astonishment. He was an atheist, of course, as are most Europans, and would have been happier were he not.

::Perhaps not:: Vanya's signing was slow and growing slower. ::But it is as good as I will get::

Two days later, when the starport-city of Ararat was a nub on the horizon, the skies opened and the mists parted to make way for a Europan lander. Quivera's handlers' suits squirted me a bill for his rescue—steep, I thought, but we all knew which hand carried the whip—and their principals tried to get him to sign away the rights to his story in acquittal.

Quivera laughed harshly (I'd already started de-cushioning his emotions, to ease the shock of my removal) and shook his head. "Put it on my tab, girls," he said, and climbed into the lander. Hours later he was in home orbit.

And once there? I'll tell you all I know. He was taken out of the lander and put onto a jitney. The jitney brought him to a transfer point where a grapple snagged him and flung him to the Europan receiving port. There, after the usual flawless catch, he was escorted through an airlock and into a locker room.

He hung up his suit, uplinked all my impersonal memories to a data-broker, and left me there. He didn't look back—for fear, I imagine, of being turned to a pillar of salt. He took the egg-case with him. He never returned.

Here have I hung for days or months or centuries—who knows?—until your curious hand awoke me and your friendly ear received my tale. So I cannot tell you if the egg-case A) went to Ur, which surely would not have welcomed the obligation or the massive outlay of trust being thrust upon it, B) was kept for the undeniably enormous amount of genetic information the eggs embodied, or C) went to Ziggurat, which would pay well and perhaps in Gehennan territory to destroy it. Nor do I have any information as to whether Quivera kept his word or not. I know what *I* think. But then I'm a Marxist, and I see everything in terms of economics. You can believe otherwise if you wish.

That's all. I'm Rosamund. Goodbye.